# THORNS OF TR

## TRAITOR'S DEATH

To : Charlotte

Hope the wait is
worth it... enjoy!

Vivienne

25/12/11

# THORNS OF TRUTH

## TRAITOR'S DEATH

Vivienne Maxwell

First published in the United Kingdom in 2011 by Lindenring Publishing
www.lindenringpublishing.com

© Vivienne Maxwell 2011

The moral right of the author has been asserted.

British Library Cataloguing in Publication Data.

A catalogue record for this book is available from the British Library.

Cover design by Claire Barker

ISBN 978-0-9569207-0-6

Prepared and printed by:

York Publishing Services Ltd
64 Hallfield Road
Layerthorpe
York YO31 7ZQ
Tel: 01904 431213

Website: www.yps-publishing.co.uk

# *Dedication*

*To My Mother*

*Always in my heart*

# *Acknowledgements*

Most notably, my friend Claire, who not only found the time between her own writing and illustrating to design the cover to Thorns of Truth but who also encouraged, supported and otherwise persuaded me over the course of a number of years and several dozen cups of hot chocolate to get the men and women of the Five Realms out of my head and onto the page.

Thanks should also go to my long-suffering family; Richard, Rick, Jay and Alex, for their patience and assistance, including advice on anything from agriculture, arms and armour to the more mundane area of grammatical editing... and whose critical comments ranged from a casual "yeah, go for it!" to an explosive "you can't *do* that!" in reference to something one of my characters said or did.

So I didn't, but they did. And, after all, this is their tale...

## *Dramatis Personae*

**ROYAL FAMILY OF THE REALM OF MITHLONDIA,**
the capital city of which is Lamortaine
Raymond★; former Prince and father to Marcus II
Marcus (Marc); ruling Prince
Linnius; his son
Linnette; his daughter

**DE CHARTREUX**
Louis (Luce); Lord of Chartreux province, the chief town of which is Chartre
Ariène (Ariena); his wife, a great beauty and reputed to be of the blood of the Faennari
Luc (Luke); their son
Rowène (Rowena) and Juliène (Juliena); their daughters

**DE VERAUX**
Guillaume; Lord of Veraux province
Richard★; his only son, recently killed in a skirmish on the northern border
Isabelle; his younger daughter, wife to Henri de Lyeyne
Céline★; his elder daughter
Joscelin; her illegitimate son, currently serving in Mithlondia's army

**DE ROGÉ**
Jacques★; former Lord of Rogé, the chief town of which is Rogérinac
Rosalynde★; his wife
Joffroi (Joffroy); his eldest son, currently Lord of Rogé
Ranulf; his younger son

**DE LYEYNE**
Henri; Lord of Lyeyne province
Hervé; his elder son
Léon; his younger son
Rosalynde★; his sister, wife to Jacques de Rogé
Gérard★; his younger brother

## OTHER ASSORTED NOBLES
Jean de Marillec; Lord of Marillec province (famous for its dark and heady wine)
Gabriel de Marillec; his eldest son
Nicholas de Vézière; Lord of Vézière province
Hal de Vézière; his only son
Gilles de Valenne; Lord of Valenne province, the chief town of which is Valéntien
Girauld d'Anjélais; a knight of Chartreux
Armand de Martine; a knight of Valenne
Alys de Martine★; his daughter, companion to Rosalynde de Rogé
Gaston de Martine; his son

## COMMONERS
Sister Héloise; a healer from Vézière
Cailen; a silk merchant of Chartre
Gwynhere; his sister, keeper of the Flower & Falcon tavern in Anjélais
Lucien; Commander of the Chartre garrison
Guthlaf, Geryth, Finn; soldiers in service to Joffroi de Rogé
Ilana; a servant at Chartre castle
Gerde; a servant at Rogérinac castle, sister to Geryth
Guy of Montfaucon (a village in Valenne); a harper, amongst other things

## ROYAL FAMILY OF THE REALM OF KARDOLANDIA,
the capital city of which is Kaerellios
King Karlen
Queen Xandra
Prince Kaslander, their youngest son


★deceased (mostly in unpleasant ways)

# PART I

# LAMORTAINE

# Spring 1194

# Chapter 1

## *A Mysterious Malady*

*Gods, grant me a little longer...*

Whenever Prince Marcus of Mithlondia had envisaged dying, it had been amidst the bloody chaos of the battlefield or, considerably less likely, in the serenity of old age, leaving his realm both peaceful and prosperous.

Certainly he had not expected to die like this; his strength ebbing a little more each day while he coughed up blood with ever increasing frequency. He was only in the middle years of his life after all, his raven hair barely marked by the silver of age. Yet despite all his efforts and the dictates of natural justice, the realm he had fought and bled and lied for over the past thirty-odd years was once again under attack, both from within and without.

He could feel the daemons even now; poised, panting with icy lust on the very brink of Hell. And possibly the only thing holding them in the freezing cold of the outermost darkness was his own increasingly tenuous grip on life. When he was gone, the daemons of death and destruction, terror and despair would rise to ravage his realm...

*Damn it, no! It is* not *inevitable,* he told himself as he struggled to haul himself higher against his sweat-soaked pillows, choking back the racking cough that threatened to tear his chest apart. *Luce will keep the daemons at bay.*

"Marc?"

Responding to the voice as much as his name, he opened his eyes and turned his aching head on the pillow, managing through his pain to find a smile for the tall, dark-haired man leaning over him. The familiar, clean-shaven countenance lightened briefly, before the warmth of affection was marred once more by a frowning anxiety.

Marcus tried to speak but found he could only cough. His companion grabbed the gold, gem-set goblet from the table beside the bed, poured a little of the herbal draught from the matching pitcher and held it out. Marcus shook his head, the slight effort taking most of his fast-failing strength.

"Do you want... to kill me, Luce?" he protested breathlessly. "There is... wine."

"I grant you this stuff smells foul and probably tastes worse," Louis de Chartreux responded with a grimace. "But your physician said that you should take this draught if you would get better. When that happens... well then we will drink our way through as many barrels of Marillec wine as you wish, Marc."

1

Marcus thought about pointing out that he was not going to get better but, from the shadow lurking behind the bleak grey gaze of Mithlondia's most powerful nobleman, he rather thought Louis knew that already. Even though he clearly retained some obstinate hope of a cure being found for his prince's mysterious ailment; a vicious wasting disease that had first struck barely a season before and against which Marcus had been fighting all winter.

Neither the royal physician nor the other healers he had consulted had been able to provide either a name for the malaise or, more importantly, a cure. But Marcus had heard them muttering when they had thought him too fevered to comprehend, heard the dread in their voices as they spoke of the "moon sickness", so called because it waxed and waned with the moon itself. From whispers of the forbidden Goddess of the Night it was but a short step to talk of witchcraft and treason but before it could reach that point Marcus had rallied sufficiently to command them all to silence.

In his heart though he feared the healers might be correct. Certainly this was no earthly malady he suffered from and the only relief he had found – and that only temporary – lay in a herbal draught brewed by the Grey Sisters of Vézière. There was a limit to how much of the stuff he could stomach but with Louis determinedly holding the goblet out he could neither find the will to refuse it nor summon sufficient strength to take it.

Hating his helplessness, but knowing also that Louis was the only man he would willingly allow to witness his weakness, he permitted his companion to slip an arm behind his shoulders and raise him sufficiently to sip from the goblet. He tasted the sweetness of honey first but it could not long conceal the metallic bitterness of the potent herbs beneath. He swallowed obediently but as the liquid trickled down his throat and into his belly, he feared he might vomit up what little he had managed to drink.

Clenching his jaw, he rested his sweating forehead against his companion's solid, supporting arm until he felt the familiar lethargy overcome his urge to purge himself. With a mutter that sounded incoherent even to his own ears he lay back against his pillows and, as Louis settled once more into the carven chair beside his bed, forced his blurred gaze to focus on the other man's face. He found Louis regarding him steadily, his lean features set in grim lines that revealed his silent acceptance of the situation. Now all Marcus had to do was get him to verbally admit the truth while there was still time to set his affairs in order.

Even so, there was silence between them for a while, Louis obviously concerned with his own unpleasant thoughts, Marcus content to husband his meagre strength in the company of the man who was closer to him – or, so said popular gossip – than a brother could have been. The irony of it was, of course, that the man the whole realm accepted as the rightful Lord of Chartreux *was*, in all truth, his brother. Or half-brother at least, Prince Raymond of Mithlondia having sired them both, although that fact had never been made common knowledge.

Feeling the draught do its work Marcus relaxed into a hazy somnolence, content for the time being simply to be in his brother's company, while memories of all they had shared drifted like sunlit clouds through his mind. Together they had fought and feasted, roistered and wenched. And although both had taken the binding oath in due course – and Marcus certainly had loved his wife – no woman had come between them. Nor had any man come close to severing the bonds of love and trust that bound them unto death.

Yet with that separation fast approaching there was no time for idle indulgence in maudlin dreams of the past. Instead Marcus forced himself to focus on the very real present and his fears for the future, belatedly assimilating the significance of his brother's formal court robes and the absence of any visible weapons.

"How went the counsel session this morning?" he enquired abruptly, his voice distressingly breathless to his ears.

Louis straightened in the comfortably cushioned chair and turned to regard him with a flicker of a wary smile.

"None so ill, Marc. We finalised the terms of Linette's binding to Prince Kaslander as you stipulated." His smile became more edged, his tone dryer. "And in all truth I do not think Karlen will object very strongly to our request that his son live here in Mithlondia with his bride. After all, the man has more sons than he knows what to do with and I cannot see him being anything other than grateful to get the youngest one off his hands in exchange for Linette's substantial dowry. The emissary to the Kardolandian court should be leaving even as we speak."

"That is good... and everything is as it should be?"

"Yes."

But Marcus knew his brother too well. He lay a moment recruiting his failing energy and then asked more strongly,

"What else, Luce?" He glanced at the light that fell through the unshuttered window, estimating the time, then back at the huge notched candle on its heavy iron stand for confirmation, and frowned. "It is not like you to leave the counsel session early, even with Joffroi de Rogé doing his damnedest to goad you into injudicious words or rash actions."

"If he has not succeeded in that these past score of years, he is not like to do it now," Louis snorted, his grey eyes glinting with a cool humour which vanished as he continued tersely, "Besides, it was not de Rogé this time."

"Who then? For gods'sake, Luce..." He ran out of breath and began to cough.

Louis snatched up the abandoned goblet and when the convulsion had passed held it once more to Marcus's lips. He drank a little, then pushed the goblet away. Accepting this unspoken command, Louis set the goblet back down but did not immediately retake his seat, choosing instead to pace restlessly about the chamber, the silver-embroidered hem of his dark blue court robe swirling around his soft-shod feet.

Marcus lay still and waited, tasting both rich wine and bitter blood. Finally Louis turned back to meet his questioning gaze, his eyes betraying some intense, inner disquiet, although his voice remained level.

"Well, you will hear it sooner or later – probably sooner if Guillaume de Veraux has his way. And the final word will be yours if the Counsel cannot come to a clear decision."

Marcus frowned at this unexpected reference to the elderly Lord of Veraux but, having made up his mind to speak, Louis had not paused.

"To put it bluntly, Marc, de Veraux has nominated his heir, as he was bound to do with Richard dead and is now requesting the Counsel to ratify that choice. Not surprisingly, given his choice, the Counsel is up in arms about it." He flashed a sharp grin. "Or would be, if swords were permitted in the counsel chamber."

"As you say, it was bound to come," Marcus replied, the words lying heavy on his tongue. "Not that I think any de Lyeyne a fitting substitute for Richard de Veraux, but however unwise it might prove to be I cannot see why the Counsel should withhold its consent. After all, there is no-one else."

"Not so," Louis struck in grimly. "Guillaume has another in mind to hold Veraux after his death."

"Go on," Marcus ordered, some inkling of what his brother might be about to say seeping like snow-melt into his mind.

Louis took an audible breath and something showed momentarily in his carefully impassive face, then was gone.

"With the death of his only son, Guillaume is saying the lands and title should by rights go to his elder, rather than his younger, daughter's son."

"Ah, I see!"

"Yes, I rather thought you would."

Marcus said nothing for a long moment, staring instead at the splash of spring sunshine that seemed to mock him with its promise of new life, and thought grimly that the first daemon had already slipped out of Hell. Finally he looked back at his brother.

"I can see why Henri de Lyeyne should take offence at what he must see as the passing over of his son's rights but surely there are some more reasonable voices in the Counsel to support de Veraux's will? It may be unprecedented but it is not outright folly."

"Maybe not," Louis replied. "But, as we both know, Joffroi de Rogé has a loud voice and not unnaturally he has raised it in support of de Lyeyne. They are kinsmen after all. Nor can any of us deny the truth of their contention. The young man Guillaume wants to name as the next Lord of Veraux is bastard-born and under the current laws of Mithlondia cannot inherit."

"Not just any bastard though," Marcus pointed out dryly. "That being so, perhaps Joffroi de Rogé and Henri de Lyeyne would like to tell me to my face why the boy I acknowledged as being of royal Mithlondian blood is not fit to

4

inherit his maternal grandsire's title. From what little I have seen of him lately, Joscelin has managed to overcome his youthful irresponsibility and is well on his way to becoming an able administrator and a soldier of some note. Indeed I had it in mind to promote him to the post of Second of the Guardians in due course. But Lord of Veraux? Well, that would be a higher honour yet. What, Luce? Why the sour face? Would you not wish to see Céline's son recognised in such a way? A Lord of Mithlondia with a seat on the High Counsel? To have a hand in the governance of our realm rather than merely perishing for it on some distant and bloody battlefield?"

His unwise burst of vehemence was brought to an end by another fit of coughing. When it had passed Marcus regarded his brother narrowly, demanding an answer with the weight of his gaze.

"Damn it, Marc," Louis snapped. "Whatever I might wish for the boy I cannot change his birth." His voice was clipped, cold, unfeeling. Only his grey eyes betrayed his pain. "Joscelin de Veraux is a bastard and scarce twenty-three years old. You try foisting him on the High Counsel and you will have open rebellion on your hands. And the gods know, you are in no fit state to deal with *that* at the moment."

"No, but you are!" Marcus retorted. "Or are you telling me that you would turn your back on Céline de Veraux's son? I thought she meant more to you than that!"

"She did! And the gods help me, I will do what I can for Joscelin. But this is not a good time, Marc! This is the year my daughters will be returning to Mithlondia. I sent them away ten years ago that they might be safe from their mother's influence. I cannot and will not risk *their* future for *his*!"

Utterly stunned by his brother's unexpected words, Marcus could only watch helplessly as Louis turned away again, abruptly halting as his attention was caught by something beyond Marcus's sight. Stalking to the window, Louis stood looking down at the courtyard below, his fingers clenched on the window frame, his face a rigid mask of control.

From the faint sounds of chiming metal, stamping hooves and shouted orders that now reached his straining ears, Marcus judged a patrol of guardians was on the point of riding out. He further deduced from the tense set of his brother's shoulders that the soldier in charge of that patrol was none other than the young man they had just been speaking of; Joscelin de Veraux, the acknowledged bastard son of Prince Marcus of Mithlondia and his long-dead mistress, the Lady Céline de Veraux.

When all trace of the riders had faded away, Louis returned to the bed, his face still carefully expressionless. Even his eyes were hooded against Marcus' searching gaze. Nor did his level voice betray any of the emotion he must surely be feeling.

"I swore long ago that I would do what I could for the boy. In keeping with that oath, I have already thrown what little influence I have with the Counsel behind de Veraux." His voice hardened. "But it will bring nothing but trouble, Marc, and you know it. You may be able to force the Counsel to change the laws of inheritance but such a fundamental upheaval will exact its own price in blood. And if Joscelin *does* become heir to the lordship of Veraux he will need to watch his back every moment, both day and night, lest his disgruntled kinsmen seek to sheath a knife in it."

"The boy is not stupid, Luce, he will know the dangers. And he has the skill with arms to defend himself from open attack from the de Lyeyne brood. Or their de Rogé kin if it comes to that."

"That may be so but there will be other, more insidious, dangers to guard against," Louis warned. "My wife for one! She will not hesitate to use all her considerable venom against him should she ever come to realise just how much Céline de Veraux's son means to me."

"Ah, but do not forget, he is my son too," Marcus reminded his brother, a thread of irony beneath the breathlessness of his tone. "As I shall take very good care to remind both the Counsel and the court just as soon as..."

He held himself still then as he felt another coughing fit coming on. But it was no good, he could not contain the harsh, tearing eruptions. The best he could manage was to muffle the terrible sounds against the sleeve of his nightshirt, all the while hoping he could hide the betraying spots of scarlet blood from his brother's keen eyes.

As he collapsed, drained of all strength and his consciousness blurring into exhaustion, he heard Louis' voice from the far side of the chamber ordering the door guard to "Fetch Master Geraint! And hurry, damn it!"

The next thing he knew his own physician was leaning over him, talking irascibly over his hunched shoulder to a woman whose face Marcus could not see but whom he vaguely supposed from her pale grey raiment to be one of the healing sisterhood. Uninterested in their argument, Marcus ignored them both, his gaze going beyond them to where Louis stood against the far wall. Even at that distance he could see that his brother's face was set, his eyes shadowed pools of fierce regret.

*Yes*, Marcus thought again, *Luce knows*; he had seen the blood and realised that there could be no hope of recovery. Now it was just a matter of time before Marcus Valéri de Mortaine, Prince of Mithlondia took the long path beyond the sunset.

But, by the grace of the Gods of Light and Mercy, that time would be sufficient to see his daughter wed and his son made ready to take over the rule of Mithlondia.

Time also to see Louis' daughters brought home from their exile in Kardolandia and safely bound to some man who would protect them from the daemons whose icy breath he could already feel cold against his neck.

6

Finally, the gods willing, time to ensure that the young man he had publicly acknowledged as his illegitimate son would be accepted by the High Counsel as the lawful heir to the lordship of Veraux.

And to Hell with Joffroi de Rogé and that flame-haired witch whose will he served.

# Chapter 2

## *Time Enough*

Marcus was unsure when he awoke how many hours, or even days, might have passed since he had fallen asleep after drinking that last filthy draught of herbs, wine and only the gods – or, more likely, the Daemon of Hell – knew what else besides. Whatever its dubious ingredients it seemed to have done its work; his limbs no longer lay as heavy as rusty iron against the feather mattress nor did he feel as though he might cough himself to death if he risked engagement in any more strenuous activity than merely breathing.

Glancing around his magnificently furnished chamber he noted that sunlight was trickling through the small, pale green panes of precious glass that filled every window in the palace but, to his surprise, Louis was not there. Instead, seated quietly in the chair beside the bed was a small woman, neatly clad in the pale grey robes and white head rail of one of Mithlondia's Sisters of Mercy.

She smiled as he stirred, the gesture easing her sombre expression and warming eyes as blue as his own. Rather than being reassured by this Marcus was assailed by a fleeting sense of shock, followed by a tug of familiarity. Did he know this woman, he wondered? On the face of it, it seemed unlikely; even in the wildest days of his youth he had always respected the chastity and dedication of those women who had chosen service to the Gods of Light and Mercy. As for the colour of her eyes, that was surely no affair of his. And yet...

"Who are you?" he heard himself asking, his voice a brusque whisper.

She hesitated a moment, then spoke in common speech, the words softly tinged with the provincial accent of Vézière,

"Pardon, Sire, were you talking to me or yourself?"

It was only then that Marcus realised that he had – solely on the basis of those unusual blue eyes – unthinkingly couched his question in Mithlondian, the language of the court and counsel chamber but not that of the ordinary folk of his realm. Hastily revising his first impression of her, he said,

"Yes, it was you I was addressing." His common speech was fluent, albeit his phrasing was still very formal. "And it is I who should seek your pardon, Sister, since I demanded to know, rather discourteously I fear, who you were – apart from being a Sister of Mercy. My wits are not yet so enfeebled as to be unable to deduce that for myself."

She regarded him steadily, seemingly not in the least discomposed to find herself conversing with the highest ranking nobleman in the realm.

"My name is Héloise, Sire," she said softly.

Héloise! Not the name he would have imagined, given her common origins, but perhaps the same man – or perchance woman – who had bequeathed her those cornflower-blue eyes had also given her that high Mithlondian name. He was halfway tempted to question her further but she allowed him no opportunity, continuing earnestly,

"The Eldest sent me to Lamortaine, Sire, when word of your continuing illness reached us, since I am – or so they tell me – the most skilled of the healers at Vézière."

"Indeed, I believe they are right in that claim," Marcus replied, a little more easily this time. "I have not been able to talk or breathe this freely since this damnable sickness, whatever it is, first assailed me. And if drinking your evil-tasting potions will keep me alive a little longer, long enough at least to achieve my purposes, you will have won my heartfelt gratitude and may name your reward. Whatever it is, I give you my word that the Lord of Chartreux will see it done."

Her steady gaze wavered a little, then dropped. She studied her slender, capable fingers a moment, then looked up again.

"I seek no reward, Sire," she said with quiet composure. "As to your recovery from whatever it is that ails you, and I must confess to being as ignorant as your own physician as to the cause..." She paused, her serene brow furrowed into a frown. "From the little Master Geraint can tell me, it would appear to be a most strange sickness that afflicts you." She hesitated again, glanced around the chamber as if she feared she were under observation and almost whispered. "It would seem to me, Sire, that this thing that is poisoning your life ebbs and flows with the waxing and waning of the moon."

She said no more but distress and fear were plain to see in the deep, blue pools of her eyes. Nor did she need to say more, he reflected; the name of the forbidden Goddess of the Night hung all too plainly in the still air between them.

"Gods!" It was the merest breath of a curse and not in any degree meant to express his disbelief but Sister Héloise evidently took it as such and hastened to say briskly,

"Whatever the cause, Sire, I shall not delude you as to the outcome."

He gave a short, harsh laugh that mercifully did not provoke another coughing fit.

"No need, Sister. I know I am doomed. It is merely a matter of how long you can stave off the demands of the Daemon of Death. So tell me the truth."

She looked at him a moment, as if measuring his strength of will, then replied haltingly,

"*If* you drink the potions I brew – and I warn you they will taste increasingly foul as I must increase their strength to prolong your life – and *if* the Gods of

9

Light and Mercy are with you, then I can give you perhaps a season of grace. Until the start of summer at best."

"That will be sufficient," Marcus muttered. "The gods know if that is all I have, it will have to be. Indeed it is far more than I expected, given how I felt earlier! Or was it yesterday? When I woke to see you arguing with my physician. The man is a fool if he would doubt your healing skills."

She smiled a little at that, albeit he thought there were tears in her eyes.

"No time for weeping," he continued abruptly. "I need to be on my feet and back in the Counsel Chamber as soon as may be." He looked at her consideringly. "Have you seen what happens when a flaming brand is tossed into a barrel of boiling pitch? It explodes and burns all in its path. Well, one of my lords has done just that – figuratively speaking, of course." He cocked an enquiring eyebrow at the healer. "You may have already heard the rumours that are presently sweeping the palace and igniting not a few old quarrels as they go?"

"Sire, I am a healer, one of the common folk. We do not concern ourselves with the feuding of your quarrelsome lordlings within the confines of the Counsel Chamber."

"And when hot words in the Counsel Chamber spill over into bloody fighting in the provinces? With the loss of innocent lives to the sword and crops to the flames? What then, Sister?"

"Then I do as all my sisters and brothers in healing do; mend what we can, pray for the souls of those we cannot help and look to our Prince to curb his warlords' heedless actions."

"Easier said than done, Sister," Marcus replied brusquely. "I have endeavoured to rule this realm with regard to common justice rather than the might of the sword for the past thirty-odd years but still there are certain lords of Mithlondia who would choose the latter. In truth, Sister, it is my darkest fear that my death will be the signal that once again blood-feuds between men, the rape of women and the pillage of property will become the accepted currency of this realm."

"Sire, you cannot prevent what will happen when you are no longer here to hold your lords in an iron fist."

"That I know. I am only mortal and that this day has come sooner rather than later changes nothing. At least I take with me the knowledge that there are fair-minded and honourable men to counsel young Linnius; Marillec, Vézière, Veraux, Valenne, Chartreux. They will stand by him and see that justice does not fail."

"I will pray that you are right, Sire," Sister Héloise said softly.

"What? You doubt any of those I have named?" Marcus queried, a touch of hauteur chilling his tone.

"No, Sire, you misunderstand me. Those names are known the length and breadth of Mithlondia, the men who bear them respected and trusted by the

common folk everywhere, not just within their own domains. I merely fear..."
She stopped, obviously unwilling to go on.

Marcus finished her unspoken thought grimly,

"You fear what I fear, Sister. You fear that those others on the High Counsel who are not so noble-hearted will seek to destroy their enemies, stabbing them in the back, poisoning the people's trust in their integrity – and all for the sake of their own greed for power and wealth. And then, when it is too late, those short-sighted, blood-thirsty fools will realise that all they have achieved is to bring this realm to its knees!"

Wearied by his passionate outburst, Marcus turned his head against his pillow to see Sister Héloise regarding him with a strange, little smile.

"You are our Prince, your allegiance quite rightly is to *all* your people. The focus of my fear is more... singular." Then before he could ask what she meant, she continued firmly. "Now, Sire, if you are to take back control of your realm – for however short a time – we should make a start. Drink this draught, then I will get your servants to bring food of a simple kind. Bread and honey, fruit and fresh water from a spring in the hills."

Marcus gave her a look of disbelief.

"*Water?*"

She smiled at him again.

"I know your fondness for the wine of Marillec, Sire, but in this case it will do you little good."

He frowned.

"You *know?*"

She gestured to the gold pitcher on the nearby table.

"I may be only a humble Sister of Mercy, Sire, but I can still recognise the scent and colour of the wine of Marillec. No other wine is so rich in hue or flavour. But for now, Sire, water it must be."

"So be it," he muttered, the tone sounding churlish even to his own ears. "I put myself in your hands, Sister."

Three days later Prince Marcus astounded the court by attending the morning session of the High Counsel, then walking with his daughter in the palace gardens during the afternoon and presiding over the celebratory feast held in the great hall in the evening. Overjoyed as most courtiers were with their prince's apparent recovery, few noticed that he spoke little and ate less. Or that his skin beneath the ruddy glow of the myriad candles and torchères was grey with strain.

Early the following morning he summoned Louis de Chartreux to his chamber and told him bluntly that it was time – and past time – that he returned to his own province.

The day was rather cool, the sky silvery-grey with a misty rain but, determined to relish the last dregs of his life, Marcus had asked Sister Héloise to open the windows before she withdrew. He was aware that she did not leave the chamber but merely slipped into the shadows on the far side of the vast chamber, thus permitting him the illusion of privacy even while she maintained her watch over him, anxious no doubt lest he overtax his strength.

Sitting on the cushioned window seat, his fur-lined mantle wrapped about him to ward off the worst of the damp chill, he passed the time whilst waiting for his brother by observing the dark-haired young captain who was drilling his men in the courtyard below, only slowly becoming aware that Louis had come to stand beside him and was also looking down at Joscelin de Veraux.

They watched the young man in silence for a while until finally Marcus shook himself from his reverie and said,

"You are late, Luce."

"I came as soon as I could, Marc..." his brother started to say but Marcus waved him to silence.

"No, I did not mean that. I meant only that you are late leaving Lamortaine this year. Usually you set out as soon as the willows begin to bud with silver and the catkins to hang out their yellow banners. But already the primroses are flowering and by the time you reach Chartre the blackthorn and wild lilac will be scenting the air."

"I always knew there was something of the bard lurking beneath your stoical royal demeanour," Louis commented with an attempt at lightness.

"And I have not even had any wine!" Marcus replied with a quick, quirking grin. "On the orders of Sister Héloise there."

Louis sent a fleeting glance in the healer's direction before leaning his shoulder against the wall by the window, folding his arms across his chest.

"So why the summons?" he enquired tersely. His grey eyes were narrowed in a sweeping survey of his brother's face and Marcus summoned all his self control, lest he betray his underlying weakness.

"I merely wished to know how soon you were leaving."

"I do not have to leave at all," Louis replied quietly. "My lady wife would be glad enough to remain here at court for the rest of her life." He snorted rudely. "It is no secret that Ariène has no taste for life in provincial Chartre and this once I am content enough to humour her."

"But you cannot remain at court for ever," Marcus said. "I have no doubt that Luc is well able to administer the province in your absence but did you not say to me the other day that this is the year that your daughters are due to return from Kaerellios? After a ten year absence will they not expect their father, as well as their brother, to welcome them home?"

Louis gave a grunt of acknowledgement and the lines that a lifetime of responsibility had etched upon his face deepened perceptibly.

"Very well. You have made your point," he said grimly. "I will go back to Chartre and do my duty there, to my people and to my daughters. The gods know I have missed them more than I ever thought possible. *Ten years*, Marc.

That is a damnably long time! And I pray that once they are returned I will have a few seasons to enjoy their company before I must bind them to some other man in wedlock."

"So you have no-one in mind?" Marcus queried.

Louis shrugged.

"No. Although there are some decent and honourable young men I can put forward for their consideration. Gabriel de Marillec for one, Hal de Vézière for another but I will leave the decision to them. I would not force them to wed where they have no sense of either respect or affection."

Marcus hesitated and then asked quietly,

"What will you tell them about Joscelin?"

All expression was wiped from his brother's face and his eyes hardened to the semblance of stone.

"Nothing," Louis said tersely. "After all, it is not as though they are likely to come into contact with a lad who is merely one of Mithlondia's Guardians."

"Not even if that lad becomes Lord of Veraux? Luce, you have to tell them something if that happens. They are blood-kin, for gods'sake!"

Louis gave a short, sharp sigh – of impatience or irritation, Marcus could not tell which.

"If it becomes necessary, I will tell them. Now, have done, Marc. Tell me instead how you are really feeling. Obviously Sister Héloise is a fine healer but even so I do not like to leave you..."

Marcus met his brother's penetrating stare with a steely tranquillity that hid his terrifying breathlessness and after a moment Louis nodded as if satisfied and grinned at some thought.

"Very well, I will go and tell Ariène we will be leaving with tomorrow's dawn. That should ensure she does not speak to me for the remainder of the day." Then he sobered. "But if you need me, Marc, you know you have but to send a messenger and I will come."

"If I need you, I will send for you," Marcus agreed. "And now, before you go, you must tell me what is needful regarding the latest mutterings in the Counsel Chamber and just what mischief Joffroi de Rogé and his cronies are plotting."

"As if they are like to tell me," Louis grimaced.

"No, but you have an instinct where de Rogé is concerned."

"As if he were about to plunge a dagger between my shoulder blades, you mean?" his brother replied, his deep voice holding more than a hint of cynicism.

"Something like that," Marcus agreed. "Just watch your back, Luce. Your lady wife is not the only viper around."

"I know. And I always do," his brother confirmed, his light tone belied by the dark awareness in his grey eyes. "The gods guard you, Marc, while I am gone."

"Ah, but you are forgetting," Marcus smiled. "I have Sister Héloise by my side so the gods will surely look kindly upon me." Adding silently, "For a season at least."

# PART II

## CHARTRE

### Spring – Summer 1194

# Chapter 1

## *Silk, Secrets and Spies*

Late on a clear spring afternoon, barely three days after the return to Chartre of its lord and lady, Master Cailen, the town's foremost cloth merchant, stood in the doorway of his shop. He appeared to be doing nothing more than staring absently at the narrow strip of speckled pale blue sky that showed above the shadowed street; mayhap calculating his profit for the day or gauging the likelihood of rain later.

In reality, Cailen's thoughts were far from such relatively mundane matters as the price of silk or even the changeable spring weather. Rather those thoughts which engrossed him to the exclusion of all else, and rendered him deaf to the greetings of the townsfolk who passed his shop, were far beyond their comprehension, concerning as they did people and events taking place far beyond Chartreux's borders.

One thing Cailen did notice about the passers-by, beyond their irritating and intrusive presence, was that on this particular afternoon there seemed to be even more of them than usual bustling about, not only along the busy length of Castle Street but throughout the town generally. Not, he considered, that that was particularly surprising in itself, given that the Lord of Chartreux was finally back in residence.

What Cailen did speculate, a little grimly, about was the reason behind his lord's extended absence. Nothing good, he would warrant. Nor was he entirely sure that Louis de Chartreux's return home at this particular point betokened anything better. More especially as Cailen viewed the recent lack of trouble along Chartreux's border with its eastern neighbour as a cause for wariness rather than rejoicing. It was now well into spring but there had been no reports thus far of any violent incursions across the Larkenlye; no armed reavers, no stolen livestock, no murdered peasants, no missing women.

Cailen was damned glad of the peace after more than a score of years of aggression but deeply uneasy as to what such quiet might portend. He did not suppose for one moment that either the man whom folk on *both* sides of the Larkenlye knew as Black Joffroy – more for the colour of his soul than his hair – or his equally ruthless brother had suffered a change of heart; merely a change in tactics.

Whatever the cause of the unexpected quiet in the borderlands, word of the Lord of Chartreux's return had flown throughout the fief and every day since then had seen the castle ward crammed with folk seeking their turn in Chartre's provincial court. That being so, Cailen had little doubt that his lord would have had scant rest or peace since he came home; likely spending all his waking hours in the great hall of the castle in an attempt to clear the aggregation of complaints and requests that his steward had been unable to deal with, or that his son had felt required his father's personal attention.

In view of that, Cailen had been more than a little surprised by the discovery that his lord had found time to slip away from the castle early that morning in order to seek him out. They had met down on the teeming quayside where Cailen had gone to oversee the unloading of a shipment of silk newly arrived from the Eastern Isles and had exchanged the briefest of conversations – perhaps no more than a score of words between them – before the nobleman had returned to the tasks that awaited him at the castle, leaving Cailen to attend somewhat abstractedly to his own affairs, heedless of the shouts, curses, crashes and seeming disorder that surrounded him.

Besides being one of the most fertile provinces in Mithlondia, Chartreux also had the distinction of possessing the busiest port in the realm. Everything from the great sea-going galleys that dealt in rare goods to the tiny fishing boats that plied their trade in the gentler waters of the Liriél river, used the docks at Chartre, and day and night the town hummed with noisy, vibrant activity. Today was no exception and several ships were in port, including the *Golden Hibiscus,* sailing out of Kaerellios and calling in at the Eastern Isles on the way to collect Cailen's precious consignment of silk.

It had taken Cailen longer than normal, possibly because his thoughts were no longer on the business at hand, but eventually he had managed to get the cloth unloaded from the ship, checked for damage (by him), checked for value (by the tax assessor) and paid the requisite amount of silver with appropriate grumbling before seeing the silk loaded, transported back to his shop and finally safely stowed away. Needless to say it had taken a disproportionately shorter time for word to fly around the town that a new shipment of cloth had arrived at the silk merchant's shop in Castle Street and towards the middle of the afternoon Cailen had caught the distinctive sound of iron-shod hooves halting outside his shop, accompanied by light, feminine laughter.

He had just finished struggling with the last bolt of cloth, quietly cursing the absence of his assistant whose job this would normally have been, and was straightening his aching back, thinking that a mug of ale and a crab pastry from the cook shop over the road would go down a treat. Some pleasures, however, were just not meant to be tasted – as those hooves proved.

Knowing himself to be unobserved, he had permitted himself a rare moment of indiscretion, his normally smiling mouth flattening into an ugly sneer. Necessity – as it had made a nasty habit of doing over the years – had conquered his personal feelings and by the time he came to the open door of the shop he was once more the unctuous and ingratiating merchant he portrayed so well.

Folding his bulky body into an awkward obeisance he had ushered into his shop the one person in Chartre – possibly in all of Mithlondia – whom he hated enough to kill without mercy.

Unaware of Cailen's hidden hostility – or perhaps merely indifferent to it – Lady Ariène de Chartreux had coldly declined his obsequious offer to bring a selection of his choicest cloth up to the castle on the morrow. Instead she had appeared to derive a certain malicious satisfaction from making him pull out every bale of linen and lawn, satin, sendal and samite that the shop contained.

Only after she and her nervous attendant – now there was a woman Cailen did feel sorry for – had minutely inspected every bolt in the shop did the Lady Ariène finally condescend to order several lengths of material, including a blue-green watered silk shot through with silver that was going to cost her lord dearly, and a double length of cheap sendal in a shade of scarlet vibrant enough to make even the stoic Cailen blink at the thought of it gracing the slender figure of Chartreux's Lady; it was, after all, a colour and fabric he would normally expect to find covering – or not, depending upon circumstance – the ample hips and buxom breasts of the dockside whores. And while he might privately consider it to be an apt choice for the Lady Ariène, Cailen had a healthy regard for the state of his skin and wisely kept his expression wooden and his mouth firmly shut.

The scarlet silk had concluded Lady Ariène's purchases and, since by that time the sun was dropping swiftly towards the uneven red rooftops, Cailen had been only too relieved to see the back of her. He had accompanied the two women to the door and waited respectfully while the bored groom hastened to help them mount. He had then wished Lady Ariène an utterly spurious good evening, promising to deliver the cloth to the castle early the following morning.

That however had been a good candle-notch ago and the lady and her entourage should by now be back within the solid sandstone walls of the castle that dominated the town from the secure heights of the cliff top above. The narrow, cobbled street outside the shop was still bustling with people, either bound for their own homes or the various taverns and cook shops of the town, but Cailen took no notice of them and they in turn spared no more than a passing word or glance for the silk merchant, merely shrugging when he did not return their greetings but continued to contemplate the sky.

Slowly, softly, the spring sun slid away into the shadows of early evening and although it was long past time for Cailen to put up his shutters and lock up for the night, still he lingered in the doorway, watching the mackerel sky, his thoughts far away...

Far from the Lady Ariène, the weather or the price of silk. Far beyond Chartreux's borders...

Far from the mildly offensive reek of salt, seaweed, fish guts and rotting crab that was wafting up from the wharf on the evening breeze. Nostrils flaring, Cailen allowed himself to succumb to the yearning for the clean, thyme-scented air of the distant province that had seen his birth and early life. In his mind he could almost hear the piercing cry of the hovering falcon instead of the harsh bickering of the seagulls as they fought over scraps on the quay.

It was at times like these – infrequent enough in all truth – that he found his oath weighing heavy on his shoulders and he wished only that he could go home. And for longer than the fleeting, furtive visits he had perforce become accustomed to. Long enough to be able to share more than a hasty drink with his brother... to see his sister settled... mayhap even take a woman of his own...

At which point in his uncharacteristically maudlin reflections Cailen gave himself a mental shake, knowing he could not leave Chartre yet. Returning to consciousness of his surroundings he noted the speckling of green and silver against the blue of the sky and decided it was time he was on his way. Reaching behind the door he plucked his mantle from its hook. Flinging the garment about his shoulders he stepped into the street, closing the door of his shop behind him. He locked it carefully, tenderly tucking the heavy key into the leather purse that hung on his belt, and set off down the cobbled street, confining himself to the casual amble that suited both his ankle-length woollen robe and respectable status as one of the chief merchants of the town.

Rather than strolling down to the Silver Swan for a quiet mug of ale as was his habit of an evening, Cailen turned his back on both castle and harbour, heading instead for the west gate of the town. He passed through the open gate with a quick nod of greeting to the guards on duty, then, rather than following the wide, tree-shaded highway, turned instead onto a narrow path that led off through the tangle of grey-green willows, honeysuckle-hung hazel and purple-flushed alders that flourished in the scrub that lay between the town walls and the river. Following this largely overgrown track he came at last to the River Liriél, which here flowed wide and serene between open meadows bordered by tall, rustling reeds. Unable to go further, the path turned and meandered up beside the quiet flowing water, coming after a league or so to the small fishing hamlet of Whitestone.

Not that Cailen had any intention on this occasion of going that far – even though on other nights it had been his accepted reason for coming this way. At such times his destination had been the Whitestone alehouse, which was well-known locally, not only for the quality of its brew but also the abundant attractions of the woman who served it. The fact that Aelfwyn wore the binding bracelet of a hulking great brute of a fisherman was cause enough to make most men take an extremely cautious approach and Cailen was nothing if not careful. If he had not been, he would not have evaded Leofric's fists for so long.

Tonight, however, his errand was such that it held his mind to the exclusion of all else, preventing any consideration of the possibility that he might enjoy a few furtive hours of casual entertainment with the energetic Aelfwyn.

As soon as he had known himself beyond observation by the guards at the gate, Cailen had drawn his constricting robe up through his belt and proceeded along the little-used path with swift strides that bore little resemblance to the ambling gait he normally affected. He remained watchful, nonetheless, though he noted nothing to cause him trouble on his side of the river and there was little enough movement on the far side of the gilded water either; a small herd of placid, cream-coloured cows grazed amongst the sweet grass and early buttercups in the meadow opposite and only the chiming of the cow bells and the calling of the curlews disturbed the still evening air. Oblivious to his presence, tall grey herons and small white egrets fished peacefully in the shallows while further out the fishermen paddled their coracles back upstream to Whitestone, gliding silently along the glittering golden path laid down by the setting sun.

Cailen's guileless brown eyes narrowed suddenly as he surveyed the men out on the river and, caution taking charge, he ducked back into the evening shadows under the trees, his mouth quirking into a grin. Just as well, he thought as he recognised the formidable frame of Leofric in the leading boat, that he had not come out with the intention of paying a visit to Aelfwyn tonight.

Abruptly, his smile tightened into a grimace as he felt the unmistakeable touch of cold steel against his neck. Obeying the implicit command he stood very still but beneath the concealing folds of his mantle his hand was reaching stealthily for the long knife he always wore. Then, just as his fingers wrapped around the hilt, he heard a low, faintly amused voice that he recognised with a distinct sense of relief, tempered by a deep irritation that he had been taken unawares.

"I warrant it is a long time since anyone caught you off your guard, Cai! Though if it were the fair Aelfwyn who was the cause of your wits a-wandering I would advise you to put her out of your mind, lest next time it should be Leofric who lies in wait for you!"

There came the rasping whisper of a sword slithering back into its sheath and, with a certain amount of self-disgust, Cailen removed his hand from his dagger hilt and brought it up to his neck. Raising his fingers to his eyes he squinted at the smear of blood on his skin.

Hearing a subdued sound – it might have been a snort of derision or a mirthless chuckle – he wiped his fingers on his robe and turned to glare through the deepening gloom at his assailant.

His hood was drawn forward to conceal his face and, like Cailen, he wore a cloak against the chill of the evening mist but there all similarity ended. Where Cailen's plain mantle concealed a robe of sober brown wool and sensible leather shoes, the folds of this man's fur-lined cloak fell back to reveal the sleeves of a fine linen shirt worn beneath a silver-embroidered tunic that fell to mid-thigh. Both sword and dagger hung from his belt and the dark blue breeches were tucked into fine leather boots, which glinted with the silver spurs of his rank.

In the silence that hung between them the other man put back his hood and Cailen found himself looking up into the familiar features of the Lord of Chartreux. The half-light under the budding ash trees was shadowy, indistinct, chancy. Nevertheless Cailen could see clearly that any trace of amusement had long since disappeared from the nobleman's eyes, leaving them a cool, enigmatic grey.

Despite the fact that there was no-one there to observe them Cailen began to bend his head to honour his lord but Louis' hand moved in a swift chopping motion.

"Not now, Cai!"

Obedient to the impatient note in the younger man's voice Cailen straightened to find his lord studying him in unsmiling silence. Finally he spoke, his voice a lethal match for his eyes.

"Far be it from me to deny you your bed sport, Cai, but I do need you in one piece. So, while I would not normally interfere in your affairs, in this instance I feel justified in doing so, more especially as you are – unusually I might add – acting like a reckless fool!" And when Cailen merely returned his piercing look in stolid silence, added irascibly, "Damn it all, man, have you not heard what Leofric did to the last man he caught swiving his woman! At the rate you are going you will end up being beaten to a bloody pulp before being tossed into the river for the fish to feast on!"

"Mayhap, m'lord, it would not be me as ended up in the river!" Cailen growled, finally provoked into unwary speech. "And how, if I might ask, did you know about me and Aelfwyn? So far as I was aware you only returned to Chartre three days ago."

"You bloody fool, it is common gossip!" his lord retorted scornfully. "My steward may be incapable of dealing with the simplest complaint but he knows all the gossip of the town. And if Cerdic knows, you can bet your life that Leofric does too! So stay away from her, Cai, before she brings you to ruin."

Cailen could not resist giving the other man a derisive glare. Evidently the nobleman saw and interpreted it correctly since he gave a grimace and continued ruefully,

"The gods know I am in no position to sit in judgement on you but I do not want to see your blood spilt for such a one as that. Bed the woman if you must but do not let her trap you into giving her more than a bit of mutual pleasure! I grant you she has as fair a face and enticing a body as any man could wish for but her heart is as cold and unyielding as stone and she will betray you without a qualm if it serves her interests best! Or do you think that after all these years of being wedded to one, I am so blinded by her enchantments that I cannot recognise another such heartless whore?"

The angry flush that had suffused Cailen's face at his lord's earlier reprimand faded away as the implication behind that bitter condemnation bit into his mind. He looked up to meet the other man's emotionless grey gaze and said in a low voice,

"M'lord, you should not say such things to me..."

The nobleman shrugged indifferently.

"Why not? You knew it anyway! As I have known for... what? It has been over a score of years now that Ariène and I have been bound... That, my friend, is a long time to live entrapped, knowing there is no escape from her web save her death or mine!"

"M'lord..."

"No, enough of self pity. That is not why I requested that you meet me here. Nor do I have much time to spare. I must be on my way as soon as I have spoken with you. At least there will be light enough to ride. The moon is almost full, the gods guard me, and the night is clear."

Cailen glanced uneasily up at the darkening sky and shivered slightly at the sight of the nearly perfect circle of the moon. Making the sign to avert evil, he looked more closely at the other man, aware that only severe need would drive any male Mithlondian – child or adult, peasant or nobleman – to travel by night under the treacherous light of a full, or nearly full moon.

"You are bound for Lamortaine, are you not?" he said abruptly, his words and style of speech suddenly less provincial, more akin to his lord's clipped speech. "I saw the royal messenger ride by just before dawn and wondered then what tidings he brought. I doubted it could be anything good."

"There is not much that passes you by, is there?" Louis replied, the hint of a grim smile in his voice. "I can only hope that you were the only one with wits awake at that god'forsaken hour." Then all hint of levity left him as he continued urgently. "Listen, Cai, this must not become common gossip but Prince Marcus has been gravely ill this last winter, although I thought him recovering when I left Lamortaine. I should not have left him else. But I fear from this summons that I was wrong. I gave him my word I would go to him if he sent for me and he would only do so if he knew he were dying."

There was a long moment of silence as Cailen assimilated these unwelcome tidings and then waited for his lord to tell him the reason he had gone out of his way to seek him out before he left.

Finally Louis sighed softly and said,

"I may well be starting at shadows but the Prince's messenger was not the only visitor to the castle today. You have seen no other strangers, Cai?"

"Strangers in plenty, my lord. Both in the streets and down at the harbour. I'd expect that, mind, with several ships put into port today. But none I saw who roused my suspicions." He looked more closely at the other man. "So who, or what, is this one stranger who is troubling you?"

Again there was silence between them. Then, rather reluctantly Cailen thought, almost as if the nobleman was talking to himself, he said,

"Perhaps my fears for Marc and my concern for my daughters are causing me to lose all grasp on common sense." Then slowly, thoughtfully, he replied to Cailen's question. "The one I speak of calls himself Guy of Montfaucon..."

Cailen felt his heart lurch at the name of that village so close to the place where he himself had been born but thankfully Louis did not seem to notice his reaction, continuing, "He claims to be a wandering harper and may be, for all I know. He has certainly demonstrated no lack of skill in playing the instrument he carries with him. Yet even so, Cai, I cannot find it in me to trust him. Something is wrong. Very wrong! But I cannot put my finger on what it is. I would have sent him on his way after giving him a meal but my lady asked that he might be permitted to stay for a few days more and the gods know that is cause for suspicion in itself!" Cailen gave a snort of agreement which Louis responded to with a flicker of a smile. "You are right! Ariène has never given more than lip service to the laws of hospitality before, particularly with regard to welcoming chance-come beggars into our hall. So why this one? Still, as I said, I could well be seeing evil where none exists." A frustrated note crept into his level voice. "Hell'sdeath, Cai! I would swear I have never met the man before and yet... there is that about him which I know I should recognise. At the same time I cannot, in all justice, throw this harper into a dungeon simply because I mislike his face or because he does not speak with an obvious Valennais accent!"

"More's the pity," Cailen grunted. "If 'twould set your mind at rest, my lord, 'twould be well worth it." He thought for a moment. "I've to take some cloth up to the castle tomorrow for the Lady Ariena and I will take a look at this stranger for you, if I can. 'Though there's precious little I can do about it even if I do recognise him. Not so long as he stays under her protection. You said he did not speak with a Valennais accent? Did you detect any accent at all to indicate where he had come from?"

"Not even a whiff of a Rogé accent, if that is your meaning?" Louis replied. "No, that would be too obvious, Cai. If Black Joffroi wanted to put a spy in my household he would not use a man so easily connected to him. But neither would I expect him to be able to persuade or even coerce a Valennais into working for him."

"No, not if this man is a Valennais," Cailen agreed grimly. He stared eastwards along the quiet river. "Still... there is some shadow lurking out there. That is not your imagination at work, my lord, for I have felt it too. Heard it in the silence of the border guards along the Larkenlye. And now this news that Prince Marcus is dying... When that becomes public knowledge, the whole realm will be thrown into disarray and turmoil. And young Linnius, is he strong enough to control the High Counsel? Pray gods the Guardians cleave to him and not to the loudest voice in the Counsel Chamber!"

"I have some faith that the Guardians at least will do their duty by Linnius, even though he comes too young and as yet untried to the rule of Mithlondia," Louis said, an odd note in his voice that Cailen could not quite interpret. It sounded not unlike a sort of grim pride. "Even if the High Commander wavers, their newly appointed Second will not. I only pray to the gods that he does not draw too much notice until he has established himself. He is not much older than Linnius himself and, for all his understanding of the politics of power and my belief that he has the courage to stand for what he believes to be right, I doubt he can yet take on the sort of opposition he will find himself facing and win."

"Who?" Cailen queried, not having heard of this recent change in the leadership of Mithlondia's army.

"Joscelin de Veraux," Louis said flatly, looking Cailen straight in the eyes, his own a piercing silver.

"What? Prince Marcus's bastard!" Cailen's tone was blank with astonishment and his phraseology correspondingly unsubtle.

"Yes."

"Well, that's a bit of dirty royal linen I never expected to be hung up for public view," Cailen muttered. "I did not realise he had been sent to serve with the Guardians. His grandsire's doing rather than his father's, I suppose?" He regarded his lord's emotionless mask with a dawning frown, trying to understand what was eluding him. "You obviously think the lad is in danger, my lord. From something other than a barbarian spear, I mean, or a kinsman's knife! Surely you do not think Lady Ariena would involve herself? I know there was some ill-feeling between her and the Lady Céline but the boy's a by-blow at best and his mother's been dead these twenty years." He hesitated, then asked, "My lord, forgive me but do you have any idea of what your lady might be about?"

"No, unfortunately I have not the slightest notion what foul web she is weaving now," Louis replied bluntly. "Or even whether she is responsible for any of the troubles currently sweeping the realm. I cannot think that she has the power to cause such a lethal recurrence of Marcus's illness, not from a hundred leagues away. Closer to home though is another matter. Hence my unease about the arrival of this harper at this particular time. To lose Marcus were sorrow enough but my heart tells me that my lady-wife will not hesitate to use my daughters to cause me yet more grief. You know I have sent Luc to bring them home?"

Cailen nodded and Louis continued,

"They will be here soon, if the sea gods grant them swift and safe passage. But it is when they arrive that I truly fear for them. Ariène knows the only power she has left to hurt me is through my children. Any of them but my daughters are most vulnerable to her spite — and she will surely know it."

He reached out suddenly and placed his hand on Cailen's brawny shoulder, his fingers tightening in a painful grip.

"If I do not return from Lamortaine... No, Cai, do not interrupt! If anything should happen to me, or to Luc, I would entrust my daughters to your guardianship. Will you accept this trust? And consider well before you do, Cai, for it will bring you into direct conflict with Ariène and that avaricious whoreson who covets both her and my lands..." Louis broke off, frowning. Then continued with uncharacteristic introspection, "You know, Cai, it is a strange thing. His soul is surely as black as the deepest pits of Hell but I could almost find it in my heart to pity him. The gods know we were never friends but since the day Ariène chose me over him he has become my deadliest enemy... even though he must surely know it was not for myself but for my wealth that she chose as she did. Yet still he hates me, with a ferocity that is matched only by his desire for her... Mark my words, Cai, one day he will succeed in his ambitions. He will see me dead. And make my wife his own. But *I* know, even if he does not, that my death will not bring him what he seeks... and by the time he does make that discovery it will be far too late. Both for him and for me. Only then, when all the golden glory he thinks to gain will be as dust in his hands, will he know why I pity him!" His voice hardened suddenly. "But neither pity nor understanding will lead me to sacrifice my daughters to his bloody ambition! Do you understand me, Cai?"

Cailen's brown eyes held Louis de Chartreux's bleak grey gaze without flinching.

"Yes, my lord, I understand you. And him too," he said grimly. "Better than you can know!"

To Cailen's relief, Louis did not question that cryptic rider merely reiterating,

"So you will accept this burden that I would lay upon you?"

"My lord, by my oath of allegiance to you I must accept your trust. Yet even without that oath I would still do this thing for you."

With that Cailen clasped Louis's proffered arm in a firm grip; not a nobleman and his servant but companions in a solemn undertaking.

"My word on it. If death or dishonour should come to you and your son, your daughters will be as my daughters. And I will give my life for them as I would for you."

Cailen hesitated a moment, aware that there was one more stage to complete for the vow to be formalised. Looking at the other man he said,

"Do you wish me to seal the oath in blood?"

Louis de Chartreux levelled a keen grey stare at him.

"You believe there is a need for blood to be shared between us two?" he asked.

Cailen shook his head.

"I do not, but mayhap you do. If that be so I will swear a blood oath to you."

This time it was Louis who shook his head.

"No, Cai, I trust you, as I always have done." He hesitated, clearly torn between the need for haste and a sudden curiosity. He started to ask a question, "Cai, I have always wondered, who are..?"

But the remainder of the words were lost as the strident sound of a horn ripped through the darkness that had fallen about them without either noticing. Both men started as they recognised the call that signified the closing of the city gates for the night and the moment for truth was lost.

Their clasp broken, Louis stepped back, pulling his hood back up over his long, silver-flecked dark hair.

"You must go, Cai, else you are like to find yourself benighted out here, and with Leofric sniffing after your blood as like as not. May the God of Light guard you, my friend."

"And you, my lord," Cailen replied, his voice tight with suppressed emotion.

He believed he could make a tolerably accurate guess at what Louis had been about to ask him before the horn had sounded and was unsure whether to be relieved or regretful that the opportunity had been lost. He had kept that particular secret for so many years now that it had become like a second skin. But he wished suddenly that he had told Louis the truth about himself and the man to whom he had sworn his first oath of allegiance, long years before he had knelt at the feet of the grey-eyed youth who had since become one of the greatest lords in Mithlondia.

Now, though, it was too late and all he could do was watch in silence as the other man slipped away into the dusk. Not long afterwards his straining ears caught the soft sounds of a horse cantering along the highway, heading for the Swanfleet Bridge. Not until the last echo had been gathered into the shadows of the silvered night did Cailen abandon his watch and return to the town.

Unlike some people, he had never been prone to premonitions. But now his heavy heart told him that he had seen Louis de Chartreux for the last time.

With which disquieting foreboding came the abrupt realisation that he had best start behaving with far more circumspection than he had been doing of late. It would help no-one if he became fish-food at Leofric's hands, least of all the two young girls whose guardianship he had now undertaken. And with that understanding came also the sudden recognition of his own ignorance in the matter of the care of any young maiden, let alone two high-born damsels who would be, when all was said and done, strangers both to him and to their own homeland.

Casting back his mind he dredged up dim memories of them as they had been ten years before; one as shy, pretty and graceful as a wood-star in spring, the other neither pretty nor graceful and as wild as one of Hell's own daemons. Not, Cailen admitted readily, that such vague impressions were of much use to him now. Ten years in the gracious and hedonistic atmosphere of the Kardolandian court must have changed them beyond all recognition; burnishing Juliène's beauty, taming Rowène's wildness. Or... maybe not?

Nevertheless those years that had gone by with the speed of the north wind, leaving him relatively unscathed, must have left their mark on them; not least in that between seven and seventeen lay a lifetime in itself. They were now old enough to be thinking of betrothal, binding and bedding. Or would they want a few more years of freedom before swearing themselves to any man? How would they think and behave, Cailen wondered in dismay. Had they inherited their father's courage and honour or would they turn out to be mirror images of their beautiful, treacherous mother?

At this moment Cailen had no way of telling what the truth of the matter would be. All he did know was that, compared to his previous task, this one would tax all his considerable talents to their limit.

As Cailen made his way back through the eerie moonlit shadows, such was his state of mind that he found that his heart was beating uncomfortably quickly in his breast and he nearly bit his tongue through when an owl swept silently down across the dark path in front of him, which now seemed longer and lonelier than ever before.

The gates had long since been shut by the time he reached the town. Despite this he experienced little difficulty in persuading the guards to unbar the smaller door set in the great iron-studded gate to allow him entry. Between the brilliant white spring moon and the flaring torchlight he was easily recognisable and a source of considerable amusement to the bored guards.

Judging from the ill-concealed grins on their faces, both the gate-keeper and the two soldiers on duty thought only that his assignation with the talented Aelfwyn had gone awry and he was returning in such undignified haste in an effort to save his face, ribs and sundry other tender parts of his body from Leofric's hammer-hard fists. Cailen ignored the ribald comments, which to his chagrin only went to prove how accurate his lord had been regarding the latest topic of gossip, and scuttled out of earshot, the perfect image of embarrassed respectability.

Once around the corner of the street, however, he straightened his shoulders and slowed his stride as he considered his next move. Despite the darkness that had so quickly swallowed up the short spring dusk it was still early and the drinking dens and eating houses would be open for a good while yet before the curfew horn sounded. Bearing in mind his lord's suspicions about the recently-arrived harper Cailen thought it advisable to conduct an impromptu round of the taverns to see what manner of strangers might be about. The harper was probably snugly settled within the castle walls but even so it was Cailen's opinion that where there was one rat, others were sure to be close by.

With the absence of any obvious two-legged rodents from the town's more reputable hostelries, Cailen found himself a quiet corner of the Swan to consume his ale and seriously consider the merits of conducting a search of the lesser drinking dens, of which Chartre had more than its fair share. Apart from the sheer impossibility of visiting them all before the curfew horn sounded, Cailen dismissed this course of action on the grounds that no man with even half his wits about him – and surely even a Rogé spy would have a grain of intelligence – would take the risk of approaching the Lady Ariène with the stench of such a place in his clothes and hair.

However by the time Cailen fell wearily onto his bed long after the midnight horn had sounded, still fully clothed and with rather too much ale swilling around in his belly, he was not feeling so sanguine. Recalling a partially overheard whisper concerning a fair-haired, blue-eyed stranger – it was mention of this unusual colouring that had snagged in Cailen's tired mind – seen down by the quay earlier, he came to the reluctant conclusion that it might prove necessary to run the risks inherent in drinking sour wine and socialising with dockside harlots after all.

Nor when he did fall asleep were his slumbers any less troublesome than his waking thoughts. Images of fierce flames and freezing mists, bloody swords and weeping women flitted around the fear-filled caverns of his sleeping mind until shortly before the dawn horn sounded he crawled out of bed, splashed cold water liberally over his face and neck and crept down the narrow, dark stairs to find something other than ale to still the complaints of his queasy belly. Only to find that his apprentice had been there before him and had left nothing in the pantry beyond the hard, inedible crusts of yesterday's bread which Cailen regarded with vocal disgust before throwing them out for the seagulls and rats to bicker over.

Thankfully, he did not have long to wait until the artisans of Baker's Lane opened their shutters and lured by the enticing scent of fresh bread Cailen summoned the energy to step outside in order to buy a couple of sweet rolls dotted with raisins and sprinkled with cinnamon – an extravagance he did not normally indulge in but felt on this occasion to be justified.

Returning to his own abode, he trimmed his already neat beard and changed his crumpled under-shirt and yesterday's stained robe for attire more befitting a wealthy merchant than a drunken sot.

Between one thing and another it was mid-morning before Cailen managed to finish loading his cart, hitch up the placid donkey and make his way up to the castle. He was as well-known to the castle sentries as those guarding the town gate the night before. Moreover they were evidently expecting him and passed him through without hindrance or question. He led the donkey towards the stable and, whilst waiting for the steward, took the opportunity for a surreptitious snoop inside.

His narrowed eyes flicked assessingly over the proud, glossy-coated horses belonging to Louis, Ariène and Luc de Chartreux, past a pair of pretty mares that were obviously destined for the young ladies of the household and then on to the less high-bred mounts kept for use by the soldiers of the garrison.

Almost at the end of the row, however, was one even Cailen could see was out of keeping with the rest of the animals in the stable; an unkempt grey mare with a ragged mane and tail who regarded his approach with sad brown eyes. A plain leather bridle and moth-eaten saddle blanket flung over the end of the stall seemed to be her only accoutrements.

Cailen would have steeled himself for further inspection save that his sharp ears caught the tuneless whistling that heralded the approach of one of the castle grooms. Hastily returning to his cart he slung the first of the heavy bundles of cloth over his shoulder and on leaving the stable, found himself confronted by the anxious steward,

"Ah, Master Cailen, there you are at last! Surely you know better than to keep Lady Ariena waiting. Gossiping with the grooms will only land both you and them in the stocks!"

Cailen embarked on a fulsome apology but the steward interrupted him with an impatient and slightly disparaging,

"Yes, yes, just hurry."

Cailen grinned to himself and, assisted by a couple of sturdy menservants, conveyed his goods up to Lady Ariène's bower, alert for any sign of Lord Louis's mysterious stranger. Despite his vigilance, he saw neither the harper nor the Lady of Chartreux – although this latter omission he regarded as a boon rather than the reverse – and having concluded his delivery and received payment from the steward, took his leave.

It was only as he was passing the partially open doorway in the high wall that surrounded the small, private garden used by the lady of the castle, that his straining ears caught the faint sounds of harp music overlaid by a woman's low, delighted laugh. He would have retraced his steps and peered through the door but with Cerdic treading almost on his heels and no further excuse to linger he confined himself to a silent curse as he continued on his way.

Over the following few days Cailen found he had neither the leisure nor the inclination to make dangerous assignations with Aelfwyn. During the evenings he prowled the taverns, drinking as little as he might and hearing precious little of interest in return for his abstinence. Nor did he ever catch so much as a glimpse of the elusive harper. From which he deduced that the Lady Ariène was determined to keep him close by her side. Nevertheless, a certain amount of gossip did leak out from behind the high castle walls, sufficient to make Cailen scowl into his ale of an evening and curse all women. Especially the wives, sisters and daughters of his fellow merchants who seemed to use his shop as a convenient meeting place where they might indulge in the latest gossip whilst picking over every shred of cloth in his shop while he attempted to preserve a guileless and amiable countenance.

He was rewarded with a wealth of rumour, some of it quite discomfortingly accurate where it touched his own former amorous activities. More than once he felt himself cringe as he caught the speculative sideways glances of certain respectable matrons of the town and cursed himself for allowing his body's need for a woman to temporarily overrule his common-sense to the extent that his private life had become public property. His more recent nightly forays into the taverns of the town were, he gathered, being put down to his desire to drown his disappointment – the word had gone out that Aelfwyn had found herself a new lover – in drink.

Cailen grimaced on hearing this and held his silence, thankful that in the way of gossip some new topic would soon rise to displace him.

To his relief this happened much sooner than he had expected and not even a week later Mistress Iorwen, the gold-smith's wife, Gundred, her sister-by-binding, and two other matrons of the town well known for their love of gossip rushed into Cailen's shop, the former obviously bursting to pass on her exciting news.

"Master Cailen," she demanded. "Do you still have that wine coloured silk I saw last month..."

"What, the one my brother said was too expensive?" interpolated Mistress Gundred somewhat maliciously, causing Iorwen to scowl at her and Cailen to intervene hastily.

"Indeed I do, Mistress Iorwen. But, if I may be so bold, what is the cause of your excitement?"

"My husband says I am to have the silk..." This with a triumphant look at her sister-by-binding before returning her attention to Cailen. "Lady Ariena sent for him first thing this morning, up to the castle. You'll never guess why."

Resisting the facetious temptation to ask whether Master Lorchan had finally been caught red-handed mixing his gold with baser metals and was destined for the stocks, Cailen contented himself with shaking his head and attempting to look intrigued.

Mistress Iorwen turned the full force of her gap-toothed smile on him and said,

"Lady Ariena has commissioned him to make a set of binding bracelets of red gold and cornelians, to be ready by midsummer, and to be engraved with the letters R and J."

Despite himself Cailen could not prevent himself taking a sudden, painful breath that, taken with the other women's squeals of excited interest, amply rewarded Mistress Iorwen's sense of importance, already bolstered by the promise of a length of wine-coloured silk.

The four women promptly embarked on a lengthy discussion of the intriguing possibilities of those initials, even as they inspected the silk in question. R obviously meant the Lady Rowena – unless it were the Lady Juliena, of course. But they could not decide to their satisfaction which of the many J's – or was that R's – among the Mithlondian nobility was her intended lord-by-binding.

Overtaken by a dark despair he could not remember ever experiencing before, Cailen could only pray to the God of Light that the man in question was not the one who had sprung with such stunning force to the forefront of his own mind. But surely not even the devious Lady Ariène de Chartreux would consider binding one of her innocent seventeen-year-old daughters to a man over twice her age? A man moreover whom Cailen had long suspected of being her own lover!

That was a sufficiently nauseating prospect in itself until Cailen abruptly remembered that the man had a brother whose given name began with R. A man whom Cailen had not seen for several years but whose reputation as a ruthless soldier and a whoremongering lecher set him on a par with his elder brother and who, even if he had been as pure and innocent as fresh-fallen snow, would still not have been a fit mate for either of Louis de Chartreux's daughters.

Then, two days later, a messenger passed through Chartre wearing the dark green and silver livery of Lord Guillaume de Veraux. That meant little to Iorwen and her gaggle of friends but, possibly because his recent conversation with his lord had brought it to his mind, he found himself recalling all the details of the old scandal involving Lord Guillaume's eldest daughter Céline and Prince Marcus, and the child born of that liaison; a son whose given name was, as his lord had reminded him, Joscelin.

On the face of it, despite his illegitimate birth and consequent lack of land and title, Joscelin de Veraux was, to Cailen's mind at least, a far more suitable match for Rowène de Chartreux than the man whose name had first struck his suspicious mind. But as he considered the matter further a niggling worm of doubt gnawed its way into his cautious approval; some deep-seated instinct surfacing to warn him that Louis de Chartreux knew nothing of this betrothal and would be furious when – or if – he learned what meddlesome games his wife was playing with their daughter's life. And all this before the poor girl had even returned to the land of her birth!

Louis, however, was not in Chartre to either contest or confirm the arrangement. Nor could Cailen go to Lamortaine to seek out his lord. The problem was not that Cailen hesitated to leave his shop, for he had done it many times in the past, ostensibly travelling in the furtherance of his business, in actual fact on his lord's errands. His apprentice had proved himself perfectly competent to run the shop in his master's absence, so long as Cailen was not gone too long. No, the trouble lay in the fact that Louis' daughters would be returning any day now and his lord had made it perfectly clear that *their* safety and happiness was now Cailen's priority. That being so, he could not afford the risk of not being in Chartre when they arrived, bearing in mind the length of time it would take him to travel the two hundred odd leagues to Lamortaine and back again.

Nor – though this was something he would not realise until later – would it have done any good if he had.

For now, all Cailen knew for certain was that he was stuck in Chartre and, whilst there, could do little more than wait with the patience of long practice and watch both the castle and the sea.

During that tense time he never managed to lay eyes on the harper even once but in the early hours of a day that was suddenly more summer than spring Cailen found himself drawn down towards the harbour. The brilliance of dawn was still in the air, giving an unusual clarity of line to the towers and battlements of the sandstone castle, the haphazard roofs of the town below and the cultivated lands that sloped away beyond, an ordered chequerboard of red soil and fields already greening with sprouting barley and peas, interlaced with hedgerows white with thorn blossom.

This early in the day the harbour was still quiet, the men from the ships and the whores of the quayside taverns still sleeping off the night's excesses, and with a grunt of satisfaction Cailen sat down on a wooden bollard, glancing by force of habit across at the beacon on South Point.

For a long moment he thought his sleep-starved eyes were deceiving him and that he was merely imagining the first flicker of a red-gold flame. Until a startled shout from behind him assured him that he was seeing true. The beacon was indeed alight and even as his gaze dropped to the pale line of the horizon, a white-sailed ship slipped gracefully around the Point and into the calm blue waters of Chartre Bay.

The ship was too far off as yet for his eyes to distinguish the swan prow or the pennant flying from the mast but Cailen *knew*; by the grace of the gods, Rowène and Juliène de Chartreux had come home at last.

# Chapter 2

## *Strangers All*

On board that swan-prowed, white-sailed ship, safely out of the way of the busy sailors, the two returning noblewomen stood on deck, one as close to the bow as she could get, gazing eagerly out over the shimmering, sun-splashed waters towards the curving line of the harbour wall, beyond which neat, white-washed, flower-bedecked houses nestled between the wide river mouth and the sandy heights behind.

In marked contrast, her sister stood at the stern of the ship, her clouded gaze never leaving the distant southern horizon until it finally disappeared from sight behind the perilously sharp-edged cliff she had heard the sailors calling Gull's Beak. Alerted by the almost unintelligible shout from the look-out stationed in the basket at the top of the mast, she finally turned to face her destination.

She glanced briefly at the pretty, sun-warmed town that so plainly beguiled her sister but her own pale, beautiful features betrayed no spark of interest. Nor indeed any emotion at all. Awareness of the great red-walled castle on the heights above had her shrinking back against the ship's rail and not even the flickering gold, blue and silver of her father's banner as it flew from the topmost tower had the power to ease the trepidation that now quivered alongside the aching sadness in her heart. Stifling a sigh, she turned and carefully walked the length of the ship until she was standing beside her sister.

Sensing her presence, Rowène reluctantly withdrew her hungry, questing gaze from the sunlit shore. They were not there yet but just the sight of her birthplace caused her to take a deep breath and smile at her sister.

"Well, Ju, there it is! Chartre! Home at last..."

"May the gods grant you joy of it," muttered the dark-haired young man who had come up in time to overhear his sister's exuberant remark.

Rowène half turned to glance enquiringly at her brother over her shoulder, her joyous smile withering at the openly sardonic expression in his grey eyes; eyes that Ju had told her, just the other day, were the exact same colour as her own. She hoped it was only colour they shared, rather than expression; she could not imagine looking at anyone as cynically as Luc was looking at her.

Still somewhat wary of the brother she had seen only briefly and intermittently over the past ten years, she made a cautious appeal,

"Oh, Luc, why the long face? Surely you are as pleased to have us home as we are to be here? We have missed you and Father so much."

Luc had not been in the best of humours since the moment when he had set eyes on his sisters for the first time since their twelfth summer but even his strained temper could not withstand the wistfulness in Rowène's eyes and voice, a wistfulness that had been present at their last farewell some five years before. Managing a smile he said slightly less acerbically,

"Of course I am glad to see you again. I was merely endeavouring to warn you that your life here is going to be very different from that to which you have become accustomed." His face darkened again as he regarded their cloaked forms. "The gods only know how I am to get you up to the castle," he muttered in some exasperation. "You cannot ride and you certainly cannot walk. Nor appear anywhere clad as you are!"

"Walk!" echoed Juliène in disbelief. "I should think not." Just as Rowène loosened her cloak so as to be able to inspect the light silk tunic she wore, saying doubtfully,

"I know we have been at sea for five days but I did not think our appearance was that bedraggled."

To her amazement her brother grabbed the edges of her long, dark blue cloak and rather roughly jerked them together.

"You obviously do not remember this," he snapped. "But in Mithlondia high-born ladies are not in the habit of showing themselves in public attired in nothing but their shifts – which, in effect, is what you are wearing. Now, for all our sakes, you will do as I say and keep yourselves covered at all times. Gods above! Do not tell me that you rode around Kaerellios dressed like that! Though, given Juliène's very obvious dismay, I suppose I can assume you did not walk anywhere."

Thus directly challenged, Juliène appeared rather taken aback and finally said, with a hint of brittle defiance,

"Of course we did not ride, Luc. Or walk. We used the litters, as everyone does there."

"Litters carried by slaves, I suppose?" Luc snapped. "That my sisters..." He bit off the rest of his comment but from the contemptuous curl of his well-formed mouth his sisters guessed that most of the things they were accustomed to do, wear and eat would find scant favour with him.

Following their reunion with Luc it had taken them very little time to discover that their only brother had matured into a somewhat brusque young man who had scant patience with the hedonistic ways of the Kardolandian court, very little aptitude for the subtle courtesies that prevailed there and no sympathy whatsoever with its long-established use of slaves. Indeed one of the biggest slave markets outside of the Eastern Isles was to be found in Kaerellios, a fact his sisters had already decided it was probably best not to remind him of.

Clearly torn between irritation at his sisters' incomprehension and frustration at his own inability to amend the situation, Luc could only relieve his feelings by swearing under his breath and stalking away, leaving Rowène to watch her brother's retreat with puzzled dismay before turning back to survey the rapidly approaching quayside.

"Do you think Father will be there to meet us?" she asked her sister hopefully. Getting no response she glanced sideways at Juliène and was horrified to see she had gone even paler than her magnolia-petal complexion warranted. "Ju, what is it? Are you feeling unwell again? Oh surely not this close to land?"

For Juliène had proved to be a poor sailor and had been sick more often than not, even though the ship's master had assured them that the sea could scarcely have been any calmer.

"No, it is not that," Juliène replied on an unhappy sigh, her green eyes filling with tears. "I just wish I could have stayed in Kaerellios. That was home. Not this place I can barely remember. I do not know how you can be so excited, so eager to be back. We are going to be strangers here, Ro. And, as if that were not bad enough, you know full well *she* will soon separate us, binding us to whichever nobleman she believes offers the greatest advantage to *her!*"

Rowène looked up, not a little startled at her sister's bleak appraisal of the situation.

"I did not realise you felt it as deeply as that. But it is in the nature of things that we must wed. And it need not all be for our mother's gain. Ju, you are so beautiful and so gentle of heart, surely some nobleman will fall in love with you for your own sake. Would you not wish for that?"

"And you, Ro?" Juliène queried, turning the question without answering it.

Rowène shrugged inelegantly and replied without rancour,

"What man of any rank would be willing to take me without a sack of gold to sweeten the deal? Aside from the fact that I can make no claim to beauty, one look at my hair would be enough to make any man think twice before paying court to me. Even in Kaerellios – and the gods know the Kardolandians are liberal enough in most things – I have heard them whisper *witch* when they look at me. In all honesty do you expect a *Mithlondian* nobleman to be more tolerant?"

The look of discomfort in Juliène's green eyes was enough to tell Rowène that she too was fully aware of the inbred wariness with which men tended to regard her flame-haired sister but after a moment she answered her honestly.

"No. Or not unless their reputation lies. Then again," Juliène offered hesitantly. "Perhaps neither of us will be bound to a Mithlondian? After all, is not all set for Princess Linette to wed one of the Kardolandian princes?"

"Or it might be that we will not wed at all?" Rowène suggested, her head tilting as she considered the idea. "Mayhap that would not turn out so ill. Perhaps I could become a healer in the Grey Sisterhood? Surely that would be better than being sold to some nobleman who would use me for his own purposes and care nothing for me."

"Ah, Ro! Now you are daydreaming indeed!" her sister remonstrated with a softly bitter laugh. "The Lord of Chartreux's daughter permitted to become a healer, living in poverty and at the beck and call of all? No, it could never happen. And I must admit I do not think I could willingly embrace that life myself; almost anything would be better than that. Having said that, if it were a choice between that and living the rest of my life in *her* shadow... I do not know."

"Well, I do," Rowène replied flatly, her gaze inexorably drawn to the red walls of the castle and the one tall tower that rose high above the square keep and long curtain wall.

"Do you suppose she has changed at all since we left?" Ju asked, her voice dropping to the merest whisper, as if afraid that the white gulls presently wheeling above them would capture her words and carry them to her mother's ear.

Rowène shivered suddenly as a chill breath of wind touched her cheek and she drew her cloak closer about her shoulders.

"Do you remember what we used to call her, Ju?"

Juliène shuddered in reply and whispered,

"We called her the Winter Lady. Oh Ro! I do not want to have to live with her again. I am afraid of her..."

"I know, Ju. And I am frightened of her too. But we must not let her see it. We must be brave – for Luc's sake and for Father's. They would not expect us to cringe and cower in front of her."

With an effort Juliène straightened her slender shoulders and forced a smile.

"You are right. And look, we are nearly there. But... gods above, Ro! What are all those people doing? There must be full half the folk of Chartre gathered on the quayside."

"Waiting to welcome you home." Luc spoke suddenly from behind them. Then he lowered his voice. "Now, when we dock, make sure you stay close to me. And for pity's sake..."

"Yes, we know, keep ourselves covered." Rowène interrupted. "Though I must say, Luc, I am grateful that Father thought to send us these cloaks. I had forgotten how much cooler than Kaerellios it is here, even when the sun is shining."

"Just wait until it rains!" Luc replied, an unexpected grin lightening his own sleet-grey eyes and rendering his lean, rather stern countenance fleetingly less forbidding.

As the ship came into the crowded, busy harbour, Rowène looked eagerly towards the quayside. At the forefront of the crowd of staring, waving, chattering townsfolk she picked out three magnificent horses; a big, dappled grey gelding and two smaller mares, one as white as starshine, the other the colour of honeysuckle. Two men whom she took to be grooms stood at their heads, their light blue tunics emblazoned on the shoulder with the silver swan of Chartreux.

"Good, news of our arrival must have reached the castle," she heard Luc mutter behind her. "I am surprised that Father is not here to meet us though."

"Yes, but... those horses," Rowène queried tentatively. "They are not for Ju and I, surely? It has been ten years since we last rode."

"It will come back to you," Luc said dismissively. Then he grimaced as he evidently remembered their unsuitable garb. "The gods know it would be easier if you could walk, dressed as you are – if dressed is the word – but that would cause even more comment. No, you will just have to do the best you can not to shame the name we share."

Rowène blinked at the sudden cold anger in Luc's voice, wondering if it was directed solely at his sisters or whether there was some other cause to arouse his ire, but did not waste her breath in a reply. Five days in Luc's company had taught her that arguing with him was next to useless. Instead, as the ship drew gently against the harbour wall and the sailors on board began shouting and casting ropes to the men waiting on the quay, Rowène concentrated her attention on the vivid sights, sounds and smells – not all of them strictly pleasant – of the land she had not seen for ten years. At last they were home.

But her pleasure, already tempered by the dismayed realisation that her sister did not share her joy, was now further dampened by an acute disappointment that their father was not there on the quayside to welcome them. Comforting herself with the reflection that he was probably busy and would be waiting for them up at the castle, she accepted Luc's hand down the narrow gangway.

He returned to the ship immediately to escort Ju but Rowène was content enough to stand where he had left her on the solid cobbles of the quayside and wait while her legs adjusted to the abrupt absence of the rolling waves beneath her feet.

"'Twon't feel so strange in a bit, maid," offered a rotund, middle-aged man in a plum-coloured robe who was perched on a nearby bollard. He pushed himself to his feet and continued amiably, "Once ye gets yer land-legs back, I mean."

Considerably surprised at being thus addressed, Rowène glanced a little askance at the man but taking in his guileless brown eyes, the hint of grey in his neat brown beard and short curling hair and his eminently respectable attire, found herself giving him a diffident smile. It had been so long since anyone had called her "maid" and, highly inappropriate though it was, it *was* the voice of her homeland. The merchant, or so she assumed him to be, bowed low and said in an appreciably less broad accent,

"By rights 'tis not my place to say it but, on behalf of all of us here, welcome home, m'lady."

"Thank you," she replied, her smile softening her features and causing the merchant to blink, his regard intensifying. Acutely embarrassed by this reaction, she glanced around for her brother and found him standing just behind her with Ju, the latter staring as if mesmerised at the restless horses, her green eyes dark with dread and her mouth set in a manner that Rowène knew reflected her deep unhappiness but which would probably appear to a stranger – and the gods knew they were all strangers here – as merely sullen.

"Cai!" she heard Luc exclaim, then continue in rapid common speech as he came over to the man in the plum-coloured robe. "Touting for business already?" And, turning back to Rowène, lapsed back into Mithlondian with something between a grin and a grimace. "This is Master Cailen. He has a very fine mercer's establishment just off the main market square in Castle Street, which I am sure you will become very well acquainted with in the days to come." And reverting to the vernacular, "Cai, as I am sure you must have guessed, these are my sisters, the Lady Rowena and Lady Juliena."

Rowène nodded at Master Cailen, who obligingly bent his stocky body in another low bow. His bearded face still wore an expression as bland as buttermilk but she caught the hint of a sharper glitter in his dark brown eyes. Perhaps it was no more than avarice; the man was of the merchant breed after all and such a one was probably always on the lookout for the chance to further fill his coffers. His interest in herself and her sister could not possibly be personal.

Still somewhat disconcerted by the contradictions she thought she had observed in the merchant, it was almost a relief to follow Luc towards the restive horses. Nodding at the groom, he stopped by the honey-coloured mare and turned to Rowène.

"Ready?" he asked.

"As I shall ever be," she muttered and held her cloak tight about her as Luc bent to pick her up in his arms and lift her high onto the saddle. She gasped and flung out a hand, twining her fingers tightly in the coarse creamy strands of the mare's mane, then looked down into her brother's questioning grey gaze and nodded with more confidence than she actually felt.

"I will be all right. But Luc, please be gentle with Ju. She is even more nervous about this than I am."

She watched as Luc settled Juliène securely on the back of the milk-white mare and was somewhat reassured to note that he stood beside her for a little while, talking in a low voice as he gentled both nervous mare and rider. Slightly envious of this bonding, she tightened her grip as her own mount moved beneath her but thankfully the groom still stood at its head and Rowène relaxed her grasp long enough to gather her cloak more securely around her. Seated on her precarious perch, with the sea breezes tugging treacherously at her mantle, she was becoming increasingly conscious that Luc had been right about the differences in raiment between Mithlondia and its southern neighbour.

Impatient now to get up to the castle and change into something more acceptable to local eyes, Rowène looked around for Luc and was slightly surprised to find he was no longer with Juliène. Rather he was standing by the grey gelding, fiddling with the girth straps and, to Rowène's mingled amazement and annoyance, appeared to have fallen into casual conversation with the silk merchant.

Or perhaps not so casual.

The two grooms were talking quietly between themselves as they stood at the mares' heads and Rowène was reasonably sure that they were paying no attention either to their young master or the merchant. She might have been likewise content to ignore them had it not been for the words she had just heard Luc utter in a low, hurried voice,

"Where is my father, Cai? I thought he would have been here."

"Gone back to Lamortaine, Master Luke. Very next day after ye left. Urgent summons from the Prince, he said. An' there's been no word from him since. Best keep yer wits about ye. There's trouble brewing for sure."

"What sort of trouble, Cai? Damn it, man, you must have some idea, else you would not have been waiting for me here like this!" she heard him hiss.

The merchant grimaced in what she took to be frustration, that same emotion spilling over into his voice as he growled something that to Rowène's straining ears sounded like,

"Don't know what sort. All I know is, yer lady mother's got herself a new lackey. Turned up here the same day as yer father left. His lordship reckoned as there was something not quite true about him but he was called away afore he could do aught about it."

"So who is he, this lackey? Quick, Cai, I cannot linger much longer."

"Aye well, he calls hisself Guy of Montfaucon. I hasn't heard him talk meself so I can't say whether his accent bears that out or not. Yer father seemed to think not. Aside from that, all I know is that he *sez* he's a harper. An' mebbe he is. But I reckon he's more than that. So watch yerself, young master. An' keep your sisters close. Ye knows how to find me when ye needs me."

With which the merchant – who suddenly seemed neither quite so respectable and definitely not harmless to Rowène's watching eyes – faded back into the crowd and Luc swung himself up into his saddle, a frown drawing his narrow dark brows together in a look that did not invite questions, even had she felt inclined to ask him any in such a very public setting.

Nevertheless, it was beginning to appear as if fending off an unwanted betrothal was not the only thing she and Ju might have to worry about and that their return to Mithlondia was far more fraught with menace than she had ever imagined it could be when she had sat watching the play of sunlight on the sparkling fountains that splashed amongst the flower-filled gardens of the royal palace in Kaerellios, wishing only to be home again.

The gauntlet of the narrow, cobbled streets crowded with townsfolk throwing flowers and calling cheerful greetings was behind them and Rowène breathed a small sigh of relief as they rode under the shadowed arch of the town gate, past the grinning guards on duty and drew to a halt in the castle courtyard. Thankfully handing the reins over to the groom who had accompanied her up from the quayside she slipped down from the mare's back into her brother's upraised arms. She waited while he performed the same service for Ju, frowning once more at her sister's extreme pallor and the dark dread that lurked in the depths of her jewel-green eyes.

But whatever was worrying Ju – and Rowène knew it was more than just fear of their mother and anxiety over some putative betrothal – there was little she could do to aid her; only love her as she had always done and help her as and when she could. She just wished she had some idea what was troubling her sister...

"Come along then," Luc's curt tones interrupted her thoughts. "It is not wise to keep our lady mother waiting."

Rowène grimaced as she exchanged a look of grim agreement with Ju, then tucked one hand into the crook of the arm her brother held out to her, holding her mantle closed with the other.

As she walked across the courtyard she looked around her eagerly in an attempt to match her hazy memories to the noisy, bustling reality of Chartre castle. All around them men and women going about their daily business paused to tug forelocks, dip curtsies or mutter shy greetings. The children, less impressionable or merely less interested in the return of the Lord of Chartreux's daughters, took little notice of their arrival but continued running and shouting amidst the scratching chickens and cursing men. From the far corner of the bailey came the clang of iron from the smithy and horses neighed in the stable block; all the sights and sounds, not to mention the smells – baking bread and roasting meat mingling with the more pungent odour of horse manure – that she had remembered in her dreams but which were now so overwhelming she could scarcely appreciate them.

Nor, as she looked around again, did she see many faces she recognised, while those she did were more worn and wrinkled than she remembered; a reminder, if she had needed one, how much life had changed in those ten years of exile, not only for herself but for those she had left behind. Pray gods her father had not changed irrevocably in the two years since he had last visited her and Ju, all too briefly, in Kaerellios.

The next moment they passed from the brightness of the early morning sunshine into the comparative darkness of the great keep. Shivering now from cold as well as tension, Rowène drew her thick cloak even more closely about her. Cerdic the steward came to greet them and she was pleased to see that he, at least, appeared little altered by the years. Then she found herself wondering whether perhaps he had changed more than she had thought; there was a twitchiness about him that she did not remember or mayhap it was only her brother's lifted black brows that caused the steward to curb his remembered propensity to gossip and chatter.

Finally, they proceeded alone up the wide shallow stairs to the upper floors where their mother's bower, their father's strong room and their parents' bed chambers were located. By unspoken consensus they halted outside the bower and Rowène exchanged a nervous glance with her sister before looking at her brother for reassurance. Luc, however, seemed almost as reluctant to enter as they were themselves, although he did manage to dredge up a crooked smile for their benefit. Visibly bracing himself, he raised his hand to rap firmly on the door. A melodic voice bade them enter and taking a collective breath they took the plunge together into the unknown icy depths.

Disconcertingly, once inside, Rowène found herself in a large, luxuriously appointed chamber shimmering with golden sunshine and sweet music. Blinking slightly after the cool darkness of the passageway, she found her gaze drawn inexorably towards the woman who sat in the high-backed chair set in the very centre of the room. She had all the grace and dignity of a queen, her uncovered hair braided into an intricate coronet that flamed like fire in the sunlight while her eyes, glittering in the pearlescent perfection of her face, were the same icy green as the gemstone that hung on a silver chain between her breasts.

*Dear God of Mercy*, Rowène thought with an uncontrollable shiver, *she is more beautiful and deadly than ever.* Then tore her eyes away before she succumbed to the dangerous enchantment she could feel tingling in her own blood and, for want of anywhere better to look, turned her gaze on her mother's companion.

The shards of cold terror transmuted into shock as her eyes fell upon the figure in the window seat. Not a female attendant making music while her mistress embroidered, but a man. A man who held a harp against one broad shoulder, his fingers abruptly stilled on the strings as his light blue eyes met hers in that first moment of mutual startlement. His lips moved soundlessly as he lurched to his feet, still clutching his harp, and Rowène became aware of her mother's silken voice saying graciously,

"Welcome home, my daughters." And in answer to a curt question from Luc. "No, regrettably your father is not here at present. Prince Marcus required his presence at court. But, as you can see, I have been very well entertained in his absence." Then, as the silent musician flushed in palpable discomfort, Lady Ariène added smoothly, "I do not believe you have met our household harper yet, Luc, but this is Guy of Montfaucon; a man of many skills I do assure you."

*What skills?* Rowène wondered bitterly. *Do his talents lie solely with his ability to make sweet music or do they extend to warming my mother's bed?*

Guy stood frozen for perhaps three more heartbeats, his gaze ensnared by a pair of cool grey eyes that betrayed all too clearly their owner's thoughts. Words of protest rose instinctively to his lips but he choked them back, knowing that he had no choice other than to allow Lady Ariène to direct the course of this meeting. But gods! Now that it had come to it he wished he were anywhere but Chartre castle. Even starving in the gutter would be preferable to the pattern of his life from this moment on – and starving in the gutter is where he would be if he did not take a grip on himself!

In the long moments of silence that followed, the Lady Ariène set a few more minuscule stitches in the garment she was embroidering and Guy managed to bring his wayward conscience under control so that when she finally looked up from her stitchery, her limpid green eyes moving slowly from her son to her two daughters before coming to rest on him, he was ready to step back into his role.

"Thank you, Guy, your playing is flawless, as always," she said lightly.

"Thank you, my lady," he reciprocated tonelessly. "With your permission then, I will leave you alone with your family. You will not want a stranger with you at such a time."

"No, stay, a little music will not go amiss. Nor, as you know full well, do I count you a stranger."

There was a distinctly discomforting intonation to her last words that told him quite plainly there was to be no escape from what was to follow.

Concealing his reluctance as best he might, Guy sank back onto the window seat and settled his harp back against his shoulder. He fingered the strings for a moment and then began to play very softly, keeping his gaze firmly on the blue infinity of sea and sky beyond the window and his ears, as best he could, deaf to everything except his music.

But he could not completely block out Lady Ariène's cool, composed tones or the words she spoke to her two daughters. Gods above! Ten years away and this was how she greeted them – as strangers that she had neither need nor desire to get to know better! No kiss in greeting. No loving embrace! As the gods surely knew, the woman who had raised *him* had had no cause to love him, yet she had shown him a far greater warmth and kindness than Lady Ariène did towards her own children, her son as well as the two daughters she had not seen since they were little girls.

He risked a glance across at the two young women, trying to gauge their reaction to their mother's cool reception. There was a subdued defiance in the grey eyes of the taller girl that heartened him briefly until he found himself staring into her sister's clear green eyes, in the depths of which he discovered a fragility that hit him harder than he could ever have expected.

Disconcerted by the flash of unwelcome sympathy he felt for the two young noblewomen, he lowered his eyes to his harp, reminding himself yet again why it was that he was here in Chartre. Reminded himself also that pity for Louis de Chartreux's daughters held no place in his liege lord's plans.

Then, just when Guy thought the worst might be over for the present, he became aware that the flow of gently mocking generalisations had become more specific as Lady Ariène continued more pointedly,

"Come now, girls, it is surely warm enough in here for you to take off those cloaks. How do you expect me to welcome you properly when you stand there looking like a pair of passing travellers?"

Disregarding his own reminder not to involve himself in the forthcoming confrontation Guy glanced up again, just in time to see one of the girls flinch whilst the other cast a look of embarrassed entreaty towards her brother who, to give the man his due, did make a valiant attempt to shield his sisters from their mother's needling.

"Madame, we have been travelling for five days and I am sure my sisters would feel more at ease in your company were they given the opportunity to first wash away the salt and dirt of our journey and change into some clean clothes."

Guy turned his head a fraction and felt the shiver in his soul as the Lady Ariène smiled. It was, on the surface, a pleasant smile but it failed utterly to warm the icy emerald depths of her eyes.

"Even so," she rebuffed Luc's suggestion with deceptive gentleness. "Surely, my daughters, you can spare me a few short moments after ten long years of absence. And, besides," she added more keenly, "I have heard so much this winter about the fashions of the royal court at Kaerellios! As I am sure you must know, Princess Linette is to be betrothed to one of King Karlen's younger sons? The binding will take place in Lamortaine this summer and I should like to steal a march on the rest of the Mithlondian ladies and see for myself how these southerners dress. You are still wearing Kardolandian court attire, I suppose?"

It was hardly a question and Guy came abruptly to his feet, with every intention of leaving the room before the revelation he sensed was coming; a revelation he knew he had absolutely no right to see. Suddenly all eyes were focussed on him; two pairs of spring green, two pairs of winter grey, with expressions that ranged from autocratic surprise to panic and from open contempt to shame. Luc de Chartreux's scorn he could deal with but the sight of the girls' embarrassment made his gut twist painfully. He looked away, only to meet the full force of the Lady Ariène's displeasure. She did not speak but the perfect arch of her delicately darkened copper brows said more than words and Guy found himself dropping back onto the window seat in defeat.

Irritated by the woman though he was, he was equally mindful of his orders and determined not to betray himself again. He therefore forced himself to resume playing, his attention once again firmly fixed on his music. He could not, however, block out all awareness of what followed.

He knew the moment the taller of the girls slowly raised her hand to undo the silver and sapphire brooch of Mithlondian workmanship that pinned her mantle. He sensed the defiant motion as she pulled back her hood and dropped her cloak, allowing it to fall into a dark blue pool that touched the very edge of his shortened vision. He heard the slither of cloth as her sister, perforce, followed her example, and found himself staring at a small, slender foot shod in the daintiest of gilded leather sandals, the tiniest of pale pink sea shell nails, a pair of delicate ankles encircled by a narrow silver anklet. If the rest of her body was so sweetly enticing…

Guy could feel his body tighten in response to that thought and dared not raise his gaze any further, knowing that for all his control he was still a man, with a man's inevitable reaction to a partially clad and beautiful woman and – the gods help him – there were two of them in the chamber with him. Gritting his teeth, he concentrated on his music to the exclusion of all else. His resolution to remain uninvolved, however, grew shakier with every passing moment and although he kept his eyes down and his fingers steady he could not help but feel the distress emanating from the two girls almost as keenly as he sensed their mother's derisive amusement and their brother's silent fury.

*God of Light*, he thought grimly, *will this damnable meeting never end?* And, not for the first time, he silently consigned his liege lord to the deepest pit of Hell for coming up with this insane scheme. Cursed himself too for ever agreeing to his own part in it.

Not that he had had much choice if he wanted to retain his freedom, his position in his lord's household and his relationship with his brothers. Nevertheless, he had always suspected that the cost to his conscience would be much higher than he was prepared to pay. Now, faced with the two innocent young women he was here to help destroy, he knew he had been right.

But it was too late by far for regrets and all that was left to him was to stay in Chartre and do what he could to mitigate the devastation that must inevitably follow if his liege lord's plans came to full and bloody fruition.

With this grim resolve hardening in his mind he inadvertently lifted his eyes and caught a fleeting glimpse of the two girls. He muttered an involuntary oath and hastily looked away. But it was too late and the image he had glimpsed would remain embedded in his memory and return to taunt him in the long dark of the night.

Kardolandian fashions were indeed different from those of Mithlondia but in his, admittedly limited, experience he had never seen anything so lovely. Those two young women, he thought in bemusement, might have stood alongside the fairest spirits of immortal legend and still not looked out of place. But then, remembering the rumours that whispered of their distant kinship with the Faennari, perhaps that was not so very surprising.

Painfully aware that his guilt damned him to a place alongside his lord in Hell but, unable to prevent his weakness, he looked up once more, feeling the impact of their appearance like a fist in the gut.

Now that he saw them uncloaked, the sisters were in truth very different from each other, although each was eye-catching in her own way.

The taller of the two was a grey-eyed girl whose thin features bore an unmistakeable – and perhaps, in the circumstances, unfortunate – likeness to her father and brother. She would have been considered handsome if she had been a boy but the de Chartreux leanness and long nose did not make for a pretty woman. To make matters even worse, her hair – dressed high on her head, bound with golden ribbons and falling in softly tumbling curls down over her shoulders and breasts – was the colour of dark flame.

Shying away like a frightened horse from the word "witch-fire" he found his gaze focussing instead on the lines of her slender body, the womanly curves exquisitely emphasised by the simple tunic of amber coloured silk shot through with golden thread. The garment was clasped at the shoulders by two filigree brooches which – shocking to Mithlondian eyes, although he doubted any male, Mithlondian or otherwise, would remain unappreciative – left bare her lower legs, arms, shoulders and throat, which exposure to the hot southern sun had imparted a faint, golden patina.

Or perhaps that colouring was simply the legacy of her Faennarian forebears and, if that were so, he really did not wish to know. One enchantress casting her silver net was more than enough for him to deal with.

Realising that he was still leering at her body in the manner of a starving beggar drooling over a honey-cake, he swallowed and forced himself to look up and into her eyes.

*Gods!*

It was as if someone had slapped him, hard, across the face. She said nothing. She did not need to. She merely returned his gaze, her eyes storm grey and shimmering with tears of shame, reminding him of what he already knew; that he was a cur of the worst kind for witnessing her humiliation in this way!

Feeling as if he had violated her with his body rather than his eyes, he hastily looked away. But this new direction was no better as his glance immediately settled on the other sister. In all truth, he hated to think of them in such an impersonal manner but he had no idea at the moment which was which. Or should that be *witch*? The gods forbid!

There was, however, no doubt in his mind that the girl whose spell he was now under was the most beautiful woman he had ever seen; the lines of her oval face breathtakingly lovely, her complexion as pure as the petals of the snow stars that flowered at each full moon, while her thick cascading hair was as dark and mysterious as midnight itself. Her birch-slender yet womanly body held no flaw that his stunned gaze could see and he silently thanked the gods that his brother was far away.

For while he, Guy, might toy with the notion that, clad as she was in glimmering sea-green silk shot through with silver, with her glossy black hair and those green eyes peeping between long dark lashes, this entrancing vision was a mermaid made mortal by some witch's enchantment, still he knew that it was just that – an illusion conjured by the words of some harper's song. *He* could contain his baser urges to disinterested appreciation. His brother, he knew, would be far less restrained.

Indeed, in a time and place where illusion was rapidly outstripping reality, the only thing that kept his thoughts safely grounded was the knowledge of his liege lord's brooding presence a hundred leagues away, waiting with hard-held patience for the bloody culmination of the twisted scheme he had devised.

Reality was the acceptance that without it neither he, his liege lord or his brother, nor any of their people, would escape the death grip which poverty had now established over their land.

Reality was the knowledge that between the two of them, Louis de Chartreux's daughters were wearing more wealth in those prettily chiming bracelets than he had ever seen in his life. Daemons of Hell! Surely it was no wonder that his lord sought those riches for himself – as well as a beautiful woman in his bed, witch though she might be!

He became aware that she was addressing her daughters again.

"So, I can see now why the emissaries to Kaerellios took such pleasure in their mission and why the ladies at our court were so affronted on their return. Thank the gods you have had the sense to hide yourselves from public view since your arrival. For now, I think it would be best for all concerned if you go to your chamber and remain there until you can appear more modestly attired. And since I doubt you have anything more respectable in your baggage, is it not fortunate that I have already arranged for new gowns for you both. With a little effort on your part they will be ready for the feast this evening. Well, do you have nothing to say, no thanks for my foresight, my endeavours on your behalf?"

"Yes, thank you, Madame."

It was the taller of the two, Guy noted, who managed to force out the words as she bent to pick up the cloaks, wrapping her sister in one with a tenderly protective gesture that touched his heart, before she hastily threw the other carelessly about her own shoulders. She seemed to hesitate and then appeared to gather her wavering courage sufficiently to ask,

"Will Father be returning soon?"

"Hardly, Rowène," replied Lady Ariène with a low, liltingly musical laugh that chilled Guy to his very soul. "Your father returned to court having spent a mere three days here and only the gods know when he will see fit to return. I have no doubt he vastly prefers to be hunting or hawking in company with Prince Marcus, not to mention enjoying the warmth of his mistress' bed, rather than doing his tedious duty by his family and his people here in Chartre. Now, go to your chamber. You will need the rest of the day to ready yourselves if you are not to disgrace yourselves and me."

Listening to this cruel dismissal Guy amended his silent characterisation of Lady Ariène from witch to bitch, then watched as the girl he now knew to be Rowène de Chartreux gave her mother a stiff curtsey before pushing her shaking sister – Juliène that would be – from the room.

Their brother lingered a moment longer, his grey eyes blazing with an intense hatred, but the Lady Ariène had already returned her attention to her embroidery and clearly had no intention of listening to anything her son might say. Accepting his dismissal with another look of blistering contempt in Guy's direction, he turned on his heel and stalked from the room, shutting the door behind him with a firmness that fell just short of a slam.

Guy rose to his feet, feeling unutterably drained and weary.

"Give me leave, my lady..."

"As you will," she agreed indifferently, not raising her eyes from the black cloth she was working on. Then, just as he reached the door, she looked up, her green eyes as hard as jade and as bright as a thousand stars in the darkest night sky.

"So, now that you have seen them, which one will you choose when the time comes? Or are you content merely to take your half-brother's leavings?"

"Madame!" he choked, in his shock reverting to the language of his birth.

"Messire?" she parodied silkily, her voice mocking his outrage, her eyes challenging his body's betrayal of his honour.

Unable to deny the implications of her words, Guy gave her the briefest of bows and fled from the room as if all the daemons of the depths were after him. *Hell and damnation!* He needed fresh air and he needed it quickly!

Almost, he wished, he had gone with his liege lord to Lamortaine and let his brother conduct this miserable masquerade here in Chartre – as he could have done just as well as Guy.

Wiping the moisture from his brow with his forearm, he caught the undeniable reek of his own sweat and behind that the delicate fragrance of roses and honeysuckle. The former he thought belonged to Rowène, the latter to Juliène, but he was not sure. Damn it all to Hell, he was no longer sure of anything!

No, that was a lie. If there was one certainty in this whole bloody mess it was the knowledge that, whether he had gone to Lamortaine with his lord in his own person or come as he had to Chartre wearing this ill-fitting guise, the end result would still be the same; his lord would win all he craved and Guy and his brother would be branded alike as ravaging wolves. The only difference between them that he could see was that *he* yet had a conscience – which even now caused him to writhe under the lash of his guilt – whereas he was unsure whether his brother still possessed – or would heed if he did – that small, quiet voice that had once guarded his soul from the icy shackles of the Daemon of Hell.

Nor would he know the answer to that question until they finally arrived in Chartre.

Breathing more easily once she was away from her mother's constraining presence Rowène followed Luc as he led the way through passages she had once known so well and up another flight of stairs, this one spiralling up inside the tallest of the towers. She was unused to such stairs – the palace at Kaerellios sprawling comfortably on one level, what steps there were being wide and shallow – but just as she felt her aching legs would seize up completely, Luc came to a halt on the third landing.

Glancing over his shoulder at them he muttered,

"Our mother has ordered this chamber to be prepared for you."

Opening the door he stood aside so that they might enter, following after them into a spacious, sun-filled chamber. The walls were hung with thick tapestries and the furnishings were comfortable if not luxurious; a huge bed, curtained in blue velvet, two chairs and a table on which sat a basin, ewer and a small silver mirror. Better than this though, in Rowène's opinion, was the wide, arched window embrasure, well provided with cushions, that gave a sweeping view out over the gleaming, silver-turquoise waters of the bay below.

"This is the best chamber in the castle after our mother's," Luc was saying. "Make yourselves comfort... Hell'sdeath! What are *you* doing here?"

Rowène fairly jumped at the escalation of fury in his tone before realising that his blazing grey gaze was fixed not on her but at some point beyond her shoulder. Turning, she saw nothing obviously amiss; the only other occupant of the room being a neatly dressed young woman – obviously a servant – who hastily dipped a curtsey as she saw three pairs of eyes regarding her with varying aspects of anger, curiosity and indifference.

"Who are you?" Rowène asked when the servant failed to answer her brother's demand.

Rising from her curtsey the woman flashed a glance beyond Rowène, then hastily lowered over-bold eyes and wiped the coy smile from her face. She started to say something but Luc's icy voice cut across her words.

"Her name is Ilana and she is one of the scullery wenches."

Cheeks burning red at Luc's contemptuous words and scorching tone, the woman yet managed a defiant reply,

"Not no more, Maister Luke. 'Twere Lady Ariena herself as said as how I was ter be tiremaid ter yer sisters from now on."

Rowène glanced at her brother, brows raised. Luc's lean face tightened even more and his cold grey eyes glittered unpleasantly.

"Do not hope for too much from your new position," he warned the young woman flatly before turning his attention back towards Rowène. "If she is in any way disrespectful, send her back where she belongs and I will find someone else to act as your maid. In the meantime though it looks as if you have a busy afternoon ahead of you and some sore fingers no doubt. I must go now but I shall look forward to the pleasure of seeing you both at the evening meal."

His final words were formal and stilted but the expression that gave light to his otherwise grim grey eyes betrayed the anxiety and affection he would not show in front of the servant.

"And where is your room?" Rowène queried softly. "Just in case we need to find you."

"The room on the floor above is mine but I intend to spend some time in the guard hall and the practice yard and I would advise you not to come there in search of me – at any time! Is that understood?"

"Yes, Luc," Rowène agreed meekly. "Until later then."

With which faintly forlorn words she stood on tiptoe to press a kiss to his clean-shaven cheek. Much to her amazement Luc returned the embrace, wrapping his arms around her in a quick, wordless hug of love and welcome. He gave the same to Juliène and then, just as abruptly, he was gone, leaving Rowène alone with her sister, their servant and the materials their mother had selected for them.

All that day they kept to their chamber; measuring, cutting, sewing and eventually trying on the garments that Ilana assured them were worn by all the high-born women of Mithlondia. The pale spring sky beyond the open window was deepening to dusky blue before they were finished and by then Rowène was heartily sick of anything pertaining to fashion and fast developing a dislike for the personal servant their mother had foisted on them. Nor had Ju provided much by way of either support or understanding. She had simply retreated to one of the window embrasures with a length of obviously expensive but irredeemably ugly puce velvet and although she had set the odd stitch or two in a desultory fashion, it was clear she had no interest in the finished article. In the end Rowène had finished sewing the gown herself, with a limited amount of assistance from Ilana.

Now both sets of new raiment were complete and, in eager anticipation of the supper horn, Rowène commenced the struggle to dress. Standing barefoot on the polished oak floorboards she looked disparagingly down at herself. At the moment she was clad simply in a sleeveless shift which was not unlike her own Kardolandian tunic in length, although in quality the fine Mithlondian linen bore little comparison to the gossamer softness of silk from the Eastern Isles.

Hearing the tap of wooden shoes, she looked up to find Ilana approaching with another garment, this one a close-fitting, long-sleeved under-gown of dark ochre-coloured wool embroidered in gold about the tight cuffs. This, when donned, proved to weigh incredibly heavy on her shoulders and dragged behind her on the floor when she walked. As if that were not trial enough, Ilana then helped her into a sleeveless over-gown of dark brown velvet, fastening a belt wrought of bronze flowers around her hips. Fine silken stockings and tightly laced leather slippers completed the ensemble but by that time Rowène felt more like a hapless lark plucked from the freedom of the sky, denuded of its natural feathers, wrapped in layers of pastry and baked in an oven.

As for the chamber walls, regardless of the fine tapestries adorning them in vibrant shades of red and green and blue, they had begun to take on the appearance of the beribboned lattices of a stone cage.

Hindered by the unaccustomed weight of her gown and her depressed thoughts, Rowène walked slowly over to the small dressing table where Ilana had unpacked, and was now pawing through, their trinkets; dainty filigree necklaces, cunningly wrought bracelets and shoulder brooches, stars of turquoise and crystal and jade strung on slender lengths of gold and silver ribbon. She ran her fingers gently over the jewellery but instinctively knew better than to suggest appearing before her mother wearing any of it. Nor did she need Ilana to tell her – with a smugness unbecoming in their own tirewoman – that it was the Lady Ariena's wish that they be dressed with relative simplicity and modesty, as befitted their youth and position in the household.

Rowène did not deign to respond to that ruling but she exchanged a look with Ju that said more than words could ever have done. Whatever web their mother was weaving, the Winter Lady had no intention of being outshone by either of her two daughters. Not, Rowène reflected ruefully, that Lady Ariène had much to fear from her but her mother might just have to yield the contest, should Ju ever shed her mantle of unhappiness and smile again. With a subdued sigh, Rowène turned away from the sight of her sister's abstracted melancholy.

*God of Light! How much longer is this unnatural brooding going to last?*

Not only was it completely out of character but Rowène had no idea what to do to help Ju get over it.

Still, worrying about Ju would not help with the immediate matter of the jewellery and, having caught the acquisitive gleam in Ilana's eyes, she was determined to lock it safely away in one of their travelling chests as soon as she found the opportunity, and then hide the key.

Turning back to the servant, she asked with the merest trace of sarcasm,

"How does our lady mother wish us to dress our hair?"

"If you will allow me, m'lady..."

Ilana paused respectfully but Rowène was not deceived; the woman would do exactly as she had been bidden by Lady Ariène, no matter what her daughters might say. Picking up an ivory comb of exquisite Kardolandian workmanship she handed it to Ilana with a shrug and sat down on the stool, resigned to whatever might come.

By the time the horn rang out for the evening meal she and Ju were ready. The long cascading tresses she had been accustomed to wearing in elaborate, tumbling styles were now confined in two neat braids, these being coiled and pinned around her head and, as a final mark of respectability, covered by a headrail held in place by a circlet of twisted silk in shades of ochre and brown to match her gown. Her head, unaccustomed to the sensation of being covered in any way, was already feeling hot and itchy. Uncharitably, she wondered if Ilana had lice.

Answering the horn that called the household to the evening meal, Rowène took one step and then another towards the doorway, feeling the heavy shrouds of her new life dragging her down into the pit of despair alongside her sister, a darkness Ju had fallen into the day they had left Kaerellios.

Now all they had left was the hope that their father would return soon from Lamortaine and that, in his absence, their brother would manage to keep them all free of whatever shadowy skein their mother was spinning. For once they were caught in the Winter Lady's dark web there would be no escape.

It was with these, and other similarly dismal, thoughts occupying her mind that Rowène, accompanied by her silent sister and followed by their maid, reluctantly made her way down the narrow spiral stairway of the Lady Tower. Progress was slow due to the necessity of moving carefully in their new gowns but finally they reached the great hall of Chartre castle, only to find it already packed with all those members of the household who had come to share in the evening meal and, at the same time, seize the opportunity to gawp at the Lord of Chartreux's grown-up daughters.

Halting on the threshold, Rowène was overwhelmed by the sea of faces turned towards her, pale masks of curiosity, wariness and awe, highlighted by the glimmering golden glow of the multitude of candles in the ceiling rings overhead and the torchères along the walls. Relieved by Cerdic's bustling approach, she followed him gratefully as he led her and Ju to their places at the high table.

Once seated, she took another, slightly more comprehensive look around the hall, comparing her present surroundings to the ones she had come to take for granted over the previous ten years. Whether it was weariness or an unexpected twinge of yearning for the familiarity of the place she had left behind, suddenly she would have given all she had to return to the light, airy halls of the pink and white marble palace in Kaerellios, with its sparkling, splashing fountains, cool, crystalline pools and trailing curtains of purple and magenta kylinia flowers, the warm, languorous air spiced with the mingled scents of jasmine and orange blossom.

Not until that moment had Rowène truly appreciated quite how different the two realms were in almost every way. And if Chartre held itself to be the pride of Mithlondia, only the royal palace in Lamortaine rivalling it for comfort and cleanliness, the gods alone knew what conditions in the other provinces were like.

Still aware of the many eyes watching her every move, Rowène kept her head high and surreptitiously glanced at her father's great carven chair, biting back her wistful sigh at seeing it empty. Dear God of Light, how she wished it had been her mother who had been away at court and her father sitting here at the high table with them! Life would have been so different for them all and Ju might even have smiled again.

The grace of the gods having been asked for the meal and all those who shared in its bounty, Rowène allowed Luc to place a slice of some roasted fowl smothered in a greyish sauce on her trencher – plates apparently being an unknown amenity in Mithlondia – alongside soft green leeks and another vegetable she could not identify. Not wanting to show her ignorance, she merely thanked him and helped herself to one of the fresh white rolls from the basket on the table. A young page boy with a timid smile poured her a goblet of some rich red liquid, so different to the pale golden wines of Kardolandia, and, under cover of taking a sip, she glanced beyond her mother in the hope that Ju had found something to suit her somewhat finicky appetite.

A vain hope, she acknowledged, as she observed her sister staring with apparent loathing at what looked like a fish, complete with tail and glassy eye, which a serving man had just placed before her. Rowène did not care for the eye herself but even so thought her sister might make some effort to eat, more especially as Ju was accustomed to dining on fish of every variety. Just not this sort of fish apparently!

Contriving to watch her sister unobtrusively during the course of the long meal, Rowène was relieved to see that although Ju rejected the fish outright and only toyed with the roasted meats she did manage to eat a little of the fresh-baked wheaten bread, honeyed sweetmeats and fruit; apples that must have been kept in store from the previous autumn and exotic fresh fruits that reminded her with an aching pang of the land they had left behind.

Her own hunger satisfied, and her anxiety about her sister temporarily allayed, Rowène finally sat back in her cushioned chair and began to study her surroundings in earnest, instinctively seeking out those things that were familiar from her childhood.

The walls of the hall were still covered with huge tapestries worked with scenes depicting ancient battles fought during the conquest of Mithlondia and equally gory hunting vistas, while from the roof rafters hung long banners of pale blue and gold emblazoned with the silver swan; the colours and device of the Lords of Chartreux. The rushes on the floor might be fresh and strewn with aromatic herbs but the prevailing smell was of smoke and sweating bodies and could in no way match the heady, openly sensual scent of the Kardolandian court.

Ruthlessly suppressing this thought Rowène glanced down the hall which was gradually emptying as the various members of the household finished their meals and returned to their duties, leaving the serving men and women to clear away the debris. Hopeful that she and Ju would soon be similarly free to leave the hall and sensing Luc's restless desire to be elsewhere, Rowène turned to look at her mother, praying that she would be showing some sign of retiring. The Lady Ariène, however, seemed perfectly content to sit there, the cynosure of castle life and, her daughter had to admit, albeit grudgingly, that the golden Lady of Chartreux filled that niche very well; of unsurpassed beauty and serenely graceful, she seemed to have stepped straight out of one of the songs of old.

Her long tresses of dark-red flame were becomingly threaded with pearled strings and showed no trace of the silver of age. An intricately-worked gold necklace emphasised the smooth, delicate whiteness of her throat, while the revealing lines of her gown clung softly to a figure many a younger woman would envy. More pearls glimmered on her golden girdle and the green silk falling about her bestowed upon the Lady Ariène something of the guise of a water spirit. Her skin, seen in the soft light of the candles, radiated a golden sheen that served to enhance the illusion she was weaving so effortlessly.

Chilled to the bone by the eldritch enchantment only she seemed able to recognise, Rowène wondered irritably why her mother was bothering when the only other person now left in the hall, save her own offspring and the servants, was her new lackey. The harper... Guy of Montfaucon, that was his name... was sitting a little way off in the flickering shadows beyond the fire. He had obviously finished his meal but was nursing a tall mug of ale or cider, staring down into its depths and looking as if he wished himself anywhere but the great hall of Chartre castle. Perhaps, Rowène thought with a certain sense of satisfaction, the harper was not so much in thrall to the Winter Lady as her mother obviously wished him to be.

Before she had time to pursue that odd thought further her mother's cold voice sliced through the increasingly uncomfortable silence like a spear of moonlight piercing the darkness of a cloudy night.

"Harper! Some music to lighten the dull mood that has taken hold here. Gods above, surely this should be a night of joy?"

Clearly startled from his thoughts, the harper put down his mug, picked up his instrument and moved his stool closer to the high table, giving Rowène the opportunity to observe him far more unobtrusively than he had studied her earlier. He was dressed in the same manner as when she had first seen him, in a shabby, short-sleeved tunic of faded blue which had surely known better days, as witnessed by the shreds of yellow embroidery still clinging about the hem and neck. Well-muscled legs were encased in breeches of faded dark green wool and – a little surprisingly, Rowène thought – high boots of soft, scuffed leather. His belt held only a distinctly empty-looking purse and a long, slender dagger in a plain leather sheath.

His short, very roughly shorn hair was an indeterminate shade between fair and mouse-brown and would, Rowène considered critically, have been much improved by a wash and the use of a comb. Despite the slightly unkempt air this gave him, his weathered features were not unpleasant to look upon and his mouth, although shadowed by the beard common to any peasant, looked gentle and accustomed to smiling. There were lines of laughter too, or possibly something grimmer, etched beside his light blue eyes and carved deep between his thick fair brows.

He was, exceptionally for one of the common folk of Mithlondia, a big man. Although not as tall as her father and brother, the harper was nevertheless solidly built, with powerful shoulders and heavily muscled arms. Not, of course, that either his build or his hair colour meant anything in itself, since it was quite within the bounds of probability that somewhere in his peasant ancestry there was a very well-diluted drop of high Mithlondian blood. But even so...

As if sensing her suspicious appraisal, Guy of Montfaucon raised his eyes from his harp and across the width of the hall their eyes met in a look that was mistrustful on Rowène's part and carefully blank on his. Then the harper dropped his gaze and, running his fingers across the bronzed wires, began to play a soft, achingly sad tune. Caught up in the poignant melody, it occurred to Rowène to wonder whether her doubts – fostered primarily by the conversation she had overheard that morning on the quayside – were in any way justified since, as she was now forced to acknowledge, the man did indeed know how to play.

The remnants of the evening meal had long since been cleared away and the trestles stacked tidily against the wall ready for use the next day. The servants had withdrawn and only the family remained in the fire-lit hall. Guy continued playing as he had been ordered but as far as he could tell it was more for his own benefit than for any of the four people seated on the dais, all of whom he was doing his best to ignore.

It was, however, almost impossible to disregard them completely. Luc de Chartreux was, to all intents and purposes, more interested in honing his dagger than the subtleties of song but every now and again his keen grey gaze narrowed in Guy's direction. Of the three women, Lady Ariène was watching him with a cool smile that gave him no hint as to her true thoughts and although the lovely Lady Juliène was clearly many leagues away in thought, the wistful sadness in the depths of her green eyes made him almost as uneasy as the outright suspicion in her sister's level grey gaze.

Idly, Guy stole another fleeting glance towards that young woman. Now clad in several layers of confining Mithlondian clothing, she appeared utterly drab, redeemed only by the flash of fire from her respectably covered hair. But he had seen, all too briefly thank the gods, another side of her and he suspected that what he saw now was merely a hastily contrived mask that only partially hid her brightness, even as pale clouds covering the moon yet left a ring of rainbow light around it to betray its presence. Or was it something more powerful? Something darker? Not simply the change in clothing but the suffocating presence of her mother that had dragged her down, temporarily turning a goldfinch into a sparrow?

Or had the enchantress hidden within the colourless young woman she had become somehow picked up on his own disgust at this whole damnable situation and was now retaliating by causing chaos in his mind?

Silently cursing his unquiet conscience he played a wrong note and with a violent effort forced all thoughts of Louis de Chartreux's daughters, and his liege lord's orders, from his mind.

As if that slip of his fingers had provided her with some unseen signal, he saw the Lady Rowène rise to her feet and, with a curtsey to her mother, politely request leave for herself and her sister to retire to their chamber, giving as excuse their weariness from their journey. Lady Ariène nodded a casual assent and then glanced around the hall, presumably looking for her son. In vain, as Guy knew well, having observed Luc make a quiet escape scant moments before.

His squire, hastily summoned to account for her son's absence, bore the brunt of Lady Ariène's displeasure with a stoical lack of emotion that must,

Guy thought with irrational satisfaction, have been infinitely irritating to her. On being questioned further, the squire permitted the merest twitch of a smile behind his beard and replied in the broad local dialect that "Maister Luke" had sent him off for the night with words to the effect that, "Where he were bound he didn't need his squire along to hold his hand nor aught else neither!"

Evidently assuming from these words that Luc was intending to visit one of Chartre's numerous brothels, Lady Ariène shuddered delicately and dismissed her son's retainer with a cool glance of distaste that effectively encompassed both men and their otherwise unmentionable activities.

Guy had been watching this encounter with a good deal of hidden amusement and was consequently rather unpleasantly surprised when the lady turned her coldly knowing gaze on him and imperiously demanded to know whether he too wished to go down into the town to seek solace with the dockside whores. Guy blinked at this unexpected question which, since he did not suspect her of having any designs on him herself, he translated into being an expedient to mask what was little short of an outright order to find her errant son.

Observing that the Lady Rowène had now descended the dais steps and was within a few paces of his stool he rose hastily to his feet, not wishing to give her any further cause to regard him with contempt. He was acutely aware that her grey eyes were watching him closely as she waited for his answer to her mother's words.

His first, instinctive, response was a blunt – and completely inappropriate, given his apparent humble position in the household – rebuttal. Instead he contented himself with the relatively mild,

"I've little taste for whores, m'lady, but with your permission I should like to go down to the town. I hear the Silver Swan serves a very fine ale."

"Go then, Guy of Montfaucon," Lady Ariène murmured, adding archly, "And enjoy your... ale."

Guy bowed low to the Lady of Chartreux and her two daughters and gratefully made his own escape from the suffocating confines of the hall. He would, he decided, conduct a cursory search for Luc de Chartreux, enjoy a mug of ale in the aforementioned hostelry and return to the castle when he was certain that all three noblewomen were safely in their beds; he had no desire to be forced into further contact with any of them that night, neither the witch he had been sent to serve nor the innocents he had little choice but to betray.

# Chapter 3

## *A Betrothal is Mooted*

The sun had barely sent its golden rays skimming across the bay the next morning when Rowène woke to find Ilana hovering over her with the unwelcome news that their mother wished to see both her and her sister immediately in her bower. Exchanging a quick glance with Ju, Rowène made haste to wash and dress, all the while wondering uneasily what tidings were so urgent that they could not wait until after the morning meal. Her first thought was that some accident had befallen their father and it was with considerable dread that she entered her mother's chamber.

Luc was there already, she saw at a glance, but there was also another man present, standing unobtrusively against the far wall, and Rowène's stomach tightened painfully until she realised it was not some messenger from the royal court but rather the harper, Guy of Montfaucon. Although what reason the harper had for being there at that ungodly early hour was more than she wished to guess. The sudden, slightly nauseating, thought occurred to her that perhaps his stated intention of visiting the town the previous evening had been nothing more than a ruse and that he had instead spent the night in her mother's bed.

An embarrassed flush mantled her cheeks as she glanced at the harper, feeling a fool for hoping his light blue eyes would tell her the truth of the matter. He returned her gaze steadily and she had the unsettling sensation that he did indeed know what she had been thinking. Placing his hand on his heart he made a formal gesture of obeisance towards her, and she thought she must be twice a fool to read denial in his eyes. But for her father's sake she had to believe him.

Before she could pursue this silent communion further, Luc abruptly drew her attention away from the harper, a certain amount of impatience in his voice as he addressed their mother.

"Well, Madame, what is this news that will not wait? I trust you have received no ill tidings from court?"

"Far from it," Lady Ariène replied serenely. "Indeed, this has nothing to do with your father but rather concerns your sister." And looking directly at Rowène, "Come child, sit with me, I have some news I think you will be most gratified to hear."

Reluctantly, her empty stomach churning most unpleasantly, Rowène sat down on the stool her mother indicated, acutely aware that the harper had moved to take the same position in the window he had occupied the day before.

Anxiety about her father temporarily allayed, she was left instead to worry about the cause of her mother's unnatural warmth towards her. She fought the temptation to chew her nails and instead folded her hands together in her lap. It was a demure and ladylike pose that at least allowed her to hide the fact that her fingers were shaking.

Then, with that complacent smile Rowène had already learned to hate, her mother said blandly,

"As I was saying, Rowène, I have some good news for you. I have arranged with Guillaume de Veraux that you be bound to his eldest daughter's son. Possibly you remember the lad? You met him once, I believe, when your father took you to Veraux with him the summer before you left for Kardolandia."

"Veraux? No... I do not recall..."

Rowène was aware that it was a less than ecstatic response but she could think of nothing else to say, her impressions of that summer having long since faded from her mind; she had been only seven years old after all. But now that she dug deep in her memory she managed to recall a few fleeting glimpses of that time; long, fresh-scented days spent among the mountains in her father's god-like company... flowers of blue and yellow and white, bright against the green of a high meadow... the sound of goat bells on the clear air... sunlight glittering on a splashing stream... a laughing, dark-haired boy...

Was that boy Guillaume de Veraux's grandson? She rather thought it must have been. But as to his given name, she could not recall it, nor anything else about him...

Then her brother's outraged voice shattered her thoughts.

"Is it *Joscelin de Veraux* you are meaning? Hell'sdeath, Madame, what were you thinking? Surely you cannot be serious in this proposal to bind my sister to that bast... base-born whelp?"

"A *prince's* base-born whelp!" Lady Ariène corrected him with gentle implacability. "Unless you mean to tell me that Prince Marcus deliberately perjured himself when he publicly acknowledged the boy as his own get?"

"No," Luc ground out, his mouth thinning and dark brows drawing together. "I am not impugning the Prince's honour. But what does de Veraux have to offer my sister except a name that is not his father's? As you well know, the lands and title to Veraux will go to Hervé de Lyeyne on their grandsire's death."

"No, I do not know that," Lady Ariène cut in coldly. "For your information, Guillaume de Veraux has made formal petition to the High Counsel to name Joscelin as his heir, despite his illegitimate birth. Yet even if that petition fails – as it probably will, given the strength of opposition to it, only your father, for some reason best known to himself, having shown any support for it so far – and the lordship of Veraux passes to the de Lyeynes, young Joscelin will not be left penniless."

"If you think Hervé de Lyeyne will toss so much as a bronze farthing in the direction of someone he has been heard to say on more than one occasion should have been drowned at birth, you are deluding yourself, Madame!" Luc retorted, his tone savage, his grey eyes blazing. "De Lyeyne is an ill-conditioned cur who does nothing to help his own misbegotten offspring, so why should he do more for the illegitimate kinsman he loathes?" He sent another scorching look at his mother. "Or are you relying on royal patronage? If so, I fear you are like to be disappointed since it seems to be generally accepted that the only thing Prince Marcus has ever done for Céline de Veraux's son was twenty-odd years ago when he publicly acknowledged him. At the same time, in a fit of remorse for his shameful disloyalty to his wife, the Prince renounced his mistress and sent her back to Veraux, along with the child, thus allowing him to forget their very existence!"

Unaffected by this tirade Lady Ariène shrugged slim, white shoulders and, in spuriously dulcet tones, said,

"What else would you have him do? Bring further shame and grief to the Princess by openly raising his by-blow at court? You do not answer. Do I take it from your silence that *you* would expect such tolerance from any woman with whom you swore the binding oath, no matter how flagrant your infidelities?"

Luc gave her back a flat grey stare but said nothing. His mother regarded him coldly for a moment or two, then said dismissively,

"It is your sister's betrothal we are discussing, not yours. And it is my understanding that Prince Marcus has recently remembered the existence of his hitherto forgotten by-blow and seen fit to promote him, with questionable swiftness, through the ranks of the Guardians. So, even if Joscelin does not in time become Lord of Veraux he should soon attain a position whereby he can keep himself, his wife and any offspring he may sire on her in some degree of comfort."

"And if this position gets him crippled or killed, as seems more than likely given the constant attacks from both north and east!" Luc growled. "What then, Madame? Another binding for my sister? Next time to some beggar you have found on the streets?"

Bludgeoned into numbness by the arguments raging to and fro above her head, Rowène was scarcely aware of the small sob of distress that slipped from her lips.

Evidently hearing that subdued sound, Luc dropped to his knees beside Rowène, taking her shaking hands in his hard grasp, swearing under his breath as he looked into her eyes.

"The gods forgive me for my careless tongue!" he muttered. Then, more reassuringly, "Listen, Ro, it will be all right. Nothing has been decided yet. Has it, Madame?"

He directed a grim look at their mother, in response to which she dropped a roll of parchment, bound with green ribbon, into Rowène's lap, together with a small leather bag, the knotted strings of which were bound securely together by a large blob of green wax. Confused and alarmed, Rowène looked from her frowning brother to her unsmiling mother.

"It but awaits your signature on the contract and the acceptance of the binding bracelet you will find in the pouch," Lady Ariène explained in cool, uncompromising tones. "Once you have done that you will be considered to be betrothed. Messire Guillaume and I have agreed that the formal blood-oath will be sworn on Midsummer's Day, whereupon your binding will be considered unbreakable."

"But… that is so soon!" Rowène gasped. "Am I even to meet this Joscelin before that day?"

"Regrettably the circumstances do not permit. The sea raiders are once again harrying the villages along the coast of Malvraine and your betrothed has been sent there in command of one wing of the Guardians. Until this matter of his grandsire's will has been settled, he remains a part of the Mithlondian army and must do his duty accordingly."

"What about Father?" Luc said sharply. "What does he say to all this?" His eyes narrowed. "Does he even know about this betrothal?"

"Naturally I sent a messenger to court," Lady Ariène replied with icy composure. "But you cannot hold me to blame if your father has not seen fit to reply nor taken any interest in his daughter's future! Instead you should be thanking me for my efforts on your sister's behalf! No? Well, in that case, I would suggest you return to your own duties and leave your sisters and I to discuss Rowène's bride clothes and organise what will be required for the binding feast."

Luc stared at his mother in impotent fury for a moment, muttering a frustrated oath under his breath. Finally releasing Rowène's cold hands, he rose swiftly to his feet and stalked from the chamber, leaving her in a state of stunned dismay that abruptly yielded to a deep embarrassment when she realised that, once again, the harper had witnessed it all.

Moon daisies and minstrels, meadowsweet garlands and mid-summer feasting, mead and Marillec wine… It was all of a muddle with blue brocade gowns and roasting boar, betrothal bracelets and binding oaths…

Rowène knew she must escape the madness of her thoughts before the fetters of insanity secured forever the door of her gilded cage. Flinging aside her embroidery, she fled from the chamber where she and Ju had been sitting, sewing in a silence that was more oppressive than companionable. Gone were the days when they had shared everything; thoughts, feelings, laughter, tears. Now, although they spent as much time together as they had ever done, Rowène felt she might just as well have been alone.

The mere semblance of solitude, however, was suddenly not sufficient; she needed to be alone in truth, in a place where she could come to terms with all the changes that had tipped her ordered – if somewhat tedious – life into turmoil.

To return to Chartre after so many years, only to find that she and her sister were now strangers in what should have been their home had been hard enough but she thought she could have overcome that feeling of loss if not for the subsequent and utterly shocking blow of her betrothal!

A betrothal her mother had quite obviously expected her to be delighted with.

A betrothal that she apparently had no chance of asking her father to stop.

A betrothal that had reduced her brother to white-faced fury.

What her sister thought about it Rowène could not tell since Ju seemed simply to have ceased caring about anything.

Not for the first time she asked herself how it was that Juliène, always so sparkling and filled with light, should turn almost overnight into the silent, brooding creature of the shadows that she had become. It was as if in leaving the brilliant skies and luminous waters of Kaerellios, she had left all the sunshine and radiance of her own nature behind.

Although – and this was something Rowène had only come to realise since their return to Chartre – Ju had stopped confiding in her even before they had left Kaerellios.

Frowning, Rowène tried to pinpoint more exactly the moment her sister had changed. She could not be certain but, looking back, it seemed to her that Juliène had suddenly become secretive and started making excuses to avoid the company of the Queen's other ladies around the same time as the Mithlondian emissaries had arrived in Kaerellios to open negotiations with King Karlen for the binding of Princess Linette to one of his younger sons.

Perhaps, Rowène hazarded, Ju had met some man then and... what? Fallen in love? No! Rowène rejected that idea immediately. Her sister could not have been fool enough to imagine herself in love over such a short span of time. Nevertheless – love or mere infatuation – something had happened that affected her deeply and caused her to change almost out of recognition.

Yet the most hurtful part about it – whatever *it* was – was that Juliène obviously felt she could not talk to her sister about it. But what, Rowène wondered in bewilderment, had she ever done to cause Ju to doubt her to the extent that she no longer trusted her with the secrets of her heart?

Feeling a blinding headache nagging at her temples – no doubt brought on by the long, lonely hours with nothing to do save sew and ponder her betrothal – Rowène continued on up the stairs, hoping that the clear, cool sea air would ease the ache in her head and her heart. Perhaps in the peaceful solitude to be found at the top of the tower she might be able to think a little more clearly, both about her sister and the betrothal she was far from certain she was ready for.

Ju had been right about that, Rowène conceded bitterly, abruptly remembering their earlier conversation and her sister would undoubtedly be next – unless the Winter Lady had some other, more terrible, fate planned for her beautiful daughter.

Unable to immediately imagine any worse fate than binding to a man she had only met once when she was seven, Rowène turned her thoughts towards her betrothed, wondering what in the name of all the gods she knew or remembered about Joscelin de Veraux that could form a foundation for their life together? Yet even as she racked her aching mind for some snippet of useful information, she found herself questioning *why* her mother should be set so obdurately on this binding, when the young man involved was neither legitimately born nor possessed of more than an outside chance of being accepted as heir to the rich lands and noble title of Veraux?

Whatever the reason – and she could not think of one that was even remotely convincing – Rowène was bleakly certain it was not out of concern for her happiness.

Arriving at the top of the narrow, circling stairs, some innate sense of awareness she had not previously suspected she possessed caused her to proceed more cautiously; easy enough to tread quietly in her soft leather slippers, holding up her trailing hems so as not to whisper a warning against the stone stairs. What she was expecting she did not quite know but when she silently emerged from the shadows of the stairwell and glanced around the small open space at the top of the tower it was to find all her guesses wide of the mark.

A man was standing there, his back to the door, his arms resting casually on the broad parapet, apparently engrossed in the breathtaking view across the busy blue waters of the bay. Not her tall, dark-haired brother, who was the only man in the castle who had the right to be there. Nor even one of the castle guards who might have some more or less acceptable reason to break the rules.

Not that Rowène had the slightest difficulty identifying the man – if only because no-one else in the prosperous and well-tended environs of Chartre castle was so poorly dressed or flaunted such raggedly cropped hair! But what in the name of all the gods was the harper doing up here? Stranger though he was to the castle, surely even he must know that this particular tower was, by tradition and custom, the exclusive retreat of the Lord of Chartreux's womenfolk. Unless...

At this point Rowène was assailed by the sudden unsettling notion that he might be waiting for someone. And that someone could only be her mother or her sister. Since she knew without doubt that it was not Ju the harper had an assignation with, that only left one person and, that being so, Rowène thought she would gladly fly back to her cage and lock the door herself rather than bear witness to her mother's betrayal of her father in the arms of this ill-bred, unkempt harper!

Hastily she made to retreat. Her foot knocked against a loose stone and sent it skittering across the roof. It struck against the wall, the small, sharp sound shattering the silence...

Leaning against the breast-high parapet, his bare forearms resting on the sun-warmed sandstone, Guy stared into the distance. There, across the gleaming sun-silvered waters, at the very limit of his sight, the far coast showed as a merest shadow of land. In truth, if he had not known it was there, he doubted he would have seen it at all. Finding his eyes watering with strain and the brisk, salt-stung breeze, he drew back a little, focussing his gaze on the harbour below where, amongst the tangled masts of merchant galleys and fishing boats, the swan ship, its white sails neatly furled, was still tied up against the quay.

God of Light, had it been only one day since he had set eyes on the de Chartreux sisters? Yet they had scarcely left his mind since; a disquieting sensation he sincerely hoped was not mutual. He had no desire to be anything more to either of them than he had been presented as; Guy of Montfaucon, a wandering harper.

He had been here in Chartre for the best part of a month now and save for the Lady Ariène who certainly knew the truth about him, no-one had given him cause to believe that they suspected him of being anything other than what he claimed to be. He had thought that perhaps Louis de Chartreux had had his suspicions; certainly his piercing grey eyes had held a worryingly sharp gleam when Guy had first arrived to beg a meal and a place at the hearth in return for his music. But the Lord of Chartreux had left later that same day and if he had passed on his doubts to anyone else Guy had seen no sign of it.

Nevertheless it had been a warning and he had taken it as such, considering carefully what he might have done to arouse the other man's suspicions since, whatever it was, he must take care not to betray himself again. Least of all in front of either Luc or Rowène de Chartreux, both of whom possessed keen grey eyes of a disconcerting similarity to their sire's.

He must remember, even when he lay down to sleep on his pallet by the hall fire, that he was Guy of Montfaucon, and pray that neither of the two young noblewomen ever asked him about his birthplace. He thought, if it were necessary, that he could convince Luc of his origins but for some reason he did not think he could lie to Luc's sisters. But what was he thinking? Was it likely that a daughter of the high and mighty Lord of Chartreux would wish to spend her time conversing with an itinerant harper of humble birth? But if, the gods forbid, either of them did, what would he tell them that would not immediately betray him for what he was?

His knowledge of Montfaucon was confined to the fact that he had been born in that small Valennais village and it was there that his mother had died, leaving him a helpless babe utterly dependent on the dubious goodwill of those fallen women who could fall no further and the unreliable charity of the knight who had refused to allow his mother entry to any respectable dwelling but who had not been quite ruthless enough to leave her to give birth in the gutter.

Whatever the circumstances of his conception and subsequent birth, Guy had few illusions that he would have lived beyond that first summer if his father had not belatedly come seeking news of his mother and, finding her child instead, had taken him far away from Montfaucon. As Guy had been told the tale – and he had no reason to doubt it – his father had ridden away with the Sire de Martine's curses ringing in his ears. Powerful curses aimed, not only at the heedless man who had caused such trouble, but also towards the motherless babe in his arms.

Carrying this knowledge with him into manhood it was perhaps not surprising that Guy had chosen to avoid not only Armand de Martine and his son Gaston but also that knight's liege lord, Gilles de Valenne, on the rare occasions when Guy had been at the royal court and had found himself in their vicinity. Nor had Guy ever returned to Montfaucon, even to honour his mother's unmarked grave.

All he had in life Guy owed to his father and, by extension, to the older brother who had allowed him to remain in the family home after their father's untimely death at the hands of Louis de Chartreux; the very same man in whose castle he was presently living and whose lady he was currently serving.

At the thought of that beautiful witch an involuntary curse rose to his lips. Daemons of Hell! She might have his liege lord utterly enslaved but *he* was finding it increasingly difficult to serve as her lackey. He could not forget the disgusted look on the Lady Rowène's face this morning when she had seen him in her mother's chamber, making it perfectly obvious where she thought he had spent the night! And although the idea made his blood freeze he knew she would not be the only person in the castle to think such a thing. He had seen for himself how easily the Lady Ariène could beguile and enthral those around her and, so far as he knew, he was the only man save for her son who remained free from her enchanted net.

Yet even as he thought it, he knew it was not entirely true. Little though he liked to admit it, he *had* come close to falling under her spell and, save for the arrival of her daughters, would now be inescapably entrapped in that unhappy state. The thought of those two innocents was as much a talisman against the Lady Ariène's wiles as a painful reminder of how close he had come to losing himself to the beautiful woman who manipulated all those around her with such lethal skill. Gods, but he wished he could see an honourable way out of this web of deceit he was caught in...

A small, sharp sound shattered his solitude and, without thought, Guy straightened and turned, his right hand starting a movement that – as he recognised the young woman standing by the stair head – he managed to curtail almost before it was begun. Seeing that she was about to flee from him he started to call out to her, silently cursing his own stupidity as he ruthlessly strangled back the words that had sprung to his lips, finally managing to choke out the same plea in common speech.

"My lady! Wait!"

At the sound of his voice she halted her flight but the expression in her grey eyes as she looked back at him over her shoulder was wary in the extreme. Forcing himself to remain where he was, with several clear paces between them, he placed his right hand on his breast and made her a low bow, his mind and tongue now firmly set in the language he must use at all times.

"Lady Rowena, I beg your pardon if I startled you but surely you must know you have nothing to fear from me."

She blinked, obviously confused by all the contradictions of language and manner that he was presenting her with. A slight frown appeared between her undarkened copper brows and she said consideringly,

"Fear you? No, I do not think I do. Although I would be a fool to admit it to you if I did! But in any case, I think it was I who startled you. You were obviously far away in thought." She swept an uncertain look over him and then, apparently deciding to give him the benefit of the doubt, asked with more courtesy that he could have expected of her given the peculiar circumstances, "What are you doing up here, Master Harper? Do you not know that the upper floors of the Lady Tower are forbidden to all men save my father and brother?"

"I did know that, yes, but I have your mother's permission to be here," Guy replied tonelessly.

"Ah!"

With that one word all the uncertainty left her grey eyes, to be replaced by the same look she had given him this morning in her mother's bower. He told himself to ignore her sordid assumption but found himself incapable of allowing her to condemn him yet again. He was annoyed with himself as much as her and consequently when he spoke his tone was sharper than he had intended.

"Damnation! It is not what you are thinking!"

"Do not swear at me!" she snapped, even as guilty colour flooded her cheeks. "My thoughts are my own affair and none of yours!"

"Not when you are thinking that I am permitted to be here by right of being your mother's lover!" Guy retorted, aware that both his tone and his words were now well beyond what might be acceptable from a humble harper to a high-born noblewoman, but unable to keep silent or couch his reply more respectfully.

Not giving her a chance to respond, he jerked back the short sleeve of his ragged blue tunic and that of the worn linen shirt beneath to reveal a broad, patterned ring of bronze set about his upper left arm – praying she would not see, or recognise if she did, the significance of the oak leaves incised on the metal – and continued harshly, "Look well, my lady, and tell me what this is!"

"It is a binding ring, I must suppose," she retorted calmly enough, the rosy flush ebbing slowly from her cheeks.

"Yes, it is," he agreed, his tone as unyielding as the black granite of his own homeland.

"But your wife is not here," she had the temerity to point out. "And men – or so I have been given to understand – have certain needs! Nor have I ever heard that a binding bracelet serves to shackle a man's desires within his lawful bed."

"Not some men," Guy agreed tersely. "But even were I the sort of man to break my binding vow, I would have to be witless as well as faithless to cuckold the Lord of Chartreux under his own roof. Nor am I some ravening wolf with a taste for soft-skinned young swan-maidens. Your mother may believe that I am capable of adultery but you need not be so foolish."

He saw the flare of temper in the grey eyes and wondered if he had pushed her too hard and whether her next words would be to call for the guards. He would not have been surprised if she had but was considerably relieved when she did not. Even so, there was more than a hint of ice in her tone when she did address him.

"I suggest you mind your tongue, Master Harper, unless you wish to lose it."

"I ask your pardon, my lady," he said quietly. "I meant no insult to you. And I swear by all the gods that my presence here today has nothing to do with your mother. Or your sister. Or you."

Thankfully, she seemed to accept his word. Even though he could see that such acceptance brought with it a recurrence of her earlier doubts. He made a deliberate effort to remove the steel from his tone and reiterated, more softly,

"I beg you to believe me, my lady."

She nodded but, if anything, now looked even more mistrustful of him.

"I do not know what to believe of you, Guy of Montfaucon," she said. There was curiosity as well as suspicion in her eyes and he knew he had to quash both.

"Believe that I mean you neither harm nor disrespect," he said, wincing inwardly even as he said the words. "It is just that I am unused to being in the company of nobly-born damsels." That, at least, was the truth.

"But what are you doing up here?" she asked again. "If you were not meeting a..." She gestured in delicate apology. "A woman."

Guy cast about for an acceptable reason but before he could come up with one he heard himself say,

"I needed to think. I thought it would be easier up here, with only the sea mews for company and the breeze blowing clean and clear."

The effect of this unintended confession was startling, causing a faint, rueful smile to touch her rose-petal lips and a hitherto unseen warmth to illuminate her grey eyes. He felt his gut clench, almost painfully, in reaction and wished to the gods he had neither given tongue to that thought nor witnessed its effect upon her. She might resemble her father far too closely in looks for comfort but there was more than a trace of her mother's feyness in her all the same. How else had she coaxed him into admitting what was in his heart? But before he could curse his weakness even more, she stunned him by saying simply,

"That is why I came too."

As if conceiving that this sympathy of thought made them friends, she moved away from the escape route offered by the stairway, three paces bringing her to the sun-warmed wall and within a foot of Guy. He caught the faint but unsettling scent of roses and his heart began to beat faster as a sense of danger burned through his blood. He took an instinctive step away from her, belatedly taking heed to the proprieties.

"My lady, it is not fitting that I should be here alone with you. Give me leave and I will go."

She turned her clear eyes on him and again he sensed the insidious caress of enchantment, reinforcing everything he had just felt; everything the fire of her hair should have warned him of long since. Damn it all, he was a weak-minded fool for forgetting for so much as a moment that although Louis de Chartreux was undoubtedly her sire, still the moon-blood of the Faennari ran within her, just as it did in her cold-hearted witch of a mother.

"My lady, give me leave," he begged again, more urgently this time.

"No, I think not," she replied, all laughter gone from her expression. "I wish to talk to you."

Seriously alarmed now, Guy took another step back, infusing a slightly coarser cadence into his common speech. Not enough to be obviously assumed, just enough to remind her of their widely differing stations in life.

"Me, m'lady? Why would you be wanting to talk to the likes of me?"

"Precisely because of who you are," she replied firmly. She eyed him for a moment or two and then asked him almost the last question he would have thought of. "Have you ever played for the court at Lamortaine?"

"I've been to Lamortaine, aye," he replied warily. "But not to play for the pleasure of the Prince and his fine courtiers. If'n I'd had the good fortune to find a wealthy patron at court, d'you not think I'd still be there, rather than wandering the highways of the realm? An' for sure I'd be able to clothe myself in something better than these rags."

"You may look like the poorest of peasants but your speech and accent betray you, Guy of Montfaucon."

*Gods!* For a moment he thought she had somehow guessed the truth about him. To his relief her next words showed that all was not yet lost, although it proved he must be more careful in what he let slip. But, Hell take him, he found it so damnably hard to lie to her!

"I do not believe," she was saying softly, "that you were born a peasant, although you have obviously fallen on hard times since."

"Certainly I have known poverty," he agreed, with total sincerity.

"I hope you will not know it again," she replied, equally sincerely he thought. "But if I may, I wanted to ask you about your time in Lamortaine. I mean, when you were there, did you ever meet my... my betrothed, Joscelin de Veraux?"

"Joscelin de Veraux?" he repeated, more to gain time to think what to say than because he did not know who the man was.

"Do not pretend ignorance," she said sharply. "I know you know who I mean since you were there when my mother gave me the news of my impending binding."

The gods knew he wished he had not been.

"Aye, m'lady," Guy agreed cautiously, keeping his accent sloppy; it would not hurt to keep her guessing as to his origins. "I knows who you mean. An' I reckon as I might've seen him once or twice."

"Then tell me, what is he like, this man to whom I find myself betrothed?"

"My lady, how can I tell what you want to know?" he asked in blank astonishment.

"Try! Please!"

"Very well," he agreed reluctantly, knowing that whatever he said would likely be wrong.

He stared out over the water again, attempting to gather his scattered wits, wondering what she really wanted to know.

Presumably, being a woman and a young one at that, she would have some interest in whether the man she was to be bound to was ill-favoured or comely. She was probably also somewhat apprehensive as to the manner in which he would treat her once they were wed. Certainly she was entitled to respect and consideration but, covertly eyeing her uncovered hair, he had to admit he did not know what Joscelin de Veraux's attitude would prove to be. If this hastily contrived binding was ever formalised, of course, and since it had not been in his lord's original plan likely it never would be. But he dare not even hint at that or she would ask even more awkward questions. So what could he tell her? He did not go regularly to court but he had spent some time in Lamortaine the previous summer and although he had not taken much notice of Prince Marcus' illegitimate son he *had* seen him and gleaned some gossip regarding his capabilities and character.

"For what little it is worth," he said at last. "I think there are worse men by far that your mother could have chosen for you. In age he cannot be much more than five years older than you. He is dark haired like his father, the Prince, and certainly the women at court do not appear to consider him ill-looking." Then added, somewhat hastily, at her sharp look, "Not that he has the reputation of a hardened womaniser, unlike some others I could name." Guy's own brother for one! He winced and hastened on. "When all is said and done, Joscelin of Veraux is a soldier rather than a courtier, as he has proved during these past few summers of fighting against the northern barbarians and eastern pirates. Hence his rapid promotion within the royal guard."

"So it is for his own worth rather than..." she hesitated and a wave of delicate colour rose in her pale golden cheeks. "As my mother intimated, his father's... influence?"

"Assuredly," Guy agreed. "The High Counsel would not have ratified his appointment as Second of the Guardians if he were not competent, no matter who his father is."

She smiled then, in relief he thought, and the warmth and light that flooded her face transformed her once more from a thin-faced, unremarkable girl into a fey and enchantingly lovely young woman. Hell and damnation! He did not need to see that now, to feel the flicker of fire flare in his blood... touch his heart... sear his soul...

Then the radiant smile faded, her grey eyes narrowed... and she was Louis de Chartreux's daughter again. And as the fresh sea breeze blew away the last rags of illusion he felt the cold sweat of relief trickle down his back.

"Why do you think my brother disapproves of him so much?" she asked abruptly, taking him unpleasantly by surprise; more especially as he had a very good idea why Luc de Chartreux disapproved of Joscelin de Veraux.

"How can I say, my lady?" Guy replied, spreading his hands in an apologetic gesture.

"Might it be because of his... um... irregular birth?" she asked hesitantly.

Guy stared at her for a moment, then gave vent to a rather mirthless laugh.

"Irregular? That must be the Kardolandian court lady talking, not the Mithlondian noblewoman."

"What do you mean by that?" she enquired, looking so genuinely bewildered that he sighed and said in a carefully level voice,

"I mean, that the attitude of Mithlondians of whatever rank is generally to despise those born to parents who, for whatever reason, never swore the binding oath. I would also add that there is no worse insult in Mithlondia than to call a man a bastard – whether or not he is by birth – simply because by that you also publicly name his mother a whore!"

He saw the shocked look she gave him and forced yet another apology to his lips.

"I am sorry, my lady, I did not mean to offend you. I should not have used such words to you but it is better that you should know."

"No, it... you did not... offend me, I mean," she replied, flushing all the same. She gave him a fleeting glance, opened her mouth to ask something else, clearly thought better of it and cast around, as if seeking a change of subject. Her eyes turned eastwards and she blurted out an unthinkable question, "Have you ever been there?"

She was looking towards the distant, dark blur of the Rogé coastline and, after a moment's indecision, Guy decided it was not worth lying. The truth, however, was not something he wished to flaunt in his present situation so he kept his tone quiet and level, as if what he was speaking of was quite normal. Although the gods knew, even a girl raised in the lax atmosphere of the Kardolandian court must guess that it was not.

"Yes, I have been there. And played in the great hall of Rogérinac castle for Lord Joffroi and his brother." Then at her look of startled astonishment – no, she was not as naïve as her attitude towards bastardy might imply – continued, with a quirk of the lips that was almost a grin. "But, as you can see, I survived to tell the tale. It is true that Lord Joffroi has no ear for music but his brother is not quite such a barbarian."

"And would you go back again?" she asked, her grey eyes sombre now beneath frowning copper brows. "Having escaped once with your livelihood and your life?"

He hesitated but the truth would serve well enough.

"Yes, I will go back. But not yet. I believe Lady Ariena wishes me to stay on until midsummer at the least. After that, who can say? And now, my lady, if there is nothing further you wish to ask of me, may I be permitted to go?"

"No, there is nothing else, Master Harper," she answered dismissively, suddenly very much the haughty young Mithlondian noblewoman he had unconsciously expected her to be before he had met her. "You may go."

When the harper had gone Rowène finally allowed herself to relax. Leaning against the wall in a manner that would have brought Queen Xandra's, as well as her mother's, recriminations down upon her head, she drew in a deep breath of the clean, sea-scented breeze. Much as the harper had done, she looked out over the glittering blue brilliance of the Bay of Chartre, hearing but not heeding the gleaming grey and white sea mews as they wheeled on sun-silvered wings, their warning cries carried away upon the wind.

For a long while Rowène just stood there, refusing to think about the harper and the strange conversation they had just shared. Instead she fixed her gaze on the view, remembering from childhood how she had loved to watch the ships sailing in and out of the bay... how the water had glimmered in the moonlight and star-shimmer of a time when it had seemed that all the days were summer and she would never have to grow up or leave the land that she loved, or the father and brother whom she adored.

Suddenly a shiver shook her slender frame, the present rushing up again on raven wings. She lifted her gaze, looking once more beyond the restless waters towards the forbidding line of the distant coast. Even when she had been a child and had been permitted to ride out with her father, she had never been closer to the borders of that shadowy land than the nearest edge of the vast beech forest that stretched from just east of Chartre as far as the Larkenlye, the river that formed the boundary with the neighbouring fief. She had been taught to regard that province and the family who ruled there with fear and dread. Nor, hearing the stories whispered about them, had it proved difficult to believe the worst of such men.

Yet the harper had told her quite openly that he had been there, might even be bound there again after midsummer. But what would take him back? She could not believe that there would be any welcome there for Guy of Montfaucon. If he had been the battle-hardened commander of a troop of mercenaries, perhaps. But not a harper!

The lords of that land had never had any use for the gentle art of music. To a man – father and sons – they dealt in rape, torture and death. For years now mere mention of their name had been sufficient to make grown men shudder and women whimper in fear. Brutal masters to a hapless people, they were dangerous men to cross in any circumstance. Rowène had only been home a day but already she had been reminded of the dark deeds committed by the Lords of Rogé, both past and present.

The previous lord had been evil enough by all accounts but it would seem that the present lord, his eldest son, was even more ruthless. His device was a black boar and, to judge by the horrific tales told of him, he was every bit as savage as that ferocious beast. Together with his younger brother, a man as steeped in villainy as himself, they had earned an unrivalled reputation, not just in the neighbouring provinces of Chartreux, Rouvraine and Vitré but throughout the entire realm of Mithlondia. A reputation that told of drunken debaucheries, vile ruttings and brutal, cold-blooded murder.

It was also common knowledge that they carried within them, like a canker, an undying hatred of the de Chartreux. Rowène shivered at the recollection of the long-standing enmity between that family and hers but told herself it was nothing more than a black shadow on the distant horizon, a cloud passing over the sun, rather than a wraith's warning. After all, the lords of that land had been trying for more years than she had lived to destroy her father but Louis de Chartreux had always proved himself more than a match for Jacques de Rogé and his brutish sons and she saw no reason for that to change now.

So rather than worrying about a man – two, if she counted his brother – she was unlikely ever to meet, except possibly in the formal surroundings of the royal court in Lamortaine as the wife of Joscelin de Veraux, she really ought to be coming to terms with her betrothal. With that thought she dropped her gaze to study the delicately wrought silver and amethyst bracelet about her arm, reviewing what little the harper had been able to tell her, matching that scant information with her vague memories of the dark-haired boy she had met once, so many years ago. She did not remember Joscelin de Veraux as being cruel or even unkind so, by the grace of the gods, life with the man he had grown into, soldier though he was, would not be as daunting as she had first thought upon hearing her mother's news.

Indeed, from a purely pragmatic point of view, there must surely be some benefits to the arrangement that would negate her very real dismay at being separated from the sister who had been the other half of herself for the past seventeen years? She thought hard for a moment but the only thing she believed she might realistically look forward to after the binding ceremony – she swallowed at the thought of the bedding that must inevitably follow that exchange of oaths – was that she would no longer be expected to live under the constant frost-rimed shadow of her mother's icy displeasure.

Nor, she reminded herself sternly, would the duties and tasks that would occupy her in Lamortaine as wife to a royal Guardian, perhaps even High Commander of the Mithlondian army in time, leave her either reason or opportunity to concern herself with the whereabouts and ambitions of a chance-come harper.

Rowène might have thought she could dismiss Guy of Montfaucon from her life as easily as blowing the down from a seeding dandelion but she soon found how mistaken she had been.

Almost suffocated by the confines of the castle and her mother's overpowering presence that seemed to seep from the very stones that surrounded her, and driven by sheer desperation, Rowène managed to persuade her reluctant sister that their best chance of escaping those bonds, even if only for a few hours, lay in the horses that their father had provided for them. Neither of them had ridden since their journey up from the harbour but the little mares had appeared sufficiently docile on that occasion to encourage Rowène's confidence that she and her sister could handle them.

Gathering her courage, she had approached her mother with a carefully couched request that she and her sister be allowed to reacquaint themselves with the lands that lay beyond the town. Somewhat to Rowène's surprise, her mother had agreed at once with but one stipulation. This condition being no less than Rowène had expected she had not argued, reckoning it a negligible encumbrance that she and Ju be accompanied at all times by one of the castle grooms.

Emboldened by this small promise of freedom, Rowène dragged her sister down to the stables early the following morning, dogged by anxiety lest her mother should have changed her mind, this transmuting into a wondrous relief when she found their mounts saddled and ready. Giddy with excitement, she turned to Ju, a laughing comment already spilling from her lips – only to have her joy abruptly curtailed as she recognised the man leading a sturdy dark bay stallion from its stall.

"What are you doing here?" Rowène asked, surprise and not a little suspicion colouring her tone.

"Waiting for you, my lady," the harper replied evenly. "And before you ask, I am here at your mother's command. She has decided that she cannot spare any of the castle grooms to accompany you but I am willing to act as your escort should you still wish to ride out."

For a moment Rowène was on the brink of stalking back to the keep but mastered that first impulse born of temper by reminding herself that it would be a pointless act of rebellion to give up what little freedom she had won. Lifting her chin, she wrapped herself in a cloak of hauteur, placed her foot in the harper's cupped hands and permitted him to throw her up to the saddle.

Under cover of arranging her skirt and reins, she watched as the man performed the same service for her sister before swinging astride his borrowed mount. Despite his size he moved easily and her frown deepened as she took note of the casual expertise he unconsciously displayed. Oh yes, she decided, the harper would definitely bear watching and she wondered yet again whether to share her doubts with Luc. Or mayhap they were all seeing shadows where none existed.

After all, what precisely had Guy of Montfaucon done to merit their suspicions? Certainly there was nothing that she personally could put her finger on.

Yet as they moved out of the castle onto the green sward beyond the western gate and he reined his mount into place slightly behind her she found it next to impossible to banish him from her thoughts; a state of mind that was rendered more acute over the following days as Ju found first one excuse and then another not to accompany her. By contrast the harper was always ready, as soon as the dawn meal had been eaten, to saddle up the golden mare and the big bay and ride wherever Rowène desired.

As each glorious, wonderful, vibrant spring day followed another she found that her wary curiosity regarding the harper's true background and motives for remaining in Chartre gradually retreated like mist before the dawn, and she came instead to anticipate the time she spent with him. Guy of Montfaucon proved himself to be an intelligent and gently humorous companion, displaying an innate courtesy and consideration for her that ultimately served neither of them well; softening her suspicions where it should have sharpened them and binding him closer to her than he had ever intended.

Yet for all the enjoyment she found in the harper's company Rowène was not unaware that she was living an existence that could never be more than a temporary – and potentially dangerous – illusion. She had the vague impression that Luc did not approve of the situation but since she saw little of him save at the evening meal and even then he seemed preoccupied with his own affairs, she chose to ignore his unspoken censure.

As for her mother, she saw even less of her, for which she was thankful. But even when they did meet, the Lady Ariène expressed neither interest in her welfare nor concern for her reputation. This being so, Rowène continued to range far and wide over the lands around Chartre, accompanied always by the harper, whom she now called by his given name as a matter of course. Naturally, he was not so familiar with her but he no longer used the formal "my lady" but called her "Lady Rowena" and never had she thought the rendering of her name into common parlance sounded so well as when spoken by his light, barely accented speech.

She had asked him once what province his accent belonged to but he had merely answered that it owed something to all the lands he had travelled through. After that she had asked him no further personal questions, unwilling to disturb the fragile sense of companionship that had grown between them or acknowledge the passing of time.

Nonetheless the seasons did not – could not – remain frozen forever and almost imperceptibly the last, lingering days of spring slipped into early summer. The delicately scented hawthorn flowers that had adorned the hedgerows so abundantly were replaced by clouds of pink and white blossom which mantled the hillside orchards and drifted beneath the hooves of their mounts like petals in a dream. In the fields beyond the now dusty roads the shoots of early barley sprang up in the warm red soil, and beneath the silver branches of the stately beech trees of Larkenlay the wood-stars and forest-bells that had once shimmered in a misty haze of white and blue disappeared in their turn. Even as the sweet young green of the canopy above changed its hue, marking the inexorable turning of the season.

As the leaves darkened so did Guy's mood. Only the fine thread of his liege lord's command bound him to his mission in Chartre and as midsummer drew closer he came within a hair's breadth of deliberately breaking that slender strand. In the end it was only the tenuous hope that he might be able to save something from the impending storm that prevented him from outright defiance.

As for Rowène, she was determined, for good or for ill, to enjoy to the full her last days of freedom before the final binding ceremony took place on Midsummer's Day; the day when she must give her loyalty and all her hopes for the future into Joscelin de Veraux's charge.

And all the while Juliène hid behind the same joyless mask she had worn since they had left Kaerellios, having not even the faintest hope that summer would better her lot. In the now frequent absence of her sister she had reluctantly been forced into closer proximity with her mother and despite her inherent wariness of the Winter Lady's power she had somehow found herself revealing the frightening secret she had not even told her sister. To her surprise – and disquiet – Lady Ariène had merely smiled her cool, enigmatic smile and counselled patience.

It was perhaps three weeks after their return to Chartre and the dawn of yet another perfect summer's morning when Rowène made her way down to the stables, in accordance with her accepted habit. She was not, she readily admitted, in the sunniest of humours, due largely to the fact that she had very nearly quarrelled with her sister. Ju had, for once, roused herself from her withdrawn lethargy. But only to point out to her initially surprised, then seething, sister the folly of her ways. The whole town, and probably half the province, was talking about her, Ju had told her bluntly. More specifically, they were talking about the Lady Rowena's custom of riding about the countryside like a hoyden. And there was worse, Ju had continued darkly, but Rowène had not been in the mood to listen.

"Hardly like a hoyden," she had snapped. "When I have our mother's sanction and the company of a groom."

"But that is just the point," Juliène had retorted, showing an unexpected exasperation. "Guy of Montfaucon is not one of the castle grooms. You know it, I know it and apparently everyone else in the province, including the cat's mother, knows it. He is a stranger to Chartreux, a wandering harper of whom we know nothing save his name. If that *is* his real name."

"Why would he come here under a false name?" Rowène had exclaimed crossly. "In the name of all the gods, Ju, what purpose would that serve?"

"You think Father does not have enemies? And some of them not so far away, as you would acknowledge if you bothered to use your wits instead of..."

"Guy has never given me any cause to doubt him," Rowène had interrupted angrily, knowing even as she said the words that she was uttering a lie, and hastened on to what she knew to be true. "He has never treated me with anything other than courtesy and consideration. And before you open your mouth on any more nasty insinuations, let me remind you that I am betrothed to Joscelin de Veraux and Guy is bound in wedlock to another woman."

"So he says!" Juliène had sneered, before adding a warning Rowène did not really need. "But true or not, Ro, he is still a man. A man riding alone with a woman. A woman who treats him with every appearance of familiarity. You make yourself very free of his name, Ro. Does he do the same for you?"

"No, of course not. Ju, it is not what you think!"

But this protest had only had the unfortunate effect of causing Juliène to lose all patience with her recalcitrant sister.

"Gods above, Ro! Do not play the innocent with me! Never mind what *I* think! We have both witnessed enough in the bathing pools of Kaerellios to know what happens when a man lusts after a woman."

"Are you saying Guy of Montfaucon lusts after *me*?" Rowène had demanded incredulously, flushing despite herself. "Oh, do not be so ridiculous, Ju! Nor, before you hint at such a thing again, do I burn for him! Yes, I like him and I take pleasure in his company. If only because he does not regard me as a witch despite the colour of my hair! He may not be of noble birth but he is an honourable man, Ju, I know he is. And I am certain he means me no harm."

Juliène pulled a face but only said,

"Go then. Enjoy his company while you can. But be careful. I have the feeling he will move on soon and I do not want to see your heart broken when he does. In the meantime, I will pray to the gods that Joscelin de Veraux does not hear the gossip and misinterpret it. Believe me, Ro, that is not the way you should start your life together, with the shades of rumour and deceit stalking at your heels."

Rowène had hesitated then, torn between common sense and her own desires. Refusing to meet her sister's gaze, she half turned away, staring with angry defiance at the cloudless blue sky beyond their window. Finally she sighed and looked back at Juliène.

"Very well, Ju, have it your way. I will tell Guy that this must be the last time he escorts me. But do not ask me to give up this day, for I will not. Not for you. Not for anyone."

"Not even Joscelin de Veraux?" Juliène said pointedly.

"Least of all for him!" Rowène had snapped. "The man, I would remind you, whom our mother chose for me. What does that say about him, I wonder?"

"Is your harper any different? No, do not rip up at me again, I am only trying to save you grief later." Tears filling her green eyes, she had continued pleadingly. "Listen to me, Ro, I beg of you. Whatever else he may be, Guy of Montfaucon is the Winter Lady's thrall and it is *her* commands he obeys in this matter. Please, Ro, all I am asking is that you take care in what you say or do."

Rowène had opened her mouth to excoriate her sister for her unwanted meddling but, at the sight of Juliène's tears, left the harsh words unsaid. Nevertheless she could not bring herself to openly admit that there might be any truth in her sister's distrust of the harper. With a huff of frustration she had turned on her heel and slammed out of their chamber.

Reckless and foolish though it undoubtedly was, she was determined to have one last day with the man who, despite her initial doubts, she now trusted with her honour and her life.

# Chapter 4

## *One Last Day*

By the time she reached the stables Rowène had regained a tenuous control of her temper – only to have her fragile composure threatened anew when she found not only the harper, attending to the business of tacking up the golden mare in her stall, but also her brother and his squire, conversing earnestly with Lucien, the garrison commander, while at the far end of the building two grooms readied Luc's big grey gelding and one of the other horses.

The first thing that struck her was the contrast in the men's garb. Guy, with the promise of another hot day heavy on the air, had discarded his tunic in favour of a threadbare shirt which, while it was scarcely acceptable attire for a member of Lady Ariène's household, looked to have the advantage of being cool. In contrast Luc was sweating in full battle gear, save for his helm, while Nick, his squire, clad in a thick quilted gambeson sewn with mail links, was carrying a long spear in his hand, a bow and quiver of arrows slung at his back. Lucien too was wearing his normal mail under a pale blue surcoat but rather, Rowène thought, because he was on duty than because he had been ordered to ride out with her brother.

Evidently hearing her soft footsteps, the soldier abruptly broke off his conversation and gave her a respectful salute, which she acknowledged with a small smile. She rather liked the dark-haired garrison commander, who was some ten or fifteen years her senior, quiet-spoken – with her at least – and who reminded her a little of Luc in some odd way.

"Lady Rowena."

For once, he had no smile to accompany his greeting and she felt a little shiver touch her skin.

"Lucien. Luc." She glanced quizzically from him to her brother, sensing from their closed faces that her arrival had been inopportune if not outright unwelcome. "Do not let me interrupt you. I only came to see if Honey was ready." Then, as the harper led the mare from her stall, "Ah, Guy! There you are. Gentlemen," She flicked another look between the three men still standing close together, silently watching her. "I bid you good... hunting."

Luc could scarcely have missed her curiosity regarding his presence in the stable, along with his squire and the garrison commander, but clearly he was not about to give her an explanation. Moving towards her, he brushed her cheek with a fleeting kiss then passed a scowling glance over the harper's informal attire, following this with a menacing injunction to ensure that no harm came to the Lady Rowena while she was in his company. He held the harper's gaze for what seemed an interminable time, then turned away, snapping an order to the grooms to bring his and his squire's mounts.

Swinging up onto the grey's back, he wasted no further time. Nodding an apparently casual valediction at Lucien, he trotted out of the stable into the castle ward, his squire following close behind. Leaving Rowène to stare after them until they had disappeared from view, wondering what they were about; they scarcely needed full war gear for a simple hunting expedition. Thinking to make enquiry of Lucien, she brought her gaze back towards him but, before she could speak, the garrison commander gave her a quick salute and retreated, rather hastily, she thought. It was almost as if he did not want to be questioned.

"Lady Rowena?" Guy of Montfaucon's light voice broke into her troubled thoughts and, turning, she found they were alone, the other grooms having vanished. "If you are ready?"

"Yes, of course…"

Her thoughts still very much on that, somehow furtive, conversation she had interrupted, she watched the harper absently as he led the golden mare from her stall, reaching out with one hand to snag the tunic he must have hung over the wooden partition while he saddled up. Before she had realised what she meant to say, she blurted,

"Leave it… if you want to."

"What?" He paused, looking both startled and confused – as well he might – and, in consequence, forgetting the formalities due between them. Then he seemed to realise what he had done, flushed and added, "Beg pardon, my lady. I do not understand."

Rowène felt herself blush in turn. It seemed to be the day for it.

"Your tunic. It is very hot today and it is early yet. You need not wear it."

"My lady," he protested, "It is scarcely fitting that I escort you attired as I am. And I would rather not give your brother any more cause for concern."

"Nevertheless," Rowène insisted, moving purposefully towards the waiting mare. "*I* say you need not wear your tunic. And I will tell Luc as much if he raises the matter with me later."

The harper muttered something under his breath but abandoned the argument in favour of his unequivocal duty which was to serve as her groom.

Perhaps because her sister's words still lingered in her mind, she found herself disquietingly aware of him as a man – of the strength of those heavily muscled arms, of his very masculine scent – as he helped her to mount. Settling herself in the saddle, she thrust those unruly feelings aside and concentrated instead upon her brother's strange actions.

"Guy?" she asked abruptly before he could move away. "Do you know where Luc is going?"

A wry smile came into the harper's light blue eyes as he stood at her stirrup, his large hand stroking the mare's gleaming, golden neck as he looked up at her.

"Lady Rowena, surely you must know that I am the last person your brother would take into his confidence. And if I were fool enough to have questioned him regarding his errand, I think it is likely that rather than answer me he would simply have slipped a knife between my ribs! Your brother, my lady, does not trust me and would welcome any excuse to be rid of me." Then, apparently taking note of her pointed look, continued thoughtfully, "But if you want me to hazard a guess I would say he has ridden out with the intention of meeting up with the rest of the Chartreux guard. If they left Kaerellios at the same time as you and your sister took ship, they should surely be little more than a day's march away."

"Yes, you are probably right," Rowène agreed, wrinkling her nose at the thought of fully armoured men marching in such heat. "Well, in that case, shall we go? I thought to take the highway west beyond the Swanfleet Bridge."

"Would you rather not ride along the coast towards South Point?" Guy asked, adding "This will surely be the hottest day of the season so far and I suspect there will be little or no breeze down by the river."

Rowène considered for a moment – it would be pleasant riding along the grassy sward at the top of the cliffs – but said firmly,

"No, I wish to go as far as Swanfleet at the least. After that... well, let us wait and make the final decision then."

"As you wish, my lady." He dropped his hand and turned to fetch his own mount but not before Rowène had caught a glimpse of the expression in his light blue eyes. An expression she found utterly unreadable and which made of him a stranger again, albeit a stranger with a face as familiar to her now as her own.

Unnerved both by that look and the flat formality of his tone, Rowène felt a frisson of unease skitter across her already raw nerves. It was not fear certainly but perhaps an echo of that disquiet she had acknowledged during her initial encounters with Guy of Montfaucon, although never once since she had come to know him better.

Or at least she had thought she had come to know him better.

For perhaps five heartbeats she actually considered cancelling her ride or asking whether one of the castle grooms was available to accompany her. But Guy had given her no real cause to doubt him and she had already conceded that this must be the last time they would ride together.

Perhaps today, if the gods were kind, she would meet her father on his way home. That was her hope, every time she rode down towards Swanfleet, and although she had always been disappointed before, she would not yield up any part of that hope, least of all because of an itinerant harper calling himself Guy of Montfaucon.

It was mid-morning by the time they reached the great sandstone bridge that spanned the wide, deceptively smooth flow of the busy Liriél river. They crossed over, nodding a courteous good day to the toll-keeper who, being quite accustomed to the sight of the Lady Rowena and her escort, passed them through without fuss, although a certain amount of speculation lingered in his gaze. An expression Rowène caught as she rode past, chin tilting haughtily in response. Yet even as she continued across the bridge she could sense the man's vulgar stare boring into her back, causing her to remember once more the warning Ju had given her.

Despite her protestations to the contrary, Rowène had not been unaware of the undercurrent of rumour that drifted upon the summer-scented breeze, much as the fallen cherry blossom had drifted under her horse's hooves. But now that Ju had brought the matter into the open she found it impossible to pretend ignorance any longer, much as she wished to do so. In her heart she knew that her sister was right and it was time – indeed more than time – that she curtailed these rides that had brought her so much pleasure, and displayed instead the circumspection due to her betrothed state. And, surely, the loss of the harper's company would cause her no more than a momentary pang, soon forgotten. That being so, for honour's sake, she had to tell him this... whatever it was between them... must end.

For his part, she doubted whether he would care that they could no longer ride alone among the orchard-clad valleys or explore the hidden pebbled coves of the sandstone coast as it curved away south towards Mithlondia's distant border with Kardolandia. He would move on. Forget her in new sights and new songs. Or return, for a while, to his own hearth and the arms of the woman who must surely be missing him. She wondered if he had any children waiting for him there but that was one of the things she had never permitted herself to ask him. Perhaps she would today since the answer would no longer matter.

Whatever *his* personal circumstances and destination, she knew that she would not forget him as easily as he would her.

Nevertheless, she *would* tell him. Just not yet!

And not when they eventually returned to the castle and were once more surrounded by people. No, she decided, she could not bear to tell him then, amidst the hustle and bustle of castle life, where there was little chance of privacy without an attendant scandal.

Perhaps when they stopped for the mid-day meal, that would be a good time? While they were still alone. And maybe – if there were none to witness – she might even coax him to touch his lips to her fingers in farewell... Yes, she decided, she would tell him then. And the gods lend her the strength not to reveal how much he had come to mean to her.

*He*; Guy of Montfaucon. A harper of humble birth but gentle heart. The only man, save her father and brother, to see *her* and not her dark-flame hair. A stranger who, from that very first moment of meeting, had looked at her with warmth in his eyes instead of that flicker of fear she so hated to see.

God of Light! She was not a witch! She had no power to enslave men against their will! She was just a woman... and not even that yet. Not really. Not until her binding night when Joscelin de Veraux would lie with her and make her his wife.

Just for one fleeting, guilty moment she wondered what it would be like to lie with the harper... before slamming the shutter on her wayward thoughts.

She knew what it would be like – the act itself. She had glimpsed that act being performed more often than she wished to remember, either behind the trailing curtains of kylinia vines or beneath the clear waters of the falls and pools of Kaerellios. She just did not know what it would feel like.

But soon – in a matter of days rather than months or years – she would find out. In Joscelin de Veraux's bed. Pray gods that he might be kind to her.

Not all men were, that she knew well enough. Neither kindly nor gentle, courteous nor considerate. Instinctively she glanced eastward along the highway towards the living wall of the Larkenlay Forest, remembering the whispers she had heard concerning the violent and brutal reputation of the de Rogé brothers. She shuddered uncontrollably as if a harsh hand had stroked her spine... coldly caressed her cheek...

"Lady Rowena?"

Guy's voice, warm and concerned, reached out to dispel the illusion that had caught her in its dark embrace.

"Are you all right? You look..." He hesitated perceptibly before finishing. "Pale."

"No, I am well. It was just... it was nothing. But I do not wish to ride that way..." She gestured along the highway towards the great green blur of beech and chestnut that covered the land between the Liriél and the Larkenlye and shuddered again. "Not ever."

Guy regarded her for a moment in sombre silence, his light blue eyes disquietingly unreadable once more.

"There is no reason why you should," he said at last. "As Joscelin of Veraux's wife you will probably live your entire life in Lamortaine." He must have noticed her grimace of distaste because he continued with a faint smile. "Oh, Lamortaine is not that bad. It is many times bigger than Chartre, yes, and I will admit that the poorer quarters stink in the summer heat like an open cesspit. But you will scarcely be living in the Marish, rather within the Guardians' quarters in the palace itself. Close by are gardens which cover many acres down to the lake's edge and the flowers keep the summer air sweet; roses, lilac, lilies and others I cannot name. What it might be like in winter I cannot tell you, but surely no worse than any nobleman's castle."

She regarded him for a heartbeat then murmured,

"Thank you, Guy, for those words. You must think me very foolish."

"No, it would be surprising if you were not anxious..."

She thought he was going to say something more but when the silence lengthened she realised he had thought better of it, whatever it had been. Clicking her tongue, she heeled her mare forwards, turning westwards onto the highway that led through the provinces of Chartreux, Liriéllon, Marillec, Viléron and finally Mortaine. There, in the royal city of Lamortaine, her father lingered yet, hunting and hawking with Prince Marcus – perhaps, as her mother had spitefully suggested, dallying with his mistress – while his daughter awaited his return with a hope that failed a little more every day.

Leaving the bridge and its inquisitive keeper behind them they rode for another league or so along the well-kept, tree-lined highway before turning aside and, passing between the rustling poplars, came to a quiet, shady place where they might stop and partake of the light meal Guy had brought with them.

Despite its proximity to the highway, the little meadow had an air of serene solitude, the grassy sward bordered on one side by the rustling screen of gently moving leaves and on the other by a shallow stream that ran flashing and glinting down to the Liriél, chuckling and chattering over round, brown pebbles with an almost unheard voice. Nudging her mare forwards Rowène saw that the water was as clear as glass, alive with moorhens and their chicks busying themselves amongst the great mats of river weed, pushing thin dark trails through the countless white flowers that shone in the sunlight with a light of their own. It was a like a place in some minstrel's tale... golden and green and glimmering with enchantment.

Perhaps it was this odd sense of recognition but Rowène felt herself shiver, acknowledging the fleeting qualm of unease that washed over her even as she leant over in the saddle, placing her hands on her companion's sturdy shoulders in order to dismount. In direct contradiction to the imagined caress of moonlight in her mind, reality lay in the warm skin, powerful muscles and damp linen beneath her trembling fingers.

The harper's hands at her waist, however, were firm and quite impersonal. Yet even as she slid down to stand suddenly breathless between him and the mare, she could see in his light blue eyes the faintest hint of disquiet... and something else... something darker...

For a wild moment Rowène was convinced that he meant to... What? To kiss her?

Would she permit such an indiscretion without protest? When she was betrothed to another man? A man, she thought in a moment of sharp and unexpected discontent, who was even more of a stranger to her than Guy of Montfaucon but to whom she would soon be bound for the rest of her life.

Scarcely daring to draw breath, unsure of both herself and him, she waited...

But if it had indeed been his intention to kiss her, he obviously thought better of it. The next moment he muttered something that could have been an apology if she chose to take it so, dropped his hands from her waist and turned to secure the horses, leaving Rowène bereft and silently berating herself for her folly.

*Gods above! What was I thinking? Of course he does not desire me!*

And even if he did, would she find such a man – a man who could contemplate breaking his sworn binding vows in such a manner – worthy of her respect or liking? The simple answer, of course, was that she would not. Yet if there was one thing she knew instinctively about Guy of Montfaucon it was that, irrelevant of his birth or present occupation, he was an honourable man and that it ill behoved her to break that integrity.

Then she smiled to herself, somewhat ruefully, as she wondered where such thoughts had come from. To the ignorant, the red fire of her hair proclaimed her to be an enchantress capable of inflaming men to grievous acts against their will! Yet, as she well knew, she had never aroused so much as a flicker of desire in a man before – let alone an all-consuming blaze! And it seemed well beyond the bounds of probability that Guy of Montfaucon would prove to be her first victim.

Reason restored, she came out of her reverie to find the harper kneeling on the flower-strewn river bank, busying himself with unpacking the bread, cheese, dried fruits and flask of watered wine provided by the castle cook.

Rowène smiled, murmured her thanks and settled down on the fragrant grass, indicating that Guy should seat himself as well. He hesitated momentarily and then settled down a few paces away, close enough to be able to share the food yet still maintaining a discreet distance; even in that secluded place, it seemed, he was unwilling to disregard the rules that would, under normal circumstances, keep a high-born damsel and a lowly harper at a distance.

For her part, given the absence of curious or condemning eyes, Rowène was more than content to sit in easy companionship with the harper, enjoying the feel of the soft, sweet-scented grass beneath her outspread skirts, smiling at the swallows as they dipped gracefully over the water, beguiled by the blue-winged dragonflies as they hovered and darted in a silent dance. In the absence of words between them, Rowène listened instead to the sounds of the meadow; the whispers of the leaves above her head, the busy chatter of the birds in the boughs and the noisy grazing of the two horses behind her.

The simple meal had long since been eaten and finding that the lazy glissade of the river was seducing her towards somnolence, Rowène withdrew her gaze from the glittering water and glanced around for her companion, knowing that if she were going to tell him of her decision it must be now.

Somewhat to her consternation she saw that, while *she* had been enjoying their last moments of solitude together, *he* had taken the opportunity to quietly remove himself and was now standing some twenty paces away, his back to her.

Something in his stance – head bent, shoulders tense, one fist clenched against an unyielding grey tree trunk – struck her hard, rendering her incapable of delivering her reluctantly prepared speech.

Dear God of Mercy, had he sensed something of what lay between them, perhaps guessed what she might be going to say? Meant perhaps to say it himself; that, for the sake of her reputation and his skin, they must no longer ride alone together like this?

Or – and she could not say whence this second, disquieting notion had come – was it something else entirely that caused his undeniable tension?

All of a sudden the sun-shot quietude of the river bank, broken only by the desultory murmur of the water and the half-heard hum of insects, seemed no longer to be a refuge but a prison. Which was, of course, a ridiculous fancy, she told herself. Almost as ridiculous as the notion that she was an eldritch enchantress and he the helpless mortal enmeshed in her power. And yet...

She cast another, narrower, look at him as he stood unmoving beneath the rippling leaves of the poplar tree, the stillness of strain showing in every line of his big body, the merest breath of a warm breeze stirring his fair hair; those ragged, lightly waving locks that barely touched his shoulders, lending him the appearance of the humblest peasant... Yes, *lent!* The realisation struck her with the force of a blow; whatever else he might be, she was suddenly certain that he was no peasant. Just as she gave the illusion of being a witch, so he had crafted his appearance as a wandering harper...

Yet, if no harper, what then was he? Whatever it was, she did not think he was happy about it. Not if the misery she glimpsed in his averted face were any indication of his true feelings.

Unable to bear the tense uncertainty any longer, Rowène scrambled to her feet and, quietly covering the distance between them, gently laid her hand on his bare forearm.

"Guy? Tell me. What is troubling you?"

He flinched visibly under her touch. Shocked by his reaction, she removed her hand from his arm and took a step back. But it was too late for retreat. Too late by far...

Guy straightened and turned his gaze towards her. The mouse-fair hair at his temples was dark with sweat and stuck to his skin, his light blue eyes were so bleak as to be almost grey and his bearded face set in such grim lines as to make him seem a stranger again. Still he did not speak and indeed he was silent so long she thought he was not going to answer her at all. She was just about to repeat her question when he finally spoke, his voice so hoarse as to be unrecognisable.

"Can you not hear it? Many men and horses. Coming down the road!"

*He* evidently believed what he was saying and Rowène found herself straining her ears in an attempt to catch an echo of what he thought he had heard.

"No... I cannot hear anything like that. Just the sound of the leaves, the river, the birds." She looked back at him in some concern. "Guy, what is it? Are you ill?"

"No," he answered tersely. "Or at least, not as you mean. Although the gods know I must have been moon-mad to have consented to involve myself in any of this. If you have any sense, you will flee now."

"Flee? From what?" asked Rowène in bewilderment, feeling the first stirrings of fear catch at her throat. There was a desperate look in the harper's light blue eyes and she wondered suddenly if he truly was... not insane perhaps but suffering some temporary affliction of the mind.

*Then* she heard it.

The sound the harper had heard in his mind now made relentless reality in her own ears.

The sound of a large troop of horsemen.

Thundering louder, ever more fiercely aggressive, more darkly oppressive with every echoing hoof beat.

Afraid, although not quite knowing why, since it could easily have been her father returning home at last, Rowène looked once more at her companion, hoping for some sign of reassurance. But without another word, he spun away from her to stand in the shifting shadows on the other side of the poplar, facing the highway, clearly waiting for the horsemen to come abreast of him.

Knowing that his advice came too little and too late, Rowène straightened her shoulders and moved to stand at his side. Close enough for the full skirt of her dark blue gown to touch the scuffed leather of his high boots. Close enough for the soft linen of his loose shirt to flutter against her cold fingers.

"Guy? Do you know who these riders are?" she asked, fear quickening her heartbeat despite herself.

Then, when he did not immediately reply, she spoke his name again, more sharply.

"Guy! Answer me! Please."

He shot her another glance but could not hold her gaze.

"Yes, I know," he said flatly, looking away.

Despite the daunting note in his voice, she might have questioned him further but at that very moment she caught a glimpse of movement out of the corner of her eye and, following the harper's fixed stare, glanced along the sun-speared roadway where a massed group of mail-clad horsemen were now emerging from the deceptive green shadows under the trees. Even so, it was not until they were within a few yards of her position that Rowène finally made out the details of the black and silver banner that floated behind the leader's shoulder.

*Gods save us!*

Scarcely able to credit what she was seeing she whirled to face the man beside her and gripped his arm, feeling the clenched muscles tighten still further beneath her trembling fingers.

"Is *this* why you told me to flee?" she demanded in a choked voice. "But how did you know? How *could* you know? Gods above, Guy! Surely that cannot be the Lord of Rogé himself? Not here, in Chartreux!"

The harper did not immediately answer and her common sense reasserted itself, offering some solace from the shivering fear that had overtaken her at first sight of those dreaded colours.

"But what am I saying? This is the prince's highway, no matter that its upkeep falls upon the Lords of Chartreux, and it is the most direct road from Lamortaine to Rogérinac. There is no reason why Lord Joffroi should not use it... no reason why he should deign to notice us. He does not know me and I doubt would recognise a mere harper who once played in his hall."

Her fearful attention was almost entirely focussed on the approaching horsemen. Nonetheless she could not fail to notice how the lines of the harper's face hardened or the way his fingers clenched into fists. Only after she had lost all hope that he might answer her babbling did he speak, his voice level once more but, astonishingly, the words that formed on his tongue were not couched in the common speech of the realm, such as he had always used in her hearing before, but the formal language of court and castle.

"Demoiselle de Chartreux, what would you have me say? Your eyes have not deceived you and that is indeed the banner and device of the Seigneur de Rogé. As to what evil... regrettably, that you will find out for yourself all too soon. Suffice it to say that Joffroi is not on his way to Rogérinac but to Chartre." His voice broke momentarily as he finished bitterly, "And may the gods damn me to the darkest depths of Hell for my betrayal!"

Rowène felt the ice around her heart slowly seep into her blood and in the last moments before the horsemen drew level with them she looked anew at her companion, realising with numb disbelief that he had been using the high Mithlondian tongue as one born to it.

"Dear God of Light, who *are* you?" she asked unsteadily, shivering with shock, her vision darkening. On the brink of fainting, it was only the uncharacteristic contempt in her companion's voice that saved her.

"Just as well your father is not here to see you now! Else he would surely think you are no daughter of his. Or do you think Louis de Chartreux would quiver like a frightened rabbit at the mere sight of a strip of cloth wrought into the semblance of the black boar of Rogé!"

Reacting more to the tone than the words Rowène felt a surge of sudden, searing fury stiffen her spine. She stood up straighter, her head held high, ready to face whatever might come. But inwardly she wept for all she had lost when the harper had revealed himself for the traitor he was, making a mockery of what she thought had been friendship between them. A friendship which, fragile and flawed though it had been had, she believed, meant as much to him as it did to her.

The gods pity her for she could not have been more wrong!

# Chapter 5

## *Warlord's Hostage*

As if only just noticing them, the leader of the horsemen raised his arm in command and the whole cavalcade reined to a halt, motionless and silent, save for the jingle of bridle bits and the swish of horses' tails; dark wraiths from some eldritch nightmare trapped within the gilded green light that dappled the highway beneath the towering trees. It was a menacing sight – and deliberately designed to be, Rowène thought, her anger suddenly stronger than her undeniable fear.

How dare this evil nobleman and his brutish minions come riding through her family's land, along the highway maintained at her father's expense, and seek to overwhelm all in their path by means of sheer arrogance and undoubted strength of arms! Even the way the leader sat his huge black warhorse, his body encased in silver mail, his features hidden behind the expressionless mask of his full-face helm, showed his dark disdain for her and anyone unfortunate enough to cross his path.

Then, with a movement that nearly made her heart halt, he raised his steel-gauntleted hands, simultaneously pulling off his helm and nudging his horse forwards into a shaft of light, giving Rowène her first sight of a broad, heavy-jawed, black-browed face that looked every bit as ruthless as the snarling boar's head outlined in silver on the breast of his black surcoat.

Seeing her watching him, his full lips quirked in something that on another man might have been termed a grin and his dark brown eyes glinted with malicious amusement. His words, however, were addressed to the man at her side. The man who, mere moments ago, had confessed to betraying her to this… this cockroach from the deeps… this monster in man's form… who, if he had ever possessed a soul, had sold it to the Daemon of Hell more than a score of years ago.

She saw his mouth open and braced herself for whatever might come out. What came was a deep, resonant voice – utterly unlike the harsh, corbie's croak she had been expecting – while his common speech proved to be fluent and perfectly intelligible. She wished to the gods that it had not been or that she could block her ears to his damning words.

"Guy! 'Tis good to see you, man. But what daemon whispered in your ear that today was the day? Or is it merely my good fortune that some affair of your own brought you out this way? So who's the lucky wench, hmm?" He cast an appraising eye in Rowène's direction, his grin widening to show sharp, surprisingly white teeth, as his gaze touched on her uncovered hair. "I never knew you harboured a secret desire to be burned, Guy! Or are you so blinded by her other charms you have not noticed the fire of her hair?"

The harper snapped something incomprehensible in a harsh language she was unfamiliar with but Rogé's lord merely raised thick black brows and continued in speech she could understand,

"Too hot for you, eh? Never mind. I dare say Ranulf can find a use for her. He's not had a woman since we left Lamortaine and I have no doubt he will take her if you lack the will – or the desire – to keep her in your own bed." The dark eyes settled on her. "Well, wench, what think you?"

Rowène gasped and shrank back under the heavy tide of revulsion that swept over her. She was dimly aware of the harper moving to stand between her and Black Joffroi's mocking dark gaze and when he spoke his normally light and pleasant tones were noticeably abrasive, for all he had reverted to Mithlondian.

"For gods'sake, Joff! Can you not at least accord the lady the courtesy due to her rank! She is neither witch nor wench but a Demoiselle de Chartreux. As I am damned sure you already know!"

Far from taking umbrage at this rebuke from his minion, Joffroi de Rogé's jocular grin widened. He inclined his head towards her in a gesture that could by no stretch be termed courteous and, with a wave of his mailed hand at the rider ruthlessly curbing a restless black stallion beside him, said with spurious benevolence,

"Since Guy would have me hold to the formalities, Demoiselle, allow me to introduce my brother, Ranulf." And to his companion in mock rebuke. "Take off your helm, man! Daemons balls! Did our lady mother teach you no manners at all? You heard Guy! This is no common strumpet whose favours you can buy with a few copper coins but one of Louis de Chartreux's virginal daughters."

There was a creak of leather and a jingle of metal as Ranulf de Rogé shifted slightly in his saddle. The helm he was wearing was of a different style to his brother's and Rowène could plainly see his jaw tighten and his lips move in some soundless oath. Reins held loosely across his thigh, he raised one heavily gauntleted fist and pulled off his battered war-helm.

"Demoiselle," he acknowledged, angling his head in the slightest of sardonic salutes.

Rowène sucked in a breath and sought to quell the nausea that flared in her belly as his eyes raked the length of her trembling body with a cool familiarity that was an insult in itself, resting with a brief flicker of something that was not ice on her uncovered hair, before finally settling on her face with an indifference that she might have found reassuring had it not also been so openly arrogant.

Even more terrified of *this* man than she had been of Black Joffroi, she raised her chin and eyed him with as much pride and contempt as she could dredge up. However alike in character they might be, he did not look anything like his older brother. Where the Lord of Rogé was as dark-avised as the daemons of night, his younger brother was fair – incongruously so – his hair, for the most part, being as pale as barley under a harvest moon, while in his eyes she thought she saw the dark blue ice of Hell itself.

Despite the revulsion she felt, Rowène refused to yield before the clear menace the man so flagrantly offered and she saw the faintest of mocking smiles touch his hard mouth as if he guessed that her mask of defiance was little more than a fragile shield to hide the fear beneath.

Beside her, the harper made a restless movement and she thought for a moment he would intervene. Glancing up at him, she saw that his light blue eyes were fixed upon the younger de Rogé with an expression that was little short of lethal.

Was that something she could use? Rowène wondered fleetingly. Some ill feeling between the Lord of Rogé's brother and Guy of Montfaucon that she could turn to good account? Yet realistically what could, or would, the harper be able to do to help her against these two high-ranking noblemen, one of whom was apparently his liege lord, the other a battle-hardened and vicious killer – unless his appearance belied his nature and reputation. And she did not think it did, not where Ranulf de Rogé was concerned.

Everything about his big, heavily-mailed body – Gods! She thought without humour, the man was built like an ox through the shoulders – to the hard jaw, mocking mouth and unyielding ice-blue eyes proclaimed that here was a ruthless marauder who took what he wanted, permitting none to stand in his way. Even the way in which he wore his very long fair hair – braided at the temples, the rest in a tangled fall over his shoulders – served to emphasise his base savagery.

She remembered how she had been curious enough to ask Luc about the length of his own hair soon after her return to Chartre, having long-since become accustomed to the way the Kardolandian men clipped their curling hair close to their heads. According to her brother, it dated back to the time hundreds of years before when the wild warriors who had crossed the Mithlain Mountains and conquered what was to become Mithlondia had worn their hair in just such a fashion and that, by tradition, any Mithlondian nobleman with a claim to warrior blood, kept his hair long. Even though most, himself included, kept it trimmed to a reasonable length and only braided or bound it for battle. There were exceptions, he had added with a crispness she had not understood at the time but did now; younger sons, landless knights and others he had not specified who were little better in status than paid mercenaries.

Ranulf de Rogé was obviously one such if his hair and weaponry were any testament. Besides the sheathed longsword belted at his side, a second sword hung from his saddle, together with a vicious looking battleaxe, the huge blade of which glittered evilly in the dappled sunlight. God of Mercy! She felt sick just looking at it! And as for the man who wielded it...

She swayed as a tide of faintness engulfed her, felt a warm, calloused hand cup her elbow and shook it off violently. In that moment, she did not know which of the three men – the two de Rogé brothers or their harper – she hated most. She just knew she could not bear the slightest touch of this man whom she had trusted; the man who had betrayed them all.

"Take your hand off me, you cur!" she hissed, relishing as he flinched perceptibly at her words the bitter satisfaction of knowing that she was capable of causing him pain. Not as much as he had hurt her perhaps but to some degree at least. The gods damn the man to the darkest depths of Hell and his masters with him!

Achingly aware from the girl's words and actions that she now understood all the implications of his presence in Chartre, the man who had been known as Guy of Montfaucon sighed and, with an unexpected reluctance, shed the harper's skin now that the necessity for wearing it was gone.

Unable to stomach the satisfied smirk on Joffroi's face, he glanced at Ranulf, observing with growing disquiet, the gleam in the dark blue eyes slanted towards Louis de Chartreux's daughter. The gods knew, Guy was not fool enough to think that Ranulf would take any notice of him if his mind was truly made up but he had to make the effort, for the girl's sake if nothing else. Guy knew, to his shame, that he could not protect both sisters. Had always known that. Had known also that the day would come when he must make this damnable choice... And now circumstance had made it for him. Keeping his tone quiet he said flatly,

"Keep away from her, Ran. She belongs to me!"

He heard, but ignored, the gasp from the girl at his side, keeping his attention firmly fixed on the man he had challenged. Ranulf, curse him, merely sat back in his saddle and regarded him with that mocking grin he knew so well, lazily gesturing to the long, double-handed sword hanging from his saddle.

"Just as well I took the trouble of bringing your blade then, Guy. You will need it if you are determined to keep the wench and against all the odds I decide I do want her. But for the time being... I will be generous and reserve judgement until I get a chance to inspect her sister!"

"Damn you, Ran..." Guy started angrily but Joffroi intervened, his voice harsh now.

"Enough! You two can fight or draw lots for the wenches as you will, once Chartre is ours. But for now..." He turned in the saddle and snapped his fingers at one of the men behind him. "Get you into your mail, Guy. Ran, bind her hands and take the wench up with you."

"No!" Guy snapped as Ranulf made to dismount. There was as much frustration as warning in the glance he divided between Joffroi's darkening countenance and Ranulf's openly mocking smile. "I will do it."

Joffroi gave him a considering look and then shrugged.

"As you will. But I am warning you now, Guy, you had best take care those bonds are tight enough that the wench does not escape to give warning of our presence here."

Guy flicked a glance at the approaching soldier who, making an accurate guess at his unasked question, hastily unwound the strip of leather binding the bundle he carried and held it out.

"Here, sir! Ye can use this fer the lass."

At the periphery of his vision, Guy saw Rowène de Chartreux start and cursed the young soldier, but silently; Geryth could not know the damage he had caused with his use of that accustomed form of address. Even as Guy watched, the young noblewoman turned her terrified gaze away from Joffroi and Ranulf and stared at him instead, a wordless question widening her eyes. Knowing that he could not answer her – or at least not here and not now – he simply took the cord from Geryth and moved towards her. Her gaze dropped to the leather thong, then lifted as she held her hands out to him in bemused compliance. Trying to ignore the wounded disbelief that lurked behind the flare of hatred in her eyes, Guy tied her wrists sufficiently securely to prevent her from working loose but not so tightly as to hurt her unnecessarily.

All too well aware that he was still treading the knife-edge of betrayal and deception, he stepped away from her as soon as he had tied off the last knot, turning to the business of arming himself. But he could not banish his awareness of her gaze as, with Geryth's assistance, he donned leather under-tunic, burnished mail shirt and black surcoat, finally kneeling to fasten the silver-gilt spurs of his rank to his heels, all the while continuing to mentally damn Joffroi, and himself, to Hell and beyond. Rising to his feet, he took a couple of stamping steps to settle his mail more comfortably.

"Guy! Catch!"

He looked up to see Ranulf lift the sheathed sword that dangled from his saddle bow, wrap the heavy leather belt around the scabbard and toss it across to him. Catching the weapon, Guy belted the familiar weight of the longsword at his hip and finally – with the utmost reluctance – turned to face the woman he had betrayed.

Only to find her staring at him as if she had never seen him before. Which, in a sense, he supposed she had not. Gone was the harper in his threadbare clothing. In his place stood Joffroi de Rogé's liege man. Silently he pleaded for her forgiveness, hoping by some miracle to remind her that he was still the same man that she had come to know over the past month. It was a vain hope, he acknowledged. The icy glitter in her grey eyes told him unequivocally what she thought about him and, breaking the wordless contact with a soundless sigh, he turned to address the waiting soldier.

"Geryth?"

"Aye, Master Guy?"

"Would you fetch my horse and that of the lady? They are tethered just the other side of these trees."

"That I will, sir, but Lord Joffroi ordered Fireflame ter be brought up from Rogérinac, so if ye was wishful o' ridin' him..."

Guy nodded. It had been inevitable after all; the final part of his transformation from humble harper to de Rogé retainer.

"Very well, Geryth. Bring him up and then fetch the others."

Rowène stared, wide-eyed, at the tall, chestnut stallion sidling impatiently in front of her. It looked, to her eyes at least, about as unscalable as a castle wall. Although – here she risked a quick glance at the broad, mailed back of the man standing nearby – she guessed he must need a horse of that size and strength to carry his fully-armoured weight. But she was not *him*...

At the moment she could not manage his name in the privacy of her mind, let alone out loud. If indeed the name by which she had known him was even his own! Then she remembered that both de Rogé brothers had called him Guy. Which meant, she supposed, that he had at least not lied to her about that – even if he had lied about almost everything else, this duplicitous cur to whom she had so recklessly given her trust and friendship!

As for mounting his horse, she did not think she could have done so even had her hands been free. How she was going to contrive now, when they were bound, she could not imagine. She spared a nervous glance at the young soldier standing at the stallion's head before becoming aware, with a sick sense of dread, that the younger of the de Rogé brothers had dismounted and come up beside her. She took one look at his dauntingly hard face and mocking, dark blue eyes and stepped hurriedly backwards, moving instinctively towards the treacherous harper. Evidently sensing her movement, he turned quickly, his good-humoured face darkening alarmingly.

"I told you to leave her alone, Ran," he reiterated tersely and, brushing past his liege lord's brother, bent down, cupping his hands for her as he had done so many times before.

She wished for a moment for the courage to kick him in the face. But all that would accomplish would be to leave her to the dubious mercy of the other men. Left with no viable alternative she accepted the traitor's assistance to scramble up into the saddle. Flushed with exertion, she blushed even pinker as he swung up behind her. He reached around her to gather up the reins and as he eased her more securely back against him she heard Black Joffroi's voice rasping unpleasantly,

"Just remember, Guy, since you have claimed her, she is your responsibility! Do whatever it takes to keep her quiet and if you let her get away from you I swear I will make you wish you had never been born!"

With that the Lord of Rogé clapped his helm back on his head, the black strands of his horsetail crest flowing down over the polished iron to mingle with the tousled spill of his own dark hair. His brother flashed her a sardonic smile and settled his battered helm on his head. She shuddered again at this sign of warlike intent and glanced apprehensively back at the man behind her but was relieved, for no reason she could define, to find him still bareheaded. Apparently sensing something of her thoughts, he shook his head slightly and murmured in her ear in the fluid, cultured tones she now expected of him,

"Despite appearances, Demoiselle, I am more harper than warrior." Then dropping his voice still lower, added. "And I will do what I can to protect you from that which must come. My word as... my word on it."

At such a blatantly false oath Rowène hunched a shoulder and turned away from him, annoyed with herself for even acknowledging the existence of this man who had betrayed her trust and given her into the hands of the two most evil men in Mithlondia.

As the horses started to gather speed, cantering easily eastwards along the highway, she forced herself to consider what their intentions might be. Surely if Joffroi de Rogé intended to hold her for ransom – which was the only reason she could think of why they should have taken her prisoner in the first place – they would return with her to their lair in Rogérinac. But Guy had already indicated that they were not bound for their own lands. So where...?

It was not until they came to the great bridge at Swanfleet and the cavalcade turned to cross the river that she began to understand that ransom was not their motive and that Chartre was indeed their intended destination. Although what fell purpose Black Joffroi and his brother had in mind there – or what part they might force her to play – she could not imagine. She only knew it would not be good.

The loud thunder of hooves as the heavily-armed troop hit the bridge brought the keeper out of his little cottage at the far end of the great span. For a moment he froze into petrified silence before abruptly recovering his wits and the use of his legs. He broke away, yelling for help, running desperately for the perceived safety of his home. Spurring his horse with a yell, Black Joffroi set off in pursuit of the fleeing man. Less than five heart-beats later, the bridge-keeper stumbled, screaming with terror, beneath the horse's iron-shod hooves, then fell silent, his head smashed by one casually cruel blow from the morning star clenched in his murderer's massive fist.

The next moment it seemed as if all the daemons of Hell had been let loose as one of Luc's small five-man patrols came unexpectedly onto the scene. There was a moment's startled silence on both sides and then one of the Chartreux soldiers broke away, bound for the castle and town, presumably to give warning of the presence of the armed raiders, while the remaining four, with yells of defiance, drove their horses straight at the intruders. With an answering shout Joffroi de Rogé plunged forwards to meet them, his men streaming after him. But to Rowène's astonishment his brother held back. Keeping his eager mount on a tight rein, he cursed as the black stallion's fretful circling caused the harper's chestnut to toss its head and sidle restlessly.

"Stay out of this, Guy, and for god's sake keep that bloody wench out of harm's way! I have a feeling we are going to need her before the day is out – and not just to warm your bed or mine."

Before Rowène's horrified mind could even think of protesting that she would rather be dead than warm either of their beds, Ranulf de Rogé had swept up his axe, just as another patrol converged on them from the other direction. Changing rein and yelling a fierce battle-cry, he rode straight at them, scything his way through his opponents with a sickening skill.

Between morning star, battle axe and a score of spears it did not take the aggressors long to overpower and slaughter the hopelessly outnumbered opposition. It was only to Rowène – shaking with fear and rage and pity in the protective embrace of a man whose loyalty placed him alongside those same blood-crazed daemons presently wreaking such destruction – that the time seemed interminable. Finally, the hideous shouting and harsh grating of metal on metal ceased... to be replaced by a woman's horrified, near hysterical, screams.

Goaded by this terrible sound, Rowène struggled frantically – and ineffectually – against her captor's iron grip in an attempt to see what was happening.

"Let me go, you beast!" she gasped.

"I will be damned first!" Then, using her proper name for the first time. "Believe me, Rowène, you do not need to witness this." The next moment she heard him snarling over her head at someone else she could not see. "Hell and damnation, Ran! Call your wolves off! Killing armed men is one thing, raping women is another! And you bloody well know it!"

"Joffroi's orders!" came back the curt reply, followed by an irritated curse. "Oh, bloody hell, Guy! The things I do to appease your conscience!"

"Bugger that! You do it for your own," Guy snapped back. But Rowène only vaguely registered his coarse words. All her attention was focussed desperately on the voice she now recognised as belonging to Ranulf de Rogé as he called off his scum.

"Finn! Edric! Gurth! Let that bloody woman alone and get to horse!"

"But, sir..."

"*Now*, Finn!"

De Rogé's intonation, which had formerly been merely clipped and cold was now so icily intimidating that even Rowène shuddered at the lethal menace contained in those two simple words and was relieved – if unsurprised – to hear sounds betokening swift obedience from the three would-be rapists.

There were a few more moments of confused noise then, finally, the steel arm banding her relaxed and Rowène was able to push herself away from the mailed body she had been mercilessly crushed against. Rubbing the bruises that the harper's unyielding grip had left on her arms and ribs, she took her first appalled glance at the hell these vile beasts had wrought... and wished she had not.

The toll-keeper lay in a huddled heap against one side of the bridge, the contents of his skull splattered indiscriminately over sun-warmed stone and the pink and white flowers of wild valerian. His woman crouched next to him in the churned, red dust of the road, clutching the remnants of her torn dress and weeping with heart-shattering intensity. The hacked and bloody bodies of the Chartreux soldiers were being flung from the bridge into the river, where they sank like stones into the depths, all save for the single man who lay crumpled in the middle of the highway where he had fallen, five black-feathered arrows protruding from his back. He they tossed into the long grass under the trees, kicking dust over the patch of bright blood he had shed in vain.

There would, she realised, be no warning for Chartre of the evil about to descend. The gods have mercy on them all!

Then, just as she thought the situation could not possibly get any closer to Hell, a young lad of perhaps eight summers came running up from the river bank. At the devastating sight that met his eyes he dropped the pole and fish he was carrying and crumpled to his knees at his mother's side. A heartbeat later, he was back on his feet, tears of shock, fear and grief tracking down his dirty face as he spat with virulent hatred and some accuracy at the looming, black-clad figure he had unerringly identified as the monster responsible for the destruction of his family.

Another man might have chosen to ignore the insult. Black Joffroi was not such a man. With a snarl, he drove his huge, snorting stallion towards the child, the blood-encrusted battle-star swinging menacingly from his fist. Terrified out of her wits, Rowène forgot her animosity for the man who held her and grabbed hold of his mailed arm.

"For pity's sake, Guy! Stop him!"

It was only after this desperate appeal had left her lips that she belatedly realised that the man to whom she had addressed it had moved to intervene, even before she spoke. She gave a sob of relief which turned into a gasp of horror as Ranulf de Rogé wheeled his black mount in order to block the chestnut stallion's advance.

"I will deal with Joff, Guy," he said curtly. "You get the woman and her brat out of the way. She will go with you easier than me. You, at least, are not soaked in her countrymen's blood as I am."

With that he spurred forwards, interposing his own wild-eyed stallion between the scared child and certain death, with barely a heartbeat to spare. Rowène could not hear what he said to his blood-crazed brother to bring him to his senses and dull the murder-lust in those blazing, dark eyes but she could only be grateful that at least the child was safe. Although, with his father dead and his mother so cruelly misused, she could only wonder what sort of existence the child would have in future.

Then she had no further time to worry about it as the harper thrust the chestnut's reins into her startled hands, dismounted and went to do as he had been ordered. Calling on one of the other soldiers to help him – she thought distractedly it was probably the same one who had helped him earlier – and using a mixture of brute force and persuasion, he managed to get the weeping woman, her sobbing child and the bloody body back into their cottage.

For a moment the thought of escape flashed through her mind. Until she looked up to find Ranulf de Rogé watching her, his narrowed ice-blue eyes still glittering savagely in the aftermath of the fight, his mouth half lifted in that taunting grin she had already learned to loathe. At which point, any reluctant respect and grudging gratitude she might have felt towards him for saving the child died in a blaze of hatred so fierce surely neither time nor distance would ever erase. He returned her gaze for perhaps five heartbeats, the emotion in his dark blue eyes unfathomable, then sketched her a mocking salute and reined his horse aside, leaving her shivering with dread, her insides roiling as if he had physically touched her.

Before she had had a chance to recover from that unnerving encounter, she felt the harper mount up again and suddenly all the ghastly events of the day overcame her fragile control. Never in all her gently-reared life had she witnessed – or expected to witness – death dealt out with such vicious intensity... Nor the violation of a woman and the near slaughter of a helpless child. She felt her stomach spasm again and retched helplessly, only dimly aware of the harper as he held her heaving body steady.

"Dear God of Light! What wrong had they done?" she finally managed to ask between clenched teeth.

"Nothing," Guy of Montfaucon said flatly as he wiped her mouth on the tail of his surcoat. "But since I doubt very much that they will be the only ones to suffer bloody agonies before Joffroi's daemons are glutted, you had best get a grip on yourself or you will have nothing left in your belly by nightfall. And, believe me, when you find out what Joffroi has in mind for you and your sister you will need something in you to be sick with!"

Not wanting to know what horrors lay unspoken behind that blunt warning Rowène swallowed the remnants of vomit down her sore throat and relapsed into silent misery.

Just over a furlong beyond the western end of the Swanfleet Bridge the cavalcade turned off the main road to Chartre town and followed the harper as he guided them along the little-used byways he had spied out in the days when he had pretended to serve the ladies of that land. In this way Black Joffroi's force avoided detection and, making a wide arc around the town, finally joined up with the highway that came up from the south. Following this road east they came within sight, just before dusk, of the western gate of the great castle of Chartre.

The drawbridge was still down but the last rays of the evening sunlight were already gilding the sky behind the high red sandstone walls, and somewhere in the distance a horn rang out for the sunset watch. Behind the battlements and across the bay the sky had deepened from mere blue to a tranquil turquoise alive with the swooping silhouettes of late hunting swallows. It was a peaceful scene, similar in its shining golden glory to any evening that had gone before. A peace too perfect to exist save in that perilous land beyond the sunset path...

An abrupt cry from the battlements warned that their approach had been observed by the guards and the great drawbridge began to rise, the creaking of chains clearly audible in the stillness of the evening. With a roar Black Joffroi spurred his horse to a gallop, his men thundering after him, the silver and black banner rippling out for all to see. But there was never a hope of reaching the bridge in time and de Rogé was forced to draw his mount to a rearing halt on the brink of the deep, stake-lined ditch that guarded the landward side of the castle.

As the big chestnut stallion likewise came to a forced halt Rowène struggled to catch her breath, grateful – despite her dislike of the man himself – for the iron arm that kept her firm in the saddle. She knew a momentary glee that the Lord of Rogé had not found it as easy as he might have thought to gain entry into Chartre until, risking a small, triumphant glance in his direction, she felt a quiver of disquiet when she saw that he did not appear to be overly concerned by this reversal. Instead of ranting and raging, as she would have expected from a nobleman of his obviously unstable temperament, he was merely sitting there, staring up at the towering sandstone walls with a dark, brooding determination, curbing his sidling, snorting horse with casual ease.

Suddenly his deep voice rang out, harsh and commanding in common speech.

"You there, open the gate!"

"Who are you to demand entry in this manner?" That was probably Lucien, Rowène decided.

"I am Joffroi, Lord of Rogé," came the arrogant reply. "And I am come from the Court of Princes in Lamortaine with tidings for the Lady Ariène, so I suggest you open this gate and let us enter, whoever you are."

"I am Lucien, Commander of the Chartre garrison," came back the uncompromising reply. "And I have no authority to allow you entry in the absence of either my lord or his son."

"Then send to the Lady Ariène," Joffroi de Rogé bellowed back, his temper beginning to slip its leash. "She will give you your damned authority!"

There was a long silence from the walls and then eventually Lucien leaned out over the battlement again. The distance was too far to read his expression but his voice was level and calm.

"I've sent for Lady Ariena but my lord's orders were plain enough. Whether in peace or armed for war neither the Lord of Rogé nor any man wearing his colours may be allowed to set foot within Chartre's walls."

At this comprehensive exclusion Black Joffroi's dark eyes flashed fire in the shadows of his helm and wrenching his horse's head around he returned to the place where his brother and harper were waiting, a little apart from the rest of the black-clad soldiers. Frustration clear to hear in his rasping tones, de Rogé growled,

"We need to get past those sodding gates and into that bloody castle."

His brother started to say something but was cut off by a vicious expletive.

The younger man shrugged but bit off any further suggestion although not, Rowène thought, because he was intimidated in any way by his brother's overt displeasure.

Now visibly irritated by the delay, Black Joffroi dragged off his helm and sat glaring at the castle, his heavy features further darkened by a thunderous scowl until, without warning, a grin of unadulterated malice swept across his face.

"I have it!"

He reined his horse back until he was level with the chestnut stallion and, pointing a mailed finger towards the sheathed dagger at the harper's side, said savagely,

"We need to send these whoreson dogs a message that we are in earnest. Get your knife, Guy, and put it to the wench's throat. One little touch against that tender white skin and I warrant that cocky bastard up there will order those gates open fast enough."

Rowène felt a return of her earlier faintness at this utterly unexpected turn of events and even through the unyielding mail she could feel the sudden tension that gripped the man who held her. And not only the harper. Although she could not see more of Ranulf de Rogé's face than the hard line of his jaw, she could hear the steel in his voice as he rasped,

"If you mean to play god with her life, you had better let me do it, Joff. At least I will not cut her throat by accident."

"Damn it, Ran!" the harper snapped. "Not that it matters what you think of my capabilities since Joffroi did not mean it anyway."

"Yes, I bloody well did," Black Joffroi growled. "And if *you* are too much of a milksop to do it, Guy, I will take Ranulf up on his offer and then it will be his prick..." He leered nastily at Rowène. "That the wench will be feeling."

"Your choice, Guy!" the younger de Rogé commented sardonically. And if he did not leer quite as openly as his brother, there was still more than a hint of carnal suggestion in the lazy glance he directed at Rowène.

Muttering another curse, the harper nudged his stallion closer to the other man and, holding Rowène firmly in the crook of his bridle arm, leant over and took a tight grip on de Rogé's mailed arm with his free hand.

"This is the last time I will say this," he gritted. "Keep your bloody hands and lascivious thoughts away from the Demoiselle."

"And if I do not?" the other queried, his dark blue eyes unreadable behind his helm. "Will you fight me? For the sake of some flame-haired witch you do not even want! Or... do you?" And when the harper continued to stare at him, without either confirming or denying his assertion, added more quietly, "This is neither the time nor the place, Guy. Now, let go of my arm before *I* am obliged to question your parentage in public and *you* are obliged to do something about it."

Whatever lay behind that softly spoken warning – and remembering Guy of Montfaucon's words to her that day on the top of the Lady Tower, Rowène thought she knew what it was — it was sufficient to cause the harper to remove his hand from de Rogé's arm. Turning to face his lord, he said flatly, "Very well, I will do it."

Scarcely able to believe this was actually happening Rowène froze as he brought his knife up towards her neck and prayed to the God of Light that his ability to handle a honed blade matched — if not exceeded — his skills with a harp.

Concentrating on controlling his mount with his knees and holding his hand steady, Guy found himself sweating profusely and praying desperately that this desperate gamble would bring about the desired end before Joffroi lost the last shreds of his precarious patience and decided that Ranulf should transform mere threat into disgusting action.

"Well?" That was Joffroi again, pitching his voice towards the upper wall walk. "Are you going to open the gates and let us in? Think well before you refuse again! Or better yet look out and see who I have here with me!" And in a lower tone, "Guy, show them what will happen if they persist in their refusal!" And reining back, Joffroi left the way clear for Guy and his hostage.

The murmur of consternation from the walls abruptly became a confusion of outcry and abuse as those now assembled finally realised the identities of the girl and the man who held her at knife point.

"Look! Gods save us, 'tis the Lady Rowena!"

"Aye, an' look who her's with! The one wi' the knife at her throat!"

"Gods above, 'tis that whoreson harper!"

"May he rot in hell, the stinking swine!"

Finally the garrison commander's voice rose above the others, roughened by a combination of rage and fear.

"Enter then and be damned to you. And may the Daemon of Hell take you if Lady Rowena comes to any harm at yon misbegotten bastard's hands!"

# Chapter 6

## *Defiance and Submission*

With much creaking of timber and clanking of chains the drawbridge of Chartre castle was slowly lowered and the gates swung open.

Joffroi crowed triumphantly and spurred his horse towards the gateway, Ranulf a little behind him. Giving silent but heartfelt thanks to the gods, Guy replaced his dagger with fingers that shook now that the crisis was over and followed the other two across the bridge and into the shadows of the gateway, the soldiers falling in behind him. The girl in his arms gave a little sigh as the tension left her and sank back against his broad chest. He suffered this in grim silence for a few moments and then bent his head to whisper in her ear,

"Get a grip on yourself, Demoiselle, and remember who you are! Unless, of course, you *want* your people to wonder if you are with me as something other than a hostage for their obedience?" And when that brought no perceptible reaction, added, "You saw how the bridge-keeper looked at us earlier! Surely you cannot claim ignorance of the gossip that whispers we are lovers?"

He felt her stiffen in his arms and guessed that she had indeed been aware that her name and his had been coupled in such a fashion — had, in all probability, known for as long as he had. But if that were so, why in the name of all the gods had she continued to accept his escort over the past few weeks, risking her reputation so recklessly?

She slanted him a filthy look over her shoulder and replied to his deliberate slander in tones of icy hauteur,

"Lovers? Are you mad! Even were I not betrothed to a nobleman, do you truly think I would take one of Black Joffroi's *lackeys* to my bed?"

Her contempt stung more painfully than he thought possible and he retaliated unthinkingly.

"Ah, but you did not know that I was one of Black Joffroi's lackeys until today, did you? If you had not discovered that unfortunate truth, the gossip would not now be false, would it? If I had wanted to, I could have taken you today, on the warm grass beside the river. And we both know it!" Then, seeing the stricken look in her eyes, he added more gently, "You should not give your trust so easily, Demoiselle, least of all to chance-come strangers of whom you know nothing."

"Nor will I, ever again," she promised in a shaking voice. "Instead I shall curse you and those two murdering monsters you serve with every breath I take

100

and only when the Daemon of Death has dragged the last one of you down to the Hell that is waiting for you, will I be free to trust again!"

The venom in her voice was not entirely unexpected but the arrow-swift pain that shot through his heart was. Guilt he had expected to feel – a heavy enough burden – but not such a crippling, *physical* hurt.

Despite this, his awareness that they were being watched from all sides forced him to keep his face blank and to take what encouragement he might from her fleeting display of emotion, chilling though it had been. He did not think he had imagined the thread of steel that underlay her bitter words of defiance and he gave thanks that she had inherited something of her father's courage; the gods knew she would need every last shred of it in order to face what must come.

He saw the spark of defiance grow in her grey eyes even as her back straightened as she attempted to put as much distance between their bodies as she could, which given the limitations of sharing a saddle with a large and fully-armoured man was not very much. It should, however, be sufficient to convince her people that she had not betrayed them by taking one of "Black Joffroi's lackeys" to her bed. As long as she never guessed that was not all he was!

Rowène might have believed the disdainful insult she had tossed at the harper but nonetheless she could not prevent his words, or her sister's, from echoing mockingly around her mind.

*Lovers!* That was what the gossips were saying of them! And he had known. As had Ju. Yet she had not. Or not that she would acknowledge. She felt a fool. And furious with anyone who had even thought such a thing. That the Lord of Chartreux's daughter might demean herself so with some nameless, low-born harper! Who was also one of Joffroi de Rogé's lackeys! Albeit a lackey who wore a sword at his hip and gilt spurs at his heels. Even so, the idea was... laughable? No, nauseating! She thrust the thought away. It came back.

Lovers? Her and Guy of Montfaucon? Never! He had betrayed her, bound her hands, held his knife to her throat at his lord's command. He had also lied to her. She did not know exactly *who* he was but she was painfully certain that Montfaucon was the last name in five realms that he could lay claim to. Guy of Rogérinac would likely be nearer the mark.

Lovers! Hah! Then, like a chill wind blasting through her mind, she abruptly remembered how he had warned Ranulf – now there was a name that grated harsh on the ear – that she belonged to *him*. To a mere harper.

Lovers? It looked as if *never* was soon to turn on its head and become grim fact. Although, she mused darkly, love was the last emotion that would enter into such an arrangement, either on her part or his.

She twisted within the circle of his mailed arm, fully intending to tell him so, but before she could utter the scathing words she caught Ranulf de Rogé's glittering, dark blue gaze. Abruptly remembering the inconceivable interest he had shown in her, she recoiled in horror from the mere thought of how that interest might be satisfied. Better by far, if she were to be forced into bed with one of them, that it be the treacherous harper rather than the blood-splattered soldier who had not, she realised now, been exaggerating in his earlier claim. At least Guy was familiar to her and, despite everything he had said and done that day, she thought... hoped... that if the gods unaccountably allowed the worst to happen and she found herself in his bed, he would be as considerate of her as circumstances allowed.

Then she gave herself a mental shake. Why was she even considering the possibility that she would end the day lying in Guy of Montfaucon's arms? Just because Black Joffroi had gained entry to Chartre by threats of violence did not mean the day must inevitably end in rape and further bloodshed. According to his claim, he was here simply as a messenger from Prince Marcus. Surely once he had delivered that message he would take his men, including his hard-eyed brother and his soft-spoken harper, and leave Chartre, never to return...

It was at this optimistic point in her calculations that Rowène became aware that the horse she was so uncomfortably perched upon had stopped moving. Glancing around she was unexpectedly relieved to see her mother standing before the door to the keep, Ju at her side, Lucien and five men of the Chartre garrison ranged behind them.

Ju, she saw immediately, was looking even more pale and wraith-like than normal and although her face was calm, her green eyes were dark with some emotion Rowène took to be fear but might equally have been something else entirely; somewhere in the past few months Rowène had lost her ability to read her sister's heart within the limpid depths of her eyes.

By contrast, the Winter Lady appeared totally in control of herself and the situation. In the silence that followed their arrival, her mother's luminous emerald eyes touched briefly on the Lord of Rogé, moved to survey Rowène with a dispassionate regard, then returned to acknowledge the now bare-headed nobleman, addressing him in common speech but with the greatest formality.

"My lord, perhaps you will do me the courtesy to tell me by what right you force entry into my home in this manner? And why my daughter should be held at knife-point by the very man whom I appointed to guard her welfare?"

"Believe me, my lady," Black Joffroi replied, a strange, dark smile gleaming in the depths of his peat-brown eyes. "I regret the manner of our entry as much as you. Nor has your daughter suffered any harm from Guy's blade, although I cannot answer for anything else he may have done to her prior to our arrival. I confess, when I first came upon them down by the river I assumed from your daughter's loosened hair and Guy's casual attire that they had been..."

He paused, seemingly lost for words to explain to a high-born lady that he had just caught her daughter behaving with all the circumspection of a dockside whore – and with one of his own men to boot! Lady Ariène, however, appeared to understand this unspoken conclusion and, ignoring the harper completely, flicked a coolly enquiring glance in Rowène's direction.

"Well, Rowène?" she demanded in a voice like sheerest silk. "Have you so soon made a mockery of the honourable betrothal I have taken such care to arrange for you, heedlessly taking a lover and permitting him to tumble you in the grass on the river bank like some peasant slut?"

"No, of course not!" Rowène denied hotly, even while she doubted the evidence of her ears. That her mother could publicly accuse her of such behaviour on no more grounds than the casual word of a man known to be their family's enemy... "I swear by all the gods, Mother, that I have done nothing wrong, whatever gossip or this... this man says to the contrary!"

Her mother smiled faintly, arching artfully darkened brows as she allowed her supercilious gaze to rest on the harper.

"And what say you, Guy of Montfaucon? Do *you* have the courage to admit what my daughter seems incapable of?" Her tone modulated, her challenge declining into reproach. "Even though, in truth, I fear some of the blame must be mine. I should have heeded her sister's warning but I trusted you neither to seduce nor force..."

"Bollocks!" the harper interrupted, his blue eyes flashing like lightning in a summer storm. "I am no more guilty of rape than Ro... Demoiselle de Chartreux is of permitting me to seduce her! As both you and your l..."

"Hold your tongue, damn you!"

Black Joffroi's roar made Rowène flinch and the harper – wisely she felt – bit off whatever else he had intended to say. The Lord of Rogé's anger was a palpable thing, throbbing menacingly in the air, wanting... *needing* to lash out and hurt someone. No-one moved. Even the horses were suddenly still. She dared not look away from the daemon that glared from those bulging brown eyes, fearing lest it break loose to lethal effect.

She could count her heartbeats, loud in the silence...

And in that silence the creak of leather sounded abnormally loud in her ears.

Slowly she turned her head, to watch in horrified disbelief as Ranulf de Rogé leaned sideways in the saddle and casually *spat* onto the cobbles, the gobbet of spittle landing just beside the chestnut stallion's huge front hoof.

She had not recovered from the shock of that disgusting show of ill-breeding when she heard, with even greater shock, his now familiar voice drawl in sardonic-edged Mithlondian,

"Flog him if you like, Joff, but do it in the morning, hmm? A pox on the wench, she is more trouble than she is worth."

Revolted as she was by both by his actions and his words, it took Rowène some moments to realise that he had – possibly at some risk to himself judging by the vitriolic glare Black Joffroi now turned on him – managed to break the ever-tightening circle of his brother's tension before it exploded into violence. Even as she watched, her breath held painfully within her breast, the fury was diminishing in Black Joffroi's face, the dangerous desire to inflict pain fading from his dark eyes.

"A pox on them both!" He agreed with a sudden, grating laugh but neither voice nor words held any humour.

Rowène shivered and then shivered again as she fleetingly caught the bleak look in the dark blue gaze of the man who had yet again risked intervening between his brother and his prey. Swallowing bile, she dragged her attention back to Black Joffroi.

"Forget your daughter's indiscretions for the moment, my lady," he was saying impatiently. "We have far more important matters to deal with. Not least, why I, of all the Lords of the High Counsel, should have been sent to Chartre at this time."

Under Rowène's bemused gaze her mother seemed to falter and one delicate white hand rose to her mouth in a rare gesture of insecurity. Her voice was scarcely audible as she whispered,

"This has to do with Louis, does it not? Is he hurt? An accident whilst hunting? Please, my lord, tell me what has happened."

"I bear a message from the Prince and the High Counsel of Mithlondia," Joffroi de Rogé replied, his deep voice heavy with formality. "And it is such that I believe you would prefer to listen to it in private."

"Very well, my lord." Lady Ariène gave him a brave, rather tremulous smile. "And I thank you for your consideration. Please, come inside. Your brother may accompany you, if you wish, but I would ask that the rest of your men wait outside. Lucien!" This last, more crisply, as she turned to look at the garrison commander. "Wait here, and remember, these men are under orders from the High Counsel and as such, their commander's authority exceeds your own." And to her wide-eyed daughter, "Juliène, come with me!" Then, obviously in response to the flash of rebellion she saw in those green eyes so like her own, added in Mithlondian. "Now, child! You may talk to your slut of a sister later, if you still wish to do so when you have heard everything the Seigneur de Rogé has to say."

Having uttered these pointed words she laid the tips of her fingers on Black Joffroi's proffered arm and glided gracefully into the castle.

Despite everything that had just happened Juliène made no move to follow her mother's command, leaving Rowène torn between anxiety and admiration as she watched her sister stand her ground; a fragile figure in sea-green silk, her gaze wide and blank as she looked first at Rowène, then at the man who held her in the crook of his bridle arm and finally at the man sitting his black stallion in tight-lipped silence, regarding everything before him with narrowed, watchful eyes.

Ranulf had heard the Lady Ariène's invitation and knew what his brother's expectations of him were. Nevertheless, he did not immediately comply with either but sat his horse for several long moments after Joffroi and the very lovely Lady of Chartreux had disappeared into the castle. He exchanged one openly antagonistic look with the soon to be ex-commander of the Chartre garrison, took careful note of the disposition of the guards that he could see and, without volition, found his thoughts wandering in a far less immediate, but eventually unavoidable, direction.

Ruthlessly he allowed his gaze to rove from the wench in Guy's arms – aware, but uncaring, that a thin face, long nose, ice-grey eyes and witch-red hair really did not make an appealing combination – to the most ravishingly beautiful young woman he had ever seen. The decision should never have been in doubt. Yet still Ranulf hesitated.

He slid one final glance at Guy and the noblewoman he had so surprisingly taken under his protection – Ranulf would have expected him to protect the beauty, on the grounds that the plain sister needed no protection – and, cursing audibly enough to make the wench colour, pulled off his helm, brushing his sweat-soaked hair back from his face. Tugging off his gauntlets, he tossed them to Geryth and, catching Guy's eye, said dryly in Mithlondian,

"We had better make haste. Joff will want both of us present to witness his moment of triumph. Best bring the wench along with you as well. It seems her sister may yet stand her friend, even if her mother has all but rejected her for acting the wanton in your arms." His sardonic tone darkened, reflecting his distaste for the whole affair. "Daemon's balls! If what has just passed is any indication of what life in this bloody place has been like, all I can say is that I could not have stood it for half as long as you have done." He forced a lighter note. "Although no doubt there were compensations if you wished to avail yourself of them. But as for Joffroi's taste in women..." He shook his head in disgust. "The daemon knows, I would as soon bed a she-wolf as that cold-hearted bitch."

"Softly, Ran."

The quiet admonition was offered in the same language but Ranulf shrugged both his own indiscreet words and Guy's warning irritably aside, turning in the saddle to bark orders at the men-at-arms behind them, swiftly making his dispositions with regard to securing the gatehouse and walls, as well as confining the garrison and its bitterly compliant commander – instinct told him he would have trouble with that one before the day was out – to their quarters.

Having made sure that Chartre castle was securely under de Rogé control, Ranulf finally dismounted and handed Starlight's reins over to Geryth with a nod of dismissal. He glanced once more at the slender beauty in the doorway, slightly surprised to find her still there since her bodyguard had long since been hustled away. He was even more disconcerted to discover that her green gaze remained as beguiling as ever and still fixed firmly upon himself. He was not overly modest about his attractiveness to women but in this case it seemed more than a little... odd.

Without conscious decision he found himself moving towards her, drawn as inexorably as the tides of the sea answering the call of the moon. The stamp of a heavy, iron-shod hoof striking the cobbles behind him broke the spell – if spell it was – recalling him to a more cynical awareness of the situation. Deliberately veering away from the beauty, he turned towards the chestnut stallion and its double burden. Standing at Guy's stirrup he looked up into the wary grey eyes of the Lady Rowène de Chartreux and said crisply,

"Come on, wench, bring your leg over and slide down. I will catch you." Then, when she hesitated, added more abrasively. "If you would rather risk a twisted ankle than accept help from one who is both murderer and ravening wolf, that is of course your choice."

Not unexpectedly she paled at his harsh words, the revulsion in her eyes overwhelming any other emotion that might have been there before. Yet despite her very obvious fear of him she held his gaze steadily for perhaps three heartbeats, glanced briefly down at the ground – the chestnut stood at least seventeen hands – then back to him, shaking her head slightly. He shrugged aside her refusal and turned on his heel.

"No, wait!"

Turning back at her choked words, he flashed a narrow-eyed look at Guy before shifting his gaze to the girl, noting – not for the first time since he had seen her – how the individual strands of red and gold in her hair seemed to dance like flames in a fire, bright and fierce against the dark blue of her gown and the black of Guy's surcoat. Against his better judgement Ranulf allowed himself to look into those clear, grey eyes once more and felt something, keen as a well-honed blade and as barbed as a fish hook, twist sharply in his gut.

Knowing that Guy was watching him closely he managed to hide his unexpected reaction beneath a sardonic smile and said, with only the barest hint of mockery,

"Even murderers can have mothers, Demoiselle, and despite all appearances mine did her utmost to instil in me the basic rules of courtesy. That she failed is not her fault but you may, in this instance, trust me to help you. As for anything else, I only ravish beautiful women. Is that not so, Guy?"

He ignored the other man's muttered epithet, aware that it had been couched in the Rogé dialect and was therefore likely to be unintelligible to anyone from Chartreux, content to concentrate his attention on the girl he was intent on baiting.

"Well, Demoiselle? Will you risk my touch?"

She bit her lip as a colour akin to wild rose petals blushed her pale cheeks, making him wonder whether perhaps she *had* understood what Guy had called him. Then he saw a look of determination darken her eyes and the next moment, before he could lift his hands to her waist, she slipped down the chestnut's side, arriving on the ground in a slithering rush.

Rasping a startled oath, Ranulf reached out to steady her, catching her as she stumbled hard against him. Unprepared and taken slightly off balance, he instinctively tightened his grip and adjusted his stance. He was suddenly, and uncomfortably, aware of the unexpected femininity of the body under his hands and the scent of the sun-warmed, silk-soft wisps of hair that snagged against the light stubble on his jaw. The unnerving, and utterly unwelcome, thought flashed through his mind that he could have held her forever.

*He* might have been able to do so – in the mythical meadows beyond the moon mayhap – but he was unlikely to mistake the shudder that ravaged her slender body for anything other than revulsion. And it was in that moment, when he felt the quiver of her soft flesh beneath his hard fingertips, that he made the decision that had been nagging at the back of his mind since he had first seen her, standing in the filtered golden light beneath the poplar trees, her red hair aflame and her grey eyes full of fear.

Gritting his teeth in a savage attempt to regain control over his body and keep his thoughts from his face, he looked up to find Guy regarding him with narrowed, watchful eyes. He might have blurted out his decision then but even as he opened his mouth, she gave a choked gasp and brought her bound hands up in a frantic attempt to free herself; evidently being held by Guy was one thing, suffering his own loathsome touch quite another!

Not that he would ever pursue an unwilling wench. Though that was something that neither she, nor her sister, needed to be made aware of. Or, at least, not yet. Guy too – for all he should bloody well have known better – did not seem disposed to trust him not to force his attentions on her. Or so Ranulf judged by the haste with which the other man flung himself down from the saddle.

As soon as he knew that Guy had a steadying hold on the girl's arm, Ranulf allowed his own hands to drop and stepped back, forcing a thread of unrepentant amusement into his voice as he drawled,

"Calm down, Guy! Even I would not rape a noblewoman in public. Behind locked doors though..." He half turned to rake a deliberate glance over the breathtakingly lovely young woman waiting by the door into the keep, before continuing mockingly, "Besides, now that I have seen that little beauty, I withdraw my claim to this one. You can have her with my good will, Guy, if you really want her. Looking at her though I have to wonder how such a homely-looking lass can be of the same blood as that siren over there? Are you sure they are sisters and this one not some serving wench impersonating her betters?"

"Of course they are sisters, Ran!" Guy snapped. "Do not be so bloody obtuse."

Ranulf nodded equably.

"Well, doubtless you would know. Though who would have thought two siblings born to the same parents could be so completely unlike in appearance when..." He caught Guy's dark, oddly defenceless look and, taking pity on the man, turned what he had been going to say. "Not that I can boast when Joffroi and I have scarcely a feature in common. And talking of our liege, we had best make haste before he realises we are keeping him waiting with our dallying out here. He has said more than once that he will have the skin off your back if you fail him in any way in this venture and my words earlier will only have reminded him of that threat. For which I apologise, Guy, but I could think of nothing else at the time to diffuse his temper."

Guy grimaced a little but they understood each other well enough without need for further words; after all, Guy was not the only one with the white welts of old lash marks scarring his shoulders.

Knowing that to linger any further would risk pushing Joffroi into another mindless rage, Ranulf turned on his heel and stalked across the courtyard towards the keep, his spurs ringing harshly against the cobbles as he walked.

Coming to a halt beside the slender yet somehow sensuous young noblewoman who waited there, he allowed the merest hint of a leer to touch his mouth. Even given her previous... odd behaviour, he was still surprised when she did not immediately shrink away from him and so took the opportunity to peruse her silk-clad body more intently, finally saying lazily,

"And you are, sweetness?"

"Juliène de Chartreux," she replied in a soft, trembling voice that reminded him of the white doves his mother had kept in the garden of Rogérinac castle.

"Show me the way then, Demoiselle. Oh, do not worry about them," he said as her long-lashed green gaze went past his shoulder. "If we go on, I warrant your sister and her lover will follow swiftly enough."

Rather than contesting his gratuitous slur against her sister's morals, she dipped him a graceful little curtsey and turned to lead the way into the keep. As he shortened his longer strides to her dainty steps he wondered if she was truly so innocent as to be unaware either of his identity or reputation; certainly she did not appear to be as revolted by – or as frightened of – him as her sister was. Or was she rather engaged in some deeper game on her mother's behalf?

Whichever it was, it changed nothing so far as Ranulf was concerned. During the course of the afternoon Guy had repeatedly warned him away from one de Chartreux sister so that left the lovely Lady Juliène to his tender mercies. And as the Daemon of Hell well knew, it would be no hardship for him to take her if, against all odds, she proved willing. If she did not... well, that was another matter and one Ranulf was not inclined to worry about until all else was settled.

Watching closely as Ranulf and the Lady Juliène mounted the steps into the keep, Guy made to follow but paused as his companion laid a hand on his arm.

"Wait, Guy."

It seemed that for the moment she had forgotten that she was supposed to hate him and had called him by the only name she knew. Looking down at her,

Guy felt again the gut-wrenching certainty that he was in over his head but by a supreme effort he kept his voice low and level.

"What is it?"

"Is it true? What he just said to you?"

"He? Do you mean Joffroi or Ranulf?

"R... Ranulf."

The name was little more than a horrified whisper but hearing it Guy hesitated and then answered quietly,

"What? That he would not have raped you in public or that Joffroi will have me flogged?"

He saw her flush at his uncompromising words, then pale at the threat of such a punishment, finally saying awkwardly,

"The... latter."

Guy looked at her without speaking for a long moment, not really seeing her, remembering instead that last day at Rogérinac before he and Joffroi and Ranulf had gone their separate ways.

"Yes, it is true. Joffroi did say that but..."

"Guy, are you coming?"

Ranulf's impatient tones, ringing out from the shadows within the keep doorway prevented him from uttering any further folly.

"Come, Demoiselle, we must not tarry longer. I would not wish to bring Joffroi's wrath down upon your head. His temper is... somewhat unpredictable, as you have seen for yourself."

"Yet still you serve him loyally?" Rowène asked sharply as she fell into step beside him. "In the name of all the gods, why?"

"Because, Demoiselle," he said flatly, walking beside her up the steps into the keep.

"Because... what?"

"My reasons are no concern of yours," he answered bluntly, needing desperately to stop this line of conversation. "Suffice it to say they seem good enough to me."

They were passing the great hall now and Guy paused momentarily to glance inside but, seeing it deserted, made for the stairs that led to Lady Ariène's bower, reminding himself grimly that she and Joffroi would not wish to conduct their dubious business in the full sight of the castle retainers, the majority of whom, despite her subtle bewitchments, were loyal to Louis de Chartreux rather than his lady.

Arriving at the bower, he knocked briefly on the door and walked in without waiting for a response. Situated as it was on the western side of the castle the comfortable chamber was still filled with the last glorious reflections of apricot and gold, rose and lilac that swept the sunset sky beyond the open window but in sharp contrast the tension in the air was thick enough to be cut with a blunt blade.

Lady Ariène was standing by the open window, hands clasped at her breast, her hair shimmering in the light like a fire-fall of flame. Her raven-haired daughter sat straight-backed on the window seat nearby, fingers clasped tightly in her lap, her eyes fixed on the floor. Joffroi was standing close to Ariène, a dark fire burning in his eyes, his hands clenched on his sword belt while Ranulf lounged by the door, his broad shoulders propped against the wall, his dark blue gaze slowly – and quite openly, damn him! – stripping the younger noblewoman of her clothes. But there was no time to worry about Ranulf's deliberately crass behaviour now.

"At last!" Joffroi growled, his patience and temper still dangerously short. "Daemons of Hell, Guy! What kept you? You can tumble the wench in your own time, not mine."

"You know damned well..." Guy's own temper flared but the Lady Ariène forestalled any further protest with a little cry.

"Seigneur de Rogé, I demand to know why my daughter is still bound like a common criminal!"

Joffroi looked momentarily disconcerted. Then he glared at Guy.

"Untie the wench but remember she is still in your charge and that I will hold you personally responsible for any mischief she might make." He turned back to his paramour. "And now, Madame..." He paused, his thick dark brows knitting in a formidable frown. "Where is your son, damn it? He should be present since this concerns his father and, therefore, him."

Guy was wryly amused to see a distinctly vexed expression mar the smooth lines of the Lady Ariène's face. Her luscious mouth thinned and a rare harsh note crept into her silvery tones as she replied with a pettish shrug,

"Like his father, Luc never tells me where he is going or what he is about. For all I know he is lying drunk in some whore's bed. He certainly seems to waste most evenings in such company. However, you must ask your spy if you would have more accurate information," she finished pointedly. "*I* am hardly in a position to know which dockside brothel he favours."

Joffroi swore and glared at Guy,

"Well, Guy, where is he?"

Grimacing at this open confirmation of his place in the de Chartreux household and avoiding looking at Rowène, he replied carefully,

"I may be wrong, but I think Madame de Chartreux is under some misapprehension concerning her son. From what I could determine of Messire Luc's activities, his frequent... visits to such... establishments is largely a smokescreen to keep those he mistrusts at bay."

"Well, I could understand that he might be suspicious of you, a stranger to Chartre, but what unlawful need would drive him to deceive me, his mother?" Lady Ariène asked, subtle and not so subtle insults dripping from her honeyed tones.

Sickened by her treachery and revolted by his own part in this misguided affair, Guy spoke more bluntly than he had originally intended.

"Because, Madame, your son is loyal to his father. And being neither witless nor open to manipulation, he is very well aware that you are not."

Lady Ariène gave him a look that would have shredded the flesh from his bones had he been in truth a wandering vagrant of common birth and her tone graduated to a coldly sarcastic formality.

"Then if you are so clever, *Messire*, tell us where Luc is now."

"And then," Joffroi added with a look of deep displeasure. "You can tell me why you have kept this knowledge to yourself for so long."

Even as Guy forced himself to return Joffroi's gimlet stare he was very well aware that Rowène had caught her breath. Although whether that involuntary action had been prompted by her mother's unexpected acknowledgement of his own status or out of anxiety for her brother, he did not want to guess.

"Messire Luc rode out of Chartre early this morning," he admitted reluctantly. "Accompanied only by his squire. Needless to say, he did not tell me where he was going or what his plans were!"

"And did you not see by which gate he left?" Joffroi asked impatiently.

"Not the town gate," Guy replied.

"So they went out by the western gate. But whither then? Damnation, Guy, getting information out of you is like wringing blood from a stone. Do not tell me that little witch there has stolen your reason as well as your loyalty to me?"

Guy shook his head, deeply reluctant to betray Rowène yet again, this time by delivering up her brother to almost certain dishonour and death, but in the end his bone-deep loyalty to Joffroi was stronger than the lighter bonds of trust she had placed on him – and which he had already broken.

"I think, although I have no grounds for this belief save my own gut feeling, that he was heading south to find the rest of the Chartreux garrison. The ones who have been serving in Kardolandia in the royal bodyguard for the past ten years and are now due to return to Chartre."

"Bloody hell, Guy!" Ranulf snorted, slanting a disgusted look at him. "I had best see about alerting our own men. Daemon's balls! What a time to let your conscience, or your cock, take control of your actions! And all for the sake of a wench I warrant you have not even bedded!"

With which he stalked from the room, leaving Guy feeling very much like a grain of corn crushed between the twin millstones of anger and guilt, whilst around him the tension in the room wound tighter with every passing moment of Ranulf's absence.

Ignoring the harper's half-hearted attempt to stop her, and with Ranulf de Rogé's crude comment still grating on her ears, Rowène moved to the window embrasure where her sister sat in strained silence. She did not understand why Ju was acting as she was – either her sister did not yet feel the same fear and hatred of these ravening noblemen and their duplicitous spy as she did or else Ju was better at concealing it – but Rowène found her sister's superficial calm almost as disconcerting as their mother's cool acceptance of this terrible situation.

As her sister moved up to make room for her on the window seat, Ju met her searching gaze briefly and gave a slight nod that left Rowène none the wiser. Nor could she ask out loud what her sister meant by it. Instead, her tongue fettered by the constricting presence of the Winter Lady and Black Joffroi, Rowène dragged the shreds of her composure back around her and waited with what courage she could muster for Ranulf de Rogé's return, it being obvious that his brother had no intention of continuing in his absence. Nor did she suppose he would allow anyone else to leave the room, for whatever reason, until he had completed his mysterious commission for the High Counsel.

Heart weighed down with an unreasoning dread, Rowène found herself watching in mesmerised fashion as the black-clad tyrant paced up and down, his glittering mail and weapons as out of place amongst the delicate feminine clutter of lute and embroidery silks as a rampant wild boar in a meadow of summer flowers. Save for the almost matching, vividly bright greens of her mother's and sister's gowns, all other colours seemed to be subsumed by the black and silver trappings worn, not only by Joffroi de Rogé but also the man who stood silently to one side of the door, his light blue eyes watching her with an expression she was at a loss to interpret.

Despite the harper's familiar presence, the fear in her heart and the nauseous churning in her belly soon became almost more than she could bear, a feeling hideously exacerbated by Black Joffroi's relentless pacing. Behind her, the light faded from clear gold, merging into the softer shadows of late dusk and still the tension in the chamber continued to mount until Rowène could almost wish for Ranulf de Rogé's return. At least then they would learn what fell fate Black Joffroi carried with him in the innocuous guise of a message from their Prince.

As if her thought had the power to summon him from the Hell that had undoubtedly spawned him, Ranulf de Rogé came striding through the door, his face set in grim lines, his sword naked in his hand, the long blade glimmering silver in the candle light, save for the point and a hand's width below it which was stained a dark, viscous crimson.

Rowène bit back a cry and, for the first time, felt a shudder run through her sister, heard her whisper their brother's name. Her only thought was, *Dear God of Mercy, is it true? Is it Luc whose life that murderer has taken with the callous cruelty that seems to come so naturally to him?*

Moving through a mist of silver and scarlet, scarcely aware of what she was doing, she came to her feet and closed the short distance between them.

"Is that my brother's blood?" she demanded, voice shaking despite her best efforts at control.

"What, this blood?" he queried lightly, effortlessly hefting the gruesome weapon, bringing the point of the blade up so that it was level with her breast and barely a hair's width away from her clammy skin.

*Dear God of Light, does he mean to murder me too? Or does he merely seek to frighten me?* Whatever his intention, if his casual control slipped for even a heartbeat, the effect would be the same.

Scarcely daring to breathe, she watched in horror as the crimson stain slid slowly down the shallow groove towards the heavy cross hilt and the fist that held it, the candlelight glinting on the coarse, pale hairs visible as the killer turned the blade, no doubt in admiration of his handiwork.

The sword was so close – and the image of it as it was thrust into her brother's flesh so real – that she felt her stomach rebel and knew that if she survived this day she would never again be able to tolerate the sight or smell of fresh blood without vomiting.

She clenched her teeth to hold back the hot, acrid bile that even now burned in her throat and forced herself to lift her eyes from the unyielding yard of blood-stained steel to meet the impervious ice-cold eyes of the man who wielded it. He held her gaze for perhaps another three heartbeats, his narrowed eyes tracing the lines of her face with an unnerving intensity, before he abruptly moved the sword away. Despite finding herself able to breathe again, she was quite incapable of either moving or looking away as he wiped the bloody blade clean on the hem of his black surcoat and then sheathed the heavy weapon with an easy deftness that simply made her nausea worse.

As if guessing at her precarious control, he grinned at her, showing a nasty array of white, wolf's teeth, and finally broke the silence that had held them all entrapped.

"Why yes, since you mention it, Demoiselle, I do believe it is your brother's blood...."

Without warning, he reached out and touched his forefinger to a point just above the neckline of her gown. The sensation of his warm, calloused finger against her cold skin made her recoil in revulsion. He smiled again and held up his finger so that she could see the drop of blood he had wiped away.

"He was proving... uncooperative... shall we say?"

"You vile, murdering hell'spawn..."

Rage finally conquered her nausea and finding her ability to move restored, if not sufficient coherence to describe the man and the feelings he roused in her, she went for his face with her nails. Only to find his fingers locked around her wrists in a bruising grip that effortlessly kept her clawing hands just beyond scratching distance of his face. Past caring what he might do to her, she continued to pit herself against his superior strength, hissing and kicking like a wild cat.

She heard him swear – words she had never heard uttered in a lady's bower before although they were obviously common enough usage for *him* – then his other arm came around her waist, tugging her violently against him. Panic-stricken, she writhed desperately in his hold, hearing but not comprehending the warning he rasped into her ear,

"For gods'sake, woman! Cease this madness, else you leave me no choice."

She felt the grip on her wrists tighten slightly, the twinge of pain bringing her to her senses.

"No choice?" she gasped, the words almost lost in the silver-embroidered, black wool of his surcoat.

"No choice but to hurt you in earnest," he gritted, low-voiced, relaxing his grasp from bone-crushingly painful to merely firm.

She swallowed and stilled against him, breathless from her struggles and bewildered by the belated realisation that he could so easily have snapped the bones in her wrists – yet he had not done so!

At the same time she became aware that everyone in the chamber – Black Joffroi, her mother, her sister and Guy of... wherever he was from – was watching her with various degrees of speculation and concern. As much as she feared the strength and violent nature of the man who held her, she dared not cease her defiant attack, even though he now held her so close she was almost suffocating under the stench of blood and sweat and steel that clung to his skin.

Forcing herself to take another breath, she closed her eyes a moment to gather her strength and then, taking a leaf out of his own book, pulled back against his suddenly slackened grasp and spat in his face, flinching instinctively as she felt him flex those long, powerful fingers.

The pain in her wrists did not increase noticeably, however, and it was with a dazed incredulity that she realised that despite the severe provocation she had just offered him, he had still not used the terrible strength she could feel leashed in the fingers that shackled her slender wrists high against his shoulder, where her own wildly-clutching fingers were now tangled in the loose lengths of his long fair hair.

Someone cleared their throat behind her and de Rogé relaxed the arm banded around her waist, dropping his hand to her hip and pushing her backwards, putting a modicum of space between them. Only then did he raise his hand. She braced herself to feel the unleashed force of his anger – one does not spit in *any* man's face with impunity, let alone this one's! – and lifted her chin, glaring defiantly into his glittering eyes. He was breathing slightly faster than normal and his face beneath the glinting gold stubble was strained but he merely freed his hair from her fingers with an impatient tug before wiping the spittle from his cheek with the back of his hand.

Ignoring her completely, he addressed someone over her head, in so icy a voice that had she not been watching his mouth she would not have recognised it as his, so far removed was it from the sardonic, drawling tones she had come to expect from him.

"I swear by all the daemons of Hell, Guy, if *you* do not tame this wild cat of yours, *I* will. And neither you nor she will care much for my methods." He looked down at her, his dark blue eyes reminiscent of the Hell he swore by. "And no, Demoiselle de Chartreux, I would not cage you. Nor even clip your claws, tempted though I am. But you may believe me when I say that after one night serving my needs you would be only too willing to mate with a man who at least understands the meaning of the word *gentleman.*"

Her throat was so tight with dread she found she could form no words to answer him but then again she doubted whether he seriously expected any coherent response – at least from her! The man he had so savagely addressed though...

"Give her to me, Ran," she heard Guy murmur and found herself released – almost flung – in the harper's direction.

She came to rest against his broad, mailed breast and felt his arms close protectively about her – and dazedly acknowledged that she had escaped lightly. Ranulf de Rogé had neither crushed her wrists nor back-handed her as he might so easily have done. Nor had he used so much force in passing her to the harper that he sent her sprawling on the floor.

Yet she could not find it in her to be grateful for his forbearance. Not when they both bore her brother's blood on their clothes and skin.

*Luc! The gods forgive me! This is all my fault! I should have told you my doubts before it was too late!*

Bitter tears burned behind her eyes and she turned her head against the harper's shoulder, trying to stifle her sobs. Distraught though she was, she yet had no difficulty in hearing – although some in believing – her mother's next words. Far from upset, the Lady Ariène sounded merely bored.

"Now that that unseemly kerfuffle is over, perhaps you will have the goodness to explain yourself, Messire. You say that is my son's blood on your sword. I may assume then that he is dead?"

"No, Madame, I fear you are under a misapprehension. Two, in truth. Firstly, it was not *your* son, although from his looks I would say with some certainty that he is indeed, as that wild-cat claimed, *her* brother. Neither is he dead. Or at least he was not when I left him."

"What a pity," her mother said coldly. "It would have been one fewer of Louis' bastards for me to deal with."

Shocked almost into insensibility by this callous statement, Rowène leant against the harper's warm, solid body, too grateful for his support to maintain her earlier avowal of hatred towards him. If only he could hold her forever...

An enraged expletive roused her from her near swoon and she turned her head to look fearfully over her shoulder.

"Enough of this!" Black Joffroi was flushed with fury and frustration. He took a deep breath and turning to the coolly unruffled Lady of Chartreux, continued in uncompromising tones, "Madame, I am charged by the High Counsel to inform you that Prince Marcus of Mithlondia is dead!"

Rowène saw her mother take a breath as if to speak but even as her lips parted it was Guy of Montfaucon's voice which ripped through the stunned silence.

"The Prince is dead? *That* was what you had planned? Gods, Joff, that is *treason!*"

Numbed by the tumultuous events of the day though she was, and not least this latest, scarcely credible, announcement, Rowène still quailed at the thought of Black Joffroi's probable reaction to the harper's accusation. But it was Ranulf de Rogé's lighter tones that sliced through her consciousness, as keen and cutting as the edge of his sword.

"Shut up, Guy! And just be bloody grateful that you chose to come here rather than…"

"Chose?" the harper practically snarled. "I did not *choose* any of this, and you damned well know it, Ran! And whatever you say, it is still treason!"

"I never said it was not!" de Rogé replied curtly. "But not…"

"Not another word!" Black Joffroi roared. "From either of you! As for *you…*"

Rowène started violently as he unexpectedly turned his fearsome fury on her.

"I suggest you sit beside your sister and stop trying to twist *my* men into *your* coils!"

Before she could choke out any response to that preposterous suggestion her mother had intervened, her voice like an icy lash.

"Yes, sit down, Rowène and strive to conduct yourself in a more seemly manner. Do you see your sister spitting at noblemen or behaving in such wanton fashion as you have done – and are still doing!"

Flushing with shame at this rebuke, Rowène pushed away from the harper and sat back down beside her sister, silently seething, eyes fixed on the hands folded tightly together in her lap. Taking her obedience for granted, her mother had already returned her attention to Black Joffroi.

"Now, Messire de Rogé, I beg you will finish what you have ridden so far to tell me. Prince Marcus is dead, you say? Well he has been ailing all winter, so that is perhaps no great surprise." She sounded so cool and indifferent, the Winter Lady in truth, Rowène thought, biting her lip as her mother continued, "Long live Prince Linnius. Is that why you have come? To carry the High Counsel's invitation to all loyal vassals to attend the young prince's crowning? That was courteous of you but it should have been my lord who brought these tidings."

"Regrettably he could not do so." Despite his words there was no regret in Black Joffroi's deep voice, only a sort of dark satisfaction. "Suspecting Prince Marcus' death to be unnatural, certain Counsellors, of whom I was one, summoned the royal physician to examine the body – he unfortunately not being in attendance during the last days of the Prince's illness. Having been dismissed by your own lord, Madame, his place was then taken by some woman who, or so de Chartreux claimed, possessed a greater skill in healing. In truth though her skills were probably of a different sort and enjoyed by your lord even as our noble Prince lay dying. Be that as it may, the physician confirmed what we had already come to suspect – that the Prince had died as a result of the deliberate administration of poison. On Prince Linnius' orders, the last person known to have been with his father before his death was duly arrested and questioned."

There was such lingering pleasure in Black Joffroi's tone as to leave none of his listeners in any doubt that in this case *questioned* was an unsubtle euphemism for *tortured*. Rowène felt her stomach rebel and pressed her fingers against her mouth. She could not, however, block out the smugly satisfied voice that continued to roll sonorously through the silence that now pervaded every corner of the chamber.

"It is now my duty to inform you, Madame, that seven days ago Louis de Chartreux was arraigned on a charge of treason and tried before the High Counsel of Mithlondia. The following day Prince Linnius signed his death warrant, together with the order that passes his lands and title to me. *I* am now Lord of Chartreux and everything and everyone within these borders is mine, to do with as I will. You, Madame, will acknowledge me as your master, your son and de Chartreux's bastard will be hanged for complicity in their father's treason and your daughters will go to my men as a reward for their loyalty!"

Inured to shock by now, the only emotion Rowène felt was a keen, piercing sorrow at this confirmation that she would never see her father again. A sorrow that left no room for dread at the fate outlined for her.

"My father is *dead*?" she whispered, tears stinging her eyes once more and running unheeded down her cheeks. Not just tortured and disgraced, though that were surely an evil enough fate, but dead!

"He died a traitor's death," Black Joffroi reiterated, with a certain amount of relish. "If you want the details..."

Rowène shook her head violently. No, she did not want to know. Ever.

But as she had feared he would, Black Joffroi ignored her unspoken plea. And not only her plea; his brother and harper had both spoken, sharply and almost simultaneously, their voices so similar in pitch she could not tell which was which.

"Damn it, Joff, enough is enough!"

"In gods' name, no, Joff!"

"I disagree," the Winter Lady's voice came clear and cold. "My daughters, Rowène especially, need to hear the truth about their father's death, so they will know once and for all that he was no god but a man just like any other. Tell them, Messire."

"Demoiselles!"

Rowène obeyed the implicit command in Black Joffroi's stern tone and, taking her sister's hand in hers, forced herself to look up, to find the new Lord of Chartreux looming before her, a singular lack of pity in his dark eyes. At the edge of her rapidly clouding vision she could just see the harper, his face pale, and beside him, Ranulf de Rogé, jaw set hard. If *they* had not wanted her to hear, it must be grim indeed.

Then Black Joffroi began to speak and the horror of noose and knife began to take shape in the swirling mist before her eyes.

"Your father, Demoiselle, went to the scaffold five days ago, escorted by Joscelin de Veraux – the man to whom you are betrothed, I believe! As all traitors are, he was hanged, drawn and quartered! And his head now sits above the palace gate. Perhaps you will see it there if ever you go to court but I doubt you will be able to recognise your father's face by then..."

All awareness of time, place and people drowned by the deep upwelling of horror and grief, it took a long time for Rowène to realise that she and her sister were alone in the chamber, although she supposed vaguely that there would be a guard posted outside the door. Glancing out of the window she saw that it was close to moon-rise and wondered dully what Black Joffroi would expect of them now.

On that thought a knock sounded at the door but before she could speak it opened to reveal a man her shattered mind barely recognised. He had shed his bright mail and black surcoat and was clad once more in the threadbare trappings of the harper Guy of Montfaucon. His boots though were still graced by the silver-gilt spurs of a higher rank and he wore his sword at his hip with the confidence of one born to it. For a moment he stood in the doorway then he asked quietly,

"May I come in?"

"As if anything a de Chartreux can say is like to stop a de Rogé!" she replied bitterly.

"I am not..."

"Not a de Rogé by blood," she said dismissively, not waiting to hear the remainder of his sentence. "But you have sworn allegiance to the Lords of Rogé, nevertheless." And when he hesitated. "You need not lie to me any more."

"I never wanted to lie to you in the first place," he replied. "Just as I never wanted to come here as Joffroi's eyes and ears. But my fealty was given long ago."

"And now that your task to spy for Black Joffroi and his hell-spawned brother is done, in what capacity do you serve your brutal masters now?" Rowène asked pointedly.

"I am come simply to escort you and your sister down to the great hall since it is time for the evening meal."

"And after the meal is done?" she asked, abruptly remembering what fate lay in store for her and Ju.

To do him justice he did not pretend to misunderstand her.

"You know the answer to that as well as I, Demoiselle. Nonetheless, I would not see you or your sister forced into any man's bed against your will. That being so, and if Joffroi holds by his threat to give you to his men, the only way

I can keep you..." he faltered slightly. "Safe is to take you to my own bed." He must have seen the uncertainty in her eyes because he continued flatly. "If you will not have me, then it must be Ranulf."

"No!"

"Then you are stuck with me and Ranulf will take your sister. And although I would hope that he will remember that Lady Rosalynde raised him to be a gentleman, I fear in his present mood there is no certainty about that."

The note of the evening horn cut across his words and when he spoke again it was with a distant courtesy,

"Come, it is time. Joffroi... your mother... everyone is waiting on you."

"No! I beg you," Rowène began, a note of desperation in her voice. "If you have any kindness in you, do not ask this of us. Surely you must see that we cannot share meat and wine with our father's enemies... men who would see our brother..." She stumbled over the word, suddenly remembering Lucien with his grey eyes and lean, gravely smiling face framed by straight, raven-dark hair. "*Brothers... dead. My sister and I shamed.*"

Although he flinched at her words, the harper did not retreat.

"Believe me, it would not be wise to arouse Joffroi's ire by further delay."

Despite the obvious warning, she did not know if she would have continued to argue but just then Juliène took her completely by surprise by rising from her seat and sweeping across the chamber to join the conversation.

"I think in this, as in so many other things we may find ourselves doing this night, we have little choice. We must face them all at some stage and it will do neither of us any good if we provoke the new Lord of Chartreux's wrath so early in his rule. Like it or not, Ro, we have to submit to these men who think themselves our masters!"

# Chapter 7

## *Victory Feast*

The evening meal – or as his elder brother had so grandiloquently styled it, victory feast – had been in progress for more than two candle-notches and Ranulf could feel the tension thickening air already over-burdened with the myriad odours of wood smoke, crushed herbs, roasted meats, Lady Ariène's perfume – that alone was enough to put him off his food – and his own sweat.

Not wanting anyone to guess how strained his nerves actually were, he was sprawled in the high-backed chair allotted to him, in a deliberately boorish manner that would have caused his mother to regard him with bewildered reproach had she been alive to see him. His father would have expressed his displeasure rather more forcefully.

His gentle-voiced, dark-eyed mother had been dead for twenty-five years, however, his father nearing twenty and the present Lord of Rogé – and now of Chartreux as well – was quite clearly indifferent to his brother's lack of manners, being totally in thrall to the bewitchingly – Ranulf used that word cautiously and only in the privacy of his own mind – lovely Lady Ariène.

*Damn it, Joff,* Ranulf thought, *need you drool over her like a starveling dog!*

Continuing to observe his elder brother's nauseating behaviour over the rim of his silver-chased goblet, Ranulf snorted in disgust and took a hefty swig of the wine. For all she must be in her middle years, the Lady Ariène de Chartreux was still flawlessly beautiful and openly sensual – well, he had always known that and could scarcely deny it now – but the very air around her shimmered like moonlight through frosted crystals and the more he saw of the wi… woman, the more he found himself disliking her.

If he were honest, there was little about the great hall of Chartre castle to give him cause for either comfort or complaisance. Underlying the quite obvious apprehension of the servants there was a subtle but undeniable reek of enchantment in the air that caught in his throat and raised the hairs on the back of his neck. Not that he should have expected anything else when not one but all three of the women within a spear's length of him carried the witch-taint of the Faennari in their blood, flaunted in the flame-red hair and jewel-green eyes of the mother while the daughters each owned one or other trait. Indeed, he was not sure which unnerved him more; the tawny-pelted wild-cat who had earlier tried to scratch his eyes out or the emerald-eyed damsel who now sat so demurely by his side. Certainly he did not trust either of them any more than he trusted their mother.

To cover his increasing unease he took another, somewhat more respectful, swallow of the rich red Marillec wine – a luxury he rarely tasted at home in Rogérinac and never on campaign – flicking a brief glance as he did so at Guy, who was sitting at the far end of the table and looking even more uncomfortable than Ranulf felt.

Not that Guy had cause to fear that his manners would let him down, Ranulf reflected. Of the two of them, Guy had always proved, by virtue of his gentler nature, the more apt pupil in Lady Rosalynde's lessons in courtesy and chivalry, whereas Ranulf had more often than not reduced his mother to tears of despair with his careless behaviour. Not that Guy had been perfect by any means, but for all he was only Lady Rosalynde's foster son she had favoured him over either of the boys to whom she herself had given life.

Ranulf had never begrudged Guy the attention he had received from Lady Rosalynde, or Lord Jacques for that matter. Nor – and here he took another gulp of wine to wash away the acrid taste in his mouth – did he begrudge the man the relationship he had obviously managed to forge with the young noblewoman by whose side he was now seated.

Or did he?

With a heartfelt curse Ranulf wrenched his thoughts from the path that led back to the gilded shadows beside the Liriél and his first sight of the Lady Rowène de Chartreux. Better by far to think of her as a witchling in training rather than the frightened but defiant young woman who had had the guts to spit in the face of the man who had deliberately led her to believe he had cold-bloodedly murdered her brother.

*Hell and damnation,* Ranulf thought with unaccustomed self-recrimination, *I should have broken her then, when I had the chance.* But he had not been able to bring himself to physically hurt her more than he had already. The best he had been able to manage had been to put the fear of the Daemon of Hell – in short, himself – into her before throwing her almost literally into Guy's arms. And he bloody well hoped Guy would be grateful to him for that action and make the most of the opportunity Ranulf had given him.

But he doubted it. Betrayal was not in Guy's nature. Which made it an interesting question as to which oath he would break faith with tonight; his binding oath to Mathilde or the older oath of allegiance he had sworn to Joffroi. Small wonder, with that choice hanging over him, the man was looking so tortured!

At the other end of the high table, Guy was asking himself much the same question – and silently cursing himself for allowing himself to be put in this damnable position in the first place. If he had thought far enough ahead he would have refused at the outset to obey Joffroi's order to come to Chartre... but he had not. Although he *had* made his reluctance plain and, as it turned out, his dubious talents as a spy had not been required after all.

Joffroi had gained everything he could possibly want – the land, the title, the revenues, as well as the woman he had lusted after for so long – by his own murderous manipulations in Lamortaine. That said, Guy thought he detected another, subtler, hand behind the events that had led up to Prince Marcus' death and Louis de Chartreux's bloody execution. Far too subtle for Joffroi, he thought grimly. Or Ranulf.

Clearly, Ran's involvement had been limited to being conveniently to hand to witness his brother's triumph. And Guy knew him well enough to know that Ranulf was no happier than he to be a captive fly dancing in the sticky web of Lady Ariène's malice. Hence Ranulf's retreat whilst in Lamortaine to the dubious delights of the Marish and his present display of self-indulgence. Even as Guy watched, Ranulf drained his second cup of wine and reached out an arm to drag the serving wench who answered his impatient summons down onto his lap.

Guy frowned but made no effort to intervene. He recognised the woman and while she might be flushed and squirming on her captor's lap, her wriggling was more for flirtatious effect than escape. He knew too that Ranulf, for all his faults, would never force himself on a reluctant woman. A belief apparently unshared by the silent young noblewoman seated at Guy's side. He caught her sniff of disgust, then shifted slightly in his seat so as to be able to look at her – something he had sedulously avoided doing once they had sat down.

He found her glaring at Ranulf with a look that should by rights have left the man incapable of tumbling a woman ever again. Through gritted teeth she hissed,

"Can you not do something? That is my tire-maid, not some cheap harlot for that... that lecher to amuse himself with."

"I hardly think Ranulf is using force to keep her there," Guy retorted, but quietly enough that only she would hear him. "And ask yourself who you would rather he took to warm his bed tonight – your innocent sister or a trollop who quite clearly has played this game often enough to know what she is doing?"

He heard her mutter something under her breath but, to his relief, she made no further fuss. The gods knew the last thing he wanted was for her to draw either Joffroi or Ranulf's attention in her direction. Not after what had happened earlier. But it was too late for that, he saw, as he glanced down the length of the table. Joffroi might be entirely enraptured by his lovely companion but Ranulf – having dismissed the pouting Ilana with a final fondle and a whispered word that had her giggling – raised his wine cup in a mocking salute directed, not at Guy, but at his companion.

Guy could scarcely miss the shudder that shook the girl's rigid body and glared a warning at Ranulf who promptly lurched to his feet and, bypassing his older brother, came to lean over the back of Guy's chair to mutter in his ear, not quite quietly enough,

"Damn it all, Guy, are you moon-mad? That wench you have chosen could freeze a man's bollocks with one look from those ice-grey eyes." Then he grinned. "Alternatively, one touch of that flame-red hair could ignite a fire in a man's loins so fierce only a taste of her honey could quench it. I wonder... which does she do for you, B..."

Guy heard the word hovering on Ranulf's lips and cut in swiftly,

"Shut up, Ran! It is none of your damned business." And, as the other straightened abruptly and turned away, added sharply, "Where are you going? You cannot..."

"Save it, Guy. I am only going to check on the guards. I will not be gone long." He paused again and glanced mockingly at Rowène. "Although I might take a few moments to warm my frozen..."

"Ran!"

"Either way, it should not take long," Ranulf commented dryly. He quirked a pale brow. Demoiselle, you should eat something. You need to keep up your strength for later."

With that he flashed her the hint of a sardonic smile and sauntered from the hall, leaving his elder brother scowling after him. Joffroi shot a darkling look at Guy.

"Where in Hell is he going?"

"Just to check the guards," Guy answered calmly. "He said he would not be long."

Joffroi's scowl deepened but when the Lady Ariène laid a delicate hand on his clenched fist his gaze was drawn back towards her without another word being uttered. Guy snorted softly in his throat. *Gods above, the man is besotted!* But then Guy had known that long before this night.

What was more disturbing was the malicious glint in those fey emerald eyes as they watched Ranulf's broad, black-clad back disappear through the hall doorway. And if her daughter's icy gaze had the power to wither his manhood, if Guy was any judge, the Winter Lady would gladly see her lover's brother eviscerated at her feet. Which left Guy wondering uneasily how she felt about *him...*

He was almost relieved when these unpleasant reflections were interrupted by a low-voiced question from his companion.

"Do you think he was serious when he implied he meant to... to..."

"What?" Guy asked blankly. He followed her grey gaze towards the doorway. "Oh, you mean Ranulf? That he had a serious intent to tumble the wench?"

She blushed in deep discomfort but nodded. Guy regarded her for a moment then shrugged.

"Probably. I cannot see why he would bother to lie about it."

An odd flicker of relief momentarily lit the darkness in her eyes.

"Then he will not need to pursue my sister if he can satisfy his... er... needs with Ilana." She made a small noise of distaste. "Not when the slut has shown herself so willing to be used in such a fashion."

Guy himself had the gravest of doubts whether her first assumption was correct, reckoning Ranulf's stamina higher than she obviously did. But neither did he think that now was the time to disillusion her. Not when, for the first time that evening, she was making some concession towards eating. Clearly not out of any pleasure in the succulent dishes set before her but with a certain grim determination to – as Ranulf had advised her – keep up her strength for what she clearly feared must still come. For her at least, even if she believed, however erroneously, that her sister might now be safe.

On that thought Guy glanced down the table to where Lady Juliène was sitting, as still and pale and ethereally lovely as a water lily in the moonlight. As far as Guy could see she had eaten nothing at all and although he could have sworn she was as relieved as her sister by Ranulf's departure, he saw something else in her beautiful face that he did not think Rowène had noticed.

The faintest flicker of desperation.

Or determination.


Contrary to the harper's assumption, Rowène was acutely aware of her sister's inner turmoil. She had felt the relief Juliène had indulged in when Ranulf de Rogé had left the hall with the obvious intention of slaking his lust in a more private place and – although she did not understand it – she had also sensed her sister's bitter fear that he might not come back.

Yet why in the name of all the gods would Ju want that lascivious daemon to return? Or was it merely that her sister thought it would be less shameful to give up her maidenhead to a ravening nobleman than one of his rag-tag soldiers? Perhaps she might even be hoping that if de Rogé did take her to his bed, he would not feel the necessity of managing the carnal act twice in one night!

Cautiously optimistic that Ju would be safe from Ranulf de Rogé's lustful attentions, Rowène picked up a soft wheaten roll and dipped it in the honey-sweetened sauce that Guy had poured over the roasted larks he had just placed on their shared trencher. The sauce she might manage but the gods knew she could not bring herself to eat those poor little birds any more than she could avoid dwelling on the situation she found herself in. Gods above! Her father was dead, her brother declared a traitor, her recently discovered half-brother a prisoner somewhere in the dungeons below the castle. Yet here she sat, at the same table as the men responsible for these monstrous acts of injustice, sharing meat and wine with Black Joffroi, his lecherous brother and his harper – if such was indeed Guy of Montfaucon's position in the de Rogé household.

But whatever his position in relation to the two de Rogé brothers she very much doubted that it was anything as innocuous as the humble harper he had played with such conviction in her father's hall during the past season. Although not nearly as well as he had played the spy, she reminded herself bitterly.

At least de Rogé – and by this she meant Ranulf rather than his elder brother, who would always be Black Joffroi to her – wore no false mask. He was what he seemed; a brutal, ruthless soldier with conspicuously insatiable appetites that he would satisfy by any means – up to and including rape! She sincerely pitied her sister – and felt guilt too in no small part – at seeing Ju forced to accept de Rogé's debauched company.

For all her doubts about the harper, Rowène had been undeniably relieved to find herself seated beside him at the high table. She might, in her first anger, have expressed a wish to see him damned to the depths of Hell from whence she need never see nor speak to him again but he was, by far, the least offensive of the three de Rogé men. Not that he was a de Rogé as such but he was a member of their household and apparently high in their favour. So who was he? She recalled how Ju had tried to warn her that the harper might not be all he seemed. How had Ju known? Had their mother perhaps dropped some hint that Guy of Montfaucon was a spy in the pay of the man who now held them all in his power?

Not that their horrible and humiliating situation appeared to trouble the Winter Lady, Rowène mused bitterly, her thoughts temporarily diverted away from the harper's iniquities and her own folly. From what Rowène could see, her mother seemed perfectly at ease. She had clearly found time since Black Joffroi's arrival to change into a magnificent gown of watered green silk that Rowène had never seen her wear before. Shot through with silver and sewn with a thousand tiny crystal beads, it shimmered and glittered with the slightest movement. Contrary to all the mores of propriety, her mother's long, flame-gold tresses fell loose as any maiden's, barely covered by the finest of gossamer silk veils held in place by a circlet of white gold studded with pearls and emeralds.

But more telling even than this outrageous flouting of convention and such flagrant display of her wealth, the Winter Lady had already removed the gold and jade binding bracelet that had been Louis de Chartreux's gift to his bride more than twenty-five years before. Seeing this, Rowène was unable to keep the anger, the disbelief and the hurt from her eyes when she looked at her mother.

Apparently unconcerned by her daughter's critical gaze, the Lady Ariène continued to occupy her accustomed place of honour at the high table, eating sparingly and keeping a careful eye on the servants, as if to ensure that her *guests* – as she had publicly named them – were attended to with swiftness and courtesy. Nor did she display any outward sign of the grief or dismay she should by rights have been suffering. Rather the reverse, Rowène thought scornfully, as she watched her mother bestowing her most dazzling smile and all her considerable charm on the blackguard seated at her right hand.

It must be obvious to the dimmest half-wit that Joffroi de Rogé was already completely enslaved by Chartreux's lady; the man could have been eating stable sweepings for all the attention he paid to his food and his eyes never left the enchantingly beautiful face of the woman beside him.

As if the moon had suddenly shattered within her skull, Rowène finally understood what this whole monstrous piece of injustice had been about. Realised too that it did not matter how many other people – from the Prince of Mithlondia down to a simple bridge-keeper – were hurt in the process, so long as Black Joffroi won the right to lawfully bed the fair Lady Ariène. Everyone else in this hall – including herself, her sister, the Lord of Rogé's own brother and his harper – were merely helpless counters in this game of lust and vengeance. *The gods have mercy on us all*, she thought fervently.

Then amended that thought; Ranulf de Rogé at least was no innocent to ride unwittingly along Black Joffroi's twisted path – as witness his eagerness to enjoy all the honeyed spoils that would go to him by right of his brother's triumph. She glanced at the hall door, wondering where the vile, lecherous beast was now and whether he meant to return to claim her unwilling sister or simply spend the remainder of the night in Ilana's bed. Pray gods it was the latter. They deserved each other, she thought venomously; a coarse soldier and a common slut.

Letting his breath out in a long sigh, Ranulf relaxed momentarily before opening his eyes. Not wanting to prolong the moment any longer than necessary he pulled back a little and glanced down, his mouth hardening in self disgust as he surveyed the woman he had just used to ease the tension that had been winding him tighter and tighter since the moment he had first laid eyes on Rowène de Chartreux.

He had taken one look into her crystal grey gaze and felt himself drowning, while the sight of that sun-shot, dark-red hair tumbling in wild disarray over her shoulders and down to her hips had set such a fire in his blood that no amount of wine he had drunk since had been able to douse the flames. He had even, Hell take him, sunk so low as to try and assuage his lust for her – the one woman he could not have – by taking his release in another's body.

Not that he thought the serving wench he had just used felt any of his unaccustomed shame. She was leaning back against the rough sandstone wall, in the same spot where he had found her waiting for him, quite obviously revelling in her perceived triumph. By contrast to her evident unconcern at their position, Ranulf was all too aware of their proximity to the great hall.

Close enough that Ranulf could hear the thrum of voices behind the sturdy oak doors.

Close enough that he could read the expressions on the faces of the two soldiers he had posted by those doors, no matter that they were carefully refraining from looking in his direction.

"Mmm."

The sound of the wench's contented murmur caused him to glance back at her, to find her looking up at him with heavy-lidded, brown eyes. Despite his earlier partial withdrawal they were still joined and now he could feel her arms tightening around him to pull him back against her sweating, partially-clad body. His disgust growing at the sight of that ample bosom pressed against the black cloth of his tunic, he took a firm step back, breaking her hold. He tucked himself back into his breeches with a grimace of distaste, righting his clothing with impatient fingers. Looking up again, he saw the wench was regarding him expectantly and, with a muttered curse, hastily dug a coin – he did not even look to see whether it was a copper farthing or silver half-noble – from the pouch on his belt and held it out to her.

Gathering her bodice together with one hand, she snatched the coin – damnation, it was a full silver noble – from his fingers and flicked her tongue over those red lips he had declined to kiss.

"Will I be seeing you later then, lover?"

"No!" he replied curtly, adding quite deliberately, "I intend to spend tonight in the comfort of a lady's bed."

Not the lady he wanted, curse it, but no-one, least of all this nosy, sharp-eyed slut needed to know that. He turned away, irritated with the wench and furious with himself...

And in his blind haste, walked straight into a stocky man clad in Chartre servant's livery who was coming along the passage from the kitchen to the hall. A full pitcher of red wine crashed to the floor and smashed into shards, splashing over Ranulf's boots and spreading like a pool of darkly shining blood over the floor.

"You bloody clumsy oaf!" Ranulf snarled in common speech. "Why in bloody hell can you not bloody look where you are going?"

"Zorry, zur," the man murmured apologetically, the local accent soft on his tongue.

Then his eyes, as hard as pebbles on the river bed, met Ranulf's irritated glare and for the merest instant before the servant quite properly lowered his gaze, Ranulf could have sworn he saw something that looked disconcertingly like recognition in the depths of the man's golden-brown eyes. Although how a Chartre serving man would have cause to recognise the Lord of Rogé's younger brother was another question entirely, given the fact that Ranulf had never before set foot in Chartre castle and what light there was in the passageway was thrown by a torch some feet behind him.

Uncertain what he was missing but aware nevertheless that something was not quite right, Ranulf regarded the man with narrowed eyes for so long that the servant started to shuffle his feet nervously, muttering something unintelligible which Ranulf took to indicate the need to get the mess cleared up.

"Well, bloody well do it then," Ranulf snapped, still irritated, and stalked down the passage towards the courtyard, reminding himself that he had been on his way to check the guards before he had allowed his body's need to over-rule his wits.

A breath of the cooler, salt-edged evening air up on the castle walls would not come amiss in any case, he thought wryly. It might even scour away the combined scents of sweat and sex from his skin before he had to return to the hall. He thought it probable that Guy would know what he had been about, in any event, but it came to him that he did not want a certain grey-eyed noblewoman to guess – even though when he had left the hall that had been exactly what he had intended.

He made his rounds of the walls and guardroom, satisfied that his men were in place and alert, and on checking the former garrison commander's quarters, found Rowène de Chartreux's half-brother to be in no danger of imminent death – or at least not from the wound Ranulf had inflicted earlier. It had certainly bled freely but was hardly fatal. That said, if the man broke the parole Ranulf had forced from him it would be a different matter entirely and death would not be long in claiming him.

For the time being, however, the bastard appeared to have accepted the inevitable – although one glance into the younger man's feral grey eyes was sufficient to inform Ranulf that this situation would not last for ever. The man hated him, that much was clear, and Ranulf thought he did not have far to look for the cause. He himself had informed Lucien of his father's fate and he did not suppose it would be long before one of his men let slip to the prisoner what Ranulf's reward for his part in this debacle was rumoured to be.

Yet even without that knowledge, it was clear that Lucien regarded Ranulf as being kin to the Daemon of Hell himself – a murderer, a reaver and a ruthless ravisher of innocents. And who was to say he was wrong, Ranulf reflected with a dark cynicism, as he made his way back to the hall. He had gone to Lamortaine knowing that Joffroi intended to bring about Louis de Chartreux's downfall by any means he could. And when the accusations of treason started flying, Ranulf had done nothing to prevent de Chartreux's death – even though he had the gravest doubts as to his guilt. Which meant that, whether he admitted it openly or not, his hands were stained with an innocent man's blood, just as indelibly as Joffroi's were.

So, a murderer – by default at least. And certainly he had been a reaver in his time. But would he go so far as to ravish an innocent noblewoman? That charge yet remained to be proven – a final test of his loyalty to Joffroi perhaps? Or of the dubious power of his own conscience!

Returning at last to the hall, Ranulf nodded to the two soldiers in the worn black and tarnished silver livery of Rogé who stood flanking the carved oak doors. Guthlaf, the older of the two men-at-arms on duty, shifted his grasp on his spear and, keeping his expression carefully blank, reached to open the nearest door while Geryth, younger by at least a score of years, avoided his commander's eyes even as he raised his fist to his chest in salute.

All of which made it very plain to Ranulf just what their feelings were. He doubted they cared about his casual and very public possession of the serving wench but both of them had seen and heard enough of his treatment of Rowène de Chartreux to give some credence to the wilder rumours that were inevitably flying about the castle.

Acknowledging their salutes, Ranulf walked past them into the hall, coming to an abrupt halt just inside, appreciating for perhaps the first time the contrast between his brother's new holding and the desolate castle where he, Joffroi and Guy had grown up together. The light from what must be two hundred candles was dazzling after the cool blue shadows of the evening sky while the fine tapestries that hid the sandstone walls and the blue, silver and gold banners that still hung from the rafters leapt upon the eye as an overwhelming riot of warmth and colour. Not that those banners would remain there for much longer, Ranulf reflected with a hint of a sardonic smile. Only as long as it took to find a long ladder and a soldier with a head for heights.

Casting aside his recollections of the dank, cheerless hall of Rogérinac castle – its damp grey walls decorated with dark mould, dusty cobwebs and moth-eaten black banners, its hungry shadows fed by the flickering light of smoky torches – Ranulf forced himself to relax and walk the length of the hall towards the dais at the far end, ignoring the surly household members dining at the lower tables.

He sent one narrow look at Guy and his companion as he mounted the steps to the dais, directed a terse nod towards Joffroi and Lady Ariène and dropped heavily into his own seat. Somewhat to his surprise the Lady Juliène immediately turned towards him, a small, strained smile on her lily-pale face and, with obvious effort, found sufficient courage to address him directly for the first time since they had all entered the hall.

"I trust all is in order, Messire? And that there has been no further trouble with the garrison or the servants?"

"No," he replied tersely. Then, feeling this to be too curt even for him, added. "All is as well as can be expected, Demoiselle, given the less than congenial circumstances."

She regarded him gravely for a moment longer, her eyes an enchanting shade of green beneath the delicate black arch of her brows and the sweep of impossibly long dark lashes, her face a pearlescent oval, breathtaking in its loveliness. He found his gaze drawn inexorably to her soft, lush lips before he forced himself to look away. Only to encounter her sister's hostile grey glare.

Easily reading the contempt in those ice-cold eyes he felt himself flush. Damn the little witch to Hell, did she think he would debauch her sister with as little compunction as he had that serving wench? If so, she would soon learn her error; he might be a lecher but he had his limits. And raping an innocent young noblewoman – either in public or in private – was well beyond them. Especially one as delicate and fragile of appearance as the Lady Juliène de Chartreux.

He yielded briefly to that steady grey stare but only in order to sweep his gaze – with deliberate insult – down over her body. She was wearing the same dark blue velvet gown as when he had first seen her and her hair still tumbled unfettered over her shoulders and breasts but now it flickered with red fire –

witch-fire – in the candlelight. Despite the unbroken ice in her gaze and his own recent exertions, he could feel his blood begin to heat again at the imagined touch of that hair on certain parts of his body. He shifted slightly in his seat in an attempt to find some ease but the movement only served to bring his eyes into contact with Guy's bleakly perceptive gaze. He sent a quick grimace of apology at the other man and resolutely returned his attention to his own table companion, hearing, as if through one of Rogérinac's notorious sea mists, her melodious voice asking him if he wished for some more wine or anything else to eat.

He managed a vaguely courteous reply but even as he watched her refill his goblet with her own graceful white hand his unruly thoughts were running wild beyond his control. Taking a sip of the rich, heady wine he studied her over the silver rim. She was most astonishingly lovely, he thought again, and the majority of the men in the hall would undoubtedly have changed places with him without a moment's hesitation. In all truth, he wondered why he was holding himself aloof from such beauty, more especially as the look of frozen revulsion that frosted her sister's clear gaze was absent from the Lady Juliène's jewel-bright eyes and her lips were curved in an alluring smile that hinted at headier kisses.

Notwithstanding that unspoken – and, he was sure, unintentional – invitation, Ranulf could not bring himself to view the night ahead with anything more than dismay and he roundly cursed the daemon – and the witch – who had taken control of his brother's mind. By rights he, Ranulf, should be with the rest of the Mithlondian army, his wits and his sword honed for battle against the northern barbarians or coastal raiders and, if he had the leisure to take a woman to his bed at all, it would be one of those hardy breed who kept pace with the army, cooking for the men when they were in camp, binding their wounds on the field and attending to their other needs as required.

Instead of which...

Silently cursing the whole damnable affair, he glanced from the beautiful young noblewoman seated beside him – she was now nibbling daintily on a peeled peach and some plump dark grapes – back down the generously-laden table at her plain-faced sister, the irrelevant thought coming to him that at least *she* looked sufficiently robust to take what was to come and not – as the Lady Juliène did – as if the very act of bedding her would shatter her into a myriad shimmering fragments of moonlight.

Had Guy already had her? He wondered where that unexpected thought had come from and considered it carefully, even as he studied the flame-haired witchling who set secret fires to burning in men's loins. Were they lovers, Guy and the clear-eyed Lady Rowène de Chartreux? But no, Ranulf could not quite bring himself to believe that. Given that there were few secrets at Rogérinac, he – in common with everyone else in the castle and nearby village – knew that Guy's binding was fraught to say the least of it. But he also knew, with a soul-deep knowledge of the man, that Guy would never be unfaithful to his wife.

Or rather, Ranulf reminded himself, he had not been unfaithful until he had come to Chartre. Now though it was perfectly clear to anyone who knew Guy as well as Ranulf himself did that, despite the Lady Rowène's superficial coldness, there still existed between her and Guy some fragile sense of trust... liking... Damnation, he did not know *what* it was. He just knew it was there. And that he was intensely jealous of it.

It was true that there had been precious little time for private conversation between him and Guy since his arrival but Guy had confessed, rather shamefacedly, that he had permitted a friendship of sorts to grow up between himself and one of Louis de Chartreux's daughters – and it had not been difficult for Ranulf to guess which one! A companionship that had drawn Guy to become more deeply involved with the woman than was wise under any circumstances, let alone the ones that prevailed now.

Not only was it not wise, Ranulf thought grimly, it was bloody dangerous! Since, not only was it looking increasingly likely that Guy would break his binding vows with that little wild-cat, he was also teetering on the edge of treason to his liege lord – as witnessed by his earlier reluctance to deliver Rowène's brother into Joffroi's bloodstained and vengeful hands.

Fighting down the surge of vomit that burned the back of his throat at the unwanted memory of Louis de Chartreux's disembowelled and butchered body, Ranulf took another swallow of the powerful wine. Cold sweat prickling at his temples, he admitted to himself that he could find it in him to share Guy's reluctance to deliver de Chartreux's only legitimate son – or even his bastard – to the same fate. Joffroi might be carrying the High Counsel's warrant for their execution but Ranulf swore to himself that if it came to that point, both Luc and Lucien would die sword in hand, not half choked to death before having their guts ripped, still warm, from their bellies and their bodies brutally carved into quarters.

As for Louis de Chartreux's two innocent daughters, surely one night with him and Guy was not too harsh a price to pay for their lives?

As the evening sky softened from lilac to lavender and the moon began to rise in her graceful dance, the elaborate meal continued to run its lengthy course until finally Joffroi's gravelled voice made itself heard,

"Ran! Guy! Are you and your ladies done?"

Startled out of his tangled thoughts, Guy exchanged a brief glance with Ranulf, then nodded silently, knowing he could not have forced his dry throat to form words even had he tried. Draining his goblet for the last time Ranulf set it down on the table, and – considering the amount of wine Guy knew he had consumed – said with remarkable clarity,

"A fine meal, and a finer wine but yes, we are finished, Demoiselle Juliène and I."

Joffroi grinned.

"Good. Because I am ready for my bed. Madame?"

He turned towards the Lady Ariène who, to Guy's astounded disbelief, actually appeared to blush. Rising gracefully from her seat, she sank into a deep curtsey which served the double purpose of publicly signifying her obedience to Joffroi's will as well as offering her lover a clearer view of the tantalising cleft between her full, white breasts. Dark eyes burning with a raw, triumphant desire he made no effort whatsoever to conceal, Joffroi put an arm around her waist and drew her in closer to his body, the easier to take her mouth in a searingly possessive kiss.

There was a general gasp of horror from those of the Chartre household who were still present, almost lost in the rowdy appreciation of the Rogé soldiers who cheered and whistled loudly. Guy – unable to watch with any equanimity Joffroi's lascivious attentions to the woman for whom he had been prepared to lie, murder and possibly even commit treason – turned his gaze towards the girl beside him. In time to see the flash of horrified comprehension in those expressive grey eyes that told him she had finally realised that her mother had never had the slightest intention of repulsing the dark warlord who now claimed possession of Chartreux and all within its borders.

Almost without volition Guy put out his hand in a gesture of compassion but thankfully before he could speak was dragged back into sanity when Joffroi released his paramour and, staring almost blindly from Ranulf to Guy, demanded,

"Well, what are you two waiting for? Surely you do not really intend to draw lots?"

Guy could not command his tongue sufficiently to make the required answer but again Ranulf proved capable of replying for them both.

"No!" He tossed the curt comment in his brother's direction. "I have better things to do with my time. Let Guy keep his doxy. I am more than content with this very lovely lady."

Saying this, Ranulf took a firm grip of Lady Juliène's slender wrist in order to raise that damsel from her seat. Guy took one look at those suddenly fearful emerald eyes, her paler than pale cheeks and knew that the moment he had actively been dreading all evening was upon him. Fists clenched, he wondered how in the name of all the gods he could go through with Joffroi's twisted scheme. Or how in Hell he could disobey his liege lord's orders without risking Rowène as well as himself...

He was recalled to reality by hard fingers digging into the taut muscles of his forearm and Ranulf's low-voiced admonition in his ear.

"Do not chance it, Guy! No wench is worth it, least of all one with no looks to speak of and witch-red hair to boot!"

The gods knew what injudicious words might have sprung from his tongue if Ranulf had given him that opportunity. Instead, he raised his voice so that everyone left in the hall could hear and continued without pause,

"Since you know your way around here better than me, Guy, you can show me the way to the bedchambers." He grinned. "Preferably one with a comfortable bed and a door that locks!"

Guy gave him an angry look but Ranulf merely tightened his grip and, reverting to the urgent undertone he had used before, hissed,

"Curse you, Guy! Make some sign of compliance before Joffroi's temper stirs again. At the moment he is too wrapped in his own lust but if you delay much longer it will be too late to salvage anything – for you or for her!" And as Guy still hesitated, added savagely, "Bloody hell, man! Just get yourself and the wench out of here. What you do behind a bolted door is your own affair. Just make damned sure there is blood on your sheet in the morning and Joff is not like to call you a liar."

At this Guy's anger died and he realised, with considerable relief, that Ranulf did not mean to obey Joffroi's depraved edict either. That being so, there might yet be an honourable way out of this whole wretched situation for them all. But obviously everything depended on whether they could convince Joffroi – and that sharp-eyed bitch now watching their quiet altercation with a coolly assessing, green gaze.

Hiding his emotions as best he could he glared into the dark blue eyes so close to his own and shook off the firm grip on his arm,

"Take your hands off me, Ran! The last thing I need is lessons from you on how to treat a woman." Then, turning to the Lady Rowène, who had risen rather warily and was now regarding both him and Ranulf with utter revulsion. "Come, Demoiselle, it is time to retire." He caught hold of her cold hand and, feeling her resistance, bent to murmur for her ears alone, "For gods'sake, do not fight me! Not here, where all eyes are upon us!" And, with a desperate harshness, "Well, Demoiselle? Either you come with me willingly or I leave you to take your chances with Ranulf!"

The girl looked up at him in sharp disbelief, then at Ranulf who obligingly gave her a leer so blatantly lewd that under normal circumstances Guy would have hit him. This situation, however, was so far from normal as to be unique. And whatever Ranulf's motives, it certainly appeared to have the desired effect. Shrinking back from the man whose attentions she obviously found utterly repellent, she flicked a pleading look at him but Guy had no leisure for mercy. With an effort he kept his face impassive and reiterated more softly,

"Ranulf or me?"

In response she laid a perceptibly trembling hand on his arm and, in poignant acknowledgement of his position and power, gave him his title for the first time.

"Very well, Messire, I will go with you. Since it is clear that the choice you offer me is no choice at all."

And with that the Lady Rowène de Chartreux allowed him to lead her the length of the hall, under the scores of watching eyes and up the stairs of the Lady Tower.

# Chapter 8

## *Moonrise 'til Dawn*

Despite de Rogé's claim to need a guide, Rowène and the harper soon outdistanced the other man – she thought he had paused to give some order to the two soldiers on duty outside the hall – and before she had quite accustomed herself to the situation, found herself outside the chamber she had once shared with Juliène and which it would seem she must now share with Guy of Montfaucon. At least for tonight. And the gods knew how many nights after. Until, she supposed, he had tired of using her body for his pleasure or his lord decreed some new punishment for her. All she could do in the meantime was pray to the God of Mercy that any such punitive action would not result in her being given into Ranulf de Rogé's hands...

*Gods above,* she thought in horror, *what must Ju be suffering now, knowing that in less than a candle-notch she will find herself in that drunken lecher's bed?*

At least, Rowène decided, *she* was not afraid of the harper or what he might do to her. Or not much. Instinct, together with her memories of the past weeks they had spent together, reassured her that Guy would never use his far greater strength to hurt her physically, even though he had already wounded her heart all too deeply by his flagrant betrayal of her trust and friendship.

Emerging from the suffocating tunnel of her dark thoughts, she found that her companion had opened the door and was waiting for her to enter. There being no choice at all in the matter, she allowed him to usher her through, then stood silently to one side, watching warily what he might do next. He shut the door firmly, muttering a surprisingly vehement curse when he saw there was no means of securing it, then stalked over to the open window where he stood staring out into the dusk. Following his line of sight across the quiet waters of the bay to the dark coastline of Rogé, Rowène felt a most peculiar sensation pervade her body as her gaze fell upon the rising moon where it flowered like a pale pink rose against the silver-dusted blue of the midsummer sky.

*Pink?*

Rowène blinked in disbelief but no matter how often she closed her eyes, when she opened them the rose pink moon was still there; a fey – and rather frightening – manifestation in the mortal skies above Mithlondia.

Moving on soundless feet, she went to stand by the harper's side, caught between wonder and apprehension as to what this eerie sight might portend. Held by the ethereal touch of a Being she had not previously believed might even exist, she forgot the sensation of abandonment she had felt when the harper had left her side so abruptly. Put aside also as best she might her very real fear for her sister and brothers and instead opened herself to the enchantment of the moment. Fragmented recollections of half-murmured songs shimmered through her mind, all tangled together with eldritch tales of the Moon Goddess, the forbidden deity of the Faennari...

But *she* was not one of the Fae, she reminded herself, reluctantly returning to reality. She was not bewitchingly beautiful, as her mother was, or an alluring siren like her sister. She was Rowène; plain of face and probably undesirable save to the desperate – or depraved! Betrothed to a man who had not seen her since childhood and who had certainly shown no haste to meet her before their formal binding – which would probably not now take place once the events of this terrible night became public knowledge.

Yet even if she discounted Joscelin de Veraux's blatant lack of curiosity about his bride, here she was, in a moonlit bedchamber with a man who revealed not the slightest sign of wishing to make love to her. Would he do it anyway, she wondered? His liege lord had commanded it, after all. But *could* he do such a thing, if he felt no desire for her?

Safely concealed in the shadows cast by the huge, canopied bed, she directed a look of narrow-eyed consideration at his broad frame, still clothed in the harper's tattered garments. He stood with his booted feet slightly apart, easily balancing the weight of the long sword that hung at his hip. He had angled his head away from her so she could not read his face but she acknowledged with wry self-derision that, even though she now knew him to be Black Joffroi's man, she felt neither fear nor revulsion for him.

Brooding uneasily over Black Joffroi's earlier statement during the course of that interminable evening meal she had thought herself resigned to becoming Guy of Montfaucon's leman rather than suffer any more unpleasant alternative his lord might devise. Although even enduring the callous defilement of Ranulf de Rogé's touch would not be as horrific, she conceded, as being used by the two score rough louts who obeyed his commands and who now made up the garrison of Chartre castle.

That said, she had not believed it would come to that. Consequently she had been shocked into silence when it did. But now that she had made her choice? The harper might not want her but she did not believe he would allow de Rogé to take her. And while she was relieved at that conclusion, she was also uncomfortably aware that her panicked agreement to share Guy of Montfaucon's bed had not been prompted solely by the dictates of necessity. Despite everything he had done... everything he was... she found her body tingling with a strange exhilaration that made her blood dance and butterflies to take flight in her belly.

And Guy? What was he feeling... thinking... That he was reluctant to break the awkward silence that lay between them was obvious but perhaps he was as disturbed by that odd, other-worldly pink orb as she? As desperately uncomfortable with their situation as she? For surely this was not something that happened to him on a regular basis, unless…

Unless this was not the first time Black Joffroi had extended his lands by twisting the law and other people's lives in order to deal with those men – and there could not be many – who were reckless enough to stand in his way, subsequently giving the subjugated womenfolk over to his brother and his harper for their pleasure. As this nauseating image formed in her mind, her tongue spoke her appalled thought out loud,

"You told me once that you were no ravening wolf with a taste for young swan-maidens! Or was that as much a lie as everything else you have told me? God of Light, Guy, have you ever told me the truth about *anything?*"

He turned swiftly as if stung.

"*That*, at least, was no lie," he said tersely, his tone imbued with a coldness she was not accustomed to hearing from him. "Far from being a ravening wolf I can assure you that, conceited though it may sound, I have never bedded with a woman who did not also want me. And, despite what you might believe after listening to my… to Joffroi and Ranulf, I am not like to start now."

She made some strangled sound that he obviously interpreted as incredulity, and continued with biting formality,

"You place no reliance on my word, Demoiselle de Chartreux? Then permit me to remind you of the reason why you may. The oath that will keep your body, if not your reputation, unsullied and fit for your binding bed." As he had done once before, he pushed back the short sleeve of his tunic, allowing the moonlight to strike sparks from the bronze ring he wore about his upper arm. "The only reason I am here with you now is…"

His head came up as if he heard something. The next moment he caught her in his arms and tumbled her down onto the bed beneath him, lowering his head and silencing whatever she had meant to say with a kiss that was neither gentle nor respectful.

Even as Rowène felt herself melt within his unexpected – but, despite everything, not unwelcome – embrace, the chamber door burst open on a wave of raucous, ribald comments and she realised with a belated, but icy, certainty what had caused his sudden surge of passion.

Cursing inwardly and fervently hoping that the young noblewoman in his arms would not comprehend the meaning of the vulgar remarks presently being bandied about above their heads – unlikely considering the extremely idiomatic terms Ranulf was employing – Guy lifted his mouth from those soft, rose-petal lips that had tempted him for so long and drew in a ragged breath.

He knew a momentary fear that he had shocked her so much that she would be unable to react convincingly to his assault but was relieved when she wrenched an arm free from his deliberately loose hold and dealt him a blow that, due to her awkward position, caught his nose more than his cheek. Eyes watering from the unexpected pain – he had been prepared for a maidenly slap rather than such a forceful hook – Guy caught her wrist before she could do any more damage and shifted his weight so that she was more fully beneath him. Fisting his free hand in the soft velvet of her skirt, he dragged it up to expose a goodly portion of her slender leg, when all he really wanted to do was check whether his nose was bleeding. It damned well felt like it.

He ignored another piece of gratuitously bawdy advice from the direction of the door, even as he grudgingly congratulated Ranulf on his ability to make the best of the circumstances in order to convince Joffroi that his orders were being carried out. He allowed Ranulf one more comment before deciding enough was enough. Looking up, he snapped a singularly crude phrase in the Rogé vernacular.

Ranulf responded to this blunt dismissal with a yelp of laughter and a brief comment in kind. Then, clapping Joffroi on the shoulder, finally contrived to draw his brother and the two women out of the chamber, pulling the door firmly shut behind him as he went.

Deeply grateful though he was for Ranulf's complicity, Guy yet remained where he was for several unsteady heartbeats, listening intently to the fading footsteps. When all was quiet again he drew in a deep breath, absently releasing his fingers from the blue velvet in order to touch the back of his hand to his throbbing nose. No, it was not broken, nor even bleeding. He sniffed reflexively and said with palpable relief,

"I think they are gone now and we are safe from further interruption. For the time being at least."

"That being so, Messire, do you think you can get off me?" the girl beneath him enquired breathlessly.

Guy glanced down at her, only then realising that she was still bearing the full brunt of his not inconsiderable weight while the hilt of his dagger must have been digging painfully into her ribs. He rolled off her body and stood, frowning as he saw the marks his fingers had left on slender wrists that already bore the purpling bruises of Ranulf's earlier – and far more punishing – grip.

"My apologies, Demoiselle" he offered abruptly. "I did not mean to hurt you. But if the gods smile on us, that will be the only price you will be called upon to pay for this night's work!"

She gave him a wry smile and tentatively touched her fingers, first to her swollen lips – the gods help him, he could taste their luscious sweetness even now – then to the reddened place on her dimpled chin where his short beard had ravaged the pale golden skin.

"I agree that is but a small price to pay," she said softly and the expression shimmering in her moonlit grey eyes was very nearly his undoing.

Knowing that he had to put some distance between them before he gave in to his, hitherto unsuspected, baser nature and took her in his arms again, he spun on his heel and strode back towards the window. It took him more than a few moments of pacing but once he had broken the spell that had kept his gaze meshed with hers, vulnerable to the moonlight and enchantment that pervaded the chamber like a subtle scent, he found it easier to regain some semblance of control. Sufficient, he hoped, to carry them both through the night with the minimum of damage – either to her virginity or his honour!

Struggling to steady her breathing and calm the frantic thumping of her heart, Rowène watched through her lashes as the harper stalked restlessly about the chamber, pausing only to light the candles – although she thought this was more as an act of defiance towards the moon than because he needed the light. Seeming at last to come to a decision, he returned to the window seat, sat down and began to pull off his boots.

Her heartbeat, which had by then started to quieten, immediately quickened again. Still not quite believing that any of this was happening, she watched as he unbuckled his sword belt and laid it carefully behind him. Her stomach lurched uncontrollably as his shabby tunic and threadbare shirt crumpled beside it. Nor could she quite prevent the nervous gasp that escaped her lips as he straightened up and turned fully towards her, the profusion of fair hair on his chest glinting gold in the glimmering candle glow.

As if from some great distance she heard his voice, no longer light and even, but raw and dark with some barely contained emotion.

"Gods! Do not look at me like that! Surely you do not think I am planning to ravish you after all!"

"Are you not?" she asked in uncomprehending bemusement, warily eyeing his half-naked body, not so much shocked as curious. He was certainly built more solidly than the slim, dark-haired men of the Kardolandian court and...

"Damnation, girl! Have you understood nothing I have said to you!" he demanded irritably. Then, in response to her startled look of enquiry, added somewhat more gently, "I give you my word that you will come to no harm in my company. But it is possible..." She saw a grimace of distaste cross his normally good-humoured countenance. "That Joffroi may take it into his head to check up on me again. So, little though I relish the prospect, if he does come back he must see enough to convince him that I am doing as he ordered." He seemed to hesitate and then added, somewhat diffidently, "If you will, you must also give some consideration between now and morning as to whether you would prefer it to be thought that I took you by force or that, for some strange reason beyond my present comprehension, you gave yourself to me without a fight."

Rowène blinked at him in a dazed way and managed to say,

"Forgive me, but I do not understand any of this. Are you saying you are willing to let it be thought that you *are* the ravening wolf I called you but without any of the..." She felt a hot flush of embarrassment rise in her cheeks but forced herself to continue. "Any of the... er... physical benefits?"

"If you wish to put it like that, then yes that is exactly what I am offering. Of course," he added dryly. "There is no guarantee that Joffroi would believe me capable of taking any woman against her will but since it is your honour I am maligning the choice must be yours."

"Messire..."

"Can you not use my given name?" he interrupted, his tone weary now rather than irritated. "After all, it came to your tongue easily enough when you thought I was nothing more than a chance-come harper of humble birth. After all this time of hearing my name on your lips it seems unnatural to be addressed by such a formal title."

"But now I know you are both more and less than a chance-come harper. Even if I still do not know how high or low your birth really is." She frowned and then said slowly, "Although by the spurs on your heels and that sword you were wearing I must suppose you are far from the peasant your hair and beard proclaim you to be."

"No," he said levelly. "I am no peasant. But then I suspect you knew I was not all I seemed long before we met up with Joffroi and Ranulf on the road beyond Swanfleet and I buckled on both spurs and sword."

She flashed him a quick glance and he continued with a rueful smile,

"I gave myself away the day you found me at the top of the Lady Tower, did I not?" Suddenly he was smiling no longer and his blue eyes were intent upon hers. "Yet you did not betray me to your brother. In gods' name, Rowène, why did you hold your silence?"

The harsh note in his voice was almost as disconcerting as his use of her given name but she answered him anyway, her gaze flickering towards the sheathed sword lying on the window seat, the silver-wired hilt and the carved chunk of amber on the pommel glimmering in the growing moonlight. She swallowed.

"That day, on the tower... you were lost in thought and before you became fully aware of where you were or who I was, I saw your hand reach for a weapon that obviously would, under normal circumstances, have been at your side, although it was absent then. And I thought you started to address me as *Demoiselle*, as no commoner would ever have done. But I told myself I must have been mistaken, misread your intentions, misheard your words." She hesitated and then confessed in a low voice. "In truth, I did not want to doubt you. Although if you had given me further cause, perhaps I would have taken my doubts to Luc. The gods know, I wish now that I had!"

"As do I," he concurred, an unaccustomed grim note in his voice.

Ignoring the shiver that trickled down her spine, she continued bitterly,

"Yet even now I do not know who or what you really are. Surely you are more to Bla... to Joffroi de Rogé than his household harper? Certainly you are high in your lord's favour since you address both him and his brother by their given names, even to the diminutives of affection." Her voice broke suddenly. "In the name of all the gods, Guy, tell me who you are! There can surely be no need for secrecy now? Not when it is *your* lord who holds the position of power over all Chartreux, myself included."

He started to say something, shut his mouth sharply and half turned away. She watched him with narrowed eyes as the barren silence stretched out between them, as bleak and dark as a moonless night on the high moors. Eventually she said dryly,

"You have asked me to call you by your given name but I do not even know if the name I have been using is truly yours."

As that accusation struck home, he finally consented to turn back to face her.

"I told you when we first met what my name was. And I told you the truth as far as I was able." They had been conversing in the high tongue but now he lapsed into the slightly accented common speech he had used with her before today. "You know me as Guy of Montfaucon, yes?"

Rowène nodded, still not comprehending.

"That is no lie – just not all the truth. To the folk of Rogé I am Sir Guy or Master Guy and although I was not raised in Montfaucon, I was at least born there. So I am, in some respects, Guy of Montfaucon."

"And your family name?" Rowène queried. "For I am very sure that you have one. You would not wear both spurs and sword else."

"No, I would not," he agreed, slipping easily back into Mithlondian. "They are mine by right of blood kinship with the knight who holds the demesne of Montfaucon from Gilles de Valenne, although I doubt that you will have heard his name." He paused, then sighed sharply before admitting with every appearance of reluctance. "In short, Demoiselle, I am Guyard de Martine."

Despite his words, he obviously expected her to recognise that name. But she had been away from Mithlondia too long and it meant nothing to her. Or did it? Something stirred in the recesses of her mind... some memory of an old feud... then it was gone, leaving her with the man and his true name.

So, he was not Guy of Montfaucon, but Guyard de Martine. She tested his name – a nobleman's name – on her tongue and then frowned, as that faint glimmer of recollection flared once more, this time into full flame.

"So how does a de Martine come to be with Joffroi de Rogé – in whatever capacity! As you yourself said, Montfaucon lies under the Lord of Valenne's jurisdiction and even I know that Valenne and Rogé have been enemies since long before I was born."

Guyard – she must remember to call him by that name now, she supposed – shrugged broad shoulders in a gesture indicative of indifference, although she doubted he was as devoid of feeling as he seemed.

"The explanation is simple enough," he replied dismissively. "But surely of no interest to anyone outside of my immediate kin."

"Please, Guyard..." she stumbled a little over his full name and he smiled crookedly.

"Just call me Guy."

She nodded, blushingly aware that he was granting her a familiarity that under normal circumstances would never be allowed to exist between them. But then nothing about this situation was normal, so she might just as well continue to use the familiar diminutive as he had indicated.

"Please, Guy, I would like to know," she repeated softly. "How you came to be wearing the black boar of Rogé rather than the silver falcon of Valenne."

"Very well," he agreed. "But stop me if my tale becomes too tedious." His blue eyes took on a distant look, as if he were looking beyond the moonshine and candlelight of this night, back over the years – how many years, she thought suddenly, wondering how old he actually was – into the dim shadows of the past.

"I suppose I must start with my mother," he said, rather bleakly, she thought. "Contrary to what you might have supposed, she was gently born, the only daughter of a relatively poor but exceedingly proud family..."

"What is her name?" she interrupted.

He frowned at her, apparently caught off balance by her simple question, then said tersely,

"Alys de... Alys." And hastened on with his tale before she could ask *Alys de what?* "Being gently born but with no dowry of her own, she was sent by her father to serve as companion to Henri de Lyeyne's sister in the days before that lady was bound to Jacques de Rogé, my mother then accompanying Lady Rosalynde when she removed to Rogérinac." He grimaced slightly, evidently lost in his tale. "It is no secret that it was not an easy binding and perhaps it was for that reason that my mother remained with her friend, not only for Joffroi's birth but to support the poor lady through the series of miscarriages and still-births that followed. And it must have been at some time during those difficult years that she... my mother, that is..."

He paused, as if uncertain what to say next. Knowing he could be blunt enough when the situation warranted it, Rowène guessed he was hesitating for a different reason.

"She met and fell in love with your father?" Rowène suggested gently, thinking how like a man to be uncomfortable with the notion of romantic love – as opposed to the tenets of honour and duty or the needs of raw, physical lust. She watched as a flicker of some fleeting emotion darkened his light blue eyes.

"Yes," he said softly. "I think it must have been love, although of course I cannot be sure." Then his tone hardened. "Knowing my father as I did, though, I doubt there was much more to it than lust on his part but perhaps I am being unjust. I would like to think there must have been some affection between them. According to my father – and I have no reason to doubt him – it *was* by mutual consent that they came together, although he did tell me that my mother was never really happy. And in the end she left him."

Rowène caught her breath at this startling admission but Guyard was not even looking at her; he was still staring into a past that clearly had brought nothing but pain and misery to all concerned. She wished she had not forced him to relive the tragedy she knew must have occurred but before she could stop him he had continued with his unhappy tale.

"Despite having no resources of her own, but unwilling to continue as she was, my mother chose to end her long service to Lady Rosalynde and to leave Rogérinac. She took the small store of silver she had saved over the years – the gods know it cannot have been much – and made her way to the court at Lamortaine, where she threw herself onto Armand de Martine's less than bountiful mercy. He, curse his vindictive soul to Hell, sent her, a gently-born lady, to the – pardon my bluntness – whores' house in Montfaucon."

He paused, regarding his knuckles, then added flatly,

"A little less than five months later I was born... And my mother died. I think the Sire de Martine would have been just as pleased if I had died too, but by the grace of the gods not all in Montfaucon were as lacking in compassion as their master. One of the other unfortunate women in that house, who had become friends with my mother, had sufficient milk for both her own babe and me. Sufficient at least to keep me alive until the day my father finally arrived. He had gone there seeking word of my mother and found me instead. As he told the tale, there was a fine litter of whelps that summer in the back alleys of Montfaucon but he knew as soon as he saw me that I must be his get, despite not knowing of my existence until that moment. Apparently my mother had not told him she carried his child when she left him, although she must have known herself, and I think it came as a considerable shock to my father."

He smiled, a shade wryly.

"I suppose I should thank the gods that I was the only new-born child in the village with hair the same light colour as his own and that the woman who was nursing me chose to do it on the doorstep of the house at the time my father was passing by. Seeing his interest in me she told him both my mother's name and the name my mother had given to me before she died – a name that I shared with my father. With both name and hair to corroborate his first instinct, he was convinced I must be his son and accordingly took me back to Rogérinac with him where he begged, or otherwise induced, the Lady of Rogé to accept me into her household. She could have left me to grow up with the hounds and the rest of the garrison's chance-fathered brats but she was a gentle-hearted lady and she had me raised alongside her own sons. Joffroi was nine years old by then and had little to do with me but by some strange twist of fate her younger son, Ranulf, and I were the same age. Born on the same day, albeit leagues apart – and in more ways than mere distance. Despite that division, we shared the same cradle, the same wet-nurse and, as we grew older, the same lessons in horsemanship and arms. Madame Rosalynde taught us manners and music – or tried to – and m... Messire Jacques thrashed us with an equally heavy hand when we were caught out in whatever misdemeanours we had tumbled into. True-born brothers could not have been closer than Ranulf and I. Despite everything, Madame Rosalynde raised me as her son and I loved and honoured her, as deeply as I would have loved my own mother had she lived."

"It was indeed kind of Madame Rosalynde to take you in and raise you as her own," Rowène said softly. "She must have been very fond of your mother to foster you with her own son."

"Indeed she was kinder to me than I had any right to expect," Guyard replied with a darkly, humourless smile. His thick fair brows met once more in that frown that sat so ill on his good-tempered face. "And certainly more generous than my father deserved!" Then he wiped all expression from his face again as he concluded briskly, "To cut a long story short, Madame Rosalynde died when I was eight and Messire Jacques when I was fifteen. Joffroi naturally became the Sire de Rogé on his death and, knowing no other loyalty, I swore my oath of allegiance to him. By the time we had grown to full manhood, Joffroi had given Ranulf command of the garrison and entrusted me with the stewardship of all his lands and revenues, and we have served him in those capacities ever since."

"And your... father?" Rowène asked hesitantly. "Is he still alive?"

He looked at her oddly and she thought he was not going to answer but at last he said quietly,

"No. He died from a spear wound, nearly a score of years ago now. A wound received at your own father's hand, as it happens."

She gasped and blurted out,

"Is *that* why you are doing this to us then? In revenge for your father's death?"

"Damn it, no!" Anger roughened his tone. "Of course I do not hold you or your sister responsible. Or either of your brothers for that matter! Nor even your father, for all it was his hand wielding the spear."

"Oh!" She swallowed. "Forgive me..."

He nodded curtly and she continued diffidently,

"Can you tell me what happened?"

He sighed, short and sharp, the sound sibilant with anger and regret.

"It was one those small but bloody exchanges that seem always to occur along the Chartreux-Rogé border. For Ranulf and I, it was our first such encounter. The gods know I wish it had been my last, but I have to tell you now that it was not. For either of us. Where Messire Jacques – and later Joffroi – led, Ranulf and I followed. As it happened that particular day, your father was out hunting with some of his men in the beech woods around Larkhill. As were we – albeit not for deer or boar – and *we* were on the wrong side of the Larkenlye. Enough said." He shrugged and turned away, a flash of uncharacteristic moodiness in his light blue eyes. "It was but a small wound my father took – a glancing scratch from your father's spear – and under normal circumstances it should have healed quickly. But it became infected beyond any care and he died."

He turned away, as if unable to look at her any longer, the daughter of the man who had caused his own father's death.

"I am sorry for your father's untimely death. For your sake, at least," Rowène said quietly, the anger and bitterness in her gaze softening slightly, tenderly tracing the tense muscles of his naked back. She *was* sorry that he had lost his father – his only blood kin – surely before he had even come of age. What she refrained from saying out loud was that perhaps his father had deserved his fate since he had been caught reaving on Chartreux land and that death from wound fever was perhaps an easier one than the cruel agonies her own father had suffered.

She also wished with all her heart that Guyard had not chosen to bind himself to a warlord as brutal and black-hearted as Joffroi de Rogé but at least she knew now who and what he really was. Guyard de Martine. Distant kinsman through his father to Sir Armand of Montfaucon and – thank the gods – no relation at all to Jacques de Rogé or his two hell-spawned sons. Albeit serving as steward to Black Joffroi and living as foster brother to Ranulf de Rogé was surely discreditable enough.

Reminded thus unpleasantly of the drunken lecher whom she had last glimpsed disappearing into the torch-lit shadows of the stairwell with her sister in tow, renewed horror rushed over her.

*God of Light… Ju!* How could she have forgotten her sister's plight, even for a single heartbeat!

"Messire de Martine?"

He turned and smiled, somewhat bitterly, she thought.

"I would rather you called me Guy."

"Guy, then," she agreed. Distracted by the odd note in his voice it took her a moment to remember what she had meant to ask him.

"Yes?" he prompted.

"My sister? Do you think... Will he... your foster brother, I mean... Will he..."

She floundered hopelessly into silence. As if sensing her need for comfort, Guyard moved a little closer, although he took care to maintain some small distance between them.

"I will not lie to you," he said, his former half smile turning into a grimace. "Never again, you have my word! As for Ranulf..." He paused, considering, then continued thoughtfully. "Judging by what he said to me earlier, I believe there is some cause for hope that he will leave your sister untouched. As it is, I have never known him to use force against any woman... But then again, I have never known him disobey a direct command from Joffroi either. If it comes to the point and he decides, for whatever reason, he has to bed her..." He hesitated, then concluded in distinctly grim tones. "If he does choose that path, unthinkable though it is... If your sister has any sense, she will yield herself to him without the need for violence and he will lose interest soon enough. He always does. And in the morning, if Joffroi is content, Ranulf will undoubtedly be heading for wherever the fighting is fiercest – north or east it will make no odds to him – leaving your sister to get on with her life."

"Some life," Rowène muttered. Then as another, stomach-cramping thought struck her, "Talking of life, what if this one night leaves my sister with a child? Will your foster brother take the binding oath with her?" She took his silence as denial and continued bitterly, "No, I thought not. He does not strike me as a man who would care over-much about anything, least of all whether he leaves my sister to bear his shame and his child to grow up fatherless. But then, what is one more... by-blow – I believe that is the *polite* term for them here in Mithlondia... you see I have learned something since my return from Kaerellios – amongst all the others he, his brother and father have no doubt sired and abandoned over the years, to starve or survive as best they can in the gutters of this realm!"

Guyard regarded her with narrowed eyes and then said with unexpected bluntness,

"Not all Mithlondian bastards end up in the gutter! Even those of de Rogé siring!"

Rowène gave him a sharp look – less for his use of the term *bastard* and more for his tone – and lifted her brows in silent query.

*Are you thinking of a child of your own*, she wondered. Was it guilt that had caused him to utter those harsh words? Yet why should she care if he could account for one or even more casually begotten offspring from the days before his binding? It was scarcely unusual, either in Mithlondia or Kardolandia – only the treatment of them differing between the two realms – and most noblemen claimed at least one. Even her own father! If only she had known that Lucien was her half-brother before today...

She opened her mouth to say something, she was not quite sure what – to remind him perhaps about Lucien or maybe to tell him that she really did not want to know about any by-blows he himself might have fathered – but he spoke first.

"No, not me, Demoiselle," he grated. "But if we are to talk of bastards – I beg your pardon, you obviously do not care for that word, I should say those of *irregular* birth. I believe that was how you phrased it during an earlier conversation we had on this subject – you know as well as I that not all such unfortunates end up in the gutter to which you now seem prepared to condemn those born out of lawful binding. You have indeed learned well since your return to Mithlondia, Demoiselle! But while there will always be some callous brutes, of whatever degree, who ignore their chance-got offspring, I can assure you that most noblemen honour their responsibilities towards both mother and child." He took a deep, hard breath and she had the fleeting impression that what he said next was not what he had originally intended to say. "I cannot help but wonder whether you would have treated Prince Marcus with such open contempt as you use towards Ranulf."

"What?" She stared at him, utterly confused. "How does Prince Marcus – the gods grant him swift passage on the sunset path – compare with that... that vermin?"

"I meant only that Ranulf, vermin and de Rogé though he be, is as little like to shirk his responsibilities as was Marcus de Mortaine. Nor is Ranulf's behaviour towards women any worse than that of our late Prince. And just remember, when you speak with such obvious loathing and contempt for any child Ranulf might sire, that Joscelin de Veraux – your own betrothed – carries a bar sinister across his device courtesy of that same Prince of Mithlondia."

"Oh!"

She glanced down at the exquisitely worked silver and amethyst bracelet about her wrist; a timely reminder that there were others involved in this quagmire of ambition and attraction besides herself and Guyard de Martine.

"Well," she murmured, struggling to order her thoughts. "It is indeed true that Messire de Veraux does seem to have risen above the perceived stigma of his illegitimate birth. But then, as you said, his father was a royal prince. Perhaps that serves to make him acceptable, to some degree at least, to his peers. Saving Hervé de Lyeyne of course..." She paused, a sneer coming to her lips. "But then I would guess *his* disapproval is motivated more by self interest than anything else, given that his kinsman stands between him and the lordship of Veraux." She returned her gaze to the man standing watching her, his face for once revealing nothing of his thoughts. "Even so – and whatever my own feeling on this matter – there *is* a vast difference between being the acknowledged, illegitimate son of Prince Marcus of Mithlondia and the chance-got issue of your degenerate foster-brother!" Rowène concluded with a fierceness that surprised even her. "I ask you this, Guy... if *you* were base-born would *you* wish to claim a de Rogé as your sire?"

For a moment there was only a frozen silence between them. She saw a flash of something that looked like pain in his light blue eyes but when he spoke his voice was flat, emotionless, icily formal.

"I cannot think, Demoiselle, that my putative paternity has any bearing on your sister's situation. I can, however, give you my assurance that there is very little possibility that she will conceive a child tonight. Despite the best part of a score of years of wenching, none of the women Ranulf has lain with has ever come forward to name him as responsible for their offspring. Joffroi has more than his fair share of by-blows. But for all his promiscuity – and the gods can attest that he has never known the meaning of celibacy – Ran has none."

"And... you?" Rowène queried hesitantly.

"No, to my sorrow, Mathilde and I have no children."

Despite his tone, which did not encourage further questions, Rowène nevertheless flashed another look in his direction. A flicker of a wry smile touched his lips and was gone.

"You are quite right, of course. I was scarcely... inexperienced when I took Mathilde to wife. But although I was never as indiscriminate as Ranulf nor as careless as Joffroi, enough women have passed through my bed to put the matter to the test. And being who I am, it is certain that had any of them felt she had the smallest chance of a claim on me she would have come to Rogérinac by now. That said, and despite the fact that in some ways it is galling to know that my seed is barren, I can still find it in me to thank the gods that I have not had to brand any child of mine a bastard! It is not an enviable fate. In Mithlondia anyway. And since I put this on," he concluded, gesturing once more to the bronze binding ring. "I have never dishonoured my binding oath to Mathilde by bedding another woman. Nor, as you should know by now, am I about to make an exception with you!"

He drew a deep breath and rubbed a hand across his forehead. He looked suddenly as exhausted as she felt. Holding out his hand he called her by the name and title she had grown accustomed to from him, although it mingled rather oddly with the language he was otherwise using.

"Alas, my Lady Rowena, there is nothing either you or I can do to help your sister at the moment. It has been a long day and you will need all your wits about you in the morning. Come, let me help you with your laces. You will be much more comfortable if you do not have to sleep in your clothes. And you really need have no fear of me."

Acknowledging that he probably spoke nothing less than the truth – and even if he did not, she had little choice but to trust him – Rowène obediently turned around so that he could reach the lacing on the back of her gown. She could feel his calloused fingers, so skilful upon his harp strings, unaccountably fumbling with the simple task and heard the undertones of frustration in his voice as he muttered,

"Damnation! I am sorry, I cannot get the knots undone... But then, I suppose if I wanted you badly enough, I probably would not bother undoing them anyway!"

Before she could even begin to guess at his intention, he abandoned the laces and coming around to face her, raised his hands to the neckline of her robe. Muttering another, obviously sincere apology, he systematically ripped the blue velvet gown from neck to hem.

Despite his reassuring words Rowène felt a sudden, sharp stab of shock and fear and, grabbing the gaping edges of her dress, held them together with trembling fingers, only vaguely aware that Guy had hastily retreated several paces and was holding his hands up, palms outwards, before him.

"Listen to me!" His voice sounded constricted, his breathing oddly harsh. "I am not going to touch you! I swear it!"

She heard him, but dimly as if through a distorting mist, and his assurance did little to still her own trembling. Amidst the swirling fog of confusion in her mind, two thoughts rang clear; that this man was a stranger to her after all and that he was under orders from his liege lord to bed her. Forgetting her trailing skirts in her rising panic, she moved to flee, trod on her hem and stumbled full against him as he caught her to him.

She felt his skin, warm and firm under her hands, the dark gold hairs on his chest soft against her fingers and his heart, surely beating faster than normal. Then she was plunged even deeper into shock as she felt something else against another part of her – something hard and unmistakeably masculine.

Growing up at the liberal and licentious Kardolandian court neither she nor her sister – nor any other woman there – could remain in ignorance of the physique or workings of the male body. Although aware of what happened between a man and his... lover – and curious to a certain extent about it – she had never been touched by such an experience. But this was different and she knew with an inner certainty that she stood more chance of touching the rising moon than of stopping this man from possessing her if he chose to do so. Still in his arms, she looked up at him, the softest of questions on her lips.

"Guy?"

He made no answer but stared down into her eyes, his bearded face set in strained lines she had never seen before, the light summer blue of his eyes almost lost in the darkness of something that could only be desire. A breeze danced across her skin and she became aware that her body was covered by the flimsiest of linen shifts and wondered when, or how, her gown had come to slip from her shoulders to puddle on the floor behind her.

Had she done that? It seemed unlikely.

Or had he? That seemed even more inconceivable!

But if he had, what would he do next? Surely his lips were closer than they had been moments before? She lifted one hand from his chest and laid it gently alongside his jaw, feeling the softness of his neatly trimmed, dark gold beard, the hard lines of clenched muscle and bone beneath.

For a moment – one heartbeat only – he was hers, caught in the same moon-spun web of enchantment as she.

The next he had thrust her away, so hard she almost fell, disjointed words falling from those lips she had thought to feel, once more, upon her own.

"No, this is not... I cannot stay!"

He grabbed his shirt from the window seat and struggled into it, ripping a seam in his haste. Perhaps the sound brought him to his senses. Or perhaps it was her involuntary cry. Whatever the cause he made a visible effort to compose himself.

"I beg you will excuse me, Demoiselle. I must... must visit the privy. Too much wine..."

He strode across the floor, barely pausing at the door to order her tersely – and a little more coherently – not to leave the room for any reason and for gods' sake to get herself decently covered before he returned.

Then he was gone, leaving Rowène to stare after him, shivering in the soft summer breeze that touched bare limbs where moments before his warm hands had lingered and recalling not only the heated look in his eyes but also his earlier kiss and the longings he had aroused in her, both then and now. And – if she were honest with herself – almost since the moment she had first looked into Guy of Montfaucon's sea-blue eyes and heard his voice. Despite everything she knew, or had suspected about him, she had been so foolish as to fall a little in love with the harper.

It had been harmless enough, she assured herself and would never have come to anything; *she* was betrothed to Joscelin de Veraux, *he* was bound to another woman. And while the knowledge of his true name and allegiance should have destroyed her naïve infatuation, she was learning through painful experience that it had not. Tears of confusion, humiliation and anger stung her eyes and she flung herself down on the window seat, rubbing the back of one hand across her tear-streaked cheeks and cursing both the Moon Goddess of myth and the man who was all too real with equal vehemence.

Dear God of Light! What had she been thinking! Had the undoubted enchantment of the night affected her mind as well as her treacherous body? Would she truly have given herself to him if he had asked? Not that he would have asked. But if he had... Well, she very much feared that she would have done. And she could only pray that *he* had not guessed that mortifying truth! For if she were to judge by his words, it would seem that she had been the only one affected by the magic – or madness – of that pale rose moon and that he had not wanted her at all.

Or... had he? For one moment, as she had stood so close against his body, his arms around her, she had thought he had felt something for her, some small flame of desire... enough at least to cause his body's reaction. She knew she had not imagined *that*!

But in the end, it seemed she had been wrong. And who was she to judge the fire in a man's blood? After all, it had been Ju who had had half the Kardolandian courtiers worshipping at her feet, sending her poetry and flowers and, in the case of one of the royal princes, thinly veiled invitations to seduction.

Guyard de Martine, however, was no dissolute southern nobleman and it was probably as he had said; he *had* drunk too much wine earlier and now needed relief from its effects. Except, when she rapidly reviewed her memories of that ghastly meal, she would have said that inebriation had been his foster-brother's problem, not his.

Ranulf it had been who had drained goblet after goblet of the expensive and potent Marillec wine, openly fondling that slut Ilana as she served him. Had she served him in some other way, Rowène wondered with disgust, in the short span of time when they had both been absent from the hall? Would that have been sufficient to complete that sort of vile transaction? Recalling things she had glimpsed in the bathing pools of Kaerellios she rather thought it had been.

Shuddering at the image – half memory, half imagination, wholly obscene – she banished Ranulf de Rogé to the edge of her consciousness lest she yield to the nausea churning in her belly, refocusing her thoughts on Guyard de Martine.

A man who – given all the available evidence and the promptings of her own heart – was certainly no lecher. Nor drunkard either since, as far as she could recall, Guy had partaken of the free-flowing wine as sparingly this evening as he had done on any other occasion when he had been in her company. Had he truly felt the need for the privy after just one goblet? Or had that just been an excuse?

As the night dragged on with no sign of his return she began to wonder whether, despite his words, he did not intend to come back. Or not before morning, when she guessed that for appearances' sake, if nothing else, he would rejoin her. At least she hoped he would. She did not much fancy trying to deceive Black Joffroi or the Winter Lady on her own. And as for facing the mocking intimacy of Ranulf de Rogé's dark blue gaze again... The thought had her fingers curling into claws.

In truth, the only person she wished to see in the morning was her sister. If Ju could just survive the pain, the fear and the humiliation of this night, Rowène had to believe that tomorrow would be better. For her and her sister at least.

As for her brothers... She did not want to imagine what might happen to Luc if he were captured; the reality of her father's fate was just too horrifying to contemplate. And Lucien... She shook her head, still uncomfortable with the knowledge that the man she had regarded as nothing more than the garrison commander of Chartre castle was in truth her father's by-blow, her own half-brother. Confused though she was, she fervently included him in her prayers to the Gods of Light and Mercy, that both he and Luc would somehow be spared the death their father had suffered. But there was nothing she could do for either of her brothers or her sister at this precise moment.

It was much later now, the night full dark beyond her unshuttered window and Guy had still not returned. Almost idly she recalled the tale he had told her and she began to wonder how it was that his father, a de Martine, had come to take service with Jacques de Rogé? Although she guessed it was not uncommon for the younger sons of noble Mithlondian families to turn mercenary and sell their swords to the highest bidder in order to support themselves, their womenfolk and any offspring they cared to acknowledge. At least, she reflected, Guy's father had cared enough to track down his wayward wife after she had left him, even though he had not known she was carrying his son until he had discovered the infant in the wh... in *that* house in Montfaucon and had taken him back to Rogérinac castle where he had been raised alongside a lord's son. It argued a certain sense of honour that Guyard the Elder had apparently passed on to his son, along with his name and the fair colouring of the Valennais.

Whereas she, Rowène, appeared to have inherited nothing from her father save certain of his facial features and, to her disgust, more from her mother than she would once have believed possible. Not the Winter Lady's peerless beauty, that was for certain, but perhaps something of her icy heart. How else could she have considered for even one moment the possibility of lying with Guyard de Martine when he was already bound to another woman and she was betrothed to another man? A man who, even if he had shown no great inclination to further their acquaintance before the binding ceremony, had nevertheless done nothing to warrant her betrayal.

Horrified at herself, she swore she would never again permit herself to behave in such a dishonourable and potentially devastating manner. She would be a good wife to Joscelin de Veraux – if he still wanted her after today – and forget that Guyard de Martine had ever touched her life.

Good resolutions and sworn oaths notwithstanding, she knew it would be a long time before she overcame the feelings of deep remorse and icy shame that consumed her now. God of Light! How could she have behaved with such wanton lack of care, either for her own honour or for his?

And, dear God of Mercy, let him not guess how brightly those dark fires of desire had blazed within her, searing her very soul...

Head back, eyes tightly closed, shoulders pressed against the rough wall of the stairwell, Guyard gradually brought his pounding heart and painfully aroused body back under control, all too aware that he had betrayed himself yet again and that he could no longer pretend indifference towards Rowène de Chartreux.

He swore almost soundlessly through gritted teeth as he remembered looking down into her wide grey eyes. Recalled too that, although she had not appeared to be afraid of him, she had certainly been shaken by what she had felt. As if with their bodies that close she could possibly have been in any doubt as to what she could feel!

Not that she could have been any more shaken than he had been! Except she was the innocent in all this bloody mess, while he was supposed to have the advantage of age and experience on his side! He only hoped she was too innocent to understand how easy it would have been for him to give in to the rampant demands of his starving body.

He swore again and straightened away from the wall, bringing his hand up to touch the talisman of his binding ring, an unyielding band of metal beneath the worn linen of his shirt sleeve, and silently thanked the gods that he had been able to hold himself back from taking that which he had wanted so desperately. Not that Mathilde would ever know if he had been unfaithful to her – or, possibly, even care – but *he* would know.

One other thing he knew with a certainty; that before he could face Rowène de Chartreux again he needed to find some relief for his frustrated desire. And since a hasty coupling with a serving wench was not a solution that found any favour with him – even if it had served the purpose for Ranulf – it would have to be the other. After all, he had become accustomed to accommodating his needs in such a fashion since Mathilde had turned so cold towards him and at least this way he did not suffer the guilt of betrayal nearly so much as he would have done if he had set up a mistress at a discreet distance from Rogérinac castle.

Accordingly he paid a quick visit to the draughty, seaward-facing privy at the foot of the tower, emerging somewhat calmer in body – even if he still could not completely banish Rowène de Chartreux from his troubled thoughts.

He paused, one foot on the bottom step of the narrow spiral of the torch-lit stairway, his left hand on the guide rope, the right braced against the cold stone. He was strongly tempted to find somewhere else to sleep for the rest of the night but the thought of leaving Rowène alone in that bedchamber, with neither bolt on the door nor the meagre protection his presence could offer, caused him to abandon that idea. That and the abrupt realisation that he would have to return before dawn anyway, if only to reclaim his boots and weapons and convince Joffroi of what must appear to be the truth.

Clad only in her shift, Rowène waited in the moonlit silence of her chamber, seated in the window embrasure, arms around her drawn-up knees, absently worrying at her finger nails until she became aware of what she was doing. Laying her cheek against her knees, she began instead to count the stars as they came out one by one, watching as the moon rose higher, paling from rose pink to the same shimmering shade of silver as the binding bracelet she kept twisting around her wrist, in lieu of biting her nails. And all the while, pointless thoughts scurried and eddied in her mind.

Where was Guy?

What in the name of all the gods was taking him so long?

Why was she concerning herself about his absence anyway? Surely she should be grateful for it?

But if he did return, how could she face him again, knowing how far from indifferent to him she really was?

It seemed an age before she heard a sound and looked around to see the door opening slowly. As she sat frozen, straining to identify the tall, broad-shouldered man who stood there, back-lit by the flickering torch on the wall behind him, she felt her hard-held courage wavering. Uncertain of his identity, the only thing she could do was wait for him to move or speak. She hoped desperately that she would not need to use the dagger Guy had incautiously left behind, but in preparation for the worst, felt behind her until her frozen fingers closed clumsily around the silver-wired hilt and she eased the blade silently free of the leather sheath.

Heart thumping painfully beneath the flimsy barrier of her shift, scarcely daring to breath, eyes straining, she continued to watch the man standing silently on the threshold. Then, just as she thought her nerves would shatter completely if he did not make some sort of move, he stepped quietly into the black and silver silence of the room and shut the door carefully behind him, saying quite calmly,

"You will not need the knife."

Recognising his voice with a rush of overwhelming relief, Rowène released her grip on the dagger hilt and came swiftly to her feet, his name rising unbidden to her lips as she took an instinctive step towards him.

"Guy! Thank the gods, it *is* you! For a moment, I admit, I was afraid. I thought it might be your lord or worse yet your loathsome foster-brother returned – although why he would wish to, I do not know. Not when he has my sister, not to mention a score of serving wenches, to debauch before he must needs turn his vile attentions to someone as lacking in looks as myself, witch-red hair and all!"

These last words were uttered in a distinctly abrasive tone and she regretted them even as she spoke. But Guy did not seem to take umbrage at her disdain of his foster brother – or wonder that she had taken Ranulf's slighting description of her to heart – and his voice was quite remote as he replied.

"No, it is only I. And you do not need to fear Ranulf. He will not touch a woman under my protection." His voice turned grim. "Joffroi now... or your mother... that is another matter altogether. Them, I believe, you would be right to fear."

Despite his solid build he moved almost soundlessly on bare feet, pausing at the foot of the dark-curtained bed before slowly approaching the window, almost as if he feared she might bolt and run like the frightened rabbit he had earlier compared her to if he made any swift movements. He might even have been right about that, she thought.

Rendered nervous by his presence yet again, Rowène sat back down on the window seat, glad to hide her trembling fingers in her lap. Not knowing quite what to expect next she was nevertheless taken by surprise when Guy casually leant his shoulder against the wall, a scant foot away from her, and without further speech, turned to look out over the dark waters of the bay, his gaze fixed on the glittering path that tempted foolish mortals towards the perilous realm of the silver-clad Goddess of night.

*Do you feel it, Guy,* Rowène asked him silently. *The eternal touch of enchantment, the silent call to that other world...*

The soft, sea-scented air that shimmered around them seemed barely more than a breath of moonlight, a cool caress across the sensitive skin of her bare shoulders, stirring her hair and riffling the ragged hem of his white shirt. It was so quiet that she could hear the muted murmur of the glimmering waves as they rippled and rushed against the cliffs below. Above, in the dark meadows beyond the moon, the stars were tiny glittering flowers, waiting for the Goddess's white hand to gather them in her shining arms, before tossing them aloft to gently settle into their appointed places again.

Even as Rowène watched, awed by the presence she had never felt before and whose power she was beginning to fear was all too real indeed, a small spark of white-gold fire rose from the eastern horizon, hung in the sky for perhaps ten heartbeats before falling and fading into the darkness. It was followed by another, then another. Three only, then no more.

"What do you suppose that was?" Rowène whispered.

"Flights of stars I have seen," Guy murmured. "And once a bright star with a shimmering tail but never have I seen the like of that before. Only the gods know what it might portend." She felt his questioning gaze upon her but she was as ignorant as he on this matter and so remained silent. "Mayhap," he suggested rather bitterly, "It marks the rise and ultimate fall of the de Rogé bloodline. In which case you may be assured that your father's death will eventually be avenged. Until then though..." His voice gentled. "Until then, there is tonight to be lived through and tomorrow's reckoning to face. I am sorry, I can think no further ahead than that."

He sounded suddenly unutterably weary and Rowène darted a quick glance up at him. As he stood, with the shadow of the window stanchion across his face, she could not determine his expression but, judging by his informal posture, the tension that had previously gripped him so tightly seemed to have dissipated and, despite his bleak words concerning portents and vengeance, he appeared more at ease in her company than he been at any other time during this hell-wrought day.

Quite clearly something had happened to soften that taut edge and in her mind she seemed to hear her mother's lightly malicious voice telling her that she was a naïve fool if she believed he had not assuaged his very obvious need with one of the serving wenches. Rowène did not think that he would have followed his contemptible foster-brother's example and chosen to enact such a hasty, sordid coupling in the shadows, yet still...

"What were you about to be gone such a long time," she asked abruptly, wincing at the flagrant discourtesy of her question.

"I... *we* needed that time apart," he replied brusquely. "And I have not the remotest intention of discussing with an innocent young noblewoman what I was doing."

"Or who you were doing it with?" she snapped, inwardly appalled at herself.

For a moment he just stared at her. Then he gave a low, mirthless laugh.

"Gods above! I thought you had a better opinion of my morals than you do of my... of Ran's. But obviously I was wrong."

He had clearly been angered by her barbed comment – one which she would have retracted if she could – but he did not give her the opportunity to apologise.

"Think whatever you wish of me, Demoiselle. I care not, since it matters not who *you* think I was coupling with so long as Joffroi believes I spent the night tumbling you! And on that note, I suggest you get yourself into that bed without further delay. It is, thank the gods, big enough that there is sufficient room for both of us to lie in it without being forced together."

"You intend to share the bed with me?" she asked, her voice rising. "But I thought..."

"But nothing!" he interrupted, the impatient edge to his voice tempered once again by weariness. "The gods know this day seems never ending but since I hope to be leaving Chartre at dawn or soon after, what I need now is sleep."

She opened her mouth but he anticipated what she meant to say.

"And before you suggest it, yes, I could bed down on the floor. It would not be the first time. Nor will it be the last. But ask yourself whether you really want Joffroi – or anyone else with a surfeit of curiosity – to open that door and find *me* sleeping on the floor and *you* still chaste in your bed?"

She shook her head wordlessly.

"No, I thought not. So, for pity's sake, get into bed. Then perhaps we can both get some sleep."

Rowène eyed him warily for a few moments and then, unable to deny either his weariness or her own, walked quickly to the bed and, lifting the heavy coverlet, slid between the cool, lavender scented sheets. Not knowing what else to do, she lay on her back; rather like a corpse on a bier she thought with a hysterical but silent giggle – except no corpse's heart ever beat as painfully fast as hers did. Gods above, what would he do now?

She realised that she was staring at him only when he said with a tired smile,

"You can close your eyes or watch me undress, it makes no difference to me. Courtesy might dictate I sleep in my clothes but that would do little to convince Joffroi that we are lovers. So if you wish to preserve your modesty, you had best shut your eyes now."

"You forget," she reminded him with an attempt at levity. "That the Kardolandians of either gender are far less enamoured of their modesty than Mithlondian noblewomen are reputed to be." Unable to prevent herself, she flashed him an impish smile. "Or have you never heard tell of the bathing pools of Kaerellios?"

"Oh, I have heard," he replied, a trifle grimly, then favoured her with a startled look. "Do you mean that you..."

"No! Or at least not the pools that you are probably meaning. I just went to bathe. I never went beyond the waterfalls, where... um..." She stopped, flushing in the darkness of the bed hangings, then tried again. "Where certain... well, most of, the noblemen and ladies of the court went to... er..."

"Indulge themselves in indecent and decadent mating practices?" he finished for her. "I believe that is how one of the more priggish Mithlondian emissaries reported it to the High Counsel not so long ago."

"Well... that is one way of putting it," she agreed with a muted giggle.

He snorted under his breath.

"Oh, I could be more blunt about it, believe me, and Ran blunter still, but

I will spare you that."

"Please do," Rowène said faintly as she watched Guy remove his remaining clothes and walk without haste around to the far side of the bed. More to take her mind off this candid view of his naked body as because she wanted to know the answer she asked, "Why is it that your foster-brother has a mind as foul as a midden — and a tongue to reflect it — when he was brought up under the same circumstances as you?"

Guyard shrugged and settled himself beneath the covers with an audible sigh of relief.

"I think perhaps you bring out the worst in him. Believe it or not, he can behave like a gentleman when he wishes to."

But Rowène scarcely attended to his answer. Instead she lay as still as one of the marble statues gracing those infamous pools, not daring to move, hardly drawing breath. Ranulf de Rogé held no place in her consciousness now — save far away at the edges of her mind where she could feel her sister's trembling awareness of him. All her thoughts and emotions were bound to the man who lay in the bed beside her, albeit with the whole width of the feather mattress separating them.

Finally he broke the awkward silence, his voice quiet and quite impersonal.

"Sleep if you can, Demoiselle. The Gods of Light and Mercy send you peace in your dreams since they cannot grant it to you in any other way."

With which faintly incongruous words he turned away from her, to all intents and purposes completely indifferent to her presence.

Rowène turned her head on the pillow, studying his broad back and strongly muscled shoulder, the powerful arm lying on top of the heavy cover, the bronze binding ring glimmering faintly in the bar of moonlight that fell across the bed. And for all she had vowed not to allow herself to succumb to the shameful pull of desire again, she could feel it in the heat that once again swept her body.

She only hoped he could not sense it too. But then, would he just lie there, breathing so calmly if he did? Perhaps he would. Unlike his foster-brother, he appeared to behave like a gentleman as a matter of course — save when his lord's orders made it impossible! When all was said and done, however, she must never allow herself to forget that, although he was a de Martine by name, he had been brought up as part of Jacques de Rogé's disreputable household.

Moving cautiously, she attempted to find a more comfortable position and finally, curling onto her side, tried to compose herself for sleep. But she was unable to settle in any comfort for more than a few moments at a time, discovering that it was one thing to share that wide, soft bed with her sister, and quite another to know the other half was taken up by a large, completely naked man. She remembered the feel of his hard body against her own before he had sought the privy — or wherever he had gone — and all at once her questions and doubts came to a head.

She sat up, heedless of her partial nakedness, her modesty preserved by the flimsiest of linen shifts.

"Guy?"

"Damnation! What now?"

He sounded tired and irritable. She gave a small, forlorn sigh.

"Nothing, Messire... it does not matter."

He echoed her sigh with some exasperation but did roll over to face her once more.

"I think it does matter," he said. "So, my Lady Rowena, what is troubling you now?"

His reversion to his old name for her rather than the formal Mithlondian title gave her the impetus to continue, although her voice betrayed her trepidation.

"Guy, I have been thinking... wondering..."

She swallowed and felt her cheeks burn, although she was reasonably sure he could not see that in the shadows of the bed.

"Wondering what? And why do I get the feeling I am not going to like this, whatever it is?"

To her considerable relief he sounded resigned now, even faintly humorous. She severely doubted whether that latter emotion would survive her next words.

"Earlier... when you said it was too much wine... Was it that? Or did you... want me? As a man wants a woman, I mean? To... to... No, I cannot say it!"

He muttered an expletive she had never heard from him before, sounding so utterly stunned that she knew her tentative hope had been wrong and that he had never, ever, thought of her in that way, even for the briefest span encompassed by a single heartbeat. Obviously curbing his desire to utter further profanities, he asked with commendable mildness,

"Would you truly have me answer that question?"

Tears of humiliation stinging her eyes, she wished she had never blurted out those dreadful words. No doubt he thought her little better than a dockside drab.

"I am sorry," she whispered. "I do not know why I thought that... let alone said it. Please... I beg you, forget it..."

Her voice broke completely and, abandoning her hold on the sheet, she hid her burning face in her frozen hands. She could feel Guy staring at her but she refused to meet his gaze. Then she felt his hands, warm and firm on her own, as he gently pulled her fingers away from her face. Even then she could not bring herself to look at him properly. Not until he said softly,

"No, I should be the one apologising. I did not mean to swear at you. It is just that you... well, you took me somewhat by surprise. There, that is better, at least you are looking at me. Now, tell me what you would have me do. I will forget you said anything, if that is your wish. Indeed the gods know it would be better for both of us if I could, in truth, forget. But this is about you. And you must obviously have wanted to know the answer strongly enough, else you would not have put aside all maidenly modesty to ask such a question in the first place."

"You must think me the veriest wanton," she murmured, still embarrassed.

"No, I do not," he smiled wryly at her, tightening his grip on her hands. "I think you are an innocent, gently-bred Mithlondian lady who has, by the grace of the gods, survived unscathed the corrupting influence of the Kardolandian court. And I would keep that innocence intact for your betrothed at all costs."

"But will *he* want me, do you suppose?" she sniffed. "Oh, not in a contractual sense, but as a woman?"

He muttered something she did not quite catch and averted his gaze slightly. Somehow the gesture merely served to depress her more. Guyard de Martine obviously found nothing about her body – clad in nothing but moonshine and almost transparent white linen – to hold his attention. His foster-brother was right, damn him! There was nothing about her to attract a man. And yet Guy had said something that sounded like...

"What did you say? Guy, please tell me."

"I said, he would be a fool not to," he muttered, this time loud enough that she could distinguish the words.

"And what is that supposed to mean? Oh Guy, do not mock me, I beg you."

"Mock you? Why would I do such a cruel thing? Especially at such a time as this, when your life is in pieces around you. I know that I have betrayed your trust but you must believe that I would not deliberately make matters worse for you now."

"Maybe you would not," she replied. "And maybe you meant no mockery. But, Guy, when no-one has ever wanted me before, how can you know that Joscelin de Veraux will be any different?"

She heard another curse hiss through his teeth and thought that she had never heard him swear so much before this night. But then the circumstances were perhaps exceptional. Certainly, she had never shared a bed – or so intimate a conversation – with him before. Or any other man for that matter.

She heard him take a deep, rather ragged breath, and could see, even in the chancy moonlight, that he was frowning.

"I do not know what happened to you in Kaerellios but it was obviously sufficient to utterly destroy your sense of self worth. Listen to me now. And *believe* what I am saying! The gods know, I would be lying if I said you were beautiful as your sister is beautiful. But there is that about you that touches a man, deep in the darkest shadows of his soul. Obviously, I cannot speak for Joscelin de Veraux but it makes no sense for you to continue believing that no man has ever felt desire for you. I know..." He hesitated, grimaced, then said with more than a hint of harshness in his tone, "I know that Ran wanted you."

She recoiled from him with an inarticulate sound of horror, an uncontrollable shudder racking her body.

"And you think I should be flattered by that? I meant a decent man, Guy! Or do you imagine I am so innocent I do not know your foster-brother's reputation..."

"No. But you are obviously naïve enough to think that is all there is to him," Guy interjected. "Believe it or not, he is not quite the daemon from Hell his reputation makes him out to be. There are worse men by far..."

"But not many, I warrant!" Rowène snapped. "Granted Prince Kaslander of Kaerellios is probably a worse lecher than your foster-brother but not by much. Or do you think I do not know what he was doing earlier this evening with Ilana? Oh no, Guy, I am not that naïve! Even an innocent like me learns swiftly enough in Kaerellios to recognise the scent of a man's spent lust, whether it be on the man himself, the woman he has used or another man..."

She was surprised by the choked sound of revulsion from the man beside her and lifted her brows at him.

"What?"

He eyed her narrowly as if suspecting she might be mocking him in her turn. Then, obviously deciding she was serious, said in a tone thick with disgust,

"Whatever perverse practices the Kardolandian courtiers may indulge in, they do not pertain in Mithlondia, thank the gods. As to Ranulf..."

"No, do not say it again! It makes me sick just thinking about it. If the only man to ever want me is a vile rutting boar like Ranulf de Rogé I would rather give up all hope of an honourable binding and become a Sister of Mercy, chaste and childless. At least that would be a useful life."

"If a somewhat severe resolution to your doubts, even were Ranulf the only man in Chartre to find you..." He caught himself and amended his words. "The only man in Mithlondia who will find you desirable."

She should have let the matter rest there but for the life of her she could not. She reached out, brushing the tips of her fingers over the warm curve of his shoulder with a touch as soft as that of a goldfinch's feather, and in a voice so quiet *she* could almost pretend she had not spoken – and *he* could mayhap pretend he had not heard – she managed two words.

"Did *you*..?"

His eyes closed momentarily, then opened them to reveal a raw honesty she belatedly wished she had not provoked.

"Damn you," he muttered between his teeth as she snatched her hand away, shocked by the tension seething just below the surface of his moon-kissed skin. "Why could you not let this thing between us lie undisturbed?"

"Ah! Forgive me, Guy! I did not mean..."

"No, it is too late for that now!"

His tone was now pure, barely controlled anger – but, thank the gods, it *was* controlled.

"You wanted the truth, so you can damned well hear me out! Yes, I wanted you earlier. I defy any man to be with you tonight, like this, and remain unmoved. And you can thank the God of Mercy who looks after innocents and fools that it is indeed I and not Ranulf in this bed with you. If you were to touch him as you touched me just now he would have you naked and spread beneath him before you could say a word."

"Ugh! Why must you keep on about that... that... whoremonger!" she finished fiercely.

"Possibly because – whoremonger or not – Ranulf is free to answer your question honestly and I am not." There was a distinct edge of frustration to his tone that made Rowène quiver a little. "However, since you would have it plain between us... and the gods know we might as well since I have already admitted that I wanted you..."

He stopped, drew a hard breath and continued in a less ragged tone,

"I thought you had come to know me a little over these past weeks. Sufficient at least to understand that I am not the sort of man who would dishonour myself and you simply to ease a lust that will be forgotten as soon as I leave Chartre." His Mithlondian was now sword-point precise, clipped, ice-hard. "Yes, I wanted you, at least as much as Ran did. But do not delude yourself that this feeling between us is anything more than a passing desire, stoked by need on my part, heedless curiosity on yours. The only difference between Ran and I is that he is free to couple where he pleases whereas I am bound, by my own choice to Mathilde and I will not break that oath for you or any other woman."

He stopped, drew his hand across his eyes, some of the ice melting from his tone.

"I will be leaving Chartre as soon as may be for Rogérinac. Perhaps as soon as tomorrow's dawn. I will return to my wife and my duties there and, Joffroi and the gods willing, you will go to Joscelin de Veraux a maid yet. Once you are his bride, it will be as if you and I had never met."

"I wish that were true," Rowène muttered. "Just as I wish that my father were still alive, my brother not a hunted man, my half-brother not a prisoner. Most of all I wish my sister had not been forced into your hell-spawned foster-brother's bed! But if wishes were stars I would be a handmaid to the Moon Goddess herself!"

With which acerbic allusion she flung herself down, jerked the covers up around her shoulders and turning her back, curled up into a defensive ball as far away from Guyard de Martine as was practicable.

It was still dark when Rowène woke from a troubled doze to find Guyard de Martine's arm lying warm and heavy across her breast as he held her close against his body. In the failing glimmer of moonlight she could see that he was still asleep, his eyes closed, his mouth relaxed. In all probability, she thought, his unconscious mind had forgotten that he was in bed with her and believed that he was holding his wife. She supposed she ought to move away but his warmth and protective embrace were oddly comforting, a barrier against the chill of the night...

It came to her then, with a sense of dread, that what had woken her was not Guy's warm breath on her cheek but the cool draught from the open door. Pale as the moonshine was, it did not illuminate the darkness beyond the bed and the night torch in the bracket out on the landing had almost burned out, giving only a dim flickering form to the figure in the doorway; a shimmering, silver-etched shadow that glided so silently into the room that for a moment Rowène felt a petrifying terror at the thought that it must be either a wraith come to claim her soul or the Moon Goddess herself.

The thing – whatever it might be – came to stand beside the bed, looking down at them. Then Rowène caught a whiff of exotic perfume and knew it was neither wraith nor goddess but a mortal woman and a hot wave of shame and disbelief flooded over her.

She moved to slip from Guy's embrace but desisted when she felt the muscles in his arm tighten and realised that he was awake too. He murmured some indistinct endearment and then, quite clearly "Rowena" as he drew her towards him, moulding their bodies dangerously close together. By some great effort of will Rowène obeyed his unspoken demand for cooperation, forcing herself to close her eyes again as if drifting back to sleep in her lover's arms, even though the proximity of his warm, masculine body and the presence of the white-clad woman beside the bed made it difficult for her to think or act with any degree of calm.

Finally, after a seemingly interminable span of time, Rowène heard the soft sound of the door closing and cautiously opened her eyes to find that she and Guy were alone again. Tense and wary once more she waited for some comment from the man beside her. But he did not speak.

He did, however, move away, ensuring that his body was no longer touching hers at any point and eventually, despite the chill in her heart, she slept again.

# Chapter 9

## *Lust Unleashed and A Witch Revealed*

It was a little after dawn when Rowène woke again to find that the golden haze of previous mornings had been supplanted, appropriately enough, by a dreary, invasive, colourless mist.

She lay on her side for a while, staring out of the open window at the drifting droplets of fog sensing, without the need to look behind her, that she was alone. Eventually, knowing she could put it off no longer, she rolled over and, as she had expected, found the other half of the wide, blue-curtained bed cold and empty. The heavy cover of blue silk, embroidered with twining tendrils of pale golden honeysuckle and darker gold roses interspersed with white swans, was smooth and unrumpled, the plump pillows unmarked by any indentation.

Had it all been nothing more than a cruel nightmare? Was her father yet alive, her sister a maiden still? Was Ranulf de Rogé merely a daemon spawned of some dark dream, Guy of Montfaucon nothing more than a wandering harper? Pray gods that might indeed be so!

Her attention caught by something out of place, she leaned over to capture the single strand of hair that had snagged in the crisp linen of the nearest pillow. Neither raven nor flame but a shade of honey somewhere between brown and gold, measuring barely as long as her middle finger.

So it was all true and the harper, Guy of Montfaucon, who was in truth Guyard de Martine, the Steward of Rogé, had indeed spent the night in her bed. And when word reached Joscelin de Veraux of that fact, as it was almost certainly bound to do, he would surely repudiate their betrothal. As precarious as his own position was, he could scarcely afford the public ridicule of being cuckolded even before his binding had been formalised. But by the time word of his rejection reached Chartre, Guy would have long since returned to Rogérinac and she and Ju would be left to the Winter Lady's mercy, the gods help them both.

*Ah, Ju! How are you faring this bleak morning?*

Rowène could sense her sister's presence somewhere nearby... sense too that she was sorely troubled in mind. Whilst the gods alone knew how sore her body must be, after a night with that vile brute! Was he still there, Rowène wondered suddenly, lying beside her ravished sister, snoring in a wine-sodden sleep? Or had Ju woken to find herself alone in the misty grey silence of dawn with nothing but a blood-stained sheet, and perhaps a long, barley-pale hair, to remind her of the man who had savagely stolen her virginity for no better reason than because his brother had commanded it.

It seemed somewhat ironical to Rowène that, regardless of the fact that Guy had not touched her and she was a maiden still, the result would be the same as if he had carried out his orders. Gently laying the hair back where she had found it, Rowène turned to cast an assessing glance at the window, and the lack of clear light notwithstanding, calculated that it must be long past dawn and, if she had not missed the horn call already, very nearly time for the morning meal.

Perhaps in his eagerness to rid himself of the memories of the previous night, Guy had not even waited long enough to eat but had already left Chartre, bound for Rogérinac and his wife, without another word to her. Nor was there any reason why he should have delayed his departure for her sake. What had she expected? A formal farewell in the great hall would have been meaningless whereas a more private leave-taking here in her bedchamber might have resulted in... what? A final kiss, his lips on hers, one last time? Then again, given the embarrassing events of the night before, perhaps it was just as well if they did not meet again. The gods knew she would not have been able to look him in the eye anyway...

An unexpected tap at the door made her jump and hurriedly drag the covers up to her shoulders.

"Who is it?"

"'Tis Ilana, m'lady. I've brung ye some fresh clothes an' clean water fer washing."

Ilana! Little though Rowène wanted to see the trollop, if she did indeed bring those items, she would not be unwelcome. In addition, she might also have tidings of Juliène.

"Enter then," she called, scrambling from the bed even as Ilana came through the door, a length of scarlet silk over one arm, a linen cloth over the other and a pitcher of warm water in her hands.

Rowène was not quite sure what she had expected of Ilana this morning. Certainly not that the tire-maid would appear still wearing the conservatively cut, blue-grey gown and white apron worn by all the castle serving women, her brown braids covered decently by a kerchief of unbleached linen. In direct contrast to her respectable appearance, however, her neck was marked quite clearly with a reddish bruise the size of a silver noble that Rowène was not so naïve as to mistake for anything other than what it was; the result of the slut's fleeting encounter with Ranulf de Rogé the previous evening.

*Dear God of Mercy, let not that vile cur have marked my sister's skin with that same vulgar brand!*

Her lip curling in disdain, she watched as Ilana poured water into the ewer then bobbed a curtsey that stopped just short of open insolence. Yes, that was more what Rowène had expected of her.

"There, m'lady, ye'll be wanting to wash, I don't doubt." The girl's tone, and the direction of her gaze, made it quite plain what she thought her mistress would need to wash away. "An' I'll just make the bed whilst ye be doing that."

She moved past Rowène as she spoke but, rather than straightening the covers, dragged the upper layers back over the end of the bed, leaving the bleached linen of the under-sheet exposed.

"What do you think you are doing?" Rowène demanded in an outraged tone – at the same time as her mind caught a frozen echo of Ranulf de Rogé's voice, speaking to Guyard de Martine, moments before they had left the hall the previous evening.

*Just make damned sure there is blood on your sheet in the morning and Joff is not like to call you a liar.*

But there would not be. Could not be. She was a maiden still and Guy had protected her honour for nothing. Next time, she knew, Black Joffroi would not leave it to chance; he would hand her over to his lecherous brother or his loutish men!

A tide of nausea rose in her throat, the light began to dim and through the numbing noise in her ears she barely heard the small sound that Ilana made. A subdued sniff... Of surprise? Or satisfaction? It was only as her wavering gaze focussed on the bed that she saw a smear of what was, unmistakeably, dried blood in the middle of the otherwise pristine white sheet.

Her bodily functions steadying, she turned hastily away before she could betray her relief to the sharp-eyed servant. Grabbing the cloth from the table she washed the cold sweat from her face and, under the meagre privacy of her shift, between her legs. Neither her blood nor Guyard's seed was there but she hoped Ilana would be content to report back to Black Joffroi and the Winter Lady the proof she had seen on the sheet.

Having finished her skimpy ablutions she seated herself before the dressing table and attempted to bring some order to her horribly tangled hair.

"I'll do that fer ye," Ilana said, coming up behind her and taking the delicate ivory comb from her hand. "Ye'll be making it worse, tugging at it like that."

Surrendering the comb with ill grace – hating the thought of Ranulf de Rogé's strumpet touching her in any way – she folded her hands in her lap and tried not to think of where Ilana's hands had so recently been...

"Have you seen my sister this morning?" she asked abruptly, both because she needed to know and to divert her queasy thoughts from the visual evidence of her servant's indiscretions. That mark, for instance...

"Oh yes, m'lady. I took her water up first, seeing as Sir Guy ordered me ter let ye sleep a bit longer," the tire-maid replied and had the temerity to give her mistress a knowing grin.

"And how did she seem?" Rowène asked, ignoring the insolence in favour of news of her sister.

"Well enough, far as I could tell," Ilana shrugged. Then, with slightly more belligerence. "An' why shouldn't she ha' bin? That Sir Ranulf, he knows well enough how ter please a woman."

"As I do not doubt you discovered from personal experience! I suppose it was he who put that disgusting mark on your neck?"

Rowène's tone would have frosted fire but the servant only giggled smugly and lifted one hand to coyly touch her neck.

"If ye're asking, did he make love ter me, m'lady, then aye he did. Give me a whole silver noble too so he musta bin pleased, don't ye think? An' I wouldn't mind letting him do it again neither, 'cept castle gossip has it he's leaving Chartre later today, along with full half the soldiers Lord Joffroy brung with him."

"Good riddance to them all," Rowène muttered. Then as a thought occurred to her added, not entirely without malice, "Rather than mourning his departure, you might find it of more use to pray to the gods that the man did not give you more than just a silver coin. Confirmed lecher that he is, he is almost bound to be poxed, do you not think?"

Ilana looked alarmed for a moment – evidently the thought that a nobleman could be so afflicted had not occurred to her – but then she shook her head and said slyly,

"I don't reckon ye'd wish that on me, m'lady, not knowing as how Lady Juliena would be taken wi' the same disease too after last night."

"I do not wish it on anyone, saving the man himself," Rowène snapped. "And if he leaves my sister alone, not even him."

"Well, like I said, word has it he's leaving terday. Sir Guy too, I heard Lord Joffroy say. An' him an' Lady Ariena be off ter Lamortaine, soon as may be ter see the young Prince. Yerself an' Lady Juliena're ter stay here though."

That at least sounded like better news, Rowène thought. Save for Guy's departure of course but then nothing could change between them even if he stayed. Lost in thought, she did not notice that Ilana had finished fussing with her hair until the servant spoke again.

"There now, I've not braided yer hair, Lady Ariena's orders. An' ye'd best be getting dressed right quick. They'll be sounding fer the morning meal dreckly. Lady Ariena said as how ye was ter wear this 'ere gown she's had made special-like. One fer ye an' one fer Lady Juliena."

At that Rowène looked up to find Ilana standing beside her, holding up a gown of scarlet silk, shockingly bright in the dull, grey light of the misty morning. Rowène opened her mouth to protest, then shut it again. What good would it achieve to tell Ilana that she would look like a whore when, quite obviously, that was exactly how her mother intended her daughters to appear.

Retreating into a grim silence Rowène permitted the smirking servant to remove her shift and help her don the gown, feeling the slippery material slither cool over her colder skin. Hands clenched at her sides, she concentrated on ignoring the softly humming maid as Ilana tightened the lacing at her back so that the shimmering silk clung smooth at hip and waist, shoulder and breast. Nor did she need to peer into the mirror to know that this gown was far more indecent than anything she had ever worn in Kaerellios.

"I s'pose ye looks well enough, m'lady," Ilana commented grudgingly. She took up a small vial of perfume but Rowène snatched it out of her hand, dabbing the rose-water on her wrists and throat herself. The wench sniffed loudly, then gave her a spiteful smile. "Shame the gown clashes with yer hair though. Lady Juliena now, her'll look proper, her will."

"My sister would look like a goddess, even in a seaweed sark," Rowène said coldly. "And now, unless you have any more impertinent remarks to make or my mother wishes you to paint my face, lest anyone fail to recognise me as Guyard de Martine's whore, I am ready to go down to the hall now."

Ilana's smirk slipped a little in the face of Rowène's glacial calm and with another, more muted, sniff she went to open the door, only to step back in surprise at the sight of the man filling the doorway. Recovering herself, she bobbed a curtsey that, for all its outward deference, yet managed to draw attention to her abundant breasts.

"Ooh, Sir Ranulf, I didn't 'spect ter be seeing ye here. Was ye a-lookin' for me?"

He spared her the briefest of chillingly indifferent glances, his pale brows drawing together.

"No, I was looking for my brother," he replied curtly.

"And why in the name of all the gods would you expect to find him in here?" Rowène interposed with cold disdain. "If he is not already in the hall, he is doubtless entertaining himself still in my mother's bed."

She regretted her impulsive words the moment they left her lips but by then it was too late; Ranulf de Rogé's gaze had already cut in her direction. Eyes that had been the cool, dark ice of northern seas when he had addressed his doxy now flared with a hot blue flame as his gaze roamed over every curve and hollow of the body now revealed by the very vulgar scarlet gown she was wearing. Icy fear doused her limbs, even as heat rose in her cheeks as his gaze settled on her breasts, barely contained within the thin silk bodice, her nipples shamefully delineated by the clinging cloth.

Not taking his eyes from her he spoke softly to Ilana,

"Take yourself off, wench, and make sure we are not disturbed. I will escort the Lady Rowena..." He put an insolent emphasis on her title. "Down to the hall when I have finished my business with her."

"Oh but, sir..."

"Out!"

The curt command had its desired effect. Ilana gave him a petulant pout and flounced out, banging the door behind her, leaving Rowène ten times more afraid than she had ever been, now that she was alone with this man who aroused nothing but revulsion in her belly, hatred in her breast and terror in the very depths of her soul.

A terror she refused to allow such a piece of fornicating filth to see! Her legs might be shaking beneath the silken canopy of her trailing skirts but she forced herself to meet the blatant heat in his eyes with an icy indifference, praying he would not divine the other, far more turbulent, emotions behind that frozen mask.

"Well, what do you want of me, Messire?" she asked haughtily. "What is this business between us that requires such privacy?"

A mocking smile curved his hard mouth, softening it not one whit.

"Oh, spare me this profession of virginal ignorance," he said, his clipped Mithlondian accent slipping into a soft drawl that made her shudder. "You know what I want of you."

He was walking towards her even as he spoke, unbuckling his sword belt as he came, casually tossing the heavy weapon onto the bed as he passed. Rowène watched him approach, holding her ground with an effort, feeling sweat break out cold on her skin. She could not evade him in such close confines, she knew that well enough. Neither did she have any weapon save her failing courage and no protection save his non-existent honour. Only the gods could help her now but considering as they had not troubled to save her father, she saw no reason why they would exert themselves on her behalf.

Chin lifted in proud defiance she waited in silence, the sound of his footsteps loud in her ears, each firm tread echoed by the ringing chime from his spurs. Inwardly she shivered, knowing that she would never hear that sound again without reliving this moment. He was perhaps five feet away when he paused to pull his tunic over his head. At which point she thought her trembling heart must stop completely and all intelligible thought froze.

*God of Light, he truly means to go through with this thing!*

Up until that moment she had not quite believed he meant to turn menace into reality.

His tunic fell to the floor, revealing the careless informality of his attire beneath; the worn linen shirt hanging loose to his thighs, untied sleeve laces dangling over his hands, the neck opening gaping wide so that the faint glimmering of grey light through the window touched the scattered hairs on his chest with pale gold… Made aware by the sheer oddity of that thought that she was staring at the man who had just climbed from her sister's bed, Rowène jerked her gaze upwards, seeking answers to questions she dare not ask. He had taken the time to shave, she saw – after a fashion at least; there was a nick on his jaw – but his hair was only loosely braided and bound. As if sensing the direction of her gaze he reached up to release the thong that held his hair, allowing it to spill free, rippling over his shoulders and down his back like ripe barley under a cloudy sky.

Then he resumed his approach, only stopping when there was barely a floor-board's width between them.

"You *know* what I want," he said again, his voice light, disconcertingly soft.

Then his tone changed dramatically, to something akin to a snake slithering over gravel; low and lethal. "And just like every other fucking whore in this castle, you are going to give it to me."

Rowène flinched – at his tone as much as the obscenity – but refused to yield him victory so easily.

"I am no whore, Messire," she said coldly.

"That gown says different," he murmured. "As does this."

He lifted his hand and ran the tips of his sword-calloused fingers lightly over the bare skin of her upper breast, down to the rising swell of her nipple. She gasped, more deeply shocked by this intimate touch than his coarse language, and took a step back, coming up sharp against the solid stone wall by the window.

"You arrogant swine," she hissed. "How dare you judge me... my sister... by the same low standards as that slut you have just dismissed."

"And why should I not?" he queried, a hint of crispness unexpectedly tingeing his otherwise sardonic tone. "As I am sure you must already have guessed, I bought the services of that slut – as you so rightly name her – yesterday evening. And a night in your sister's arms cost me what silver I had left. Why should you be any less mercenary?"

"I am not... I do not..." Words failed her.

"You do not want my money?" he queried, openly mocking. "That is just as well since, as I said, I have none. Which means, my sweet, you will simply have to take what pleasure you can of me in return for the pleasure I intend to take of you."

"The moon or the mist has addled your wits, Messire, if you think I will either give or take pleasure from you." And as he lifted his hand again. "No, do not touch me, lest you want me to vomit over you."

He regarded her for a moment, his dark – very dark – blue eyes narrowed, and she dared to think it might be possible to reason with him after all. A heartbeat later she saw his mouth twist in that sardonic smile she hated.

"And you truly expect me to be taken in by this show of reluctance? Oh no, Demoiselle, I am not so easily made a fool of twice in such swift succession."

She frowned up at him, trying to piece together his meaning. It sounded as if...

"You think this is all a ploy on my part? That in reality I welcome your... your attentions?"

"Do you not?" His mouth tightened into a cruel, predatory smile that showed his teeth and made her think of a ravening wolf barely held in check. "Granted, I do not expect you to admit openly to burning with a lust as fierce as mine for you. You purport to be a lady after all. Nevertheless, and for whatever reason, you *will* let me take you, however and wherever I wish." He swept another look down her rigid body and his voice dropped to a more caressing pitch. "Although judging from the way your body reacted to my touch a moment ago I could be forgiven for thinking that secretly you are itching to feel the weight of my cock in that sweet place between your legs..."

"I... do... not!" she managed to gasp before his arms came around her and his mouth came down on hers; rapacious, brutal and fully as arrogant as she had accused him of being.

Trapped by the sheer size of him, panic-stricken by the hard heat of the tall, broad body effortlessly holding her against the wall, Rowène struggled frantically, managing at last to drag her mouth free from the brutal pressure of his lips and the rough invasion of his tongue. Revolted, frightened, her wits in utter disarray, she tried to bring her knee up into his groin but his legs were too firmly pressed against her trembling limbs, trapping her from thigh to ankle, so close she could feel his booted feet through the soft leather of her shoes.

Then she realised that while one of her arms was caught within his unyielding embrace the other was still free and, without further reflection, she brought her hand up, raking her nails – such as they were – down his face.

"You bloody little bitch!"

There was surprise, anger and the promise of retribution in his voice and the blue fire flaring in his eyes was undoubtedly fuelled by temper rather than lust. He fell back a step but was nevertheless quick enough to prevent further attack – although shock at the damage she had wrought had caused her to stop struggling even before his fingers clamped about her wrist. Frozen, she watched as he pressed his cuff against his cheek for a moment. Then, as he dropped his arm again, her gaze left his face, to stare at the three crimson smears that stained the linen. His shirt was not white after all, she thought stupidly, it was the pale dirty grey of snow just before the thaw...

There was no thaw of the ice around her heart. Or in those narrowed eyes that were slowly lifting from his own study of his blood-stained sleeve to settle on her face, with an expression that informed her that the leashed wolf she had seen before was about to slip its self-imposed shackle. Aware though she was of the dangerous nature of the feral animal she had inadvertently roused, Rowène made no further effort to escape. She could only stare up at his face...

At those eyes, mere slits of blue ice glittering savagely between lashes that were barely darker than his mist-silvered pale hair.

At the dull glimmer of barley stubble below his hard jaw-line; a reminder, if she had needed one, that he had obviously been too hung-over to shave properly that morning.

At the three livid, blood-beaded lines that scarred the weathered skin of his left cheek.

And through the terror that numbed her limbs and held her heart, she felt a sudden surge of joy that she had at least managed to mark the beast, so that all who saw him would know what he was and what he had tried to do to her...

How long they remained like that, she could not have said... perhaps one heartbeat, perhaps a score... but then she saw the white lines of tension around his mouth deepen and her brief feeling of exultation flickered and died, leaving only fear and the fragmented flotsam of thought and memory. Gods above, what had she been thinking of to rouse the de Rogé wolf from its sated slumber?

An icicle was melting somewhere in Hell, trickling freezing cold water through her mind and with it a voice. In her present state she could not even put a name to it; it sounded like the voice of the man before her but that could not be right, a wolf would not give warning of its own savage nature. Then she remembered, it had been Guy, speaking about her sister. *If she has any sense,* he had said. *She will give him his way without a fight and he will lose interest soon enough. He always does.*

But it was too late now to consider the wisdom contained in that warning and apply it to her own situation. Far, far too late. All she could do now was hold herself still under de Rogé's dark – there was barely any blue left now, she saw with a shiver – gaze. But it was not just his eyes. His smell was all around her, deeply unpleasant and unlike that of any other man; feral almost, vaguely herbish, overlaid with the pungent odour of fresh sweat.

As if it were not enough that he must assault her senses of sight and touch and smell, her lips were still tender from his bruising… she would not call it a *kiss,* and the taste of him lingered in her mouth, a vile mélange composed of the residue of last night's Marillec wine and something else she could not even guess at that rendered his mouth so foul she nearly retched.

His voice came harshly as his breath skimmed her ear, his warm lips nuzzling her neck and she realised that at some stage she had closed her eyes in order to shut out the horror of his presence.

"I do not normally couple with bitches but in your case I will make an exception."

He nipped the soft skin of her neck, his sharp teeth unnervingly gentle, and her eyes flew open in shock, just in time to see his head lifting away from her shaking body, the brush of his long barley-pale hair against her shoulder making her shudder. *Gods, why does he have to be so fair? A daemon should be dark!*

But it was not the first time she had thought that and quelling her mind's indignant howl, she forced herself to look past his deceptive fairness and study the brutal lines of his scarred face. He was frowning a little, his pale brows drawn together but it was not anger she saw in his blue eyes.

"Is that truly how you wish to play this game, wench? A bit of Mithlondian rough after your soft Kardolandian lovers? Just as well, perhaps, since we do not have time for more than the briefest of tumbles before Joffroi starts wondering what in Hell is keeping me."

She blinked at him, wondering if amongst all the vulgar innuendo she had heard him right. It had been her impression from what he had said to Ilana that he had come up here looking for his brother, but now it sounded as if Black Joffroi had sent him…

Then all coherent thought was swallowed by nausea as he bent his head again, laying a line of burning kisses beneath her jaw and down her neck towards her breast. She felt his tongue lick, his lips suck, his teeth nip at her flesh and it was all she could do not to faint from horror and revulsion. Dimly, through the encroaching black mist, she heard him groan... something about roses more potent than wine, and made one last effort to free herself. Surprisingly he lifted his head and relaxed his hold on her. She felt the mist begin to recede a little under the frail advance of hope.

"I beg you, Messire, do not do this," she pleaded, trying to see the blue of his eyes through the greying fog. If she could just fix on something, perhaps she might not faint.

"I have a name, damn it!" he rasped on a shortened breath, bringing one hand up to fondle her breast. "Ah! Rowène, so sweet... Gods, you will never know how much I want you."

"Messire, I do not want..."

"Use my bloody name, will you!" he growled and suddenly she could see him... see his eyes, searing in their intensity but holding a hint of vulnerability.

Taking heart from this and thinking perhaps that compliance with this one minor demand might serve her better than defiance had done, she forced her tongue around the hated syllables of his given name, though it came out a bare breath above a whisper.

"Ranulf, please..."

She had been going to continue with *let me go. I do not want this.* But he gave her no time to utter that protest, sweeping her off her feet, one powerful arm braced behind her shoulders, the other beneath her knees and before she had time to either struggle or plead further, she felt the softness of the bed at her back rather than the harsh sandstone of the wall. His name came more naturally to her tongue this time and definitely louder.

"Ranulf, no!"

"Yes!"

His contradiction was swift and short, more than a shade breathless as he wrestled with one hand – the other had returned to shackle her straining wrists – to loosen the lacing of his breeches, yank down her bodice and slide her skirts up around her waist, baring her legs to the cold, moist morning air. He dragged his shirt out of his way with an impatient oath and then she felt the unsubtle demand of his knee forcing her legs apart...

And abruptly she yielded.

Obviously he was not going to heed her verbal protest and, having already had a taste of his physical strength, she knew that however fiercely she fought him, he would win in the end.

She thought she was resigned to his possession but even so the grunt of triumph he gave as he pressed between her spread legs made her stomach revolt anew.

*Sweet God of Mercy, please, let him not kiss me again! I cannot bear it!*

Her chin burned, her lips felt swollen, her throat undoubtedly bore the blood-bruises left by his earlier ravages and she knew she would be sick if he touched her anywhere with any part of his mouth.

Closing her eyes, she waited tensely for the final, irrevocable invasion, praying that it would not hurt too much and that it would be over as swiftly as his words implied; a quick tumble, that was what he had promised her. Then he would be gone, leaving only nightmare memories of his overwhelming size, his brute strength, the pungent reek of him and the bitter taste of his mouth.

She heard his voice; a man's hoarse murmur, a wolf's throaty growl.

"Rowène, sweeting, open your eyes."

*No, I cannot! I am a coward. I cannot look into his eyes and see not a man but a wolf about to…*

She felt his fingers tighten warningly about her wrists as he repeated his words, this time as a ruthless command she dared not disobey.

"Look at me, damn you! I want to see in your eyes that you know who I am as I take you."

Forcing aside tears of pain, shame and confusion she slowly opened her eyes, blinking to bring him into focus when she found him much closer than she had expected. He was leaning over her, his thick, fair hair falling about his face like mist-pale barley straw, brushing her naked breasts with a touch as soft as a thistle's down. His eyes were darker even than before, the merest ring of blue around midnight black, and every harshly carven line of his lividly-scarred face was tight with tension, a sheen of sweat dewing his temples and upper lip.

"Have you seen enough yet?" His voice was a low, bitter-soft rasp. "Take your time, sweeting. I want you to be in no doubt of who I am or what I mean to do to you."

Was it an order? Or – an odd thought given the situation – a plea?

Whichever it was, she found herself responding. She forced her gaze from his faintly flushed face, down towards that portion of the heavily muscled chest she could see through his gaping shirt and then wished she had stopped there rather than venturing any lower. But it was too late and now that she had seen, she could not look away.

This was not something half glimpsed through the flowering vines and distorting waterfalls of those infamous pools of Kaerellios. There was nothing hidden here, nothing of softness, nothing to encourage hope that this act might bring pleasure rather than pain and a soul-deep shame. She swallowed back bile but did not look away, trapped by the stark reality of ragged white linen, rough black wool and blood-suffused flesh. Against the rumpled linen of his shirt, she could quite plainly see his fingers wrapped around his rigid male member as he stood between her naked legs, her own flesh startlingly pale against the coarse black cloth of his breeches.

*This* was who he was… *this* was what he meant to do to her. How could he possibly think her to be in any doubt as to his identity or intentions? He was Ranulf de Rogé and quite clearly he meant to take her like the whore he had called her – although the gods alone knew why or how he had come to that conclusion – without bothering to do more than remove his tunic or unlace his breeches.

Stunned by this realisation and shamed anew, she brought her gaze back up to meet his eyes, meaning to make one final attempt at reason.

"Ranulf…"

His name turned from plea to scream as he suddenly thrust full into her. Her body shattered into shards of white pain and she felt herself crashing down into the icy darkness of Hell.

Behind her, as she fell, she heard his voice, sharp in a startled expletive, followed by a guttural groan that could have been her name or merely another oath.

She thought she felt something soft brush across her face… mayhap his hair as he bent over her? Or calloused fingers, unbelievably gentle against her cold cheek. Whilst *there*, in the very centre of her pain, she could feel him still, as he held himself tense and unmoving within her.

And with her last, barely conscious, thought she wondered why he did not finish it. Now that he was there and surely the worst was already over…

Unwillingly slipping from the blessed refuge of darkness, she became aware of the damp morning mist upon her cheeks an aeon before she sensed the pale grey light beyond her closed eyelids. Recollection seeped slowly through her dazed mind and she kept her eyes firmly closed, every other sense stretching out; listening, feeling, straining to catch any trace of his distinctive smell… all the while praying fervently to the Gods of Light and Mercy that he had abandoned her while she lay unconscious. She did not care that he would have left her exposed and shamed… *Just let him be gone!*

Silently, stealthily, exploring her surroundings with tentative, trembling fingers, she found that she was lying along the length of bed, with some part of the heavy silk cover draped over her. No, that must be wrong! She had been on the edge of the bed…

Her fingers tightened convulsively on the sheet and her toes twitched, confirming her initial impression. She made no effort to understand it but it was true. Whoever had moved her fully onto the bed had also rearranged her gown so that she was once more decent – or as decent as that piece of flimsy frippery allowed – and then laid the cover over her.

She wondered who could have come in and done such a thing? She hoped it had not been Ilana. Then another, even more unpleasant thought struck her. Perhaps the person who had performed that task had already been in the chamber? Shock rippled through her at the suspicion – unlikely though it seemed – that it might have been de Rogé himself and the thought of his hard hands on her body caused her to cringe.

But that was foolish! He had already dragged her gown down her breasts and up her legs. Why should he not repair the disarray he had wrought in the pursuit of his lust. As for the other disgusting things he had done…

A sudden recall of just exactly what he had forced on her caused her entrails to knot anew, twisting into ever tighter coils as she unerringly recalled her last conscious glimpse of him; blue eyes blazing with a searing heat, the fingers of one hard hand clenched around the shrinking flesh of her thigh, the other about his own rigid flesh, a single heartbeat before he had thrust into her...

With that she became fully aware, for the first time since she had returned from the darkness, of the place where he had been. That part of her where – for however long or short a time – he had bound them together in hatred and lust, forging an unbreakable shackle by the mingling of her blood and his seed.

*Dear God of Light*, she thought, self loathing sending pragmatism flying, *can I ever forgive myself for yielding? For not fighting to the end?*

Against the heartless brute who had callously looked on while her father died in agony and who would no doubt do likewise to her brothers if the occasion arose. The same man who, only the evening before, had tumbled her tire-maid before going on to ravish her sister.

And if she could not forgive herself, she certainly could not forgive *him* for what he had done. Ever! Nevertheless, she knew she must put this morning behind her. Not forgotten – oh no, never forgotten – but overcome.

To which end she must rouse herself and play the part expected of her. She shifted in the bed, wincing in discomfort, finding her body achingly sore in that place where he had penetrated her so roughly. How long had he remained within her, she wondered suddenly, grunting like the wild boar of his family's device, his skin and hair slick with sweat, until at last he spent himself. The image was so nauseatingly real she nearly retched.

She had to admit to being puzzled though. For if that foul beast had indeed taken his rutting to its inevitable conclusion, why could she not feel any trace of his... spilt seed? Either on the sheet or her skin? Not that she had more than a hazy notion what it might actually feel like, but surely she should feel something?

Cold and slimy if he had left her some time before... Or still warmly wet with his own body heat... She felt her stomach heave again, as her mind abruptly brought up those facts from the collection of uninhibited confidences shared with her by one of Queen Xandra's other, more knowledgeable, ladies. Feeling she must move or vomit where she lay and being *almost* convinced that she could hear no sound other than her own breathing and the faint, far-away rushing of waves against the cliffs below, she dared to open her eyes.

And found she had been wrong – in one thing at least!

She was not alone.

*He* was still there. The wolf himself. Ranulf de Rogé.

Standing by the window, his back to her, his forehead resting against the arm he had braced against the window support in a pose that caught painfully at her heart because, for a single heartbeat, she thought it was Guyard de Martine standing there. But there was, the gods help her, no mistaking the length of that barley-blond hair. Even though it was no longer falling unfettered over his shoulders but instead had been ruthlessly confined into one long tail by a single twist of leather at his neck.

Beyond binding his hair back, however, he had clearly made little effort to order his appearance. He must have retrieved his sword from the bed since it stood upright against the wall beside the window but his tunic still lay on the floor in a puddle of black and silver, his shirt hanging loose, save where it clung to his back and shoulders, the worn linen dampened by the tiny droplets of mist that drifted in through the open window – or, she thought bitterly, the sweat of his previous exertions.

At the sight of him, still in a state of casual undress, as if he did not care who saw him like that or what they might think he had been doing, Rowène felt a flash of violent hatred such as she had never known before. But it was not an emotion she could sustain for long. And once it had gone she did not know what she felt, beyond an ice-cold desire for retribution – no matter how long it might take to achieve.

More for her family's sake, she realised, than her own. Since, whatever this man had done to her personally – and it had not been pleasant – it was over and nothing anyone said or did now could change the fact that he had broken her maidenhead. She might argue that she had been forced – a dubious argument at best – but she doubted whether that would keep Joscelin de Veraux from repudiating their betrothal. As for de Rogé himself, well he was a soldier after all and she thought it likely that brute force formed an all too common part of his dealings with women.

She wished that he would simply finish dressing and go, leaving her alone to compose herself as best she could. But if *he* did not leave, she knew she would have to move; she could not lie in bed all day bemoaning her lost virginity. She would still be expected to present herself in the great hall and sit at the high table, to share the morning meal with the new Lord of Chartreux and that most beautiful and cold-hearted of enchantresses, the Winter Lady herself.

Her only hope and consolation was that, if the gods were kind and took pity on her, her sister would be there too.

*Gods, Ju!*

How would they face each other now? Would they be able to comfort and commiserate with each other over their shared shame and perhaps rediscover their former closeness? Or would the events of the previous night and this morning drive an even deeper wedge of silence and misunderstanding between them?

And then there was Guy! Was it too much to hope that he might already have left the castle? To hope that he would never know what had taken place in this chamber after he had left it? He had warned her what would happen if she handled Ranulf wrongly. And she had, she admitted bleakly, mishandled him very badly indeed. In which case would Guy hold her to blame for what had occurred, rather than his foster-brother...

The distant sound of a bell clanging dully through the fog recalled her wandering thoughts, causing her to take a steadying breath and set her jaw. Pushing back the heavy silk cover she sat up, sliding her legs over the side of the high bed.

Obviously hearing the rustle of movement, the man at the window turned swiftly. She had the fleeting impression of dark-shadowed blue eyes in a face so leached of colour beneath the weathering of sun and wind that it most nearly resembled the pale linen of his shirt, the bloody tracks of her nails on his cheek standing out with startling clarity.

But it was first and foremost his extreme pallor that gave her pause. He looked, she thought in shock, almost as sick as she felt!

"Are you all right?" he asked abruptly, his once light tones lost under the layers of gravel and flint. Then answered himself before she could speak. "No, of course you are not all right. How could you be? What a bloody stupid thing to ask the woman I have just *raped!*"

She gasped at that final, harsh word. Gods save her, it sounded even more vicious spoken in his raw, rasping tones than in the secluded privacy of her own mind. She did not refute his accusation however. Not only because it was at least partially true but because she did not know what to say to him in the wake of his violent actions and her own lack of resistance. One day she might be able to think clearly but just now her wits were still wandering within a seemingly endless thicket of tangled thorns.

As the silence drew out between them, she became aware that he was subjecting her to a searching scrutiny, although his own eyes remained carefully guarded. Unable to move, she returned his gaze, wondering for a moment whether that flicker she half thought she glimpsed in the dark blue depths might be... regret? Or guilt?

But no, this was Ranulf de Rogé, she reminded herself; nobleman, warrior, drunkard and defiler of women. Whatever it was she thought she had seen, it was surely neither regret nor guilt. Far more likely it was impatience at her lack of response. Even so, he remained by the window, at least six feet away from her and made no sudden movements, exercising a restraint she would not have guessed him capable of and for which she found herself obscurely grateful.

Finally deciding that she could not remain perched there like a wounded animal facing the hunter who has brought it down, she stood, rather too quickly, found herself swaying and reached out to grab the nearest bedpost.

"Sit down," he ordered tersely. "Before you fall down and I am obliged to pick you up and return you to your bed."

She glanced up nervously but, despite his threat, he had not moved from the window, his scarred face still set in that emotionless mask that had replaced his former uncontrolled violence.

"It is probable that Joffroi will be sending someone to search for us before another candle-notch," he went on, glancing towards the door. "But I can give you a few moments to compose yourself. If such a thing is possible."

Doubting that a few months, let along a few moments, would be sufficient to allow her to regain her equanimity, she ignored his order to be seated but retained her grasp on the bed post, fearing her legs might collapse under her if she let go. She found she could not take her eyes from his parchment-pale features and did not know whether to be surprised or appalled when she heard herself saying,

"Was it you..." She swallowed to moisten her dry throat. "Was it you who... made me decent and put the cover over me?"

"Yes."

She thought he would leave it at that but after a moment he continued.

"I did not think you would want anyone seeing you like that, witnessing what I... had forced you to do. To which end, I also..." He glanced down at his hands then back at her. "Washed your..." He hesitated, grimacing, then finished with a delicacy she wished he had exhibited earlier. "Washed you where it was necessary."

She felt herself flush, deeply uncomfortable with the thought of him performing such an intimate task and averted her gaze from his hard blue stare.

"I am aware that I must be the last person in five realms you would want to touch you." His voice was suddenly alive with emotion again. "But I had to do something! There was enough blood – on you, on me, the bed-cover, even my shirt, damn it – that even the most dull-witted servant would have guessed what had happened between us."

"But surely..." She swallowed again and regarded him uncertainly. "Surely that is inevitable?"

A muscle clenched in his jaw.

"Not inevitable, no. And I cannot think you would wish to make it public, the cost to you being almost as high as it would be to me. For my part, I have no intention of telling anyone what passed between us. And certainly not my brother."

She frowned at him, unsure of his meaning. Then dismissed it as irrelevant when there was a far more visible impediment to their keeping this secret. And, she had to admit, it would be better for her if they could. But it was just not possible.

"Much though I might wish to, Messire, I do not think this is something we can keep hidden."

"Damn it! Do not call me that! Not now! Not after..." He took a step towards her as he spoke and she felt herself flinch. He halted immediately, his dark blue gaze momentarily unguarded, allowing her a glimpse of all the conflicting emotions seething beneath the pale mask of control he now wore.

"It is all right," he said tautly. "I will not touch you again. My word on it, if that means anything to you after what I did. But in return for my belated attempt to behave like a gentleman, I suggest you tell me why in Hell you would wish to ruin yourself by speaking out."

Relieved by his promise not to touch her but unable to physically form the requisite words, she concentrated on what she could answer.

"You asked why we cannot conceal this... this..."

"Rape!"

He supplied the word that she could not bring herself to speak out loud. She nodded, swallowed back another surge of bile and said unsteadily,

"Your face."

"What?"

"Your face, it tells its own tale. Look in the mirror if you do not believe me. There is one on my dressing table."

As if suddenly remembering, he raised his hand to his face, fingering the raised welts on his cheek and for a moment he seemed undecided whether he wanted to look or not. Then, striding to the table, he picked up the mirror.

"Hell and damnation!" He laid the glass down again, his jaw set. Then, for the first time since she had opened her eyes to find him still there, his mouth twisted into the barest hint of that sardonic smile she was coming to recognise. "Not that I do not think you had good reason for doing it, Demoiselle Chaton, but I could wish you had kept your claws to yourself. It will make it much harder for me to keep you from paying the price for my mistakes."

"Your mistakes?" She queried, wondering in some bewilderment what had prompted him to call her *kitten* rather than something more vicious. "I thought this was exactly what your brother had ordered you to do. And as far as I can see, you would gain no benefit from remaining silent for my sake. Rather I should have thought you would find yourself doubly rewarded once he knows that you have bedded both my sister and myself."

"I doubt that," he replied with a faint grimace. "Besides I have no desire to take credit for either action, albeit for vastly differing reasons." He touched his cheek again, his mouth tightening.

"Does it hurt?" she asked. And then wondered where those words had come from.

"No, not really." He shrugged broad shoulders dismissively. "It is just... Wait! There must be a way around this. How if I say I tried it on with some serving wench and it was she who scratched my face? After all, not every woman in this bloody castle can be as easy to lay as your so-called tire-maid."

"One would certainly hope not," Rowène agreed, somewhat tartly. "But even so, it will not work. No servant in her right mind is going to refuse a nobleman of your high birth. Not when it lies within your power to have her whipped or even cast out to beg in the streets."

"And here I was, thinking it was me the wenches wanted," he replied, the faint quirk to his lips curving into a slightly more genuine smile. "Rather than the few coins in my habitually-empty purse or to escape a beating. I do believe you have a ruthless tongue to go with those claws, Demoiselle Chaton."

She glanced from the three bloody welts on his face to her ragged, bitten nails and frowned.

"You say that... and I know I did. But *how* did I mark your face like that? Look at my nails. Do they look like claws to you?"

She held them out towards him and, after a wary look at her face, he accepted her unspoken invitation to close the distance between them, approaching her much as he might a wild cat, uncertain as to whether it meant to pounce or flee.

"No," he agreed after the most cursory of inspections. "I do not see how you could inflict such deep wounds with those nails. Have you always bitten them?" he asked with a grin. Then abruptly sobered. "Or is it just since you met my brother and I?"

"No, I have always done it," she confessed, even as she wondered why she was telling him, of all people. "Queen Xandra frequently despaired of me. In Kaerellios, you see, every part of a woman is supposed to be beautiful. I failed her miserably and not just because of my nails," she finished, wishing she had kept quiet. But he did not take the opportunity to mock her lack of physical beauty. Instead he merely said, somewhat acidly,

"I warrant your sister made a more apt pupil."

"Yes," she agreed without rancour. Then something – the gods only knew what – made her say. "Mes... Ranulf. Would you let me try something?"

"When you call me by my name like that, sweeting, you can try anything you wish," he murmured, a hint of mischief lifting the bleak darkness from his eyes, and she could suddenly see why Ilana – and all those others he had bedded – might have gone with him by choice rather than necessity. The next moment any hint of light had fled his eyes. "Forgive me, Demoiselle. That was uncalled for on my part. Nor need you force yourself to call someone you must loathe by name. I should never have asked..." He caught her look. "Demanded it of you in the first place."

Momentarily at a loss as to how to reply in the face of what appeared to be genuine contrition, the best she could manage was a helpless shrug. Then, pulling herself together. "No matter, Messire. It is done now and I only wish to forget. As to the other, you have given me your permission to do as I will with you and that is all I need. No, you need not look so apprehensive. I am not going to hurt you. As if I could!" She had muttered these last words but he must have heard them nonetheless.

"Oh, I think you could hurt me very much indeed. And without any effort at all," he told her.

She flashed a suspicious glance up at him but could read no mockery in his dark blue eyes. What was the man implying? It was not the first time that de Rogé had hinted that he stood to lose as much by this encounter as she did, but she could not think how. He was a Mithlondian nobleman, after all, and could probably get away with any crime he might chose to commit, up to and including cold-blooded murder! And ra… forced carnal knowledge of a woman was hardly a hanging offence. Or at least she did not think so.

Pushing aside the faintness that came on her with memory of the carnal encounter he had so recently forced on her, she said with as much firmness as she could muster,

"Just stand still, if you please." She took a step towards him, then another. Taking a deep breath, she took the last step that separated them. "I have to tell you that I have no idea if this will work. But it may…"

With that, and ignoring the almost imperceptible quiver that ran through him as she raised her hand towards his face, she gently touched the first blood-encrusted scratch with the tip of one visibly trembling finger, striving to ignore the resurgence of nausea as she felt his warm skin against her frozen flesh. Holding his wide, wary gaze with her own, she persevered, managing – or so she thought – to hide the shivers of revulsion that ran through her as she traced the length of each swollen weal. She started slightly as she accidentally touched the softness of his eye lashes, shying away from the sharp flecks of pale gold stubble along his jaw, trying not to recall the sensation of that same stubble pricking like tiny thorns against her skin, at cheek and neck and breast.

Instead she concentrated on completing her self-appointed task of healing, reminding herself that she did this for her own sake rather than his. Because she could not risk anyone guessing who had given him those scars and why…

When she was done she stepped unsteadily away from him, wiping her fingers as unobtrusively as possible in the folds of scarlet silk and studied his face, while he remained where she had left him, still as a stone figure.

"What was that all about?" he asked at last. "Since I cannot think from the look of repugnance on your face that you found it easy to touch me like that. In fact you look as if you might throw up yet."

"No, I am not going to do that," she said, swallowing back bile. "But you are right and it was not easy to touch you of my own free will, not after… Well, not after."

"Believe it or not, it was no easier for me," he said softly. A hint of something, not quite a smile, not quite a grimace, touched his lips. "Although possibly not for the same reasons."

She did not understand but merely sighed.

"Alas, I think I have put us both through Hell for nothing then. My apologies, Messire. I do not have the gift I hoped I might, merely the curse of the Faennari."

"I do not want to know what you might mean by such cryptic utterances," he replied. "But obviously my face tells the same story as it did before. That being so, and as we still have to face the curious eyes waiting for us below, I can only suggest you leave me to make what explanations as seem fit to me. I would claim your sister was the culprit, if I could, but Guy has already seen me this morning and would know I lied. So I will just have to convince them it was some other unwilling wench who caught my fancy and hope Joffroi does not choose to pursue it further." He must have caught the expression of doubt on her face because his voice turned impatient. "Do you *want* your name to be dragged through the mire of common gossip? No, I thought not. And I certainly have no desire to stand trial for your rape."

She gave him a disbelieving glance,

"So that is what you meant earlier? Gods above!" She clenched her still shaking fingers in the skirts of her gown and a thread of bitterness ran through her tone. "That is about as likely as my being able to mend what you have broken!"

"No, trial or not, you will never be a maid again," he agreed. "You know it and I know it. But for all that, there are ways around it. Just ask your mother if you do not believe me. And if you follow her instructions better than your sister did, Joscelin de Veraux will never guess you do not go a virgin to his bed. And before you start tearing yourself apart over deceiving the man, just remind yourself that I gave you no choice in the matter. If you wish to tell him that I have taken what should have been his, that is, of course, your right. Do you mean to be faithful to him?" he asked abruptly.

"That is no affair of yours, Messire," she snapped. "But if Joscelin de Veraux is still prepared to honour our betrothal after word reaches him of events here in Chartre, then of course I will be faithful to him." But it was more by instinct that she answered as she did. Her attention had been caught by his brief mention of her sister and although she was not of a mind to ask him what he meant by it, she was resolved to ask Ju when she saw her next. For surely he could not have meant what she thought he did...

Before she could follow that unforgivable suspicion any further, his voice broke into her disquieting reflections and this time there was a distinct flare of frustration in his tone.

"Damn it all to hell, *why* could you not have been what I thought you?"

"What?" Confusion turned to anger as she belatedly caught his meaning. "You seek to blame *me* for this mess because I was not the... the whore you thought me?"

"I never thought you were a whore," he snarled. "Yes, I know what I said but I did not mean it like that. I only thought..."

"Thought what?" she demanded when he bit his words off..

He met her gaze briefly, then turned away, staring out of the window.

"What did you think? You might as well tell me. It cannot be worse than what you have already done to me."

"Very well." He did not turn around but she could hear his reply; low, level and utterly devoid of anything approaching shame. "I did not believe you were... experienced. But I did wonder... oh to Hell with it!" He smashed his fist against the wall. "To be blunt, I thought it within the bounds of possibility that Guy had already had you!"

"And you supposed I would... would welcome you as well?" She could hardly believe her ears. "Dear God of Light! If that is not putting me on a par with a whore I do not know what is! And if the way in which you treated me earlier is commensurate with the way you treat the women you normally pay to share your bed, the gods know I pity them with all my heart."

That stung him, as she had meant it to.

"Believe it or not," he grated, his eyes blazing blue as he whirled to face her once more. "I am not usually quite that brutal. Even with whores! And as you so rightly say, having taken my money, they have no choice but to accept what I give them! But I do *not* abuse them," he added through his teeth. "Only the Daemon himself knows what drove me to act as I did with you."

"Well it could not be lust!" Rowène muttered, trying not to consider in what ways his behaviour might differ when he lay with the whores he normally paid to service his needs. She saw that he was regarding her with a rather odd look, almost as if he had not quite heard her right, and added somewhat defensively. "Well, you said yourself that you did not find me attractive. Plain-faced and with witch-red hair to boot! Although..." She hesitated. "Although Guy would have me believe differently."

"And what might that be?" he queried. "Guy is not infallible but he can be too damned perceptive at times."

She flushed.

"He told me that you lusted after me. *I* cannot help it if he read you wrong on this occasion."

"And do you not perhaps think that my recent actions proved him right?" de Rogé asked grimly. "Or at least partially right. It *was* lust, yes, I admit it. But if your sister had not roused my bloody temper..." He broke off and she seized the opportunity to ask,

"Speaking of my sister... Did you do to Ju what you did to me? Merely because you are incapable of controlling either your lust or your temper?"

"Your sister?" He gave a short, mirthless laugh. "Oh no, I refuse to take responsibility for that one. Wine, witchcraft, that bloody, eldritch moon... something else besides my own lack of control was at work last night. If it had been left to me, your sister would have slept the night away as chastely as you obviously did with Guy."

About to express her contempt for his inability to take responsibility for his own disgusting actions, Rowène paused, abruptly remembering the strange, bitter taste that had befouled his tongue. And his eyes... She glanced up at him, but his eyes were clear, no longer the extreme dark blue, almost black, that she remembered from earlier.

Gods above! Could it be... Had someone – and it could only have been her mother – drugged his wine? But in the name of all the gods, *why?* What had the Winter Lady hoped to achieve by it?

But if that was so, was it also possible that the last dregs of that drug, whatever it had been, had still been clouding his judgement this morning? After all, according to Guy, his foster-brother was not in the habit of using force in order to secure his bed-mates. And if she could bring herself to trust his word, Ranulf himself had said much the same thing, except he had openly admitted to using money when his personal charms failed. Which must be most of the time, she thought uncharitably. But Ilana...

It was at this point that Ranulf's voice broke into the morass of conjecture and doubt that was swamping her mind.

"Rowène?"

"I thought we had decided on a certain formality between us," she said, aiming for a cool disdain but uncertain as to whether she achieved it. "So I would prefer you not to call me by my name. Or sweeting. Or chaton."

"I have already said I do not expect you to use my given name," he agreed. "And in public I will respect your wishes. But in private do you not think *Demoiselle de Chartreux* to be an overly formal mode of address? I may regret... I *do* regret the manner of it," he corrected himself. "But I have nonetheless been more intimate with your body than any other man. Damn it, woman, think what we have just done!"

"Do not remind me!" she exclaimed. "I told you, I wish only to forget it!" Her voice dropped so that she was talking more to herself than him. "Though I fear I never shall."

He muttered something that sounded rather like "Nor I" but although she flashed him a sharp glance he said nothing more. She eyed him warily for another moment or two, then continued.

"I said I wanted to forget it but there is something I must ask you. You said... you said there was... *blood*. But what about... I mean, did you..?"

He regarded her for a long moment, stony-faced, after she had floundered into embarrassed silence.

"If you are asking what I think you are asking, the answer is *no*." A muscle showed briefly white in his clenched jaw. "No, I did not spill my seed in you. Could not, if you must have the truth." He gave her a flicker of a grim smile. "I may have raped you – or as near as makes no odds – but in return you have managed what no other woman has done and reduced my once proud prick to something more nearly resembling an impotent worm."

She felt herself flush even more at his words, then realised that – coarse and sardonic though they might be on the surface – there was a hint of something else beneath, something darker, more vulnerable.

"I have no doubt you will recover soon enough," she retorted, not sure whether she believed her own words but thinking it was probably better if he did – at least while she was still in the same room as him and his uncertain temper.

"I bloody well hope so!" he said with a fleeting grin. "I do not much fancy living the next thirty-odd years of my life in celibacy like some puling Brother of Peace. And now, given that you have stopped shaking and there is a bit of colour in your face, I think we should go down. I know you do not want to but we will have to face them all at some stage. Better surely at a time of our choosing rather than Joffroi's or your mother's."

She nodded mutely, thinking that even Ranulf de Rogé's company seemed preferable at the moment to that of Black Joffroi or the Winter Lady. Taking her consent for granted, he was already moving, swiftly and decisively, tucking his shirt into his breeches. There was a damp patch on the front tail of his shirt, she saw. Was that where he had washed away her blood? It seemed all too probable. He bent to snag his tunic from the floor, pulling it over his head, tugging the garment into place. Finally he buckled his sword belt around his waist and looked across at her.

"Are you ready?"

"As I am like to be," she replied, trying to make her voice as steady as his.

He strode across the chamber towards the door, the faint, chiming echo of his spurs making her choke on her memories. Evidently catching the sound, small though it had been, he stopped abruptly and looked at her more closely.

"Are you sure?"

Swallowing back her apprehension, she nodded and drew herself up proudly. For a moment she thought she detected a flicker of relief and even approval in the dark blue eyes before the shadows came down again.

"I should have said this before but I feared that it might truly make you ill. But it still needs to be said before we are done."

She looked at him, caught a little off guard by the grim pitch to a voice that had gradually been regaining its customary lightness. She saw that he had gone rather white again and it came to her, like a blast of icy wind, what he meant to say.

"Please, Messire, do not say it. I know what you are thinking and it is not possible. You yourself said you did not..." She boggled over putting it into such plain speech as he had used but he obviously understood.

"I know what I said. And I know what I did not do. But the way the daemons of Hell have been dogging my footsteps since I stood by and watched your father die a traitor's death, it could very well happen – even though by all the laws of nature it should be impossible. And if you should find yourself..."

"No!" It was almost a shout, passionate in the intensity of its denial. "No," she repeated in a slightly less hysterical tone. "It will not happen. You have my word."

To her surprise he went even whiter at that.

"Gods!" His voice was raw. "I know I hurt you but do you hate me so much? That you would murder an innocent babe before it had even drawn breath, simply because it has the misfortune to spring from my seed?"

"No," she whispered, shaken by his reaction, despite her dislike of him. "Or at least... I do not think so. But it will not come to that."

"But if it does," he insisted. "I need you to swear that you will tell me."

She saw he was not to be put off and, since she could not foresee the situation ever arising – if he had told the truth about his inability to complete the act, and she could not see why he would lie about such a thing – said in a resigned tone,

"Very well, you have my word." Then, as a flash of foreboding struck her, "Did you make Ju swear the same oath?"

"No," he replied curtly.

"But why?"

"Perhaps because your sister is a duplicitous witch. Or perhaps because I am a callous bastard who does not care. Take your pick."

She looked up at him, a frown creasing her brow.

"But you would care if *I* carried your..." She swallowed. "Your child?"

"I did not say I would *care*," he pointed out. "I merely said I wanted to know. To which end, since I am leaving Chartre as soon as Joffroi gives me permission, I will give you some token... something you can send to me..."

"Could I not just write?" she asked impatiently. Then as a thought struck her. "Or are you not sufficiently literate to read..." Her voice trailed off as he gave a bark of laughter.

"Oh, I am literate," he replied. "Just. But that is not why I suggested some other form of message. Think for a moment, Demoiselle. How would it run, this infamous missive you might have to write, a missive I might not be the only person to read? Something like this maybe... To Ranulf de Rogé from Rowène de Chartreux, greetings. Following the unfortunate events of midsummer last I find myself swelling with your bastard and..."

"I trust I could be a little more discreet than that," she interrupted crossly, stung both by the truth of his words and his slighting reference to the life he might have started. "And how can you speak so cold-bloodedly of what would be your own child?"

"Because it would be true," he replied tersely, any hint of humour leaving his strained face. "Best accustom yourself to it quickly, since there is nothing I can do about it. Except wed you, of course, if de Veraux will not. But somehow I cannot see you consenting to take the binding oath with the man who watched your father die, slept with your sister and who will hang both your brothers if the opportunity arises."

"No." It was the merest whisper.

He regarded her more closely, blue eyes dark shards of steel.

"Or would you? No, do not throw up on me! It was a reasonable enough question. Would you consider it, if only to save your child from a lifetime of taunts and insults?"

"No." Her voice was stronger this time. "If there is a child... and I pray to the gods that there is not... still I will not bind myself to you, thus cursing a poor, innocent babe with a father like you... a name like yours..."

"Better, I would have thought," he retorted. "To grow up a de Rogé rather than the nameless bastard of a traitor's daughter! But I can see your mind is made up. That being so, do you even want me to acknowledge the brat, if there is one, and support it – and you? Not," he added with a humourless smile. "That I am likely to be in a position to offer such support for very long once the High Counsel gets wind of..."

"I do not want *anyone* to get wind of *anything*," she snapped, hysteria looming again. "Not the High Counsel, not... anyone else in this wretched realm."

As her voice rose, he came to stand in front of her and gripped her shoulders, his hard fingers digging into her flesh. He lowered his head until he was staring directly into her eyes.

"And you think *I* do?" he snarled. "In gods' name, Rowène, what do you think will happen to me if my seed takes root inside you?"

She blinked at him, lost for a moment in the Hell she saw behind the surface blue of his eyes. For a moment his name hovered on her lips but before she could speak it, he muttered an impatient oath at her lack of response, and released his grip.

"Never mind! Forget I said anything. Suffice it to say, if the unthinkable happens, the choice will be yours. If you wish, I will acknowledge the child and support it for as long as I am able..." He broke off, with a grimace. "And when that is no longer possible, I will see that my brother takes over the task."

"Your brother?" she repeated. "You cannot tell me that Black Joffroi would care about the fate of any... any by-blow you might sire. For that matter, does he even care about his own?"

"No," de Rogé said shortly. "In truth, the only reason Joffroi supports his own bastards is because Guy handles his revenues and attends to that particular task. But then I sincerely doubt that you want Guy – that was who you meant by *anyone,* was it not? – getting wind of this brat until it becomes necessary! *If* there is a child. And that, sweeting, is the reason why I said a written message should be the last resort, why we must arrange matters otherwise between us." He pondered a moment, frowning heavily, then seemed to come to some sort of decision. "I do not have it about me just now but I will give you my cloak pin before I leave Chartre. It was my father's and so far as I know there is no other like it in all of Mithlondia. Return it to me if, against all the odds, you find yourself... breeding. As for the messenger... you remember the soldier, Geryth? For all he is one of my men, you can trust him to do your bidding and to treat you with a modicum of respect into the bargain."

"And if there is no cause to send to you? Surely you will want your pin back if it means so much to you?"

He hesitated a long moment, then shrugged irritably.

"Keep it! It may serve some useful purpose for you one day. Now, are we agreed?"

She felt that she should argue further but could not muster the strength to do so and then the muffled blast of a horn drifting eerily through the mist informed them both that the time for discussion was gone. Giving de Rogé a curt nod, she walked past him, heading towards the door, the silken whisper of her trailing skirts overlaid by the faint chime of his spurs as he fell into step beside her. He was just reaching past her to lift the latch when, with the briefest of knocks, the heavy oak door swung inwards.

# Chapter 10

## *Brothers in Blood*

A man stood in the shadows of the stairwell. A tall, broad-shouldered man, booted and spurred, a sword at his side. A stranger clad in a tunic of fine leaf-green wool, intricately embroidered with gold and silver and black. Yet not quite a stranger...

Through the swirl of sea mist that suddenly permeated the chamber and confused her vision, she heard the voice she had once thought of as sunlight on water exclaim,

"What in Hell are you doing here, Ran?"

And heard the slightly deeper, slightly darker voice of the man beside her say,

"What in Hell do you think I am doing!"

"I do not know. That is why I asked," came back the edged reply.

A hand clamped on her arm, holding her steady – obviously de Rogé thought she was about to faint but she was not... was she?

"I was looking for you," de Rogé was saying. "To tell you that Madame Ariène is requesting your presence in her bower before the morning meal. But judging by that tunic, you have already seen her."

"Yes, curse it! Even so, Ran, you can scarcely have needed more than a quick glance to ascertain that I was not within. Yet despite my repeated warnings to stay away from the lady, I find you here, behind a closed door, with her. So for how long, Ran? A moment? A candle-notch? Long enough to be the cause of some distress to her since she is obviously on the brink of swooning. And take your damned hand off her!"

"Daemon's balls, Guy! What are you implying?" Ranulf's tone was curt and coldly furious and exactly as it should have been if he were indeed being unjustly accused. But he did take his hand from her arm.

Not sure whether to be glad or sickened by his ability to lie under stress and shamed anew, Rowène fought her way free of her faintness and took a deliberate step back from the two men where they stood on either side of the doorway; one in the grey morning light, the other in the darker shadows of the stairwell.

"I should have thought it obvious what I was implying," Guy was saying tersely, his tone so similar to his foster-brother's that Rowène could not help but blink.

"Damn you, yes!" de Rogé snapped. "But just ask yourself this. When, over the past fifteen-odd years, have I ever tumbled a woman you had warned me away from? *Never,* as you bloody well know! And even if I had not had my fill of the trollops in this cursed castle do you think I would trouble myself over a skinny, red-haired, whey-faced wench who would sooner scratch my eyes out..." There was the barest hesitation as he seemed to realise what he had said before he hastened to cover his mistake. "As open her legs for me! Besides, do you really think I would want to lay an untried virgin? No, thank you, I prefer my wenches soft and willing and experienced, as you should know by now." The abrasive note left his voice, to be replaced by a silken sneer. "But perhaps she *was* willing for you, *Brother*?"

She had thought the fog gone from her mind but realised it had returned, cold and chill, with that one sneering phrase. She heard Guy growl, "Shut up, Ran!" and de Rogé give a short, incredulous laugh but paid little heed to his actual words, though the few she caught made a horrible sort of sense.

"Bloody hell, Guy! ... all night ... still have not told her! ... even I would not ... a wench under false pretences but you..."

"Be quiet, both of you!" she cried. Then, addressing the terrible void as both men, rather surprisingly, fell silent, she demanded, "Tell me what?"

"The truth!" de Rogé offered tersely and suddenly the mist was gone, both from the room and her mind. She could *see* his weathered features quite clearly now and, for many reasons, wished she could not. There was an oddly disquieting look in the dark blue eyes that rested on her own – surely pale – face. Without turning his head, he spoke sharply to the other man, "Come into the light, damn it, so she can see you properly."

Spurs chinked as Guyard de Martine took a single long step into the pale golden-grey light that now suffused every corner of her chamber. Everything he had ever told her of his life flashed through her mind but her heart refused to accept what reason insisted must be the truth...

She continued to stare from one man to the other. Although they had seemed, in that first frightening moment to be identical, there *were* subtle differences. Of similar height and build, the resemblance was quite startling, now that they were both clean-shaven. But the eyes of the man to her right were the soft light blue of the summer sky and his newly-washed hair gleamed dark gold like ripe wheat in the sunshine. By contrast, the eyes of the man on her left were the dark blue of winter ice and his roughly-bound hair made her think of stooked barley under a harvest moon.

Finding herself utterly incapable of meeting Guy's bleak gaze for more than a heartbeat, she chose to turn instead towards his foster-brother for disillusionment; hard, ruthless and predatory though he undoubtedly was, he was also – for the moment at least – a shield against the man who was causing her such unrelenting pain. Only one faint hope held her heart from tearing apart completely and it coloured her tone as she almost pleaded with the one man she knew would not lie to her, unaware in her distress that she was once more using his given name rather than a formal title.

"He told me he was named for his father but how can that be if he is..?" But she could not say it. She shook her head. "Who is he really? Tell me, Ranulf!"

She saw de Rogé jerk slightly at the sound of his given name on her lips. His pale brows frowned a warning at her even as he shrugged and said, with a barely passable imitation of his normal mockery,

"Come, Demoiselle, you are neither blind nor deaf. Nor even particularly stupid, I should say. You heard me call him *Brother*, did you not? Or did you think that was merely a term of affection? Or courtesy? Yet you must know me well enough by now to know that I do not pay lip service to either." She saw him skim a look of dark irony at the other man. "You may as well tell her, Guy. You are the one who spent the night with her and, when all is said and done, it is hardly my place to reveal your lineage to her."

She saw Guyard de Martine slant a searching look at his foster-brother but Ranulf de Rogé's bland countenance and sardonic smile were giving nothing away and, with a short, sharp sigh he said,

"You are right, Ran. I should have done this long since but I thought I would be gone from here before the need must arise. And, but for Joffroi's cursed whims, I would have been."

He took a deep breath and turned to look at Rowène. She realised she was shaking again, anticipating what she knew he would say. She scarcely needed the confirmation of his words.

"Ranulf *is* my brother. *Half*-brother to be precise. And I *was* named for my father. That was no lie. As to my mother, her name *was* Alys. The Demoiselle Alys de Martine. And although she was Madame Rosalynde's companion she was also my father's mistress. My father being no mere mercenary, as you must have guessed by now, but Lord Jacques Guyard de Rogé. I am their bastard." He took another breath and his drawn face hardened, only his light blue eyes showing any emotion. "I am sorry, Rowène, I know I should have told you before now but perhaps, when it comes down to it, I am just as feckless as my father – and brothers – when it comes to women. Not least for not discouraging your belief that I came by the de Martine name honourably but I could guess well enough what would happen if you knew I was Jacques de Rogé's by-blow and, fool that I was, I did not want you to look at me as I had seen you look at Joffroi and Ranulf. With hatred, revulsion and fear, simply because I was a de Rogé too, and base-born at that."

With every word he had spoken echoing dully in her ears, she could manage no words in reply, her heart frozen within her breast, her mind numb.

There was nothing wrong with her vision, however, and even as she watched, she saw him grimace and glance at his half-brother.

*Dear God of Light, Ranulf is his brother!*

Not merely by affection or usage but his brother *by blood*. And Guy was nothing more than the illegitimate son born of Jacques de Rogé's adulterous liaison with his wife's companion. Their *bastard*, Guy had said, with a blunt lack of emotion that had struck her almost as painfully as the revelation of his father's name. Yet he was a by-blow who had not – as so many noblemen's by-blows were – been cast aside or forgotten. He had been brought up alongside his true-born brothers. And she had thought herself in love with him. With a de Rogé! She would have given herself to him for love. Instead she had allowed Ranulf – his own brother – to take her by force! Gods! She felt as if a thousand thorns were piercing her heart...

She came out of her pain-induced daze in time to hear one of them – she could not even tell which one by this time, she was so overwrought – say in a worried tone,

"I think I must leave her to your care. Since I cannot think, from the look in her eyes, that she will be able to tolerate my company just now – or ever again perhaps. Will you do this for me?"

"I will," came the curt reply. Ah! Those were Ranulf de Rogé's clipped tones. "If not for you, then for the sake of the woman who was mother to us both."

"She would have been sorely disappointed in me, I fear," Guy sighed.

"And doubly so with me," his brother muttered. "Go on, Guy. She will be safe enough with me, my word on it. But will you fetch her sister in my stead? I will take Demoiselle Rowène down to the hall immediately, since I do not doubt Joffroi will spitting blood by now at our continued absence."

"Yes, I will escort Demoiselle Juliène down," de Martine replied. "It will be better thus. She, at least, has never cherished any false illusions about me."

His brother watched him go, muttering something that sounded like,

"No, but I fancy you have your own delusions regarding her."

Then he looked back at Rowène, his frown deepening as he scanned her face.

"Why do I get the impression that while I might have hurt you in the worst possible way a man can physically hurt a woman, Guy has just broken your heart? You loved him, did you not?"

There was no sympathy in his voice; no warmth, no comfort. Rather, his voice was as flat and calm as a snow-melt tarn on some distant, bleak moor, the very lack of emotion in it whipping her trampled pride into life once more.

"If I did, Messire de Rogé, I do so no longer. In truth, I think I hate him even more than I hate you, if that is possible!" She lifted her chin and regarded him steadily; tears, if she allowed herself to shed them, could come later when she was alone once more. "And you are wrong. At least *he* only lied to me. What *you* did to me... to my sister... can never be made right!"

Belatedly her conscience reminded her that he could have left her to be discovered by Ilana or even, the gods forbid, her mother. And he *had* promised that he would try to keep their brief but disastrous union from becoming public knowledge. For his own sake as much as hers but at least he had offered her some protection when he need not have bothered at all, since she could not believe that the High Counsel of Mithlondia would arraign – let alone hang – a nobleman for rape. Even if he believed it himself. And clearly he did…

"Demoiselle de Chartreux?"

The formal mode of address did indeed sound odd after all that had happened between them but even as she responded to his sharp tone and broke free of her dark reverie, she gasped as her wits belatedly caught up with her eyes.

"Now what are you staring at?" he asked irritably. "Are you looking for the differences – or mayhap the similarities – between Guy and myself? In looks at least, we are generally held to be mirror images, both of our father and each other, although assuredly Guy is not the womaniser Jacques de Rogé was."

"Whereas you most definitely are," she snapped, although much of the venom had gone from her voice and when she spoke again there was a distinctly pensive note in her voice. "You *are* very alike. Save that his hair is a darker gold, and shorter of course. And his eyes are a lighter blue."

"His legacy from his mother, I suppose," Ranulf replied quietly. "Since our father's eyes were the same colour as I have been told mine are. As for the length of his hair… well, admittedly he has never worn it as long as I do but assuredly it was no shorter than Joffroi's until the very day Guy left Rogérinac to come here. He is a nobleman's son, after all, not some nameless serf with dirt beneath his finger nails and wool where his wits should be."

Accepting this without comment, Rowène continued to study him, wondering how she could have been so blind – wilfully so, perhaps? – as not to see before this morning just how alike they were and seeking any small differences that would set the two men apart.

"There is a scar on your cheekbone," she said suddenly, her hand half lifting towards it. "Just below your right eye…"

"A barbarian arrow some five years ago." He grinned. "I had lost my helm and was lucky not to lose the sight in that eye as well. Or the eye itself! I doubt the wenches would have come to my bed quite so eagerly if I had and the whores would certainly have charged more."

"And your nose looks like it has been broken at some time," she continued, disdaining to notice his crude reference to the women he had bedded.

"A tavern brawl. What else would you expect from a drunken whoremonger?" he responded, so sardonically that she wondered if he might be lying to her.

She saw a muscle twitch slightly at the corner of his mouth, reinforcing her belief and drawing her attention in that direction. She felt suddenly as if she were standing beneath an icy waterfall and barely aware that she was speaking, whispered,

"And your mouth… Gods above! There is no softness there at all…"

"There could be," he murmured, blue eyes darkening as he spoke, taking a step towards her. "For you, I would be as gentle as the rose petals that scent your hair."

She swallowed and took a wary step backwards, fear arising anew at this abrupt shift in the tension between them, and instinctively wrapped her arms around herself as a shiver coursed through her aching body. Instantly the incipient warmth died from his eyes, leaving them a cool, frosty blue that was little short of ice.

"A simple *no* would have sufficed," he snapped. "I do know the meaning of the word, little though I have given you cause to believe it. Come! It is time and more than time that we joined the others in the hall. I would not care to wager on the outcome should Guy think to look in on his way back down with your sister and find us still here. I doubt I can deflect his suspicions again. Or at least not without an outright lie this time. And I will not lie to Guy."

Even as he said this, his brows drew together in a puzzled frown and some of the hardness left his voice.

"That said, I am damned if I know why he accepted the implication earlier that I had not molested you, given the evidence you left on my face!" He put up his hand to touch his cheek, then spun towards the table in order to snatch up the mirror.

"Daemons of Hell!" he muttered, staring wide-eyed into the silvered glass.

The next moment he let the mirror drop, and – heedless of the expensive glass shattering about his booted feet – spun to face her once more, something that looked oddly like fear flickering behind the frozen disbelief in his eyes.

"Bloody, damned Hell! So it *is* true! You *are* a witch! One of the cursed Faennari indeed. And I took you by force! Gods' balls! No wonder my cock withered in you. And I always thought that was just part of the legend."

"What *are* you talking about?" Rowène demanded, even as she flushed at the sudden spate of profanity. "What legend?"

"That any mortal man who took one of the Faennari by force would be cursed to impotence for the remainder of his life. As you have cursed me!" he continued with a snarl. Then, his temper cooling as rapidly as it had flamed, "Not that I did not deserve it! Hell'sdeath, I would have flogged and gelded any of my own men who raped an innocent! How then should I think to escape unpunished? And, for all you have your father's face, your hair proclaims you a witch. Or a witchling at least. Gods aid me! I should have guessed at the power you have been hiding when I first saw how you had marked my face, since by rights you should scarce have raised a welt with those nails, let alone drawn blood. But, damn it all, I did not want to believe you might be a witch in truth." He regarded her grimly. "And now you have healed me I can doubt the evidence no longer."

"Ranulf..."

"No! Just listen!" he interrupted her, his voice harsh once more. "I know nothing about the limits of tolerance in Kardolandia, but here in Mithlondia we destroy what we fear! Rowène, I watched your father die and, though I am damned for saying it, I do not want to watch you die too – whatever you have done to me!"

Shaken, both by his words and the intensity with which he uttered them, Rowène struggled not to show her disquiet. She hated him for his involvement in her father's death, she disliked him intensely for what he had done to her sister and was not sure how far she trusted him as regards herself but she did not think he had lied to her yet and had no reason to start now. Unless...

"Is this your way of punishing me because you think I cursed your... er..."

"Cock?" he suggested, the darkness lifting from his eyes as a hint of a strained grin touched one corner of his mouth. "Prick?"

"Manhood, I was about to say," she interrupted hastily before he could suggest any further vulgar alternatives.

"Whatever you want to call it, I do not suppose you would consider healing it as you did my face?" he enquired, the dark blue eyes icy no longer but gleaming with laughter and something else... a heat she recognised, though he kept it partially hidden behind the humour. "I will swear not to tell anyone and I doubt it would take much effort on your part. Just one stroke from those clever fingers of yours...

Rowène flushed as she caught his meaning and her glance dropped involuntarily to his groin.

"I think not," she replied tartly. "I am sure it will not hurt you to remain celibate for a few months." Ignoring his horrified expletive she continued, "Besides, I am not convinced that your... um... inability to... er... complete the act was anything to do with me or some insubstantial myth of the Faennari. Unlikely though it sounds on the surface, it might just have been your conscience!"

"A de Rogé with a conscience?" he mocked, obviously completely recovered from his former state of shock... or fear... or whatever it had been. "Surely not."

"Oh, believe what you will," she said irritably. "But I am *not* touching you *there...*" She waved a hand vaguely in the direction of his groin. "I may have left Kaerellios without personal knowledge of a man's body but I was not completely naïve even then and, eldritch curses notwithstanding, I can guess how your..." She gestured again.

"Manhood?" he suggested, still grinning.

"Cock!" she retorted. Then winced, wondering how that coarse word had come to be issuing from her own mouth, and finished somewhat unsteadily. "Would... er... respond."

To her continuing consternation, de Rogé greeted her alarming descent into vulgarity with open amusement.

"Try it, sweeting, and we will see what happens." Then his face settled into harsher lines as all softening traces of laughter drained away. "No, on reflection, I believe you are wise to keep your hands to yourself. I really have no wish to be forced to stand witness at your trial and know it was my word that condemned you. Not after the harm I have already done to you."

"You are truly serious then, about my being a witch?"

"You must admit that the evidence is against you, Rowène." Both tone and words were bleak. "Both my face and this..." He raised one hand to lightly touch his fingers to her hair, accidentally brushing her cheek as he smoothed a strand back from her face. Surprisingly, she found she did not flinch at the touch but was grateful nonetheless when he took no further liberties, simply allowing his hand to fall away again.

"But if what you say is true," she said slowly, her brow furrowing. "About Mithlondia's attitude to... witches... to those with..." She grimaced and lifted a hank of sadly-tousled hair. "Witch-red hair... how is it that my mother is still Lady of Chartreux, accepted at court?"

"Because, despite her fey beauty, the fire of her hair and the unusual colour of her eyes, she has never openly been accused of any evil," Ranulf replied stonily. "Because by virtue as her position as the wife of the man who, after Prince Marcus himself, was perhaps the most powerful nobleman in Mithlondia, was nigh untouchable. And though Louis de Chartreux is dead," he concluded grimly. "She has enticed my brother into her web in his stead and I fear she will not release her hold on him until she has sucked all the usefulness out of him, as she did your father. Then she will destroy him and seek a new..."

A faint chink from the stairwell – as of a nobleman's spurs ringing against the stone steps – caused de Rogé to break off what he was saying and glance towards the door.

"Damnation! That will be Guy on his way down with your sister. For both our sakes this ends now! Once beyond this chamber you are on your own." He snorted softly under his breath and finished wryly, "Although I am sure, if you let him, Guy will do what he can to protect you until he has to leave. The less contact you have with me, however, the better it will be for both of us..."

"Now that," she concurred swiftly. "I will not argue with, Messire de Rogé."

"Unless..." He added dryly, with a pointed glance towards her flat belly. "It becomes necessary." Then, so softly she was not sure that she had heard him right, "Rowène."

She stared at his mouth as if the word might still linger on his lips, until another metallic chink made her start and look up. He, however, was still staring at her stomach.

"I have already told you, there will be no... it will not be necessary," she reiterated, pushing aside all thought of that horrifying possibility.

She needed to see Ju. Needed to assure herself that her sister was... not *well*.

195

How could any woman be well – either in body or soul – who had spent a whole night with the ravening wolf who now trod at her heels? She pushed aside the sudden, unlooked for and curiously bitter thought that perhaps de Rogé had not acted the wolf with her sister...

Another thought slipped into her mind; another pebble tossed into the mirrored pool of reflection. A pool wherein she could actually *see* a fair-haired man and a dark-haired woman lying together in tangled embrace. She could *hear* his voice, murmuring something... perhaps asking the woman to call him by his given name in those heated moments before he joined his body to hers...

Sweating and shivering she jerked herself from the trance... illusion... whatever it had been and forced the last remaining traces of mist from her mind. She saw a pair of dark blue eyes regarding her from beneath knitted pale brows and, hand pressed to her mouth to contain her nausea, brushed past him.

Whatever had happened just now – and from the pain presently splitting her skull she hoped it would not happen again – and whatever had happened last night, she needed to see with her own eyes that her sister had survived the experience, rather than having to take the word of their sluttish tire-maid or the man who had, in whatever form – lecher, lover, wolf – lain with all three of them.

In the event, Rowène was unable to either see or speak to her sister, Ju having first locked herself in the topmost chamber of the Lady Tower and then refused Guyard de Martine's request to come down to the hall.

That was worrying enough in itself – although de Martine had assured her that Ju had sounded coldly determined rather than hysterically tearful – but without her sister's company, the morning meal proved to be an even more nerve-racking experience – if such a thing were possible – than the feast of the evening before. At least then Rowène had been clad in her own modest – if somewhat the worse for wear – attire, rather than being forced to appear before all and sundry draped in the flamboyant indecency of scarlet silk, a colour very nearly matched by the flush that mantled her cheeks as she took her seat at the high table.

Finding herself flanked by Guyard de Martine on her left and Ranulf de Rogé on her right, she scrupulously avoided contact of any sort with either man but an awareness gradually grew in some dark hollow of her heart that their very presence, hateful though it was, provided her with a shield against the lewd looks and coarse comments of the other men in the hall; the servants having taken the measure of their new steward and the soldiers reading retribution in their commander's icy blue gaze should they dare to treat the vulgarly-clad woman between them as anything other than the high-ranking noblewoman she had been until her father's attainder.

There was, regrettably, little that either man could do to quell their ebullient elder brother.

It was abundantly clear to everyone in the hall – from scurrying servants and bleary-eyed guards to the nobles at the high table – that Black Joffroi was in an exuberant mood that morning, the dark fire in his deep brown eyes banked, yesterday's all too tangible lust satiated for the present. Indeed he was in such a high good humour that he took his brothers' late arrival at the meal table with no other outward sign of displeasure than a brief, glinting glance. And he had barely allowed them to take their seats before loudly demanding to hear the details of their nocturnal antics.

To Rowène's disgust, de Rogé – had she ever willingly thought of him by his given name? – appeared only too ready to comply with this edict, and even though much of the colourful language he employed to describe his encounter with her sister was as foreign to her as Kardolandian would no doubt be to him, she grasped enough of his meaning to wish herself deaf. Despite her embarrassment at his lewd recital and a burning anger that he could speak of her sister in such terms, she felt an odd mingling of relief and guilt when she realised he meant to keep his word and say nothing about the time he had spent with her.

As for de Martine, when Black Joffroi enquired of him, with a sly smile that revealed a certain level of suspicion, as to how his half-brother's night had gone, he merely replied tersely that "It was done", adding, in an uncharacteristically surly growl that was more convincing than any explicit exposition would have been, that he never wanted to speak of it again.

Rowène just caught a glimpse of the odd grimace that twisted Ranulf de Rogé's hard mouth at these words but Black Joffroi openly guffawed and appeared to accept without further questioning that his half-brother possessed, as he rather vulgarly phrased it, more steel in his sword than he had previously supposed. Notwithstanding this acknowledgement he sent a smirking Ilana to fetch down the sheet from her mistress's bed. Rowène could sense de Rogé stiffening beside her as the impact of this order struck what passed for a conscience with him, and could only pray he had thought to clean the bloodstains off the coverlet as well as his shirt hem.

For vastly differing reasons she did not dare look directly at either of the men flanking her but sat in a misery of embarrassment until Ilana finally appeared, smugly displaying the bloodstained sheet over her arm. With that Black Joffroi's last doubts as to his half-brother's virility and obedience appeared to be laid to rest and he applied himself heartily to his meal once more.

Watching the trickle of ale that escaped his mouth and dribbled down his heavy-fleshed jowl – darkly shadowed even though he could only just have shaved – Rowène winced and could not refrain from glancing at the woman seated beside him, wondering how her mother could tolerate, let alone welcome, the man's boorish company, not only at her table but also in her bed.

It came as something of a shock to find those cool, green eyes fixed on her in return, as the Winter Lady surveyed her daughter with a penetrating objectivity that was as unnerving as it was unwanted. Rowène had the odd, flashing thought that had she been the cat de Rogé had called her, every hair on her body would be standing on end. Nevertheless she forced herself to meet her mother's shrewdly assessing look with a blank defiance that she hoped might serve to hide her deep sense of shame. After all, what would it matter to her mother whether it had been Ranulf de Rogé or Guyard de Martine who had taken her maidenhead when it was irrevocably done?

Her mother's delicately-darkened brows arched at this sign of intransigence but she said nothing, transferring her interest with a subtle shift of her lashes to the two fair-haired men beside her. Only too glad to be released from the Winter Lady's keen eyes, and wishing it were possible to escape the tense atmosphere of the hall altogether, Rowène dropped her gaze. To find that one of the men had surreptitiously placed a small almond pastry before her while her attention had been elsewhere.

Little though she felt like eating, Rowène picked it up and with an effort managed to swallow some of the sticky, flaky pastry. Normally she loved the sweet delicacy but today she nearly choked on it – although it would seem that she was the only one in the hall who had any trouble keeping her food down. Her mother was eating daintily but steadily whilst Jacques de Rogé's three hulking sons ate as if this might be their last meal.

In contrast to the excesses of the night before, the morning meal was a simple affair. Fresh wheaten rolls, pastries studded with raisins and nuts and dripping in honey, the last of the previous autumn's apples and Kardolandian peaches and grapes from the trading vessel that had docked in the harbour two days before. For the men, with their more substantial appetites, there was also an array of cold meats, cheeses and Chartre ale.

Abandoning the sweet pastry, Rowène nibbled at a piece of crusty bread and sipped at the crisply scented cider a nervous serving man poured for her. Although she did not look at him and the hand that held the pitcher was steady enough, she could smell the faint odour of fresh sweat on him and knew he misliked the company as much as she did. Keeping her gaze firmly fixed on the bleached linen of the table covering, she murmured a word of thanks but before the servant could retreat, she heard de Rogé mutter something to him that was both curse and warning combined.

Tension began to knot her muscles anew but the servant merely mumbled an inarticulate response and slipped away without drawing de Rogé's ire further, and she took a deep breath to calm her trembling nerves. Her equanimity was far too fragile a thing to take any more violence this morning and although she knew she had had no choice but to come down here, she felt physically sick when she considered her own cowardice. How could she sit here like this, flanked on one side by a man who had lied to her with every word he had spoken and on the other by the man who had – by his own admission – used her worse than he would have treated a whore. While not six feet away the swine who had openly gloried in bringing her father to his shameful and agonising death ate like a starving boar and ogled her mother over his ale cup.

Yet her sister, whom she had always considered so fragile and delicate, had found the courage to refuse to come down. Of course, Ju had had the advantage of being able to lock herself in Luc's chamber, giving Guyard de Martine the choice of either taking his half-brother's battle axe to the solid oak door or leaving Ju there until hunger overcame her defiance. He had chosen the latter course and, with one of his brother's men guarding the stairway, had left her to her own devices.

But Rowène had not had that option. There was no lock on her chamber door for one thing and even if there had been, de Rogé would never have permitted her to remain there. He might, for reasons of his own, be prepared to keep silent regarding his violent rape of her maidenhead but assuredly he would not let her escape his older brother's clutches. Damn him – Ranulf, she meant – to the darkest pits of Hell!

And his brother and half-brother alongside him!

*Would Jacques de Rogé have been proud of his sons*, she wondered venomously, *and consider that they had lived up to his own vile reputation.*

Indeed, she thought, they had exceeded it! For while their father might have indulged himself with relatively petty border reaving, between the three of them, Joffroi, Ranulf and Guyard had personally violated, or been complicit in violating, almost every law of Mithlondian society. They had lied, connived at and committed murder, theft and rape.

Yet here she sat, in her wrongfully-hanged father's hall, and accepted their presence in her life without demur. What did that make her? Perhaps she was the whore her mother had presented her as; after all, had she not agreed to exchange her honour for Ranulf de Rogé's silence? And had she not been fool enough to fancy herself in love with Guyard de Martine? Gods!

A fierce flood of poisonous hatred coursed through her, directed not only at the three de Rogé brothers but also, in part, at herself. Her burning gaze focussed on the eating knife beside her plate and, almost without volition, her fingers curled around the hilt, gripping so tightly it would have hurt had she been in any state to feel anything other than the black hate and bitter self-loathing that held her.

What might have happened next she had no way of knowing. But before she could turn the knife on herself, or anyone else, steel-strong fingers flecked with pale gold hairs closed around her wrist and a sardonic voice murmured in her ear,

"I am not so careless as to leave a honed blade within your reach but I suggest you drop it all the same."

Her grip tightened convulsively and in response he let her feel the strength that lay in his own fingers; sufficient to remind her what he was capable of but not enough to truly hurt her. She glanced up at his hard, brutally unyielding features and found herself wondering, quite irrelevantly, why she had ever imagined the Daemon of Hell was wrought of darkness, when surely he must possess the same glittering ice-blue eyes, iron-hard mouth and pale hair of the man before her.

"Let me go," she said quietly. "You have made your point."

He held her gaze a moment longer, then relaxed his grip. Draining his ale, he shoved his chair back and stood up, snapping his fingers with careless arrogance at the nearest serving man.

"You! Yes, you! No need to piss yourself, man, I am not holding a grudge for yesterday's accident. My boots have had worse than wine spilt on them before now. Just go and find the soldier called Geryth and tell him to bring all my gear immediately. To the stables, mind, not the hall."

"Aye, zur."

The hapless servant jerked a bow and scuttled off. Rowène watched him go, cringing inwardly at the manner in which he had been addressed, whilst attempting at the same time to ignore the content of de Rogé's mocking comment. By contrast, Black Joffroi was ignoring the servant whilst regarding his brother with amused interest.

"Spilt wine on your boots, did he? And you let him off without a whipping? Do not tell me having a noblewoman in your bed is making you soft, Ran? It is supposed to have the opposite effect."

De Rogé grunted something under his breath that sounded to Rowène remarkably like *a pox on all witchlings* as he shot her an unreadable glance, then turned his gaze towards the high windows beyond which the fog appeared to be roiling as thick as ever.

"I have more important things to do, Joff, than flogging some half-witted servant, especially if I am going to get away today."

Black Joffroi did not reply immediately, seemingly more intent on stabbing a thick slice of cold beef with the point of his knife than debating the weather with his brother. Lifting the meat to his mouth, he bit off a hunk with vicious relish.

"You are somewhat over-eager to be away, are you not, Ran? I thought Demoiselle Juliène's charms would surely hold you here a day or two longer?" The comment was ungraciously uttered around a mouthful of partially chewed meat. "Or even that serving wench you were tupping between courses yesterday?"

"You know me, Joff," his brother replied easily. "Wenches have their place and purpose but I would just as soon be with the rest of the army at this time of the year. Besides, you gave Linnius your word that I would be bringing our men up to Lamortaine as soon as we were done in Chartre and you are perfectly capable of dealing with Luc de Chartreux without my help."

"Oh, I will deal with him right enough," Black Joffroi growled. "I will hang him from the castle walls – just as soon as *you* lay the bastard by the heels. So the sooner you catch him, the sooner you can ride north." He directed a malevolent glare at his half-brother. "Of course, if Guy had not been so bewitched by de Chartreux's sister that he let the whelp out of his sight in the first place, you would have been able to leave as soon as you wished."

"Do not credit the little wild-cat with more charm than she actually has," de Rogé said tersely, overriding whatever angry protest his half-brother might have been about to make. He flashed a dismissive glance in Rowène's direction and continued with a more casual intonation, "Oh, come on, Joff, admit it. Guy has done everything you ordered, even to breaking his precious binding vow in order to bed a traitor's daughter. He deserves to be allowed to return to Rogérinac and make his peace with Mathilde. And if I am to discover de Chartreux's whereabouts for you before I hand over command of the garrison to Guthlaf, I had better get to it."

He brought his gaze back to his half-brother who had also risen to his feet.

"I take it you are leaving now, Guy?"

"I would have left sooner if I could," de Martine replied, his tone indicating a certain underlying irritation although Rowène could not tell what had caused his temper to spark. "Unlike you, Ran, I have no duties to hold me here and the harvest to oversee at home. Provided that foul murk lifts, I can be across the Larkenlye by noon and back in Rogérinac in three or four days. If not," he shrugged broad shoulders. "I shall, at least, be on my way."

Rowène saw him hesitate, as if meaning to say something else, then visibly abandon the notion. He nodded towards his elder brother and sketched a half-bow in her mother's direction.

"Madame." And then, taking Rowène by surprise, made her a deeper bow. "Demoiselle."

Heart pounding under the influence of a myriad conflicting emotions, she turned her head away, refusing to acknowledge either the man or the warmer feelings he still aroused in her, then flinched as a hard hand her flesh recognised with nothing but revulsion grasped her arm firmly, just above the elbow, and that sardonic voice she hated spoke above her head.

"Joff! I have it in mind to visit de Chartreux's bastard whelp before I leave and, with your permission, I would take Guy's doxy down with me. I imagine it will have a salutary effect on the misbegotten cur when he sees his precious half-sister wearing whore's scarlet. And while he will know he cannot change what happened to her last night, the possibility that he may yet be able to save her from having to service the rest of the garrison might just prove a more gainful method of persuading him to talk than the rack or hot iron."

Hearing – but not quite believing she had heard his arid speculation aright – Rowène gaped up at him in horrified disgust, almost as unaware of his hand hauling her to her feet as she was of Black Joffroi's grunt of approval.

"And after I have broken *your* bastard brother, Demoiselle" de Rogé added with a sneer, his grip on her arm tightening warningly as his icy blue gaze finally dropped to meet her frantic one. "I might even grant you the favour of bidding farewell to *my* brother, always supposing Guy is still here by the time I have finished with you. The stables may not make so snug a setting for a final fondle as your bedchamber but it is considerably better than a stinking dungeon cell." She saw him flash a taunting grin at his flushed and furious half-brother before returning his attention to her, his dark blue eyes narrowed and cruel, his voice a mocking drawl. "Then again, since I have never known my tight-laced brother to do anything so uncouth as tumble a wench in the stable straw, you may just have to make do with me."

Rowène felt all the blood drain from her face as she absorbed the threat, both to Lucien and to herself. She might have lost all hold on consciousness then had it not been for the painful grip he had on her arm and the fleeting hint of white tension beside his leering mouth that seemed to contradict the casual coarseness of his last words.

Finding herself, some moments later, in the chill, misty damp of the castle courtyard with no real idea of how she came to be there, she wrenched her arm from de Rogé's slackened grasp just as Guyard de Martine grabbed hold of his half-brother's arm from the other side and said in a tone of hard-held temper,

"Now will you tell me what in bloody hell that was all about? If I did not know you considerably better than Joffroi does I would have laid you out in the hall rather than giving you this chance to explain yourself."

"I should not have to explain," de Rogé grated, temper flaring in his own eyes. "But since you have obviously given your wits into this little witch's keeping, I will. You know Joff! Know how quickly his temper can turn ugly. And while I may have defended your actions in the hall just now, the truth of it is that if you had not lost track of de Chartreux in the first place, I would not now be in the damnable position of having to torture the only other man in this bloody castle who might know the details of where he has gone to ground."

"And if the threat of torture does not work, you would use an innocent girl to break him?" de Martine exclaimed, staring at his half-brother as if he had never seen him before. "His own gently-born sister?"

"Gently-born, I grant you. But innocent? I think not," de Rogé sneered. Rowène felt his gaze crawling over the exposed flesh of her shoulders and upper breasts, saw the heat flaring in his eyes as he deliberately followed the waving mass of her dark-flame hair as it tumbled wildly down, only partially obscuring the scarlet-limned outline of waist and hip and thigh. "Does she *look* innocent to you, Brother? I should rather have said she looks like a high-priced strumpet touting for custom. *Your* custom, if she has any sense."

"Damn you, Ran! Are your wits still sodden from an excess of Marillec wine or are you simply out of temper because you cannot ride north yet?" his half-brother demanded. "Either way, you know damned well that whore's gown was her mother's idea. I never bedded her."

"There is a blood-stained sheet that says different."

"The sheet was *your* idea!"

"Yes, but neither our brother nor hers is aware of that little piece of trickery," de Rogé pointed out, his tone low and exceedingly dry. "And if you want to keep it that way, I suggest you keep your mouth shut and let me use her as I see fit. After all, I am the bloody garrison commander, not you, and if I have to strip the wench naked in order to wring the truth out of de Chartreux's arrogant bastard or take her in front of his eyes, I will do it! This castle and the power it represents means more to our brother at the moment than almost anything else and if it is snatched from him due to negligence on my part or folly on yours, then neither of us can expect any mercy. The fact that we share the same father will not stop Joffroi from laying your back – or mine, if it comes to that – open to the bone! Not to mention handing the wench over to the garrison if I cannot find her brother."

Already struggling against the horrors raised by his words, she could not help the flinching of her flesh when de Rogé suddenly put out a hand and dragged her around to face him. His dark blue eyes were hard and bright, containing some message she could not read. He shook her slightly, not enough to hurt but enough to remind her of the danger she was in.

"Well, wench? What do you think? One man – me – or two score rough men-at-arms? Which would you reckon the less evil fate, hmm?"

"Offer her that choice again and I will break you, brother or no!" de Martine snapped, stepping between them. "And if it comes to a flogging, my back will heal. And so will yours, Ran. Broken maidenheads, on the other hand, do not mend, whether it be one man or two score."

His light blue eyes narrowed and as Rowène followed his gaze she too took note of the sudden pallor that reduced de Rogé's mist-sheened skin to the colour of old linen, and caught her breath in fear that de Martine might guess what his half-brother had done. Then breathed again when he said slowly,

"Gods above, Ran, surely after all you said to me, you did not go so far as to rob Demoiselle Juliène of her virginity?"

"No!" de Rogé said coldly. "I did not." Rowène saw him glance up but the Lady Tower was still hidden behind the clinging swathes of white mist that obscured one side of the castle from the other. "Bloody well ask her next time you see her, if you do not believe me." Then, returning his attention to his half-brother, continued unpleasantly. "Let me get this straight, Guy. You would stand for a flogging rather than see a traitor's daughter given over to the garrison for their common use?"

"If I had to," Guyard replied evenly. "As would any man with any claim to honour. Whatever her father's crimes, real or imagined, she is innocent."

"Just as well, for all our sakes then, that I was bred to be a soldier rather than a milksop."

Clipped and honed as sharpened steel, de Rogé's words sliced through blood, bone and flesh to stab Rowène's heart with ice. She paid no attention to his half-brother's crude, one word reply, being totally overwhelmed with the realisation that she had completely misjudged the depths of the wolf's ruthlessness; not only had he already had Lucien tortured but he was now prepared to use her in the most degrading way possible if by doing so it would cause her half-brother to betray her brother's whereabouts and plans.

And it was with this man... this ravening wolf... that she had made her hell-spawned bargain of silence. Gods! Luc would disown her without hesitation if he ever guessed what she had done...

She could not say what distracted her attention from the low-voiced, increasingly acrimonious argument that continued to rage over her head but glancing around the eerie emptiness of the mist-hung courtyard, she belatedly realised that they were not the only people there. She might only be able to hear the guards as they patrolled the surrounding walls and towers but she could see the servant as plainly as the droplets of moisture that clung like silver spider webs to the pale hair and black-clad shoulders of the daemon beside her.

She peered cautiously around de Rogé's bulk, almost expecting to find the serving man gone; just one more strange manifestation of this increasingly surreal morning. But he was still there, although he was not one of the household servants she recognised. He was nevertheless clad in the de Chartreux livery, his short, greying brown hair curling around his face... She blinked. Surely that round, guileless face should more properly belong above a cloth-laden counter in a prosperous merchant's shop. But unless Master Cailen had a twin brother, surely this was he. Yet what in the name of all the gods was he doing here, in a secured fortress where no-one was permitted entry or egress without authorisation from the new Lord of Chartreux or his garrison commander?

The man did not have the appearance of someone whose wits had gone wandering nor did he seem to be doing anything untoward and yet... Steady brown eyes met her own for a heartbeat but she did not have time to decipher the message they contained before the servant... silk merchant... spy perhaps... was gone, hidden again by the breeze-blown rags of drifting white mist.

A forceful oath uttered in a rasping undertone caused her to start, abruptly recalled to an awareness of the two quarrelling curs and the bone they were bickering over. She shivered uncontrollably, although whether that ripple of gooseflesh was caused by the cold sea mist coalescing on the bare skin of her arms, the ever-present fear for her siblings or simple revulsion at the thought of Ranulf de Rogé forcing himself upon her again, she could not have said. She shivered again.

"You are cold," she heard him say. And supposed he spoke to her, his voice as chill and devoid of colour as the mist that swirled around them. Then, definitely not to her. "Ah, Geryth, there you are! You took your own sweet time getting here."

"Sorry, sir, yon half-wit of a servant you sent to find me would have had me off on a wild goose chase. 'Twas purely luck I heard ye and Master Guy arg... um... talking."

De Rogé muttered another curse, then snapped,

"Here, Guy! You are the one who is insisting the wench be treated like a piece of expensive glassware rather than a flesh and blood woman. Cover her up and be done with it while I get into my gear."

Feeling almost as fragile as a piece of expensive glassware, Rowène surrendered to the reassuring gentleness of Guyard de Martine's hands on her shoulders. She could not shut out the presence of the mailed soldier or the fact of de Rogé arming himself so close beside her but she did her best, focussing instead on the light blue eyes that regarded her with such concern. She felt his hands, working swiftly to wrap the thick black cloak around her trembling, goose-fleshed shoulders, finally securing the heavy silver brooch in the folds at her neck.

"There, at least you are decently covered now," he murmured. "And I cannot believe Ranulf means you harm, whatever he might say."

"And Lucien? I know he..." She jerked her head at de Rogé's broad back. "Hurt Lucien in some way yesterday, but did he really torture him?" she whispered, honeyed pastry and sharp cider churning uneasily in her belly.

De Martine darted a glance over her shoulder and shook his head.

"Not as far as I know," he said, keeping his voice low. His mouth thinned in a manner that reminded her of most unpleasantly of his half-brother and the clean-shaven line of his jaw hardened. "But I would not encourage you to hope for too much. I think, in this instance, Ranulf is entirely capable of such brutality, if he judges it to be necessary."

"And yet you insist he means me no harm!"

"I cannot answer for his intentions towards Lucien but if Ran truly meant to use you in such a vile manner as he indicated, he would not have given you the protection this offers," de Martine muttered, gesturing at the black and silver mantle, his dark gold brows drawing together in an expression that suggested he was quite as confused by the contradictions of his half-brother's behaviour as Rowène was. "Circumstance may have falsely branded you a whore but there is not one of Ranulf's men who would take liberties with you now."

Something in his words suddenly struck clear through her confusion, ringing like a bell in the dark, frightened recesses of her mind. She angled her head in an effort to see the brooch that pinned the mantle on her left shoulder; quite obviously a man's accoutrement, round and wrought of silver, the width of her clenched fist. She could not make out what pattern or device it might bear but obviously it was distinctive enough to mark her out as Ranulf de Rogé's property.

It had belonged to his father once, he had told her, but was now his. He would leave it with her, he had gone on to say, that she might use it as a means to send a message to him if it proved necessary.... And the messenger... She looked up sharply to catch the guarded speculation in the hard but not overtly vicious features of the young man she tentatively identified as yesterday's banner-bearer and horse-holder. Geryth? Yes, that was his name. The one she had been told she could trust to carry her message...

It was at that very moment that she met Ranulf de Rogé's coolly assessing blue gaze and realised suddenly that whatever other evil he meant to accomplish this morning, the main reason behind this nerve-racking game they had all been playing had now been fulfilled. Though it still remained in the balance as to whether he truly was ruthless enough to use her against Lucien. His older brother obviously believed he was. Just as plainly his half-brother did not. For her own part, she did not know what to believe any more.

Nor was she granted the time to make up her mind as, without warning, the white swathes of fog parted to reveal a plume of smoke, dark against the soft blue of the morning sky, bright red-gold flames licking the wooden shutters which had been flung wide against towering sandstone walls. Even as she stared up in disbelief, Ju appeared at the topmost window, her face contorted in terror, her mouth open in a distraught scream.

# Chapter 11

## *Fire and Steel*

"Fire!"

The startled shout emanated from a soldier standing guard on the near wall, and was quickly taken up and repeated as servants and assorted retainers who had been keeping discreetly out of sight of the arguing noblemen, suddenly poured into the courtyard.

"Fire! Fire in the Lady Tower!"

"Gods! Ju!"

Spurred from her numb sense of disbelief by the realisation that her sister was in danger Rowène picked up her scarlet skirts and dashed across the slick wet cobbles of the courtyard, back towards the main door into the keep. She heard a startled curse and a shouted order behind her but paid no heed, such was her desperate fear for her sister. Paid no heed either to the jingling echo of heavy footsteps behind her, so intent was she on reaching her goal.

She felt a hand catch at her arm but twisted away, dislodging the imperfect grip. The contact, brief though it had been, nevertheless proved disastrous. Already off balance, she felt the smooth leather soles of her indoor shoes slip on the fog-greased stones of the bailey, recovered herself with a panicked gasp... then went crashing to the ground, the full weight of a large, mailed body crushing her against the uneven cobbles. She heard his breath harsh in her ear, saw a tendril of pale hair fall past her cheek, smelt sweat, steel and beneath that a faint hint of some elusive herb, and knew who had felled her.

"Damn you," she wept. "Let me go."

"Not until I... have your word... you will not... do such a... bloody stupid... thing again!"

He was breathing heavily, whether with exertion or emotion she could not tell. Neither seemed particularly likely.

But then she was not thinking very clearly herself, so how could she judge him? She thought she might have hit her head as she fell since one of her temples was throbbing painfully. Her ribs felt as though they were broken, her cheek was uncomfortably flattened against the gritty, unyielding surface of a broken cobble and she could scarcely breathe – let alone utter the promise he had demanded.

All she could do was lie helplessly beneath him, enduring his weight and the painful pressure of his metal hauberk, the chain-mail links bruising her skin even through the layers of silk and wool, watching in despair as smoke and flames gushed from one window after another, starting with the lowest and climbing ever higher towards the battlements of the Lady Tower where she had once stood and talked in the sunshine with a wandering harper.

Then, between one rasping, painful breath and the next, the window of the topmost chamber was empty save for the fiery daemons leaping in their grotesque dance of death. Of Ju there was no sign.

Did that mean she had been rescued? Or even now lay overcome with smoke, consumed by flame? Either way Rowène could do nothing to change her sister's fate.

Her captor appeared to realise this too and rolled away from her with a grunt and a curse. Standing up, he ignored her mew of mingled pain and relief at his abrupt transfer of weight, leaving it to his half-brother to help her up. Trembling slightly, she straightened her gown and absently brushed the damp grit from her face and hands, deciding without any especial interest that perhaps her ribs had not been broken after all, since she could now breathe again.

Then again, at the moment, she did not really care if Ranulf de Rogé had broken every bone in her body as well that other, secret, part of her he had shattered earlier that morning. She could not even see the tower now for the tears that blurred her vision but it did not matter. Ju was gone; she knew it by the icy emptiness that filled the place where her heart should have been, and so she wept. Not only for all those she had lost but also for herself; her father was dead, her sister was no more, her brother was a hunted outlaw and her half-brother, whom she had never had the opportunity to know, would die simply because he was her father's son.

With all that gone, what was left in her life now? A castle that was no longer her home, a mother who had given her over to be used as a whore and the ravening wolf who had used her as such. The man whom she had thought she loved could no longer protect her since he would be heading as soon as he might for his home and wife. Whilst as for the man whose binding bracelet she wore... she glanced down at her bruised wrist and saw that the delicate silver band Joscelin de Veraux had given her was still there; flattened and bent awry by the force of her fall, but not yet broken.

Was that an omen? She wondered distantly... Before being jarred back into a disconcerting realisation that what had felt like an aeon of sorrow and loneliness had been in truth little more than a few moments. Barely long enough, in fact, for Guyard de Martine to fold her limp, unresisting body in his arms. He was now questioning her in an increasingly concerned voice but she could scarcely hear him over the roar and crackle of the flames, and the yelling and screaming of frightened servants as they ran between well and keep, trying pathetically to stem the blaze, their movements hindered by those others who simply stood and wept in disbelief.

The only thing she heard with any clarity was the stream of increasingly filthy curses issuing from Ranulf de Rogé's lips as his narrowed, grimly calculating gaze moved from the fiery tower to the soldiers uneasily pacing the outer walls, their attention clearly more on the flames sweeping the keep than their own duties. Because she was watching him, she saw the moment awareness hit him of what was going to happen.

She had not known herself until she saw the vivid flash of blue in his eyes as he turned to yell a warning. But by then it was too late!

The gate tower went up in a shower of red and gold a heartbeat before the gate shattered in a thunderous roar of splintered oak and black, choking smoke. The nearest guards were flung from their feet, little more than bloody rags of flesh and torn metal and, as the smoke cleared, there came an earth-shuddering thud as the drawbridge went crashing down. Then, out of the medley of hammering hooves, startled shouts, clashing steel and the roar of flame, one sound rose clear above the rest.

The war cry of Chartreux. Luc had come.

Pulling free from Guyard de Martine's arms, Rowène darted a look of pure defiance at the mail-clad man now delivering terse orders to an older man in a battered hauberk who nodded quick comprehension and broke away at a run, yelling as he went. As if sensing her gaze, Ranulf de Rogé turned back towards her, his blue eyes sweeping her with a savage look that held a surfeit of suspicion, fury and behind that, the knowledge of what he had done to her.

"If... *when* Luc wins, he will hang you, you know that?"

She could not say whether she meant it as a warning or a promise of retribution. Either way, de Rogé did not reply, merely saying tersely to his half-brother,

"For gods'sake get her out of here, Guy. And look to yourself, the wildcat has claws and will not hesitate to use them on you if all her other wiles fail."

He clapped his brother briefly on the shoulder and turning away, grabbed at the reins of the wild-eyed black stallion Geryth had had the presence of mind to hastily saddle and bring from the stables. Jamming his helm on his head, de Rogé swung up into the saddle and wrenched the stallion around to block the charge of a man in de Chartreux colours. His sword sang from its sheath, its cold glitter dulled by the miasma of smoke and mist as it swept around to meet his opponent's blade.

Ears still ringing from the raw metallic chime as the blades met, Rowène flinched at the force of impact but could not look away, seeing nothing beyond the huge black stallion and the black and silver bulk of the man who rode him. Frightened almost beyond clear thought, she moved by instinct out of reach of the massive iron-shod hooves, but she was still close enough to hear the sickening grunt of effort as one of the men broke through the other's guard, followed by a horrible choking sound she had never heard before. A stream of crimson splattered the grey cobbles beneath the dancing black hooves, riveting her horrified gaze. But before she could look up again a strong hand closed around her own, dragging her, sobbing and stumbling, from the path of the battle.

Finding herself thrust inside a stable full of white-eyed, stamping horses Rowène drew in a breath that tore at her chest and grabbed the nearest partition to steady herself. She glanced towards the doorway, her heart nearly halting at the sight of the man who stood there, sword drawn, warily eyeing the mêlée in front of him.

As well he might, she thought, as her trembling legs gave way and she collapsed into a pile of straw. Despite the sword, a weapon she had every confidence he could handle with the same lethal skill as his more violent half-brothers, de Martine was otherwise unarmed, his mail the gods only knew where in the castle. And although he was clad in leaf green rather than black, the very quality of his tunic, the glittering embroidery about neck, sleeves and hem would mark him out as a de Rogé, even if his clean-shaven face – with its unmistakeable resemblance to the younger of his two half-brothers – did not.

She had thought she hated him but the sudden stabbing anxiety for Guyard de Martine told her that, like it or not, she was as terrified for *his* safety as she was for her brothers'. Whichever way this battle went, whoever won, someone she cared for would pay with their lives. If the unthinkable happened, both her brothers would perish. If Luc won, he would hang all three of the de Rogé brothers without compunction. Black Joffroi certainly deserved to die, she thought vindictively, as to a lesser extent did Ranulf, but Guy...

Rowène drew in a deep, sobbing breath, the peaceful scents of dust and hay, horse and dung a stark contrast to the chaos that had erupted beyond the relative haven of the stable. Moving quietly so as not to distract the man in the doorway, she rose to her feet and slipped along the roughcast wall until she could see what was happening – and then wished she had not!

*God of Light have mercy on them all!*

The fog had now lifted completely and there was no possibility of deceiving herself as to the nature of the maelstrom that swept through the courtyard; a swirling vortex of rearing horses, yelling men, flying arrows, the flash of spear and sword, the crimson splash and spray of blood, the terrifying screams of pain, often cut short by death, all overlaid by the curses, taunts and grunts of the living.

Amidst the chaos her frantic gaze alighted on a familiar figure astride a big grey gelding. Luc! Thank the gods, he was safe yet. Beside him, his squire carried a spear from which streamed a pale blue and gold pennon emblazoned with the silver swan of Chartreux and all around them, ranged about the courtyard and walls, the men who followed him fought and fell. Nor was it just those Chartreux soldiers who had spent the last ten years serving in the Kardolandian king's bodyguard. Rowène also saw men she recognised as being part of the garrison who had been taken prisoner the day before but who must have somehow managed to escape their confinement.

But everywhere she looked, dividing and surrounding the Chartreux men, the soldiers who owed their fealty to Black Joffroi.

She could not see Ranulf in the confusion of blue and gold, black and silver, but she knew that if he had survived that first encounter – if that had not been his life's blood she had seen splattered across the cobbles at her feet – he would be where the fighting was fiercest, looking for either of her brothers, carrying their death in the yard of steel in his hand, secure in his knowledge that his own half-brother guarded her; their final bargaining counter if all seemed lost.

For a moment Rowène closed her eyes, her fear and nausea further chilled by this sudden insight into Ranulf de Rogé's coldly ruthless mind. Had she really thought he had had her safety in mind when he set his half-brother to watch over her? Of course he had not. He had said it himself, he would use her as he saw fit. To service his own vile lusts. To break her half-brother. Or, as now, as a hostage to the gods of chance. She was nothing more to him than a means to an end. Damn him!

She closed her eyes and imagined him, naked and freezing, chains of ice about his wrists, his skin seared by the Daemon's cold breath, his precious manhood hanging shrivelled and shrunken throughout the eternity he would spend shackled in the deepest ice pit Hell could offer.

Satisfying though such an image might be, it brought only a temporary alleviation of her fear and beyond the relative calm of the stable, the slaughter and destruction continued to rage unchecked. She told herself that the nightmare of not knowing what was happening was worse by far than the blood-splattered reality could ever be. Desperate to reassure herself as to Luc's safety, she opened her eyes once more, breathing a sigh of relief as she saw that he was still alive, still mounted, and – although surrounded by Rogé soldiers – competently holding his own. She saw at least two black-clad men fall to his sword while another was struck by the grey's flailing hooves.

It was in the slight lull that followed these deaths that she saw Luc glance around the bailey, as if seeking something or someone. Saw too the moment when his eyes locked onto hers and narrowed in wild fury. Sheathing his bloodstained sword, he snatched the spear, its pennon long since torn away, from his squire's hand and spurred his horse straight at Guyard de Martine, the foot-long iron point aimed with lethal accuracy at the other man's unprotected chest.

Unable to help herself, Rowène screamed a warning and saw the moment when Guy, already engaged in fending off a Chartreux foot-soldier's attack, finally realised the danger bearing down on him. He flung himself aside with barely a foot to spare and regaining his balance, backhanded Luc's spear aside with sufficient force to send the weapon clattering from her brother's fist. Gods! If her heedless action caused Luc's death, she would never forgive herself!

But no... he was all right. She watched as her brother tugged on the reins, turning his steed aside and shouted an order to the foot soldier that this was *his* kill. Sliding to the ground, his fingers closed on his sword hilt, and he swept the long blade at his opponent's unprotected head in a scything blow that would have killed him outright, had he not brought his own weapon up just in time. The blades clashed, grated and separated, but Luc was only partially successful in parrying Guy's next attack, cursing as it broke through his guard and sliced a raking gash up his sword arm, sprinkling yet more crimson droplets over the reddening stones of the courtyard. Rowène bit her lip and dared not take her eyes from her brother, lest he be killed.

He seemed to have matters under control, however. Tightening his grip on the slippery sword hilt, he aimed a cut at his opponent's chest, this one coming close enough to slice through the finely woven cloth, although it fell a hair's breadth short of drawing blood. Stepping back, Guy's boot slipped in the trickle of something noisome, and as his guard dropped, Luc drew his arm back for the final killing blow.

"Luc, no!" Rowène screamed.

Visibly dragging himself from the red killing fury that had engulfed him, Luc stared at her, grey eyes widening in blank disbelief.

"You cannot kill him!" she reiterated, stepping warily between the two panting men.

"Not kill the bastard who raped my sister?" Luc exploded, eyes narrowing once more to merciless steel as he glanced from the sliver of scarlet that showed between the parted folds of the black mantle she wore to her unbound, uncovered hair and the very visible abrasion on her cheek. "Hell'sdeath, Ro! Have you run mad? Even if I could not see the result for myself, I *know* what happened here last night! Just as I know now who this bastard scum really is! Or do you mean to deny that too?"

"No, why should I?" Rowène cried, fisting her hands in the folds of the black cloak, heedless now of the garment's ownership, seeking only to conceal what lay beneath. "Yes, he is Jacques de Rogé's son. But I swear by the God of Light he never touched me!"

Her brother's eyes narrowed still further, as if to say *if not him, then who?* But to her relief he did not ask the question out loud. Instead he allowed his sword point to drop very slightly as he warily reassessed the other man. Narrow dark brows lifted and then he said derisively,

"So that is the way of it? Incapable of bedding a woman, is he? Perhaps his tastes lie in other directions. I hear they have a lot of sheep in Rogé!" He swore as a nearly spent arrow hissed past his ear and, with a final glare that promised retribution when his sister was not around to stay his sword, added through gritted teeth, "You owe my sister a life. Remember that, Bastard."

With that he grabbed at the gelding's trailing reins, hauled himself back into the saddle, wheeled the grey and plunged back into the heart of the battle again.

Rowène watched him go, fear for him once more replacing the disorientating determination that had impelled her to prevent him from taking Guyard de Martine's life. She turned to the man beside her, not knowing quite what she meant to say, but his attention had snapped back to the swirling tide of the battle.

"Get back inside!" he ordered brusquely without looking at her. "And this time stay there! No matter what happens!"

Swept by a storm of contradictory emotions, Rowène stumbled back inside and sank down onto the pile of straw, no longer caring whether it was clean or not. All she could do now was pray...

It was the silence that finally restored numbed nerves and sound-deadened ears to some sense of awareness. Scrambling to her feet, Rowène lurched to the stable door. She had to know who had won the battle for Chartre castle – or even how much of it survived for the victors, whoever they might be, to crow over...

She felt her heart drop away into the depths of despair at the sight that met her eyes. In a clear blue sky marred only by a few shreds and wisps of smoke that leaked from the split and blackened stones of what had once been the Lady Tower, the sun soared hot and high, shining down with a merciless brightness onto a courtyard choked with the bodies of the dead and dying – men and horses – of both sides.

Neither wanting, nor even capable of believing the evidence of her burning eyes, she drew in an unwary breath and found herself gagging as the mingled stench of blood and ordure, smoke and sweat – the whole foul spectrum of violent death – hit her stomach.

"Gods, Luc!"

But there was no way of telling where his body might be if he was dead and she was almost certain he would not wish to be among the captured living. There was a small knot of them, she saw, gathered by the whipping post next to the south wall, their arms bound behind them. More were being herded or dragged there, depending on their ability to move independently, by soldiers in de Rogé black. She did not want to go over there and face the truth but knew she had no choice if she would learn Luc's fate.

Having come to this frightening decision she took a step in that direction, only to be brought up short by the grip of a hard, calloused hand on her arm. She would not have been surprised to see the Daemon of Hell himself come to collect the souls of the dead but as it was it was only Guyard de Martine.

Not that he resembled in the slightest the gentle harper she had once known. He had sheathed his sword but the evidence of the violence he had engaged in lay all about him; Rowène counted four crumpled bodies at least and his once fine leaf-green tunic was liberally splattered with blood, some of it quite clearly his!

His short fair hair stood up in wet, dark spikes and his clean-shaven face was drawn and streaked with sweat and dirt. A deep frown was carved between his dark blond brows and his mouth held a white, grim tension that echoed the pain in his light blue eyes, the source of which was not hard to find. Rowène peered at the long, ugly gash that had opened his sword arm from wrist to elbow and fought nausea. And if that were not enough she thought there must be another wound on his thigh, although it was difficult to tell how serious it might be since it was partially concealed by the skirts of his tunic.

Evidently he saw the horror in her eyes but completely misinterpreted the cause. Before she could verbalise her first instinctive offer to help him, he had loosed his hold on her arm and now leant back against the stable wall, struggling with his one sound hand and wounded arm to tear a strip from his shirt to serve as a makeshift bandage.

"I am sure you would rather see me dead at your feet, together with both my brothers," he grated. "But if you can bring yourself to bind up my arm I will not hold that desire against you."

"Your brothers, yes," she agreed bitterly, stepping forwards. "You... perhaps not."

Coming closer, she resolutely finished ripping a broad strip from the bottom of his linen shirt and bound the torn flesh of his arm as best she could. But when she would have knelt in order to get at the wound on his thigh he warded her off with his good hand.

"Leave it! It is not fitting you do this... just give me the bandage."

"As if I had not already seen you naked and shared a bed with you!" she reminded him briskly as she brushed his protest aside, folding the torn cloth of his breeches away from the wound. She did not think there was any debris caught within but knew there was little enough that she could do for the time being save bind it. Later, she – or perhaps one of the other castle women – must cleanse and tend it properly but for now all she had was what slight power she had inherited from the Moon Goddess of the Faennari and if she could waste it on Ranulf de Rogé, assuredly she could spare some of her care for his half-brother.

Gently and as unobtrusively as possible she ran her fingers along the wound, then pushed her straggling hair out of her eyes and staggered back to her feet, feeling as if she had lived ten lifetimes in one morning.

"There, it is done. If the gods are kind," She did not think she dared invoke the Moon Goddess in his hearing "You will not take a wound fever and, like your father, die at the hands of a de Chartreux." She hesitated then forced herself to address the issue she had held in abeyance whilst she tended her family's enemy. "Guy? Do you know what has happened to Luc? Or Lucien?"

"No," he replied, his voice rasping across her raw nerves. "I have no idea. But if I were you I would be praying to the gods that neither of them yet lives to suffer the revenge Joffroi will enact upon them for this day's work. Because, believe me, he will be furious! As to yourself, for gods' sake, do nothing to draw his temper down on you, since I doubt extremely whether he will listen to either Ran or myself while his blood is still hot."

Rowène nodded but her stricken gaze was already flitting over the crumpled dead and the wounded living, searching for her brother and half-brother. The sound of Black Joffroi's smoke-hoarsened voice roaring from the top of the steps that led into the keep made her start, her gaze flying from the assembled prisoners to the huge, black-armoured, blood-soaked beast who was now unquestionably Lord of Chartreux as well as Rogé.

"Luc de Chartreux! Show yourself! Beg for mercy on your knees and I will let your men live! Defy me still and I will hang every one of your miscreants from the walls of this castle, alive and as naked as the day they were born, and you can watch while the seagulls peck at their eyes and genitals!" A moment of silence, then his deep voice rang out again. "Ranulf! Where are you, man?"

"Here, Joff."

Another voice so changed she would not have recognised it and, in spite of her companion's warning to remain inconspicuous, Rowène could not restrain the sob of horror these words aroused in her, the realisation that Ranulf de Rogé had survived the carnage merely making her even more nauseous.

"Right, Ran!" That was Black Joffroi's voice again, issuing his hoarse orders. "Get the first of the prisoners strung up and keep going until de Chartreux comes forward or they are all dead!"

Rowène started forwards with a whimpering moan and felt Guy drag her back against him, his filthy, blood-streaked hand coming up to cover her mouth. From that uncomfortable imprisonment she watched as one of the Chartreux prisoners – she thought it might have been Luc's squire Nick, although it was difficult to tell – spat defiantly at the nearest black-clad soldier, only to be brutally kicked in the ribs by a man in rent mail she would never have recognised as Ranulf de Rogé save for the tangle of pale, blood-matted hair spilling over his shoulders and half-way down his back.

Struggling to free herself, she heard Guy swear as he tightened his grasp but a murderous rage had now burnt out her fear and she no longer cared what happened to her. Despite his wounds she found she could not break his hold and reluctantly had to yield to the knowledge that she was no match for his greater strength – just as, in other circumstances, she had not been for Ranulf's – and, gasping for breath, she abandoned the struggle even as Black Joffroi's taunting voice rang out again.

"Well, de Chartreux, are you not willing to stand up and die for your men? Or do you wish to prove yourself as much a spineless, gutless worm as your father did when he went to the scaffold, begging on his knees for his life!"

Despite Joffroi's jeering demand the prisoners under guard by the stable wall continued to hold their silence. Guyard only wished the woman in his arms would follow their example since she was now almost choking with suppressed rage as well as lack of breath and he was hard put to hold her one-armed.

Rapidly reviewing his options he muttered another heart-felt curse and, tugging Rowène unceremoniously with him, limped over to his older brother. Joffroi regarded him for a moment in silence, his dark eyes unreadable, his heavy jaw set hard.

"I am in no mood for mercy," he warned. "So save your breath, Guy!"

"As if I would be fool enough to ask," Guyard replied roughly. "But it is quite possible that you are wasting your time, Joff, and that de Chartreux is already beyond your reach. The gods know there are enough dead or dying men out there."

Joffroi swept the courtyard with a look of black disgust, muttering curses as he chewed at his lip.

"Very well," he growled, coming to a decision. "Ranulf! Here, man!" And when their brother came over, a look of enquiry on his filthy, blood-streaked face. "Hurry up and get this scum sorted between carrion and gallows-meat and then Guy can get his doxy to pick out her brother!"

"My do...?" Guyard echoed, belated comprehension being swiftly replaced by incredulous distaste. "God of Light, Joff, you cannot expect her to do that! Not knowing that her word will see him handed over, first to the torturer and then the hangman!"

Joffroi merely laughed callously.

"Given a choice between identifying her brother or going first to Ranulf's bed and then to the rest of the garrison when he leaves, she might decide to co-operate. And since you are more familiar with the whelp than either Ran or I, I will need you to verify her identification." He gave the girl a malevolent look. "I do not trust Louis de Chartreux's daughter as far as I can see her. How you do it is up to you but mark this, Guy, I am making you responsible for finding Luc de Chartreux before you even think of leaving for Rogérinac. Ariène would do it, of course, but I would not willingly subject her to any further distress this day."

"Indeed, and where is the Lady Ariène?" Guyard asked, suddenly curious as to why she had not appeared to witness her lover's triumph, since – notwithstanding Joffroi's reluctance to upset his paramour's delicate sensibilities – he had little doubt that the Lady Ariène was perfectly capable of identifying her son and thus sending him to the gallows far more cold-bloodedly than he ever could.

"She was in the tower when the fire broke out," Joffroi replied, continuing to glare darkly at her daughter. "She must have inhaled too much smoke before I could get her out and she is still in a deep swoon. Her maids are looking after her in the hall now. As for the green-eyed bitch who set that fire, all I can say is that it is a damned shame that she is already dead since I would fain burn her alive myself!"

"What green-eyed bitch?" Guyard asked blankly. The only green-eyed bitch he could think of was Ariène de Chartreux – not that he was rash enough to say so to his besotted brother.

"Oh, come now, Guy. Not you too!" Joffroi growled just as Rowène dragged her mouth free from his slackened hold long enough draw sufficient breath to say pointedly,

"I think you will find your foul-mouthed brother means my sister by that discourteous description."

"But surely you cannot think it was Demoiselle Juliène?" Guyard asked in disbelief. "For gods'sake, Joff! She must have been one of the first to die in that inferno!"

"Well, that fire did not start itself," Joffroi replied moodily. "And it could not have been your doxy because she was with either you or Ran the whole time, although I do not doubt she would have burned the place down around our ears if she could have managed it!" he finished darkly, glowering at what had, just that morning, been a fitting symbol of the wealth and power of the new Lord of Chartreux but which now appeared of less worth and stability than the slowly disintegrating fortress Jacques de Rogé's three sons had grown up in.

"Hell and damnation, Guy! What a bloody mess! And neither you nor Ran need have any thought of buggering off to Lamortaine or Rogérinac or anywhere else until this place is secure and habitable again. Sod the prince and sod the harvest. I need my garrison commander and my steward here!"

With which blistering assertion Joffroi stalked off across the courtyard, heading for the place where Ranulf was grimly supervising his men as they ordered the living from the dead, presumably to give him the unwelcome news that rather than leaving that day to join the rest of the Mithlondian army as he had planned, he would be remaining in Chartre for the foreseeable future.

Once Joffroi was out of earshot Guyard cautiously loosened his grip on Rowène's wrist, although he did not release her completely. He shot one look at her tear-stained face and hastily looked away again.

"Come along, we may as well get this over with. This is one task I would not hand over to your mother, even should she choose to step out into this shambles."

Rowène returned his gaze with all the hatred he had expected. Her mouth curled contemptuously as she said unsteadily,

"I wish now I had kept quiet earlier and let Luc kill you when he had the chance! He spared your life and in return you are going to betray him to a dishonourable death!"

Guyard set his jaw but said nothing, either in confirmation or denial of Rowène's bitter accusation, merely hauling her alongside him to the grisly task awaiting them. He was utterly weary of this whole bloody business as, once again, he found himself treading the fine line between his sworn duty to his brother and the demands of his own conscience.

Picking his way as best he might between the sprawled bodies of the dead, he determined to start his search with the living. Reaching the area where the prisoners were being kept under guard he paused to survey the score or so of men sitting or lying in the full glare of the noon-tide sun. Despite their defeat they were an arrogant lot, and he had little doubt that Joffroi would order Ranulf to hang them all before the day was out, whether he succeeded in his quest to find Luc de Chartreux or not.

Flashing a rapidly assessing look over them Guyard was relieved to see that most of the faces were unfamiliar to him. Although not all. He was also as certain as he could be in the circumstances that Rowène's half-brother Lucien was not one of them, although he did recognise Luc's squire, Nick, who was hunched over, nursing what was possibly a set of broken ribs. As casually as possible he allowed his gaze to go beyond the wounded squire, passing disinterestedly over the unconscious man who had been flung down in an untidy sprawl of limbs beside him.

And swore silently as he heard the sudden, sharp intake of breath from the girl at his side. Frowning, he risked another look at the insensible man. Even from this distance it was plain to see that he had taken a nasty cut to his head and how he had escaped death Guyard did not know, since if the amount of blood matting the black hair and masking the left side of his face was any indication, he should have been dead long before now.

Fortunately for his purposes, Ranulf's men had stripped the prisoners of their mail and weapons before binding them at wrist and ankle, and if the unconscious man had once worn a nobleman's spurs, these had long since disappeared into some rogue's pouch and were unlikely ever to be seen again. There was nothing left to define the man's rank save for the length – and possibly the colour – of his raven-dark hair. But *that* was surely enough to identify him, curse it!

Guyard rapidly reviewed his options then, after another fleeting glance to ascertain that Joffroi was nowhere in sight and that Ranulf was sufficiently occupied with his own unenviable task, limped over to the single soldier who had been left to keep an eye on the prisoners and said crisply,

"Ah, Geryth!"

"Yes, sir?"

"Look after Lady Rowena for a moment, will you. I want to speak to one of the prisoners."

"What? Ye want me ter look after...?"

Geryth gulped and turned an alarmed eye on the young noblewoman, her fiery hair tumbling in wild curls around her pale, smoke-smudged face, bright against the black of her borrowed mantle. His troubled brown eyes fastened on the heavy silver brooch at her shoulder before returning reluctantly to meet Guyard's impatient gaze.

"Ye wants me ter look after a wi... Your... Com... The lady?" he repeated.

"Yes, you!" Guyard said firmly, having followed the young man's false starts with increasing irritation. "Damn it, Geryth, you said it yourself. She is a high-born lady, not a witch! Or anyone's leman. Not mine. Not Commander Ranulf's. Now, take her arm, treat her with the care and respect you would wish for Gerde and all will be well. But, for gods'sake, do not let her go!" he warned. "Lord Joffroi will have your balls, and mine, if she escapes."

He handed Rowène into Geryth's charge and, had the situation not been so serious, he would have been tempted to laugh at the wary manner in which the soldier took possession of her wrist, flinching quite visibly as he felt a lock of that flaming hair brush his bare hand; ample evidence that the young man was still more than half convinced that he was manhandling a dangerous witch who would curse his manhood as soon as look at him! Not that Guyard believed such old wives' tales but then again, he supposed wryly, even a myth must have some basis in fact.

He kept the unlikely pair under observation for a moment or two but Rowène appeared to have accepted her change of circumstances without demur and Geryth was plainly too agitated by his new charge to worry about anything else, least of all what Guyard might be about.

Left with the freedom to carry out his tentative plan, Guyard began to pick his way amongst the prisoners. He sensed rather than saw Rowène's sudden, convulsive movement – presumably she had seen her brother and feared what he, Guyard, might intend to do – but he continued to make his halting progress, in seeming random fashion, through the men, stooping every now and again to peer into a scowling or pain-racked face.

Finally he stopped beside de Chartreux's squire and rather painfully dropped to one knee beside the unmoving body of the man Joffroi wanted to hang – if not worse. The prisoner was lying partly on his side, in the same position as Ranulf's men had thrown him, his face almost hidden by a mixture of blood, caked dirt and hair. Twining the sticky dark hanks around his fist and, bending lower until his broad back was almost certainly obscuring the view of anyone who might be watching, Guyard quickly sliced through the hair at neck level, losing the shorn strands as best he might down the back of the other's tunic. Straightening slightly, he spared one brief, antagonistic glance for Luc's squire, saw the flicker of confused comprehension in the other man's brown eyes and braced himself.

With a growled "Let him alone, you bloody bastard!" the squire spat with considerable accuracy into Guyard's face.

Even as he raised his bandaged arm to wipe his wet cheek his ears caught the distinctive jingle of spurs and he cursed silently. Damn it, he did not need Ranulf caught up in this folly too. He pushed to his feet as fast as his wounded leg would allow but there was little he could do to prevent his brother's sorely-tried temper from exploding into violence. He winced as Ranulf hauled the burly squire to his feet as easily as if he had been a rag-doll and backhanded him across the face, the viciousness of the blow only ameliorated by the fact that Ran had already discarded his mailed gauntlets and in all probability inflicted as much pain on himself as he did his victim.

"Learn to use some respect, scum, when you speak to my brother!" Ranulf snarled before releasing his hold on the prisoner who promptly collapsed into a groaning, cursing crumple of limbs.

"There was no need for that," Guyard murmured. "I asked for it when all is said and done."

"Do you think I do not know that," Ranulf snapped, absently shaking his smarting fingers. "Otherwise I would have broken his neck!" He looked around the grim scene, taking in Geryth's obvious discomfort at his commander's sudden arrival and the white-faced young woman whose wrist the lad was still holding. Then he returned his gaze to his brother, paying no attention to the prisoners at all.

"So... any sign of de Chartreux?" Ranulf queried, holding Guyard's eyes.

Guyard hesitated, flicked the briefest of glances to make sure Luc's face was completely hidden by his squire's fallen body, raised his eyes to meet Ranulf's narrowed gaze and shook his head.

"No. I thought it might be this one..." He nudged Luc's limp leg with the toe of his boot. "But it is not."

"Well, by the looks of him he is near dead as makes no odds anyway," his brother replied with a disparaging glance of his own. "And Joff wants a living man he can make an example of, curse it." He swore again, more savagely, and raked back the escaped strands of sweaty, tangled hair that framed his equally filthy face and were obviously irritating him as much as the situation. "Do not get me wrong, Guy," he said in a voice meant to carry as far as Geryth and his charge and any of the men-at-arms within earshot. "I do not give a toss one way or another but it would mayhap have sweetened Joff's temper if we could have presented him with Luc de Chartreux. Damn it all, Guy, I wish I had never laid eyes on this cursed place! And have you heard the worst of it? Joffroi now wants me to stay here and oversee the rebuilding of this witch's den."

"Never mind, Ran," Guyard forced a lighter note into his voice. "I am sure being left in charge of Chartre will have its compensations – the wine here is better for one thing! But I suggest you stay away from the dockside brothels unless you want to catch the pox!"

"Speaking from experience, are you?" queried Ranulf with a grin that was not quite as chancy as his previous remarks. "After all, you were here in Chartre for... how long? A month at least? Plenty of time to sample the local whores."

"You know damned well I did nothing of the kind," Guyard retorted, although without any particular rancour; this being an old argument between him and his brother and one which would be more than familiar to any of the soldiers who might still be listening to them.

"More fool you then," Ranulf gibed. Then the bantering note left his voice as he cast another disgusted look around the shambles of the courtyard. "We may as well get this finished. Bring the wench and we will go and look through the bodies. He has to be here somewhere and the mood Joff is in he will keep us all here until they start rotting. We need to find de Chartreux, and since you say he is not alive, he must be amongst the dead."

Guyard briefly considered remonstrating against the necessity of forcing a delicately-reared young noblewoman to inspect a succession of gruesome bodies but the dour set to Ranulf's mouth did not encourage argument and, with a grimace, he relieved Geryth of his prisoner.

Rowène's dilated gaze *had* been fixed on the crumpled bodies of her brother and his squire but as Guyard's fingers closed about her wrist she started violently and frowned up at him. He could see that she was unsure what to conclude from his actions or from those parts of the conversation she had been able to overhear between Ranulf and himself. He tried to convey some measure of reassurance in the light pressure of his fingers and was relieved when she allowed him to lead her without protest along the untidy line of bodies that Ranulf's men had made. He did not, however, fail to note that her steps were growing ever more unsteady as they progressed past the mutilated corpses while her face, already pale with strain, was beginning to take on a distinctly greenish tinge.

When Ranulf halted about half-way down the line, Guyard stopped too, shot a keen glance at his brother's set face and then looked down.

"Well?" Ranulf queried with a callousness Guyard was completely certain was feigned. He bent as he spoke and withdrew the thin knife he kept in his boot, making some show of pausing to clean the blood and dirt from under his fingernails. "Is this him?"

It was evident that anything else aside, he had as little wish as Guyard to waste his time inspecting shattered, stinking corpses and wanted to get this unpleasant task finished as soon as possible. Or at least that was impression he generated. Guyard experienced a moment of doubt; he believed Ranulf knew what he was about – and even agreed with his actions – but it behoved them both to tread exceedingly carefully in this matter.

Dropping his gaze, Guyard skimmed a wary glance over the blood-soaked figure at his feet; hair the colour of a raven's feathers a dark spill against the dirty cobbles, one grey eye staring up at the sweet summer blue of the sky from the raw wreckage of a once handsome face. He found himself totally unable to speak lest the bile burning at the back of his throat spew forth but he managed to catch his brother's eye, giving him an infinitesimal nod.

He saw Ranulf glance towards the girl standing between them, a muscle twitching in his clenched jaw, a look that was frighteningly close to indecision flitting through his dark blue eyes. The next moment he had regained control of his face and said, with a note of terse indifference in his voice that might have fooled Guyard had he not known his brother so well, and if he had not already seen that other expression in his eyes,

"Black hair, grey eyes, what is left of the face looks like Louis de Chartreux! Well, wench?"

"What?" she whispered faintly.

"Open your eyes, curse you, and look!" Ranulf snapped, darting a warning glare at Guyard as he opened his mouth to protest his brother's brutal speech. "I do not have time to pander to your sensibilities."

Slowly the girl forced open the eyes Guyard – and probably Ran as well – knew she had shut after the first body, took one look at the ravaged features of Lucien of Chartre, retched helplessly and brought up what little there was in her stomach all over Ranulf's boots, causing him to swear viciously enough to make Guyard, let alone a gently-reared young woman blench, before snarling,

"Take her away, Guy, before I treat her as she deserves! Wine I can put up with but not vomit!"

"Gods above, have some pity, Ran!" Guyard snapped, his eyes on the white-faced, weeping girl.

With an effort that shot sheer agony up his sword arm, he lifted her shaking body in his embrace, afraid that she might swoon at any moment. He looked up to meet his brother's narrow, glittering eyes.

"A word of advice," Ranulf commented in biting accents. "Dump the little witch with her bitch of a mother and get one of the castle women to tend those gashes of yours properly. Then ride out of this accursed place before the sun has set. With half his new property gone up in smoke Joffroi will need you in Rogérinac, wringing what profits you can from this summer's harvest, though doubtless he will expect me to stay here and whip the servants into line in your stead. As for Luc de Chartreux..." He hesitated, then straightened his shoulders, almost as if anticipating the sting of a lash. "It is probably best if I tell Joffroi that the whelp is beyond his vengeance. He will take my word more readily than he will yours, since of the two of us I am not the one bewitched by a traitor's daughter and Joff knows it."

He flicked a disparaging glance at the girl he thus maligned but there was something else – some fleeting shadow of emotion – behind the careful mask of indifference that Guyard could not quite identify. Nor did Ranulf give him the opportunity to discover what it might be.

"I am not like you, Guy," he continued sardonically. "And never have been. One woman is much the same as another as far as I am concerned. So long as they keep my bed warm and do not bother me between beddings, that is good enough for me."

Worn with fatigue, stress and in a considerable amount of pain, Guyard allowed his long-standing vexation with his brother's casual approach to women to finally get the better of him.

"One day, Ran, you will meet a woman who will mean more to you than that. A woman you will want to share your life, not just your bed. And unless you make some effort to change your ways, I doubt very much whether she will have you."

"Daemons of Hell, I hope not!" Ranulf retorted, his gaze returning to the now quiet girl in Guyard's arms. "Not for me the cosy hearth fire, the bonds of binding, or worse yet a brat I never wanted…" His voice faltered momentarily then he went on. "Who will take his mother from my bed and expect me to act as a father should." There had been an odd, bleak note in his voice as he said these words but when he lifted his gaze, there was only mockery in his eyes. "No, Brother, that is not for me, even if it might be the sum of your ambition." He cocked his head. "Perhaps Joff was right when he said that all these peculiar notions of yours stem from Father's allowing you to spend so much time playing that bloody harp and talking to the minstrels at court, rather than tumbling the serving wenches or practicing your sword skills with the rest of us."

He gave a snort of disgust and turned sharply away. Guyard let him go. He knew Ranulf was not so lacking in finer feelings as his words might indicate. Knew too that he would regret that final ugly flash of temper. Just as he obviously regretted the part he had been forced to play in this bloodbath.

Not that he, Guyard, was blameless. He too must take some responsibility for this bloody mess. He had brought unhappiness and havoc to more lives than his own when he had come to Chartre and he could mend nothing by staying. The best thing he could do now – in fact the only sensible thing left to him – was to do as his brother had advised and ride back to Rogérinac and Mathilde, leaving Rowène in Chartre in Ranulf's charge. He only hoped she might be able to find some peace eventually and that when gossip reached Lamortaine – as it inevitably would – Joscelin de Veraux would deal fairly with her. But if he had no power to influence her betrothal there was yet one thing he could do for her before he left.

"Ran! Wait!"

His brother swung round to face him, his blood-streaked face set in uncompromising lines. Then something flickered in his bloodshot blue eyes and he strode back towards Guyard.

"Give me the wench," he said brusquely. "You cannot carry her with that arm of yours. You have already bled through the binding and milksop though you may be, you are still my brother and I do not want your death on my conscience."

"I did not think you had one," Guyard gibed, handing his burden over with barely concealed relief.

"Neither did I," Ranulf muttered with a darkling glance at the pale face of the nearly unconscious girl in his arms. Then, on a different note. "What did you call me back for anyway?"

"The prisoners. If Joff is not set on hanging them all perhaps they could be put to better use. You mentioned the need for money and I happen to know there is a trading ship from the Eastern Isles down in the harbour. Or there was yesterday. If it is still there…"

His brother's eyes narrowed as he considered the situation.

"I do not doubt that Joff would still prefer to hang the lot of them," he said, his blunt words serving to still the feeble struggles of the girl in his arms. "If only as an example to the rest of the Chartreux folk that it is not wise to antagonise their new lord. On the other hand," he continued dispassionately, shifting his hold. "I think I can make him see the disadvantages of pushing our young Prince too far, too fast. And while de Chartreux is dead, his influence gone, Jean de Marillec and Nicholas de Vézière are still respected members of the High Counsel and, I would judge, both capable of making a nuisance of themselves in a number of ways, not least in turning Linnius against us if Joffroi is not very careful. That being so... that is not a bad idea of yours, Guy!" His voice turned crisp. "I will send Guthlaf down to the harbour straight away to speak to the ship's master. And I will speak to Joff, suggest that he sells the prisoners for what he can get and though I doubt that rag-tag lot will fetch much in their present condition, even a handful of silver is better than more dead bodies. Especially in this weather!"

"And Demoiselle Rowène?" Guyard asked, smitten by a sudden qualm.

"I will look after her," Ranulf promised, a shade grimly, Guyard thought. "At least whilst I am in Chartre. I do not know what will happen to her when I leave and I can hardly take her with me on campaign." He gave Guy an evil grin. "Or can I? No, I see from your face that you do not like that idea! Well then, she will have to stay here and take her chances and, I suppose, it is always possible, although unlikely, that de Veraux may be induced to accept a soiled bride. No, you cannot hit me Guy, not while I have a wench in my arms." The levity left his voice abruptly and he was grimly serious again. "Until then, however, I will do what I can to keep her safe – if not from me at least from that ice-blooded bitch whose bloody web we are all caught in. Go home, Guy, you have done all you can here. Mathilde and the harvest await and that is more than enough trouble to deal with, without worrying about..." He hesitated, then added in the Rogé vernacular. "About this poor lass. And you have my word, I will not touch her."

Knowing that this was the best he was likely to achieve – and somewhat reassured by his brother's concluding words – Guyard nodded his agreement and, with a pang, limped away.

# Chapter 12

## *A Promise Given and a Farewell Taken*

Matters, perhaps not unnaturally – given that there was nothing either natural or normal about this whole accursed affair – did not go quite as Ranulf had hoped when he had decided to back Guy's plan.

By the grace of the gods and the most pragmatic arguments he could put forward, he did eventually succeed in persuading his irate older brother that a public perception of mercy towards the defeated Chartreux soldiery might be more advantageous than mass slaughter – especially when such a seemingly magnanimous action would put some much-needed silver into his almost empty coffers.

Moving swiftly before Joffroi could change his mind – and reluctant to have Guthlaf held to blame if his act of deliberate deceit went wrong – Ranulf had escorted the prisoners down to the harbour himself, then sat watching impassively from the dockside as they were loaded onto the slaver's ship and shackled in the stinking hold. The ship, he was assured by the grinning, dark-skinned captain, would sail on the very next tide.

The sun was still high in the sky, albeit slipping westwards rapidly, when he returned to the castle. He found Guthlaf supervising the clean-up operation amidst much cursing from the men-at-arms detailed to remove the reeking bodies, and Guy leaning against the mounting block outside the stables, arms folded across his chest, an uncharacteristic scowl knitting his thick fair brows while he waited – or so Ranulf guessed – for his horse to be readied.

Although, since Ranulf knew his brother was perfectly capable of saddling his own mount...

"What has that ungrateful wench been about now?" he asked brusquely. "Someone has put you in a temper! And do not waste your breath telling me that *she...*" He dared not speak her name. "Is not behind it."

Guy pushed off the block but did not look at him, his heavy frown being directed towards the ruins of the tower and the partially damaged keep.

"Not Rowène," he muttered, the mere sound of that name on his brother's tongue stabbing Ranulf deep in the gut. "Or at least," Guy amended. "I do not think so. The order came from Joffroi so no doubt Madame Ariène is behind it."

"Behind what, damn it?" Ranulf demanded.

But this time Guy did not answer him at all, merely turning his head to indicate the stable door through which a sullen-looking groom was now leading his chestnut stallion. And behind that another man. Geryth – *his* bloody man-at-arms when all was said and done – holding the reins of another horse; the pretty, honey-coloured mare Ranulf recognised as the mount Rowène had been riding the day before.

Comprehension hit him like a blow in the belly and he swore with a savage intensity that took even him by surprise.

"For once, Ran, I agree with you," Guy said in biting tones before adding bleakly, "The gods help me, what am I going to do with her in Rogérinac? Even aside from the ramshackle state of the castle itself, Mathilde is bound to take her in dislike."

"Because, gossip being what it is, your wife is bound to hear that you spent the night in another woman's bed and will accordingly believe that woman to be your mistress?" Ranulf asked, his gut tightening into a knot of pain he did his best to ignore. Nevertheless, he thought it entirely possible that Mathilde would recognise immediately that Rowène de Chartreux was no virgin. The addition of that undeniable fact to the inevitable rumours would give Guy's bitch of a wife cause in plenty to put the blame for that deflowering firmly on Guy's shoulders – where it definitely did not belong – thus bringing yet more disharmony to his brother's binding.

*Hell and damnation! What a bloody tangle! And bugger all I can do about it!*

Telling the truth was unlikely to cause Mathilde to look upon Guy with any more favour and would only serve to drive a wedge between him and the brother whom he had always regarded as the other, better, half of himself. As for Rowène de Chartreux, he could only pray that three seasons from now she would not give birth to a child of his seed – however bloody impossible such a bloody awful consequence of those few fleeting moments of fucking madness should be!

Some instinct he had not known he answered to drew his gaze up towards the warm harebell blue of the afternoon sky, where the palest hint of a silver face looked down on him, causing a wraith-cold finger of premonition to shiver the length of his spine.

Daemons of Hell! Perhaps all that nonsense his wet-nurse had muttered concerning the forbidden powers of the Moon Goddess of the Faennari had some substance after all! He had never paid much heed to old Hilarie's stories but after his experiences of the previous night and the hellish morning that had followed, he was suddenly less inclined to scoff at such legends of the immortal maidens of forest, stream and sea as he dimly remembered; sprites, sirens and enchantresses, all with hair like dark red flame...

As if that thought had called them up – he spared a scowling glance up at the pale moon – he saw two women coming towards him. Two women whose uncovered hair flickered like flame. The Witch herself and the witchling she must have in training!

Despite the appalling stench of spilt blood and voided bowels that clung to the still foul cobbles over which they trod, both women appeared composed, if rather pale. But whereas the older woman's pallor merely served to emphasise her unearthly beauty, her daughter's unnatural lack of colour was – or so Ranulf surmised as they came nearer and he caught his first clear sight of her face – the result of shock rather than her cold-blooded manipulation of the situation.

Her thin face was so completely bloodless... her grey eyes so utterly empty of all expression...

He had seen them like that once before but when? Memory hit him as he saw again the look in her eyes the moment he had brutally forced his way into her body, shattering her soul in a single heartbeat...

Daemons of Hell take him and bind him! What had he been thinking to do such a thing!

Fighting to conceal the cramping pain of guilt that shot through his gut – he had raped her, he must not also betray her – he dragged his gaze from her face, feeling a moment's irrational relief when he realised that, despite everything, she was still wearing his mantle, the distinctive silver brooch secure on her shoulder.

The pain eased a little more with the realisation that – to judge from the disgruntled expression on the youth's face – Geryth was to be part of the escort accompanying her to Rogérinac. He would, however, make sure of that and have a private word with Geryth before he left.

Repressing the urge to double over – the pain, although less, was still there, mercilessly twisting and knotting his guts – he told himself that all was as well as could be in such a damnable situation. And perhaps it would be a better resolution – for him at least, and maybe even for her... for Rowène, if she went to Rogérinac under Guy's care.

Once away from Chartre *she* might forget the man who had raped her and *he* might possibly come to forgive himself for the terrible wrong he had done an innocent young noblewoman.

*On my death-bed*, he thought grimly, and turned to bark an order at the glowering groom to ready his own mount.

He would escort them as far as the Swanfleet Bridge, he decided, and make his formal farewells out of that green-eyed, cold-blooded witch's hearing. To Guy he need say little, he knew, but he wanted to make sure that Rowène de Chartreux remembered her promise to him!

The sun was dipping towards a pale silver horizon as Rowène and her black-garbed escort finally approached the Swanfleet Bridge.

She had left the smoke-blackened, blood-soaked ruins of her home in a state of almost total apathy, her only emotion a sort of vague gratitude that she would not have to travel to Lamortaine – as had briefly been considered – in company with Black Joffroi and the Winter Lady. Even remaining in Chartre under Ranulf de Rogé's brutal rule would have been preferable to that.

Instead, she was being sent away with the man she had once thought herself in love with, leaving her birthplace for his home, where his wife would be waiting for him. Was that better or worse than being left with his ruthless half-brother, she wondered, but without much interest in discovering the answer to that or any other question that slipped almost unnoticed through her dazed mind.

She had travelled the quiet green lanes aware of nothing save the weight of dark depression that lay heavy on her heart. She did not hear the larks piping in the soft blue of the late afternoon sky nor smell the pale gold fragrance of the meadowsweet that frothed against the legs of the men's mounts as they passed. Her ears were still filled with the crackle of fire and the sounds of battle, her eyes blinded by the memory of blood – blood against stone, blood against flesh, blood everywhere – while her nose was overwhelmed by the fiercely masculine aroma of hot horse, oiled mail and stale sweat; none of the men of her escort having had the time to wash. Or perhaps they were so accustomed to their own foul odour that they no longer noticed it.

Yet, with that thought, she realised she was beginning to turn her attention outwards once more. Why else should the rank stink of her escort cause her discomfort? At the same time her proximity to the scene of yesterday's initial bloodshed caused other feelings, sharp as dagger points, to slice through her determined indifference, shredding the shield she held over her soul.

For the first time since she had stood, coughing against the smoky smitch of the great hall, and learned that she was to leave Chartre for Rogérinac under Guyard de Martine's escort she became truly aware, with all her senses, of the two men who rode, one on either side of her. Silent though they were she found she could ignore them no longer, hate and despise them both though she did.

She knew the reason for Guyard's presence but, dear God of Light, why was his half-brother riding with them? And how far did he mean to go?

She had heard enough of various people's hastily contrived plans to know that de Rogé had been ordered to remain in Chartre, overseeing the building work and the governing of the province in his older brother's stead while Black Joffroi and her mother travelled to Lamortaine to seek Prince Linnius' approval of their binding. Not that Rowène entertained any doubts that the new prince would give it.

Whatever had happened in Lamortaine to cause Prince Marcus' death, precipitate her father's execution and ultimately engender the dark madness of the past two days, she knew her mother was at the core of it. The Winter Lady might have been a hundred leagues from Lamortaine at the time, serenely stitching new raiment for her lover, but her power ran deeper than mere distance. And Black Joffroi *had* been in Lamortaine, Rowène reminded herself grimly, together with his debauched and degenerate brother.

Alerted by the change in timbre as the horses moved onto the bridge, she clenched her jaw against the onset of nausea, hastily averting her eyes from the ugly splotch on the parapet that marked the site of the toll-keeper's murder but suddenly felt she could go no further. Before she could draw rein however, the man riding on her left evidently sensed that she was about to baulk and leaned over, grabbing the mare's reins in his gauntleted hand.

A startled, angry protest rose to her lips but catching a glimpse of the steely expression glinting in his dark blue eyes Rowène swallowed the words and allowed de Rogé to do as he would, turning her face sharply away from him and a yard or two past the gruesome stain he wordlessly released his grip on her reins and she found she could breathe again.

As they continued across the bridge, the broken beat of their horses' hooves loud in the quiet of early evening, Rowène forced herself to concentrate on the peaceful scene before her rather than the violence that had taken place here and been following her since. A fleet of white swans floated with gilded grace on water that mirrored exactly the serene tones of the lavender sky. Egrets and herons fished in the darkening shallows as they had always done although, unusually, the busy Liriél was empty of all craft save for a small fishing coracle moving slowly upriver, paddled by a burly man and a slight youth.

Rowène watched them idly for a while, only gradually becoming aware that her regard was being returned in full measure by the fishermen and, as renewed shame at her situation washed over her, she turned her gaze away.

Yet, despite her lingering misery and embarrassment, some fleeting impression nagged at her consciousness. There was something about the two people in the coracle... something familiar...

Abruptly she returned her now intent gaze to the fishermen, studying them for whatever it was that had caught at her awareness. Something that was not quite right...

It took several heartbeats but all at once she caught the elusive memory she had been searching for as she recognised in the nondescript features of the older man those of the servant she had seen in the castle courtyard just moments before chaos had exploded all around her. The same man who had smiled benignly as she and her sister squabbled good-naturedly over the merits of the various silks on display in his shop in Castle Street. The same man Luc had spoken to the day they had returned from Kardolandia.

Yet what was Cailen of Chartre – she could no longer think of him as either silk merchant or servant – doing paddling a coracle on the Liriél at sunset? Or a more pertinent question might be, not *why* – for the answer to that was obvious, since what sane person would willingly remain in a town under the dubious governance of Ranulf de Rogé – but whether it was the coincidence it seemed that this particular man was fleeing Chartre just as she herself was riding by?

She was still frowning over this peculiar puzzle when something about the elfin features of the youth in the coracle suddenly caught at her heart, causing it to soar and quicken with a desperate joy as she realised that Ju had not, after all, perished in the flames that had consumed the Lady Tower.

Thanking the gods for that mercy, Rowène felt a dizzying relief flooding her body, some small part of her own despair lightened by the painful hope that one day she and her sister would be together again. Yet, even if they never met again this side of death, at least she would carry the knowledge with her into Rogé that Ju was still alive and travelling with a man whom Rowène believed most fervently would stand her sister's friend.

In any event, she knew she must do nothing to jeopardise *their* chance of freedom by inadvertently alerting any of her escort to her sister's presence. Not that she feared the half-dozen soldiers riding behind her, engaged as they were with their own gripes and jibes, but the noblemen flanking her – intimidatingly large in their mail and probably considerably more alert than their men – might well prove a dangerous bar to her sister's attempt at escape.

Cautiously she raised her eyes from the glittering silver-gilt river, glancing first towards Guyard de Martine, and permitting herself a small exhalation of relief when she saw that he was staring straight ahead, his light blue eyes surprisingly grim for a man returning home to his wife. Though possibly Guy would not have raised the alarm even if he had recognised Ju.

His half-brother though... that was a different matter entirely.

Steeling herself, she turned her head, meaning to take a quick peep beneath her lashes to see what de Rogé was doing. Only to flinch involuntarily as she encountered his stark dark blue gaze, fixed upon her with an intensity that turned her bowels to water. Almost as if the ice in his eyes had touched her skin she felt fear freeze her blood, numbing her mind and piercing her heart. Fear, not for herself, but for her sister. Dear God of Light, she could not live with herself if she allowed Ju to fall back into this wolf's hands. But how to keep his attention on herself, without stirring his suspicions even further, and away from the coracle on the river?

She did not think he would recognise Ju in her present guise, not when he believed her dead, but Rowène was not prepared to gamble her sister's life on the possibility that a dissolute piece of Hell-spawned filth such as de Rogé had proved himself to be, did not also have the wit or imagination to see through a witch's illusion. Not that it had been all illusion; the fire had been real enough and Rowène did not herself understand how Ju had escaped. She assumed that Cailen must have been involved somehow and that there had been no need for the dark enchantments of the Faennari. This evening, though, with the moon beginning to rise...

Her senses fairly tingled with the glittering, quicksilver glamour of enchantment. At the same time, she felt a strange sadness wash over her. Ju had obviously allowed the Winter Lady to teach her more of the subtle skills and elusive beguilements of the Faennari than Rowène ever wanted to master. Or had even believed existed. And de Rogé had called *her* a witch!

Holding his penetrating dark blue gaze as best she might, she felt a flash of familiar panic when she saw the already brutally hard line of his jaw tighten even more, the tense alertness pervading his big, mailed body becoming an almost tangible force.

*Dear God of Light, he suspects something!*

For surely nothing else would cause the reaction she sensed in him. But what to do to distract him? Heart hammering, mouth dry, Rowène felt her mare move uneasily beneath her and allowed her reins to drop.

She heard de Rogé curse with his usual coarse fluency as her mare's sudden unhindered display of skittishness caused his own temperamental stallion to sidle beneath him but at least it served to keep his attention away from the river. Bringing his mount back under control with an ease she knew she could never match, he leaned over to grab the mare's trailing reins, handing them back to her with a scathing glance and an impatient injunction to his half-brother to keep a closer eye on "the fumble-fisted wench" since her equestrian skills were "obviously more suited to riding a donkey."

As he settled back in his saddle, Rowène risked a sideways glance at the river and was relieved to see that the Liriél's smooth surface was now empty, save for the white swans still gliding gracefully down the darkening waters towards the sea.

Coming at last to the far end of the bridge, de Rogé reined to a halt and signalled the soldiers to ride on and wait a little way off, while he and his brother exchanged a few last, low-voiced words. Rowène made no attempt to listen but nudged her mare a little apart from the men, gazing back over the river towards the town. But it was hidden already in the darkening shadows of night and the castle – looking oddly unfamiliar without the tall height of the Lady Tower – showed black against an indigo sky. Would she, or Ju, ever return? she wondered. Somehow she did not think so – or not for more years than there were presently stars in the sky. Looking up, she could count perhaps twenty of the tiny twinkling gems, with more being born with every heartbeat...

A soft metallic chink made her start nervously – gods, how she hated that sound! – and as she glanced around she saw that de Rogé had swung down from his horse and was, to her horror and disbelief, walking straight towards her.

Trying not to shrink back as the man came to a halt at her stirrup, she forced herself to look down at him. Dear God of Mercy! Had it only been yesterday that he had stood thus, looking up at her, mockery and indifference in those eyes set in a stranger's face, framed by neat braids and a smooth spill of barley pale hair. Now, on the other side of that chasm of fire and blood, lust and fear, he was no longer a stranger to her. Not outwardly anyway. She knew every blemish on his weathered face; the small white scar beneath his right eye, the disfiguring ridge across his otherwise straight nose. Her gaze took in the matted, filthy hair straggling loose from its single binding. Moved along the line of his hard jaw, coarsened by a day's growth of glinting stubble. Then, when she could avoid it no longer, she looked full into those unyielding dark blue eyes.

As if this was what he had been waiting for, he finally spoke. The other men were out of earshot but he nevertheless pitched his voice low and when she heard what he had to say she understood why.

"You still have my mantle and the pin, I see. And you will remember your promise?"

She nodded, unable to speak for the revulsion surging in her throat. *God of Mercy, let me not be carrying his child... spawned in that Hell... of hatred on my side, drug-induced lust on his...*

"When is your flux due?"

"What?" She had heard the words but could not believe he had spoken them. She had not expected such blunt directness, even from him. Closing her eyes, she prayed that when she opened them again he would be gone. Or would at least stop asking her such...

"You heard me! So *when*, damn you!"

"Today... tomorrow." The words stuck in her throat.

"So you will know soon? Open your eyes, Rowène, and bloody well *look at me!*"

Nausea surged up at those words, so similar to those he had spoken just before he had... no she would not think of it again! She swallowed and obeyed his command. His face was strained and entirely without colour, his pallor reminding her that he wanted such an outcome as little as she did.

"Yes... I will know soon," she managed to whisper. "And... and I will send Geryth to you if... if..."

She could not complete the thought but then he did not need her to. He nodded, his face still tense, although now there was a hint of a flush along his cheekbones. She hoped... *needed* him to simply turn and leave her now. But he gave no sign of moving.

"What? What more do you want of me?" she demanded unsteadily. "If you have something to say, please, say it quickly before your half-brother arrives."

Evidently understanding her meaning he raised his voice to a more ordinary pitch and allowed his normally clipped Mithlondian to slip into a sardonic drawl.

"Oh, one last thing, wench. Do not test my brother's good nature too far and, if you would ever hear yourself being addressed as Madame de Veraux... stay out of Guy's bed!"

She blinked at this piece of seemingly pointless irrelevance, then pulled herself together as she caught the warning that flashed in his dark blue eyes like lightning across a stormy sea.

"As if I needed either your insults or your advice," she sniffed disdainfully and added in a tone that fairly reeked of sarcasm, "Fare you well, Messire de Rogé. I pray to the gods that we never have cause to meet again."

"Believe me, Demoiselle de Chartreux," he replied with a thin, cold smile. "You cannot hope for that any more fervently than I."

With that he reached up and, in a move that took her entirely by surprise, caught her clenched fingers in his, carrying them to his now unsmiling mouth in what could only be the cruellest parody of the courtesy expected of a gentleman to a high-born lady. Shocked, revolted and utterly unnerved by the warmth and softness of his lips, she gasped and snatched her hand away.

Yet, fleeting though the contact had been, the memory remained branded into her shrinking flesh long after the man himself had been left behind.

Standing alone at the end of the Swanfleet Bridge, the black stallion's reins held loosely in his hand, Ranulf watched with narrowed eyes as his brother, the girl Guy had wanted and *he* had taken, together with their armed escort disappeared into the dark golden dusk that lingered under the silver-grey boughs and dark green canopy of the Larkenlay beeches.

Only when he could no longer see or hear any trace of them did he give vent to – for him – a mild oath and, settling his buttocks against the warm sandstone parapet of the bridge, allowed his gaze to be drawn back towards the irregular jumble of roofs, walls and towers of the town and castle that were now his responsibility.

*Damn Joffroi to the depths of Hell!*

If not for his brother's ill-judged and temper-sparked decision to appoint him Governor of Chartreux in Joffroi's absence, he would be well out of it by now, several leagues north at the least, heading for the summer's fighting. Instead of which...

*Hell and damnation!*

Although he was considerably more literate than he had allowed de Chartreux's daughter to believe, he still knew next to nothing about merchant guilds or charters, harbour fees, taxes or tally rolls. Or the procedures and punishments of civil justice. His training and experience were purely military; he commanded Rogérinac's garrison when he was at home and led the de Rogé levies in the royal army when summoned by the Prince and High Counsel – in effect every summer for the past eighteen years.

However, he strongly doubted that such experience would be sufficient to enable him to efficiently govern the second wealthiest province in the realm. Not that he had a choice. Joffroi, being fully as stubborn as any pig, wild or domesticated, would never retract his hasty decision. It was also the only means, short of ordering his flogging, by which Joffroi had been able to express his displeasure at Ranulf's less than wholehearted support in the matter of Louis de Chartreux's attainder and death. But, *damn it all to Hell*, what else had Joffroi expected of him? He was a soldier, not some lily-livered, soft-handed, slimy-tongued schemer.

But simply because he was what he was, he had always carried out his liege lord's commands, even though he had not, in the past, particularly agreed with some of them. Certainly he had not approved of, or enjoyed, any part of this campaign against Chartreux – with the possible exception of the mêlée earlier that day when he had been fighting against men whose skill and training matched his own.

Yes, he had sworn a blood oath to bring about the downfall and death of the man responsible for his own father's early demise. But that had been an oath given by a hot-tempered fifteen-year-old boy under his elder brother's goading and he had certainly not envisaged at the time that eighteen years later he would go to Lamortaine in fulfilment of that oath, only to find he bitterly regretted ever making it.

Still cursing both his brother's black temper and his own weakness, Ranulf withdrew his vexed gaze from the sight of the distant towers in favour of one last sweep of the empty river, thinking his first step on the morrow must be to acquire an efficient clerk and an accurate map of the province of which he was now Governor.

This close to midsummer true darkness would not fall for some time. Nevertheless it was late enough that all hint of liquid bronze light had now seeped away, abandoning both sky and the smooth dark silk of the water. Taking with it too all signs of life, save for an owl that floated past on the soft white wings of silence, sending an odd shiver down his back.

Forcing aside that wraith-touch of foreboding, he remained where he was a little longer, hoping that the very serenity of the scene before him might calm some of his nameless – or not so nameless – fears. Instead it merely served to exacerbate a temper that had never been particularly placid and which had been rubbed raw by the events of the past ten days – not to mention what had happened in the misty grey dawn of this hell-cursed day!

*Today*, she had said. Or possibly, *tomorrow*. Whichever it was, he would know soon. But what in the name of all the gods would he do if she did – by the evil design of some fey power that had the force to overturn the natural laws – carry his child?

All the way down from the castle he had been fighting against consideration of that impossibility. Struggling to come to some sensible decision should impossibility become reality. As they had ridden across the long span of the Swanfleet Bridge nothing else had impinged upon his thoughts. The entire citizenry of Chartre could have been escaping up river and he would not have noticed – or cared if he had. He had been aware of nothing save the steady beat of his heart as it counted down the moments until he must watch the innocent girl he had forced into womanhood disappear into the golden dusk of that summer evening, not knowing whether or not the seed of his rape had taken root within the untouched body he had possessed so brutally.

Cursing more viciously still, he reached up to jerk the thong from his hair, unable to bear the feeling of being bound in any way. The long pale strands hung heavy over his shoulders, coarsened by sweat and matted with dried blood, bringing him little by way of relief. Rather, the raising of his arm had had the

234

contrary effect of making him realise just how much he stank! His thoughts turned briefly towards hot water, fresh linen and the hard green soap made by the Grey Sisters of Silverleigh but even the desire to be clean again could not hold his mind for long.

Instead, the soft caress of the sea-scented breeze on his unbound hair became the harsh pressure of a rough hemp rope about his neck. The stones of the bridge beneath his booted feet became the creaking wooden boards of the scaffold. And as Faela, the brightest of all the evening stars, glimmered into life above him, the night call of a shriek owl became the far off cry of a new-born babe. A babe with its mother's grey eyes and its father's pale gold hair...

Sweating and shivering, Ranulf wrenched himself from the illusion, swearing savagely under his breath. Curse the little witchling, was this *her* work? This spell that had almost unmanned him? But no. She... *She* had a name, he reminded himself, although no-one would ever guess he knew it, careful as he had been only to call her wench or wild-cat or witchling in anyone else's hearing. But she... *Rowène...* had sworn it would not happen; that there would be no child. He had to believe her, else he would go mad with the waiting. He wished now that he had told her to send Geryth back to him, whatever the answer. Then at least he would know that all was well.

And if it were not?

She would tell the truth, of course, of that encounter in the misty grey light of this morning's dawn. He accepted that. It was not the sort of thing that could be kept quiet, even though Rogérinac was well removed from Lamortaine. Word would reach Joscelin de Veraux sooner or later that Rowène de Chartreux was swelling with another man's child and the bastard would be hammering on the gates of Rogérinac castle as soon as the campaigning season was over, if not before, demanding justice for the brutal mistreatment of the woman to whom he had once been betrothed. For all they had fought in the same campaigns Ranulf did not know Prince Marcus' by-blow particularly well but he did know how dearly the younger man held his honour.

Nor did he think many of the other members of Mithlondia's nobility would be prepared to ignore his actions if they were made public. Joffroi might think he had the High Counsel under his control but Ranulf doubted his brother's influence was so extensive as to convince its members to regard an innocent young noblewoman's rape as an acceptable, if regrettable, consequence of Joffroi's seizure of Chartre. The subsequent swift and bloody suppression of Luc de Chartreux's rebellion would probably cause some mutterings among the Lords of the Counsel but, Ranulf thought, it would be condoned rather than condemned outright.

And even if the Counsel — for some peculiar reason beyond his imagining — did not take the punitive action against him that it should, *he* would still know that what he had done to Rowène de Chartreux was neither forgiveable nor acceptable. Even now, he still had no clear idea *why* he had done it! Yes, he had felt a flare of desire for the girl when he had first seen her, her hair gleaming like red flame in the gilded green light under the trees by the Liriél. But he had known, even then, that she was not for him. Not only by virtue of Guy's protection but by the revulsion she had so obviously felt for him. Nor, by the time he had seen her the next day, a slender creature of flame – from the fire of her hair to the glow of her gown – blazing bright against the grey chill of dawn, had he felt any need of a woman, his normal needs having been fully sated the night before.

Yet still he had wanted her. Had felt himself burning for her. And because of that fire, which she had so unwittingly lit in his loins, he had ruthlessly taken her, heedless of her protests. Concerned only with the slaking of his own criminal lust, seduced by the scent of roses more heady than Marillec wine that misted her silken skin, and the sound of his name on her tongue, he had ignored her protests and in pursuit of a half-forgotten drunken oath, had made her his, reckless of his own fate.

Well, it had not brought him death. Or at least not yet! But a part of him had died just the same. Even now his manhood hung limp and shrunken, devoid of even the smallest ember of banked fire. Oh, he still wanted her. He had proved that when he had taken her cold fingers in his and brought them to his mouth. Gods! He had wanted so desperately to taste her lips... but had known he could only get away with the briefest contact with her fingers. And only then by making that gesture into the grossest of mockeries. Yet, in spite of his care to conceal his desire, he had felt his brother's curiosity start to coalesce into suspicion. As for the woman whose hand he held, he had not needed to look into her eyes to read her revulsion; the shiver of her soft, rose-fragranced skin had already told him exactly how she felt about him.

She hated him! Quite justifiably. But he knew, even if she did not, that vengeance lay within those cold, clenched fingers. He had forced himself on her. And he would surely pay for that crime, one way or another. Sooner or later. Sooner, if there was a child to prove his guilt.

Would she come to watch him die, he wondered mordantly, having first stood witness at his trial and faced the inquisition of the High Counsel? Not that he would deny her accusation. How could he? He was guilty and he knew it. But later, after they had passed their sentence of death on him, would she come to stand at the foot of the scaffold, his child in her arms, her clear grey eyes his last sight before the Daemon of Hell claimed his body as well as his soul!

Eyes the clear, silvery grey of an upland tarn, of mist in the moonlight, of steel in the sun... He could see them now...

Except these eyes were not set in a young woman's thin, pale face but in the lean, weathered features of a man in his prime, silver barely feathering the dark hair at his temples. A man who stood upon the gallows, exchanging a few final words and the merest flicker of a grim smile with the man who had escorted him there; a young man whose face appeared shockingly sallow against the black of his hair. A man who had, quite obviously, wanted to be there, in the main square of Lamortaine, as little as Ranulf himself did.

And if it had not been for Joffroi's bloody-mindedness in tracking him down, forcibly sobering him up and then hauling him bodily from the brothel where he had deliberately drunk himself into a state of insensibility, Ranulf would not be sitting here now, alone in the dark and dwelling on every mawkish fancy that took possession of his mind! Never mind rose-petal lips and rose-scented skin! He could still taste the stale residue of the Marillec wine he had drunk the previous night, thick and foul upon his tongue. But not as vile as the memory of that day in Lamortaine...

Was it then? Ranulf wondered. At the very moment when he had met Louis de Chartreux's steel grey gaze? That he had felt that first stab of... disloyalty was perhaps too strong a word, but certainly disquiet, that the brother who held both his oath of allegiance and his affection had chosen this path? Ranulf had offered to challenge de Chartreux to single combat while it was still at the trial stage but Joffroi would have none of it. It had to be this way, his brother had insisted. De Chartreux must be seen to die a traitor's death. Ranulf had acquiesced perforce and put it out of his mind.

Until the moment when he had looked from the grimy cobbles beneath his feet towards the scaffold and found his gaze meeting that of the condemned man. There had been a spark of recognition in de Chartreux's grey eyes... a scornful acknowledgement of Ranulf's presence at his brother's side... condemning him as he stood there, for his mindless complicity in a witch's twisted schemes.

Sick from the gut-rot wine he had consumed to excess in the taverns of the Marish and with his head pounding as if it were being hit by the same mallet that had hammered the nails into the scaffold, Ranulf had still felt the pull of that cool grey gaze and, much though he had wanted to look away, he had not. He had forced himself to return Louis de Chartreux's stare without flinching.

Forced himself to watch as Joscelin de Veraux stepped aside, his place being taken by that of the black-hooded executioner.

Forced himself to watch as Louis de Chartreux died the bloody and agonising death reserved for all traitors.

When it was all over, the crowd dispersed and the square empty of all save de Veraux, a small contingent of guards, a weeping Sister of Mercy and the bloody parts of the dismembered corpse which were even then being hauled away for display above the city gates, Ranulf had turned to his brother. He had had the vague thought of excusing himself with some flippant comment but the gloating look in Joffroi's dark eyes had proved too much. Without a word he had turned away, seeking out the relative privacy of a nearby alleyway where, helpless to prevent himself, he had vomited up everything in his stomach, cursing himself for a weak-bellied milksop as he did so.

It was not as if he had not seen dead men before. He had. Many a time.

Wounded men, dying men, tortured men. He had seen men slaughtered by sword and spear and axe, trampled under iron-shod hooves, ripped apart on the rack, seared by hot iron. He had killed his share of men... although, the gods be his witness, never a woman and never a child! Or at least not wittingly. He had had men hung at his command and watched them die without compunction. But never had he taken pleasure in it.

Nor had he this time, his lack of enthusiasm bolstered by his doubt that Louis de Chartreux had been guilty of anything worse than loyalty to the prince he had loved as a brother.

Just as Ranulf had always been loyal to his brother. But he had never had the slightest interest in Joffroi's political manoeuvrings and, in truth, would have preferred to continue to distance himself from them now. Unfortunately with that one look into a dying man's grey eyes, something had shifted in his soul. And he had ridden south to Chartre with the uneasy feeling that, whether he admitted it or not, his life as he had known it was about to change in some unforeseen way and that his allegiance to Joffroi had been dented, if not yet irretrievably damaged, by the events in Lamortaine.

Well, he mocked himself, as he straightened off the parapet and swung up onto Starlight's broad, black back, his life had changed already – and might well change even more drastically in the next few days.

*Today,* she had said. Or maybe *tomorrow...*

Guyard de Martine kept his small six-man troop moving steadily through the night, grateful for the long summer dusk. Watching warily as the huge pale golden orb of the moon rose in a sky speckled with stars like a starling's breast, he could not repress a shiver – as if, perchance, a wraith had danced upon his grave. Remembered, much against his will, the fey pink moon of the previous night and the confused emotions and events it had heralded.

He glanced at the girl riding silently by his side but Rowène continued to ignore him, as she had done ever since they had left the Swanfleet Bridge and turned east along the highway towards Rogé; a route he had told her, only the morning before, she would never be called upon to travel.

Later though, when the moon turned to silver in a sky that seemed to hold the brightest stars ever born and still they continued to ride, Guyard found himself obliged to take her before him on Fireflame. It was either that or stop for the night and he was unwilling to risk that whilst they were still within Chartreux's borders. Once settled, she had soon drifted into sleep, supported by the strength of his arm and wrapped in the warmth of his brother's mantle.

He frowned a little then, considering Ranulf's odd behaviour that morning when he had, with apparent carelessness, given Rowène his cloak; a guard against the chill of the fog and the lascivious looks her indecent scarlet gown had been bound to elicit. Fair enough, perhaps, but why had he not reclaimed it later and given her something else? Ranulf so rarely acted the part of the gentleman his mother had raised him to be that Guyard had been inclined to be suspicious of his motives even at the time. The violence of subsequent events had driven it out of his mind and now it was too late to ask him what he had meant by it.

But he had problems enough of his own to worry about without prying into his brother's uncharacteristic behaviour. Not least among these problems being how, in the name of all the gods, he was going to convince his wife – and himself – that the girl presently sleeping in his arms was not his leman, never had been and never would be. The best he could manage at the moment was a conviction that if he could only rid his mind of the beguiling images that rose in the fevered moonlight of his imagination, his body might possibly be trusted not to betray him.

Emerging from the cover of the beechwood, they crossed the Larkenlye in the cold, drizzling rain of yet another grey dawn and Rowène opened her eyes to find herself on the Rogé side of the river, still held in the comfortingly strong curve of a man's bridle arm, a fold of his cloak between her cheek and the chilly discomfort of the mail shirt he was once more wearing. Yet, looking up at his tired, unshaven face, all she could think of was how much he resembled the man she hated so vehemently.

"The gods damn you to hell, Guyard de Martine," she whispered wearily. "And your cursed brothers with you."

# Part III

# ANJÉLAIS-SUR-LIRIÉL

## Summer – Autumn 1194

# Chapter 1

## *Upriver by Coracle*

The sun had almost gone from the river, the curlews were quiet again but her companion continued to wield his paddle with slow, even strokes, each dip of the paddle taking them another foot, another yard, eventually a furlong, then a league, perhaps two, away from Chartre. Away from that unyielding, flame-haired enchantress who had given her life; the witch she and her sister had called the Winter Lady.

Telling herself this, Juliène strove to still her shivering, control her breathing, steady her heartbeat. And with each almost silent stroke of the paddle wielded with unexpected skill by the man behind her, she found it easier, felt the frost about her heart melt into the molten bronze of the sun-streaked waters she floated on.

But with the familiar gone – cold though it had been – what was left but a deep-seated misery and an even icier fear. She was alone, adrift in a life where she knew no-one, not even her guide and companion, and had no notion what the future might hold, save that it was certain not to be anywhere near as pleasant and civilised as her life had been to date.

The change in her social status aside, she realised she had never been alone before, never called upon to make her own choices, to determine how her life might run. Of course, this newly discovered freedom depended largely on whether she could get far enough away from her mother and Lord Joffroi. And it was entirely possible that this new life would consist of nothing better than begging in the gutter. *Not* an attractive prospect, she owned, but perhaps no worse than the one she had left behind. Only now, when she was on the verge of escape, was she beginning to see just how far she had fallen under the Winter Lady's power since her return to Chartre.

She had always been more than a little open to the influence of Ariène de Chartreux. She realised that now. Had always feared it, to a greater or lesser extent. For some reason she had never fathomed, her father had always seemed closer, more openly affectionate, towards her sister; had taken greater care of Rowène, shown more pride and delight in her achievements. As much, almost, as he professed for his son's. Or so it had seemed to a very young Juliène. Not that her father had ever neglected her or ignored her. There was just something in his eyes when he looked at her, something that hurt her even then. Something she had never quite forgotten.

A coolness, a wariness... she could not say exactly what it was. Just that it slumbered there, in the hidden depths of his grey eyes; the same translucent grey as Luc's eyes. And Rowène's.

Perhaps that was it, a much younger Juliène had thought one day, as she sat watching her reflection in her mother's silver mirror while the Winter Lady combed and braided her hair. Save for the raven darkness of Juliène's straight, shining hair, there was nothing about her that reminded her of her father, brother or sister. She looked nothing like Louis de Chartreux, not in the way that Luc and Rowène did.

Even one of the stable boys resembled her father more closely than she herself did, she had reflected, torn between hurt and spite. She had noticed him just that morning when she had accompanied her father, Luc and Ro to the stables for their daily ride. She had watched the others leave – she did not ride herself, being frightened of the huge, unpredictable beasts – and had turned to find one of the stable lads looking at her curiously as he leant on the pitchfork he had been using.

He had short, straight, black hair and grey eyes, a thin, sun-browned face and a long nose. He was the son of one of the castle laundresses and the groom who had now disappeared about some task in the depths of the stable, calling as he went for the boy to follow him. Juliène had barely registered his name at the time. Her only thought was that he looked just like Luc, if somewhat older.

Upset, but not quite knowing why, she had scowled at him, her eyes flashing disdain to cover her own hurt that she had been left behind and must spend the morning in her mother's company. The boy – Lucien, his father had called him – had looked away almost immediately and, with a small sense of bitter satisfaction, she had assumed as much of her mother's haughty expression as her softer countenance would allow and swished from the stables, her silk gown lifted a little away from the floor from which he had just swept all traces of wet straw or dung.

Now the boy who had once worked in the Chartre castle stables and who had risen to become the garrison commander was dead. Indeed, she had been more than a little surprised to find him still alive when she returned from Kaerellios, since she had known for years that his death was inevitable; had known his fate even before she had heard her mother utter those cold, condemnatory words the day Joffroi de Rogé had come to Chartre. Almost as long in fact as she had known that Lucien was not the groom's son at all but her father's by-blow. She had seen the implacable hatred on the Winter Lady's face that day, ten years ago, when she had blurted out her observations regarding the stable lad and her mother had told her, not *who* but *what* Lucien was. She had been so frightened by her mother's reaction that she had never told Rowène what she had learned about the boy.

It had not been many days after that incident that she and her sister had been sent to Kaerellios and Luc had gone away to continue his weapons training at

Marillec, Lucien accompanying him in the capacity of groom and body servant, and she had put all thought of him from her mind. Now though...

She wished that Lucien had not had to die. He was, after all, her half-brother. Not that she felt any particular sorrow, only an impersonal pity for a young man's death before his time, and perhaps a little shame that she could feel nothing deeper. But then, she did not really know what she felt about her father's death. Nausea, certainly, that he had died in such a terrible fashion, but grief? She supposed she grieved for him. She had loved him as much as she could. As much perhaps as he had loved her. And she thought again that he had never seemed to love her as he did Luc and Ro. How he might have felt about his bastard son she did not know and wondered briefly if Lucien had even known the Lord of Chartreux was his natural father, then shrugged. It did not matter; they were both dead now.

As perhaps... no, *probably*, Luc would be soon! If the Winter Lady had deemed an illegitimate stable boy a threat to her plans, how much more would Louis de Chartreux's legitimate son and heir be? By the grace of the gods Luc had survived the battle for Chartre castle but even if he overcame his wounds, the sea journey, the overseer's lash and eventually contrived to escape the shackles of slavery and return to Mithlondia, neither the Winter Lady nor Black Joffroi would knowingly permit him to live.

Tears burned in her eyes at the thought of all Luc must be suffering. He might always have been his father's favourite but Juliène had never held that against him. To her he was simply her big brother, to be adored and honoured above all others. He had been openly affectionate to her in the years before they had all left Chartre and he had several times over the ten years of her exile made the long journey from Mithlondia to Kardolandia in order to visit her.

She had never understood why her father had sent her and Ro away. Was it because he feared the Winter Lady's influence on them, young and vulnerable as they had been? He had gone to some trouble to protect all his children, Juliène admitted grudgingly, placing Luc and Lucien under Jean de Marillec's guardianship and sending herself and her sister many hundreds of leagues south to the King of Kardolandia's court.

She did not know what might have motivated Jean de Marillec to accept such a charge but King Karlen had driven a hard bargain. Fifty of Chartreux's finest soldiers to form the nucleus of the royal bodyguard and train up the pleasure-loving Kardolandian men into an effective army should the self-styled Emperor of the Eastern Isles attempt to incorporate the rich but ill-defended city of Kaerellios into his trading empire. The bargain to hold for ten years.

What Juliène had not realised, although she really should have done, was that the ten years of that agreement also marked her own time in Kaerellios. She had thought – or rather she had not thought at all, merely taken it for granted – that she would remain at court, as one of Queen Xandra's lady companions, in due course wed a Kardolandian nobleman and spend the rest of her life there amidst the bright blossoms and warm, fragrant breezes, under soft blue skies and within sight of the fascinating turquoise-blue waters of the Eastern Sea.

She would have been happy never to have returned to the harsh life that awaited her in Mithlondia; to be either hunted down as a traitor's daughter or, if she chose to abide with her mother, to live with the knowledge that she was little better than a witch herself. In Kardolandia she had been looked upon as a beautiful and alluring woman and treated accordingly. Many men had made overtures towards her, had invited her to bathe with them in the warm, clear waters of the pools of Kaerellios. Revelling – fairly innocently – in her power, she had accepted none of them. Until...

No! She would not think of him. Not now. The lover she had been forced to leave behind. She had told no one about him, not even the sister who had, over the ten years of their exile, become the other half of herself.

But she had not been able to conceal her secret from the Winter Lady and the first time Ro had left the castle to go riding, the harper in attendance, she had been summoned to her mother's chamber, where the Lady Ariène had coldly revealed all the truths she had seen in the mirror of her daughter's emerald eyes. Juliène had been too depressed and frightened to deny any of them. Her mother had waited only to make sure that Juliène felt the full weight of what she had done before telling her what she must do about it.

Her mother had not mentioned Joffroi de Rogé by name but Juliène had known that some dire threat loomed close. Just as she had known that Guy of Montfaucon was somehow tied to that doom. Waking one day from a formless nightmare, she had known that this must be the day their fate would be decided. Accordingly she had braved her mother's icy displeasure should she learn of Juliène's loose tongue and her sister's quick temper and tried to warn Ro that the harper was not all he seemed.

Alas, Ro had not been of a mind to heed her – no doubt fancying herself in love with the soft-spoken, blue-eyed harper – and so Juliène had let her go, turning instead to her own concerns. She had spent that last lovely summer's morning brewing a potion under the Winter Lady's instructions. The same potion she had subsequently slipped into Ranulf de Rogé's wine during that short time when he had been absent from the great hall, checking the guards or tumbling the serving wenches or whatever it was that he had been doing.

As for what came after... Juliène shivered slightly, pretending it was the chill of approaching evening rather than her own memories. What was done was done and she would not think of it again. Those memories belonged back in the castle she had succeeded in escaping. She only wished she could have bought her sister's freedom as well as her own.

Despite herself, she had been shocked by the sight of her sister and her accompanying escort as they crossed the Swanfleet Bridge. But at least one of Juliène's crushing fears had been alleviated by the sight; distressed her sister might have been at being seen attired as she was and riding in the company of two of the victorious de Rogé brothers but at least she was alive and, Juliène thought, unharmed. She had caught a glimpse of scarlet silk as her sister moved and guessed it to be the twin of the gown her mother had sent to her but which she had never worn and had left to perish in the flames of the Lady Tower along with her old life. Of more consequence perhaps had been the observation that Rowène was still wearing Ranulf de Rogé's black mantle, causing Juliène to wonder rather uneasily what, if anything, *that* might portend.

There was nothing, however, that she or Cailen could do to rescue Rowène from her captors and indeed they must go warily themselves if they were to escape the attention of the man Cailen had already heard mentioned as the new Governor of Chartreux. They had drawn into the shadows near the shore and through the low branches of the trailing silver willow she had watched de Rogé take his farewell of his half-brother, then seen him exchange a few, private words with her sister that greatly increased Juliène's anxiety, for why should the man be troubling her in such a fashion? She could see too, even at that distance, that Ro was greatly agitated, either by his words or his touch. He had had the temerity to kiss her sister's hand in farewell and Juliène waited in some glee for the slap that would surely follow. To her amazement Ro had held her temper and, having scrubbed de Rogé's kiss from her hand with the tail of his own cloak, had nudged her mare past the man and back towards the highway.

The troop had then disappeared eastwards, leaving de Rogé alone on the bridge. Juliène had thought it might be safe to move again but Cailen had merely shaken his head and remained still. Only when he heard the steady hoof beats crossing the bridge and fading into the darkness on the western side of the river did he take up his paddle again.

Now, far enough upstream from the Swanfleet Bridge for it to have disappeared from sight long-since, Juliène sat huddled on the narrow bench of the small craft, seeing not the star-strewn emptiness of eternity above her but remembering, with an odd sense of dislocation, the strange silken sheen of the sky before night's black wings had come sweeping down. She had had a gown once of that exact shade of molten bronze; she had been wearing it the day she had met and fallen in love with the man she had thought to wed, the man to whom she had, with loving recklessness, given her body when he asked that gift of her. The man she had been forced to leave in Kaerellios, with nothing more than a hasty farewell and his sworn promise that he would journey to Chartre to find her again.

Juliène wanted to believe that he would come – in spite of the memory of her mother's cool laughter at the notion. Yet even if he did come, how would he ever find her again? She was going... well, she was not quite sure where she was going. But at least, she reminded herself, she was with someone who would help her. She thought. Hoped.

Her sister was certainly not in as optimistic a position.

Forcing back the aching pain that she had lived with since leaving Kaerellios, Juliène finally broke the tranquil peace that lay with such exquisite fragility over the moonlit river. She thought they must be the first words she had spoken since leaving Chartre.

"Did you see my sister, Cailen? Riding amongst those gutter-scum?"

"Aye, my lady, I saw her."

"Well, at least I know that she is alive, even if she is still keeping company with that treacherous hound of a harper. His half-brother may be a swine but at least a woman knows where she is with him."

Her companion grunted something under his breath that sounded like,

"Aye, flat on her back with her legs spread wide or pressed up against the nearest wall," but then before she could take issue with him added, "Do not be too quick to judge Guyard de Martine, my lady. He may look uncannily like his half-brother but, as you have observed for yourself, he lacks Ranulf de Rogé's honed edge. I only hope I do right to trust him with your sister for the time being, but my first duty is to you."

Something about his words or his grimly determined tone – either were disconcerting enough coming from a merchant of increasingly dubious provenance – caught at her attention and she turned her head to look at Cailen.

"Why should you have a duty to either of us? We are nothing to you. Who *are* you, Cailen? And where you are taking me?"

Apparently detecting some hint of the panic underlying the puzzlement in her voice, Cailen rested his paddle a moment before saying sombrely,

"As to duty, I swore an oath to your father to see you and your sister safe should anything happen to him. As to where I am taking you, I have already told you. We are going to Anjélais-sur-Liriél, a small village some leagues up river. Once I have seen you safe in my sister's care I intend to follow Lady Rowène to Rogérinac and, if possible, bring her out of that place before Guyard de Martine is tempted to make rumour reality."

"You mean the rumour that he is her lover?" Juliène asked unhappily. "I should perhaps not say this of my own sister but I am not sure that is merely a rumour. His brother did try to tell me that he... de Martine I mean, would not break his binding vows but I am not sure I believed him. Not having seen the way Ro watched the man when we all thought he was nothing more than a common harper. And seen the way *he* watched her in turn when he thought he was unobserved."

Cailen grunted under his breath, although whether that was in response to Juliène's comment or the effort of paddling again, she could not tell.

"Hmph. Ranulf de Rogé's reputation as a lecher is indisputable but so far as I know no-one has ever – justifiably, at least – called him a liar. In which case your sister is undoubtedly a maiden yet and safe enough with Guyard de Martine for the time being. On the other hand it would probably not be wise to put too much faith in his honour since he is, after all, a man. With a man's desires and a man's needs. From what I have seen of him, I think you are probably right and he is not entirely indifferent to your sister's charms. That being so, only the gods know how well he can keep his distance from her in the days to come. Hence the urgency of getting you to safety, so that I may go after her."

"Safety?" Juliène repeated, her soft voice husky with the strain of holding back the tears that suddenly choked her throat. "I do not think either Ro or I will ever be safe again."

For a moment Cailen hesitated then laying the paddle down once more, allowed the little boat to drift along on the current towards the bank, placing an avuncular arm about her slender shoulders. At his comforting touch Juliène lost all pretence at control and gave way to tears, sobbing uncontrollably against his broad, sturdy chest.

Finally, when her tears had washed away some of the foul taint that the events of the previous night and that day had branded on her soul, she straightened and said unsteadily,

"Thank you for your patience, Master Cailen. Ro always used to say I wept too easily."

"Sometimes you need to weep," Cailen's gruff voice came soft from the darkness. "And I think this is one of those times. The gods know I wept myself when I heard that your father was dead – and in such a manner!" His tone hardened. "One day I will go to Lamortaine and find out for myself how he came to be put under attainder for such crimes. Treason and regicide? Ha! Black Joffroi must have been cup-shot when he thought of that one! That or bewitched!"

Juliène peered at her companion but what with the deep dusk and the shadows under the trees she could not see his face with any clarity.

"You think Joffroi de Rogé had a hand in my father's arrest and attainder? I know de Martine accused him of that but you are saying it was by deliberate design, rather than just seizing the opportunity when it presented itself? And that my mother helped him?"

"Well, whether it was by chance or design, no-one else in Mithlondia hated Louis de Chartreux enough to contrive his death!" Cailen replied grimly. "But either way, I cannot understand how your father came to walk into any snare of Black Joffroi's setting or once he had, how the High Counsel could have been so foolish or so blind as to permit such a blatant injustice."

"You do not think that, perhaps, it might have been true?" Juliène asked hesitantly. "I mean, if Prince Marcus *was* mortally ill, might my father not have thought to ease his passing and spare him any more suffering?"

Cailen's voice came harsh from the darkness,

"I will make allowance for the fact that you are young, that you have been away for ten years and that you do not know the full tale. But *I* know it and I tell you this – your father would never have betrayed, in any way, the man he loved as a brother. He would have taken his own life first!"

249

They passed the night in uneasy slumber, wrapped in their cloaks on the river bank. For Juliène it was a bitterly uncomfortable experience, a far cry from the feather beds and soft linen sheets she was accustomed to. This close to midsummer, the nights were not cold but the ground was hard and the place where she was lying seemed composed solely of tree roots and sharp stones. Grimly she reminded herself of the alternative.

She had fallen asleep eventually from sheer exhaustion somewhere between midnight and dawn and awoke to find herself bruised and chilled, her cloak damp with dew. Stumbling to her feet she brushed dirt and debris from her clothes, washed her face and hands in the river and, after pulling her cloak about her with trembling fingers, managed to relieve herself with some discretion. Rising and ordering her clothing, she began to look rather anxiously around her for her guide.

Cailen, she thought several long moments later when he finally stepped, almost silently, from a ragged screen of scrubby hazel bushes hung about with honeysuckle, appeared disconcertingly at ease for a fugitive and a town-bred merchant at that! She was also more than half convinced that she could detect a hint of merriment in his warm brown eyes as he perceived her own discomfort. Annoyed though she was that the merchant should find anything amusing in their situation, Juliène refrained from snapping at him and managed a tight smile in greeting, to which Cailen responded with an irritatingly cheerful grin and a broad Chartreux accent.

"An' the gods' greeting to ye this fine morn, Lady Juliena. I must ask yer pardon that there be only yesterday's bread an' river water fer yer meal. But once we reach me sister's home there'll be food a-plenty fer the both of us."

"How much farther?" Juliène asked, sounding pathetically plaintive even to her own ears and wondering why Cailen had apparently forgotten his former facility to pronounce noble Mithlondian names properly.

But it was better, she supposed, to consider her companion's inconsistencies than the lack of appetising food. Her empty belly growled quite audibly and she reached without further complaint for the small loaf of hard rye bread Cailen held out to her.

"Oh, another day at the least," he replied to her question, squinting at the river between the silvered green of the sheltering alder and willow trees. "'Twill be hard work paddlin' upstream, fer sure, but better'n riskin' the highway. Less'n I miss me guess Black Joffroy an' yer ma'll be leavin' Chartre terday. They'll be lookin' to fix Prince Linnius's early agreement ter their binding I don't doubt. An' I reckon as how ye'll not be wantin' ter be seen by either on 'em," Cailen replied, lapsing even more deeply into the dialect of the countryside; almost as if, Juliène thought, the farther he went from the city, the more layers of the silk merchant he shed. "M'sister's village lies right on the river so us'll not miss it if us stays wi' the water. An' though the place be full of busybodies and tattletales I doubt us'll stand out enough ter warrant attention from Sir Girauld or any passin' gentryvoke. There's no reason, arter all, fer 'en ter connect a scruffy looking lad like yersel' wi' the beautiful Lady Juliena o' Chartre."

He pondered a little longer, then continued more thoughtfully and certainly less idiomatically,

"I wonder how much truth there is to the rumour I heard just before we left the town, that Black Joffroi has made his brother Governor of Chartre in his absence. It could well be... And yet, even if 'tis true, I suspect Ranulf will have enough trouble on his hands keeping order throughout the province to spare a thought for hunting down fugitives from his brother's rule. More especially as he, in common with everyone else, must believe you to have perished in the fire."

"Ro knows I am alive," Juliène pointed out, fascinated despite herself by her companion's ability to lapse from colloquial to unaccented common speech almost between one breath and the next.

"Aye, but she's not likely to tell anyone, is she?" Cailen retorted. "That said, I think we would do well to take a few further measures to protect your true identity. An inn just off the main highway between Chartre and Lamortaine is mayhap not the best place to flaunt yourself for all to see, not unless you want to bring the new Governor of Chartreux down on you."

"Dear God of Light, no!" Juliène muttered, aghast at the possibility. "I never want to see him again."

She was aware that Cailen was looking at her rather searchingly but she refused to meet his eyes. She knew that he was remembering – as how could he not? – the room where he had found her the day before. Knew too that he had recognised the scent of stale sweat and spilt seed that had lingered in the rumpled linens on the bed and which, taken in conjunction with the tear stains on her face, had been enough to convict Ranulf de Rogé of rape in Cailen's mind.

She could still feel his eyes on her, hard as pebbles, and for a heartbeat she wavered. But she could not afford to let her guard down and so held her silence with a grim determination. Finally she heard Cailen say, with something that was not quite a sigh.

"I should not have thought it of him." He shook his head. "But obviously I was wrong."

She made the mistake of looking up then and in that moment he caught her gaze, his own eyes as bright and lethal as a swooping falcon's.

"You know that one day he will hang for what he did to you," he said flatly. It was not a question.

Juliène flinched and hoped that Cailen could not read her guilt and the doubts that grew stronger with every league that distanced her from the Winter Lady. But Ranulf de Rogé was surely culpable of crimes other than the rape Cailen believed he had committed against her and more than deserved the fate her companion had laid out for him.

"So be it," she said, her voice as merciless and chill as that of the Winter Lady herself.

It was early in the morning of their second day on the Liriél when Juliène noticed an increase in the amount of traffic on the river, small fishing coracles similar to their own weaving around the bigger, shallow-draughted boats that traded up and down between Chartre and the lands farther north, carrying all manner of goods from the busy port to the city of Lamortaine and the towns in between. Interested despite herself by the variety of craft making use of the river, she only gradually became aware that Cailen, who could remain silent for leagues at a time, was talking again, grunting a little with the effort of conversing at the same time as paddling upstream against the strong current.

"We are nearly to my sister's village. Time now to put the past behind us if we are to save our skins, since neither regret nor the hope of revenge will feed our bellies. As from two days ago, there is nothing in Chartre I wish to claim and your name is best forgotten. In such circumstances it would be little short of madness for me to continue calling you *my lady*." He looked across at her and a flicker of irrepressible humour lit his eyes as he continued, "From now on, if you are willing, you will be my brother's daughter."

She looked at him, a trifle startled, then nodded. After all, what choice did she have? He grinned at her.

"So we are agreed then? That being so, you will need a new name. What say you to..." He paused, eyeing her with pursed lips. "What say you to Freyda?"

"Absolutely not," she replied with a moue of distaste.

"How about Hildegarde? Or Hildebrun? Hilde for short?"

She shook her head, smiling slightly, for she could not suppose him to be serious since his brown eyes were fairly glinting with laughter.

"What about Liena?" she suggested.

He shook his head.

"Too much like your own name and certainly not common enough."

Grudgingly she admitted that he was right.

"I know," he said after a few moments of more serious cogitation. "What about Nell? Your second name is Eléanor, is it not?"

"Yes, but how did you know that?" she asked, disconcerted as always by the previously unsuspected depths to his knowledge.

"Never mind how *I* know that. Would Ranulf de Rogé have cause to know it?"

"No. Not unless my mother told him."

Cailen shook his head.

"Why would she? Unless," he eyed her keenly. "She has some reason to suppose you still alive. Do her powers extend so far as to sense your heart's life?"

"I do not think so," Juliène said slowly, terror welling up inside her at the mere thought. "Surely, Cailen, that is not possible?"

"For an ordinary woman, no. But your mother carries the power of the Faennari. As do you and your sister, muted though it is by your father's Mithlondian blood. And that reminds me, I meant to warn you that you must be careful how you use what power you do possess." He was entirely serious now. "With those green eyes of yours, it would be all too easy for someone to levy a charge of witchcraft at you."

"But I do not *have* any power," she said rather irritably. "And I am not a witch."

"Hmmm." He was regarding her with that keen falcon's stare again and she struggled not to show her discomfort. Gods above, he really was the strangest man; one person one moment, another the next.

"So who are *you* going to be now?" she asked, as much to deflect his knowing look as anything else. "Since obviously you can no longer be a silk merchant."

To her relief he grinned again, the intensity of his golden-brown gaze diminishing into a merry twinkle.

"I think I shall be..." He paused, evidently considering. "Ah... how does this sound? Henceforth I shall be Gaelen of Anjélais, a humble tavern keeper, with a taste for good ale and roving adventure. In truth, I never much cared for Cailen of Chartre, he was always far too staid and respectable! And you will be my brother's daughter, come to live with me and my sister for a bit."

"But do you really have a brother?" Juliène asked curiously. The newly renamed Gaelen gave her another glinting look, this one considerably keener.

"Never doubt it, maid! His name is Hilarion and as he lives a long way from here no-one will know if you are his daughter or not. As my sister will no doubt tell you, he's a cold-hearted bastard so no-one would suppose it odd, even if they did know him, that he has sent you to stay with Gwynny. Not when it saves him the bother of dealing with all the problems that arise from having the care of a pretty, young daughter of binding age. Gwynny tends to be a tad biased in her opinion where Hilarion is concerned," he added judiciously. "But for my part I do have a certain affection and admiration for the man. The gods know it can't be easy dealing with our father on a daily basis."

"Do you have any other kin I should be aware of?" Juliène queried rather apprehensively, striving to get her new family straight in her mind. "You mentioned your father?"

Cailen... no, Gaelen regarded her consideringly for a moment or two then said,

"Aye, my father is still alive but for now you need not worry about him. As I said, he lives with my brother in the far north-west of Mithlondia. In the province of Valenne to be precise. You're looking blank, maid! Do you not know anything about that land and its lord?"

He looked a question but Juliène merely shrugged.

"I have been away from Mithlondia for ten years and I remember little of what I was once taught. If there is anything I should know about Valenne and its lord, you will have to tell me yourself."

"Oh, I dare say it can wait," he replied with another lurking smile. "For the time being, all you really need do is remember that we are now Gaelen and Nell, once of Valentién – the chief town of Valenne – but now of Anjélais. Look, there! The river dock. Just keep your head down and your mouth shut. I will just settle up with whatever weasel Sir Girauld has put in charge of collecting tithes and then we can be off to the Flower and Falcon."

Obediently Juliène pulled her hood tighter around her face and lowered her head.

"Sir Girauld?" she queried softly. "Who is he? If he is one of my father's men surely he would help us?"

"Aye, 'tis true he was given tenure of Anjélais and the surrounding land by your father and he was loyal enough while your father was alive. But for all that he would be a fool to stick his neck in the noose now, in defiance of the new Lord of Chartreux. Or its Governor. In any event he is too fond of fine wine and comely wenches to risk outlawry for your sake. You can look for neither help nor compassion from him."

"You seem to know much of what goes on outside the walls of Chartre town," Juliène commented curiously. "Do you visit your sister often?"

"Not as often as Gwynny would like," commented Gaelen wryly. "But I hear things, even in Chartre town. Now, quiet..."

This, as the coracle gently bumped against the weed-stained sandstone of the river dock. Gaelen secured the small craft and clambered out, leaving his companion to scramble up as best she might. For a moment Juliène nearly uttered some scathing remark. Then, remembering her appearance was that of a peasant youth rather than a gently-bred damsel, closed her mouth and struggled after Gaelen, who was by now engaged in trading cheerful insults with the small, narrow man – he did have something of the look of a weasel, Juliène thought – who seemed intent on extracting as much hard coin from Gaelen as possible. In the end he had to be satisfied with three bronze pennies and the promise of a fine river eel for his supper.

Once out of earshot of the satisfied official Juliène turned to Gaelen, regarding him with a new respect,

"Can you really catch him an eel?"

"I doubt it," Gaelen grinned. "Alas, I cannot claim fishing to be one of my skills. But I am equally sure I can find a man who does before this evening is out. Now," he drew a deep breath. "Onward. For a mug of the best ale south of the Lenne."

# Chapter 2

## *The Flower and Falcon*

"Where is your sister's tavern?" Juliène asked, looking curiously about her at the haphazard crop of thatched cottages – complete with thriving vegetable patches and livestock in the form of tethered goats, the odd inquisitive chicken and several aggressively vocal ducks – that straggled along beside the lane that led away from the river in the direction of the castle she could just see perched on the hill that rose above the river valley to the east. To judge from the smudge of smoke that drifted against the hot blue summer sky above the profusion of chestnut and plane trees the main part of the village lay that way too.

"The Flower and Falcon is just off the village square," Gaelen commented, obviously reading her thoughts. "See, if we just walk up the lane aways..." And then, some time later. "Well, there 'tis."

Juliène, who had been concentrating on picking her way through the assorted rubbish of the narrow, stony lane, now looked up, filled with an eager curiosity to see the tavern that was to be her refuge, *if* Gaelen's sister agreed to take them in.

It was a fair-sized building, she noticed, or at least it was compared to its neighbours. Long and low, with some sort of climbing plant running rampant over its slightly tatty frontage; one of the shutters of the tiny dormer windows was hanging loose and the lime wash had clearly not been freshened in recent years. Peering through an archway at the near end of the building she saw a small, grass-grown courtyard with a covered well, backed by what Juliène took to be disused stabling, while over the arch itself hung a faded sign depicting a fierce-looking falcon clutching a branch of flowering thorn in its talons.

Despite these indications that the place had seen better days, the tavern had a homely, pleasant feel to it, made all the more welcoming by the most deliciously tempting smell of fresh-baked bread and frying bacon wafting through the open door.

Juliène's stomach gave a loud – very loud – gurgle, causing Gaelen to chuckle.

"Not long now, maid."

At those cheerfully casual words, Juliène felt her heart lighten a little. Not that the sensation lasted more than a couple of heartbeats, as it occurred to her, not for the first time since he had told her their destination, that Gaelen's sister might not be so willing to welcome her as her brother believed. Striving to put these doubts aside she limped after Gaelen, her limbs still bruised and stiff after two nights sleeping on the ground and two days sitting in a cramped little coracle.

Coming closer to the tavern entrance she found the scent of food in strong competition with the reek from the gutter that ran down the middle of the lane, and into which someone in the opposite house had just flung the contents of their chamber pot. Recoiling instinctively, she felt a resurgence of apprehension as she realised someone was coming out of the tavern.

This turned out to be a plump, respectable looking woman dressed neatly in a gown of dark mulberry wool, her hair completely hidden by a coif of unbleached linen. She was vigorously engaged in brushing dirt from the tavern into the lane with a birch broom and took no notice of the man and the scruffy youth at his heels.

"Good day, Gwynny," Gaelen said quietly.

At that the woman looked up, her deep brown eyes widening with a shock which blossomed wonderfully into the warmth of love. She whispered something – his name maybe, although it was not one Juliène was familiar with – and, dropping the broom, flung herself into his arms, crying and laughing and scolding all at the same time. Gaelen tolerated this for a few moments then put her gently from him, searching her face.

"Why, Gwynny, what's all this? 'Tis not like you to fuss."

"I feared you were taken prisoner or, worse, dead," Gwynhere muttered, seeming somewhat ashamed of her emotional outburst. Gaelen frowned a little and said sharply,

"Then you have heard? About what happened at Chartre?"

"Aye, we heard. Oh Cai, 'tis dreadful! His lordship dead, the young lordling too. One of the little maids perished in a fire that 'twas said nigh on destroyed the castle and t'other taken back to Rogérinac to be held for a hostage."

"How do you know all this?" Gaelen asked, his darkening frown turning his amiable countenance formidable. "'Twas scarce two days ago it happened."

"Lord Joffroy spent the night up at the castle, on his way to court." Gwynhere paused and then added tonelessly. "He had Lady Ariena with him."

"Well, he would have," Gaelen growled. "Look, Gwynny, the road is no place to talk about any of this. And neither the lad here nor I have eaten much since yesterday."

Mistress Gwynhere lifted her hand to her mouth.

"I'm sorry, I wasn't thinking. Come on in..." She glanced at him and, appearing to understand her unspoken question, he gave a grin.

"I am Gaelen of Valentién, for the moment. But your brother, always."

She gave an answering smile, albeit tinged with wistfulness.

"I'm glad that at least never changes," she said softly. "As for Gaelen... Yes, I can get used to that, I think. But Valentién? Do you think it wise to claim that name, considering the man who is now Lord of Chartreux? And have you heard? He has publicly named his brother – Sir Ranulf that is – Governor of Chartreux in his absence."

Gaelen shrugged.

"Yes, I knew. But do not worry, love. I do not intend to do anything to draw either Joffroi or Ranulf down on us while we are here. And perhaps, when my task here is finally done, it may be that we may think about going home, Gwynny."

"Home? Oh Cal..." She caught herself before Juliène could guess what name she had been going to speak. "Gaelen, I mean. Are you sure? And what is this task you must finish?"

Her brother flicked another wary glance look up and down the road.

"Let's get inside, Gwynny, there is much we have to talk about. It is not so simple as just packing up and leaving. As I said, there are things I must do first."

"Yes, come inside. I'll get you and your companion..." Here Mistress Gwynhere directed another, somewhat puzzled, look at Juliène, as if something about her appearance struck her amiss. "Something to eat and drink."

With which, she picked up her abandoned broom, ushered them inside, bade them make themselves to home and bustled off.

Juliène stared about her with some interest – and not a little relief that the first hurdle had been passed. There was no-one else in the tavern this early in the day and everything was clean and well-ordered, with the smell of lavender and rosemary underlying the inevitable aroma of ale. She sank down, rather diffidently, onto a stool near one of the tiny, horn-paned windows.

"This is the first time I have been in a tavern," she whispered to Gaelen.

"You'll grow accustomed to it soon enough," he commented laconically. Then, lapsing into a dialect that was far more provincial than his sister's, added, "This 'ere be yer home fer now an' 'ee'll 'ave ter behave like a country maid 'stead o' one o' they gentryvoke. Larn ter talk like Gwynny do, an' 'ee'll be a proper tavern wench afore a se'enight's out."

"Tavern wench?" frowned Gwynhere as she came back with three mugs of cider. "Nor do I talk like that I'll have you know!"

"No, you are not quite as broad as that," Gaelen replied with a grin, returning to the parlance Juliène had become most accustomed to hearing from him, his common speech only faintly coloured by some accent she could not quite place; certainly it was not the local Chartreux idiom.

"And you do still have need of an honest wench to help you around the place, do you not?" Gaelen asked coaxingly. "Leastways I don't see the luscious Aldith hereabouts, unless you're keeping her out of my sight?"

"Yes, I do and no, I'm not," Gwynhere admitted with an exasperated sigh as she eyed her brother sceptically. "Though I've yet to learn that *you* can help me find an honest anything." There was more than a hint of tart suspicion in her voice as she continued, "Aldith never would tell me who fathered her babe."

Gaelen managed a hurt expression that Juliène, for one, did not find particularly credible. She doubted his sister was any more convinced and Gwynhere, she thought, must know her brother considerably better than Juliène did.

"I told you before, Gwynny, that it weren't me," Gaelen protested. "Look, do you really think I am that careless or so lacking in consideration for you, my only kin in this..."

"Oh, enough! Enough!" Gwynhere interrupted. "We can argue this one 'til the ale runs dry. For now, where are your manners? You've not even introduced your..." Again that curious look at Juliène. "Companion yet."

"No, well, I was waiting for you to shackle your sisterly disapproval of my morals sufficiently to welcome one who needs your help."

Gaelen eyed Gwynhere's quick flush and then glanced at Juliène where she sat stiffly on her stool.

"Stand up, lad," he said with a grin, "and meet my sister, Gwynhere of Valentién. And this, Gwynny, is your new tavern wench."

"Wench?" Gwynhere looked from Juliène – slight and undoubtedly effeminate of appearance despite her masculine attire – to her stocky, boisterously robust brother. "Are you mad or am I?"

"Neither," Gaelen grinned. "Meet Nell, your brother's daughter."

He reached up to tug the hood from Juliène's head, releasing the long midnight-dark braids to uncoil over her shoulders as far as her waist. For a heartbeat or more they sat in silence, Juliène held quiet by a desperate fear of rejection, Gwynhere in total, unmitigated shock. Juliène started to stammer some sort of apology but Gwynhere ignored her, turning her stunned gaze in her brother's direction.

"She is your *daughter*? Good God of Light, Cal! Why didn't you tell me before! She must be all of sixteen summers old! And what do you mean by dragging her around the countryside clad in such an unseemly manner? Truly, I think you must be mad."

"Calm down, Gwynny," Gaelen said soothingly, albeit still with that glimmer of laughter deep in his eyes. "And why must you instantly think of me? You do have another brother, after all."

"Sweet God of Mercy! Not Hilarion!" she exclaimed, her cheeks suddenly the same colour as the linen that framed her face; a reaction that caused Gaelen to regard his sister with a frown, all notion of teasing abruptly fled.

"Aye, Hilarion. And why not? Do you think he is any different to the rest of us in his dislike of celibacy."

"I know he is not!" Gwynhere replied with something of a snap. She glared at her brother. "Just tell me the truth now, without any more of this unseemly jesting. Whoever she is, can't you see the poor maid is nigh to dropping with fatigue! And hunger too, no doubt."

With which she reached out and drew the astonished Juliène into a warm embrace that encompassed the scents of ale, fresh-baked bread and the promise of safety.

"There, child, whoever you are and whatever either of my brothers might have said or done to turn your life upside down, you are safe now."

To the best of Juliène's knowledge her mother had never given her a hug in all her life and, although she knew her sister loved her dearly, gestures of affection had become rare between them of late. Her fault, Juliène acknowledged with a dull ache of regret; she had been so enmeshed in her own despair at leaving Kaerellios that she had shunned the loving support Ro had repeatedly tried to offer. Now, though, Juliène found herself so weary and so utterly confused that, unfamiliar though the notion of comfort might be, she took momentary refuge in Gwynhere's arms, feeling the tears of loss gather in her eyes again.

Tears she had forfeited any right to shed! Pulling back she managed to say, "I thank you for your kindness, Mistress Gwynhere, but I am well enough." She glanced at Gaelen who was watching them both, his expression quite unreadable. Jolted back into remembrance of all he had done for her, she added, "And I would ask you not to judge your brother too harshly, vexing though you must find him. He saved my life when he brought me out of Chartre castle and I can only hope he has not brought danger down on you by bringing me here."

"Chartre *castle*?"

Startled, Gwynhere looked into her brother's watchful falcon's eyes.

"What in the name of all the gods is going on? Cal, is this child Hilarion's daughter or not?"

"No, but that is what we will tell anyone who asks. As to who she really is," Gaelen continued grimly. "You told me that you had heard about the fire and that it was known that one of Louis' daughters had died in that blaze. Well, what no-one else can possibly know was that it was me who set the Lady Tower in flames, in order to cover my tracks and those of the young woman I brought out of the castle with me."

"And this is she?" Gwynhere said, although it was barely a question. "The one who was supposed to have died in the fire?"

"Aye, this is the Lady Juliène Eléanor de Chartreux," he replied. Then his voice roughened. "And I tell you now, Gwynny, that if either Black Joffroi or Ranulf or, worse yet, her whoring witch of a mother discovers she is yet alive, they will tear Chartreux apart to find her."

"She cannot stay here long then," Gwynhere warned. "Lord Joffroy and Lady Ariena may be gone but that still leaves..."

"Ranulf, yes," Gaelen agreed. "And for all his womanising, I have never doubted the sharpness of his wits. You are right, she cannot stay here long. She needs a safer refuge than Anjélais can provide."

"So you will take her to Lord Gilles then?"

"Yes, just as soon as I can," Gaelen agreed. "But I dare not take the time to travel to Valentién and back at the moment. As you know, her sister has been taken to Rogérinac and I must get her out of there as soon as may be. There now, Gwynny, I have told you everything. You know who you are dealing with and the very real dangers involved! So... can I leave her here in your care?"

"You did not need to ask," Gwynhere said simply and Juliène could hear neither hesitation nor doubt in her reply. "Come, child, you must eat. And then we will set about clothing you more respectably. Life here will be hard for you, I don't doubt, but the gods willing, I can keep you from harm until Ca... Cai... my brother can take both you and your sister to a more certain refuge with Lord Gilles."

Juliène started to open her mouth, to dispute these dispositions of her person, to protest the necessity of leaving Chartreux for Gilles de Valenne's territory. But in the end she said nothing, having no choice for the moment but to trust herself to this brother and sister of whom she knew next to nothing but who seemed genuine in their determination to help her. And if Gaelen were successful in freeing her sister from Rogérinac and she and Ro were to be reunited...

On the one hand, Juliène felt such a leap of hope at that prospect as to defy all words. On the other she scarcely knew how she would manage to look her sister in the eye, so many secrets and half-formed suspicions now lying between them; sharp thorns hidden beneath the fragile white flowers of truth.

They assuaged their hunger in the small but scrupulously clean kitchen of the tavern, the back door open onto the grassy yard, the morning sun glowing on the bright orange marigolds spilling from a pot by the door and never had Juliène been so grateful for a meal, simple though it was. The bread was still warm from the oven, the bacon hot and flavoursome, the cider that washed it all down crisp and cool.

Immediately after they had eaten Gaelen disappeared. Neither his sister nor his putative niece asked him his errand, Gwynhere merely adjuring him to take care. Left alone with Mistress Gwynhere, Juliène felt a moment's panic but the older woman smiled warmly and said with quiet cheerfulness,

"Come along then... Nell." She stumbled slightly over the name, as if thinking she should not be so familiar with her noble guest but when Juliène made no obvious demur continued with thoughtful determination, "We must find you something more suitable to wear before we do anything else. Are you handy with a needle, my... Nell?"

"I can embroider prettily enough," Juliène replied, somewhat ruefully. "But if you are asking whether I can sew a straight seam or darn a hole in my stocking, then no, I am not handy at all. My sister is more practical than I am, by far."

"She will need to be, I am thinking," Gwynhere commented as she led the way from the kitchen, up the narrow, dark stairs towards what was likely her own bedchamber. "I'm afraid there's not much by way of comfort waiting for her at Rogérinac."

"You have been there?" Juliène asked, her curiosity aroused.

"No, not me!" The appalled tone of Mistress Gwynhere's voice strongly suggested she had no desire to venture there either. "But Ca... Gaelen, has been there on occasion and from what he says of the place I'm not surprised he wants to get your sister out of there as soon as may be. The keep's nigh to falling down and as for the ruffians that live there... aye well, you don't want to be hearing tales of gloom and doom when your poor sister's got no choice but to be there. But at least Gaelen did say that she was with Sir Guy, did he not? I reckon he'll see your sister's all right."

"What do you know about Guyard de Martine?" Juliène queried in some surprise, wincing as she caught the note of unconscious hauteur in her voice. She had not meant it like that at all but fortunately the other woman either did not hear it or chose not to take it amiss.

"I only know what everybody else in Mithlondia knows," Mistress Gwynhere replied, rather more airily than Juliène thought credible for a sister of Gaelen of Valentién. "That he's Lord Jacques' base-born son by Lady Alys of Montfaucon. And for all he's half-brother to Black Joffroy, I believe him to be a gentle man at heart. So don't you worry, Lady Rowena will be safe enough with him." A wisp of doubt seemed to dim her sunny confidence for a moment. "Not that there's aught any of us can do about it if she's not." Then shaking off whatever thought had clouded her mind. "Now, let's see what we can do for you."

Juliène spent the rest of the morning – aided by Mistress Gwynhere when her normal chores permitted – cutting down and sewing back together a set of clothes for herself from the garments the older woman pulled from the clothing chest in her chamber. They were much of a height but Mistress Gwynhere's bones were far more comfortably covered in flesh than Juliène's willow-slender frame. The garments themselves were such as would be worn by any respectable provincial matron. Well cared for and stored with lavender to keep them fresh, Juliène could not repress the suspicion that Gwynhere had given her what were her best feast-day clothes and so tried to avoid giving any impression of disdain. Nevertheless they were far from anything she was accustomed to.

She had thought it trial enough to exchange the light silks and gauzy linens of Kardolandia for the weightier velvets and brocades she had worn in Chartre. But Mistress Gwynhere's garments were made of serviceable wool in sober shades of mulberry and dark leaf-green, the linen shifts and nightgowns being of a far coarser quality than Juliène had ever imagined possible to wear next to her skin.

Still, she had no choice if she were ever to shed her boy's garments. Indeed she thought she would rather dress in the humblest rags than continue to wear the rough breeches and thick tunic in which she had lived, slept and sweltered so uncomfortably for the past two days and nights. Not that her new garments bore any resemblance to beggar's rags but they were certainly very different to anything she had ever worn before.

She looked, she thought, craning her head to observe herself as she stood in the tiny, low-ceilinged chamber that was to be her own, just like a peasant wench. Which, she supposed ruefully, was what she was supposed to be.

Despite Gwynhere's urging she had refused to cut her long hair to a more modest length but had promised to keep it pinned up and out of sight under the unflattering linen cap she now wore. Her feet in wooden clogs were bare but she had only worn stockings since she came back to Chartre and did not mind their lack now, although she did fear blisters from her new footwear. The shift she wore irritated her soft skin, especially where it was bound close to her breasts by the tightly-laced black bodice. A dark green, ankle-length skirt of heavy wool completed the attire of the Flower and Falcon's latest serving wench. She tugged her bodice up a bit higher and thus garbed, she went down to show Gwynhere what she had accomplished.

It was not, however, the friendly mistress of the Flower and Falcon tavern whom she found in the kitchen but Gwynhere's far more dangerous brother. Catching the sound of her wooden clogs on the slate floor Gaelen stopped what he was doing and looked up abruptly, the faint surprise on his bearded face subsumed almost immediately by intent interest, his amber-brown eyes narrowing and his mouth pursing in silent consideration. Putting down the knife and whetstone he had been using, he gestured her towards the open door.

Ruffled by his silent appraisal though she was, Juliène nevertheless stepped obediently into the light and permitted him to continue his perusal, unable to quite restrain her nervous twitch as he grunted slightly under his breath at something that obviously struck him awry.

"What is it?" she asked, wondering what she had forgotten or whether her sewing skills were so blatantly lacking that even a man could notice their deficiency. She tugged self consciously at her bodice again. "Is it this? Am I not respectable enough? It is rather revealing, do you not think?"

"You're a tavern wench, you're not supposed to be *too* respectable." There was no lewdness in his voice, only a fine thread of something that sounded like regret. "No, leave it, 'tis fine." He exhaled deeply and shook his head. "You're a lovely looking maid and no mistake. I'd not be surprised if you don't have all the men in Anjélais tripping over their feet to be served their ale by you afore the day's out. Just keep out of Sir Girauld's way, aye?"

"I cannot help how I look," Juliène pointed out. "And you need have no fear that I shall encourage any man, be he noble or peasant, to go any further than looking. I had a surfeit of drunken, lascivious louts in Chartre!" Then regretted her rash words when Gaelen's thoughtful gaze took on the hard sheen of polished agate.

"I take it you're meaning Ranulf by that?" he asked, his voice low and grim.

She thought of not answering but finally nodded. Gaelen grunted again.

"You obviously know about him and that tirewoman of yours then?"

She was so relieved that he had not asked about de Rogé's experience with herself that she replied without thinking,

"Yes, I could sm... that is, he made no secret of it. But how do *you* know about it?"

"Coupling in a public passageway is scarcely discreet," Gaelen commented dryly.

She goggled at him.

"What? You mean you actually *saw* him and Ilana... ugh!"

"Quite," Gaelen agreed, still watching her rather more keenly than she cared for. "Wasted a pitcher of good Marillec wine and soaked his boots for him at the same time."

She smiled slightly then sought hastily to divert his thoughts from that night... the night she could not remember without a shudder... the night she had lain with a man she did not love.

"Please, Gaelen, can we not forget that night?"

"If you think you can, I am agreeable," Gaelen replied, greying brown brows lifting slightly. Then, resuming his normal expression. "Neither Gwynny nor I will mention it to you again."

"Thank you."

"Unless it becomes necessary," he added, grimly overriding her gratitude. He did not need to specify why it might become necessary; she already knew. Gods forgive her, how could she not know?

Swallowing back the resurgence of dread, she asked,

"So what is it about my appearance you do not approve of? Obviously something caught your eye, something wrong?"

He did not answer immediately but bent to the bucket that Gwynhere had left by the door. Dipping his finger in the cold, grey ash he swiped a streak across Juliène's cheek and temple. Standing back he grinned at her as she fought against the instinct to wipe her face clean of the grime.

"'Aat be better. Now 'ee looks like 'ee might ha' done some proper work. A bit of weedin' in Gwynny's veg patch, work up a bit of a sweat an' git zum dirt un'er yer nails an' I reckon as 'ee'll do. But first, come 'ee into the tavern, maid, an' pour I a mug o' zyder. Get 'ee used to it afore the men come in from the fields."

"When will you go to Rogérinac," she asked over her shoulder as she walked from the kitchen into the main room of the tavern.

"First light tomorrow," he replied, dropping the accent. "For today my duty is solely to you. To make damned sure that any lecherous-minded local knows that Gaelen the wanderer is back for good and that his womenfolk are no longer without protection. Not," he added with a grin. "That Gwynny has been without defence since her man died. Very handy with a broom, she is. And none so luckless with an ale pitcher neither."

"Skills I will be sure to acquire," Juliène assured him gravely, although her eyes smiled.

Skills more practical and more honest than any of the dubious accomplishments she had learnt at the Winter Lady's instigation. What need had she now to know how to twist the truth for her own ends? How to incite lust and corrupt honour?

How to seduce a man with her body or brew a potion to steal away his will? Indeed she hoped she would never need to make use of such power ever again. Once was more than enough.

Thrusting aside memory of that one occasion, she forced herself to smile at her companion – a dazzling smile to cover her creeping sense of shame.

"Come on then, Gaelen, teach me about cider and ale."

# Chapter 3

## *A New Life*

Juliène woke the next morning in an unfamiliar bed, to the sound of swallows in their nests outside her tiny window and the knowledge that Gaelen must already be gone, heading out alone and in the gods only knew what guise, to save her sister from Guyard de Martine. Yet did Ro even want to be rescued, she wondered, or would she rather stay with the man as his mistress, shameful though such a position would be?

*Had* they been lovers at Chartre? Juliène asked herself for perhaps the dozenth time. She had thought not but now, remembering her sister as she been the penultimate time Juliène had seen her – the morning after Ro had spent a night alone with Guyard de Martine – she was not so sure. And there had been something in de Martine's eyes as he had looked at her sister that had brought forth an answering awareness from every raw emotion Juliène had ever felt... together with the conviction that if de Martine and her sister were not lovers already, they would be soon. In which case should she hope that Gaelen reached Rogérinac before that happened? Or not?

She sighed, her thoughts turning away from her sister and back towards the practical difficulties of her own life. She was alone, save for Mistress Gwynhere; a fugitive from her mother by choice and a tavern wench by necessity, waiting for the gods to determine how her life would run from here.

When first she had returned to Mithlondia, a little under a month before, she had been convinced that she would never survive the transition from life as lady-companion to the Kardolandian queen, with all its attendant luxuries, to that of a Mithlondian nobleman's daughter. But at least in Chartre she had still been surrounded by the trappings of power and privilege. And she had had her dreams to sustain her.

As she did still, she reminded herself firmly. Kaslan had promised that he would follow her to Mithlondia, that he would find her again, wherever she was, and make her his in every way. Her mother had scoffed at the notion when Juliène had told her, her belief in her lover inevitably wavering under the cool amusement in the Winter Lady's knowing green gaze, before stubbornly making a recovery. Yes, men seduced women and abandoned them all the time but Kaslan was not of that ilk. Juliène knew that as surely as she knew her own heart. He had said he could come north to claim her and so he would.

Obviously he would seek her first in Chartre but surely he would not believe she had perished in the fire; his heart would tell him otherwise. So he would spread his search wider. And, gods willing, he would find her. As for her, situated as she was in a village that touched both the main highway and the Liriél River, she was well placed to wait for him, hidden from those who sought to use her for their own ends.

Her determination notwithstanding, it proved no easy matter to turn the Demoiselle Juliène Eléanor de Chartreux, pampered lady-in-waiting to Queen Xandra of Kardolandia into Nell of Valentién, serving wench of the Flower and Falcon tavern in Anjélais-sur-Liriél.

To start with, Juliène found it difficult to understand, and in turn speak, the broad dialect used by the locals. It did not help either that most of the other women of the village viewed her with no great kindness – she was a "vurriner", after all, coming as she supposedly did from the far-off province of Valenne – and had it not been for Gwynhere's unwavering patience and her own belief in Kaslan's love, she might have yielded more often to the tears of desolation that came in the darkness of the night as she lay on her hard bed, coarse linen sheets and rough woollen blankets pulled high against the menace of mice, bats and spiders. At least, thanks to Gwynhere's determined efforts to keep her home clean, there were no lice to further torment Juliène's soft skin or crawl through her hair.

Nor, she discovered after a few days, was Gwynhere the only person in Anjélais willing to ignore the strangeness of her arrival and treat her with kindness.

She had been standing outside the butcher's shop, idly watching as Gwynhere haggled with the red-faced merchant over the price of sausages. The morning was already hot, the air dusty and she would have been even more uncomfortable had it not been for the welcome shade provided by the great plane trees that marked out the square. She was just wondering how much longer Gwynhere was going to be when she was surprised – and not a little alarmed – to find herself accosted by one of the other villagers, a buxom young woman with a basket over one arm, a merry smile and light brown curling hair which was obviously too springy to remain properly confined beneath her cap.

Her initial alarm being somewhat allayed by the girl's cheerful tone and sunny smile, they had fallen into a somewhat one-sided conversation under Gwynhere's amused, if watchful, eye. Despite Juliène's incomplete command of the Chartreux dialect, she understood enough of the young woman's speech to ascertain that her name was Helge and that her father kept the Three Sygnets, the tavern at the other side of the square. Grateful as she was for this first sign that she might one day be accepted in the village, Juliène had even managed to return Helge's exuberant overtures of friendship, although admittedly in a much more restrained manner.

Yet even with the unstinting support she received from Gwynhere and Helge, life in Anjélais continued to prove itself a constant round of difficulties of every variety. Nonetheless, every morning Juliène awoke and thanked the gods for their mercy, even though by sunset she was often reduced to despair and given to wild thoughts of returning to Chartre.

Only the thought of the man who was now Governor of Chartreux held her back. If Guyard de Martine had still been in Chartre, she might have ventured to return, believing that she could manipulate his compassion into protection. His half-brother, however, was a completely different prospect and she feared Ranulf de Rogé too much to go back, the memory of the blunt language in which he had couched his rejection of her, not to mention the dangerous look in his eyes as he surveyed her naked body, warning her that she could expect no mercy from him.

The days continued to pass and in spite of her almost constant weariness and occasional bouts of self-loathing mingled with formless terror, Juliène came to accept that Gwynhere's kind-hearted welcome of her was perfectly genuine and, in return, a determination was born in her that the Valennaise would never regret the generosity and affection she had shown towards the Winter Lady's daughter.


Still summer drifted on and life continued much as it ever had in Anjélais-sur-Liriél. Travelling merchants and other itinerants brought tidings that were eagerly listened to and then shrugged aside as having no bearing on the harvest in the fields or the depth of cider in the barrel. Nevertheless in this way, Juliène learned something of what was happening within Mithlondia.

In far-off Lamortaine young Prince Linnius was said to be finding his feet, presiding over the first binding of his reign with one hand and promoting his illegitimate half-brother to High Commander with the other. Meanwhile, somewhat closer to home, a de Rogé continued to live in the half-ruined castle in Chartre and govern an unquiet province by martial law. Juliène heard rumours of violence committed by both sides – stealthy murder by the Chartreux partisans, answered by swift and brutal reprisal from de Rogé and the soldiers under his command.

There was, however, no sign of Gaelen returning from Rogérinac.

And still Kaslan did not come!

Would he even recognise her if he did, she wondered sometimes, looking down at her hands, once as soft and white as lily petals, now cracked, calloused and just plain ugly. Hands that had formerly undertaken nothing more strenuous than her embroidery, now swept and polished, washed crockery and clothing, baked bread, seasoned stews and poured ale and cider by the barrel.

Almost without her noticing, Midsummer – the date on which her sister should have celebrated her binding with Joscelin de Veraux – came and went, life in Anjélais continuing at its own slow pace, following the flow of the river and the ripening of the crops in the field. She even ceased to notice Gaelen's continuing absence – although she did worry about her sister's welfare. Missing Ro as she did, Juliène came to rely on Gwynhere in a way she would never have believed possible and as the days passed so her guilt grew at the way in which she was deceiving the woman who was more of a mother to her than the Winter Lady had ever been.

As for Gwynhere, she found herself torn between anxiety over her brother's whereabouts and concern at the changes she observed in her guest. Always pale and slender, the young noblewoman was becoming whiter and thinner with each passing day. The cause might merely be weariness – it was no easy life at the Flower and Falcon – or it could be distress on her sister's behalf.

Or it might be something else again.

Before he had left for Rogérinac, Cal – he was always Cal to her in the quiet of her mind – had confided something of his thoughts regarding the Lady Juliène's experiences at the hands of the man who was now Governor of Chartreux and as the weeks went by Gwynhere began to fear that her brother had been horribly accurate in his surmise. But she said nothing to the girl. Fond though she had become of Juliène, and in spite of her belief that the young noblewoman had come to trust her to a certain extent, she still did not feel there was sufficient intimacy between them that she could ask outright whether Ranulf de Rogé had forced her into sharing his bed.

All she could do was keep an increasingly anxious eye on her "niece", at the same time praying to all the gods that, for once in his life, her infuriatingly acute brother might be proved wrong. Failing that, she could only hope that Juliène would trust her with the truth before it became obvious to everyone, thus giving the villagers one more cause to gossip about the newcomer. And gossip, as Gwynhere well knew, was never less than painful.

Meanwhile danger continued to stalk the highway and roam the streets of the larger towns of the province – bringing death by blade, arrow, noose or fever – though it did little to disturb the cheerful tedium of life in Anjélais. Until one day, completely without warning, it arrived and with such force as to lay waste not only to the new life Juliène had begun to build for herself but also to destroy what remained of her old one as well.

It was autumn and in the crisp brightness of early morning, Juliène stood in the small orchard behind the Flower and Falcon, pegging wet laundry on a dew-spangled line.

Her hands were as rough as those of any peasant girl but quick and competent at their task. Her small, slender feet in the heavy wooden sabots were wet from the droplets of dew that clung like tiny glittering jewels to the grass and dampened the hem of her green kirtle while her dark hair hung down her back, bound in one thick braid and partially covered by a kerchief of unbleached linen.

She sang a little as she worked, a slightly plaintive love song Guy of Montfaucon had played one afternoon when he had been summoned to entertain her mother and herself as they sat in the small, walled garden of Chartre castle, the scent of sun-warmed honeysuckle heavy on the air. The melody had caught at her heart in some strange way and Juliène had persuaded him to teach her the words; some lovelorn nonsense about a mermaid and a mortal man which she strongly suspected the harper of making up to flatter her, since in his version of the song the mermaid's tail of shimmering green matched the emerald of her eyes and her long shining hair was black as a raven's wing. She had enjoyed that rare afternoon spent in the harper's company – usually he was with her sister – more than she liked to admit but it had not been repeated. Instead his brothers had come to Chartre...

Her voice died in her throat and in the silence that thrummed as loud in her ears as the frantic beat of her heart, she heard a familiar voice behind her.

"Oh, Nell, don't stop! 'Twere a right pretty song 'ee were singing though 'tis not one I've heard afore. From Valenne, is it? An' what's one of they mermaids then?"

Shaking off her memories, Juliène turned to smile at the newcomer but neglected to answer her question as to the origin of the song or explain that a mermaid was a fey woman of the sea. The less said about any of the Faennari to superstitious villagers the better, especially given the colour of her own eyes.

"Helge. What brings you here so early in the day?"

"Surely ee've not forgot, Nell? Us be gwaing blackbreeing."

"Oh yes, of course I remember... but I will have to finish my chores first. Gwynny..."

But suddenly Juliène could not remember what she had promised to do for Gwynhere. Or even who Gwynhere was. Breaking out in a cold sweat, she reached for the nearest branch to steady herself and clamped her mouth tight shut. Helge, evidently realising that something was drastically amiss, squinted short-sightedly at her.

"What be wrong, maid? 'Ee do look a mite green! Not bin eatin' eels, 'ave 'ee?"

Juliène started to shake her head in denial then brought her hand up to her mouth as she struggled to contain her nausea. She could not do it and, with a muffled apology, she fled for the privy, leaving Helge to follow if she wished.

Emerging cautiously a little while later from the noisome shelter, she took a deep breath of the fresher morning air and tried to still the trembling in her limbs. Looking around, Juliène was not surprised to find Helge waiting for her, the former speculation in her friend's hazel eyes replaced by certainty.

"'Ee's breedin', bain't 'ee?"

Juliène stared at her, wondered whether to deny it, then said unsteadily,

"I think I must be. Though it might be something I ate."

"Not likely," Helge snorted. "Mistress Gwynhere's the best cook an' alewife for leagues around. Even me own faither cain't deny that, much as 'e'd like to! So 'ow long 'ave 'ee been pukin' like this then?"

"Not long," Juliène replied, her voice tight with the effort of containing both nausea and emotion.

"An' I'll wager as 'ow 'ee've missed yer last two fluxes," Helge said decisively, causing a hot rush of blood to darken Juliène's otherwise pale cheeks, even as she nodded in embarrassed affirmation. "Not much doubt about it then," her friend concluded knowledgeably. "Come mid spring I'd say, 'ee'll be in the straw and cursin' some man to Hell an' back agin."

"Never mind back again. When he gets to Hell he can stay there with my good will," Juliène retorted, not entirely speciously. She hesitated then prompted by a diffident curiosity, said, "You don't seem particularly shocked, Helge! Nor even very surprised that I am... er... breeding and neither man nor binding bracelet in sight."

"Don't make a ha'pence of difference to me, lovedy," Helge said with a grin. "But I s'pose that's why your faither sent you all this way down yere... outta sight, outta mind like. All I'll say is, just be thankful Mistress Gwynhere's got a kind heart." Adding rather caustically. "An' if'n that's the sort of faither he be, Nell, 'ee be better off wi'out him!"

Juliène choked on a spurt of laughter at this robust summary of her situation. She was surprised but very relieved that Helge did not seem to think any worse of her. She *hoped* Gwynhere would prove to be equally complacent but was inclined to doubt it. As for Gaelen's attitude when he eventually arrived with her sister, she really had no idea what it might be.

And Ro? What would she say?

*God of Mercy,* she prayed. *Let Kaslan come soon...*

But Kaslan was thousands of leagues away and beside her Helge was still chittering on.

"... bit o' dry bread in the mornings, that'll settle yer belly proper, or so Goody Nan allus says. An' her's had nine brats, so her did oughtta know."

"If she's had nine, she ought to know better!" Juliène exclaimed. "I tell you, this is one too many for me!"

"Aye well, mebbe make 'ee think twice afore 'ee says aye nex' time," Helge commented, adding with a sly look and a crooked grin, "Though there's times when a maid thinks twice an' still says aye. Jus' depends on the man doin' the askin'. What do 'ee reckon to that there new lordling in Chartre then? Lord Joffroy's brother I heard he were?"

Juliène gave a shudder and said forcefully,

"Believe me, as far as the Governor of Chartreux is concerned, he could go down on his knees and *beg* and the answer would still be *no*."

"Aye well, mebbe not 'im then. But I reckon as how 'ee'll sing a diff'rent tune when 'tis the right man doing the beggin'," Helge offered, her grin widening even more to reveal slightly uneven but otherwise healthy looking teeth. "'Ow about 'im up at the castle? Sir Girauld? 'E comes down to the tavern now an' again and Fritha... 'ee knaws the maid I means, mouthiest wench up at the castle... well, her sez as 'ow 'e's got the biggest..."

"Helge!" Juliène broke in, her appalled intervention marred by a sudden gurgle of laughter.

Mistress Gwynhere was all that was kind but it seemed so long since she had been with another girl her own age and although Helge could never, ever replace her beloved sister at least she could share a gossip and laugh with her, at the expense of the men around them. And if Helge was prepared to stand her friend, it would not do to alienate her now. Pushing aside her troubles for a moment, she therefore responded as expected and asked with a sigh, "All right, Helge, the biggest what?"

The other girl gave an answering snicker and said,

"I knawed 'ee couldn't be as lackin' in interest as all that, e'en wi' a babe in yer belly..."

Juliène's smile dimmed at this reminder of her situation but fortunately Helge was well into her flights of fancy regarding Sir Girauld's sexual prowess and physical attributes and took little heed of her companion's gradual withdrawal into her memories. Even as they collected baskets and shawls Helge continued to chatter.

Juliène listened with half an ear while her fingers were busy among the brambles but the wraiths of the past continued to flit through her mind. She tried to hold fast to the good memories, those of her lover; tall, slim and handsome, a young man with short, black, curly hair and laughing dark eyes. Only to find the illusion displaced by the image of another man; older, harder, with long, fair hair and an unreadable dark blue gaze...

Two men with absolutely nothing in common.

Nothing save that they had both been intimate with her body; one with love, the other with something that had felt very much like hate.

# Chapter 4

## *Noble Visitors*

Returning to Anjélais village around noon with their baskets full, their clothes snagged with prickles and burrs and their hands scratched and stained with blackberry juice, Juliène and Helge found the folk of the village gathering in the market square.

"What be all the fuss then?" Helge asked the nearest bystander, an elderly man with surprisingly sharp old eyes.

"Zum vurrin lordlings or sech be ridin' this way. Leastways that's what young Jarec sez. 'E were out t'other side o' the village, s'posed to be exercisin' Sir Girauld's hosses, though I reckon as how 'e were checkin' his snares, more like. Anyhow 'e comes drashin' back yere like all the daemons in 'ell were arter 'e, spoutin' zum nonsense or t'other that zeems like it might acherly be true fer once. Look'ee there!"

Following his jutted chin and bright glance, Juliène was astonished to see a large group of riders making their way at a walking pace between the cottages that formed South Street. Not that travellers were a rarity in Anjélais – the village did straddle the road that connected the province of Rogé and the port of Chartre to the rest of the realm – but it was unusual to see a cavalcade quite so impressive as this one.

Merchants and messengers, hunting or hawking parties from the strongholds of Anjélais or nearby Liriéllon were all to be expected but not since Black Joffroi, Lady Ariène and their escort had passed that way at the beginning of summer – and Juliène had not witnessed that event herself – had such a large and diverse group appeared to enliven the quiet tedium of Anjélais-sur-Liriél. Naturally the villagers were both keenly interested and mulishly cautious about these new arrivals and Juliène smiled to herself at the thought that they would be able to gawp and gossip about the strangers for days, if not months, to come.

Nonetheless caution won out over curiosity and Juliène found that she and Helge were the only ones brave – or foolish – enough to linger in the open. Even the old man who had been their informant had hobbled out of sight, plainly distrustful of any large group of armed men. Juliène herself was torn between retreat – lest it be the Governor of Chartreux himself – and remaining where she was in the sudden overpowering hope that it might be her errant lover. Jarec *had* said they were "vurrin"; although she did accept that to a lad born and bred within the walls of Anjélais castle, anyone hailing from farther away than the next village was likely to be considered foreign. Helge, moreover, was staring as if mesmerised at the approaching riders and it would prove difficult, if not impossible, to coax her away.

Confident in her ability to conceal herself – should it prove necessary – behind the broad trunk of the plane tree under which she and Helge were standing, Juliène returned her attention to the two riders at the head of the cavalcade. They were both "lordlings", that much was obvious, but there any similarity ended. One was a big man, mounted on a huge black stallion and clad in serviceable mail, his dark cloak thrown back over his shoulders to allow ease of access to the sword that hung at his side and...

Panic flared as Juliène realised that she knew that horse. Recognised too beyond all doubt the bearing of the man riding it!

Heedless now whether Helge stayed or went, Juliène had already turned to flee when something about the other man jerked her to a halt. She turned back for another look, desperate to escape but constrained to stay by some overpowering tug of familiarity.

Clearly a courtier rather than a soldier, young and handsome, his lean, lithe body was shown to advantage by his light raiment. A soft white linen tunic bordered with a swirling pattern in blue and green exposed long, graceful, golden-brown limbs. A mantle of some shimmering turquoise material fell with casual elegance from his shoulders. Two wide silver bands glinted about his wrists and, save for a jewel-hilted dagger in a gilded sheath, he did not appear to be armed. Neither did it seem that he was a horseman by choice, clearly being content to rely on the groom walking beside him to control the placid dappled gelding he was seated upon.

Behind him, a sturdy dark-skinned man bore a huge banner that flashed in the noon-tide sun. Not the chilling black and silver of the present Lord of Chartreux but bright gold and deep blue, reflecting the sky that arched over his head and the blazing golden sun that so brilliantly embodied the youngest Prince of Kardolandia.

*Goddess be praised! He has come for me, as he swore he would.*

There was no power in the five realms that would make her hide now although she felt a momentary qualm that Kaslan should see her like this, looking like a peasant wench, berry-stained, sweaty and unkempt...

Then another thought intruded as it occurred to her to wonder why he should be travelling the highway to Lamortaine and in such a fashion? She had expected him to come to Mithlondia, it was true, but surely he should have come alone, not counting a servant or two. But this...

Frowning uncertainly, Juliène glanced down the full length of the cavalcade, past the standard-bearer to the untidy gaggle of pack animals laden with all manner of bundles and baggage. They were accompanied by a couple of vitriolic Mithlondian drovers and several unhappy-looking Kardolandian servants dressed in short kilts of sea-blue linen and very little else, while around and behind the baggage train and the servants rode another group of men, as grim in appearance and as well-armed as their leader, all of them wearing the badge of the black boar.

Recognition of this hated emblem brought a further flurry of slamming shutters and the occasional insult shouted in the local dialect, a reaction which, Juliène observed, caused Kaslan to glance apprehensively at his companion, but de Rogé gave no sign of noticing the stir he and his men were causing. He sat easily in his saddle, reins held loosely in one hand, sword hand resting lightly on his thigh, his bored glance apparently moving neither left nor right. Yet not for one moment did Juliène – nor, she was sure, did any of the hidden villagers – make the mistake of supposing the man to be unmindful either of where he was or the bone-deep hatred that surrounded him; too many men had died for him to take chances.

As for Juliène, just the sight of his face as he drew closer was enough to make her gut churn with a sudden return of her earlier nausea and vanquish the warmth that Kaslan's proximity had engendered as if it had never been, leaving only despair. Ducking back into the shadow of the tree, she found herself wondering frantically how, in the name of mercy, the gods could have permitted this to happen? Why, out of all the men in the five realms, did these two have to ride into Anjélais *together*?

The one man she had wished to see above all others; the lover to whom she had given herself so freely and whose child she now carried. The other, who had... no, she would not think about that night, not when her true love was so close.

Yet how was she to speak to Kaslan? That would be difficult even without the added complication of de Rogé's presence. She had little doubt as to her fate should he recognise her but attempted to reassure herself with the thought that there was no reason for him to be suspicious of a simple village girl. As far as he was concerned the Lady Juliène de Chartreux was dead and once Kaslan realised who she was, surely he would protect her. When all was said and done, he was a Prince of Kardolandia whereas Ranulf de Rogé was a mere landless Mithlondian soldier, little better in rank – despite his noble birth – than a paid mercenary! Well, that might be a slight exaggeration, Juliène thought, but it made her feel better.

She had just decided that she would make herself known to Kaslan as soon as he drew level with their tree when she became aware that Helge was busily preening herself, one eye cocked towards the approaching noblemen, who were now scant yards away.

"Ooh, I wonder who they be?" Helge muttered excitedly as she tried to scrub the blackberry stains from her scratched fingers. "Do 'ee think they'm headed fer the castle fer to see Sir Girauld? 'Twould be a cruel shame if they was just to pass through, don't 'ee think?"

"Yes... no," Juliène replied abstractly as she calculated how long she had before she must make her move.

"Oh but look at them, Nell, don't 'ee think they'm good looking? An' dressed so fine an' all."

"If you say so. But Jarec was right for once. They *are* noblemen, Helge, and men like that..." Her words dwindled away but it scarcely mattered since Helge was not listening.

"So, who do 'ee think they be?" Helge repeated. "One of 'em's vurrin for sure. An' t'other one, 'e'll be one of the new lord's men, don't 'ee think?" Her hazel eyes widened and some of the sparkle left them. "Mayhap even the Governor hisself!"

The words rang heavily in Juliène's ears and she said tautly,

"Look, Helge, I don't want to sound like a croaking old crow but just be careful of the one in black."

"Oh, an' why's that then?" Helge asked, curiosity flaring at the unmistakeable warning note in Juliène's voice. "Sounds like 'ee does knaw him."

"Not like you mean!" Juliène lied. "But yes, I know enough. If you must have it, Helge, that *is* the Governor of Chartreux, Black Joffroi's younger brother."

"Oh!" And then, "Do 'ee think 'e be as much of a monster as they say?"

It was hard to tell whether Helge was genuinely afraid or merely excited.

"He's a vicious brute!" Juliène snapped. Then before Helge could question her further, "The other, I think, from the banner... I think he is one of the Kardolandian Princes."

Helge's eyes widened even more and she started to say something in an awed squeak but Juliène did not hear. She was listening in the silence of her mind, hoping to hear the echo of Kaslan's whispered reassurance the day they had parted; that he would come to Mithlondia and find her again. Surely that moment had come and he was even now searching for her. His joy when he found her would be boundless. And how much deeper would that joy become when he learned she was carrying his child!

He was nearly level now. It was act now or lose this one chance to secure her own happiness and an honourable future for her unborn babe. Drawing a deep breath Juliène made to step forward, prepared to risk the revelation of her identity to her family's enemy in order to be reunited with the man she loved. She was sure... it had to be now... and yet...

Still she hesitated, glancing desperately up at the sky. But it was too close to noon, the sun unyieldingly bright in a high blue autumn sky. It would be hours yet before the moon rose and until then Juliène was on her own.

But was not the power of love greater than the silver skeins of deceit spun by the Goddess of the Night?

Not fully convinced of this wisdom, and with her ears filled with the noisy jingle and rumble of the cavalcade, it came as something of a shock to Juliène to realise that she could actually hear her lover's voice. Yes, it *was* him, his

Mithlondian fluent albeit touched with a faint Kardolandian accent. And yet…
she had not known he could speak her language so well. Certainly he had never
used anything other than Court Kardolandian when he had been with her.

"…Must be past noon, Messire. Can we not stop in this place for some
refreshment? I grant you it does not look much but I thought I saw an ale house
just back there. Or we could ride on up to the castle. Surely this knight, this Sir
Girauld you told me about, would make us welcome?"

"I… *you* cannot afford the time," de Rogé replied, his curt voice rasping
unpleasantly across Juliène's ears after Kaslan's mellifluous golden tones. "As for
drinking the stuff you would get in a midden like this, if you could not stomach
the wine from the castle cellars last night you will never swallow the horse piss
the peasants around here brew and call ale."

She winced. Gods above, his language was every bit as crude as she
remembered it. As for Kaslan, was that the faintest hint of peevish complaint she
could hear in his voice?

"Messire, I would remind you that I am a Prince of Kardolandia, not one
of your rough troopers. The meal I was served last night was execrable and the
wine was worse. I had a draughty, ill-lit hole to sleep in, on a bed a Kardolandian
slave would disdain and which I would swear was infested with vermin of every
sort and even…"

"I have already apologised for the state of the castle, your highness," de Rogé
interrupted, the words sounding as if they came through gritted teeth. "But I
did warn you when I met you down at the harbour that, due to events entirely
beyond my control, little of the castle is fit to be lived in. And I can assure you
that you were much better housed last night than either myself or my men."

Kaslan grimaced at that and slanted a sideways look at his host, his tone
becoming a degree more conciliating as he replied,

"I suppose, under the circumstances, I should not complain, considering
as you gave up your own quarters to me. Not to mention lending me your
doxy by way of compensation. She was skilful enough, I will say that for her,
and made up in some measure for the lack of other comforts." Kaslan's faintly
lascivious grin submerged into a scowl of annoyance. "That consideration aside,
Messire, I have had to tolerate being woken up before it was even light by your
damned workmen shouting and banging out in the courtyard, not to mention
the fact that the wench took fright when she heard you cursing your half-witted
steward and ran off before I could taste her a third time. If that were not enough,
you barely gave me time to stay my stomach's rumbling before insisting we get
on the road. Since then we have been riding without pause and I, for one, am
thirsty and hungry enough to risk whatever the locals, if they can be persuaded
to come out, can produce by way of food and drink. The gods know it cannot
be worse than the meal your cook served up last night. And, considering that
you were wrong about your doxy's skills, you may well be mistaken about the
quality of the ale they brew here."

Despite Juliène's deep dismay at Kaslan's casual mention of the woman he had bedded the night before, she realised that this would likely be her only opportunity of talking to her lover before he disappeared who knew where. She glanced up at de Rogé, willing him to make some sign of acquiescence to the wishes of the man who so clearly outranked him. Instead she saw the look of slightly irritated boredom in his dark blue eyes intensify and, as his mouth tightened, she knew with a sinking feeling that he was about to refuse Kaslan's request.

Just as she was wondering in nervous desperation whether she should risk stepping in front of the horses – the black stallion, in particular, scared her almost to the point of swooning, with its huge iron-shod hooves and a cold fire in its eye – de Rogé flicked an appraising look around the square and abruptly reined in level with Juliène and Helge. Shaking with both hope and fear – of which the latter was easily the dominant emotion – Juliène drew a deep breath and took a step forward.

"You, wench!" de Rogé demanded in common speech. "Is there a decent tavern hereabouts?"

At the sound of his voice, rough and impatient, Juliène froze. Forgetting everything the Winter Lady had taught her, she could find neither courage nor coherent response to his demand. As from a distance she heard him curse, the words muttered in Mithlondian this time, before he repeated his original question in halting Chartreux patois, evidently in the belief that neither of the women he addressed had understood his question, clear though it had been.

Tongue-tied as she was, Juliène did not know whether to be alarmed or grateful when Helge collected herself and, producing a tentative smile, dropped into a curtsey that wittingly or otherwise gave both horsemen ample opportunity to admire her best attributes. Now as Juliène well knew, sight of those assets never failed to get the Anjélais men drooling, but to her surprise – given what she knew of his attitude towards women – de Rogé proved to be made of sterner stuff, his glance merely skimming Helge's endowments before returning his irascible attention to Juliène.

Why did he expect an answer from her, she wondered, rather than Helge? Was it that she had inadvertently done something to arouse his suspicion? Then she forgot the anxiety de Rogé had incited as she became aware that Helge's charms had found a far more receptive audience than the boorish Governor of Chartreux. A rip-tide of hurt flooded through her at Kaslan's open appreciation of another woman, even while her own attention was forcibly wrenched back towards the man she had once – oh so foolishly – thought she could bend to her will.

"Bloody hell and damnation!"

Juliène flinched as his words sheered through her thoughts. Ranulf de Rogé, it seemed, cursed as fluently – and as unimaginatively – in common speech as he did in Mithlondian.

"I swear if I do not get an answer from one of you, I will have you both flogged for whoring on the prince's highway. I said, is there a tavern in this sh…"

The leashed violence in his tone made Helge jump and, simultaneously, released Juliène from her frozen stillness. Giving a quick peasant's bob she cut across his final word.

"Aye, m'lord. Beggin' yer pardon, m'lord, but there be two taverns hereabouts." She added another "m'lord" for good measure and then, unable to gauge his expression with her eyes discreetly downcast, sent a fleeting glance up at his face. This, however, proved to be a mistake.

"*Sir* will do," de Rogé said flatly, some fleeting emotion flaring in his eyes as green met blue for a single heartbeat.

His eyes narrowed and his gauntleted hand clenched on his thigh even as Juliène hastily broke the contact. Even without looking, she sensed his frown. Then, as he seemed to remember the reason they had stopped in the first place, he said tersely, "Well, do not just stand there, wench. Ale and food for us all."

"Aye, sir, at once," Helge agreed with alacrity. She gifted both men with a dimpling smile before catching hold of Juliène's arm and saying firmly, "Come on, Nell, us'll go to Faither's place. 'Tis nearer…" She lowered her voice. "Even if the ale bain't as good as Mistress Gwynhere's. They'm not to knaw that."

Refraining from mentioning that Chartreux's Governor was already expecting a liquid his horse might produce, Juliène allowed Helge to pull her towards the Three Sygnets.

Once removed from de Rogé's immediate vicinity, her fear-dulled wits started working again. This was the chance she had prayed for, the chance to make herself known to Kaslan. All she needed were a few moment's privacy…

So intent was she on planning how she might accomplish this that she paid scant attention to her friend's giggles or whispered speculations. Nevertheless, as she reached the Three Sygnets she could not prevent herself from obeying the impulse that prompted her to look back at the two men whose presence had cast her into such turmoil. De Rogé was just dismounting, the movement light and easy despite the weight of his mail. He had not lost one whit of that arrogance he wore as casually as he did his…

She blinked, caught a glimpse of a memory only to lose it again. Surely something about the man was not the same… But then it was gone. That thought… or memory. But no matter. She had more important things to worry about…

Juliène glanced beyond her enemy, seeking the reassurance of Kaslan's beloved face. A hint of a smile touched her lips as she watched him slide from his mount with an uncharacteristic lack of grace. As she knew well, horses were not much used in Kaerellios and it seemed that the Prince was suffering from assorted aches in unaccustomed places from the unusual exercise.

Not to mention his exertions with whichever slut he had spent the night with! De Rogé's doxy, Kaslan had called her, but that did not mean much.

The smile faded from her face, replaced by a shadow of pain and then a frown of anger, this latter directed not so much at Kaslan as the man who had supplied him with the strumpet in the first place. Damn him, did he think to turn Chartre castle into a brothel? But then after what Gaelen had told her, and what she had guessed, of de Rogé's uninhibited behaviour with Ilana the night of their victory feast, what else should she expect of a lecherous whoremonger? But that Kaslan should behave likewise... well, damn him too for accepting de Rogé's offer of a wench to warm his bed.

With that betrayal in the forefront of her mind she asked herself whether she could face speaking to him now. And what if she did, and made herself known to him, only to find that Kaslan had already learned the incontrovertible truth; that the woman he loved – and probably now believed to be dead – had spent a night in Ranulf de Rogé's bed. Juliène fully expected Kaslan to be enraged and hurt by that piece of perfidy but surely she could convince him that she had been given no choice in the matter...

"Nell! Come on!"

Helge's voice brought her back with a jolt and she hastened after her friend, still worrying about the likely result of revealing herself to Kaslan in this place, in her present guise and, worst of all, under Ranulf de Rogé's dark blue gaze. A gaze that, as she knew to her cost, could be either menacing or mocking, depending on his mercurial humour at the time.

A large, gold-tinted leaf drifted down from the venerable plane tree above him, then another, and another. Ranulf eyed them moodily and shifted his weight restlessly, the distinctive crunch and skitter of the brittle leaves beneath his booted feet a warning in his ears. Leaning his shoulders back against the solid trunk of the tree, he muttered a more than usually vitriolic curse under his breath. Autumn already and here he was; still stuck in Chartreux, the campaigning on the Malvraine coast as good as over as far as he was concerned. Perhaps it was just as well he did have the province to govern, he reflected grimly, since he could not risk returning to Rogérinac while Rowène de Chartreux was still there. Best to wait it out in Chartre. At least there he had sufficient work to keep his mind occupied and his body exhausted.

Surprisingly, he had found some unlooked-for satisfaction as, day by day, Chartre castle rose anew from the blackened ruins. On the other side of the coin, he had the feeling that the province itself was only kept from slipping from a state of subdued hostility into even more widespread violence by a wary regard for his vicious reputation – a reputation that had been further blackened by rumours of the rape he had committed at Chartre – and a fear of even more savage reprisals when their new lord returned from Lamortaine.

Not that such an event was in any way imminent. Joffroi had recently written to Ranulf from Lamortaine – that was one messenger who had managed to get through unscathed, probably due to the fact he was displaying the royal colours rather than the black boar of Rogé – advising that he would be remaining at court for some few months longer as Prince Linnius required his counsel. He had ended his letter by confirming that he was more than satisfied with his brother's grip on Chartreux.

His governorship thus endorsed there should have been nothing to cause this undeniable tension he felt within himself; a violent gut-wrenching tension that he had so far been unable to ease. He had considered various remedies but had reluctantly concluded that losing himself in a wine jug would be both irresponsible and dangerous in the present volatile situation while finding relief in some willing woman's body was possible only in his imagination.

He glanced down at the plain red-bronze brooch he had picked up one day in a Chartre metal-worker's shop. He had needed something to pin his cloak and the fact that the burnished metal was almost the colour of a wild-cat's pelt – or Rowène de Chartreux's hair – had had nothing to do with his choice. It had been cheap and that had been all that mattered. Even so, she had been very much in his mind as he stowed the crude semblance of a leaping cat into his purse and though there had been no word from her since that bitter farewell by the Swanfleet Bridge – and enough time had gone by that she must *know* – still his gut cramped whenever he thought of her in the dark reaches of the night when he lay restless and aching, praying to the gods that he might one day forget that moment of madness when he had...

No, damn it, he would not return to that treadmill of desire and regret. He had done what he had done and now must pay the price. He might not have sired a child on a red-haired, grey-eyed witchling – at least he fervently hoped that was what her silence meant, rather than that some accident had prevented her from sending word – but he was still incapable of bedding any other woman, as his one humiliating visit to an anonymous dockside brothel had proved. That had been several weeks ago now, just after she... Rowène... had gone from Chartre and the tension that coiled deep in his gut and burned impotently in his loins had been growing more unbearable with every day and night that passed.

And then, as if his own bodily frustrations and the mental and physical demands of governing a rebellious province were not enough to try his temper, Prince Kaslander of Kaerellios had suddenly arrived in Chartre demanding fine wines, succulent viands, clean sheets and soft pillows, together with the expectation that Juliène de Chartreux would be there to share them with him.

He had been surprised, and not a little irritated, by the Kardolandian's arrival, the message advising him that Princess Linette's betrothed was expected to land at Chartre and should be sped on his way to Lamortaine as expeditiously as possible having reached him only *after* the agitated harbour master had sent up to the castle to tell him there was a "right royal princeling" on his dock demanding the attendance of the Lord of Chartreux or his representative immediately. Ranulf had just returned to Chartre after a week long tour of the province and had been hot, dirty and tired. He had nevertheless resisted the temptation to verbally flay both hapless messengers and had duly hauled himself back into the saddle and ridden down to the harbour to soothe the royal ruffled feathers as best he might.

Exercising considerable restraint over his sorely-tried temper he had made the first of many apologies for the delay in meeting his highness, for the state of the castle, the quality of the food... the wine... the accommodations... He had also felt obliged to give his unwanted guest a blunt but colourless account of the death of Prince Marcus, the subsequent attainder of Louis de Chartreux and the ensuant events, including the unfortunate demise of Juliène de Chartreux in the same fire that had destroyed or otherwise affected much of the eastern end of the castle. He had, however, refrained from mentioning the manner in which the Lady Juliène had spent the last night of her life.

Far from expressing dismay at her death, the Kardolandian Prince had seemed to accept the situation with a greater degree of equanimity than Ranulf thought he himself might have done had the situation been reversed. Indeed Kaslander had shown far more interest in the serving wench who had brought his wine than the tragic death of the woman he had blithely admitted to seducing in Kaerellios. Still simmering with disgust, at both Kaslander and himself, Ranulf had muttered a blistering curse and set himself to make the best of the situation that had been forced on him.

Aware from the start that his brother's reputation as Lord of Chartreux and Counsellor to Prince Linnius was resting on *his* manners and actions, Ranulf had done his best to make his unexpected guest welcome, wining and dining him on the best Chartre could provide and putting his own quarters at his disposal, together with the use of the wench Kaslander had been so taken with.

Ranulf himself had slept little – and alone – in what had once been Lucien of Chartre's bed, waking before dawn and determined to set the Kardolandian Prince on his way to the royal Mithlondian court at Lamortaine with all speed... whether Kaslander liked it or not. And he had not!

At the recollection of the Kardolandian's horrified attitude to his early awakening, scant meal and introduction to his current mode of transport, Ranulf's simmering annoyance eased somewhat, leaching into sardonic amusement as he watched his royal charge make himself as comfortable as sore buttocks and stiff limbs allowed. Ranulf had already noticed, with a contempt he barely bothered to conceal, that as soon as they had stopped Kaslander's swarm of servants had hastened to unpack soft rugs and plump, feather-filled cushions from one of the packs. These then being arranged under a silken canopy set up beneath the plane trees of the square so that the Prince would be able to enjoy some measure of comfort, for a while at least.

With a snort of disgust Ranulf turned his attention towards the more serious problem of calculating how many more days he would be required to waste riding escort to this pampered Kardolandian princeling. Already he had been obliged to break the day's journey before it had barely started and Namarillien, the town where Ranulf had planned to spend the night, was some ten leagues farther along the road.

The sooner this unwanted duty was done, the better he would be pleased. And if he managed not to lose his temper with his royal bloody highness while he was doing it he would have pulled off a feat even Guy would have to acknowledge had been a commendable action on his part. And, the gods knew, he had accomplished little else since coming to Chartre that could be considered even remotely worth while. If Prince Kaslander would only keep his mouth shut, Ranulf thought grimly, and refrain from mentioning either of the de Chartreux sisters he might just achieve his aim of keeping his temper and the Prince might make it out of his jurisdiction in one piece. And good riddance to him, with his airs and graces and his tedious boasting of his many conquests!

But at least his bragging had served one purpose and Ranulf now knew who Juliène's unnamed lover had been, although he had no idea which of them he felt the most contempt for; the Kardolandian prince for being so blithely untouched by his paramour's death, the innocent young noblewoman – and yes, he did her the reluctant justice of believing her innocent at that stage – for succumbing to Kaslander's blatantly practised seductions. Or himself for allowing himself to be manipulated by wine and lust into...

Abruptly becoming aware that he was wallowing once more in fruitless memories, Ranulf unfolded his arms and straightened away from the smooth trunk, casting an assessing glance around the square. His men were all dismounted and looked as if they had been waiting for their ale for some time. Impatient at the delay Ranulf was on the point of sending Guthlaf to hasten the process when he saw that intervention would not be required after all.

Stepping confidently across the square from the direction of a tavern that boasted a green sign painted with – Ranulf narrowed his eyes – three rather stubby-necked cygnets, came the bold-eyed lass who had offered them refreshment in the first place. Eyeing the way her hips swayed as she walked, Ranulf thought cynically that she would make a suitably sensual armful should there be the opportunity for Kaslander to accept her very obvious offer. Nor, having been subjected to the Prince's conversation since the previous afternoon, did Ranulf have many doubts as to the outcome.

Daemon's balls! He had thought himself a womaniser – after all, what else was there to do at Rogérinac in the winter except fornicate with the serving wenches? He could only spend so much time hunting for deer or boar, practicing his sword skills with Guthlaf or playing fox and geese with Guy.

Or at least he had been known as a womaniser, until a certain grey-eyed Fae had withered his manhood. Hell and bloody damnation! *Why* had he ever touched her?

Even with the father of all hangovers, he had known that the hatred she justifiably felt towards him for his part in her father's death was insurmountable, known too that she was under his own brother's protection. Yet still he had not been able to stop himself from touching her. And, ultimately, from forcing her to yield to him.

And now he would never bed a woman again. Unless...

Unless he could persuade her to touch him of her own free will...

Oh yes, he could really see that happening, he mocked himself savagely. Rowène de Chartreux hated him. Despised him. Feared him. And with good reason. Was it likely then that she would ever touch his limp and impotent prick from choice? Hell'sdeath! Assuredly she would not!

Save, perhaps, just before they executed him. He knew that it was not uncommon for men convicted of rape to be castrated before they were hanged. If the High Counsel offered her the chance to emasculate him, would she do it? Did she hate him enough to take a knife to his balls, cut off his cock? It would be the supremest of ironies that she would heal his manhood and deprive him of it almost with the same touch.

Restrained from clutching at his threatened genitals only by the returning awareness that he was standing in the leafy square of a quiet village in Chartreux rather than the bleak Place of Execution in Lamortaine, Ranulf thrust aside his recurrent fear and attempted to turn his attention towards the problems he could deal with.

Still trying to shake off the last lingering effects of the illusion, Ranulf watched with a frown of unfeigned irritation as the wench approached Kaslander and offered him a brimming tankard, together with an openly provocative smile that made her hazel eyes sparkle invitingly. As Ranulf had expected, Kaslander made not the slightest effort to decline the implicit offer. Rather he smiled as he rose to his feet, his dark eyes warming with the first sparks of serious interest. Accepting the tankard he murmured something in heavily accented common speech that Ranulf did not catch but which caused the peasant wench to blush and nod. Whereupon Kaslander gestured at the rug and drew her down beside him.

Ranulf raised his brows in resignation but rather than wasting his breath in a pointless protest about the delay, looked first to make sure his men were being served and then for his own ale. And in so doing, caught the expression of white shock on the other girl's face as she saw her friend and the Prince sharing far more than a tankard of ale. Perhaps, Ranulf thought cynically, she had had an eye to him herself. The next moment, however, she had dragged her stricken gaze away from Kaslander and, as she looked directly at him, Ranulf found himself staring into a pair of eyes of such an exquisite and unusual shade of jewel green that all sensible thought abruptly stalled.

No, it could not be! The only other young woman he had known with eyes like that had perished in the flames that had consumed the Lady Tower; a death he would not wish on his worst enemy. And, whatever else she had been, Juliène de Chartreux had scarcely been that.

And yet... No, there could have been no escape, even for a witch, from that terrible pyre. So how in Hell could he possibly imagine otherwise?

But then, he reminded himself harshly, he had done little else but imagine impossible things since his parting from Rowène de Chartreux. Imagination was all he had left to warm his cold bed and his even colder dreams.

Unaware of Ranulf de Rogé's internal battle – indeed she had not even been aware of meeting his gaze – Juliène strove with everything that was in her to control the terrible burning pain in her heart. Averting her eyes from the agonising sight of her lover with another woman she walked blindly towards the man standing under the nearby tree, his broad shoulders resting against the trunk, arms folded across his mailed chest. Then, abruptly realising where her feet were taking her, she glanced up quickly, in a belated attempt to gauge his mood.

He had discarded his helm, she saw, and the dappled sunlight glimmered on the neatly-braided, partially-bound fair hair but left his hard, clean-shaven face in shadow and she dared not stare, still wary of the possibility that he might somehow recognise her. She had no choice now but to approach him and, knowing how it put her at a disadvantage when dealing with the suspicious and irritable Governor of Chartreux, made a desperate attempt to expunge all emotion from her heart. She was not entirely successful and pride warred with common sense as she fought to control the almost overwhelming urge to empty the brimming mug of ale she was carrying over Kaslan's handsome, treacherous head. Failing that, she thought she would derive a certain amount of pleasure from flinging the contents full in Ranulf de Rogé's all too knowing face.

Shaking slightly with the effort of containing her destructive emotions she stopped in front of him, prudently lowering her gaze to conceal her green eyes.

"Yeralezur," she mumbled in her best peasant patois.

"What?"

Holding out the tankard with hands that trembled only slightly she repeated her words more distinctly, her gaze fixed on his booted feet.

"Yer ale, sir."

She watched with wary surprise as he stripped off his mailed gauntlets and tucked them under his belt. Then he spoke again, in the softly rasping voice that still haunted her memory. Three words only in common speech, the last words she would have expected of the man she remembered.

"Thank you, Mistress."

Whether it was his unexpected courtesy or the touch of his warm, calloused fingers on hers, Juliène could not have said. She gave a sudden gasp of shock and loosened her grasp on the heavy mug. Only the fact that he already had a tenuous grip saved it from spilling completely. As it was a goodly portion of the ale splashed over him.

He muttered one startled expletive and, with the vivid recollection of how vicious his temper could be, Juliène turned and fled.

Ranulf watched her go with a frown. Guy might call him an arrogant idiot – and the gods knew that was true enough where his actions towards a certain grey-eyed young noblewoman had been concerned – but he was not nearly so witless as to be unaware of the hatred and distrust with which he was regarded by the men of Chartreux. Until now though he had not realised the depth of fear the majority of ordinary women of the province might feel for him, more especially as the serving women employed at the castle had long since ceased to tremble at his approach or shrink away if he addressed them.

That said, it was clear that his reputation as a ruthless despoiler of innocent maidens must still hold sway in the countryside. And who was he to argue with that truth? The plain and simple fact that no woman had been molested, either by him or any of his men, since he took over the governorship of Chartreux did not absolve him of his own secret guilt. But, damn it all to Hell, was he never to live down that one vile action? No matter how many other women he kept safe, would he never be able to sleep without *her* stark white face haunting his dreams or hearing his own name echoing in the long dark watches of the night as a silent scream of pain.

Cursing himself, he wrenched his thoughts back to *this* day, *this* place. Cold sweat was trickling down his back and he wondered how long he had been lost in memory and what might have occurred during his absence of mind. His bleak gaze swept rapidly around the square but his men, apparently well aware of the dangerous state of his smouldering temper, were behaving with an unusual degree of circumspection towards the older woman who was busily serving the soldiers, drovers and Kardolandian servants with bread and ale.

He swallowed his own ale with a grimace – it was not, he told himself, horse piss, but not far off – then tipped the bitter dregs on the ground. He glanced at the Prince but Kaslander was still engrossed with his companion's charms and appeared to have every intention of idling away the rest of the day in such fashion.

Vexed by the delay though he was, Ranulf knew there was little he could realistically do to hasten matters. That being so, he found himself actually considering calling the older woman over and ordering another mug of whatever it was he had been drinking. At the same time, he eyed the group of men gathered around her, wondering whether he ought to intervene, even if he did not want another drink. But although clearly a respectable matron of the village, she appeared to be having no difficulty holding her own with his men. A plump, smiling woman in her middle years, she was comely enough but too old for him by about twenty years. Guthlaf, however, seemed unusually taken with her. He hid a grin at that, since Guthlaf had rarely been taken with anything in skirts in all the thirty-odd years Ranulf had known him.

He did not know what it was but something suddenly struck him as odd about the group. Looking more closely he noticed that one of his men was noticeably absent from the knot of restrained conviviality gathered around the woman.

Damn the man, he knew he should have sent him back to Rogérinac again but Finn had sworn to mend his ways and Guy had been only too glad to be rid of the trouble-maker. So now he was Ranulf's problem again! Swearing in irritation and the beginnings of anger, he stalked over towards the men. All laughter and talk died abruptly at his approach, the woman taking several hasty steps to one side, as if she had heard of his reputation and feared him accordingly. Caught on the raw, his voice snapped crisply into the silence.

"Finn? Where is he?"

A couple of the younger soldiers shifted uncomfortably, while another snickered knowingly. Then, as Ranulf's gaze arrowed in his direction and Gunnar found himself standing alone, he muttered,

"He went off that way, sir, down that lane there. Said he were going for a piss, but I reckon he was following that wench. You know, one of the ones what brought the ale."

"How long since he left?"

"Long enough to have caught up with her, sir, if that's what he meant to do."

Ranulf heard the little sound of distress the village woman made and glanced her way.

"Your daughter?" he asked tersely.

"My brother's daughter, sir." She caught her breath. "I beg you, sir..." Her voice choked off.

"I will find her for you," Ranulf assured her flatly. And to his second-in-command. "Guthlaf, stay here and look after Mistress..."

"Gwynhere, sir."

"Mistress Gwynhere. The rest of you, finish your food and ale. And keep out of trouble."

Then silently cursing everybody from the absent trooper to his brother for sending the man back to Chartre and himself for not having done something about him before, he tossed his mug at the nearest man-at-arms and set off towards the lane, his mouth set in a grim line. The last thing he needed at this delicate moment was for any of his men to be found forcing themselves on a local woman.

The men watched as he strode off, muttering amongst themselves and largely ignoring the ale-wife who had been serving them but who was now hovering anxiously beside the man designated to look after her.

"Uh-oh, the Commander's fair riled up about this," Sweyn said suddenly.

"Aye, I don't give much for Finn's chances if the Commander do find him with a wench," Gunnar added with a certain relish, Finn not being universally popular with his fellows away from the battlefield.

"He never used to be like this," Alun complained in a disgruntled fashion. "The Commander, I mean. Liked his way with a wench same as the rest of us, aye?"

"Providing the wench was willing," Guthlaf's gruff tones cut through the general murmur. He was the oldest of the company and by virtue of experience and length of service under the de Rogé banner, second-in-command of the troop. Unlike Finn he was generally respected and the soldiers tended to listen when he spoke. All eyes turned on him as he continued steadily, "Sir Ranulf's never turned a blind eye to rape and each and every one of you bloody well knows it."

"Mebbe not but he's starting to sound more like Master Guy every day. More's the pity," Alun retorted. Then added slyly, "Mebbe he's been bewitched."

"Watch your mouth, Alun! You start tossing words like witch around and you won't last long in this troop. If Lord Joffroy don't hang you, Sir Ranulf will. But you're right in a way. Something did happen back when we took that cursed castle," Guthlaf continued thoughtfully, adding in such a low voice that probably only the woman standing close by him heard. "Something that changed him."

"We know what happened well enough," Sweyn grinned and made a lewd gesture with his hand. "Commander Ranulf, he got to bed that there Lady Juliena – now that was a woman I wouldn't have minded taking down in the straw!"

"Aye," Gunnar chimed in. "I remember her. Soft white tits and shiny black hair down to her arse. Hey, lads, d'ye think he had her sister too, that red-haired Lady Rowena?"

"Na. Commander likes 'em plump and pretty," Sweyn said dismissively. Then grinned. "Like that saucy serving wench someone told me he had first off. He wouldn't have looked twice at that Lady Rowena. Left her to Master Guy, didn't he?"

"Aye, but Sweyn, 'twere the Commander what brought her down to the hall the next day, not Master Guy. Ain't that right? Who else was on duty that morning? Guthlaf, you remember, don't you?"

"Of course I remember!" Guthlaf said irritably. "I was there, same as you!"

"But did he have 'em both, d'you think?" Sweyn demanded.

"Shit! I don't know," Guthlaf snapped, even more irritably. "What I do know is that it ain't any of your nevermind, nor mine."

"Aw, come on, Guthlaf. Ye can do better'n that!"

"All right then, you want to know what I think? Well, for starters, I reckon as how you all ought to keep your fool tongues from waggin' about your betters, unless you want to find yourselves tossed into the nearest midden. As for the rest of it, I've known Master Ranulf since he were born, which is a damn sight longer than any of the rest of you can claim. I've known him in all his moods and tempers, but I misdoubt I've ever seen him so wild as he was that night. Aye, it was him what brought Lady Rowena down to the hall, her looking as white as a wraith and him like he wanted to puke. But as to what you filthy-minded runts are thinking, it ain't so. He wouldn't ha' touched her, her being Master Guy's lady so as to speak. Now I don't know what happened, no more than the rest of you do, but unless you really want to fall foul of Commander Ranulf an' Master Guy both, you'll keep your noses out of it from now on and your tongues from flapping about what don't concern you. An' if you didn't know before today, you do now, to keep your breeks tightly laced until you are bloody sure the woman you want really is willing."

There was a general murmur of agreement at this and then Sweyn's voice made itself heard.

"Aye, well. You mebbe right in some of what you say," he admitted reluctantly. "But at least at Chartre we got to *fight*! An' even if they weren't back then, most of the castle wenches are willing enough now. Riding escort to that pretty-boy there though..." He nodded and spat. "'Tain't my idea of fun at all."

"Nor Master Ranulf's neither," Guthlaf replied. "And that ain't helped sweeten his temper on top of everything else. Come on, lads, I've an idea we'd best be ready to move when he comes back." Only then remembering the ashen-faced, middle-aged peasant woman standing nearby, he cleared his throat and added awkwardly, "Take no notice of the men, Mistress. Nor me. 'Tis just their way when they'm bored, like they are now. They don't mean nothing by it."

"And your Commander? Sir Ranulf? What does he mean by it, hmm? Even though you defend him, you don't seem very sure what happened."

"Mebbe I don't know for sure, Mistress," Guthlaf said stoutly. "But one thing I do know. Master Ranulf, he wouldn't hurt a woman. Not then, at Chartre. Not here, today. And may the daemons of Hell take me if I'm proved wrong."

"Daemons of Hell!"

Ranulf cursed under his breath as he paused to get his bearings. Finn had not been in sight anywhere near the top end of the alley, where he might with some slight justification have been found. That only left the crowded square – where quite clearly he was not – or further down the winding lane that, Ranulf assumed from its direction and general aspect, led down towards the river.

Hoping he was not wasting his time on something that had all the appearances of becoming a wild goose chase, Ranulf continued on down the narrow alley, one hand on his dagger hilt. He was pleasantly surprised to find the lane widened after about a hundred yards or so where a couple of well-maintained cottages on his left faced a homely looking tavern on his right.

The Flower and Falcon, he saw from the recently repainted sign – the sight of the white thorn blossom clasped in the talons of a fierce-eyed falcon causing him to frown momentarily as a thought, too fleeting to catch, skittered across his mind. He wondered absently if the ale might be any better there and paused long enough to look through the open door – not for ale but for the missing trooper – but the only person he could see in the gloom was a bulky looking man he took to be the tavern keeper since it was certainly not Finn.

Ducking back outside he continued as quickly as he might down the lane, which soon narrowed again to a six-foot width divided by a central gutter, presently overflowing with fly-covered filth. His nostrils flared, not so much at the smell, to which he was largely inured, but the place itself. A narrow and noisome alley was not the place he personally would have chosen to pursue a seduction but knowing what he did of Finn's sensibilities – or lack of them – he doubted the other man would care.

A candle-notch later Ranulf found himself at the end of the lane and stepped out into sunshine and cleaner air, having passed nothing larger than a couple of fast moving rats on the way.

Then he saw them; Finn and the woman. The soldier had the wench backed against a broad-trunked tree close to the river bank, her skirts dragged up to reveal slender white legs. And there could be not the slightest doubt that she was an unwilling participant in this coupling, struggling and weeping as she was.

For a heartbeat Ranulf stood frozen, seeing not golden-yellow leaves and the tranquil river beyond but a canopy of dark blue velvet and a pale blue silk coverlet embroidered with white swans and yellow flowers. And against that background white thighs spread wide, a flash of dark-flame hair and a scarlet silk dress. He heard neither the dry rustling of autumn leaves nor the distant sounds of the river but rather a woman screaming something that sounded like his name.

No, not his name! And not her voice!

Another woman. Another man. But the same vile act...

Dragging himself back from the mist-cold Hell of memory he shook his head to clear it and realised that what he could hear was a different woman's tear-choked voice sobbing incoherently, overlaid by the soldier's panting breath as he struggled to subdue his prey. Striding forwards Ranulf yanked Finn away, turning his back on the girl to give her the opportunity to pull down her skirt and straighten her torn bodice, while he channelled his own shamed guilt and fierce frustration into fury against the younger man.

"Finn! What in Hell's name did you think you were doing?"

The man caught his balance with some difficulty, his breeches being tangled around his knees but, having put his clothing back to rights, looked up with a somewhat aggrieved grin at Ranulf.

"I'd ha' thought t'were obvious."

Then, apparently recognising the warning flash of temper in his commander's eyes, he hastily wiped the leer from his face and amended his form of address.

"Didn't mean no harm. Sir. 'Twas just a bit of fun wi' the wench. Lord Joffroy..."

"I am not Lord Joffroi," Ranulf snapped. "And even if my standing orders were not plain enough for you, Finn, the bloody woman herself was saying no."

"But, sir..." Finn started in protest.

"Enough," Ranulf broke in, his voice ice cold. "Not a se'ennight back I had one of Chartre's most respected merchants flogged for abusing one of the dockside whores. And when I told the townsfolk I would hang any of my soldiers I found guilty of rape, I meant it. You can count yourself fortunate that I caught up to you before you could sheath that over-ready prick of yours. Now get back to the square and tell Guthlaf I want the men ready to move out as soon as I get back."

Recognising that it was time to retreat while his skin – or any other part of his anatomy – was still in one piece Finn contented himself with saying sulkily,

"I know what 'tis – one law fer me an' another fer you. But if ye wanted the wench fer yerself all ye had ter do was say so."

"I do not want her, you dolt!" Ranulf exclaimed in exasperation. "But that does not mean I will stand by and permit you to force an unwilling maid."

Finn stared at him for a moment, a gamut of emotions playing across his flushed face, before he turned away, muttering something Ranulf did not quite catch.

"*What* did you say?" he asked, a dangerous edge to his voice.

Finn stopped dead, then turned slowly and stood looking back at him. Evidently he recognised that he had overstepped the mark but equally he had meant whatever it was he had said.

"I said, sir, that I'd be willin' ter bet a month's pay that she's no maid! An' that even if she were... well, ye're not above using force yerself! We all know what ye did to Lady..."

Not giving Finn the chance to speak her name out loud Ranulf backhanded him savagely, drawing blood from nose and mouth and very nearly felling the other man to the ground. Breathing hard, he snarled,

"You know nothing of what I might have done to..." He scrabbled for control, belatedly realising he did not know which of the noblewomen Finn might have been about to name, and continued coldly, "To the lady. But mark my words, Finn, if you mention either of Lord Joffroi's wards, in my presence or out of it, I swear by all the daemons in Hell you will wish you had never been born. Now get back to the square."

As Finn moved away, one sleeve held against his bleeding nose, Ranulf turned slowly to face the peasant girl on whose behalf he had intervened. She was huddled against the tree trunk, one cheek pressed against a piece of flaking bark, in a manner that must, he thought, have been extremely painful and her whole body was shaking helplessly. Her cap had been torn off and her very long, very dark hair hung in a tousled plait down her back. Her skirts were still somewhat awry, revealing dainty ankles and part of a slim, bare leg. He could see a red graze on her shoulder where her shift had been pulled aside in the struggle and there was a bruise on her arm.

Despite these minor injuries and the girl's obvious fear and shame, Ranulf knew it could have been far worse for her and undoubtedly would have been if he had been much later arriving. He thanked the gods he so rarely prayed to that he had been in time.

But where had the gods been the morning Rowène de Chartreux had needed protecting from him?

With an impatient oath Ranulf dragged his mind out of the circle of pointless recriminations he had been fighting against for the past season and, addressing a point somewhere beyond the girl's shoulder, spoke tersely in common speech, keeping his translation formal.

"I apologise, Mistress, if you have been hurt or frightened. Perhaps you will allow me to escort you back to the square."

She did not lift her eyes. Neither did she move away from the tree or stop trembling. But she did manage to shake her head. Ranulf gave a shrug of indifferent acknowledgement at her rejection of his offer.

"As you wish, Mistress, but if you will accept my advice in lieu of my escort, do not wander off on your own again whilst my men are in town since, although I can have any man flogged or even hung for rape, it is not going to do you much good after the event."

At that the girl glanced fleetingly over her reddened shoulder and said in choked accents,

"I beg of you, sir... please, just go away and leave me alone."

"I do not think you should be left on your own," Ranulf answered slowly, his eyes travelling beyond the tree to the fast-flowing river. "And I feel in some part responsible for you, seeing as it was one of my men who brought you to this pass." He paused, eyeing the slender, shaking body pressed against the tree trunk, seeing how she had turned her face away from him again. Summoning a gentler, more persuasive tone he said, "Perhaps you should let me take you back to your family. Your... ah... father's sister I believe she said she was, is waiting for you in the square. She will be most anxious for your safety."

"I... No. I cannot go with you!"

Angered by her stubborn refusal to accept his aid, especially when it had been offered in good faith, Ranulf took a step towards her and said harshly,

"I can assure you, Mistress, that I mean you no harm despite what you might have heard of me." At that she did look at him, a fleeting glance only between long dark lashes but with eyes so green he felt the hairs on the back of his neck rise as if kissed with an icy breath.

"What I have heard of you?" she repeated unsteadily.

"You do know who I am, do you not?" Ranulf said; it was scarcely a question.

The girl nodded anyway and, although she still would not meet his eyes, a small, malicious smile touched her mouth.

"You're the Governor of Chartreux. Brother to our new lord, him what wed the Lady Ariena. Word is that Lord Joffroy's left you here to tax us into poverty and whip us into obedience while he's off making merry at court with his high-born whore!"

"There may well be some justice in what you say," he agreed, eyes narrowing. Then, putting a certain amount of steel into his voice, he continued, "As well as a lot of bloody damned lies. Time will tell which is which, Mistress. Now come back to the square before I lose what little patience I have left!"

With that ultimatum issued he took another step towards her, wondering as he did so why he bothered. Certainly not from compassion. Which left only the ever present sense of guilt...

# Chapter 5

## *The Governor of Chartreux*

Observing Ranulf de Rogé's determined approach Juliène shrank even closer to the tree trunk. She did not think he would hurt her physically but neither did she think she could trust herself to him. She had seen the momentary suspicion in his gaze when she had so foolishly allowed him to see the colour of her eyes and she dared not allow him any closer. Then, just as she was wondering how she might best rid herself of his unwanted company, she heard a gruff voice growl belligerently,

"What be gwaing on yere then?"

Recognising with an overwhelming relief the voice she had given up all hope of ever hearing again, Juliène gave another sob and, leaving the comparative safety of the tree, pushed past de Rogé and flung herself into the newcomer's arms.

"Gaelen!"

Her head resting against his sturdy shoulder, she looked up in time to see the look of cold fury he bent on the younger man and with a complete disregard for their relative positions in life snarled,

"The gods damn you to Hell, what have you done this time?"

"I have done nothing, churl," de Rogé snapped, evidently missing by some great good fortune the significance of Gaelen's last two words. "Since you obviously count preventing her rape at the hands of one of my men *nothing*. I have not laid a finger on her! Nor would I have done even had you not arrived when you did. And just who in Hell are *you*, that you demand an accounting of me?"

Ignoring the blatant menace in the nobleman's rasping tones, Gaelen looked him in the eye and replied steadily,

"I am Nell's uncle. My name is Gaelen of Valentién."

"Valentién?" De Rogé's eyes widened momentarily and then hardened to blue ice and his tone slid from rasping menace to silky suspicion. "As in the Flower and Falcon tavern, I suppose. A little far from home, are you not?"

Gaelen shrugged, not appearing to be intimidated in the least by the other man. He stared fearlessly back at him, his brown eyes as hard as the stones at the bottom of the nearby river. Juliène thought he was not yet actively hostile but clearly it would take little more by way of pressure from de Rogé to make him so.

"I'm a free man," Gaelen pointed out in tones as bland as milk once the cream has been skimmed from the top. "Able to come and go as I please within the realm. As is my brother's daughter here." He glanced down at Juliène, held securely within the curve of his arm, and asked quietly, "It is true, lass? He has not harmed you?"

She risked a fleeting peep over Gaelen's brawny arm and judged from the look on his face that de Rogé's temper had now cooled, fury at Gaelen's insolence having been succeeded by relief that he could now hand over responsibility for her to her family. Becoming aware that Gaelen was still regarding her in some concern, she said hastily,

"No, it is as he said. He did save me from the other one. *He...*" She shuddered and could not bring herself to complete the sentence. Gaelen nodded,

"'Tis all right then, lass. Ye're safe now." He raised his eyes to meet de Rogé's narrowed gaze and some of the aggression left his face as he said with palpable reluctance, "It seems that I owe ye thanks... sir. 'Tis not every nobleman as would interfere. When all's said and done, the lass is only a tavern wench and the likes of ye only notice such as her when it suits yer own needs."

"She reminds me of someone," de Rogé muttered, his thoughts plainly many leagues away in both time and place. "A girl I once..."

"Then take your guilty conscience to her," Gaelen snapped, anger once more flaring in his speech, together with a certain piercing gleam of interest in his eyes. "And leave Nell to her own kind. Sir."

"I thank you for your advice," de Rogé said flatly, his eyes narrowing once more at Gaelen's tone. "Good day to you, Mistress."

With which curt valediction he turned on his heel and strode away, the autumn sunlight glinting on the spurs on his heels, his dark cloak flaring out behind him with the swiftness of his passage. Only when she was certain that he had gone did Juliène draw a deep breath of relief and turn her gaze back towards the man in whose arms she still sheltered.

"Thank you, Gaelen. I do not know what I would have done if you had not come. Although," she added reflectively, "I think he meant it when he said he would not have hurt me. Rather I feared that he might recognise me."

"I think you're right, lass," Gaelen conceded. "I've said it before, I know, but although Ranulf de Rogé may be a black-hearted cur in many ways, he is no liar. The gods know that must be his only saving grace!" His tone softened. "Come along, lass, I'll take you back to the Falcon. Best to keep you out of that hell-hound's way, I think. You heard what he said; that you remind him of someone. I'd not trust his non-existent conscience over his duty to Black Joffroi when it's your life and freedom at stake!"

"No, I am sure you are right," Juliène agreed dully. "At least where his sense of duty is concerned. But I must go back to the square," she added more firmly. "And please, Gaelen... please do not ask me why."

"'Tis not because of de Rogé?" Gaelen demanded, his voice a low growl of displeasure.

"No. This has nothing to do with him," Juliène replied. "But, we must hurry. I think he means to leave as soon as he can and I have to speak to Ka... the man he is escorting."

She turned quickly away before Gaelen could ask her more and as she hastened up the lane towards the village her only coherent thought was that she must, somehow, speak to Kaslan before he left Anjélais and tell him all that had happened since they parted. Ah gods! If only she knew what de Rogé might have said to her lover about the night they had spent together!

Meanwhile Ranulf was in no mind to waste any more time in this miserable excuse for a village. Expecting to find on his return to the square that the Prince and his escort would be ready to go, he came to a stunned halt when he realised that his expectations fell well short of reality and that the simple canopy Prince Kaslander's servants had originally erected had erupted into a full-blown tent.

"What in the name of bloody Hell..."

He glanced questioningly at those of his men who were lounging nearby but though they all straightened immediately, the only one who made any effort to meet his disbelieving glare was the man who had taught him everything he knew about soldiering and now acted as his second-in-command.

"Well?"

Guthlaf responded to his irate demand with a grimace and a shrug.

"I did try to tell him, sir, as how you'd be wanting to be on your way as soon as you got back but well... you can see how much notice he took."

"I am sure you did your best, Guthlaf," Ranulf replied, his clipped tones revealing his exasperation. "And in all truth, I should not expect you to gainsay any royalty, let alone this particularly pampered example!" He turned his annoyed gaze towards the tent. "I suppose the wench is still in there?" he demanded.

"Aye, sir."

Ranulf swore again, more or less under his breath. Then, returning his attention to Guthlaf,

"I see Finn is back. Do not lose him again! And while you are about it make sure all the rest of the men are here and ready to move out as soon as I can prise his royal bloody highness out from between that wench's legs. The gods send *she* does not have an angry uncle or father lurking somewhere nearby. That would be all I need!"

He took a long step towards the tent and something flickered behind Guthlaf's normally imperturbable dark hazel gaze. Apparently unable to stop himself the older man blurted,

"You're not meaning to go in there, lad?"

Ignoring the familiarity that only slipped out in moments of extreme stress, Ranulf glanced at his former mentor and said satirically,

"You have some reason for thinking I should not?"

Guthlaf visibly swallowed his misgivings and met Ranulf's sardonic gaze with the hardiness born of long practice and the unacknowledged, but very real, bond between them.

"You know as well as I do what his highness is about and he won't be best pleased to be disturbed. Prince or no, I'm thinking there's a viper underneath all that gilding. That being so, do you really want him for an enemy once he reaches Lamortaine and the snake pit of the royal court?"

Ranulf shrugged dismissively.

"Snake is probably right but I can take care of myself! You just get this rabble organised!"

"Aye, sir!"

Evidently recognising the impossibility of changing his commander's mind, Guthlaf snapped off a salute and, raising his voice, began shouting rapid orders to the rest of the troop who hastened into action, casting aside empty mugs, the inedible rinds of cheese and last crusts of hard rye bread. The clink of bridle bits and the creak of saddle leather assuring him of their compliance, Ranulf left them to Guthlaf and, striding over to the voluminous gold and blue tent, grasped the flimsy panel that did duty as a door covering. It was warm and so incredibly smooth he could feel it snag against the rough skin of his fingers.

Something in that sound... that touch... hit him hard and he stood stock still, staring blindly at the crumpled folds in his hand, feeling once again the tingling in his fingers as they brushed against scarlet silk, as warm and pliable as the woman's breast it covered...

Dropping the cloth as if it burned him, he shook his head violently. *Hell's death!* He had to get that witchling out of his head before she drove him over the edge of reason into the dark chasm of utter madness! Fighting the memory of terrified grey eyes and rose petal skin – and peripherally aware of Guthlaf's curious glance – he raised his hand to the panel again.

Only to hesitate once more as the sounds from within brought him a vision of Kaslander and the wench, writhing and gasping as they coupled amidst the soft cushions. Judging from the intensity of those noises they would be done soon enough and Kaslander would be ready to move on – to another town and another wench, if the impression Ranulf had formed of the Prince's character was not entirely adrift.

At this rate, he thought in moody exasperation, they would be lucky to reach Namarillien by dusk and the border with Marillec was at least another three days' ride on from there. After that Ranulf did not give a toss if Kaslander bedded every wench he saw between Rocque-Miriél and Lamortaine; the Prince would no longer be within his jurisdiction and it would be some other poor sod who would have to deal with his untrammelled taste for women and any by-blows he might sire along the way.

*Gods!*

His gut clenched in the way that had become only too familiar to him over the past season, whenever some chance word or thought had reminded him of the by-blow to whom he himself might have given life!

With a deliberate effort he pushed that thought aside, instinctively reaching up to touch the bronze brooch on his shoulder; seeking reassurance that his brutality had not gone so far. *Could not* have done, else he – and probably the whole realm – would have heard by now.

Rather than dwell on his memory of the appalled revulsion in Rowène de Chartreux's grey eyes at the thought that she might bear his child, he forced himself to consider the probable dismay on Jean de Marillec's self-righteous countenance when he realised that his well-ordered province would never be the same again after the amoral and licentious Kardolandian prince had passed through it.

His temper somewhat restored by the thought of de Marillec's discomfiture, he stepped back from the tent, meeting Guthlaf's anxious look with a wry smile and a shake of his head, indicating that he had changed his mind about interrupting the royal amours. Ignoring the older man's clear relief, he walked over to his fretting stallion, stroking the sleek black nose and neck and murmuring inconsequential nonsense as the horse's huge head butted affectionately at his chest.

With a final pat he turned away, his gaze colliding with that of the burly man he had met down by the river and who had, for whatever unfathomable reason of his own, now made his way up to the tree-shaded square, his young kinswoman – Nell, he had called her – close by his side. The wench looked even more pale and distraught than she had done earlier, if such a thing were possible, and her gaze was unwaveringly fixed on the blue and gold tent. Despite her beauty – and Ranulf would have been the first to admit she was both lovely and desirable – it was her uncle who held his attention.

He had the nagging feeling that he should know the man. Had the equally uneasy thought that he was missing something vitally important and blindingly obvious. By his own admission, the man came from Valentién and he *had* spoken with a Valennais accent. Yet Ranulf's instinct tied him to Chartre... Surely he had seen him that first night... or had it been the following morning...

He swore silently as the memory slipped away, like water along a sandy shore, leaving nothing more than a darker line on the sand to show where the tide of thought had touched before turning in retreat. Still frowning, he caught a whisper of sound behind him and turned to find Kaslander emerging from his tent, the girl just behind him, flushed of face and bright of eye, attempting in acute, if belated, embarrassment to tame her tangled brown curls into some sort of order.

"Are you ready to move on now, your highness?" Ranulf asked, his voice cold, level and lethally courteous.

"As soon as you like," Kaslander answered magnanimously, the grin that quirked his full lips indicating that he knew full well just how irritated Ranulf really was. "After all, it would not do to keep my lovely betrothed waiting. But are you sure *you* do not wish to linger here any longer? I do not mind waiting if there is a wench you fancy. What about that one there?"

He nodded carelessly in the direction of the young woman standing within her uncle's protective embrace. Disregarding her obvious horror and shock, the Prince added maliciously, "A good swiving would work wonders for your temper, Messire."

Keeping from his face the bleak knowledge of his current inability to swive any woman, Ranulf held Kaslander's dancing, dark gaze for a moment before saying with wintry indifference,

"I have not the slightest interest in bedding the wench, your highness. And to judge from her expression, the feeling is mutual."

Kaslander shrugged,

"It was just a thought," he grinned. Then the smile faded slightly, to be replaced by a look of growing interest as he surveyed the peasant girl. "I must admit she is not to my taste but there is something about her..." His expressive black brows twitched together as he surveyed her, from crumpled cap to ill-shod feet, his gaze lingering on the pale, tear-stained face and those stricken, dark-lashed eyes. Then abruptly his face cleared and he laughed. "I have it! Tell me, Messire, does she not remind you a little of Juliène de Chartreux?"

"What?" Ranulf directed a fleeting glance at Nell of Valentién but his mind was not really attuned to any chance resemblances between a dead noblewoman and a humble village wench. "No, I cannot see it myself," he said dismissively before turning his interest where it really lay; namely how fast Kaslander's servants could dismantle and reduce the frivolous mass of silk, wood and rope to portable baggage again. "And even if I did," he continued coldly. "I hardly think that would justify any further delay, not when I am the one most likely to be held accountable by the High Counsel of Mithlondia for your tardy arrival in Lamortaine. Nor, I am sure, would you wish to offer any insult to Princess Linette, such as might be perceived in your apparent lack of haste."

"Half a day's delay, nothing more," Kaslander said airily. "Set against the fact your princess will have me for the rest of her life. But the sooner you get me beyond Chartreux's border, the sooner you can return here, eh Messire? That said, if you desire a more willing, not to mention more voluptuous bed mate, I would not bother stopping here at all but head straight back to Chartre and the luscious Elena."

Ranulf must have looked as blank as he felt since Kaslander continued,

"You know, the doxy I had last night. I am sure she said she was your woman normally."

"Ilana," Ranulf corrected coldly. "And no, she is not. I had her once, that is all, the night my brother took possession of Chartre."

"Gods above!" Kaslander stared at him in disbelief. "You have been Governor of Chartreux for what? Three months? Do not tell me you have been sleeping alone all that time?" Kaslander eyed him with clear mockery in his black eyes. "By all the gods, I would never have taken you as one with this Grey Brotherhood I have heard about!"

"Nor am I!" Ranulf snapped. Feeling that he might have over-reacted, he forced a lighter note into his voice and continued, "There are brothels aplenty in Chartre town when I feel the need."

Kaslander grinned.

"Each to their own, Messire. Myself, I do not think I will care much for your Mithlondian brothels – filthy, verminous places, I was told by one of the noblemen who visited Kaerellios in the spring; a Messire de Marillec, I believe? Your Ilana, though! Ah, she was hot and skilful enough, even by Kardolandian standards. You will no doubt have heard of the pools of Kaerellios?" He seemed to take Ranulf's grunt for assent and continued expansively, "You cannot know what you are missing until you have sampled those delights! But tell me, Messire, was not this Ilana once tirewoman to de Chartreux's daughters? By the gods, she could have taught Juliène a trick or two! You would not have thought it to look at her but when I finally coaxed her into laying with me it was like making love to a block of ice! Perhaps I should have tried her sister instead. What do you think, de Rogé? Would she have proved to have the fire in her blood that the flame of her hair promises?"

Ranulf stared at the other man, sick to his gut at these crude reference, not only for Rowène's sake but also – reluctantly and perhaps for the first time – on behalf of her dead sister; no woman deserved the treatment this bastard had meted out to her. Setting his jaw, Ranulf swallowed back bile and managed to choke out, with what he hoped was sufficient indifference,

"I have neither the leisure nor desire to discuss either of them. Now, if you are ready, your highness..."

"No, I am not yet ready, Messire. And I must confess to being somewhat curious as to your reluctance to talk about either lady. As you know, I have no such qualms regarding Juliène or our time together." He paused and a sudden flare of mocking interest lit his dark eyes. "Or perhaps you are keeping quiet because you are hoping that I do not know that you and she were lovers?"

Ranulf could feel a muscle twitch in his cheek and, seeing this small betrayal, Kaslander's grin widened even more.

"Oh yes, I know you took Juliène to your bed the night Chartre fell into your brother's keeping. Ilana was only too eager to tell me everything that transpired that night and the events of the following day. But do not fear, Messire, I have no intention of laying a claim for dishonour against you with your High Counsel when I finally get to Lamortaine. It means less than nothing to me that Juliène shared your bed. And as to that, I must suppose you found her as lacking as I did since she lasted only the one night there!"

"Your highness, Juliène de Chartreux is dead," Ranulf said flatly, clinging to the shreds of his temper with difficulty. "And whether or not it is true that we were lovers, it is scarcely a fitting subject for casual conversation. Anywhere! Let alone here, in the heart of her father's fief!"

Kaslander glanced around at the folk who were gathered beneath the plane trees; the Rogé soldiers, his own servants, the watchful villagers who had gradually been gathering.

"Surely none of these peasants understand the high tongue?" the Kardolandian prince said dismissively. "Or would care if they did. Furthermore, need I remind you that Louis de Chartreux is dead! Hanged, drawn and quartered for the traitor he was! It is *your* brother who is lord here now. Juliène and her red-haired bitch of a sister hold no sway." There was real venom in his voice when he spoke of Rowène de Chartreux but before Ranulf could react to it, the prince's tone had reverted to its smooth mockery. "Correct me if I am wrong, Messire, but as I understand it, Demoiselle Rowène has had to lower her lofty expectations considerably since I knew her in Kaerellios. Or is it not true that she is now living openly in Rogérinac as your bastard half-brother's leman?"

Ranulf bit the inside of his mouth and concentrated on the metallic taste of blood rather than the cold, white pain that stabbed through his heart. He had not thought it visible but something must have shown in his face because Kaslander grinned once more and exclaimed,

"Ha! So it *is* true! And just as obviously that truth does not sit well with you! Why, did you want the bitch for yourself?"

"No, I did not," Ranulf grated, the falsehood bitter as bile on his tongue. He saw Kaslander watching him, black eyes bright with mirth and wondered if the bastard had guessed that he was lying.

"In any case you should be grateful to me," Kaslander went on. "At least I warmed the ice maiden up for you. I tell you now, if one of my companions had not laid odds I could not get her to melt enough to open her legs for me, she would have frozen your balls off when you tried to bed her! But I must own to a certain vulgar curiosity, Messire. Tell me, *did* she benefit sufficiently from my brief tuition to give you satisfaction?"

He cocked one dark brow but Ranulf declined to make any reply and Kaslander continued, as if determined to find the thing that would finally goad him into losing his precarious hold over his temper.

"I wish now I had made more of an effort with her sister but just one look from those ice-water eyes was enough to chill me through to my soul." He evidently saw something in Ranulf's face for the other brow shot up and he said softly, "So... not one but both sisters, hmm? Hence your obvious fury at having to give the surviving one over to your half-brother?"

"Whatever happened at Chartre, it is my affair and I will not hold it up to public scrutiny," Ranulf grated, his hands clenched in an effort to prevent himself from smashing his fist into Kaslander's fine-boned, far too good-looking and openly mocking face. Satisfying though such an action might be it was one that would, at best, land him in irons and, at worst, cause a serious diplomatic rift between Mithlondia and Kardolandia. Moreover, whatever happened to him, it would ultimately serve no meaningful purpose since it would neither restore one sister to life nor mitigate his own vile actions with regard to the other.

He could not, he reminded himself grimly, afford to follow his own personal inclinations towards verbal or physical violence against Kaslander. Joffroi had waited too many years to gain the lordship of Chartreux and the Lady Ariène as his wife to display any tolerance towards his younger brother should Ranulf cause Joffroi to lose either land or lady through some intemperate act of discourtesy towards Princess Linette's betrothed. Moreover he did still have to travel with the man for another two, probably three, days.

Fighting to keep his ill temper from becoming any more apparent than it already was, he said with forced courtesy,

"Your highness, as you can see your servants have now finished packing up your things and my men are ready. That being so, I must insist that we leave immediately. Prince Linnius, your betrothed and the entire High Counsel of Mithlondia await your arrival."

Evidently realising he was not going to succeed in provoking Ranulf into any further indiscreet admissions, Kaslander accepted a leg up from one of his servants and settled with a visible wince onto the quiet gelding's back. Breathing a sigh of relief, Ranulf reached for Starlight's reins and swung up into his own saddle. Curbing his burning desire to set spurs to the stallion and outride his tiresome royal charge, he began barking swift, incisive orders at servants and soldiers alike. Within moments the village was behind them and they were trotting along the tree-lined highway, heading for Chartreux's border with Marillec.

Glad to be gone though he was, Ranulf nevertheless carried two memories away with him from Anjélais-sur-Liriél. One was of the speculative suspicion in the Valennais' pebble-hard gaze. The other was the look of utter misery in the green – yes, they had been green – eyes of the young woman he had heard named as Nell of Valentién.

Despite his preoccupation over the following days with the necessity of keeping his royal charge moving steadily northwards – alas, not as quickly as Ranulf would have liked but without leaving any more ill feeling behind him than was inevitable when dealing with a promiscuous and petulant young princeling – those nagging feelings concerning Gaelen, Gwynhere and Nell of Valentién remained with him and he had still not decided what he intended to do about them by the time he retraced his steps a se'ennight later.

With this uncharacteristic state of indecision plaguing him – and although it would have been entirely reasonable to halt there, it being nearly dusk by the time he and his men reached the village – he chose not to stop in Anjélais. His sharp ears detected a certain amount of subdued grumbling from the men as they rode behind him but he ignored it, continuing down the highway for another league or so before indicating they would make camp in a sheltered meadow beside the Liriél, not far from the place – had it only been two seasons ago? – he had come across Guy and Rowène, standing side by side, so close they were almost touching, beneath the green-gold shade of the poplar trees.

It had taken but one stunned glance at her dark witch-fire hair… one fleeting glimpse into the depths of her clear grey eyes… to know that he was lost! And he had been falling into the depths ever since!

Later, much later, he lay rolled in his cloak beneath one of the poplars, listening to the dry rustling of the dying leaves and watching the dizzying blaze of stars across the autumn sky. Eventually, lulled by the near silent song of the river nearby, Ranulf fell asleep. Only to be haunted by the same nightmares that had stalked his dreams for the past season; dreams that left his soul shackled in chains of ice, his mind troubled and his body on fire, desperate for release.

To Hell with it all, he thought sourly as he awoke to cold feet and the glittering discomfort of a crisp, white-gold dawn, he would ride to Rogérinac and somehow get this thing… this flame, this madness that bound him to Rowène de Chartreux… Gods above, even *he* did not know what it was… could not put a coherent name to it to save his soul from the Daemon of Hell. But whatever it was, he was determined to see it rooted out and destroyed, once and for all.

Then, when he was done with *her*, he would return to Anjélais-sur-Liriél and, by whatever means necessary, prove the validity of his suspicions about one Gaelen of Valentién and the green-eyed beauty he called his brother's daughter!

Unaware that she had woven herself so dangerously into Ranulf de Rogé's thoughts, Juliène lay abed, watching as pale wisps of light from the huge dark gold moon limned every shadow in her narrow little room with stark precision. Normally she kept the shutters closed against the stink of the gutter outside or the possibility of bats flying in, but tonight she had felt the need to *see* the moon, to *feel* the power of the Goddess of the Faennari, even if she herself could not wield it.

Curling herself in a ball against the chill of the early autumn night she tucked her feet into the folds of her nightgown and wondered drearily if she would ever sleep again. She had not really slept, she thought, since *that day*; the darkest day of her life. Not even the day Chartre had fallen to Joffroi de Rogé's predatory grasp had been so full of despair for at least then she still had hope to sustain and steady her.

But now she lay, utterly without hope of any sort, so tired her skin itched but sleepless for all her fatigue, scattered images flitting with unwelcome persistence across her weary mind; Gwynhere's anxious face… Gaelen's barely repressed anger… Helge emerging from the blue and gold tent, lips swollen, her neck marked with the bruises of passion… herself pressed painfully to the tree trunk as the man Finn tugged at her skirt and fumbled with her breasts... the sudden flicker of doubt, or recognition, in the dark blue eyes of the man who was now Governor of Chartreux...

It was all too much and she tried to push some at least of those memories aside, in order that she might make some coherent attempt to consider how her life might run from now on. Her efforts availed her nothing though and her troubled thoughts continued to race around and around, drawing into ever tighter circles of despair and panic, starting from that disorientating moment when Helge had first put into words her long suppressed fear.

*'Ee's breeding, bain't ee?*

God of Mercy, it was true! She *was* carrying a child!

She had shied away from that possibility ever since a chance remark by her sister as they sailed up the coast towards Chartre had awakened her to an awareness that lovemaking carried its own consequences. And she had taken what steps she could against such a consequence arising. Had prayed that it might not be so. Yet not half a day after finally accepting that she was pregnant, she had watched the man who had fathered her child ride out of her life without so much as trying to speak to him.

Why, oh why, had she done that?

Because, much though it grieved her to admit, she had suddenly seen him for the worthless wretch he was and even lower in the scale of humanity than the man by whose side he had ridden into Anjélais. And the gods knew, not many men fell as low as Ranulf de Rogé.

She should have listened to her sister when Ro had tried to warn her against Kaslander – although the gods knew Ro had not listened to her when Juliène had tried to warn her about the harper. Still, she hated it that Ro had been right about Kaslan. Almost as much as she hated the man himself; with a black and bitter hatred that was the dark reflection of the love she had once felt for him.

How could she have been so foolish as to wilfully misinterpret his sweet cajoling? How could she have believed he meant to make her his bride? The fact that, by such a binding, she would have become a Princess of Kardolandia had meant something to her, it was true, but much less than the belief that Kaslan had loved her above all others. She saw again the tender look in his dark eyes as he held out his hand to lead her away from the open licentiousness of the courtiers at play in the pink marble pools to the sweet privacy of a flower-hung bower. Damn him, he had seemed so sincere, so intensely in love with her!

Intense maybe, but with lust not love, Juliène told herself, the memory of his careless conversation with that other misbegotten lecher returning to dispel the illusion. But she had not known then the perfidy of men and when Luc had unexpectedly arrived in Kaerellios to escort her back to Chartre she had only been persuaded to leave by Kaslan's promise that he would follow her north. Well, he had certainly kept that promise, she thought bleakly. Not to seek *her* out but to celebrate his betrothal to Princess Linette of Mithlondia.

She squirmed as she remembered how she had yielded her virginity to Kaslander in the implicit belief that they would be betrothed. Well, now she must pay the price for her naivety. Yet even if he had not been in the process of contracting a binding to Princess Linette – she remembered now seeing the Mithlondian emissaries in Kaerellios but had thought nothing of it at the time, being too intent on keeping her meetings with her lover a secret from her sister – she knew now that Kaslan would never have wed her. He was a Prince of Kardolandia; he would naturally take for his bride a woman whose royal birth matched his own, not a mere nobleman's daughter. Particularly not when that nobleman had just been executed for high treason.

She supposed she *should* feel some pity for Princess Linette, since it was obvious to her that Prince Kaslander of Kardolandia would never change his ways. Indeed she doubted the concept of fidelity to one woman was within his comprehension, be they legally bound or not. But it was not pity she felt. It was jealousy; fierce, burning, destructive. Jealousy not only of the unsuspecting Linette but of that slut Ilana. And of Helge whom she had thought her friend. Fury was there too but behind it all, crowding ever closer, shrill in her ears, the terror of what would happen to her when the truth were known.

*Dear God of Mercy, I feel so alone! Ro, I need you!*

For she had to believe that her sister would not turn her back on her if she knew the truth.

Unfortunately – for perhaps fortunately, Juliène no longer knew which it was – that was not a matter that could be put to the test. Because that was the other blow she had sustained, the same day she had lost her love...

When all had finally grown quiet again, the noblemen and their escort gone, Helge having been hauled, weeping, back to the Three Sygnets by her irate father – although knowing Master Cenruth, Juliène had supposed that he had been angered less by what Helge had done than because she had not profited more by it – Gwynhere had turned to her brother and asked the question Juliène herself should have asked had she been thinking of anyone save herself!

"Gaelen, where is Lady Rowena?"

The Lady Rowena, Gaelen had reported tersely, was still in Rogérinac. Or at least he assumed she was; despite all his efforts he had been unable to get into the castle to confirm that for himself. He would go back again, he assured his anxious sister, but for the present he wished to remain in Anjélais and learn what he might of how matters stood in Chartreux under its new Governor. Lord Gilles, he had added pointedly, would certainly wish to know as much as Gaelen could find out for him.

Gwynhere had not looked happy at that, Juliène reflected, but then neither had she appeared particularly eager to return to Valentién either. For her own part, she had been disappointed that Ro had not come, of course she had been. But she sensed that her sister had her own moonlit path to follow and if that led her into the arms of Guyard de Martine, well so be it. Unless...

Well, unless her sister proved to have more sense than she herself had displayed, more sense than to give herself to a man who could never wed her. *The gods go with you, Ro.*

On the one hand, Juliène wished she might have been given the opportunity to make her peace with her sister before their paths had divided like this, wished desperately for her sister's loving support. Yet at the same time, there was relief that Ro had not come, for how would she ever have been able to face her sister with Kaslander's child in her belly?

When would it begin to show? Juliène wondered with a sudden resurgence of panic. How much longer would it be possible to hide her condition? Not long, she feared. She had not yet found the opportunity to tell Gwynhere but knew she must do so soon. For one thing, Helge knew, and though the other girl would not mean to let it slip, it was inevitable that she would. For another, if this awful sickness continued to take her unawares, sooner or later Gwynhere would guess at its cause. Better by far for Juliène to tell her first.

Yet what would Gwynhere do with that knowledge? Juliène hoped rather desperately that Gwynhere would not abandon her. Gaelen neither, not when he had sworn an oath to her father to keep her safe.

The only question that lingered in her mind was whether she should tell them about Kaslander or allow them to assume – as they most assuredly would – that the child she carried was the result of the night she had been forced to spend with the man who was now Governor of Chartreux. After all, she thought, *that* was the reason why she had lain with the man. And at the time, with her mother whispering words of poison in her ear, it had seemed the only way forward.

Now she was not so sure...

His reputation made of him a dissolute lecher from whom no woman was safe. And by his own admission, he was little short of heartless, without regard for the women he used to slake his lusts and utterly careless of any by-blows he might sire along the way.

Yet it had been Ranulf de Rogé who had saved her earlier today. The last man in Mithlondia whom she would have expected to step between an unknown village girl, in whom he had no sexual interest, and one of his own men.

Looking back, she knew she had been a fool to have left the square alone but, unable to bear the sight of Kaslan and Helge together, she had fled blindly, not even thinking that she might be followed until it was too late. Even Gaelen had not known she had been in danger; he had only come down to the river because he had been following de Rogé, suspicious of his reasons for being in the lane.

But none of her mental meanderings made it any easier to reach the decision she must make before morning.

Did Ranulf de Rogé's one good deed on her behalf balance out all his other foul crimes – against her father, her brothers, and possibly even her sister? And his reputation was so besmirched already that one more implication of rape and careless impregnation would not matter? Not when she had no intention of telling anyone save Gaelen and Gwynhere.

De Rogé himself would never know and it *was* true, to a certain extent; she had not coupled with him by choice and although he had taken what precautions he could to avoid such a consequence, she doubted such methods were infallible. What only she, and the Winter Lady, knew was that he had had as little choice in the matter as she herself had been given. And it was not as if he had found no pleasure in it!

For her own part, Juliène had expected to find his touch a terrible violation after Kaslander's loving but she had been prepared to tolerate it. Except it had not been terrible at all. Even so, she regretted most bitterly the acts she had been compelled, by circumstance and her mother's bidding, to commit.

# Chapter 6

## *Dark Wine and Darker Memories*

Without volition, her thoughts returned to that fateful morning when she had taken the final, but quite deliberate, step into the Winter Lady's silver web...

Despite opening her eyes to the wondrous promise of another golden summer's day, Juliène felt neither lightness of heart nor body, waking as she had from a night of disturbed dreams, only to find her head throbbing with pain and a heavy cramping in her lower belly, such as would normally presage her flux.

If physical discomfort were not trial enough she then had to endure her sister's transparent eagerness to be out of the castle. Already made deeply uneasy by her mother's mysterious hints, Juliène determinedly put aside her own troubles for long enough to remonstrate with Ro about her habit of riding out each day in company with the harper, a habit which Juliène knew was beginning to cause more than a few scandalous rumours. The end of it all had been a rare and heated quarrel culminating in her sister storming out, leaving Juliène to her own devices.

Having watched first Luc, then Ro, ride out of the castle – the former accompanied by his squire, the latter by the harper – Juliène spent the morning with her mother. Save for the time when she went alone to the small, secluded corner of the walled garden where the Winter Lady cultivated her special herbs; plants whose uses Juliène was reluctantly beginning to understand. She gathered what was necessary and then returned to her mother's bower to cut and crush and brew, finally straining the resultant clear potion into a tiny silver vial the Winter Lady handed to her, together with one of her rare, approving smiles – the sort that made Juliène shiver inside.

A short-lived approval, as her mother quickly dismissed her, ordering her to take a leisurely bath and wash her hair, then to put on the green silk that became her so well. And not to forget her perfume. Not the sickly one that smelt of honeysuckle, her mother had added coldly, but the one she herself had given to her; the one that contained the rare essence of moonflowers, distilled at the full of the moon when the Goddess of the Night was at her most powerful.

Juliène was only too eager to change out of her stained gown and even managed to shed some of her tension in the warm, scented waters of her bath. Not that the crude wooden tub could compare in any way to the wonders of the marble pools of Kaerellios. Nor did it help to take her mind from its constant brooding over her physical separation from Kaslan or the more subtle separation that had arisen of late between herself and her sister, but she was at least clean again.

She left the tub only when the water had cooled beyond comfort and proceeded to dry herself unaided; not wanting anyone to witness her actions, she had earlier dismissed the sharp-eyed tire-maid. Once dry, she anointed herself carefully – the inside of her wrists, her neck and between her breasts – with the scent from the crystal bottle her mother had given her. She sniffed cautiously at one wrist and wrinkled her nose. *Essence of moonflowers indeed!*

Yet even as she dismissed it as pale and insipid, she felt the scent seeping into the warmth of her skin, taking on a life of its own, arising heady and sensual, twining around her mind, opening her eyes to another place. An enchanted place where white lilies drifted on dark waters in the moonlight... and lovers lay naked together beneath the stars...

Dropping her wrist abruptly, she turned and drew in deep breaths of the clean sea breeze that blew in at the window. For a moment she hesitated, tempted to plunge her wrists back into the now cold and scummy bath water... to scrub her neck and the soft hollow between her breasts until the delicate white skin was red and raw... to wear instead the light golden fragrance of honeysuckle that she had chosen for herself and made her own.

But in the end she did not have the courage to defy her mother's command. The Winter Lady was the only person who could help her now and she dared not go against her wishes in any way.

Dressing herself carefully in the close-fitting green silk gown her mother had designated, she went to sit by the open window where the warmth of the afternoon sun and the soft sea breeze could dry her hair. She sat there for a long time, concentrating on drawing the delicately carved ivory comb through the long dark skeins, patiently working out the tangles. Trying desperately to ignore the unyielding chill of the silver vial secreted beneath her gown, she continued to comb her long hair – as black as midnight and as straight as her sister's was unruly – until it had captured the texture and sheen of spun silk, all the while wondering *where* her sister was. To her certain knowledge Ro had never been this late returning to the castle before.

Had some accident befallen her and her companion? Or, despite all warnings, had she fallen for the gentle charms of a wandering harper, ignoring the fact that he wore another woman's binding ring about his arm?

Whichever it was, Juliène decided, as soon as Ro returned she would go to her and somehow make it right between them. No matter what she herself had done, no matter what she feared her sister might have done, nothing must be allowed to come between them ever again.

The darkness in her heart lightened a little by this decision, she laid down the comb and rose to her feet. And it was then that she heard the first distant shout from beyond the walls. Something in that sound caught at her heart, dripped fear and dread into her soul as venom from a serpent's fangs. Forgetting all sense of decorum, and ignoring any possibility of danger, she hastened towards the chamber door and jerked it open, recoiling when she found Ilana outside, her face flushed with excitement and the barest hint of fright.

"Lady Ariena says as how ye're ter meet her in the entry hall, m'lady. Right now."

"And what is all that commotion I can hear?" Juliène demanded. "What has happened? Is it... Gods forbid, is my sister hurt?"

"Oh no, m'lady," Ilana replied with more of a smirk than Juliène thought appropriate. "'Tis the Lord of Rogé, m'lady, with a whole troop of soldiers. An' Lady Rowena's with them, with that harper fellow. Only he don't look like a harper no more, m'lady. More as if he were one of Bla... I mean, one o' Lord Joffroy's men. But ye must come now, m'lady."

Taking a deep breath, knowing instinctively that this was the moment her mother had been preparing her for, Juliène went down the tightly curving stairs as fast as she might in her trailing skirts, one hand on the cool, smoothly polished stone of the central support, the other skimming along the rough guide rope. She paused at the bottom in the hopes of calming her uneven breathing and thundering heart but Ilana was still urging her to hurry. Accordingly she straightened her shoulders and walked quickly down the passageway, past the great hall and on towards the main door, finally gliding down the steps into the courtyard where her mother was waiting, as poised and beautiful as a flame lily in the golden dusk.

Evidently hearing Juliène's soft footsteps, she turned, her green eyes lighting with a satisfied smile that almost, but not quite, warmed her daughter's cold heart.

"Ah, there you are! Quickly, child, come stand with me and we will welcome our visitors together." She waited until Juliène stood at her side and then, apparently reading her apprehension, said soothingly. "You have no need for anxiety. All will go as I have planned and no man – save Joffroi of course – will look upon your beauty and remain unmoved. Indeed, child, you might even have your sister's lover at your feet if you wish to take him from her."

Juliène swallowed and shook her head; she could not betray Ro in such a fashion. Indeed, she wished quite fervently that she had not been so weak-willed as to become enmeshed in this web her mother had so skilfully woven. Especially when she looked up to see a troop of heavily armed men pour through the open gateway and into the cobbled courtyard; like an unstoppable tide of black water edged with silver spray. She caught sight of the black boar pennant rising above the amorphous mass of men and horses and Ilana's remark and her mother's comments belatedly took shape and form.

Black Joffroy. *Lord* Joffroi; the Black Boar of Rogé.

As to the man himself, Juliène had little difficulty identifying him, even before her mother addressed him. Nor, having been clearly warned away from him by the Winter Lady, did she care to pay him too much heed. All her attention was fixed on her sister, seated on a huge chestnut stallion, held captive in a man's mailed arms. In spite her mother's and Ilana's hints, it took Juliène a long, long moment to realise that the man clad in the black and silver livery of Rogé was no ordinary soldier but the harper, Guy of Montfaucon.

As the conversation progressed she found herself watching the play of emotions across his face. A face that had become so familiar to her that she had almost ceased to notice it. An open, good-humoured face with eyes of a soft, light blue and a neat, dark blond beard; an attractive face for all it was not handsome as Kaslander's was. The Winter Lady's words returned, making her wonder whether perhaps she could draw him away from her sister. But no, despite Ro's quite obvious antipathy towards him, Juliène knew that the harper was not for her. Guy of Montfaucon had clearly chosen to champion her sister and whether they were lovers or not, Juliène would not interfere between them.

Which left her with... who? One of the men who fought under Joffroi de Rogé's banner? A common soldier! No, after all her mother had said, she could not believe the Winter Lady would sacrifice her most beautiful daughter in that way. But if she would not waste Juliène on a worthless nobody, who else was there? Dimly she heard her mother's silken voice saying,

"Very well, my lord. And I thank you for your consideration. Please, come inside. Your brother may accompany you..."

*Brother!* The word burned like cold fire into her mind. Joffroi de Rogé's brother. That would make some sense and at least he was a nobleman. But which...?

"Juliène, come with me!"

The sharp command broke through her thoughts and she turned towards her mother, a question flashing in her eyes. She did not hear the words that issued from her mother's red lips. Of more import was the direction of the Winter Lady's hooded green gaze as her mother silently answered her unspoken question.

Tracing that sly sideways glance, Juliène gazed in blank disbelief at the man clad in serviceable mail who was sitting his huge black stallion a little apart from the other soldiers. He had not yet removed his helm and she could see little of his face, save the direction of his arrogant, assessing gaze. But it did not really matter what he looked like, she reminded herself. *This* was the man she must deal with. He might be hideously scarred beneath that helm and a hunchback to boot – although she did not think he was, judging by the way his mail hung on his broad-shouldered frame – but she would still have to find a way to deal with him without showing her revulsion.

Then he moved, pulling off his helm, and she drew in a quick breath of relief. The gods knew he was not particularly good-looking but neither was he utterly repulsive. Indeed, save for a certain granite hardness to his features and a rather unpleasant mocking glint in his dark blue eyes, she might have passed him in the street and never given him a second glance. His hair, braided and bound, was long, appeared slightly coarse in texture and was dark with sweat where his helm had been, the rest of the length being fair – that broad term that encompassed everything between the dark gold of honey and the same silver gilt as that piece of Mithlondian coinage termed a noble. But whichever it might be, it was nothing like Kaslan's soft, dark curls and she bit down on her lip to control her panic.

She *had* to do this thing! And, what is more, *do it well*. Not only for herself but because the Winter Lady had commanded it.

Her heart felt suddenly as heavy as a lump of ice in her breast as the realisation dawned on her that this was why her mother had been prepared to help her. Not to save her daughter from public disgrace – how could she ever have been so foolish as to believe that! Rather, the Winter Lady needed, for whatever unfathomable reason, to bind Joffroi de Rogé's brother – or was that brothers, Juliène wondered, glancing from the warrior to the harper – within the silken silver skeins of the Faennari.

She became aware that the man, Lord Joffroi's brother – had she ever heard his name? – had ceased his silent study of the castle defences and seemed now to be engaged in assessing the availability of any beddable women within his line of sight. She had seen that look in the eyes of too many men over her years at the Kardolandian court to mistake it now and she could not afford to let this moment pass without using it to her benefit.

Emptying her mind of everything but her mother's instructions, she fixed him with a steady gaze, making it as luminous and mysterious as lay within her power. He held her eyes for a moment and she felt his interest flare. He took a step towards her but, just as she thought she had him hooked, he broke the tenuous contact, moving instead towards his brother – if brother was what Guy of Montfaucon was – and her own, clearly terrified, sister.

Torn between relief and frustration, Juliène watched the interaction between the three of them, waiting for the opportunity to catch the dark blue eyes of the man she had no choice but to ensnare. Finally it came and this time, although he looked away and continued his casual conversation with the harper, she knew she had him. A few moments longer and he came striding across the courtyard towards her, his eyes still cool and faintly wary but with a hint of heat that gave her some hope that she might yet succeed.

"And you are, sweetness?"

His voice was lightly mocking but with an underlying rasp she had heard a thousand times before in the pools of Kaerellios. She had always ignored that invitation when it had been directed at her, save when it had been uttered in Kaslan's deeply sensual tones, but now she made her voice soft and enticing as she gave this Mithlondian warrior her name.

She bent her knee in a deep curtsey but even though she kept her own gaze on his spurred boots, she could feel the last of the ice melting from his blue eyes as his gaze was drawn down towards the white swell of her breasts beneath the clinging green silk and the scented shadowy hollow between them. When she thought he had looked his fill she straightened and, obedient to his prompting, turned to lead him into the keep, trying desperately not to think about the twisted path she had set her feet upon.

She sat through the ensuing debate in her mother's bower in a daze, paying very little heed to the words spoken. She did not need to listen to know that her father was dead and her brothers condemned to the same fate. She did not care about Lucien but a small flake of ice chipped away from the casing around her heart as she tried to imagine Luc gone from her life. If there was anything she could have done to prevent his death she would have acted without thought for herself. But glancing around her – from Joffroi de Rogé's heavy, dark features to the blood-tipped sword in his brother's hand to the icy glitter in the Winter Lady's unyielding green gaze – she knew that, whatever she did or said, Luc's doom was already set in stone.

She did not even notice when they all left the chamber and had only the vaguest sensation of Ro wiping away her tears. When had she started weeping, she wondered numbly, and for whom was she weeping? Her father, her brother or herself? She did not think any of her tears were shed for her sister's sake; she had seen the care Guy of Montfaucon displayed for her and she knew Ro would come to no harm at his hands. Nor would he permit any other man to hurt her sister; it did not need the sight of the spurs at his heels or the sword at his hip to convince her of that. She was, she realised with pin-prick sharpness, more than a little jealous and shuddered at that horrifying revelation. How had such a dark and bitter division arisen so quickly between her and her beloved sister?

But she knew how. The Winter Lady's poison had slipped insidiously into her heart, diluting her father's honour and courage with the subtle sorceries of the Faennari until now she was fit for nothing save to become her mother's tool. Nor could she blame anyone else for her situation. She, and she alone, had wrought her doom by her own weakness. All that remained was to make what she could of her place in the Winter Lady's shadowy realm of hidden power. She would be her acolyte, her apprentice, and in time she would come to be as powerful as her mother. In the quiet stillness of her mind she heard the word *witch* whispered – and shivered.

The colour of her eyes notwithstanding, she had no desire to be a witch. No desire to wield the sort of power that destroyed realms and brought men to their knees. All she wanted was for her lover to come and find her and put his binding bracelet about her wrist. Her mother had mocked that hope and disdainfully denied that he would keep faith. But Juliène knew Kaslan better than the Winter Lady ever could and she had faith that he would honour his promise to her. All she needed was a little time. And if her actions this night would buy her that time... so it must be. She wished it did not have to be so.

Still in that numb state between despair and determination, she suffered her sister's sympathy in silence, hiding her own sorrow deep within her heart even as she washed away the ravages of her tears. The Goddess knew, she could not allow anything to mar the fragile power of her beauty tonight, lest she fail at this first test.

A simple enough test in all truth. All she had to do was seduce Ranulf de Rogé into taking her to his bed. The twist would be to convince him that he did it from his own will, not hers!

So when she heard her sister arguing with Guy of Montfaucon, pleading with him not to make them eat at the same table with the very men who had seen their father executed and who would watch their brothers die with as little compunction, she had chosen to intervene, the words forming on her lips with frightening ease, like dewdrops freezing to frost under the first moon of autumn. *Although in truth it is barely midsummer*, she thought, on a ripple of rising hysteria which she ruthlessly repressed.

"I think in this – as in so many other things we may find ourselves doing this night – we have little choice. We must face them all at some stage and it will do neither of us any good if we provoke the new Lord of Chartreux's wrath so early in his rule. Like it or not, Ro, we have to submit to these men who *think* themselves our masters!"

She flinched inwardly as she heard herself using the affectionate diminutive of her sister's name, almost as if she had abrogated the right to use it and yet she did love Ro most dearly, even though it felt as if she were betraying her with every word she spoke. As for the rest of it, her final words had been accompanied by a breathless quiver of something that was half dread, half – the Goddess help her – bitter anticipation; if she had to do this thing, then let there be no more delay. It was nearly moonrise already, surely it must be time.

But no, first must come the evening meal; a veritable victory feast, she had no doubt. Yet even as she walked down with her sister to the great hall, in her mind she was counting off the candle-notches until she and Ranulf de Rogé would be alone. Or at least she hoped her mother had such arrangements in hand; she did not think she could conduct a seduction of a possibly reluctant man without at least the trappings of privacy. Even the pools of Kaerellios had possessed a few bowers, curtained with gossamer silk or flowering kylinia vines, to give the illusion of seclusion to those few who preferred to conduct their amours away from the public gaze.

But would a rough Mithlondian warrior care about such a trivial matter as privacy? Juliène had grave doubts on that score, doubts that were only exacerbated by de Rogé's subsequent behaviour over the course of the elaborate meal that followed.

Despite being seated beside him at the high table, Juliène found herself a little at a loss as to how she should proceed. De Rogé appeared to care more for the wine than for the food and more for the attentions of the wench who filled his goblet than the noblewoman at his side. Ilana, she saw with some surprise, had taken up the role of serving woman for the evening. A role that appeared far more suited to her talents than that of tirewoman had ever been, Juliène thought with an inexplicable surge of spite. The gods knew she did not *want* Ranulf de Rogé and had he not been hers, by the Winter Lady's will, she would have sent him to Ilana's bed without a qualm.

Yet for the moment she held her peace, steeling herself against the moment she must draw his full attention back to herself. She watched him from beneath her lashes as he drained his goblet for a second time, then raised the cup in an unmistakeable demand. He had merely flirted with Ilana the first time she had refilled his goblet but this time when she approached he pushed his chair back from the table a little way and pulled the woman down onto his lap, fondling her with a complete disregard for Juliène's presence, even going so far as to draw her shift down over her shoulder and loosen her bodice. Although to judge from her giggle, any protest Ilana made was more for show than of any actual substance.

Hiding her unexpected flash of embarrassment – this, after all, was nothing compared to the indiscretions she had witnessed at the royal Kardolandian court – behind a thin veneer of haughty disdain, Juliène fixed her gaze on the untouched roasted partridge on her platter and wondered whether she had completely misread the heat in de Rogé's dark blue eyes when he had looked at her earlier.

From the corner of her eye she glimpsed a plump breast cupped in a large hand, the dark nipple tightening under the rough caress of calloused fingers. Feeling slightly sick, panic beginning to swirl cold in her belly, Juliène reached down to surreptitiously touch the silver vial beneath her belt, the breathless relief she felt serving in some measure to steady her at this solid reminder that she yet retained some control over the situation.

She took a small sip of the rich red Marillec wine and, as the heady fruity flavours touched her tongue, she knew suddenly what she must do. It would take little more than a heartbeat to implement her plan but she doubted she could do it with de Rogé so close. Even though he did not appear to be taking any notice of her, she did not trust lust to entirely blinker that piercing blue gaze of his.

Not surprisingly, considering the way Ilana was writhing on his lap and doing a little unsubtle fondling of her own, the lines of his body were taut with tension. And while that tension might just be caused by something as simple and straightforward as sexual desire, it could equally well be the warrior's instinct for danger that kept his body alert and ready to act. He was still wearing both sword and dagger and Juliène had no doubt that in his current taut state he would use either on her should she provoke him sufficiently. Better perhaps if he could disperse his obvious tension in another direction. But, please gods, not here at the high table, with everyone watching...

Just as she felt she could endure it no longer, she felt rather than heard de Rogé murmur low in Ilana's ear. The next moment the woman had slipped from his lap, adjusting her dress with as much aplomb as the boldest Kardolandian courtesan. She walked down the dais steps and the length of the hall, head up, hips swaying, knowing the majority of male eyes were fixed on her in avid and vociferous envy of the fair-haired nobleman still lounging at the high table, a slight flush mantling his cheekbones.

Juliène cared nothing for that. All that mattered was that in the slut's preoccupation with her perceived triumph over her mistress, Ilana had neglected to remove the almost empty jug of wine from the table. Disdaining to notice either the servant's exit or de Rogé's obvious state of arousal, Juliène permitted herself a subdued surge of satisfaction as she regarded the chased silver mouth of the pitcher.

Whether Ilana had responded to the silent message Juliène had been whispering in her mind was questionable but at least she had done what Juliène had wanted her to. It only remained to distract her dining companion for the three heartbeats she had calculated would be sufficient for her purposes. On that thought, she began to whisper another silent suggestion in her mind but it did not work quite in the way she had intended. Instead of following the strumpet from the hall, de Rogé leaned forward in his chair and fixed his gaze on someone at the other end of the table. The harper? No, her sister, damn the man to Hell!

She saw him lift his goblet in a patently mocking gesture, rising to his feet with a swift, somewhat unsteady movement – gods! surely the man could not be drunk on three goblets of Marillec wine, potent though she knew it to be – and finally made his way out of the hall, pausing to exchange a brief word with the harper as he went. Juliène watched him go with a certain amount of relief, tempered by an acute and hideous fear that he did not mean to return.

She caught her mother's cool green gaze, shivering as one delicate brow arched in a subtle sign of the Winter Lady's displeasure and, feigning a confidence she was far from feeling, reached for the pitcher, as if to pour herself a measure of wine. The light from the enormous circular candle-holder overhead caught and flickered with red flame as her mother tilted her head in the most infinitesimal of nods and Juliène breathed again.

As she had thought, three heartbeats more than sufficed to empty the contents of the silver vial into the remnants of the dark red wine but the candles had burned down another notch before Ranulf de Rogé returned to the hall and resumed his seat. Disregarding the unmistakeable reek of sweat and sex that clung to his skin and caught sharply in her nose, Juliène turned to him with what she hoped was a convincingly strained smile. Not that it was far from the truth, she reflected distractedly; her heart was nigh to collapse under the onslaught of so many conflicting emotions and all the stars she had ever seen were shooting painfully around inside her skull.

She heard herself ask him something meaningless to which he replied with an indifference that sent her even closer to the edge. Then he looked away again.

Goddess help her, she *had* to hold his attention!

Sheer willpower on her part dragged his gaze first to her face, then to her lips. Yet even so, she could feel him fighting her allure with every beat of his heart. He looked away again, back towards her sister. Ro was staring at him with such a depth of ice in her grey eyes that even Juliène shivered. Whatever de Rogé felt for her sister – and it was becoming increasingly obvious to Juliène that he did indeed feel something – it was clear that Ro regarded him as nothing less than the personification of the Daemon of Hell.

Juliène saw de Rogé shift slightly in his seat – perhaps even he could be rendered uncomfortable by the glittering, honed-ice edge of her sister's disdain – and she seized the moment to draw his attention back towards herself.

"Will you have some more wine, Messire?" She gestured towards the gracefully curved shape of the silver pitcher. "Or perhaps some more food?"

Not waiting for his reply and holding his gaze with her own she reached out for the pitcher, pouring the red wine into the silver goblet by his hand. Then she sat still, watching him. For a moment she thought he hesitated, then he lifted his hand, his calloused fingers curving about the stem of the innocent silver vessel. The candlelight glinted gold off the hairs on the back of his hand as he lifted the goblet slowly towards his hard, unsmiling mouth and Juliène thought she might scream just to break the tension of the moment.

*Drink. Drink.*

Finally he touched the silver rim to his mouth, his dark blue gaze still locked with her own. Almost without volition she moistened her lips. At once a spark sprang to flame behind the ice in his eyes and he tilted the goblet higher, his lips parting. She watched him sip, sensed the dark red wine lying warm and heavy on his tongue... slipping down his throat to set a fire in his blood. Sensed too that his desire was stirring once more... Only this time, Goddess help her, it was focussed on her.

For a time he seemed to forget the goblet in his hand, so intent was his interest, and her limbs began to tremble under the almost unbearable strain. But if she broke his gaze now, she knew the moment would be lost, never to return. And she had to ensure that he finished the wine.

*Drink. Damn you, drink!*

Whether obeying her silent command or the promptings of his own senses, he lifted the goblet to his mouth once more, taking another sip. Rather than swallowing immediately he seemed to hold the liquid upon his tongue. Savouring the sensual sweetness of the wine or...

*Goddess*, she thought with fresh panic, *let him not taste the bitter memory of the herbs I used to weaken his will and inflame his baser urges.*

Cold as ice now, she forced herself to hold his gaze steady, willing him to drain the goblet to its dregs. She curved her lips into what she hoped was an enticing smile, her eyes holding out the promise of passion. She saw his own eyes darken in response and knew he understood what she was offering him – or rather what he thought she was offering him.

Yet even at that stage, she sensed that he was still fighting against the desire she roused in him and she silently cursed the steel-strong force of his will. What would it take to make the man crack?

Then, with a movement so swift, so abrupt she almost missed it, he tossed back the contents of the goblet and set it down with a decisive click.

*Goddess be thanked, I have done it! He is mine now, to do with as I will.*

Not daring to allow her relief to show, she reached out with seeming casualness towards the silver dish piled high with the exotic fruits of Kardolandia, selecting a peach and a small bunch of sweet, black grapes with trembling fingers. She felt his eyes upon her as she nibbled on the succulent flesh, but after a moment he looked away, frowning in her sister's direction.

Juliène did not care. It did not matter now where he looked or what thoughts he harboured for Ro. Or Ilana. Or any other woman in Chartre keep. He was hers now and it would be her bed he came to tonight.

Her euphoria at achieving this first part of her plan waned considerably as she contemplated the next stage, the enormity of what was to come making what had gone before seem a trifling affair. After all, what was drugging a man's wine as set against performing with him such an intimate act as must follow?

It had been different with Kaslan. Once he had overcome her natural diffidence, it had been so easy to give herself to him. They had been lovers in the truest sense of that word.

But to do *that* with a stranger? With *this* stranger? The sweetness of the grapes turned sour in her mouth and she nearly retched as she tried to swallow.

*Goddess help me, how am I to do this thing? And do it so well, he does not guess that he is not the seducer?*

She slid a sideways glance at the man beside her, taking in details she had only vaguely noticed before, details that only served to depress her further.

Compared to Kaslan's lithe slenderness, de Rogé was a hulking ox of a man. She had thought that perhaps the bull-like width of his shoulders was merely a product of the mail hauberk he had been wearing earlier but now, clad in a simple, if somewhat shabby black tunic devoid either of insignia or all but the barest shreds of silver embroidery, he looked just as big, if not bigger. Ox or not though, he had apparently taken the trouble to wash before the meal – for which she was truly grateful – even though the beneficial effects of that had largely been negated by his recent exertions with Ilana.

But at least his hair was clean and proved to be even fairer than she had previously suspected. Part-braided at the temples, the remainder was allowed to fall free over his shoulders, reaching more than half way down his back, longer than his older brother's by far, a thick, unruly tumble of pale gold – similar in colour and texture to the mane of her sister's palfrey, she thought uncharitably. After years of being accustomed to the shorter styles prevalent at the Kardolandian court it seemed... effeminate almost.

She slipped another surreptitious glance at him and abruptly changed her mind. There was absolutely nothing soft or feeble about any of the de Rogé men, least of all this one. Not when a broken nose and a small but prominent white scar on his cheekbone were added to an unyielding, slightly thin-lipped mouth and a hard jaw line that not even the smattering of pale gold stubble could disguise. Nor did she believe the body beneath those plain garments would be any softer. While as for his soul... she had the morbid fancy that if he possessed one at all, it would prove to be just as ruthless as his ice-cold, dark blue eyes.

What would it be like to lie with such a man... beside him... beneath him? Take him into her body in the most intimate of acts? With thoughts of that inevitable coupling whirling in her aching head, she could not trust herself to eat another morsel, fearing she might vomit in earnest.

And yet, she attempted to reassure herself, Ilana had survived such a coupling – she could see the slut serving down at the far end of the hall now, seemingly none the worse for being so used – and, if his unwholesome reputation bore even the faintest resemblance to reality, she knew there must have been countless other women over the past score of years. She might not have taken much note of Mithlondian gossip in general but she had heard much since her return about the de Rogé brothers. Joffroi would have to curb his appetites after today, she thought with the first flicker of humour she had felt all day, if indeed he meant to wed her mother. As for Ranulf, he could bed every wench he saw after tonight and she would not care, as long as she survived and never had to see him again.

Then she corrected that blithe statement. Every woman save her sister; Ro deserved better than a black-hearted lecher like Ranulf de Rogé. And perhaps, Juliène thought, she might even have found it. Glancing along the length of the high table, past de Rogé, her mother, his brother and her sister, Juliène acknowledged a wisp of envy as she studied the harper's familiar features which were now set in rather bleak lines. She wondered idly what he would look like without the beard – not unlike the man beside her, she thought, not for the first time since she had seen them together.

*Guy of Montfaucon? Hmm...*

But whoever he was, his attitude towards her sister was distinctly protective and she could not help but envy Ro. Until the moment, that is, when the harper reached out a hand towards the bread basket and the short sleeve of his ragged tunic rode higher up his heavily muscled arm. The candlelight sparked red and gold against the broad bronze band just above his elbow and Juliène tasted the bitterness of truth in her mouth. Yet even so, there was a grimly determined look in his light blue eyes that told Juliène that whether bound or not, kinsman or no to Joffroi and Ranulf de Rogé – and she was now almost sure that he must be – Guy of Montfaucon was an honourable man and if he had taken Ro under his protection, then protect her he would, with his life if need be.

It must be wonderful to inspire such regard, Juliène thought. Kaslan loved her, that she knew, but she had the niggling suspicion – born no doubt of the Winter Lady's cool scorn – that the love he had for her was not of the order that would cause him to lay down his life for her and that...

"Ran! Guy! Are you and your ladies done?"

Joffroi de Rogé's deep voice shattered her musings, causing her to start nervously and bite the inside of her cheek.

Attempting to gather her wits and her courage, she paid scant heed to Joffroi's very public claiming of her mother's lips, concentrating instead on the thread of tension she could hear underlying Ranulf's curt tones as he rejected his older brother's facetious comment about drawing lots.

"I have better things to do with my time than draw lots. Let Guy keep his doxy. I am more than content with this very lovely lady."

Responding to the firm grasp of his fingers about her wrist she rose to her feet, suddenly too terrified to move or even think. Her gaze flew to Guy of Montfaucon, pleading silently with him to somehow stop this moment... turn it back... change time itself... He met her eyes steadily, allowing her to read both defeat and regret in those summer blue depths before finally accepting that he could give her no direct aid, he closed his eyes, fists clenching at his side.

The next thing Juliène knew Ranulf was drawing her briskly towards the far end of the table, pausing beside the harper. She could not hear everything he hissed in Guy of Montfaucon's ear but she did catch a few salient phrases, one in particular causing a resurgence of her earlier panic.

"What you do behind a bolted door is your own affair. Just make damn sure there is blood on your sheet in the morning and Joff is not like to call you a liar."

What did that mean? For Ro? Or for her? She had no way of knowing what de Rogé was implying but whatever the harper thought he meant, it caused relief to flicker almost unseen in his eyes as he glanced from Ranulf to her. It was the briefest of looks, then he turned his attention towards coaxing her sister out of the hall.

De Rogé watched them go and then followed in an outwardly leisurely fashion, albeit there was nothing relaxed about the grip he retained on her wrist. He paused outside the great hall for a few words with the middle-aged man on guard duty, nodded to the younger one and then turned to her.

"This is your home, Demoiselle. The least you can do is show me to our chamber."

The blue eyes looking down at her appeared unnaturally dark and not a little forbidding but that might just have been due to the uncertain light from the torch on the wall behind him. Then again, it might be the effect of the herbs she had recklessly added to his wine. Either way, she had no choice but to continue along the path her own folly and her mother's cunning had laid down for her.

"This way, Messire," she said, keeping her voice soft and low, leading him through the torch-lit passageways towards the arched opening at the base of the Lady Tower.

He released her wrist as they ascended the narrow, curving stairs but she could feel his presence close behind her and, behind him, she could hear his brother's heavy steps accompanied by the faintest trace of her mother's subtle yet powerful perfume.

Coming to the chamber she had formerly shared with her sister, she would have carried on had not Ranulf suddenly caught at her wrist again, forcing her to endure his own and his brother's bawdy would-be witticisms even as she tried not to look at Ro where she lay, trapped beneath the harper on the bed. Despite her faith in Guy of Montfaucon's integrity she suffered a severe shock at the scene; it looked uncomfortably like ravishment in deed as well as name and she was still worrying about that when she heard Black Joffroi bidding his brother a jocular good night and he and her mother descended the stairway again.

Drawing a deep breath she turned her back on the now closed door of the bedchamber and continued on upwards to the room at the top of the tower, the chamber that had once been Luc's but which the Winter Lady had prepared for her. On reaching the heavy door, however, she found herself unable to move, either forwards to the conclusion of this never-ending day or to turn and flee down the stairs to despair. Either way would bring dishonour and she knew not which would ultimately be more shameful.

In the end she had no choice. Taking hold of her wrist again, Ranulf de Rogé drew her inside – not aggressively but certainly firmly – and shut the door behind them, the sound of the bolt grating home as loud and harsh as a corbie's croak.

# Chapter 7

## *Witch by Moonlight*

With the door shut fast behind them, de Rogé released her wrist and – of all things he *could* have done – spoke in a level, perfectly emotionless tone,

"Are you cold? Or merely frightened of what I might do to you?"

*Goddess, yes!*

Not cold, but certainly frightened. Not enough to turn aside from this course of action but enough to know just how wrong it could all go.

"Neither," she replied steadily, lifting her chin and drawing courage and power from the celestial symbol she could glimpse through the open window. It glimmered like an enormous pink pearl against a cobalt sky and must surely be an omen; a sign that the Moon Goddess was with her... that all would be well.

Somewhat to her surprise de Rogé did not move away from the door. Instead he leaned back against it, arms folded across his chest, his shadowed blue eyes holding a hint of a wild, dark fire that greatly alarmed her, even though it was she who had deliberately fanned it into flame.

*Goddess, give me the strength – and the subtlety – to handle this daemon I have unleashed!*

She had expected him to pounce on her as soon as they were alone behind that bolted door and was disconcerted to find him making no such move. Instead he continued to lean against the impenetrable oak boards, his gaze sweeping over her, from the toes of her dainty little feet clad in the green silk slippers that matched her gown to the almost transparent gauze of the pale green veil that overlaid her raven tresses. She had been confident that she could direct the course of this encounter but now found herself desperately uncertain about everything, even her own appearance, with which she had taken such care.

"You are very beautiful," he said suddenly. "And very desirable."

Despite the words Juliène did not think from his tone that he meant them as a compliment. Nevertheless she dipped him a curtsey, the fragrance of moonflowers drifting gently on the air as she swayed, graceful as a mountain birch in the summer twilight.

"Thank you, Messire," she murmured.

"A very beautiful, desirable noblewoman," he continued, his stance not changing one iota, although it was certain that his eyes had followed every movement of her body. The fire in his eyes burned darker and wilder for a moment, then settled into little more than a glowing ember as he finished flatly,

"You are also doubtless a maiden still. Not to mention being young enough to be my daughter."

Despite the panic that abruptly took wing, beating frantically in her breast, Juliène held her silence. She did not think he was so many years older than her as to make such a thing possible but was not about to argue the point with him. And as for the matter of her virginity, that was certainly not up for debate.

"That being so, what I want tonight..." de Rogé paused, fair brows lifting, his hard mouth twisting into the most fleeting of sardonic smiles. "What I need tonight... is something *you* unfortunately cannot give me."

"And what might that be?" she enquired, keeping her voice soft when all she wanted to do was scream in vexation.

He grimaced again, then said curtly,

"A woman I can fuck tonight without thought for tomorrow!"

*Good God of Light! Did he really just say what I thought he said?*

Shock rippled through her even as he continued remorselessly,

"A woman I can walk away from in the morning and feel no guilt over..." He broke off, mouth tightening in his gold-dusted jaw.

"A woman like Ilana, I suppose you mean?" she asked, with more than a hint of contempt.

His mouth relaxed slightly and lifted in another derisive smile, but whether he mocked himself or her, Juliène could not tell. Goddess help her, what was she to do now? It was quite obvious that he had no intention of loosing his lust on her voluntarily – and given the concentration of the drugged wine she had managed to get down him she had thought it would be over and done with by now. But how to overcome his steel-hard control when the potion the Winter Lady had assured her could not fail very palpably had?

As she hesitated, irresolute and turning over varying schemes of increasing desperation in her head, de Rogé finally pushed off the door, his hand lifting to rub his eyes as if his vision had suddenly blurred. He walked, somewhat unsteadily, towards the window and sat down heavily on the stone seat. He looked, Juliène thought as she eyed him narrowly, as if he might pass out or vomit at any moment – and neither of those options appealed to her.

The slick of sweat on his face caught in the silvery-pink shimmer of the moon as he bent forwards and the unexpectedly horrifying notion that she might have poisoned him slithered icy and insidious through her mind. Followed by the even icier realisation that he would be of little use to her dead. Knowing she had to do something, but uncertain as to what exactly, she knelt at his feet and peered uncertainly up into his face.

"Messire? You are unwell?"

He sent her a brief, brittle glance between narrowed lashes, his breath rasping heavy and uneven against the stillness of the night, then dropped his head again.

"No," he gritted. "I am well enough. A griping in my belly, nothing more."

"You do not look well to me," Juliène offered doubtfully. "Can I not get you something to ease the pain? Some wine?" He winced and she hastily amended her offer. "Water then?" At that he grimaced outright, shaking his head even as he pressed one hand hard across his belly.

Notwithstanding his refusal, Juliène looked around the chamber but neither of them had thought to kindle a light and in the chancy glimmer of the moon it was difficult to see anything beyond the man beside her and the bed behind her. Then her roving gaze fell on the clothing chest against the far wall beneath the courtyard window and the pewter pitcher that rested on the polished surface. She gathered her skirts, intending to rise, but halted as a large, cold hand clamped about her arm.

"No more wine," de Rogé grated. His lips were compressed into a thin, bloodless line, his pale blond brows knit, sweat glimmering at his temples and on his stubbled jaw. He shook his head, unable to speak for a moment, then managed through clenched teeth, "A pot... would be of... more..."

He stopped, sweat running freely down his pallid face, then lurched around and, leaning out of the open window, retched convulsively, vomiting up what seemed like everything he had eaten or drunk that evening. Juliène scrambled to her feet with more swiftness than grace, thinking dispassionately that it was fortunate he had chosen that window rather than the one that gave onto the courtyard; at least there was only the thrift-covered cliffs and the sparkling sea below.

She stood uncertainly for a moment, watching his heaving shoulders and listening to the ghastly noises that made her own belly clench in a mingling of appalled disgust and the very faintest trace of reluctant guilt – *he* might have been the one who had over-indulged in the strong Marillec wine but *she* had been the one who had contaminated it with the gods only knew what herbs of her mother's choosing – then decided it was probably in her own interest to render him what assistance was possible.

Finding a folded square of rough linen on a shelf she dampened it in the liquid in the pitcher – it seemed only to be water but she felt vaguely that she should take nothing for granted any longer – and wringing it out, carried it back to the window where de Rogé was now slumped on the seat, his head thrown back and resting against the side wall of the embrasure. His eyes were closed, his face a nasty shade of pale, and an unmistakeable reek of vomit clung about his person.

Trying not to breathe in any more of the sharp stench than necessary, Juliène knelt beside him again.

"Messire?"

At the sound of her tentative tone, he slowly opened his eyes and regarded her with a blank lack of recognition that frightened her almost more than the sudden, and probably unnatural, violence of his illness. In the light of the moon – the fey pink now fading imperceptibly to true silver – his eyes lacked all but the barest ring of blue, being mere bottomless pools of black shadow in which she could read no emotion whatsoever, not even the lust he had displayed earlier.

"Here... this might help."

She held out the damp cloth but, when he made no move to take it, edged close enough to wipe his face and hair with an unsteady hand.

*Goddess help me, now what do I do?*

Certainly this was not the way she had envisaged this seduction... ravishment... possession... unfolding. By now, it should be over, her virginity unimpeachably lost to a de Rogé. Instead it appeared that she had rendered the man incapable of anything more strenuous than merely breathing – and by means of the very potion that should have made him malleable to her wiles. The best she could hope for under the circumstances was to somehow get him into the bed and trust that if he woke up beside her in the morning he would believe the obvious had occurred between them. A few judicious tears, a little blood on the sheet and all would be well. Better yet, there would be no necessity for her to give herself to him at all...

Indeed, Juliène mused with a mildly questioning glance at the ambiguously smiling face of the moon, this might even be a better resolution to her problem than the Winter Lady's plan. All she had to do...

She froze, the cloth falling unheeded from her hand, as she felt his arm band around her waist and pull her suddenly stiff body closer to his. Panic flared in her breast and she shot to her feet, then took... or tried to take... a step back.

But there was no yielding in the arm that held her and, even as her thoughts scurried, fled and then regrouped into recognition of what was happening, she felt de Rogé's other hand slid up the silk-covered length of her leg, briefly cup her bottom, then continue on up, stroking over her hip, to her breast.

She cast another look at the moon, the last vestiges of her pink raiment now all but washed away by the glitteringly bright, hard-edged silver light that suddenly seemed to Juliène to hold more of malice than encouragement. She felt almost as if she had been betrayed by that distant deity who ruled the star-scattered reaches of the night – even as she acknowledged that what she had planned for the man now nuzzling at her nipple had been as perfidious as anything the Daemon of Hell might have enacted.

De Rogé's hands and mouth were moving even more purposefully now, rough against her silk-cool skin and trembling, moon-touched flesh. She heard him make a guttural sound low in his throat but knew that this time it was the wrenching groan of growing desire not the warning of incipient illness. With an effort she made her body pliable in his arms, leaning into him, instinctively giving his mouth access to the delicate curves of shoulder and neck, wondering as she did so how much he would remember in the morning.

Should she make some show of reluctance? She did not want him to remember her as a wanton wench but rather as a frightened, *virginal*, young noblewoman. Yes, some sign of dismay would be appropriate, she decided, and on the thought pulled back abruptly just as one hot, heavy hand moved from her buttock to glide down her leg and up again, only this time beneath the meagre armour of her clinging gown.

His other arm was still at her back, his fingers incredibly freeing the careful knot she had made when she had laced her gown up earlier. Goddess save her! Even more than half drunk on Marillec wine, drugged with the Winter Lady's herbs and ensnared by whatever dubious powers of enchantment she had inherited, the man still made appallingly swift work of his business.

Or had done.

She became aware that she was trembling quite noticeably and that de Rogé's fingers had stilled. The abrupt removal of his warm mouth from her breast allowed the cooling night air to dance over the damp silk of her bodice and caused her tautened nipple to tingle. She gasped at the unsought sensation and took another step back.

Unbelievably he let her go, his hands dropping away.

"I will not hurt you," he said, his voice low but holding some small trace of the lust that burned unguarded in his drug-darkened eyes.

"Will you not?" she whispered, swallowing away the shameful sensations that still shimmered through her body.

She had been prepared to give her body to de Rogé for expedient's sake but had not expected to enjoy the process. Not when she had no particularly pleasant memory of Kaslan's possession. She had found the gentle warmth of his lips on hers sweetly pleasant until the moment he had thrust his tongue into her mouth and the shock of that invasion, followed by the further shock as he took her body, lived with her still. She had expected it to be far worse with this drugged and drunken stranger and yet...

Confused and trembling, she glanced over his shoulder at the serenely smiling face of the moon but if she expected answers from the enigmatic Goddess of the Faennari she did not find them. Instead she heard de Rogé say roughly,

"Believe it or not, I do not force women into my bed. Nor do I hurt them whilst they are there."

"Serving wenches," she muttered, finding a sneer from somewhere. "And... and..."

"Serving wenches and whores?" he rasped. "That is my standard, you would say? And you would be right, for the most part. Nevertheless, I *do* know what it is to lie with a virgin. To give her pleasure as well as pain."

Juliène swallowed again, fighting against the onslaught of cold, unrelieved dread rather than... But what had he just said? Before she could think, she had blurted,

"How do you? Know, I mean?" The incredulous words, *You? A de Rogé!* remained unspoken but hung between them nevertheless.

He gave the merest breath of a laugh.

"I may not be in the habit of seducing young, beautiful, virginal noblewomen but I do have some limited experience."

"At court?" She was incredulous still but curious now as well. And not a little wary. She had not counted on him having experience of such matters as broken maidenheads and the discovery that he did was most unwelcome; she would have to be doubly cautious when he took her.

"No, I have kept away from the women at court since the time I was seduced at the age of fifteen by a noble lady who shall remain nameless. She was some years older than me and wed – although I did not know it at the time I went to her bed – to one of the fiercest warlords of the realm. And no, it was not your father! But I learned more than one lesson that night. Lessons that still hold true, I might add. As to my more recent experience with virgins... back in Rogérinac, my..." He paused, evidently searching for a suitable word.

"Mistress?" Juliène suggested, slender dark brows arching.

He grimaced, hesitated and then gave an off-hand shrug.

"Not the word I was going to use but it will suffice, even though that term implies a permanence that is unlikely ever to exist. As she understands." He frowned. "I hope." He gave another dismissive twitch of his shoulders. "What I meant to say is that she was most definitely a maid when she came to me and if she had any complaint as to the part I played in the loss of her virginity, I have not heard it."

As if the unfortunate woman would dare make complaint – to him or anyone else – if she was, as Juliène supposed she must be, one of the peasant girls local to Rogérinac. Or perhaps even a servant in the castle itself; she had already observed de Rogé's facility for fornicating with the Chartre serving wenches and did not believe he would show any more restraint in tumbling any of his brother's serfs if the urge took him to do so.

His explanation, such as it was, clearly having concluded, she expected him to resume his interrupted seduction but once again, he took her by surprise. Pushing abruptly to his feet, he strode across the small, square chamber to stare out of the other window, at the moonlit courtyard below or the tall walls where his men patrolled, leaving Juliène to glare at his broad back.

Now what ailed the man? Could it be that when he had so gracelessly expelled the contents of his stomach he had also purged his body of the herb that was supposed to make her task easier. Be damned to him if that were so!

She was still turning over various choices of action in her mind when he turned back to face her. When he did not immediately break the silence between them she seized her chance and, although all she really wanted to do was swear at him and *order* him to take her to bed, she kept her voice soft and enticing, even venturing to use his given name for the first time.

"Messire... Ranulf..."

"Do you know what your sister and my brother are likely doing now?" he interrupted moodily, his tone as much as the question taking her completely by surprise.

"My sister and your..?"

"Brother. Yes, you heard me right."

Gods above! So there *was* more to the harper than he had been prepared to admit to and this then was the source of the likeness she had observed between him and Ranulf de Rogé. It mattered little to her but, dear God of Light, such knowledge would devastate her sister.

"So Guy of Montfaucon is your brother," she heard herself say coldly. "Base-born, I assume, and obviously as lacking in morals as you are if he can contemplate lying to my sister with one breath and making love to her with the next."

"Making love!" De Rogé gave a low, softly scornful laugh. "You truly think *that* is what he is doing?"

"You do not think he would ra... ravish her?" Juliène asked with genuine horror.

"Daemons of Hell! Of course he would not rape her!" de Rogé snapped. "Guy is far too bloody honourable to break his binding vows in your sister's bed, let alone take her there by force. Indeed, I would be willing to wager my stallion, my sword and all hope of a speedy departure in the morning that he is even now as far away from her as he can get whilst still remaining in the same room. It will be a bedding in name only," he added as she stared at him blankly. "With a bloody – and no, I am not swearing – sheet in the morning to placate Joffroi."

"And is that the fate you intend for me?" Juliène asked. "But you have no binding vows to keep. Do you?"

"No. And no desire to take them either. What I do know is that Joffroi's orders in this matter run close to madness and I have no desire to hang when the High Counsel learns that I have forcibly deflowered a young noblewoman at my liege lord's command."

"You think the High Counsel will care what happens to me?" Juliène asked with a sudden bleak bitterness. "Those same noblemen who impeached my father for a crime he could never have committed? Who declared him and my brother guilty of treason? The same men who watched my father die a traitor's death? Why would they care what happens to me? Or to my sister?"

"Believe me, they would care soon enough if it came to their attention that you – or your sister – had been raped, either by me or Guy."

"But if it were not *that*?" Juliène asked, unable to utter the terrible word lest it become real. "I believe Ro fancies herself a little in love with your... with him. I think she would give herself to him willingly enough and you cannot tell me that he is indifferent to her."

"No, Guy is not indifferent but whether your sister was willing or no, he would still be held to have debauched her," de Rogé retorted. "Nor would he do it." He smiled grimly from the shadows and crossed his arms over his chest. "It seems, Demoiselle, that I have more faith in my brother's integrity than you have in your sister's bewitchments."

"Ro is not a witch!" Juliène snapped, stung by the mockery in his voice and wondering how she had managed to lose control of the situation so badly. "She is good and gentle and..."

"And as such would make a far more fitting mate for Guy than the bitch to whom he is already bound," de Rogé finished, his smile twisting awry. He took a step away from the window and reached for the buckle of his sword belt. "Get you to bed, Demoiselle, and sleep without fear. I will not touch you and in the morning I will play my part before Joffroi with as much conviction as I am able."

"But where will you sleep?" she queried, still wondering how she might turn this to her advantage. If he shared the bed with her there was still a chance...

"On the window seat or the floor, it matters not to me," he shrugged, his very indifference destroying her last frail hope. "Thirty years living at Rogérinac, interspersed with nearly a score of years of border campaigning has left me with the ability to sleep in the most uncomfortable of places. And, as the door is bolted, no-one is ever like to know."

*Damn, damn, damn!* The man obviously meant it! Now who would have supposed a de Rogé would be concealing so much as a spark of honour behind his black reputation?

Juliène glanced once more at the rising moon but the last lingering traces of mystic pink had long since faded. Nevertheless, she could not let this chance wither without making one final, desperate gamble. And it was not entirely a gamble, she assured herself; his earlier lust had not been feigned. If she could just rekindle it...

Reaching behind her, she tugged at the knot de Rogé's fingers had already loosened. She felt the silk slip over her shoulders and caught it just before it could slither down over her breasts. She shook back the tumbling, dark fall of her silken hair, an action that both revealed her body and released the heady, beguiling fragrance of moonflowers into the suddenly breathless stillness between them.

"Bloody hell!"

The muttered words shredded the silence and even though he still stood in the shadows beyond the edge of the moonlight she could sense how desperately he was fighting to control the dark, destructive lust that blazed anew in his drugged blood.

One more spark and he would be lost to it.

One last chance for her to step back and let this moment go. Ro would stand beside her in her shame, she knew that now, almost as if her sister had whispered the words in her ear. And Kaslan would surely come for her.

*I do not have to take this path!*

And yet... the Winter Lady wished it. It was as if an icicle pierced her soul, dusting her heart and mind with a sparkling frost – fragile, brittle, dazzlingly beautiful – that cleverly concealed the utter darkness beneath. As her mother's cold voice spoke with painful clarity in her mind, ousting her sister's gentler whisper, Juliène accepted that there was no possibility of escape. She had to do this and do it *now*.

Setting aside all emotion, she released her grip and allowed the gown to slip unhindered down her body to pool around her ankles, leaving her clad in nothing more than the sheerest of shifts spun of silver moonlight.

De Rogé said nothing but the catch in his breath was clearly audible.

Smiling, she took a dainty step out of her puddled gown and, untying the ribbon that held the neck of her shift, allowed that to drop too, wreathing her ankles in mist.

Moonlight silvering her white limbs she took another step towards the man who stood motionless in the dark shadows at the other side of the chamber, his breath harsh and uneven, as if he had just fought – or was still fighting – a battle. She could not see him clearly, just his silhouette against the unshuttered window, but even so she sensed his eyes following her every movement.

Silent as enchantment itself she stepped around the foot of the bed, gliding gracefully past him in a drift of fragrance and reached to pull back the bedcovers.

"What is that...scent? And what in Hell do you think you are doing?"

His question came in a constricted voice she scarcely recognised as his.

"Moonflowers, Messire," she murmured over her shoulder as she set a knee on the mattress, then turning to face him again, lay back against the piled pillows. "From the Goddess's own garden. Do you like it?" She did not wait for his reply but continued with a smile, "As for your other question, I am simply doing as you bade and going to bed. Was that not what you wanted me to do?"

The inarticulate sound that issued from his mouth was somewhere between a grunt and a growl and Juliène was hard pressed not to recoil as he emerged from the shadows, stripping off his tunic and shirt as he came. He paused by the bed, breathing heavily as he stared down at her with burning eyes.

"I swore to myself that I was not going to do this! That trollop I had earlier was good enough for me. She served her purpose. Or so I thought. But now..." Then even more savagely, "For whatever reason, you want this as much as I do! So do not complain afterwards that you received more than you bargained for."

With that he sat down heavily on the edge of the bed, wrenching off boots and breeches, and before Juliène had time to draw breath or think better of pushing him beyond the bounds of his endurance, he was lying beside her, unashamedly naked, fully aroused and terrifyingly beyond her control...

He reached out to drag her close against his battle-scarred, iron-hard man's body and she muted a squeak.

*Goddess save me, he is nothing like Kaslan! Why did I ever think he would be?*

Nor did his subsequent possession of her bear any resemblance to that of her former lover's and she realised, in some near hysterical state between bemusement and bitterness, that de Rogé had been telling nothing less than the truth when he had claimed he knew how to give a virgin pleasure as well as pain.

If only, she thought in a moment's flashing regret as his knowing hands caressed her body, she had been the virgin he obviously still believed her to be. But regret was irrelevant to her need and the Winter Lady's shadowy schemes. All Juliène could do now was to ensure that he never knew that he had been duped – for she feared he would not react kindly to such usage. And only the Daemon of Hell knew in what direction his black temper might explode or what form his vengeance would take.

She had thought him totally out of control and was almost relieved when she felt him hesitate, even though his position – lying warm and heavy between her legs, his weight partially held on his forearms – did not indicate a change of mind.

"Are you sure?" he murmured.

This was it then! The last possible moment to turn aside from this thorny path she trod. She saw again the Winter Lady's icy, emerald eyes glittering behind his own strained, dark gaze... and nodded. The best she could hope for was that he would not remember that she had given her consent to this.

Then it was too late to change her mind. Within a heartbeat he had shifted his weight, reaching down between them. Knowing what must follow, she set her teeth and looked away.

Contrary to her expectations, he did not thrust into her in one violent movement but entered her slowly and more gently than she had supposed a man in the grip of such a powerful lust could. She thought he hesitated again when he was sheathed as far as he could go but then, when he began to move more purposefully, she concluded in a flood of relief that she must have been mistaken.

*This*, she thought fatalistically, was what she remembered from Kaslan's lovemaking. The relentless thrusting, the roughening, panting breaths, the torn sob of release at the end, the hot gush of a man's seed.

What she had not remembered – what she had never experienced with Kaslan – was the overwhelming sensation of her own surrender to pleasure and a soaring flight into the star-splashed darkness of a moonless night.

And what she failed to realise until very much later, when she woke briefly in the dark watch before dawn, to find herself lying in a cold and disgustingly damp puddle of... *something*, was that – unlike her first lover and partially drugged though he had been – de Rogé had made very sure that he had spilled his seed on the sheet and not in her body.

Damn the cur to Hell, it had all been for nothing!

# Chapter 8

## *Whore by Morning*

The next time Juliène woke it was to the sound of what sounded like water splashing onto the courtyard cobbles. Was it raining? she wondered drowsily. No, she thought rousing a little, it was far heavier than any summer rain could possibly be and not outside either. Mayhap it was Ilana pouring her washing water into the ewer? But it sounded too close even for that... as if it were coming from right beside the bed.

Curious now, she opened her eyes. And just as quickly shut them again.

*Gods above! Not Ilana. And* not *her washing water!*

Yet even as she felt her normally magnolia-pale cheeks flush the colour of Queen Xandra's blush roses she knew there was no way she could erase the image of the man, long, tangled, fair hair hanging half-way down his naked back – thank the gods he *did* have his back to her – standing less than a yard away, casually relieving himself in the chamber pot beside the bed.

Finally the embarrassing sound ceased – she had not realised quite how much wine de Rogé had drunk the night before, or how much of it his body had retained despite his purging – and he muttered something concerning his other bodily functions that she would much rather have not heard, followed by the rustle of cloth as he pulled on his clothes and stamped his feet into his boots.

An awareness of her own vulnerability caused her to keep her breathing soft and steady, waiting for the heat to fade from her cheeks, while at the same time she took stock of her shockingly naked limbs, tousled hair and an undeniable tenderness in a place she did not want to think about.

God of Mercy, would Kaslan ever forgive her for allowing another man to take what should have been his alone? And how was she to face de Rogé now? With angry accusations of ravishment? Or with tears of shame? She did not much fancy playing such a wretched role, but concluded that it would be more profitable, and less dangerous, to arouse this man's pity rather than incite than his ire.

Her thoughts interrupted by a sharp and quite shockingly explicit expletive, she peeped warily at him through her lashes. He was standing on the far side of the chamber shaving with the aid of his dagger and the cold water in the pitcher. It looked to be a painful process and he swore again as he nicked his jaw. He dabbed at the cut with his shirt sleeve, ran a cursory hand over the lower half of his face, then dropped the knife on the table and moved to unbar the door.

Realising that they were about to have company, Juliène eased the cover discreetly up over her heated cheek and prayed that whoever it was, it was neither Ro nor their mother. The way her nerves had been worn raw by last night's coupling and this morning's discovery, she knew she would not be able to cope with either the Winter Lady's questioning gaze or her sister's sympathy.

Eyes closed, she could only listen, first to the subdued creak as the heavy oak door swung on its iron hinges, then to the quick tangle of murmuring voices. One, quite obviously, belonged to the man with whom she had spent the night, grating harsh on her ears as a blacksmith's file on iron.

The second was that of a woman. Not a noblewoman but a servant, her superficially respectful tones underlain with curiosity and a hint of insolence. Of course, she thought, recognising the voice – Ilana, her own tirewoman and one-time mare to de Rogé's stallion. The slut was saying something about water for washing, new clothing sent by the Lady Ariena. Juliène did not bother to listen too closely, frozen in the warmth of the feather bed and uncomfortably aware of the surface similarities between herself and that cow-eyed little strumpet.

Then she heard a third voice, recognising it with an odd lurch of dismay. Firmly the owner of that voice dismissed the servant then addressed de Rogé, more than a hint of disgusted disbelief underlying the cultured accent.

"You did it then? I was sure that you would not; staked my own honour that you retained some semblance of such honour in you. Damn it, Ran, I thought I knew you!"

"Maybe you do. But you know bugger all about what happened here last night," de Rogé retorted. "That being so, I suggest you take yourself back to your own *innocent virgin...*" There was such a very definite sneer to these last words as to make Juliène shiver again despite the comforting warmth of the bedcovers. "And leave me to deal with mine as I see fit."

Even as she cringed involuntarily, Guy of Montfaucon's voice slipped around her like a supporting arm, firm and reassuring, though he kept his voice low, obviously believing her to be still asleep.

"Then you did not... She *is* virgin still?" He sounded doubtful.

His brother gave a harsh, humourless laugh.

"Hell and damnation, Guy! I have never known you so eager to believe the worst of me. Even so, I have no intention of telling you what she and I might or might not have done together last night! Hardly the act of a gentleman, hmm?" Then his voice hardened. "A word of advice, Guy! Stick to harp songs and harvest tithes and leave me to take the path to Hell in my own way. Now get out of here. There are some things I need to settle with her before I come down for the dawn meal. After which, I am riding out of here. If you are wise, Guy, you will do the same and allow Joffroi to enjoy the fruits of his victory unhindered by your mealy-mouthed moralising."

"Very well, Ran." Juliène thought that the other man sounded regretful rather than angry. "I will leave you to stew in your own ill temper, for the time being at least."

Sounds of booted steps upon the polished floorboards, the sharp snick of the heavy iron latch being raised and she thought he had gone... And was consequently badly shocked when Guy of Montfaucon's dangerously quiet voice proved her wrong.

"I will see you in the hall shortly then, with Demoiselle Juliène. And whatever else you do, Ran, for gods'sake treat her with a modicum of consideration. Remember, she is a noblewoman waking to find her world in pieces, not one of your usual trollops casually resuming her chores after a quick tumble in the hay or a furtive grope in the dark anonymity of the stairwell."

"The last time I groped any woman in the stairwell I was a fumbling fourteen-year-old desperate to poke my prick into any wench who would have me, and hay brings me out in a rash," his brother replied, lightly sardonic. Then something shifted indefinably in his tone. "Do not worry, Guy. I will treat her with all the *consideration* she deserves."

Juliène bit her lip at that, not liking at all the dark edge she detected to those words. Goddess, surely he had not guessed at the truth she had sought to keep from him? She stiffened, her fingers clenching around the sheet as he continued flatly,

"Oh, and Guy..."

"What?"

"I would not trust that grey-eyed witchling of yours with anything you hold dear, least of all your precious honour. Mark my words, she will destroy you if she can and she will use whatever means available to her to achieve that end. You are a de Rogé – by blood if not name – and she is a de Chartreux. There will never be peace between us, especially now with her father's blood on our hands."

"You may be right, Ran," his brother conceded with a sigh. "But it is not likely she will get the chance to ruin me. Like you, I am leaving after the dawn meal and she will be going with Joffroi and her mother to Lamortaine to conclude her binding with Joscelin de Veraux."

"You do not sound over eager to let her go to another man," de Rogé's voice observed, mockery replacing menace once more. "Are you sure you have not had her, Guy? If not last night, then on one of those long rides when you were serving as her groom?"

"Rot in hell, Ranulf!"

There was a fierce and unaccustomed anger in Guy of Montfaucon's voice, emphasised by the use of his brother's full name, but below that anger was something else, something Juliène could not quite identify.

"Undoubtedly I will." De Rogé was clearly indifferent to the prospect of his eternal damnation. Then he said, more pointedly, "But I also note you have not answered my question."

"No more than you did mine," his brother snapped and stalked from the room, the door not quite slamming behind him.

"Well, that was interesting," de Rogé muttered. Then in a louder voice, "Do you not think so, Demoiselle?"

Even as he sneered that final word – and long before Juliène could collect herself sufficiently to ready herself for the coming confrontation – he had crossed the room and wrenched the bedcovers from her naked body, leaving her quivering with shock and fear, inadequately concealed behind her dishevelled black hair, cool grey droplets of mist settling on her goose-fleshed skin.

His narrowed, dark blue gaze raked over her with a cutting edge of hard-held disdain.

"Get up!" he ordered curtly. He bent and picked up the shift she had discarded the previous night. Balling the soft white linen between his hands he flung the garment at her as if tossing a piece of rubbish on a midden. "Put that on before I drag you from the bed and dress you with my own hands."

Concluding he did not mean to be gentle with her if she delayed obeying his commands, Juliène tugged her shift over her head and scrambled out of the bed. She saw de Rogé's blue gaze flick past her shoulder and his hard mouth twitched into something that was definitely not a smile.

"I see I was right," he remarked.

Unable to prevent herself, Juliène glanced behind her, following the direction of his coldly assessing gaze... over the bed with its rumpled linen sheet, the pristine whiteness marred only slightly by the stain of his spilled seed. In sharp contrast, the bright crimson smear of a virgin's blood was glaringly absent.

*Goddess save me!*

Her mind shivered under the icy penetration of her mother's displeasure, realising now – when it was too late – that she had failed to carry out her instructions to the full, exchanging as she had all grasp on reality for the unsuspected pleasures offered by a stranger's body. Her mind stammered silent excuses in reply to the Winter Lady's taunts but the simple fact was that all their plans now lay in disarray at her feet and de Rogé could no longer be in any doubt as to her state.

"I did not think I was mistaken at the time," he said, eyeing her sardonically while she tried not to betray her discomfort. Then his mouth quirked into a smile that mocked himself as much as her. "But I was too sated to worry about it then."

His grin widened into knowing appreciation and his brows lifted in such as way as made Juliène long to strike him.

"You were good. Very good indeed. Better indeed than most of the professional whores I have lain with over the years. And almost as honey-sweet as the lass who gave herself to me before I left Rogérinac."

Juliène knew she had just one chance to change his mind. She opened her mouth to refute his words... to accuse him of taking her by force... to explain why there was no blood, a childhood accident perhaps... anything to cast some shade of doubt in his mind... but he over-rode her with a controlled curtness she found more crippling to her wits than actual physical violence would have been – even though in some small corner of her mind she was grateful that, despite his ruthless and bloody reputation as a fighter, he did not seem inclined to take out his anger against her with his fists or his belt.

"If you know what is good for you, you will keep your lying tongue between your teeth. There is nothing you can say that will convince me that you are not the most devious and manipulative – if alluring – little harlot it has ever been my misfortune to bed." Something flickered in his dark blue eyes as if some thought had occurred to him and he said with a chill cynicism, "I suppose I need hardly ask whether your sister is cast in the same wanton mould?"

"Ro!" Juliène blinked in shock at his corrosive accusation and unthinkingly told the truth. "No, of course she is not like..."

Realising what she was about to say, she made to retract the words but it was too late. De Rogé's eyes were now almost the colour of moorland slate and a muscle twitched white in his hard jaw.

"Pure as the dawn dew, you would say?" He snorted. "That is about as credible as my being named as the next Lord of Valenne!" Abruptly the mocking drawl left his tone and his voice was once more clipped and business-like. "How much?"

"How much?" Juliène repeated, disorientated by the swift shift in direction and tone.

"Never mind," he muttered, his hand dropping to his belt. Yanking loose the strings of the soft leather pouch that hung there, he tossed it at her. "That is all I have so it will have to be enough. Take it. And then I never want to see or hear from you again."

She stared down at the small bag at her feet, feeling the blood rise hot in her cheeks again.

"You think I..." She swallowed, experiencing all the shame he no doubt intended her to. Then on a sudden flare of steadying defiance. "I do not want your money!"

"Well, if you are holding out for my name, I can tell you now that every icicle in hell must needs melt before I put a binding bracelet on the wrist of a de Chartreux whore."

"As if I would wish to wed a piece of de Rogé scum," Juliène hissed with perfect sincerity. "But then I do not need to lower myself so far since no sane person would expect me to swear a binding oath with you, given your exceedingly unwholesome reputation." She gave him a malicious smile. "A reputation that will perversely stand in my favour since, while *you* may deny it, the rest of the realm will find it all too easy to believe you took my maidenhead by force."

On an impulse, she stooped and swept up the little bag, weighing it on her palm, making the few coins within clink and jingle. She lifted her chin and stared down her nose at him.

"On second thoughts, Messire, I *will* take your coin. And I shall tell anyone who asks that you gave this to me lest I should find myself with child from this night."

His eyes widened in sudden comprehension and he took a step towards her, his knowing gaze sweeping her still slender form.

"So that is it! You are pregnant and your lover has deserted you – and who can blame him, the gods know I would do the same in his position – and now you seek to shift the attention away from your own shame by putting the blame onto me! Well, good fortune to you in that endeavour!"

Not understanding quite what he might mean by that, she looked warily up at him, a question in her eyes. A question he did not hesitate to answer.

"When planning an ambush, Demoiselle, always survey the territory first."

"And what is that supposed to mean?" she demanded, apprehension and cold sweat trickling down her spine.

"It means," he replied flatly. "That if you proceed with your plan, you will be the first woman ever to lay public claim that I have planted a brat in her belly."

She thought about the possible implications of that statement for a moment. Then,

"You mean you are *impotent*?" she blurted.

"Scarcely that," he laughed. "Or have you forgotten already what we did last night?"

She could feel her face flushing again and strove to overcome her shame at the memories he roused whilst at the same time absorbing the impact of the information he had tossed so casually in her face.

"I did not mean it like that," she gasped, feeling she was once more losing what little control over the situation she might have exercised. "I meant only that you would have me believe that you... that your... your seed is... barren? In the name of all the gods, what man would make a public claim of that sort?"

Evidently seeing and correctly interpreting her consternation, he gave her a singularly nasty grin in reply and said with a shrug,

"*I* would, if necessary. And mayhap it is the truth. Or then again it might simply be that I am more careful than most men – if not *where*, then at least *how* I sow my seed." Then all amusement left his voice and he continued with a coldness that carried its own conviction, "Be that as it may, one thing is not in doubt. To whit, that even had I a score of bastards to my name, I would sooner die under torture than acknowledge any brat you might bear within the next..." He swept another brutally assessing glance at her flat belly, slender waist and softly rounded breasts. "Shall we say... two seasons... as my get!"

"Even so, Messire," she retorted, struggling for the upper hand in this increasingly wayward conversation. "You and I both know that if I bear a child next spring, it will be believed to be yours, even if it is not. And we will see then how well, given your reputation, you can live down a charge of ravishment and abandonment!"

For a moment he just stared at her, dark blue eyes narrowed to glittering slits. Then without warning, he laughed again, curt, harsh and utterly without humour.

"Do your worst then and be damned to you! And the gods help you – or your sister – if either of you cross my path again!"

With that he turned abruptly, long hair flying, spurs chiming, and snatched up his dagger from the table. Instinctively Juliène recoiled, more than a little afraid that he meant to stab her, but he slid the blade with controlled violence into the sheath on his belt and, with one final contemptuous glance, stalked from the chamber.

He did not bother shutting the door behind him and the echo of his spurred and booted feet as he descended the stone steps, together with his terse instruction to the guard at the base of the stairway, lingered in her shaken mind long after the man himself had gone.

Left on her own, Juliène glared at the open door for several long, frustrated moments, clutching at the bedpost as her suddenly quivering legs threatened to give out beneath her. Eventually, however, some semblance of sense returned to her mind and she forced her trembling limbs to carry her across the polished boards towards the door. Her hands were still shaking quite noticeably but she pulled the heavy door closed and shot the bolt, locking out every man or woman, noble or servant, who might come seeking her. Then, all strength gone for the moment, she slumped against the door, wondering what in the name of the Gods of Light and Mercy she was going to do now.

One thing was certain, she could not stay there forever and after perhaps a score of heartbeats she resolutely straightened and, moving to the wash-stand, tossed de Rogé's shaving water out of the nearest window and used the warm, clean water and honeysuckle-scented soap that Ilana had brought to wash her face and inner thighs, scrubbing with the rough linen towel until all trace of his touch had gone.

Clean again, she realised she could no longer ignore her need to relieve herself. Recollection of de Rogé's use of the chamber pot earlier made her wince in disgust at the thought of using the same vessel but, looking desperately around the small, square chamber in hopes of a viable alternative, she saw something that had escaped her attention before. A narrow little door, set in the east wall and partially concealed behind a faded tapestry – she vaguely thought she could see a pair of swans swimming on a lake, a many-turreted castle in the background. The privy behind the door was of more immediate interest, and though she thought it would be cramped indeed to judge from the dimensions of the door, it would be infinitely better than using the pot.

Moving swiftly now, she lifted the heavy cloth and put a hand to the small iron ring. But no matter which way she twisted it, nor how hard she pulled, the door would not budge. She wondered if the constant damp of the sea air had made the unpolished wood swell and stick to the frame. Or possibly the door was locked – there was a keyhole after all – though she could not imagine why Luc would bother to lock his privy! And if he did, surely the key would be somewhere handy!

She glanced around, but as far as she could see there was no key and, with the situation becoming increasingly exigent, she was reduced to making use of the chamber pot. Reluctantly and with rigid distaste, and only after pouring the eye-wateringly, malodorous contents out of the seaward window. Emptying the pot for a second time, she remained kneeling in the window embrasure for a few moments, wondering for a moment if she might be sick – she had heard that sickness in the morning was not uncommon when with child – but the clean coolness of the salt-sharp mist proved efficacious, even though the dismal grey shrouds that clung to the sandstone cliffs did nothing to lighten her depressed spirits.

Thrusting the pot back under the bed, she searched for, and eventually found her brother's comb. Returning to the window seat, she attempted to tidy her tangled black mane – not a chore she normally undertook herself – finally managing to braid it into two thick plaits. She thought at one stage that she heard a sound... a muffled cry... from the chamber below and voices... Her sister's, she was almost sure, and a man's too low to be identified though she tentatively supposed it to belong to the harper. Or, as she now knew him to be, one of the cursed de Rogé brothers.

Curious now, and not a little disquieted, she leant perilously far out of the window, straining her ears. But she heard nothing more. Perhaps, she told herself in an attempt at reassurance, it had been nothing more than a sea mew calling through the mist to its mate.

By this time the cold damp of the morning had penetrated the fine linen of her one garment, chilling her skin most unpleasantly and providing a reminder – although she scarcely needed one – that she could not remain in her shift for the rest of the day. Accordingly she forced her battered mind to consider what choices she had. She had two and neither held much appeal. She could either go down to the great hall wearing yesterday's green silk – now irretrievably crumpled after a night on the floor and bearing a dirty boot-mark withal – or the gown of scarlet sendal that Ilana had brought up as a gift from her mother.

How, Juliène asked herself bitterly, could the Winter Lady have known in advance that her daughter would fail in her bid to manipulate Black Joffroi's brother? That, despite the potency of the potion Juliène had brewed so carefully, she would fail to bring him to his knees?

Or... and here was a thought; perhaps she was simply reading too much omniscience into her mother's actions out of her own guilt. Perhaps, after all, she was being given a free choice. Wear the green gown and proclaim herself an enchantress worthy of the Faennari. Or don the whore's scarlet in token of her failure...

But before she could pursue that dismal thought further, a soft snicking sound from the far corner of the tower room – as of a key in an oiled lock – made her look up, all other emotion leaching into stunned amazement as the door of the privy slowly opened out into the room.

# Chapter 9

## *An Unexpected Ally*

Eyes fixed on the door – and whatever else it might be, she doubted that it was solely or even primarily a privy beyond those rough planks – Juliène came to her feet and darted towards the bed, concealing herself behind the bed hangings. It was an inadequate hiding place at best but, scantily clad as she was, she did not feel bold enough to openly confront this intruder, whoever it might be. Her speculations were wild indeed, ranging from the Winter Lady or one of the de Rogé men, to a complete stranger or her absent brother, the latter appearing the most likely; after all, this was his chamber and it was his privy.

Trying to breathe quietly – difficult when her heart was beating so very loudly – she waited, watching with mingled hope and dread, as the flickering shadows thrown by a torch carried by an unseen hand danced along the north wall and then steadied as its bearer – to judge from the noise – thrust the brand into a wall socket located just within the doorway.

Her heart now thudding even more erratically in her breast, Juliène waited, gripping the bedpost tightly.

A man clambered sideways out of the narrow opening, puffing a little with exertion, straightened and turned. Disappointment flooded her breast since she could see at once that the intruder was not her tall, raven-haired brother. This man was much shorter, his cropped, curly hair a grizzled brown, his burly frame clad in blue-grey servant's livery. Then the stabbing ache of disappointment faded into bemused surprise as she abruptly recognised the man now carefully closing the door behind him.

"Master Cailen!" she gasped in disbelief. "What in the name of all the gods are *you* doing here?"

The merchant started at the sound of her voice and almost dropped the key. He glanced towards her, brown eyes widening as he took in her state of undress, then narrowed again as he regarded the rumpled bed that stood between them. A heartbeat later he seemed to recall his own business and, having locked the door through which he had just entered, dropped the key into his purse and returned his attention to her – although this time his bland gaze fixed itself on a point somewhere beyond her shoulder.

"Lady Juliena. What're ye doing in Maister Luke's room, if'n I may make so bold as to ask?"

She saw his glance flick around the chamber but there was, thankfully, nothing to betray the fact that Ranulf de Rogé had spent the night with her. Cailen did not seem to notice that she had not answered his somewhat impertinent question but instead continued brusquely,

"I takes it you're not wanting to bide here with they Rogé whoresons in charge?"

"No," she agreed cautiously. "At least, not if there is any way in which to leave the castle undetected." And with a pointed look behind him. "As there obviously must be, if your own presence here is any indication. What *is* beyond that door? *Not* a privy, I take it?"

Cailen favoured her with a penetrating look as if wondering how much to tell her, then replied,

"'Tis a stairway, m'lady. Secret, of course. Leads down to the cellars it do. Then another passage takes ye down through a series of caves to the beach. But 'tis not an easy path an' only passable when the tide be out. I come up it yestere'en an' I've been in the castle since, hence the clothes." He gestured at his servant's livery, the silver swan of Chartre embroidered on his breast. "I even took a turn servin' the wine fer the feast las' night," he finished with a grimace.

She blinked at little at that remark but said only,

"When you say secret, who else besides you knows about this hidden way?"

"Only your father and your brother, my lady."

"Well, if you were in the castle last night you must undoubtedly have heard what happened in Lamortaine?" she said somewhat harshly. "That my father is dead? My brother a hunted man. And that Black Joffroi is now Lord of Chartreux as well as Rogé, his ruffians spread throughout the castle."

"Aye, m'lady, I heard," he said grimly, suddenly looking utterly unlike the genial merchant she had once thought him. "And I am doing what I can to honour your father's last command by getting you and your sister away from this nest of hell-spawned vipers. The question is, do you trust me enough to come with me?"

Juliène hesitated but, the question of trust aside, she could think of no cogent arguments for remaining in the castle with her mother and the de Rogé brothers, and at least one very persuasive reason for disappearing. She nodded briefly.

"Very well. And my sister?"

"I will do my best, my lady. Do you have any idea where she is now?"

"No, I am sorry. I... we were separated..." She felt a slight flush of colour rise in her cheeks. "You say you were in the hall last night? Then you must know what happened... who my sister spent the night with?"

He nodded, looking grimmer than ever and she continued with some difficulty.

"I have not yet been allowed to see her this morning but I think you may find her still in Guy de Rogé's keeping, either in the chamber on the floor below this or in the great hall."

"He is Guyard de Martine," Master Cailen corrected her absently. "Not Guy de Rogé." Then his gaze sharpened on her once more. "Now, my lady, listen to me. I will be as quick as I can and shall bring your sister to safety if I am able. But even if I cannot, there are some things I must attend to before we leave. I want you to stay here and bolt the door again after me. Let no-one in, save for your sister or myself. And do not leave this room until I return. Oh, and whilst I am gone, you would be well advised to find some of your brother's clothes to wear."

"*Men's* clothes?" Juliène queried, aghast.

"Less noticeable than emerald-green silk or that piece of scarlet mischief," Cailen retorted, gesturing at the gown lying over the end of the bed. His brown eyes hardened. "I remember the day your mother came into my shop and bought that material. I wondered then what she wanted it for but I would never have guessed it was destined for her daughters." And as he set his hand upon the door, she heard him mutter something that sounded like a curse on all heartless witches. Or bitches. It was difficult to tell.

Seeing him draw back the bolt and cautiously ease open the door, Juliène dismissed her own trivial concerns over clothing and curses and hissed,

"Master Cailen! There is a guard at the foot of the stair, I am sure. And I do not know where any of the de Rogé brothers might be now. You will be careful?"

"That I will," Master Cailen reassured her with a flicker of a smile over one burly shoulder. "Although I doubt I will have any trouble with the guards and what nobleman really looks at a servant, after all? Even when said servant spills wine all over his boots." He hesitated perceptibly and then said in a soft growl, "But if it should happen that I do come to grief, then I want you to get out of the castle while you still can, down the stairway to the beach. Here, I will leave you the key. Once away from Chartre you must follow the highway west until you come to the village of Anjélais-sur-Liriél. At the sign of the Flower and Falcon you will find my sister Gwynhere. She will help you. Tell her that I am lost and that she must take you to my father. She will know."

Juliène barely had time to nod before Cailen slipped swiftly and silently from the room. She stared at the closed door for a moment, the key gripped unnoticed in her hand, bemused not only by the sudden flow of information but by the language it had been proffered in. Although the man had begun by using the common speech of a Chartreux merchant, that accent had gradually disappeared and there had been a clarity and command in his later delivery that indicated that he was not what he had originally appeared.

More intriguingly perhaps, while she had already come to the conclusion that, despite Ranulf de Rogé's casual naming of Guy of Montfaucon as his brother, the harper was only a base-born sibling to Jacques de Rogé's legitimate sons and would therefore have no right to the name of de Rogé. Cailen, however, had *known* what his true name was – not a piece of knowledge in keeping with his position as a provincial merchant. Except that he was, by his own admission, not just a merchant but a man who had been high in her father's confidence.

Still pondering these anomalies, and wondering with wavering hope whether Cailen might truly be able to rescue her sister – and what she would say to Ro if he succeeded – Juliène proceeded to ransack her brother's clothing coffer for suitable raiment. Not that she expected to find anything that would fit since Luc, although lean was a very tall, well-built young man, considerably broader in the shoulder than herself, with a correspondingly long length of limb.

Finally she managed to clothe herself after a fashion, her dainty frame swamped from shoulder to knee in a tunic of dark green wool, with soft leather breeches held up by a belt that went twice around her slender waist before it could be buckled. None of Luc's boots or shoes could be made to fit and as emerald-green silk slippers looked too bizarre for words, it was with bare feet that she began to nervously pace the small room, trying to assess how long it had been since Cailen had left, her ears straining for any indication that he had been captured.

It was not a distant soldier's shout that almost made her heart stop, however, but a sound considerably closer to hand; a firm knock on the door and a nobleman's cultured voice to accompany it. She shot a fearful glance at the door, assuring herself that she had indeed shot the bolt after Cailen's departure.

"Demoiselle?"

Ah! Guy de Ro... No, Guyard de Martine. Thank the gods it was not his half-brother returned to further torment her. *He* would have no hesitation whatsoever in taking a battle axe to the door if he had a mind to haul her out but she recognised with that sharp sense of perception she had perforce had to cultivate, that his half-brother was cast in a far less violent mould.

"Demoiselle?"

The voice was darker now, considerably terser and the fist that struck the oak boards sounded alarmingly more aggressive. Perhaps the man would resort to a battle axe after all!

"Demoiselle! Are you all right?"

"What do you want, Messire?" she called, putting some anger into her voice, and not a little measure of disdain; it would do no harm to let him know that she was aware of his tainted lineage and, as a direct corollary, despised him for it.

"I am come to escort you down to the hall for the morning meal. Your mother commands your presence there, along with that of your sister."

"Then go and escort her," she snapped back. "Since it is she whom your lord has made you responsible for. *I* am no concern of yours."

There was silence for perhaps five heartbeats, then de Martine's voice came back, level enough but a shade ragged about the edges, she thought.

"I have given your sister into Ranulf's charge. She has no use for my company just now."

"In other words, *Messire de Martine*, she has discovered that you have been lying to her these past few weeks," Juliène concluded, adding with overtones of malicious sarcasm, "But merely about your paternity, I wonder? Or is there some other seemingly trivial detail you have been keeping from her?"

Another long moment of silence... then something that might have been a sigh.

"Ran told you, I suppose? But no, there is nothing else, trivial or otherwise. Now, will you please open this door and come down to the hall. I can understand your reluctance to see my brother again after last night if he..." He cut himself off, quite obviously changing his mind about the wisdom of discussing his half-brother's actions or her putative virginity when almost anybody might be lurking within earshot. Instead he continued firmly, "Your sister needs to assure herself that you are as well as might be. For her sake, will you not come down?"

"And can you guarantee my safety if I do?" Juliène asked derisively. It was easy to be brave, she thought, with a bolted door between them. "Guarantee also that Black Joffroi does not have worse in mind for me than I have already suffered at your..." She hesitated, wondering suddenly whether Guy was older or younger than Ranulf. "Your other half-brother's hands."

"You have my word that I will keep you as safe as is within my power," de Martine replied, a certain amount of exasperation creeping into his – until now – reasonable tones. Then his voice dropped, became more muffled, as if he were leaning closer to the crack of the door. "And for what interest it might be to you, Demoiselle, Ran and I are the same age. To the day."

As were she and her sister, she completed the comparison he had refrained from drawing.

Except that while Ranulf de Rogé and Guyard de Martine might share a birth date and a father, they quite clearly did not share the same mother and that made all the difference to...

"Demoiselle, I am waiting," came the clipped reminder from beyond the stout door.

"And you can wait until the Moon Goddess herself comes down to walk among us," Juliène replied coldly. "No, Messire, I will not come down. Not for your asking. Not for my mother's command. Take that message to your daemon-spawned brothers and tell them that I curse both them and you to the darkest depths of Hell."

With that she turned and stalked over to the seaward window, standing with her arms held tightly about her shaking body, her eyes staring blindly into the mist. She thought he might argue or take out his palpable frustration on the door with his fist or feet. But he did neither and if he sighed or swore at her intransigence he did it too quietly for her to hear him. The only thing she did hear was the soft clink of his spurs as he slowly descended the stairs, not pausing on the landing below but continuing on down to the bottom.

Left alone once more Juliène returned to her reckoning of the passing moments but it was, at best, a futile exercise, more especially as she could not make even a guess at the height of the sun through the impenetrable white fog.

344

All she knew was that it seemed a very long time.

Where was Cailen? What was he doing? Had he been captured?

And Ro? Dear God of Light, how was *she* faring?

Juliène had little doubt that her sister would have been taken down to the hall by now and she felt a small sense of sick shame that she had left Ro to fend for herself in such lethal company as she would find there, an emotional ache echoed by the physical pangs of hunger gnawing at her belly. Not that she thought she could have eaten even had there been anything by way of sustenance in Luc's sparsely furnished room.

The mist was lifting a little, she observed, as she glanced restlessly out of the window a little while later. She could see the tufts of thrift, as pale a pink as last night's moon, clinging further down the cliffs, the occasional white flash of a sea mew's wing, the pallid blur that was the pale gold chariot driven by the God of Light. Perhaps she might be able to see something out of the other window now...

Walking quickly past the depressing disarray of the bed she peered cautiously out of the courtyard window, starting nervously at the sight of Cailen crossing the empty expanse of wet cobbles below, apparently heading for the garrison's quarters.

*God of Light, the nerve of the man! And God of Mercy watch over him and keep him safe.*

Wondering what he might be about now – and increasingly irritated that he was risking himself down there when he should have been helping her and Ro escape – she gripped the cold stone of the window stanchion and leaned out, the better to watch his progress.

Something else caught her eye and she forgot about Cailen completely. Just beyond the tattered fringe of the mist, three figures... indistinct but there was something familiar about them...

Then the white shreds drifted back to reveal two big, fair-haired men – no mistaking *them!* Even though one was clad in black, the other in leaf green, they were so alike in face and form they could have been twins. And the third figure, standing between them, considerably shorter and slighter... A woman, whom on first glance Juliène would have taken for a harlot with her loose hair and scarlet gown, save that she knew Ro too well to think she would whore herself to either of the men who stood alongside her. Or at least not now she knew the truth about Guyard de Martine.

Abruptly realising that they would be able to see her as easily as she could see them, Juliène shied back from the window but she could not resist peeping out again, ears straining in an effort to catch what was being said below. It was too far to hear individual words but the rising tones of anger in the two very similar male voices told her quite plainly that the brothers were arguing. And with a heat she would not have expected of either man; de Martine being normally so even-tempered, de Rogé so coldly controlled.

Almost as if he had heard her speak his name out loud, Ranulf de Rogé glanced suddenly up at her window and she hurriedly shrank back beyond his line of sight and by the time she dared to look out again he was shrugging into his armour with the assistance of one of his soldiers while his half-brother – armed but not yet armoured – was tenderly wrapping her sister in a large black cloak.

Sagging back against the wall Juliène felt suddenly overcome by a great wave of desolation and loss, deep enough to drown in. For by his actions Guyard de Martine was making it clear to any watching eyes that Rowène de Chartreux – traitor's daughter or not – was under *his* protection, which while that might keep Ro safe meant that for all his sympathetic words to Juliène a short while before, he was not likely to prove susceptible to *her* wiles. She had known it before, of course, but seeing it before her like that... And if Cailen failed her too...

A subdued knock at the door brought her head up, making her heart skitter and tossing the indulgence of self pity out of the window. Swallowing, she crossed to the door.

"Who is it?" she asked, wary even though she knew that two at least of the de Rogé brothers were down in the courtyard. That still left Black Joffroi or worse yet...

"Cailen, my lady."

For a moment she hesitated but she really had no choice but to trust that he had returned alone and without coercion. She drew back the bolt and let him in, eyeing the small bundle in his hands with curiosity.

"What..."

"Quickly now, my lady, we've no time to waste. I've set a fire in the room below and intend to set one here as well. The whole tower should be in flames soon. A little diversion to keep their attention off the main gate and a signal to your brother to begin his attack. Are you ready to leave? If Lord Luke is successful then you will be back here before you know it. If he fails, then I must get you as far away from Chartre as possible."

"Lord Luke?" she repeated blankly. Then in a different tone. "Luc? He is coming? But a fire, you said? Let me help."

Working together, she and Cailen made swift work of setting the room ablaze. She derived more than a passing satisfaction from watching as the flames leapt to devour the dark wood bed posts, the heavy blue canopy and curtains, and especially the stained linen sheets, until all evidence of de Rogé's spilled seed and her own lack of virginity were lost in the conflagration.

By this time the chamber was beginning to fill with choking smoke but she ran past the hungry flames and searing heat of the burning bed to the courtyard window and leaned out, needing one last glimpse of her sister. She wanted desperately to reassure Ro that all would be well but knew that such an assurance was far beyond her limited powers.

The only credible thing she could do in the circumstances was scream. So she did.

Ro heard her. Looked up, terror contorting her face. For a heartbeat Juliène held her sister's gaze, trying to convey everything that lay in her heart. Then saw Ro begin to run, obviously frantic with fear, towards the door to the castle.

*No!*

She did not know whether she screamed the word aloud or only in her mind. Her heart was burning in her breast and she was sobbing in earnest now. Then she realised that one of the men... no, all three of them, though de Rogé was in the lead, had taken off after Ro... she could hear him yelling after her sister – not Demoiselle or wench but her *name* – shouting at her to stop... Now he was at her sister's heels... had caught her wrist, taken her down under the full weight of his mailed body.

Juliène felt the shock in her own body.

*Gods, Ro! That must hurt!*

She winced in sympathy and began to breathe again, weeping a little, in relief she thought; at least Ro was no longer in any immediate danger. Not from the fire anyway... Ranulf de Rogé might be another matter!

Feeling Cailen's imperative hand on her arm, she drew back from the window, more tears searing her eyes and scouring her cheeks.

"How can I leave, Cailen? Knowing I am abandoning my sister to that scum!"

"You have no choice," Cailen stated flatly. "And neither do I! Now follow me. And take care. Even with the torch it will be dark and the steps are narrow and steep and slippery. All either of us can do now is pray to the God of Light that your brother wins this fight."

But Luc had not won and by mid-afternoon Chartre, castle and town alike, found itself irretrievably under de Rogé control. Within days all of that vast fief would be theirs.

Emerging from the clinging darkness of the caves onto the sunlit shore – the fog had lifted completely whilst they had been travelling the secret way, surprising them both when they emerged onto the pale pink pebbles – Juliène and Cailen made their cautious way along the beach towards the town.

They found a place to hide in one of the warehouses down by the harbour and were thus well placed to endure the pain of watching as a small band of soldiers led by Ranulf de Rogé herded the pitiful remainder of the Chartreux garrison down to the dock where a ship – its red sails, black-painted hull and double bank of oar ports revealing its eastern origins – was getting ready to sail with the next tide.

Juliène would probably not have recognised Luc in the limp-bodied, blood-drenched, barely conscious man being dragged on board, fitted with shackles and subsequently tumbled down onto the rowing deck like a rag doll, had it not been for Cailen. This time when the tears came, she wept until she could cry no more.

"He *will* come back," Cailen promised her grimly.

But Juliène did not believe him. No-one escaped from the rowing benches of a ship like that. Save they went to the slave markets of Kaerellios or the Eastern Isles. Such would be an evil enough fate for a fit man; how could a man as badly wounded as Luc be expected to survive such a hell?

Yet from within that black whirlpool of clawing fear and deep pain, a single thought floated free, light as a breeze-blown leaf. How in the name of all the gods had Luc managed to escape identification as the outlawed son of the former Lord of Chartreux? And who had shorn off his long dark hair, likely saving him from the traitor's death that had been decreed for him? A fate that still awaited him if, against all odds, he should survive festering wounds, the overseer's lash and slave shackles to return to Mithlondia?

She doubted she would ever learn the answers to those questions but for the moment she cared little as to *how* or even *who*? Luc was *alive!* And Cailen had said he would return!

*Sweet God of Mercy, let it be so...*

It was late in the afternoon, the sun darkening from gold to bronze in the smoke-stained sky beyond Chartre castle, before Cailen returned to the warehouse from yet another foray through the streets of the town. He was now clad in nondescript brown rather than his stolen servant's livery and carried a small sack tucked under his arm. This proved to contain a pair of sturdy leather shoes that very nearly fitted Juliène's feet, together with some bread, cold sausage, a hunk of hard cheese and a flask of ale.

He bound the shoes on Juliène's sore feet himself – the green silk slippers had not survived the journey through the cave – made her eat and drink a little and then informed her with a hint of a sly smile that he had "acquired" a small fishing coracle in which he intended they should make their escape from the town. The owner of the coracle was, alas, in no state to notice or report his loss until the morning at least. By which time the thief and his lad would be well upriver of Chartre and beyond the justice of the new Lord of Chartreux, should he even care to investigate the theft of a mere fishing coracle when he had other, more important, matters to see to. And, since Leofric would get his boat back in due course no-one would be the loser – save perhaps the man Black Joffroi had installed as Governor of Chartreux.

Juliène regarded the burly man with some suspicion, aware from his tone that he had not told her everything by any means. But she really could not find it in her to care either about some obscure Chartre fisherman or the newly appointed Governor of Chartreux – whoever he might be – not after all she had gone through since sunset the previous day. So she had not enquired further, content to leave their escape in Cailen's obviously competent hands.

Which is how, some little time later, she came to be crouched uncomfortably in a flimsy fishing coracle, clutching a paddle she did not know what to do with, and accompanied by a former silk merchant who – she observed, quite without surprise by that time – actually did.

She arrived at Swanfleet just as her sister and her accompanying escort rode over the bridge; a piece of fortuitous timing that enabled Juliène to bid Ro a silent farewell and invoke the blessing of the gods on her path, wherever it might take her.

And, from what Juliène could see, that path was taking Rowène to Rogérinac under the escort of Guyard de Martine...

# Part IV

# ROGÉ

# Summer – Autumn 1194

# Chapter 1

## *Across the Larkenlye*

It was barely dawn when Rowène awoke to grey drizzle, muted birdsong, bodily discomfort and memories she would just as soon forget. Becoming painfully aware that she was still held close to a man's mailed body, the acerbic words slipped past her lips before she could recall them.

"The gods damn you to Hell, Guyard de Martine. And your cursed brothers with you."

He looked down at her for a moment without speaking, then raised his unencumbered arm, signalling to their escort that he was calling a halt to that seemingly endless nightmare ride. She struggled to straighten cramped limbs sufficiently to sit up, peering blearily at the surrounding countryside – or what little of it she could see through the misty rain – before finally raising her eyes past his stubbled jaw to meet his wary blue gaze.

He looked tired from the long night ride but, surprisingly, managed to find a faint smile for her. "I can understand your feelings, Demoiselle," he said, with a cool formality that made her want to hit him. "But now is not a particularly good time to give tongue to them. For your information, that was the Larkenlye we just crossed. You are no longer in Chartreux but over the border in what is my home land and, believe it or not as you will, I am the only thing standing between you and further dishonour. Unless, of course, you are willing to rely on Ranulf's soldiers abiding by the rules of chivalry as laid down by Prince Marcus."

"Those gutter dregs?" Rowène did not even have to look at the six men of their escort to formulate an opinion. "Hardly!"

"Well then, you have little choice but to put your trust in me again. And bear in mind, if you will, that I like Joffroi's decision to place you in my charge as little as you do yourself." Then the illusion of calm cracked as he continued with more than a hint of irritation in his voice. "The gods know, this is the last thing I need at the moment and, unless I miss my guess, Mathilde will go out of her way to make life in Rogérinac seem like the antechamber of Hell for both of us!"

"You are forgetting that, thanks to you and your depraved half-brothers, my life is already in ruins," Rowène snapped back. "Why should I care whether your wife makes your life miserable?" Then, as she belatedly remembered that he could have made her life far worse if he had actually done as his elder half-brother had ordered – as his other half-brother *had* done – she managed to choke out some sort of apology. "Forgive me, I did not mean that quite as it came out. And if I have made life more difficult for you, I am sorry about that too. Especially since – and you probably do not want to hear this – accompanying you to Rogérinac as a hostage is vastly preferable to the alternative. I do not think I could have gone with my mother and..." She made a sound of disgust deep in her throat.

"And Joffroi, to the Court of Princes at Lamortaine," he finished for her, his blue eyes bleak. "No, I admit it would have seemed unbearable to watch them together and to be expected to smile and dance at their binding feast. But I still think it would have been better if you had been able to remain in Chartre."

"You would rather I had stayed in Chartre with... with that... that *monster?*" Rowène asked incredulously.

"If by that you mean Ranulf, then yes I would," Guy replied tersely. "You would have been as safe with Ran as you would be with me..."

Rowène did not even attempt to answer that naïve remark. The gods knew, there was no answer she could make, save for the truth and that she would not tell unless there was no possible alternative. Such as if she should find herself carrying Ranulf de Rogé's rape-spawned child.

"And if you had stayed in Chartre I would not now have to confront my wife with the woman everyone believes to be my..." He clearly sought for a civilised word and finally settled on "Mistress at my side!"

"Well, you could always try telling her the truth!" she snapped.

"I doubt she would believe me if I did," he replied dryly. "Not when gossip will give me the lie. And do not think she will not hear it! It will be at Rogérinac just as soon as we are!" He tilted his head, indicating the men-at-arms riding behind them.

Rowène made another inarticulate noise under her breath and, hunching her shoulder, turned her head away from him. There was not much to see through the thin grey rain. The meadowsweet and willow herb that in Chartreux would be standing tall and proud, cream and pink, was here wet and straggling, bent under the weight of water. The track – surely this could not be the main highway to Rogérinac? – they were splashing along was more squelching mud than solid stone and the only livestock she could see was a shaggy, ochre-coloured cow who stood lowing unhappily as she cropped the poor grass beneath the meagre shelter of a dying elm tree.

Left to his own reflections Guyard shook his head, less in answer to Rowène's words than his own thought that even if Mathilde believed him – which was by no means certain – he did not dare trust her with that knowledge. Fortunately, he was spared the need to pursue that unpalatable thought further when the rider he had sent on ahead came back at a weary canter.

"Well, Geryth?"

The young soldier reined his mud-splattered, dark bay gelding in beside the chestnut stallion.

"'Tis as ye thought, sir, from the state o' the Larkenlye! They've had a fair amount of rain whilst we've been gone. Reckon we was lucky the bridge was still in place, 'cos there's no sign of the bridge over the Tawne and ye can't even see the coast road for water."

Guyard glanced up at the grey sky and grimaced.

"More rain to come by the looks of it. We will have to take the higher road across the moors and pray to the gods the rain does not change to fog. One thing is certain – we cannot stay here."

"An' that's fer sure," Geryth muttered.

Guyard gave him a sharp look but did not take issue with the youth's tone and sullen expression. He was well aware that Geryth resented being ordered to return to Rogérinac, added to which he was undoubtedly wet, weary, ravenous and eager for what dubious comforts Rogérinac castle could offer. As were they all, Guyard thought grimly, feeling a trickle of rain water slide down the back of his neck, as cold almost as the iron links of his mail shirt.

Feeling Rowène shifting uncomfortably in his arms, Guyard glanced down at her and said quietly,

"A couple of leagues further on, just before we start the climb up to the moors, there is an ale house. It is not much by the standards you are accustomed to but it will give you the chance to rest and get some warm food inside you." He hesitated and then continued, "And since you are now awake, perhaps you would prefer to ride your own mount?"

"If you remember, I never asked to be carried around like a piece of baggage," she snapped, obviously stung both by his tone and his comment, although such had not been his intent.

Sighing slightly at the incomprehensible ways of women, Guyard called Geryth to bring up the mare and transferred Rowène from his saddle to her own. Irked by the blatant curiosity of the watching men his tone was more curt than normal as he said,

"You will not do anything stupid will you, Demoiselle, like try to escape? I gave my word to my brother that I would bring you safe to Rogérinac and that I intend to do."

For a moment she frowned at him, as if wondering which brother he meant but she did not ask and, apparently as aware as he of the avid eyes watching them, gave a tiny shrug of acquiescence.

"You have my word. At least for the moment." She gave him a slightly mocking, wholly mirthless smile and – he thought, as much for the benefit of the listening men as himself – added in common speech, "I would far rather continue as *your* unwilling mistress than take my chances with your half-brother's gutter sweepings!"

Guyard was strongly tempted to point out that she was his mistress, willing or otherwise, in name alone but the keenly listening ears of Ranulf's "gutter sweepings" made that inadvisable. At present the Lady Rowène's only protection lay in the men's mistaken belief that Guyard was, in all truth, her lover. That and the silver brooch she wore pinned to the shoulder of the black mantle she still wore.

With a curse directed impartially at all women, Guyard nudged the stallion with his heels and, followed by the Lady Rowène and the half dozen men of their escort, headed towards the moors.

Before they had gone more than a few furlongs down the road, Guyard's forebodings about the weather were fulfilled. Larger, heavier, colder drops of rain began to fall, drenching the riders and rendering the muddy track almost as dangerous as the now impassable road that – save for the section that ran through the marshes – was better maintained and easier to travel, leading as it did eastwards along the rim of the coast before following the line of the dark granite cliffs north towards Sarillac, Black Rock Cove and eventually Rogérinac itself.

The difficulties of the road demanding that she give most of her attention to her mount, Rowène found little time to study the countryside through which they were passing but from what little she could glimpse between showers it made a bleak prospect. Through the sweeping silver-grey veil of rain she caught brief glimpses of hills rising on her left, bare of trees or habitation. To her right it was merely grey. Signs of life were few and far between; a small flock of dark-spotted sheep here or a pair of wild-looking black cattle there.

Wistfully she remembered the colourful lands of Chartreux; the sunlit fields of ripening wheat, splashed with the vivid red of poppies, the healthy-looking brown and cream cows in the green fields, the hedgerows overflowing with flowers. The swallows swooping in graceful flight overhead, wagtails strutting cheekily in the dusty roadway, blue skies vibrant with lark-song...

The only bird call Rowène expected to hear in these barren, desolate lands would be the keening cry of a hunting hawk.

Honey's hooves slipped, for perhaps the dozenth time, on the mud-slimed stones of the track and she decided she would be better served by concentrating her attention on getting where she was going, rather than mourning what she had lost – or worrying about the future. Her flux had not come overnight. The gods send it start today, even though travelling as a virtual prisoner in company with seven men, all enemies to her family, in a land where she was a stranger, was the last situation under which she would have wished to deal with such a personal matter. The alternative, however, was beyond contemplation.

She shivered, then forced aside her very real fear of the future for the more immediate hope that Guy had not mistaken the distance to the inn. Ten years of basking in the flower-scented sunshine of Kardolandia was no preparation for the bone-chilling damp of Rogé and she wondered gloomily what – if this was mid summer – winter would bring by way of snow-storms, icicles and howling winds?

Unless, that is, Joscelin de Veraux came to claim her as his bride before then. Given the implied proviso that he cared enough to come for her in the first instance... and that, once having found her, he was prepared to take her as she was – since she did not think she was capable of pretending to be a maiden still, as Ranulf de Rogé had rather snidely suggested she should do. Then, if de Veraux were prepared to accept another man's leavings – and she rather thought she would prefer him to think she had taken a lover in Kardolandia than live with his likely reaction to de Rogé's brutal possession of her – and if he had the courage to face down the scandal that was bound to ensue... and if Black Joffroi and her mother were prepared to honour the terms of the betrothal and release her from their guardianship...

There seemed to be an insurmountable number of *ifs* and no way of finding a speedy resolution to any of them. Not to mention the most important *if* of all... the one she was trying desperately not to think about but which kept creeping back, slithering like a venomous snake through the silence of her mind. The one tangible fact that would render all other ifs instantly irrelevant.

*God of Mercy,* she thought for perhaps the thousandth time, *let me not be carrying his child.*

In her present state of despair, she thought she would rather die!

# Chapter 2

## *Mud and Mulled Ale*

It must have been close to mid-morning – and still raining heavily – when Guyard drew his mount to a halt outside a grey stone croft thatched with heather. A miserable-looking apple tree grew to one side of the door, the flowers long since withered and with no sign of having set into fruit. Turning to look at the shivering noblewoman he had undertaken to escort to Rogérinac, he experienced more than a flash of concern as he observed the dull lack of awareness in her clouded grey eyes.

Kicking his feet free of the stirrups he slid down into the ankle-deep sludge of silt that did duty as a yard and caught hold of the mare's bridle, bringing the animal to a halt, noting absently how the horse's pale golden hide was so darkened by rain as to be almost the same colour as the sodden hem of the black mantle that trailed over the streaming, mud-flecked flank. Stroking the mare's wet neck he frowned up at his brother's hostage, speaking her name just loud enough to catch her attention.

"Demoiselle de Chartreux?" And when she did not respond, said a little louder, "Rowène!"

She started slightly and dropped her blank gaze to his.

"This is it, Demoiselle. This is the ale house I told you of. The Apple Tree. If you would dismount I shall see what comfort I can obtain for you."

She regarded him so strangely that he began to wonder whether it was merely weariness or an active dislike of him that kept her from availing herself of his assistance. Then suddenly, between one heartbeat and the next, her expression unfroze and she came down into his waiting arms. Not wanting to set her down in the mud he simply carried her to the nearest bit of firm ground, too swiftly for her to voice a protest.

"My apologies, Demoiselle," he murmured as he lowered her to her feet and turned towards the door. "Undignified but better perhaps than the alternative."

Hearing the unmistakeable splash and clatter of a group of travellers pausing outside his ale house, Anlaf of Applelea cautiously opened the door a crack and then slammed it shut in instinctive alarm. The sight of half a dozen or so sweating, mud-splattered horses accompanied by the same amount of heavily-armed men led him to mutter into his beard and wish he had gone up on the moor to cut peat after all.

A second hasty peep through a convenient knot-hole at the leader's face did little to dispel his unease. Nor was he in any doubt as to his likely fate should he not make haste to serve these horsemen with the food and ale they would undoubtedly demand. Demand, but probably not pay for; Black Joffroy and his men having strange ideas about things like that. Gathering his failing courage he set his hand to the latch and flung wide the door.

"Welcome, welcome, come ye in out the rain. 'Tis most welcome ye be."

The man in the dripping, dark green cloak threw him an irritated glance and said curtly in unaccented common speech,

"I doubt that. Now, cease your grovelling, man, and get out of the way. We can scarcely come in with you blocking the doorway!"

"Oh aye, fer sure," Anlaf reiterated as he backed further and further into the dim interior of the ale house until his backside was nearly in the fire. "Now how mayst I serve ye, master?"

"I need feed and stabling for eight horses, hot food and ale for myself and my men. And I hope you have a good fire burning; we are all soaked to the skin."

The other men had crowded into the room now, which suddenly seemed far to small to hold them all as they pulled off sodden cloaks, cursing the weather and each other and stamped their wet boots, splattering mud everywhere. Their leader did none of those things but he did push back his rain-soaked hood and straighten warily, his short-cropped hair brushing the cobwebs that clung to the dark rafters. Anlaf stared at that hair; darkened by rain though it was, it was undoubtedly fairer than was commonly seen in Rogé. But not unknown, he reminded himself hastily. And since he could hardly mistake the black boar on the soldiers' tunics, he could only suppose this man to be one of Jacques de Rogé's by-blows – the gods knew the old lord had seeded enough throughout the province. Unless...

"I apologise for the mess but we do need to get warm and dry before we go on."

The man's clipped tones interrupted Anlaf's speculations, confusing him more. He was using common speech all right, but the very precision of his delivery, weary though he obviously was, advised Anlaf that he was no peasant.

"Oh, and I also require some mulled wine and something fit for a lady to eat."

"Wine?" Anlaf's mouth fell open and his voice rose as he forgot his former conjectures as others, even more lurid, opened out before him. "Lady?"

"Yes, lady," the other man confirmed, an unpleasant glint that was purely de Rogé in his light blue eyes.

Then he stepped aside, allowing Anlaf's first confused, then bemused, gaze to fall on the person standing behind him; a young woman wrapped in a black mantle, its thick folds hanging wet and heavy about her, secured on her shoulder by a round, intricately-worked brooch the size of a man's fist. Anlaf swallowed hard, staring. He recognised that circle of silver, as would any man who had known Lord Jacques de Rogé in whatever fashion.

Torn between caution and curiosity, Anlaf raised his gaze until he was looking into a pair of clear grey eyes that seemed able to read whatever foolish thoughts were writ across his face. A small, somewhat bitter, smile touched her pale lips and, raising her ungloved hands, she pushed back her hood. Anlaf felt himself pale and he took a hasty step back, only just missing the fire. The room was not well lit – a couple of rush dips and the fire – but even with this lack, the young woman's hair still flickered as red as the flames on the hearth, falling over her shoulders in wild, gold-shot disarray.

Gods save him! What was toward here? A woman whom even the most pragmatic and unimaginative of men would flinch from as a witch, standing in *his* ale house, wearing Jacques de Rogé's silver brooch on her shoulder and accompanied by one of his bastards...

Who was even now stripping off his wet gauntlets and eyeing Anlaf with exasperation, his irritation clearly not held in check by very much at all.

"Well?" he queried tersely as he tossed the gloves onto the nearest table, where they landed with a soggy slap.

Anlaf opened his mouth but no words came out. Instead he watched as the man held out his bare hand to his companion and, when she took it, brought the... young woman – Anlaf refused to utter the word *witch* even in his mind, lest such thought make it true – closer to the meagre fire. This he stirred into more vigorous life with a couple of judicious prods with his booted foot before courteously helping the woman to remove her dripping wet cloak, thus revealing a gown of such vibrant colour and revealing cut that Anlaf could only blink in amazement.

Gods save him again! Not only a witch but a harlot as well!

Forced from his palsied trance by the steely impetus of the man's light blue glare, Anlaf gathered his scattered wits sufficiently to make some sort of reply to the order he had almost forgotten about under the successive shocks.

"Aye... mulled wine fer the... the... lady. An' somethin' t' eat. Of course, of course, master. I'll set me good wife t' tend t' it straight away. An' something fer yerself an' the men... see t' the horses!"

The dark blond brows lifted and the faintest of smiles replaced the frown on the other man's face as, half turning, he spoke over his shoulder.

"Finn! Connor! Geryth! Go and help Master Anlaf here with the horses."

"Aye, sir."

As three of the soldiers stumped back out into the rain, Anlaf could not help himself.

"Ye knows me name? Sir?"

"Certainly," the man replied with a pleasant if weary smile. "As I know to a bronze farthing the tithe required of you by Lord Joffroi and how you settle it. Your heather beer makes a welcome change from the normal ditchwater we drink at Rogérinac, so let us have some now before my men perish from thirst and the lady from cold."

"At once, sir."

Anlaf fairly scuttled from the suffocating confines of the crowded public room, wiping his sleeve across his sweating face as he went. What, he wondered, would his wife make of all this?

He found Aethelfryth in the kitchen, red-faced with temper or heat, stirring oats and water in a pot over the fire.

"I heard!" she snapped as Anlaf came into the room. "Though how his high an' mighty honour 'spects food fer that many mouths in the time it takes ter snap his fingers, 'tis more'n I can say! Good thing the bread was already a-bakin'. Not but what I'd like ter know who he thinks he is anyhow!"

"Aye, well, 'tis not his lordship hisself, thank the good gods," Anlaf offered placating. "I'd say from his face an' manner o' speakin', that this'n must be one o' the old lord's bastards. But that's better'n havin' Black Joffroy hisself out there, surely?"

"Ye think?" Aethelfryth snorted sarcastically. "Ye tell me, where's the diff'rence atween the old lord an' any o' his hell-spawn?"

"Aye, well, fer sure," Anlaf agreed distractedly, still labouring under the stress of dealing with the quantity and possible quality of his unexpected customers. "Anyhow, his honour wants mulled wine as well as the food an' ale so ye'd best hurry up an' see ter that first!"

"An' since when is honest ale not good enough fer one o' Lord Jacques' bastards or that scum he's got wi' him?"

"Nay then, 'tis fer the lass as came in wi' them. An' though her did give me a fair ol' fright when I first seed her, 'twas jus' the firelight on her hair belike. An' as fer the gown, well, I'm thinkin' she can't be no more than some sad-eyed slip of a lass wearin' some other strumpet's scarlet by mistake," Anlaf offered with unexpected tolerance. "I wonder how her comes to be wi' him, poor lady."

"Don't be more of an idiot than ye can help, Anlaf! An' we ain't got no wine, 'twill ha' ter be mulled ale. Good enough fer her surely..."

Aethelfryth gave the porridge a vigorous stir.

"'Cos there's no *lady* either in Rogé or wi'out who'd be caught dead wi' the likes of Black Joffroy or his brothers, whether by-blow or legitimate get, an' ye can be sure of that! Likely 'tis jus' some doxy yon bastard picked up along the road an' brought along ter warm his bed fer a bit. 'Twas ye as said her were wearin' a colour no woman'd wear save she'm a whore." Then, seeing that he was wavering, added caustically, "An' if that bain't enough fer ye, ye knows yerself what they'm like! Lechers all, man nor boy, don't make no odds! Ne'er a Rogé who weren't, far back as I can remember. 'Tain't natural ter think as how any o' Lord Jacques' sons 'ud be any diff'rent from he, now would it?"

Anlaf scratched his sparsely covered head doubtfully. Normally he would have agreed with Aethelfryth but this time he was not so sure. Although the young woman... girl really... had been garbed in a red silk gown that left precious little to the imagination and no respectable kerch covered her indecently vibrant hair, the hand he had glimpsed in her companion's hard, proprietorial grasp, had been slender and soft, as a lady's should be, albeit unnaturally reddened from contact with cold rain and leather reins. And then there was that unfathomable look in those clear grey eyes...

No, despite everything, Anlaf did not think she was either witch or whore and he felt an unexpected twinge of reluctant pity for her. Enough to make him hope that the man she was with would not do as gossip said was custom with Black Joffroy and his only legitimate brother and give her over to the male servants and soldiers of the Rogérinac garrison when he himself had no more use for her.

A rising murmur of voices from the main chamber jolted him from his ruminations and he set about drawing ale for the men, leaving Aethelfryth to attend to the rest of the order – which she did with very bad grace. He was on his third trip, this time for another pitcher of ale and more mugs, before she was ready. Curious to see her reaction, he followed her as she swept into the main room of the inn, surging confidently through the press of large, loud, muddy, masculine bodies in search of the woman she had already stigmatised as a strumpet.

Anlaf knew the exact moment that his wife's baleful gaze fell on the young woman by the hearth and – if he had not been so concerned as to how much these ruffians were going to cost him – he would have found the transformation laughable as the indignant belligerence left Aethelfryth's stance and she said with brusque warmth,

"Yer ale, mistress. 'Tis not wine, no much call fer that hereabouts, but 'tis hot at least."

"Thank you," came the soft reply. "You are very kind."

Already doubting, Aethelfryth now appeared completely taken aback by this unexpected evidence of gentle manners in anyone keeping company with a de Rogé, bastard or otherwise, and continued with something of a stammer,

"An' there's oatmeal porritch cookin', if'n ye'd fancy it... m'lady?"

The young woman nodded and murmured something in a grateful tone that was too quiet for Anlaf to catch but which caused Aethelfryth to bob an ungainly curtsey before bustling back towards the door to the kitchen. Pushing past Anlaf she hissed,

"I allus knew yer wits were in yer ale kegs! O' course her's a lady. Any fool can see that! Now get out o' me way so as I can see 'bout getting' some food inter her. Poor lass, her looks half starved an' chilled t' the bone! An' the gods pity her, aye, if hers bein' made ter share that bastard's bed against her will."

It was some time after noon – not that there was sufficient daylight in the tavern by which to judge – and Rowène was still sitting on the stool by the fire where Guyard de Martine had ushered her... how long before? She did not know, having lost all sense of time or place. What she did know was that she must try to snatch what rest she could – the warmth of the hearth wall at her back made that easier – so as to be as ready as she might be for the hard ride ahead. She even allowed herself to indulge in the dubious hope that once safely within his half-brother's territory Guy would not force the pace quite as much as he had through hostile Chartreux.

But, if nothing else, this break had given her the opportunity to try and order her thoughts without the distraction of cold rain down her neck or her mount losing her footing in the mud of what passed for a roadway in this benighted region.

A quick glance around the room informed her that the men had been fed and provided with ale and, having consumed this with all the finesse of starving beasts, were now slumped on stools or sprawled on the even harder earthen floor in various stages of slumber. The ale house could never have been large but packing it with half a dozen soldiers had definitely had the effect of making it seem cramped to bursting, while the homely scents of ale and cooking had been quickly overborne by other, more rancid, odours.

The fire had finally picked up and now blazed quite brightly with the unexpected sweetness of apple wood – she vaguely remembered seeing a half-dead tree beside the croft as they halted – but most of the smoke curled around the rafters rather than escaping up the inadequate chimney, further thickening air already heavily laden with moisture from their drying clothes and stifling with the pungent aromas of wet wool, damp leather and male sweat. Her nostrils flared slightly and she wondered in some disgust whether she would ever be rid of that overpowering and uniquely masculine reek.

Breathing as shallowly as possible, she glanced warily around at the men with whom she must make this journey. She knew three of them by name now but, with the exception of Geryth – who was quite clearly the youngest of the group – they appeared all too depressingly similar in attitude and appearance; swearing, spitting, crude-mannered brutes with craggy, bearded faces and shaggy, cropped hair of varying shades of brown. Even Guy, for all she knew him to be of a nobler breed entirely, seemed little different at this moment from the men under his temporary command. In appearance at least; she had never known him spit and had rarely heard him swear – although she did not doubt he could be as coarse-tongued as his half-brother when the occasion warranted it.

Pushing away this dispiriting conclusion she dropped her gaze towards the quiescent figure at her feet, studying the man with a painful concentration; fighting to see past the shining mail hauberk, the charging boar picked out in silver thread on his black tunic, imagining his fair hair long enough to spill over his shoulders and his face without the two-day growth of wheaten stubble that glinted on his jaw. What she saw, however, only reinforced her fear that Guyard de Martine *was* a de Rogé, in all the ways that mattered.

Nevertheless, she could not prevent herself remembering, with a certain wistful despair, those sweet spring days they had spent in each other's company, riding the flowering lanes and orchards of Chartreux, in that enchanted time when he had been merely Guy of Montfaucon and she his Lady Rowena. If only he could have remained that harper...

Then she pulled herself up short, knowing that she must not allow herself to forget that – for all the gentleness he had shown her then and the courtesy he had given her since – he *had* been complicit in her family's destruction. That he was, by his own admission, as deserving of her enmity as either of his more violent half-brothers.

As she watched, his broad brow creased in a deep frown and his mouth tightened in a hard line, causing Rowène to wonder if he truly was asleep. Perhaps, she thought grimly, his conscience would not let him find rest from the shadow of the dark deeds he had connived at. Certainly he seemed far from finding any peace in slumber, even though his need to escape the exhaustion that lay claim to his mind as much as his body was plain enough to see.

Or perhaps he was not thinking about the events of the past two days and nights but rather about his forthcoming reunion with his wife! What was her name? Rowène was sure she had heard him mention it... Marianne... Maude... no, Mathilde, that was it. The woman Guy had said would make their lives into something resembling the ante-chamber of Hell. It did not sound an inviting prospect and she wished with some fervency that Black Joffroi had given some thought to his half-brother's feelings before putting Guy in charge of his hostage, considering that, so far as he knew, Guy had done everything he had been commanded to do.

That said, Rowène knew she was not entirely innocent in this matter. *She* had made no protest when informed that she was to accompany Guy to Rogérinac, her acquiescence based on the simple and purely selfish belief that she could not bear to remain in Chartre with the man who had forced himself on her. She had given no consideration at all to the damage her presence – given her current mode of dress and the power of gossip – was likely to cause to Guy's binding but now, when it was too late by far, it came to her that this was a poor way to repay the man for his consistently honourable behaviour towards her.

*Almost* she wished that she had stayed in Chartre and taken her chances with Ranulf. Ravening wolf though he was, what could he do to her that he had not already done? Nor was this escape from him likely to prove other than temporary if her fears – and his, she amended reluctantly – were realised, since if she found his seed had taken root inside her, she would find herself dealing on a personal basis with Ranulf de Rogé again, whether she liked it or not. Even, a small cold voice whispered in her mind, if it were only to watch him hang!

She swallowed her nausea at the thought but could not control the cold sweat of fear and revulsion that prickled her skin despite the warmth of the fire. Yesterday had gone. And it must be past noon of today. But there had been none of the familiar signs she had learned to look for. Not the heavy, sluggish feeling that usually overtook her lower limbs. Nor the dull ache that nagged in her belly. Yet now she would welcome the insidious agony that more often than not accompanied her monthly flux. Just let it come and she would never again complain at this curse the gods had inflicted on all women.

*Tomorrow.* Gods willing, it *must* come tomorrow.

But if... *when* that happened, she must be prepared. And this might be her last opportunity to talk to another woman before it did. Somehow, Rowène resolved, she must find a way to speak privately to Mistress... she could not remember the woman's name although she had heard Guy mention it... And she could only hope the woman would prove to be sympathetic, Rogé vassal though she was. If Rowène were to explain how she had come to leave Chartre... no, better perhaps not to mention the place she had come from... she must just tell the woman that she had lost all she possessed in the fire that had ravaged her home and that her flow was due any day now. And surely she would be able to help; difficult though it was to judge age in this dim light, she had not seemed past the age of child bearing herself and must surely have some rags to hand for her own use.

Mind made up, Rowène rose abruptly and, with a wary glance at the snoring soldiers, eased past the recumbent figure at her feet. Then, just as abruptly, stopped, as he said very quietly, in Mithlondian.

"Where are you going?"

She glanced down, startled, then seeing him wide awake, looked away in acute embarrassment.

"Do not make me answer that, I beg you."

He frowned and gathered his legs beneath him in order to rise. He was on his knees and about to stand when she hissed,

"No need for you to get up. I only wish to speak with the ale-wife."

Ignoring her first words he pushed to his feet and she bit back an unladylike word, no doubt acquired during the course of her unfortunate acquaintance with Ranulf de Rogé, damn the man! But now his half-brother was standing in front of her, a slight frown knitting his dark blond brows.

"I do not wish to sound discourteous, but why would you want to do such a thing?"

She huffed a little in exasperation and hoped the poor light hid the reddening of her cheeks.

"Women's matters, Guy! *Please* do not ask me to explain further! And I need to... visit the privy – or whatever passes for it here – before we leave."

She saw a faint flush that was not the reflected glow of the fire touch his own cheekbones.

"I must apologise, Demoiselle," he said formally. "I have given little thought to your comfort. You must speak up if you need to p... er... pause awhile once we resume our journey."

Indeed, she recalled, they had *paused* – was that really what he had been going to say? – only once since crossing the Larkenlye. It had been an embarrassing experience, the thick tangle of briar, bramble and hawthorn notwithstanding. Mayhap his own recollection of that occasion was the cause of the grimace that crossed his face.

"I am afraid it will be even rougher travelling over the moors and with very little by way of... ah... comfort. Although I will, of course, ensure you what privacy I can."

There seemed nothing much to say to this so instead she reiterated with soft urgency,

"Thank you. And may I speak with Mistress...?"

"Aethelfryth." He grinned. "It does not render well into Mithlondian." Then, more seriously. "Are you certain you do not wish me to come with you? I am not entirely... ignorant of women's matters."

"No! I mean, I am sure you are not!" she said, badly flustered now. "But I can manage."

He frowned, whether at her denial or her determination, she could not tell.

"Aethelfryth speaks the common tongue well enough but the Rogé accent can be a little hard to understand," he warned her.

"I will manage," she assured him again, trying for a smile. "And if I discover that I need a translator after all, be assured that I will come and find you."

"You may be right," he said with a thoughtful glance in the direction of the kitchen. "In that you will manage better without the hindrance of my presence at your side, the barriers of language notwithstanding. Aethelfryth and Anlaf know *what* I am, of course. Looking as I do, there is scarce a chance that they would not. But folk hereabouts are not easily disposed to either trust or aid any of Jacques de Rogé's sons."

"And what about the women who keep company with your father's sons?" Rowène queried uneasily, aware once more of the misleading nature of her attire.

He sighed and shrugged.

"Just tell Aethelfryth the truth..."

"The truth?" she gulped, feeling herself blanch.

"You need not tell her that Joffroi had your kinsmen murdered, your sister and yourself given over to be ravished by his brothers," he said grimly. "All you need do is tell her that you are not with me by choice and she will guess the rest for herself. The de Rogé reputation has been well earned."

"It has indeed," she whispered, the bitterness on her tongue inevitably recalling the vile taste of Ranulf de Rogé's mouth on hers.

Holding back her nausea with an effort, she lifted her chin and stalked towards the kitchen in search of Mistress Aethelfryth.

They left the Apple Tree towards the middle of the afternoon.

It was still raining but more lightly now and there was a pale glimmer overhead where the sun rode high beyond the drear grey cloud cover. Guyard took it as an auspicious sign and determined to press on. Men and horses having been made ready, he ordered Geryth to bring the Lady Rowena's mare as near to the ale house door as possible. This being done, he helped her to mount, frowning slightly at the residual dampness of her gown and mantle as Geryth led the mare to one side and went to get Fireflame.

He turned, still frowning, to find Anlaf at his elbow. Reminded that there was one matter still to be attended to, he reached for his purse and was astounded to see the man reverting to the servile tone he had greeted him with earlier.

"Nay, sir, don't... I beg ye... haven't we treated ye right? Food, an' ale, an' stabling an' all."

"What?" Guyard said blankly. Then, realising how his actions had been interpreted, he sighed impatiently. "I am not going to slaughter you like an autumn pig, you fool." He took a couple of coins from the pouch hanging from his belt and held them out to the tavernkeeper, who stared at them as if he had never seen silver nobles before. Very likely he had not.

"Take them, man, I need to be gone. Rogérinac is a damned long ride this way."

Anlaf started out of his daze, snatched the coins as if fearing they might disappear like moorland mist before the rising sun and stood clutching them as he looked from the six mailed soldiers to the scarlet-clad, black-cloaked young woman, then back at Guyard himself.

"I'll be wishin' ye a safe journey then, Sir Guy. Ye an' the lady."

Guyard eyed the smaller man curiously.

"You were not sure when we arrived who I was but you know now. Did L... did the lady tell you my name?"

"Nay then, sir, don't ye be blamin' the lass... lady, I mean an' beggin' yer pardon as not to reckernise ye at once..." Here Anlaf darted a surreptitious glance upwards, no doubt at Guyard's raggedly cropped hair. "But tis well known hereabouts as there's only one o' the old lord's sons as ever paid fer his ale or..."

He darted another look at the girl huddled on the honey-coloured mare but did not finish the thought aloud. But Guyard did not need him to. He knew well enough what Anlaf would have said; that he was the only one of the old lord's sons who would have treated any woman clad in such shameless fashion with the courtesy he had shown. Guyard said nothing, however, merely giving the other man a brief, understanding smile and, taking the chestnut's reins from Geryth's hand, swung up into the saddle.

Then, with the lightest touch of his spurred heels, he nudged the stallion into a walk, taking the narrow, treacherously-muddy track that led up to the treeless heights of the mist-drenched moors, the others falling into line behind him.

# Chapter 3

## *Rough Lodgings at Rushleigh*

It was almost dusk – grey, damp and drear as the day itself had been – when Guyard and his men descended like a pack of starving wolves onto the little village of Rushleigh, if the huddled collection of half a dozen decaying cob hovels could be so termed.

Whatever its official status on the Steward of Rogé's tithe rolls, there was no welcome in the faces of the thin, raggedly-clad peasants who peered cautiously out from behind their hide-covered doorways, although none of them would be so foolhardy as to show open resentment. Holding the weary stallion still in the muddy centre of the circle of huts, Guyard waited until the headman of the village had made his reluctant way towards the threatening mass of sidling, stamping horses, finally raising fearful eyes to the hooded riders.

"Aye, sir?" he quavered.

"We seek food and shelter for the night," Guyard responded, his tone, despite himself, flat and hard. He had been riding for the better part of a night and a day, most of that time in foul weather, and was weary past the point of consideration. He saw the headman flinch at his voice and taking a guess at the cause of the other man's obvious unease, dragged back his damp hood and said,

"I know it is much to ask but just do your best."

"Sir Guy!" The headman's eyes widened in belated recognition and his tone warmed a little. "Ye're welcome, o' course."

"And the men, Eadwyn," Guyard reminded him implacably.

Dislike flickered darkly in Eadwyn's dull eyes as he glanced at the black-cloaked men looming out of the dusk but he nodded agreement. He had no choice but to make them all welcome, and he knew it. But it was likewise obvious that he was wondering what Guyard de Martine might be doing commanding a pack of his half-brother's wolves. He saw Eadwyn's gaze fixed bitterly on the black boar banner that flapped wetly from the spear just behind his shoulder, the headman's lips moving as if calculating how he and his fellow villagers were going to be able to feed and house so many hungry men and horses.

Guyard was willing to allow the headman a few moments to think but, when nothing further was forthcoming by way of a decision, fatigue forced him to take matters into his own hands.

"If you and your folk are willing to accept one man per each household, no single family need bear all the inconvenience. We have some food with us but even a bowl of pottage by a warm hearth would not come amiss on a night such as this."

"Aye, Sir Guy, as ye will," Eadwyn confirmed, albeit he still looked deeply unhappy about the arrangements.

"And, of course, you have my word that your womenfolk will not be troubled by any discourtesy from my brother's men," Guyard commented, his chillingly clear tones suddenly loud enough to be heard by even the most distant and selectively deaf among his escort.

Eadwyn's gloomy countenance lightened slightly at this assurance.

"My home is yourn fer the night, Master Guy, if that be yer need," he offered, warming further.

"For which I thank you, Eadwyn," Guyard replied with weary courtesy. He swung down out of the saddle, tossed his reins to Geryth and turning to Rowène, held up his hands.

He could see from her face that she had had ample opportunity whilst he had been talking to Eadwyn to assess the dismal place he had brought her to but she said nothing in reproach. Moving stiffly, she put her hands on his shoulders and, as she had done so many times in the past when he had served as her groom, allowed him to lift her down. Feeling her tremble, he slipped his arm around her waist, guessing her legs would be unsteady after so many long hours in the saddle. Moreover the ground itself was slippery, covered with a layer of malodorous mud. He felt her stiffen against his hold but ignored her silent protest, preoccupied as he was with the startled distaste that had appeared on the headman's face when he realised that it was not a wholly male company he was being asked to provide hospitality for.

Setting his jaw against the peasant's obvious shock Guyard answered the other's unspoken speculation.

"Eadwyn, this is the Lady Rowena who is travelling with me to Rogérinac. If you would be so kind as to take her to your hut where it is warm, I will see to the men."

He helped her to the edge of the mud then watched as she followed their disapproving host, darting an uneasy look over her shoulder at him as she stepped cautiously into Eadwyn's hut. Returning his attention to the men he gave orders for their disposition, adding a brutally explicit reminder of what would happen should any of them even attempt to molest any of the village women.

Finally the muddy circle was clear of men and horses and he felt able to see to his own comfort. Lifting the door skin on Eadwyn's hut, he ducked into the dark, smoky, cramped interior, thanking the gods that at least it was dry inside and relatively warm. Once his eyes had adjusted to the dim light he found Rowène perched uncomfortably by the fire on what was likely the only stool in the hovel, warily watching as a withered, toothless old crone muttered to herself on the other side of the small fire while a younger – but equally worn and thin – woman turned oatcakes in the embers.

Despite the young noblewoman's best efforts at a courteous façade Guyard could sense the uneasy pity she clearly felt for these humble people whose home she had been forced to invade. Not to mention discomfort on her own behalf. As the door skin fell closed behind him, her head came around and a look of profound relief lit her eyes. Standing up, she took the few paces that lay between them, her cloak pulled tight around her.

"Messire de Martine..." As always, it was a shock to hear her addressing him so formally but he supposed in the circumstances it was probably wiser. "I need to go outside."

"But you have only just come... Ah!" Belatedly he took her meaning and held back the door flap for her to go out, saying with a rueful smile, "I am at fault again. You should have reminded me sooner."

He might have followed her but she said softly,

"I will not be long, Messire. There is no need for you to accompany me."

"Just do not go too far away," he said warningly. "It will be full dark soon and there are other wolves prowling these parts besides the two-legged variety that ride with us."

She gave him a sharp look but nodded her understanding. Despite his belief in her common sense, he continued to watch covertly as she picked her way through the kale, turnips and other greenery of the rough vegetable garden. It was difficult going but there was more light than he had supposed there might be, the rain having finally stopped and a faint glimmering of moonlight seeping through the silvered sable of the clouds to shimmer over the huddled hovels.

Lowering his gaze from the mist-ringed moon and glancing around the vegetable plot, he was disquieted to realise that she had disappeared from sight and every whispered rumour he had ever heard concerning the uncanny powers of the Faennari slithered serpent-like down his spine. Heart pounding, he kept from plunging into the barred black and silver shadows only by an effort of will, waiting uneasily for what seemed an age – but was probably no more than the few moments necessary for her to relieve herself – only to have his blood chill once more as an elusive figure came towards him and then disappeared again, moving as soundlessly as any wraith.

He had started to mutter an involuntary prayer to the gods when he heard a startled cry, followed by something that sounded distinctly like a word more reminiscent of the stables than the wraith world, as the figure stumbled over something in its path and the illusion of enchantment was instantly dispelled. Cursing his own folly – for this was no fey wraith but a mere mortal maid – he watched as she emerged fully from behind a wall of tall, leafy beans and made her way between two irregular rows of cabbage plants.

He did not think she was aware that he had been keeping an eye on her and was on the point of discreetly retreating into the hut when he noticed that she had paused at the edge of the garden and appeared to be scanning some low-growing plants with a keen interest. She even went so far as to bend and examine one of them by touch, bringing her fingers up to her nose to smell. Whatever it was, it was evidently not what she was seeking. She shook her head and straightened, moving swiftly back towards the hut.

"Demoiselle?" he queried softly as she came level with him. "Are you quite well?"

Even in the dubious moonlight her face registered her surprise and he mentally castigated himself for an insensitive idiot. Was it likely she would be feeling well after the events of the past two days and the night in between. Sleeplessness and saddle sores were likely to be the least of her ills.

"I have a slight headache, Messire," she replied, her low voice matching his in formality. "That is all. I was merely looking to see if there were might be any medicinal herbs in the garden."

"I will ask Eadwyn if you like. He will know if any of the women of Rushleigh grow or know about the use of such plants. If not, I am afraid the nearest healing house is on the other side of the High Moors, three days' ride at the least in this weather."

"Indeed, I am surprised there is any such establishment in Rogé at all," she replied, somewhat shakily he thought. "But do not trouble yourself about the herbs. It is a trifling ache and will be gone by morning, I am sure."

He could not really see her face as she brushed past him, the moonlight being chancy and the firelight within the hut little better, but he thought she looked pale. Paler even than a day of arduous travelling should have made her. Plainly her headache was worse than she would have him believe. Equally plainly, she did not wish him to make a fuss. Unlike Mathilde, he thought a shade grimly, who would have taken to her bed until the healer arrived and left everyone else to fend for themselves in whatever manner they chose.

Despite his better judgement, he continued to watch the young noblewoman with an intensity that seemed scarcely proper in the circumstances. She resumed her seat beside the fire at Eadwyn's gesture, giving him a small smile of thanks in return. Then, as she looked back towards the door, Guyard made her a slight bow in acknowledgement of her unspoken request and, securing the heavy skin, made his own way back to the fire. Dropping to his heels in the rushes beside her stool, he gratefully accepted the bowl of barley and bean stew the old woman handed him and proceeded to eat. It was poor enough fare, thin and nearly tasteless, but it was at least hot and he had eaten far worse in his time.

Although, he sincerely doubted as he surreptitiously observed the Lady Rowène, that she had *ever* experienced such fare. Nevertheless she made a gallant effort – as much, he thought, from a natural courtesy to the folk who had shared what little they had as from hunger – but in the end she glanced at him and shook her head, a pleading look in her grey eyes.

"I am sorry, Guy," she murmured, formality apparently forgotten. "I can eat no more. But I do not want them to think me ungrateful. Perhaps you could finish it, you must still be hungry."

"A little," he said, keeping his tone prosaic. "If you are certain you do not want any more?"

She shook her head and unobtrusively handed the bowl to him, eyes lowered so he could no longer read their expression. She had eaten even less than he had first thought, he realised, uneasily. The bowl was still three quarters full; perhaps her headache was worse than she was prepared to let on? Or perhaps she was just too weary to eat?

Whichever it was, he was determined that she would eat a more substantial meal tomorrow morning. It was a long, hard road they had to travel, the High Moors between Rushleigh and Rogérinac being notoriously lethal towards those – beast or man – who were weakened by injury or sickness and he knew he could ill afford to lose Joffroi his hostage, even setting aside his own disturbing feelings for Rowène de Chartreux.

The simple meal done, Guyard became aware that Eadwyn was nervously addressing him.

"Your pardon, Eadwyn, what did you say?"

"Only that, if it please ye sir, me an' Hilde'll sleep by the fire. Ye an'... an' yer lady would mayhap be more comfortable over there." On the bed, was what he meant but, thank the gods, had the wit not to make a more direct reference to it.

Guyard glanced rapidly from Eadwyn to the young noblewoman, wondering whether she might actually comprehend something of the Rogé dialect. He did not think he was imagining the blush that touched her pale cheeks with rose, although it was difficult to be certain of anything in the dim light. Regardless of this, he could sense her growing unease, if only because he shared it in equal measure. This was the moment he had known must come ever since Joffroi had told him of the change in plan that meant the Lady Rowène de Chartreux would be placed in his charge rather than Ranulf's.

Reverting now to the Mithlondian tongue he said in a quick, low voice,

"You may not have understood, Demoiselle, but Eadwyn is offering us the use of his bed for the night." He saw apprehension flare in her eyes, and hastened to lay her fears to rest. "I say 'us' but you must know that you will be quite safe from me." He gave her a hint of a wry smile. "Even were I free of any binding vow, I do not think I should perform well with an audience."

He saw her flash an assessing glance from him to Eadwyn, to the hut's other occupants, then back to the bed-place itself. This was made up of a solid wooden bench on which was laid a mattress which he guessed would be stuffed with straw or bracken – if they were lucky. This, in turn, was covered with a rough woollen blanket and what looked like a sheepskin, the whole being redolent of grease, grime and lice. She gave a perceptible shudder – of distaste rather than fear, he thought – and replied softly in the same tongue that he had spoken in.

"Thank you, Messire, but I would rather suffer the discomfort of the floor than share the dubious comfort of that bed – either with you or the vermin that undoubtedly thrive there."

Guyard felt his mouth twitch into a half smile but said seriously,

"I can understand your feelings, Demoiselle, but I think you must put them aside. Eadwyn has offered us his bed in all courtesy. He may only be a peasant but this is his home. Do you wish to dishonour him by refusing his offer, merely because you are too proud to risk the advances of a few fleas?"

This time Guyard had no difficulty in interpreting the flush that stained her cheeks. With a slight, shamed nod she signified her agreement and he turned at once towards Eadwyn to express polite thanks, both for himself and on the Lady Rowena's behalf.

His grudging offer having been accepted, Eadwyn muttered something to the two silent peasant women and, taking no further notice of their noble guests, the three of them shuffled to the far side of the banked fire, huddling all together under a couple of ragged blankets. At the same time Rowène moved to sit on the low bed, fingering the covers piled on the hard, narrow frame with an expression midway between disbelief and resignation. Weary though he was, Guyard tried not to make his tone too abrupt but feared he failed.

"I would offer you my mantle as a blanket if it were not still sodden," he said. "Nor is your own cloak likely to be any drier so I am afraid you have no choice but to risk the fleeces. I am just going to step outside so why do you not make yourself as comfortable as you can in my absence. Unless," he hesitated. "You wish to..?" He left the question open.

"No." She shook her head, then asked with a note he could not quite interpret, "Are you really going to sleep here with me?"

"We shared your bed in Chartre," Guyard reminded her dryly. "And you came to no harm then."

He thought she sighed.

"It is true enough what you say. Forgive me, Guy. I am just tired."

"I know," he said gently. "So the best thing you can do is take your wet things off and get beneath the covers where it is warm. Sleep without fear if you can. I will be gone a little while since I need to check that the men and horses are settled. I will try not to waken you when I return."

He took his time doing the rounds of the soldiers' billets, making sure that none of the peasants had been given cause for complaint, checked that the horses had been cared for and were hobbled securely within the protective ring of stone and thorn that guarded the village and its livestock from incursion by wolves and foxes. He had no idea where the latrine pit might be and had no intention of stumbling around looking for it in the dimpsy, diffuse light of the rain-soaked moon so he contented himself with a quiet piss beside the fragrant hawthorn hedge before returning to the headman's hut.

Once inside he refastened the door skin and stood listening to the soft breath of the banked fire and the snuffling, chesty snores of the three peasants huddled close to its meagre warmth. Eadwyn had thoughtfully left a rush light burning for him and with the aid of this tiny flame he felt his way towards the bed, moving as quietly as his spurred boots would allow. Despite his caution he tripped over the stool, unseen in the shadows. Cursing under his breath, he set it upright, his very next step bringing his foot up against some other impediment he had not seen in the gloom. Exploring with his fingers, he discovered it to be a discarded mantle, the frail, flickering flame of the rush dip behind him waking glimmering echoes of starlight from the heavy object still pinned in the dark, wet folds.

He glanced at the bed, where the piled blankets and furs made an untidy haven of comfort, and permitted himself a faint, almost tender, smile. His Lady Rowena might not make public display of the arrogance normally to be found in a noblewoman of her high birth but it was obvious that she was accustomed to having servants picking up after her and caring for her discarded garments. Clearly it had not occurred to her that if *she* did not set her cloak to dry, no-one else would, and consequently that it would be next to useless as a shield against the weather come morning. Or perhaps she had merely been too weary to think further than a good night's sleep.

In either case, he could not leave her to wake to wet clothes. Picking up the mantle he reached up to hang it from the rafters, draping his own alongside it. Catching another glimpse of the silver brooch he found himself questioning, not for the first time, why Ranulf had made that utterly uncharacteristic gesture of protection. Wondered too what had made Rowène de Chartreux accept.

Frowning now, he sought out the shape of her in the darkness but all he could see was the pale oval of her face amidst the dark coverings. Her soft, even breathing was barely audible and, despite all the questions churning in his mind, he found himself hoping, for more than one reason, that she was in fact asleep. He had vivid recollections of the night they had spent together in Chartre and had no wish to repeat any part of that uncomfortable intimacy. Or rather, if he were truthful, he wished to take those first tentative intimacies to their natural conclusion. And if he had been free, he might well have done so, the girl in the bed being willing.

As it was though...

He lifted his hand to touch the binding band about his arm then, gritting his teeth, sat down on the stool to pull off his muddy boots. Undoing his sword belt, he set it carefully beside the bed and stood to wriggle out of his mail shirt. Finally he draped his rust-marked, sweat-stained gambeson over the stool along with his mail and straightened, stretching his muscles. It was only then that he remembered the wounds he had sustained the day before. Amazingly, although both sword arm and upper leg were stiff, neither appeared to be hurting as much as he would have expected. He was too tired to worry about it though, and beyond making a note to check his bandages in the morning, put the matter out of his weary mind.

He hesitated over the remainder of his clothes but both tunic and breeches were damp and he knew better than to lie down to sleep in wet clothes. Shedding his outer garments, but retaining his shirt as a sop to propriety, he hung the damp clothes up to air. He pinched out the rush-dip and slid cautiously beneath the coarse blankets, easing himself tentatively towards the enticing warmth of the slumbering woman – but not so far as to allow his body to touch hers – and within moments had drifted into the dreamless depths of sleep.

Not more than a candle-notch later, Rowène woke from her own dark dreams, disorientated and alarmed by the sudden touch of a muscular, *male* body against her own and for the space of five soul-shattering heartbeats she knew only a terrible sense of suffocating, blinding panic.

But when the man beside her made no further move – aggressive or otherwise – she slowly drew in a deep breath, exhaling in painful relief when she failed to detect the distinctive stench of sweat and steel, blood and bitter herb that was uniquely Ranulf de Rogé's. Only then did she recall her earlier conversation with Guyard de Martine and realise the identity of the man who shared her bed.

*Guy!*

With the warmth of that thought caressing her heart, she allowed her fear-frozen limbs to relax just a little. For a while she lay still, just listening to his deep, slightly ragged breathing, unconsciously lulled into acceptance until the point when, as she felt his back come to rest against hers, she was able to see his gesture not as a threat but more as a means of sharing warmth. Although it was summer she had been chilled to the bone during the long day's ride in the Rogé rain – often it had been as hard as hail, occasionally waning to a seeping drizzle, but always wet and always raw – and she guessed that for all his hardihood, Guy was as cold as she herself had been before the weight of the thick sheepskins had finally warmed her.

Calmer now, she allowed herself to relax another few degrees, turning her head slightly to breathe in the warm scent of the man at her back. Strongly masculine though it undoubtedly was, she did not find it unpleasant. Nevertheless she was still wary – a direct result of her hideous experience at Ranulf de Rogé's hands – and she was only too painfully aware that a fine linen shirt and a thin silk gown would make a pitifully inadequate barrier should Guyard de Martine choose to act as his half-brother had done. Fortunately for her nerves, his sleep remained deep and untroubled and eventually she relaxed completely, remembering then, with tears in her heart, the treacherous feelings she had once held for this man. Feelings his half-brother had irrevocably destroyed by his brutality.

But perhaps it was better that way, Rowène told herself; better for everyone that Guy should be nothing more to her than some chance-met harper. Except there had been nothing of chance about their meeting. Nor was he a commoner, though he clearly had a harper's skills. He was, moreover, her enemy; made so both by his own deeds and his half-brother's ruthless rape and not for one moment must she forget that latter fact. She could not afford to allow herself to be beguiled by Guy's kindness nor succumb to her own tentative feelings for him.

Not only because he was already bound until death to another woman but because she was terrified that she might be carrying his half-brother's misconceived babe. Another full day had gone by and still she had not bled.

*God of Mercy, let it be tomorrow.*

Yet, even with such troubled thoughts tumbling unchecked through her mind, she still found Guy's solid presence reassuring and finally she fell asleep, to dream of a golden moon and the promise of a passion she had never known.

Guyard woke early the next morning to find the soft warmth of a sleeping woman in his arms and his loins heavy with unfulfilled desire. He lay for a while, telling himself to get up and go about the business of the day. His baser self took no notice, whispering instead that it would not matter if he broke his binding oath – he was already guilty, in name anyway – for the ephemeral pleasure of making love to Rowène de Chartreux.

The alluring sensation of her slender body in his arms was both torture and bliss, as was the certain knowledge that he could take her if he wanted to. He remembered the need implicit in her words to him in the darkness of that night they had shared in Chartre... the honeyed sweetness of her mouth that he had tasted so briefly... He could not help but believe that if he chose to kiss her again, now in the quiet warmth of this dark bed, that he could take it further... to the point where, if neither of them came to their senses, she would welcome him into her body...

*Gods!*

With that thought the heat in his loins escalated to an excruciating peak. Shuddering at the ease with which he had fallen into the whirlpool of desire he forced his thoughts elsewhere – to the upcoming harvest... to the tasks awaiting him in Rogérinac... to his wife, for gods'sake! But although he could control his thoughts to some degree he could not control his body and, in an attempt to ease the discomfort of his erection, he tried to move away from the woman who had caused it. But with a sleepy, indistinct murmur she only snuggled closer in his embrace, dragging a low groan from him as his arms tightened around her.

In the end it was only her trust in him – a trust it would be so easy to destroy – and his own strained sense of honour, that kept him from making love to her.

When Rowène woke the next morning it was to find herself alone once more.

As alone as she had been two mornings before. Dear God of Light, was it really only three days ago that Chartre had fallen into Joffroi de Rogé's blood-splattered hands? To Rowène it felt like a lifetime!

She had spent the night with Guyard de Martine on that occasion in unmolested safety and the only difference she could see between that awakening and this one was that now she found herself, not in her own well-appointed chamber of Chartre castle but in the miserable poverty of a Rogé peasant's hut.

There was, of course, one other extremely pertinent difference. Here she was safe from assault by Ranulf de Rogé!

Hearing a cock crowing discordantly from somewhere nearby, she raised herself on her elbow and glanced towards the open doorway, guessing from the sparse fall of rain-washed light that it was not long after dawn. Early though it was Eadwyn and his women must already be out and about their daily chores. As to when Guyard had left she could only speculate but the place beside her where he had lain was cold and no trace of his presence remained – not even a short, dark blond hair.

Which was not to say that he might not return at any moment. Or the headman. Or any of the soldiers of their escort, come seeking orders from their temporary commander. That thought in mind, Rowène hastily scrambled out of bed and desperately tried to smooth and otherwise tug the tawdry scarlet gown into some semblance of respectability. A lost cause, in truth, since it was an inescapable fact that she must look like a whore just risen from her bed. The irony of that image being that, thanks to the man everyone believed to be her lover, she would still be as innocent and virginal as the first starlit snows of winter. What no-one here could possibly know was that, due to his brutal half-brother's actions, she was not. Not only no maiden but she was very much afraid...

It was at this point in her scattered thoughts that Guyard de Martine ducked back into the hut. He spared one fleeting glance at her flushed face, disordered gown and tumbled hair before fixing his gaze on the wall just behind her and addressing her with his usual courtesy. She thought she could detect a tinge of red to the weathered skin above his cheekbones but by contrast his voice was blandness itself.

"Good morning, Demoiselle. I trust you slept well? There are oatcakes and honey beside the hearth for you and a beaker of milk. I suggest you eat it all, it will be another long day in the saddle." He cocked his head. "How is your headache?"

"Head..? Ah, yes..." She dredged up a smile from the depths of the still, grey pool of despair in which she was slowly drowning. "It is much better, thank you."

She saw that he was regarding her with a sceptical expression in his light blue eyes and, touched that he might be worried about her, gave way to the impulse that swept through her. Stepping closer, she raised herself up on her toes and brushed a kiss – of gratitude, of reassurance, of... she knew not what – across his mouth, feeling his lips warm and soften under hers as, undoubtedly against his better judgement , he allowed himself to respond.

It was the very briefest of embraces, barely even a kiss she told herself, but even so the taste and touch of Guy's lips was nothing like her nightmare memories of his half-brother's mouth. Not ruthless and cruel as Ranulf's had been, but sweet and heady as summer mead. And she sensed that Guy was as lost as she to the unexpected enchantment of the moment...

Until the sound of footsteps squelching in the mud outside the door brought them both to their senses!

Even in the uncertain grey light in the hut Guyard could see the look of shock that flashed across the young soldier's face before he hastily dropped his gaze to his boots. Guilt and embarrassment at his own unguarded response to Rowène de Chartreux's kiss caused him to snap with unusual harshness,

"What is it? And wipe that damned look off your face before you answer me!"

Geryth flushed at the rebuke but his face, when he finally looked up, was suitably blank.

"Sorry ter int'rupt ye, sir," he managed to get out. "But ye did say as how ye wanted ter know when the men were ready ter ride."

"Yes, I did." Guyard agreed in clipped accents, annoyed with himself more than the other man. "Go and tell them to mount up. We will be with you in a moment."

"Aye, sir."

Geryth risked one last puzzled, almost disbelieving, look from Guyard to his companion, then turned and trudged off through the mire, obviously deeply disturbed by what he had witnessed. Guyard waited until he had gone and then he dropped the arm that had somehow folded itself around the girl's slender waist. Declining to bring up the matter of the kiss, he said as emotionlessly as he could,

"Hurry and eat, Demoiselle. As I said, we have a long way to go and your next meal is likely to be worse than your last."

He waited until she had seated herself on the stool and made sure she had at least begun to nibble on the oatcakes dribbled with heather honey, before moving to pull the black cloak from the rafters, pleased to find the woollen cloth nearly dry. From the corner of his eye he saw her take a swallow of the milk before hastily setting it down again. He was not really surprised; he had not expected her to find the taste of goat's milk appealing, hence his deliberate reticence in telling her from what animal the liquid had originated.

Realising after some moments that she was not going to eat any more, he scooped up the remainder of the oatcakes and, wrapping them in the square of linen he carried in his purse, tucked the packet into the otherwise empty pouch. Impatient now to be away, he dropped the mantle around her shoulders, leaving her to wrestle with the heavy silver pin.

What in the name of all the gods had prompted Ranulf to make that gesture, he wondered yet again. No altruistic motive, of that he was sure; he knew his brother better than that. *But then, why?*

For a moment he hesitated, on the brink of asking her quite bluntly, but changed his mind and said simply,

"If you are ready, Demoiselle, we should be gone."

Having finally managed to secure the pin on her shoulder, Rowène nodded and rose to her feet. Only then did she appear to notice that although his sword hung at his hip he had not resumed his mail shirt.

"No hauberk, Guy? Is that wise?"

He shrugged, ignoring her use of his given name though his belly muscles clenched in answer to it.

"This is Rogé, my home land. What need have I for the protection of mail? The only enemy I have here is you."

"Gods above! I am not your enemy," she said impatiently and therefore, he thought, sincerely.

"That is not what Ranulf believes," he said wryly.

"And I suppose it is entirely inconceivable that your arrogant half-brother might be wrong in his reading of my character?" she queried icily, taking him aback with the force of her dislike.

Under contemptuously raised copper brows, her frosted grey eyes regarded him – and, by extension, his brother and all Ranulf's doings – with disdain. Then, when he merely chose to stare stolidly at her without reply, she swept past him, head held high. Out of the smoky hut and into the open area at the centre of the half-dozen tumbledown hovels, where the soldiers of their escort waited, jesting and grumbling casually between themselves. The horses, rested and restive, churned the muddy ground to a slippery mire, watched by the distrustful, hate-filled eyes of the gathered peasants while a couple of scrawny brown chickens, indifferent to the identity of the horsemen, pecked voraciously through the pungent piles of dung almost under the huge, stamping hooves.

Contrary to Guyard's half-formed supposition, she barely hesitated at the edge of this sloppy sea before gathering up the trailing lengths of both mantle and gown, rewarding the two soldiers who were keeping a desultory eye open for their commander with a flash of scarlet silk and a clear view of slender white ankles. Ignoring the ripple of muted awareness and the intensity of the masculine attention suddenly riveted upon her – and before Guyard could pick her up in his arms, as he had been on the point of doing – she stalked heedlessly through the ankle-deep muck heading for the spot where Geryth stood gaping at her, clutching the reins of her mare and Guyard's stallion, both animals now brushed clean and gleaming in the pale morning light.

It was, Guyard noted entirely without surprise, raining again.

Rain or not, he had to do something to retrieve the situation. And bloody quickly, before the impetuous noblewoman in his charge ended up on her silk-covered arse or the soldiers forgot the fact that she was supposedly *his* woman even while she wore Ranulf's distinctive black and silver trappings. Gathering his wits he strode rapidly after her, ignoring the unpleasant squelch and suck of the mud around his booted feet – the gods knew the sturdy leather was better protection from the quagmire than her own soft shoes. Even so he did not catch up to her until she halted beside her mare and then there was little he could do save wordlessly offer his laced hands for her foot. She gave him a mute look in which cold anger and resentful gratitude were clearly mingled but, as he had guessed she would be compelled to in the end, availed himself of his proffered assistance.

Grimacing at the state of her ruined shoes and trying not to think about her dainty, if exceedingly dirty, ankles and mud-splashed legs, he threw her up into her saddle. Wiping his filthy hands on the tail of his already soiled cloak, he checked the mare's girth strap and handed her the reins, not waiting for any thanks she might feel obliged to make. Turning away he retrieved Fireflame's reins from Geryth's slack grasp and, ignoring the stares he could feel heavy on his shoulders, put one muddy boot in the stirrup and hauled himself up, settling solidly in his saddle.

It was going to be another bloody long day – with an even more difficult night at the end of it!

He had already made his thanks and farewells to Eadwyn earlier so now he paused only long enough for Geryth to mount up before giving the headman one final courteous nod and setting his small company into motion.

Whatever other uncertainties might cloud his mind, he was in no doubt that the villagers of Rushleigh would be unreservedly glad to witness their departure. For all their surface respect for him, he was still Black Joffroi's bastard brother and therefore untrustworthy, while the soldiers accompanying him were as welcome as pestilence or crop-blight – even though Guyard had never done anything to deserve their distrust and the Rogé soldiery were regarded elsewhere as a necessary and lethal fighting unit in Mithlondia's army.

At the same time Guyard was equally certain that, for the second time in as many days, he and Rowène had provided enough fodder to keep folk happily gossiping until long after harvest time. A fact he did his best to forget, despite its tendency to intrude upon his mind at odd times during the day, rather in the manner of an intermittent, and unreachable, itch between his shoulder blades.

# Chapter 4

## *"Does it do Nothing but Rain in Rogé?"*

Despite the depressing drizzle that fell all that day, Guyard found that they made steady if slow progress and managed to cover a goodly distance, leaving Rushleigh several leagues behind by mid-day. The rain made visibility uncertain and all the rough tracks that criss-crossed the moors looked much the same but he knew his way well enough, having ridden all over Rogé's rough terrain during the near score of years he had served as Joffroi's steward.

They had been climbing by imperceptible degrees all day, each slope down to a treacherous, gushing stream being succeeded by a longer, steeper haul up to the crest of the next hill but by his reckoning they should reach the far edge of the Low Moors by nightfall. That was when the real problems would start; the rolling, bracken-clad lower lands being gentle indeed in comparison to the stark crags and fells of the High Moors. Two days' hard travel, he thought grimly, his gut tightening. Two days for him or the men of their escort, that is. With a gently-raised and exhausted young noblewoman in their midst, however...

He shook his head. Such difficulties as they encountered would have to be dealt with as they arose. There was nothing he could do to change their situation; the coastal road had clearly been impassable and this was the only other way to reach Rogérinac. Shying away from the thought of Rowène wet, miserable and cold, hungry and heart-sick from the loss of her home and kin or, worse yet, suffering injury or even death due to his decision to take this road, Guyard put his mind to planning for the journey ahead.

Even without delays from accident or injury to any horse or rider, rations were going to be short. They carried some in their saddle bags – raided from Chartre castle's storeroom – and water would scarcely be a problem but hamlets where they could obtain more provisions were few and far between on the Low Moors and practically non-existent on the higher reaches and hunting for fresh meat would only delay them further.

Viewed realistically, they could not reach Silverleigh and the settlement of the Grey Sisters on the birch-covered eastern slopes of the High Moors for another three days, mayhap four if this infernal rain did not let up. Once past Silverleigh, however, it was all fairly good riding, downhill through the oak woods of Howe, Hembury and Ham until they reached the barley strips of the lowland fields and finally, say one more day of travel, they should see the black cliffs of the eastern coast and, rising above them, the solid bulk of Rogérinac castle. The gods knew he would be more glad than he could say to reach it with both his charge and the six men of their escort intact.

On that thought he half turned in the saddle to look back down the line, pleased to see that five of the men were riding with an orderly discipline that reflected some credit at least on Ranulf's training. Young Geryth, still looking vaguely uncomfortable, was holding to his position at Guyard's left shoulder, the black boar pennant hanging in sodden folds from his spear tip, now and then flapping wetly as a rising gust of wind caught it. Cold though it was, perhaps the wind would blow the rain away and give them some sight of the sun; that would make all the difference to the journey facing them. Encouraged by the prospect, he glanced to his right where the Lady Rowène rode beside him, meaning to say something of the sort to her.

She had pushed her hood back from her face, presumably that she might better see where she was going, and countless glittering droplets of misty rain clung amidst her wind-tumbled tresses so that it seemed as if a thousand tiny, sparkling diamonds were strung along each fine dark copper thread. Her soft mouth was set in a determined line and in a pale face that borrowed the translucent sheen of sunlit pearls, her eyes – her one shining beauty, he had always thought – glimmered between dark lashes, reminding him of a mountain lake he had once seen; deep yet clear, and as dangerously beguiling as the moon itself.

*Gods! No, I cannot... will not... fall for her!*

So he told himself as his heart contracted with a pain he had never suspected he might feel and whatever words he meant to have spoken to her died on his lips. Hastily he turned his gaze away before she could either see how deeply he had become entangled in her silvered snare or guess at the vulnerability of his emotions.

He shifted uneasily in his saddle but could not forebear from glancing at her once more, hoping that he had mistaken that unwanted, arrow-swift, sword-sharp, *bloody complicated*, surge of love for something as plain and unvarnished as lust. That at least could be dealt with simply enough and would wreck neither his life nor Mathilde's and would leave Rowène de Chartreux mercifully unaware of his feelings.

Hearing the creak of saddle leather and sensing Guy's regard, Rowène withdrew her eyes from her dispassionate survey of the drear grey hills, glimpsed through the even drearier grey rain, in order to meet his troubled gaze. She wondered vaguely whether she looked as wet and drawn and weary as he did and concluded, without really caring, that she probably looked a good deal worse. Her stomach, empty of all but the single oatcake she had managed to swallow – the mouthful of goat's milk, ugh!, and the smear of honey really did not count – grumbled hungrily and with an abrupt movement she jerked the wet hood back over her damp hair.

"Does it do nothing but rain in Rogé?" she snapped, irritated as much by her inability to read the thoughts and emotions behind her companion's level gaze as the weather itself.

At that – admittedly somewhat petulant sounding – demand he shrugged, a smile dawning in his eyes, banishing the clouds so that of a sudden they were the same clear pale blue of a rain-washed spring sky.

"No, Demoiselle, it does not always rain in Rogé," he said, the same hint of humour playing around his firm mouth. "And sometimes the sun even shines." A gleam of sympathy tempered his amusement with compassion. "I know that Rogé can never compare in your eyes to Chartreux or even Kaerellios, and indeed at the moment it does not appear to have either use or beauty to recommend it, but still it is my home land and I am bound to it. Even though I was not born here."

She saw him glance around at the barely visible hillsides, his smile fading and his mouth hardening into a grim line, uncannily reminiscent of the half-brother he resembled so closely – in looks if not character. When he spoke again, she had the impression he was talking to himself more than her.

"The year has been dismal so far here in Rogé. The winter the worst I can remember, the spring cold and wet and now in midsummer the coastal lands are flooded again, the moors a quagmire. It certainly does not bode well for our chances of a good harvest this year."

"Harvest?" Rowène permitted herself to borrow some of his despised half-brother's irony. She glanced around at the rising moorland, barren brown for the most part, with here and there a patch of dull purple that hinted at early flowering heather or the livid green of a moss-covered bog. "What do you find to harvest in this god-forsaken land? Or must I suppose that heather and bracken are good for something? Not forgetting the few scraggy sheep I have glimpsed. They certainly do not look of much use, either for their meat or their wool."

"Rogé is not all heather, bracken and sheep," he commented mildly, lifting his gloved hand to brush the raindrops from his face. He had not shaved during the past two days and his jaw was rough with a dark gold stubble. He looked sufficiently like the harper Guy of Montfaucon that she could almost forget that he was half-brother to the bastard – the bastard by nature, that is, rather than birth – whose cloak she still wore.

Oblivious to the direction her thoughts had taken, he continued,

"There are some tracts of fertile farmland nearer to the coast that sustain oats and barley and, as you discovered last night, most of the peasants grow vegetables to supplement the field crops."

"I should think they might, since I am certain Black Joffroi levies a heavy enough tithe on those same standing crops," Rowène retorted.

"As do all Mithlondian lords," Guy pointed out equably. His light blue eyes glinted back at her as he ended softly, "As your father did."

Stung by his gibe, together with the vexing realisation that it might actually be the truth, she sought for some other weapon to throw at him.

"Speaking of tithes, Messire de Martine, is it not a steward's duty to assess and collect his liege lord's due?"

Guy shrugged, either indifferent to, or determined not to react to, her baiting.

"As you say, Demoiselle. And yes, as you know very well, I am Joffroi's steward."

"No doubt it is very convenient for him to have his half-brother acting as his steward?" Rowène queried somewhat scornfully.

"It works, Demoiselle," Guy replied, this time with something of a snap crisping his cultured tones. She thought he would let the matter drop there but after a moment he continued, almost as if compelled to defend himself and his half-brothers. "If you believe that Joffroi, Ranulf or I grow fat and rich while our folk starve in poverty, think again, Demoiselle. You have seen my gear, you are *wearing* Ran's mantle, for gods'sake!" His dark blond brows twitched together as if he were still perplexed by that anomaly but to her relief he did not ask. Instead he continued flatly, "Can you look at that... look at me... and tell me in all honesty that either Ran or I flaunt the appearance of wealthy men?"

It was true, she supposed. She remembered the shabby raiment he had worn when she had first seen him. Up until this moment she had assumed that he had donned his oldest garments to complement his humble role but was now forced to consider the possibility that the frayed and threadbare linen shirt, patched breeches and scuffed leather boots were his normal attire. Clothes he wore on a daily basis, in and around Rogérinac. God of Light, the grooms who mucked out the Chartre castle stables were dressed better than Jacques de Rogé's by-blow! And what about his half-brothers? Lord Jacques' legitimate sons? Black Joffroi had seemed to be clothed finely enough but as far as his younger brother went...

She felt surreptitiously at the black mantle that covered her from wet hair to muddy shoes. It had once, she thought, been good cloth, the yarn tightly woven, thick and warm, the natural grease of the sheep's wool rendering it proof against all but the heaviest soaking. Now it was thin, discreetly mended in some places, not so discreetly in others; the work of different hands, she guessed. There was a hint of silver stitching about the edges but, as with Guy's garments, the embroidery was more a memory of a woman's loving fingers than anything substantial.

But she did not want to consider Ranulf de Rogé in any way, shape or form. Not his penniless state, nor his relationships with the women of Rogérinac, nor the possibility that he had... No! Definitely not *that*. Remembering with an effort the subject at hand, Rowène returned her gaze to the man riding easily alongside her and remarked cynically,

"I would not expect the harper Guy of Montfaucon to come calling at Chartre castle clad as befitted the Lord of Rogé's half-brother! That would hardly have served your ends."

"Think what you like, Demoiselle," he retorted. "But in truth I have little more by way of wealth – in gold or lands – than if I really were an itinerant

384

harper. When all is said and done, Guy of Montfaucon was not so very different from.Guyard de Martine."

"Except that penniless harpers or base-born stewards do not carry swords of the quality of the one you own," she said more sharply, nodding at the silver-wired sword hilt at his side, regretting the dig at his illegitimacy almost as she spoke.

He looked back at her, his head held at a proud angle, a flicker of pain in the depths of his light blue eyes, rising impatience roughening his normally pleasant voice.

"The sword was a gift from my father, at a time when Jacques de Rogé was as wealthy as Louis de Chartreux. In those days he could afford to arm all his sons properly, his *bastard* as well as his legitimate get. But that was many years ago now and if you were thinking to find comfortable halls and fine living in this poor land, you will discover your error soon enough. We all of us have to work for our bread with whatever talents we have, hence Ranulf is Joffroi's garrison commander and leader of our levies when summoned to battle and I am his steward and sometime harper, finding that those skills came easier to my hand than that of sword or spear, even though my father did his best to have me trained as a warrior." He snorted softly. "I do not doubt he would have been grievously disappointed in me had he lived past my fifteenth summer."

"Well, I sincerely doubt whether your elder brother shares that disapprobation," Rowène commented caustically. "Else he would not have trusted you as he did when he sent you to Chartre. In truth, I think he does very well out of your loyalty to him."

Guyard watched her grey eyes blaze disdainfully and sighed inwardly at the grim thought that the next four or five days would be difficult in more ways than one – since, even in the unlikely event that the weather cooperated, on present showing the Lady Rowène de Chartreux most likely would not! Not that he thought she lacked genuine grounds for her dissatisfaction with the men who accompanied her but there was nothing either he or she could do to amend the situation until they reached their destination. And while he was perfectly prepared to converse in a civilised fashion with her, he had no intention of being drawn into any further discussion of the situation that pertained in Rogérinac – despite the strong temptation to tell her that it was a relationship that worked both ways.

While it was undoubtedly true that, in him, Joffroi had a steward he could trust not to cheat him – and at very little cost to his coffers except in food – in return, as there was no law that said Joffroi was required to provide for the bastard his father had got on his wife's gently-born companion the fact remained that Joffroi had continued to keep his half-brother in his household at a time when the Rogé revenues were barely sufficient to cover the taxes due to the crown, let alone maintain his own appearance at court, feed a household of servants and equip the troop of soldiers he was expected to send to Lamortaine every spring.

The common folk might grumble at the taxes demanded of them, the other nobles of Mithlondia might suspect the Rogé coffers were not as full as they might have been but only Joffroi, Ranulf and Guyard knew how far into penury they had really fallen. And the fact that Joffroi had continued to retain both him and Ranulf at Rogérinac under such impoverished circumstances argued a bond of affection and loyalty that most people would have believed the Black Boar of Rogé to be intrinsically incapable of...

Hearing a sound – something between a sniff and a choke – he dragged himself out of the deepening morass of his thoughts to find the Demoiselle de Chartreux regarding him, open contempt and incredulous comprehension in her clear grey gaze.

"God of Light! *That* is why your brother – your older brother, that is," she added hastily. "Wanted Chartreux so desperately! To replenish his empty coffers!"

"That and the fact that he has hated your father and lusted after your mother for more years than I can remember," Guyard answered, his voice quiet but edged with warning nonetheless. "And now, Demoiselle, I think you and I have gone as far down this path as it is wise to go. Whatever the rights or wrongs of it, Joffroi is still my liege lord and your mother is about to become his lady." Simultaneous with those words dawned a bemused realisation of how that binding would affect the relationship between him and this young woman. "Gods above! Once their binding is formalised and their child born, you and I will be accounted kin... by law at least."

"Child!"

He watched as what little blood there had been in her fatigue-pale face seeped away, leaving her skin wraith-white, and he wondered if she were about to swoon. Frowning in concern, he leant over and grabbed the reins from her slackened grasp before the mare could respond to her rider's lack of attention.

"Yes, a child," he repeated, keeping his voice low. "Surely you had considered the possibility? Joffroi wants a son – a legitimate one! – who can inherit the lordship of Rogé. And now Chartreux." He cast another swift glance in her direction and smiled through his teeth, acutely aware of the men at his back; although they were unlikely to hear his words, they all had eyes in their head and tongues to gossip with later. "You may be of child-bearing age yourself, Demoiselle, but that does not make your mother so close to her dotage as to be incapable of presenting Joffroi with a healthy child."

"No, I know that... I just..."

She swallowed and turned her head away, clearly fighting to recover herself. He saw her fingers rise, unconsciously he thought, to touch the silver brooch on her shoulder. Then, seeming to realise what she was doing, she dropped her hand with a shudder of something he could not mistake for anything other than revulsion. As if the movement served to bring her back to her senses, she straightened and turned back to him, her face now perfectly composed.

"My mother and Black Joffroi?" Her tone was as light and cold as the very snowflakes of Hell but trembling ever so slightly. "Gods above! Just the thought of anyone coupling with your brother..." She faltered more perceptibly. "*Either* of them – and the child such a vile act might produce – makes my stomach turn!"

"I suppose that is natural enough," he replied. Then, more firmly, "But it is a situation that you must accustom yourself to. Whatever the rights or wrongs of it, your father is dead and Joffroi very much alive. Prince Linnius *will* give his consent to the binding with your mother. Indeed, I think he has little choice since the whole realm will know soon enough that they are lovers."

"Were they lovers before my father's death?" she asked suddenly.

He considered lying but he had sworn an oath to himself never to lie to her again.

"I do not know for certain," he said quietly. "But yes, I believe they were."

She did not, he observed wryly, look in the least surprised. Just nauseous and very young. Repugnant though he found the situation himself, it was not an emotion that he could allow her to wallow in and she needed to be reminded that her own position was not so very different.

"Just remember, Demoiselle, that in view of the gossip following in our wake, you too are likely to be held up to public pillory for taking a de Rogé to your bed."

He shot a quick look over his shoulder but Geryth – the only one of the escort close enough to overhear – had dropped back out of earshot and, responding to the fear and horror he perceived in her eyes, Guyard continued hastily,

"Yes, I know we are not lovers in truth. But we have shared a bed, not once but twice, and although I grant you had little choice in the matter either time, we will both be damned, in most people's eyes at least. That being so, I would ask you to bear in mind that you are not the only loser from Joffroi's desperate gamble. *You* are left with your virtue intact but a reputation so soiled as to warrant Joscelin de Veraux's repudiation of your betrothal. *I*, on the other hand have gained the unwanted – and unmerited – brand of adulterer and the possibility that my wife will never talk to me again, let alone allow me back into her bed. You and I may know the truth of the matter but the good folk of Mithlondia will not. Nor will they perceive any difference between Joffroi's relationship with your mother, and our own situation. To put it bluntly, Demoiselle, your mother is bedding the man who brought about your father's death and gossip will be no kinder to you."

Rowène raised appalled grey eyes to meet his bleak gaze.

"Do you think I did not already know that?" she whispered. "I know there is little difference between my mother and me..." Her voice steadied and hardened. "Save one."

Guyard nodded, thinking he knew what she was about to say.

"There is that at least. Since we have never lain together, you cannot be further reviled for giving life to child who carries the tainted de Rogé blood.

You should thank the gods for that small mercy, Demoiselle."

"Yes," she agreed, her voice a mere echo of a whisper. "I should do, should I not?"

The words continued to echo mockingly in Rowène's mind long after Guy had fallen silent. *Gods have mercy! A child who carries the tainted de Rogé blood,* he had said. Not *his* child, no... but she very much feared his half-brother's seed might already have taken root.

She had worn the cloth pads Mistress Aethelfryth had provided her with since leaving the Apple Tree and had checked them with febrile eagerness every time she had paused to relieve herself but the bleached linen remained obstinately unbloodied. She repeatedly assured herself that it had only been two days — although it sometimes seemed like a lifetime since Ranulf de Rogé had first raised that horrific possibility — but unlike Juliène, whose flux was so irregular as to defy prediction, her own flow had always followed the moon's cycle to the day.

Yet now, for the first time ever, her flux was late and although there could be other explanations for that... the shock of recent events, the... But she could not think of any other reasons, remembered only that de Rogé's... She sought for an acceptable word but heard only the sardonic murmur of his voice uttering those crude alternatives and chose one at random. So... his prick then... had already been wet at the tip when he had thrust into her. And although he had denied spilling his seed, she knew mischances did happen; again, she had life at the Kardolandian court to thank for such unwelcome knowledge.

That being the case, and as she was now two days late by her calculations, she knew she must at least acknowledge the possibility that she might hold the lives of three people in her hand; her own, de Rogé's and the... She could not bring herself to call it a babe, not when she considered the daemon whose spawn it was. Yet could she bring herself to rid herself of it? Even if she could think how to do so without anyone knowing? If she were in Kaerellios it would be no problem... a word in the right ear... a sufficient amount of silver... a dark chamber and a sharp implement...

She shuddered at the thought, thankful that she was not in Kaerellios and though she doubted she could have taken that sordid path even if she had been, yet what was the alternative? Shame for her and the babe... and death — or so Ranulf had implied — for its father? There must be another way. But what? Then it came to her... a discreet conversation between two of Queen Xandra's ladies which she had barely heard at the time and never dreamed she would need to pay attention to. A single scarlet seed, one had assured the other, that was all it would take.

But Rowène did not know anything about medicinal herbs or poisonous seeds and if it was a Kardolandian plant, as she suspected it must be, she doubted that any healers she might contrive to speak with — Guy had mentioned that there was an enclave of the Grey Sisters somewhere in these bleak moors – kept such a lethal thing in their stores. They were sworn to preserve life, the Sisters of Mercy, not connive at the murder of unborn babes. Even if that babe were the unwanted, illegitimate offspring of a murderous, ravening wolf named Ranulf de Rogé!

A murderous, ravening wolf who had seemed genuinely appalled at the thought that she might do such a thing. *I know I hurt you but do you hate me so much?* he had asked, his dark blue eyes stark with horror and disbelief in a face blanched white to the lips. *That you would murder an innocent babe before it has even drawn breath, simply because it has the misfortune to spring from my seed?*

Was she capable of such a thing? She had denied it at the time but was very much afraid that she might be.

Then again, she told herself, it had only been two days. Her flux could well come before night-fall; she had felt twinges of a familiar ache low in her belly since just before they had paused to eat and rest the horses somewhere around the middle of the day. Perhaps by the time she dismounted again, she would see some visible signs that her prayers had been answered.

Despite this tiny flicker of hope, which was all she had to sustain her, the remainder of the day seeped by in ever-increasing misery, ice-cold drops of rain water slowly penetrating every layer of woollen cloak and silken gown to chill her clammy skin, while the chafing of the wet saddle left her stiff and sore in places she had no wish to think about, let alone mention to Guyard de Martine.

The mere thought of Guy, however, served to recall his earlier words and her reaction to them. Those words had cut far too close to the bone – although he had been talking of their own relationship, not the one that he could not know existed between her and his half-brother – and she had very nearly betrayed herself. As it was, she found the thought of Guy knowing what his vile half-brother had done to her almost more humiliating than the memory itself.

Yet memories were supposed to be ephemeral, lacking in all physical substance but she could still *feel* in her flesh the tearing pain of de Rogé's violent possession of her... the searing touch of his...

No! She *would not* recall those terrifying moments, either in her mind or with her body.

She would dream of happier times. Of riding in the warm sunshine, under blue skies, down leafy lanes... through the Chartreux orchards, pink and white petals catching in her hair and her horse's mane... Guy brushing them away, his light blue eyes smiling up at her, just before they darkened and he turned hastily away...

No, she must not think of that either! Guy was bound to another woman and there could be nothing between them now but the cool distance of gaoler and hostage.

Yet she had to think of something to divert her attention from the chill of her aching limbs and the hideous, heart-sick fears that still swirled in the darkness of her mind. Thoughts of her father and her brothers merely made her want to weep and she had no wish to recall those lost ten years in Kardolandia. Despite having all the comforts appertaining to one of Queen Xandra's lady companions, she had never quite felt that she belonged there. Unlike Ju, who had quite obviously revelled in the life she had led.

*Ah, Ju!*

She lifted her face to the misty drizzle, allowing the rain to wash away her tears. Then, incredibly, she sensed something… the tentative touch of her sister's mind perhaps, and turned to look back over her shoulder. But she could see nothing, the west was veiled in glimmering grey. Nor could she feel anything now, the quicksilver sensation of contact having gone as swiftly as it had come.

*Where are you, Ju?*

She flung the question into the mist-drenched silence behind her but, receiving no answer, faced forwards again into an identical swathe of shining rain, her thoughts humming in her head like tiny bees. Had Master Cailen, whoever he really was, managed to get her sister to a place of safety?

Or – and this thought stung like a wasp's sting – did Ju still flee through the wide lands of Mithlondia in fear for her life?

Another thought occurred to her; not a wasp this time but a veritable hornet! What if Ju should find herself with child? It was scarcely impossible. De Rogé had made no secret of the fact that he had lain with her sister – and their tire-maid too, for that matter. Gods, she felt sick! – before forcing himself on her. He had also made it quite plain that he would take no responsibility for any child born of his… coupling with Ju. Or presumably, that other one, though he had not mentioned it specifically.

Whereas he had *demanded* to know the truth if she, Rowène, should discover the gods had played them both false and breathed life into a child *she* did not want and *he* could not support and whose very birth would – or so he had appeared to believe – bring about his own death. A child who, by rights, could not have sprung from that single heartbeat when…

But no! She remembered now, with another nauseated lurch of her insides, that it had been more than one… nearer ten… a score of heartbeats even… during which *he* had remained deep in her body, even as the world had exploded into white shards of ice before her eyes.

After that, all had turned to darkness and she knew not what had occurred then. He had insisted that nothing had happened. That after that one tearing thrust his manhood had withered into the semblance of an impotent worm. That he had had no chance to spill his seed.

But *she* knew – and guessed he did too, although neither of them had spoken openly of it – that he had been – she gave a grimace of disgust at the memory – wet before he entered her. She had *seen* him, seen that monstrous thrusting *thing*, flushed dark with blood. And the single droplet... no, a trickle... of some thick, pearly white liquid... his...

*Gods! His seed!*

And he had put that seed in her body and left it there to take root!

Curse him! *That* was why he had been so insistent that she tell him if she were with child. He had *known* what he had done! *Must* have known, since he, understandably perhaps, had been far more in control of his wits than she at that point in time. Yet even she had suspected, in the recesses of her shattered mind, the significance of what she had seen.

So why in the name of all the gods had she not washed his seed away when she came back to a consciousness of where she was and what he had done? She had heard enough of Queen Xandra's ladies gossiping to know what to do after lying with a man if there were to be no consequences of what was essentially a coupling for mutual pleasure.

So... had it been because she had experienced no pleasure – only pain and humiliation – that she had not thought such preventative action necessary? Had she, in her naivety, believed that the gods would not permit an innocent babe to be born of such a father's vile crime? Or was it that de Rogé's unexpected presence in the room when she finally emerged from the black shadows that masked the entrance to Hell, had so scattered her wits that even simple common sense was beyond her?

Then again, she did not think she *could* have stripped and washed under his knowing blue gaze. Although why *he* had not forced her to take such measures, she did not even pretend to understand. He was, without doubt, the most brutal man she had ever met but he was *not* a stupid one! With his years of experience and intimate knowledge of the workings of women's bodies, he had to be aware of the means by which whores – whether the high-born courtesans of Kaerellios or Lamortaine or the common harlots he himself used – protected themselves from the curse of a man's seed.

A whore! That is what they would call *her*, she thought with a flash of bitter anger, regardless of the truth of the matter. Ranulf de Rogé's whore! And with his brat in her belly she doubted she would be welcome anywhere in Mithlondia, save possibly Rogérinac. Since surely not even Black Joffroi would refuse house room to his own brother's cast-off whore and their unwanted bastard! No, that was not the issue. Rather it was the certainty that she could not bear to live within the same confines – she had no idea how large or small Rogérinac castle might be – as Guy and his lawful wife!

Yet what other choice would she have? De Rogé had seemed convinced that he would hang for her rape although it was by no means certain that she could stand up before the High Court of Mithlondia and attest to that. For though she had initially fought to preserve her virtue, she *had* yielded at the end. Not because she wanted what had seemed inevitable but that it might be over quicker. But would the members of the High Counsel – all men – view that submission from her point of view? It seemed unlikely. Moreover, she did not think she possessed the stomach to watch him hang on her word, not when she suspected he had been almost as much a victim as she of the Winter Lady's poison.

So, where did that leave her? It seemed extremely unlikely that he would be willing to take the binding oath with her, even did she feel capable of swearing such a rigidly unbreakable vow to honour a man she hated. Nor – unless he turned mercenary and sold his sword to the highest bidder – did he have any money of his own to take her elsewhere in the realm, whether he wed her or merely kept her with him in whatever capacity suited him; mistress, drudge, nursemaid to his child.

It occurred to her that if he did adopt the life of a mercenary and kept her with him, he might conceivable want to bed her again, if she were conveniently to hand; a notion that made her feel faintly sick until she had the cheering thought that he was unlikely to remain faithful to... what was it he had said of her... ah yes! *A wench like her with no looks to speak of and witch-red hair to boot.* As a solution to her problem, it had a certain appeal. *She* – and the child he had fathered – would have some measure of security but without the necessity for her to yield her body to de Rogé's brutality more than a few times. *He* could bed with whomsoever he pleased without having to placate a jealous wife or mistress. And best yet, mercenaries were not noted for living into their dotage!

But it would never happen, she acknowledged with a sigh. She did not know much about Ranulf de Rogé – save that he was a wolf by nature, a womaniser by inclination and a warrior by training – but she did not think he was in the least likely to turn his life upside down or break his oath of allegiance to his brother for the sake of a woman he had called both wild-cat and witch. Even if there proved to be a child of that cursed coupling.

Another stabbing pain in her stomach brought her back to her surroundings and waves of relief washed over her, hot and cold by turns. Thank the gods, her flux had come. Her fears had been for nothing. There would be no child and perhaps in a year... or ten... or twenty... she could forget she had ever seen the evidence, let alone felt the searing touch, of Ranulf de Rogé's lust.

Yet, even with this modestly encouraging thought to lift her spirits, by the time Guy finally called a halt, just as grey day was washing into charcoal night, she was so stiff with fatigue that she almost fell from her horse into his arms. And so chilled that she made no protest when he carried her into the dubious shelter of a deserted shepherd's croft set in the lee of a few stunted thorn trees.

# Chapter 5

## *Night at the Shepherd's Hut*

While the soldiers of their escort were tending to the horses at the far end of the long, low croft, Guy set about kindling a fire. Taking the opportunity offered by the men all being occupied indoors, Rowène limped back outside. Not only did she have a desperate need to relieve her bladder, she also wanted to inspect her linens before it was too dark to see.

Later, as she sat huddled by the small but cheerful blaze, finally beginning to feel the blood warming in her toes and fingers once more, she found herself smiling into the flickering red-gold flames. Her flow had not started in earnest but there had definitely been spots of blood on the linen pad. Her grateful thanks to the Gods of Light and Mercy were silent but utterly sincere and in her relief she even considered briefly how she might get word to Ranulf and put him out of his uncertainty. Could she ask Guy to send Geryth back to Chartre? But what reason could she possibly give that would not arouse his suspicions?

She was still wrestling with that problem when her attention was diverted towards the men gathering with rowdy enthusiasm around their own fire. There had been three sheep peaceably grazing near the croft when they arrived and Guy had given orders for one of them to be slaughtered. The choicest parts of the luckless animal were now being cooked – toasted or roasted, Rowène was unsure – to the accompaniment of much merriment from the men, who were clearly looking forward to something other than the eternal oatcakes to eat.

Rowène too was heartily sick of that particular item of what appeared to be the Rogé staple diet but when Guy presently knelt beside her and offered her a piece of mutton – scorched on the outside, raw in the middle – she found that despite her rising spirits she could not quite bring herself to eat it. Something about its appearance, or the smell perhaps, turned her stomach.

Guyard watched without surprise as the young noblewoman's thin features first paled in revulsion, then flushed in embarrassed apology as she looked up to meet his eyes. He shrugged and smiled to show he had taken no offence at her rejection of the food he had brought. Nevertheless he was concerned by her lack of appetite. By his reckoning she had eaten two oatcakes, a handful of dried raisins and a sliver of cheese since dawn and it had been a long and miserable day, both in terms of the weather and the rugged countryside over which they had been riding.

Ignoring the loud grumbling of his own empty belly, he put the lump of meat down in the embers of the fire where it would stay warm – and possibly cook a little more thoroughly – and turned to rummage in his saddle bag. Drawing out a fist-sized hunk of hard yellow cheese, he removed his knife from the meat, wiped it clean on the leg of his breeches, cut a thick slice of cheese and placed it between a couple of crumbling oatcakes.

Raising his brows, he looked a question at his companion. She smiled her thanks for his consideration, causing his heart to miss a beat, and took the cheese and oatcakes from his hand, the involuntary caress of her soft fingertips warming his blood against his will. Unable to look away, he watched her take a bite of the rough repast. Then, knowing from experience how difficult it would be to swallow the dry biscuits unaided, reached for his water flask.

"Here, take a drink," he murmured. "It will go down easier that way." He grinned at her hesitation. "No need to worry about good manners here, Demoiselle. Expediency is more compelling than courtesy in this situation and I shall not care if you drink with your mouth full. Every man here knows how dry stale oatcakes can be. And now, if you do not mind..."

He gestured with his knife towards the now sizzling lump of mutton.

She nodded and reached for the flask, taking a cautious sip, then a larger swallow when she realised it was water. Far from fresh, and thick with the dark tang of peat and leather though it was, it was clearly more palatable than this morning's offering.

"It is only water," he confirmed with a smile, spearing the mutton on the end of his knife. "Not goat's milk."

"Thank the gods for small mercies," she retorted and he thought he had never seen anything so wonderful as her unshadowed smile. Sweet as honey, reckless as a falcon in flight, as bright as a meadow of buttercups in the summer sun... As beguiling as a shooting star and as unconsciously enticing as only a woman who has given her heart to a man can be. At this unexpected thought, his own heart stumbled in his breast.

*Gods above! Surely she does not fancy herself in love with me?*

Not after all that had happened between their two families. Between the two of them!

It was grim enough that he knew himself not indifferent to her... recognised how easily she stirred his desires and heated his blood. But it was just lust on his part. Or so he had told himself earlier this very day. And the day before. And countless days before that. Since the first moment he had seen her in fact. And if he continued telling himself that, it would continue to be true.

He forced himself to take a bite of the tough meat, chewing stolidly. It was not so bad, he thought. Hot at least, although it would have been improved by salt. And for being cooked all the way through. Still, it was better than starving and Rowène had just eaten the last of his oatcakes. It would be foraging and hunting tomorrow, he thought. Not that the men would mind but it would delay them further.

"I beg your pardon?" He swallowed a mostly chewed piece of meat and looked across at his companion.

"I asked," she said, smiling demurely at him and setting sparks of heat skittering down his spine and up his legs to meet at his groin. "Do you yourself drink goat's milk?"

"I would as soon drink goat's piss," he confessed, with a flush for the coarse word he was not swift enough to retract, but she only grinned back at him in such carefree fashion that he could not help but smile with her.

There was, of a sudden, a peace and a companionship between them and he thought that Rowène was as aware of this shift in feeling between them as he. He glanced towards the other fire, wondering if the men were still watching them, but for the most part they appeared at ease and were content to ignore, for the time being at least, their lord's brother and his hostage. This deep within their own home province, the soldiers had removed such items of their gear as they could and, much as Guyard had done the night before, had hung cloaks and tunics alongside the dusty cobwebs on the rafters to dry. Sprawled around the warmth of their fire, five of them were relaxing with knuckle bones or other relatively harmless amusements.

Only Geryth sat slightly apart, regarding Guyard and Rowène with a fixed and frowning stare. Rendered more than slightly uncomfortable by the younger man's glower, Guyard returned his attention to Rowène just in time to catch her yawning.

"You are worn out," he said ruefully. "As are the rest of us."

"It does not show on you. Or them!" she replied, glancing towards the men, and he saw that for once there was no open animosity in her eyes. She lowered her voice. "Is Geryth all right, do you think? He does not seem to be so..." She fumbled for a word. "So at ease as the others. Or even to be a part of their group."

"No. But then he and Finn get on together about as well as a wild-cat and a wolf." He caught her startled look and wondered what there had been in his words to warrant it but did not ask. "It was Ran who sent Finn back to Rogérinac and although I know his reasons for doing so I cannot fathom why he should send Geryth in the same company. Ran knows as well as I that there is likely to be trouble between those two one day."

Perhaps if he had not been watching her closely he would not have seen the shadow deepen in Rowène's clear grey eyes at the mention of his brother's name – a dark flicker of movement like a fish suddenly disturbed at the bottom of a lake, gone almost before it could be glimpsed – but she only said,

"Why did..." She did not appear to be able to speak his brother's name or be willing to acknowledge their kinship. "Why has Finn been sent back to Rogérinac?"

"As punishment," Guyard said simply.

Her slender copper brows drew together in a frown then arched questioningly at him.

"For what?"

"For his attempted rape of that woman at the Swanfleet Bridge, the day..."

"Yes, I remember that day," Rowène interrupted. She had gone rather pale again, he saw, and he cursed his thoughtless tongue for reminding her of those events. Only four days ago, it seemed like another life, another realm. "But why would... he... Ranulf, I mean..." She finally managed to choke out his brother's given name. "Why would he bother to punish one of his men for that? When he is little better than a ravening wolf himself!"

"What nonsense!" Guyard spoke curtly. "Ran is no wolf. Neither does he permit the men under his command to behave in such a way as to merit that description. Finn is lucky to escape with banishment back to Rogérinac; Ran usually has such offenders flogged. Or hanged, in the worst extreme, in accordance with the laws of Mithlondia."

Some sound – it could have been a whispered "Gods" or simply a sigh – slipped past her lips but too quietly for him to be sure and, as suddenly as it had arisen, his flash of temper was gone. Remembering all she had gone through over the past four days, he would not have been surprised had she descended into outright hysterics. Instead, aside from an understandable determination to think no good of any of them, and Ranulf in particular, she had given him no trouble, revealing an underlying thread of steel in the otherwise soft and womanly fabric of her body.

The gods knew, the conditions under which they were travelling were enough to try the hardiest man's endurance, let alone a pampered young noblewoman. Much as he loved his homeland, Guyard would be the first to admit that the unseasonably harsh weather they had been enduring for the past three days had been appalling, even by Rogé standards. But to a girl raised under Kardolandia's brazen blue skies, where the air was burnished by the sun, warmed by caressing breezes and cooled by sweetly splashing fountains, this unending rain must seem like an evil jest perpetrated by the dark daemon who held sway over the frozen depths of Hell. Yet she had uttered little by way of serious complaint and had attempted to eat the unfamiliar and largely indigestible provisions presented to her.

Unwillingly he compared her once again with Mathilde, only to acknowledge wryly that there was no point of similarity between them. If it had been Mathilde who was the hostage... captive... prize of war... call it what you will... every man in the escort party would have been made aware that she was a woman and needed to be treated as if she were made of spun glass.

Not that Guyard was not intensely aware that Rowène was a woman – entirely so in that shocking scarlet mockery of a gown, now revealed as she reached out to the growing warmth of the fire. He doubted the men at the other fire could see anything but he could not quite prevent his eyes from straying nor from remembering the lissome form, the small but perfect white breasts, the slender ankles he had glimpsed and even touched that morning before mounting...

*Enough!* he told himself, shifting in sudden and acute discomfort. He had been sitting cross-legged beside her but realised now that was perhaps not the best of positions; his breeches were growing uncomfortably tight across his groin and, worse still, Rowène had evidently caught his slight movement and was now looking at him, smooth copper brows raised enquiringly while her soft mouth quivered in a secret smile. Almost as if she knew what had caused his condition and was amused by it. But no, he confirmed with a quick look, there was no malice in her eyes and he felt marginally less embarrassed. If no less attracted!

He risked another glance in her direction, watching how the firelight flickered like tiny red-gold flames up and down every fine silk strand of hair that rippled over her br...

No, damn it! He was not going down that path again, his blood was heated enough already! And in the morning, he promised himself, he would find her a comb and get her to do something with that wild, tumbling mass of witch-red hair and then conceal it safely beneath her hood. His blood cooled a little at this reminder of her Faennari forebears and he found himself actually considering the notion that she might be attempting to bind him to her – as her mother had bound his elder brother. If so, he was making it damnably easy for her, forging his own shackles in the dark fires of lust.

It *was* lust, he reiterated yet again, and could only be glad that neither of his brothers were there to witness his weakness. Joffroi would not understand his dilemma and Ranulf would merely be amused that he should be so helpless to deny an emotion he had freely admitted to but rarely acted upon, even in those long gone days before he had met and wed Mathilde. He had never felt at ease visiting brothels – and in fact could number on the fingers of one hand how many times he had done so over the years – and, what is more, Ran knew it.

Yet he wondered what his brother would counsel him to do now. Take Rowène to his bed if she were willing to accept him as her lover? Or slake his lust with one of the whores in the brothel in Sarillac that Ranulf normally patronised when he was at home? Or return to his cold binding bed in the optimistic belief that Mathilde would welcome him there?

But if he could not contemplate breaking his binding vows and becoming an adulterer in truth as well as name for Rowène de Chartreux, neither did he think he could make love to his wife whilst wanting another woman. And absolutely nothing would induce him to lie with a woman he had had to pay to take him into her bed.

*Damn it all to Hell*, he thought as he rose abruptly to his feet.

"I am going outside for a bit," he said out loud and stalked off, willing to wager anything that it was still raining.

It was! But at least the cold rain on his heated flesh brought him some initial sensation of relief. Nor did it take him long to achieve a complete, if momentary, release from the tension that had held him in its unforgiving grip throughout the day.

*This*, he thought grimly, leaning back against the damp stone wall of the croft, and breathing deeply of the cool night air, scented with hawthorn, rain, bracken and sheep dung, *is beginning to become a habit.*

Rowène looked up with a wary smile as Guy walked back through the door, relatively but not entirely certain what had prompted his abrupt departure nor in what frame of mind he might return. She had thought – possibly naively, she supposed – that they had reached an accord, a truce that would allow them to travel together in some amity.

Moreover, released at last from her own bleak mood of despair, she recognised the truth of what he had said to her earlier; that the Guyard de Martine who journeyed with her now as her unwilling gaoler was still the same man who, as Guy of Montfaucon, had served her as both groom and protector and had, in some strange way, become something as close to a friend as was possible in such a situation.

Yes, he had betrayed her but she could now accept that he had had no choice but to do so under the terms of his oath to his brother. Nonetheless he had not hurt her in any way. Nor would he ever, she knew. Neither was he responsible for the deaths of either of her brothers, Lucien in battle, Luc on the rowing bench of a slave galley. Though mayhap Luc was not dead…

She had been distraught at the time but, looking at it more calmly, felt the first tiny, tentative flicker of hope. For all the time Luc had breath and a heart beating in his breast there was the possibility that he might surmount the trials of slavery and escape to a life he might live in freedom and honour. She did not care if he never returned to reclaim the birthright that had been stolen from him, just as long as he was safe. But if he did come back to Mithlondia and managed to avoid the hangman's noose long enough to exact his vengeance on the bodies of the de Rogé brothers, she prayed he would show mercy to Guy at least.

She had little faith in that happening, however, and an uncontrollable shiver ran through her. So real was the image of Guy dying on the point of Luc's blade that it was somewhat disconcerting to hear his voice, light and quiet as normal and totally unmarred by even a hint of the pain-filled groan she could still hear echoing in her mind.

"I think you would be wise to get out of those wet clothes before you catch a chill."

"What?"

She started and blinked away the bloody vision, focussing instead on the pair of light blue eyes barely a foot away, regarding her with growing concern. He had dropped to his heels beside her and just the sight of his face, as familiar to her now as her own – the dark gold stubble on his jaw glinting in the firelight, the underlying etching of good humour visible despite the deeper lines of fatigue and tension – returned her fully to reality.

"I said, you should get out of those wet clothes before you take a chill," he repeated patiently. "You were shivering when I came in and there are no sheepskins here to keep you warm tonight."

"No fleas either," she observed wryly, scratching at a bite on her arm. "And the shiver had nothing to do with my wet clothes," she assured him, certainly not intending to tell him what had really caused it. Instead she continued as pragmatically as she could, "Whilst I would welcome the chance to rid myself of this harlot's rag, I have nothing to wear in its stead. Unless you think there is something here I might use?"

Lifting her brows, she swept an expressive glance round the restricted quarters of the small, stone-walled croft, taking in the men lounging by the other fire, almost silent now as weariness overtook them, the shadowed, cobwebby corners and smoke-blackened rafters now hung with the soldiers' gear like untidy laundry, and the dark space beneath the low roof. Then looked back at him with limpid expectation.

She watched his lips move soundlessly, before he once more turned to delve into the nearby saddle pack. Curbing the urge to be even more overtly sarcastic, she eyed him curiously, wondering what else, besides his harp and the odd oatcake, that capacious leather pouch might hold. She would not have thought that he had had time to pack so thoroughly in the confusion of that last day at Chartre; certainly she had brought nothing away with her, not even the rags and bindings that were so necessary now that her flux was about to start.

Hugging her joyous relief close, as she had done all evening, she kept still, absorbing some quiet pleasure from watching him... the play of muscles in his broad back and shoulders, the way the flickering light tipped each short strand of his dark blond hair with bright gold. She wished she had seen him before his ruthless elder brother had ordered him to cut it so short that now it barely touched his shoulders.

*He has never worn it as long as I do but assuredly it was no shorter than Joffroi's...*

A lightly mocking voice whispered in her mind and she shook it away. Nevertheless she was glad his hair had never been as long as Ranulf's - she had a fleeting memory of a long, rippling fall of coarse pale gold, as pale as moon-bleached barley - and bit her lip until pain ousted memory. She would not think of *him*. Would no longer have to remember what he had done to her. She was free of him. Free of that gut-churning fear that she might still carry something of him inside her. And once more she thanked the gods for their mercy...

"Demoiselle?"

She forced herself to focus once more, staring in silence at the garments he had laid before her, recognising the threadbare linen shirt, faded blue tunic and patched dark green breeches she had become so accustomed to seeing on the big frame of the harper, Guy of Montfaucon. Perhaps it was that juxtaposition of memory and emotion that caused the name by which she had known him then to rise to her tongue.

"Guy?"

Oddly he seemed to know what she was asking, although she was not sure herself. He smiled without the normal trace of shadow in his eyes. She thought he had forgotten they were not alone, that he was bound to another woman, that she...

"Lady Rowena."

He spoke softly, using the name he had called her by in those days before reality intruded. Then his voice changed and she knew he was aware once more of all − or at least some of − the things that lay between them.

"Forgive me, Demoiselle. I..."

Yes, she thought sadly, the awareness was there; in the slightly hoarse note in his voice, in his choked off words, in the way the darkness returned to his eyes, like cloud shadows skimming the sunlit sea, dulling the blue to grey.

His gaze slid towards the men at the other fire, then back again, and the moment was gone. She sighed silently and strove for practicality again.

"I cannot wear your clothes, Messire. In case you had not noticed, I am a woman and you are a man. More than that, you are a very large man and I am... not."

"I am well aware of that fact, Demoiselle. I am also fully aware that my clothes stink of horse and sweat but I can do nothing to change either the size or the smell. They are, however, dryer than your own garments and that is the important thing here."

She eyed his own damp clothing speculatively.

"I am sure it is but does not your advice apply equally to you, Messire? No, I think I had much better stay as I am and let you change out of those wet things. After all, if I catch a chill, nothing much will happen except that Black Joffroi will be deprived of his hostage. On the other hand, if you catch a chill, who is going to get us down off these god-forsaken moors?"

"I am in no danger of catching a chill," he retorted, evidently unconvinced by her reasoning. "You forget that I am more accustomed to these conditions than you are and, unlike you, I have never known anything else."

"Spending ten years in Kardolandia does not mean I am utterly feeble," Rowène exclaimed in some disgust. "And you are confusing me with Ju when you worry about my health. She is the one Queen Xandra called her white lily, because she was always so pale and bruised so easily. She is the one who does not travel well. She even felt sick sailing back up the coast from Kaerellios to Chartre, when the sea was as calm as the river at Swanfleet!" She looked at him steadily. "On the other hand, I know the Queen once told one of her other ladies that I was as tough as a kylinia vine."

"I do not know what that is," he said. "But even so, you *will* change into dry clothes and you *will* be warm again."

There was not the slightest hint in his face that he would yield to whatever arguments she might put forward, so in the end Rowène simply nodded and reached for the garments. It was only as she took them that his mouth lifted in that gently humorous smile she loved and his blue eyes lightened with rueful laughter.

"The Queen was wrong. Oh, not about your sister perhaps, although I cannot be sure – I have not spent so much time in her company as I have in yours. But you... No, not a vine, although I do not doubt you have the power to bind a man to you, heart and soul, so tightly he could never escape, if such were your wish."

She was not sure whether to be offended by that assessment or not but did know that she would have been more flattered had he chosen to liken her to something else – almost anything would be preferable to being thought as tough and *useful* as the ubiquitous Kardolandian vines!

"So what, if not a kylinia... or, I suppose, ivy would be the nearest equivalent in Mithlondia?" she asked.

"Something tough. Something a little sharp perhaps?"

He was grinning now, she saw, permitting himself to enjoy the tentative friendship that had once existed between them, in spite of the apparent social chasm between a low-born harper and a high-born lady. Other shadows lay between them now, of course. Not so much the illegitimacy of his birth but more the name and blood of the man who had sired him. That and the seemingly unbreakable bonds that tied him to his half-brothers; the two men who, between them, had wrought death and destruction in almost every aspect of her life and that of her siblings.

Nonetheless, she sensed that between her and Guyard de Martine there existed some small warmth of feeling, some measure of wary trust. And if there could be nothing more than that between them – and she was not sure she could ever permit any man, even Guy, closer after her recent experiences – then she would be content with that.

She saw that he was looking at her, perhaps wondering at her silence, and rallied her wandering wits sufficiently to say,

"Something tough but sharp? What were you thinking of? A thistle perhaps?"

"No, for thistles I can walk upon and squash."

"A nettle then?" she grinned back at him. "They have a sharp sting."

"Not when the castle cook has boiled them down into soup!"

"Ugh!" She pulled a face, not sure whether he spoke in jest or not. "Truly, you eat nettle soup at Rogérinac? What sort of place is it that you are taking me to?"

"My home, Demoiselle, you know that. As to the soup... well, you will have to wait until we get to Rogérinac. But as to your likeness..? Wait here."

He broke off, stood up and walked away without another word, leaving her staring after him. He left the croft momentarily, returning to toss something into her lap. Looking down she saw it was a small, slender twig, its bark dark and slick with rain, each tiny branch bearing a delicate crown of pale petals and, beneath and almost hidden, some very sharp thorns.

"Oh!" She could think of nothing else to say and, in any event, Guy did not seem to need a response.

Walking over to the other fire, he spoke to the men, pleasantly but in a manner that did not brook argument, ordering them to wait outside until called. Somewhat to her surprise, in view of the prospect of a renewed soaking, they rose to their feet immediately, amiably enough, although one of them made some remark under his breath – likely lascivious to judge from his tone – which Guy silenced with a flat look that promised retribution if the man persisted. The soldier – she thought it might have been the one called Finn; the one Ranulf had sent back to Rogérinac in lieu of flogging – gave her an unfriendly look but otherwise kept his mouth shut as he stumped off out into the dark wet of the night, closely followed by Geryth and the others.

Guy followed them to the door, closing it after them, but kept his back towards her. Always the honourable gentleman, she thought with wry amusement as she attempted to reach the lacing on the back of her gown. To no avail, of course, Ilana having tied her up tighter than a chicken ready for the spit. Not knowing whether to be irritated or embarrassed, she addressed his back.

"I am sorry, Messire, but you are going to have to help me."

"Are you sure?" he asked, glancing over his shoulder at her. "The last time you let me near your laces I proved myself a most unhandy lady's maid."

"As if I would care if you did tear this gown," Rowène retorted with subdued violence. "I hate everything about it and would be glad never to see it again."

He hesitated a moment longer, before muttering something under his breath and striding back to her. Despite his deprecating words regarding his lack of skill, it took him less than five heartbeats to undo the knot, whereupon he did not linger but resumed his post at the door.

Quickly, for despite the fire and the combined warmth from both men and horses, the air still shivered with unpleasant clamminess against her skin, Rowène peeled the damp gown from her body and quickly pulled on the loose – exceedingly loose – linen shirt and blue tunic, the former falling somewhere in the region of her knees and the latter even lower, rendering the necessity to don a man's breeches almost superfluous. If she had been ten years younger and a peasant lass instead of a nobleman's daughter, it might have been acceptable if not respectable. Or serving as one of Queen Xandra's companions; her court clothes being considerably less concealing than her present attire.

She was not, however, either a peasant or a Kardolandian courtier. As she was well aware, she was in Mithlondia now and she did not much fancy Ranulf's rough soldiers staring at her legs. It was bad enough that their commander had seen them... stood between them. Indeed she still bore the dark purple bruises on her thigh where his fingers had gripped...

She set her jaw, refusing to give way to emotion, and forced the memory away. It did not matter now, she told herself resolutely. The bruises would fade – were already fading, she had noticed, the purple turning to green and yellow – and when they had finally disappeared, Ranulf de Rogé would likewise be gone from her life! Her flux would come, if it had not already started, and then she need never see nor communicate with him ever again.

His half-brother, however, was another matter...

"You can turn around now," she murmured. "I am quite decent, though I will need something to keep the breeches up."

He turned. Slowly, as if he feared she might not have been entirely truthful. Then the wariness in his light blue eyes was abruptly gone, to be replaced by open amusement – she did, she supposed, look rather bizarre; so much for her reputation as an enchantress!

"Save for the colour of your hair, you look rather like a ten-year-old boy wearing his elder brother's gear and trying to convince his father he is grown enough to ride out with the men of the garrison."

She cocked her head at him, wondering if he spoke of himself. Or...

*No!* She would not think of *him!*

Clenching her fingers in the cloth of the tunic, she found her attention drawn to the frayed and faded threads of embroidery she had noticed before but never really studied. There was not much left, a few shreds of yellow and black but nothing, thank the gods, to suggest the de Rogé device. Neither had she taken much notice of the small gold motifs on the leaf-green tunic her mother had sewn for him and which he was still wearing, despite its rather disreputable appearance but now, curiosity aroused, she looked more closely. They looked like...

"Oak leaves?" she asked doubtfully. "But why in the name of the gods would my mother embroider oak leaves on your tunic?"

Brows raised, he said dryly,

"Surely you understand the significance of that? Or do you mean to tell me you no longer recognise the devices of your own countrymen?"

"Oh, I can recognise the black boar of Rogé well enough," she retorted. Then waved one hand in mute apology. "Chartreux's silver swan, of course. The white horse of the princes of Mithlondia. But apart from that, no, I am afraid I have forgotten. Those ten years in Kardolandia... Oh, Guy! It was too long an exile for a child. I tried to remember everything... our language... our songs and tales. But banners were just so many pretty colours to me and once I was home..." She paused, shrugged and smiled shyly at him. "I had other things to think about." Then when he did not respond as she had hoped, continued more seriously. "So, tell me about the oak leaves?"

Guyard shrugged.

"It is simple enough. Armand de Martine's device is a golden oak tree, hence the oak leaves." He gave her a small, rather bitter smile. "Mathilde embroidered them on that tunic you are wearing in the early days of our binding, when there was still the money to waste on such fripperies. And now, your mother has done the same, except she used gold thread, the gods only know why when she openly despises me."

Rowène glanced again at his tunic but the green cloth was so smeared with mud, and other things she preferred not to think about, that the embroidered borders were barely visible. Nevertheless, she thought she could see another colour alongside the gold.

"Not just oak leaves," she commented darkly. "Surely I can see black boar as well?"

He did not look at his tunic, merely said wryly,

"Not black boar, Demoiselle, merely a bar sinister, the significance of which I am sure you must understand."

She eyed the device emblazoned on the pennant fastened to the spear standing against the wall nearby but said no more. Despite her time in Kardolandia, she understood well enough what he was saying; that although the black boar was his father's device he had no more right to use it than he did the de Rogé name.

"Yes," she said quietly. "I understand."

"I thought you would." He gave her the merest flicker of a smile. "Very well then, Demoiselle, if you are ready I will call the men back in. Then, if you wish to... er... have a moment in private outside, that would be the time to go. In the meantime I will find you a belt of some sort and make up a bed for you. It will only be a couple of saddle rugs but better than the floor."

"Much better and I will take you up on your suggestion. And... I do thank you... Guy." She spoke uncertainly, wishing to cover her unthinking lapse, truly sorry that she had ever mentioned the oak leaves, since she had not meant to throw his illegitimate birth in his face yet again.

*Why,* she wondered as she hastened outside, *do I always seem to say the wrong thing?*

Not just to Guy, but to his half-brother as well.

# Chapter 6

## *The High Moors*

They left the shepherd's hut early the following morning and after a reasonable night's sleep, curled back to back with Guyard de Martine beneath the covering of two rather smelly and tattered saddle blankets, Rowène was wooed into a spirit of mild optimism. This had its source, not only in the fact that the drenching rain had lifted into the very lightest of drizzles, but in the fresh spots of blood that stained her linens.

And when, a little after sunrise, the drizzle drifted away completely, leaving a clear, sparkling summer's morning, Rowène felt almost as if her soul could break free of her body and soar high in the endless blue of the sky, to mate with the wild spirit of the falcon whose lonely cry she could hear but not quite see.

Ahead of her loomed what she supposed must be the High Moors, although to her eyes they appeared more like mountains; great, almost sheer-sided slopes, clothed in the green of grass and heather and bracken and the darker shades of pine. Looking back over her shoulder, she saw that the distant west was still washed with grey, but where the sun shimmered against the rain arched the most brilliant and delicate illusion she had ever seen; its colours so soft yet so clear as to seem both real and unreal. A perfect bridge between the mortal world and the fey lands beyond, a bridge built not of stone but of multi-coloured light. A bridge between the past and the future.

A past that had witnessed her forced coupling with a man she hated and a future where she would be free of all fear that there would be anything, save the merest wisp of fading memory, to bind them together.

"Are you all right?"

Guy's low-voiced query brought her firmly back to the present and she turned to face him with a smile that contained all her joyous wonder at the beauty now revealed around her, all the gaiety of her youth and the unshadowed warmth of her feelings for him. A smile so glorious that she saw him blink in amazement before he smiled back at her.

"Yes, I can see that you are," he answered his own question. Then lifted his free hand and gestured about him. "Look! I told you Rogé was not all grey rain and bedraggled sheep. It has a wild beauty of its own."

*As do you*, his eyes seemed to say, although his lips did not speak the words.

Nor should she expect him to, bound to another woman as he was. She looked away, suddenly depressed again, and it was in that moment that she heard another voice speaking in her head; a low voice, heavy with desire and reckless in its urgency, *Ah! Rowène, so sweet... Gods, you will never know how much I want you.*

"No!" she said fiercely, not realising she had spoken aloud until she heard Guy saying in some bewilderment.

"I beg your pardon?"

She forced a smile and recollected herself.

"Forgive me, I did not mean this..." She gestured around her. "This unexpected beauty of moor and sky. It was... something else."

"Something you do not wish to tell me about?" he replied, although it was less a question than a statement.

"Something I *cannot* tell you about," she answered. Then, as she saw the flicker of suspicion in his light blue eyes, she added hurriedly, "Women's matters, Messire."

As she had known he would, he immediately halted that line of conversation, instead saying with some exasperation.

"Oh, to Hell with formality until we reach Rogérinac. I wish you would call me Guy, as you used to."

She smiled at him, a little mischievously, mentally banishing his hell-spawned half-brother to the past where he belonged.

"Only if you call me by my given name, as *you* used to."

"Rowena or Rowène?" he asked, lifting an enquiring brow.

"I suppose it had better be Rowène," she sighed. "I can never be Rowena again, however much I might wish it." Then, before he could say anything else, exclaimed, "Oh! How lovely. I have never seen its like before."

For as the track bent around the side of the hill, they emerged into a long, steep-sided valley, at the bottom of which, almost at their feet, lay a sinuous strip of silvery water about a furlong in width, the end of which could not been seen, disappearing as it did around the curve of the next green hillside perhaps half a league away.

"Lac Linne, or Lach Linny as the locals would say. It is probably the largest of the waters of the High Moors but you will pass by at least two others before we reach Silverleigh."

"How long is it?" she asked absently, still amazed by its unexpected beauty; the unruffled serenity of its surface that reflected so imperfectly the colour of the sky, being a far darker and deeper blue, almost indigo.

It was quite different from either the pellucid blue waves that lapped the white sands of Kaerellios or the glinting, green-bordered waters of the Liriél. It was a shade, she thought on a fleeting flash of memory, most nearly the colour of Ranulf de Rogé's dark blue eyes!

She waited for, but for the first time did not feel, the nauseous dread she had been accustomed to suffer whenever she thought of the man. But why did she not? Perhaps it was because he was so many leagues away now that she could no longer feel any trace of his presence. Or perhaps it was that, looking around at the wild moors over which he must have hunted many times... looking into the indigo depths of Lac Linne, she had realised that she need never fear seeing his eyes looking out at her from the face of her own child. She was free of him and he could go to Hell in whatever way he chose. While she...

Well, she was determined to enjoy whatever span of time, no matter how short, the gods might care to allot her with his half-brother. A man whose eyes, she saw as she smiled back at him, were the same warm and wonderful blue as the sky that sheltered them both.

Thankful for the improvement in the weather, Guyard pressed on more swiftly, heading steadily eastwards alongside Lac Linne. They halted at mid-day and found enough driftwood on the lake shore to start a fire, then shared a meal of oat stir-about and fish, difficult to eat without burning tongue and fingers but a welcome change in fare all the same, the soldier who had been lucky enough to catch them being the recipient of much boisterous ribbing from his fellows and a spectacularly sweet smile from the Lady Rowena that caused him to colour to his ears and hastily retreat from her vicinity.

But it was remarkable, Guyard thought, how everyone's spirits had been lifted by the sunshine, even Geryth coming out of his extended fit of the sullens until a typically coarse remark from Finn regarding the lad's sister had caused a reversal in his short-lived bout of good humour. Had they not all been mounted by that time, Guyard would not have been surprised if Geryth had gone for the other man with his fists. But if not today, then one day very soon, violence was going to erupt between those two. In the meantime all any of them could do was enjoy the fine weather while it lasted.

Which was not long at all. Indeed by the time they left the lakeside in early afternoon, the washed sheep's-wool clouds were already turning a more natural shade of dirty grey and the sunshine was becoming sporadic to say the least. By mid afternoon it had disappeared completely, being replaced by a fine misty drizzle that penetrated clothing and defied vision.

In spite of this, they had little choice but to continue and at least the track was plain before them, leading as it did alongside the gently lapping shores of the lake, this being now as grey as the rain splashing into it and it was getting damnably difficult, Guyard thought irritably, to tell one from the other.

They stopped for the night in the pine woods that clothed the hills between Lac Linne and Lac Dimérac – or as the taciturn moor folk called it, if they spoke of it at all, Lach Dim. And then it was usually only to frighten their children, by telling them that the Daemon of Hell would rise up out of the pool and grab them if they did not behave! But it was not just among the credulous peasants or their children that it had earned such a terrible reputation. Despite having hunted over every foot of these moors in years past, neither Guyard nor Ranulf would camp within sight of the unnaturally still, darkly unruffled waters of the pine-shadowed mere. It might not be the Daemon's drowning pool as local legend whispered but it was sufficiently unnerving for all that to stand on its shores in bright sunlight and see not a glimmer of gold reflected anywhere upon its malevolent sable surface.

Clearly as affected by the atmosphere – and the legend – as Guyard himself, the men were noticeably quiet and subdued, both in camp that night and during the early part of the following day, uttering neither jest nor jibe as they passed beneath the dark green branches of larch and pine, their horses treading almost soundlessly over the thick layer of fallen needles, the chink of bridle bits loud by comparison.

As for Rowène, she had not appeared to sleep at all, tossing and turning with a restlessness that had only eased when Guyard had, with a great deal of resignation and a certain measure of guilty pleasure, taken her into the circle of his arms. Then the situation had been reversed! She had settled into a deep and apparently untroubled sleep and he had slept only fitfully before finally awakening in the damp dawn in a state of aching arousal.

Neither she nor the men had found much to say over the morning meal of oatmeal stir-about and raisins and to a man – or woman – had been openly eager to break camp and get away from the silent woods, even though the trees themselves provided some shelter from the rain.

The men knew all about the reputation of the pool, of course, but Guyard was disquieted to observe how oppressively the heavy, clinging mist and dark, dripping pines seemed to weigh on Rowène's spirits. Her grey eyes were dark with shadows and her face showed him emotions he did not think were entirely due to the dank weather or the lowering trees. Could she sense the looming menace of the dark mere? She was – if the colour of her hair told truth – of the blood of the Faennari and he was beginning to fear she had inherited something of their power too. Or was it something else? Something more mundane and mortal?

Breaking the silence that bound them all – men, horses and hostage – in a complicity of unspoken dread, he said quietly,

"Are you all right?"

She looked across at him, her eyes pools of fey glimmering grey, her long lashes dark copper spikes against her pale, rain-wet skin.

"All right? No. I... Guy, I do not like this place. It feels..." She glanced around her at the close ranks of the tall trees, their dark green figures clothed in ragged raiment woven of ancient mist. Harper though he was, he did not much care for that thought. Or Rowène's answer. "*Wrong* somehow." She shivered and, as if seeking protection – either from the mist or her thoughts – drew her cloak more closely about her, the silver brooch on her shoulder catching his eye and causing his unease to grow.

"Is that all?" he queried, his dissatisfaction both with her response and her continued wearing of Ranulf's gear, making his tone sharper than he had intended. "You are not feeling unwell?"

If anything, he thought, she went even paler at that, although she shook her head in denial.

"No. I am well enough." Then, with a perceptible effort, she released her convulsive grip on the mist-silvered black cloak and peered nervously off through the trees to their right. "Where are we, do you know?"

"Of course I know." Guyard managed a crooked smile. "Surely you do not think I have managed to lose us all in the mist?" Then, when she merely blinked at him, added reluctantly. "The locals call this place the Dim Wood and over there, a little to the south, lies Lac Dimérac. It is... a strange place, I will admit. But we pass no closer to it than we are now."

"And thank the God of Light for that," she murmured. "I never thought to say this but I think I shall actually be glad to see Rogérinac. At least – or so I assume – your family's stronghold comprises four or more solid walls, a roof that does not leak, a bed with proper linens and a kitchen that produces something other than oatcakes, burnt fish and raw meat."

Guyard winced inwardly at her optimism but said nothing to disabuse her of such odd notions.


Once away from the eerie woods around Lac Dimérac, the whole troop, Guyard included, breathed a collective sigh of relief and by mid-day the men's spirits at least had been somewhat restored despite the continued poor weather. There had been no sign of the sun's chariot today but about a furlong beyond Dimmerleigh the mist had turned to rain which, although unrelenting, was not particularly heavy and made sight of the track and the rocky-stepped slopes to either side possible.

That had been earlier, however. Now it was scarcely possible to see a dozen paces in any direction and the stunted thorn and rowan trees that leaned precariously over the muddy track were hung with shreds of the same white mist that blanketed the distance from view or clung to mail, cloth and any exposed flesh. Looking down at his bare forearm, Guyard could – if he had wanted to waste his time in such a fashion – have counted the individual droplets that clung to each fair hair and he felt the chill seep through his skin into the very bones beneath. Uncomfortable though such a sensation was, having lived all his life in Rogé's frequently inhospitable climate, it was one he was accustomed to. Rowène, on the other hand...

As he had done with increasing frequency as the morning wore on, he glanced towards the young woman riding beside him and was dismayed to see that, even though they had left the maleficent environment of Lac Dimérac, her face was still unnaturally pale, all colour gone even from her rose-petal lips, her grey eyes regarding him with a stark lack of expression that frankly terrified him.

She was shivering too, despite the fact that she was wearing all his own spare clothing as well as his brother's mantle.

Pitching his voice so that it would carry no further than her ears, he spoke her name but she gave no sign of having heard him and he could detect not the slightest flicker of awareness to ameliorate the terrible emptiness behind her eyes.

His anxiety growing with every furlong, Guyard kept his small troop moving for another league, keeping an unobtrusive but ceaseless watch on the young noblewoman until finally, seeing her sway in the saddle, he manoeuvred his mount into a position level with the mare. Reaching out, he wrapped an arm around her waist and dragged her onto his own saddle where he could keep her from falling if she lost consciousness. Settling her firmly into the crook of his bridle arm and cradling her close against his chest – he would give her what little warmth his body yet retained – he eased Fireflame forwards again, gesturing to Geryth to take charge of the mare.

Even as they continued to traverse the high, barren plateau, Guyard was considering with an uncharacteristically profane desperation where, and how soon, they might find shelter for the coming night. Preferably something more substantial than the dripping pine woods of the previous night or the deserted shepherd's hovel of the night before that and he cursed again the unseasonable weather that had caused the Tawne to burst its banks.

If it had not been for that circumstance they could, once they had passed the marshes, have travelled with relative ease and moderate comfort along the coast where all the larger settlements were situated, including the town of Sarillac; modest in size and wealth by comparison with Chartre but where he was assured of a welcome from his and Ran's old nurse.

Instead, he was stuck on the High Moors – deserted save for the magnificent red deer and the odd solitary hawk – in some of the poorest weather he could ever remember experiencing, together with six grumbling men-at-arms and a gently-bred noblewoman whom he very much feared was on the brink of falling ill, if she had not already succumbed. All it needed now was for one of the horses to go lame or his wounds – to which he had scarcely paid any attention since leaving Chartre – to start festering…

Two days later Guyard was seriously worried indeed.

None of the horses had gone lame, Finn had not succeeded in provoking Geryth into a murderous rage, they had passed the lach at Archenlay in an unexpected but nevertheless extremely welcome spatter of sunshine and, having reached the loneliest and loftiest point of the High Moors, were now descending steadily towards the lower, more civilised lands of eastern Rogé.

Nor, when Guyard had finally found the opportunity to check them, had his wounds festered from lack of care. Indeed he had been surprised, considering the reckless neglect with which he had been treating them, to find them healing well.

Too well, he thought with a shudder, remembering that although it had been Rowène who had initially tended his wounds in the aftermath of the fighting, it had been her mother who, at Joffroi's request, had finally washed, anointed and bound the deep gashes in forearm and thigh. Was it by the bewitchments of the Faennari that his wounds had healed so quickly? He did not know but resolved once they reached Silverleigh to get them looked at by one of the Sisters of Mercy.

But that was not the most pressing of his reasons for wishing to reach Silverleigh soon. Glancing down for perhaps the thousandth time, he scanned the drawn face and blank eyes of the young noblewoman he was once more carrying before him on his saddle. She had, to his certain knowledge, neither spoken nor eaten in the past two days and had left his side only when directed to, in order that both he and she might attend to their personal needs. Otherwise they had not been separated. By night he had slept with her in his arms, sharing blankets and body heat, while by day he held her in the crook of his bridle arm as they rode.

Without exception, the men were all convinced that they lay together as lovers. Guyard had heard them discussing his uncharacteristic behaviour amongst themselves but had ignored it since he did not think they had meant their crude comments for his ears. Under other circumstances, he might have taken issue with their belief that he had finally broken his binding vows and taken a traitor's daughter to his bed, making the Lady Rowena de Chartreux his leman. But he had held his tongue. The men would believe what they wished, regardless of anything he might say, and although he knew such false aspersions would inevitably come to his wife's ears, for the moment he could not find it in him to care. He was far too anxious over Rowène's health to worry about the damage to her reputation. Or his own. And it was for her sake, rather than his, that he wished to reach Silverleigh without further delay.

It was late in the afternoon when, dimly through the cool, bracken-scented mist, Guyard thought he heard a fragile, shimmering sound. He shook his head, more than half convinced he had imagined it but looking around, he found that Geryth had come up level with him, a slight grin – the first for days – on his mud-splattered face.

"'Tis all right, Master Guy, I can hear it too."

"The bells of Silverleigh, do you think?"

"Must be. 'Tis only the Grey Sisters as hang bells outside their gate. Let's hope they don't recognise ye, sir, an' ye was thinkin' of askin' their help fer the Lady Rowena."

The lad aimed a pointed look at the young noblewoman in Guyard's arms and he nodded without replying. He did not need to, Geryth knew as well as he did the situation they were riding into.

Sworn to live peaceably and give aid to any who asked, there yet existed a considerable depth of ill will between the Sisters of Mercy who struggled to maintain their presence at Silverleigh and the Lord of Rogé whose land their settlement was situated upon. Forbidden by Mithlondian law from having the women forcibly removed by his soldiers, Joffroi had been obliged to allow them to remain but had taken his revenge by harassing the Sisters in any way that occurred to him and demanding from them payment of a tithe far in excess of anything that might be deemed reasonable.

This dispute was now of several bitter years standing and Guyard could only hope that the Sisters would not refuse to honour the terms of their oath of healing simply because the man who came to their gate as a supplicant was Black Joffroi's brother. Grimacing at this thought, he glanced down at the girl in his arms and knew that the choice had been taken out of his hands and that he must beg, on bended knee if necessary, the Sisters' goodwill for a woman in distress, even one who was – temporarily and unwillingly – a member of the hated Lord of Rogé's household.

Indeed her condition appeared to have worsened, he thought, even in the score of heartbeats since he had last checked. She was now slumped against his chest, eyes closed, a vivid and unhealthy flush colouring her previously pale cheeks. Awkwardly he raised a hand, tugging off his glove with his teeth, so as to be able to gauge the temperature of her heated cheek and forehead. And felt an icicle of fear pierce his heart. Not only was she soaked to the skin and chilled by the latest drenching shower of rain, she was also burning with a fever and, to judge by the cleft between her coppery brows, tormented in some other way he could not fathom.

Again he heard the distant chiming and spared a moment to address a silent prayer of thanks to the God of Light for giving him this chance to redeem himself. Silverleigh's Sisters of Mercy, reluctant though they might be, were the only source of help or shelter he was likely to find before dark. There was a village, with a tavern of sorts, about a league further down in the valley, where he and the men could rest for the night. As long as the Grey Sisters agreed to succour Rowène, he and the others could fend for themselves.

Nudging Fireflame with his spurs and following the sound of the bells, Guyard left the track that descended to Blackoakleas, guiding the stallion along another, less well-used trail that wound through sprawling heather, low-growing bilberry bushes and scattered birch trees until, with a suddenness that caught him by surprise – on his quarterly visits to Silverleigh he normally rode straight from Rogérinac and thus approached from the east – they came upon a dry-stone wall and in it a wooden gate that Guyard personally considered would prove little hindrance to any predatory animal, let alone the two-legged wolves who obeyed the Lord of Rogé's orders.

As if in direct contradiction to such grim thoughts, the rapidly strengthening wind brought him the same delicate ringing and chiming that had guided him here and, glancing at the white birch that stood beside the gate in solitary and slender grace, he found the source of that distinctive sound; amidst the gently fluttering green leaves hung a multitude of tiny bronze bells.

# Chapter 7

## *Secrets Shared at Silverleigh*

Guyard regarded the bells in grim silence for a moment then reined to a halt. He looked over his shoulder and, catching Geryth's eye, nodded meaningfully at the gate. The young soldier hesitated, appeared to steel himself and then dismounted. Walking up to the gate he pounded on the rough timbers with the butt of his spear and when this produced no perceptible response, raised his voice in a shout loud enough to raise the dead, let alone a community of peace-loving women.

Finally, after what seemed an interminable wait, the gate was pulled open and a small figure swathed in a simple, pale grey robe, face framed by the distinctive white headrail of the Sisters of Mercy, came to stand on the threshold. She said nothing, either in greeting or question, but Guyard could see her eyes – blue as cornflowers and utterly lacking in welcome – travelling from the faces of the bedraggled but nevertheless well-armed troopers at his back, touching momentarily on the pennant dangling damply from the now upright spear, pausing for slightly longer on the huddled form of the nearly unconscious girl in his arms before finally rising to meet his own impatient gaze.

Only then did she speak, her voice low and, in other circumstances, would probably have been quite musical. Now however it was merely cold, with an underlying note of strain; no question then that she had failed to recognise the device on the pennant, or possibly his own features, although he was very sure that he had never seen *her* before this day. Certainly she was not the Eldest with whom he had dealt regularly – and with increasing acrimony – over the past few years.

"You called?"

Her common speech was very slightly tinged with an accent Guyard did not recognise. Nor could he help but suspect that the lack on any honorific – even a blandly impersonal "master" or "good sir" – to be a deliberate omission. "Have you perchance lost your way on the moors and require direction? I must tell you that you are a long way from the comforts of Rogérinac if that, judging by your appearance, be your destination!"

The biting tone of this final remark left him in no doubt that she was aware of his identity – or, if not his exact relationship to Black Joffroi, that he was at least a part of the Lord of Rogé's household – and despite himself, Guyard found the low voice with its faintly ironical undertone more than a little disconcerting.

However he was in no mood to be put aside, and in a courteous but firm voice he replied,

"Yes, I did call. I have need of shelter and the aid of someone skilled in healing for my... the young woman who travels with me. Perhaps, Sister, if you would permit me to speak to the Eldest this matter can be settled without further delay?"

"The Eldest is currently in Lamortaine, bringing a charge of unlawful abuse against the Lord of Rogé, his garrison commander and his steward, if that information be of any interest to you," the woman replied, her tone still cold and apparently not in the least intimidated by the presence of seven armed and ruthless men at the gate of a defenceless community of healers.

"Not at the moment, no," Guyard replied tersely. "I have made known to you my plea and it is one which I do not believe you can refuse to grant, no matter your opinion of me personally, Sister..?"

Ignoring his invitation to name herself, she merely looked at him as if he had just crawled out of a slimy pond and continued in that same cool, faintly disdainful, voice.

"So, who is this young woman and how does she come to be in your company and thus need our aid?"

"Her name, if you must have it, is Rowena," Guyard replied, increasingly impatient with these questions but sensing that if he did not answer them, any hope that he had of gaining the healer's cooperation would be lost. Steward of Rogé though he was, his position would avail him nothing in this place, more especially if what she had just said about the Eldest was true. "She is in the unfortunate position of having lost her home and almost all her kin a se'ennight ago and has been travelling with me, and under my protection, since."

"And what ails her, apart from such prolonged contact with a pack of Black Joffroi's wolves?"

He opened his mouth but she gave him no chance to speak.

"Just tell me this, has she been physically abused either by you or them?"

*Gods above,* he thought in astonishment and growing anger, *does the woman have no fear?*

Of him? Or the "wolves" at his back? Or the violent-tempered lord whose device they all rode under?

"She is suffering from grief and five days of this unseasonable weather," he snapped. "Nothing more. Certainly she has not been raped, if that is what you are implying, Sister! Neither by me nor any of my brother's men!"

"I ask your pardon but it was an understandable assumption," the healer replied imperturbably, her penetrating blue gaze once more levelled at the armed and mounted men at his back.

It was at this moment that Guyard felt a movement from the girl in his arms, almost as if she knew herself to be under discussion. Her head moved restlessly against his shoulder, dislodging the black hood that had formerly concealed her

415

hair. Guyard saw the healer's blue eyes glance up and widen in shock. Wet and bedraggled though Rowène's hair was, the long, loose lengths much tangled by travel, its wild flame subdued, the colour was undeniable. And to those of a superstitious disposition…

"What did you say her name was?" the obviously shaken healer demanded.

"As I have already told you, Sister," Guyard replied with a touch of impatient hauteur; now, if ever, was the time to make use of his position and lineage. "Her name is Rowena. Now are you going to fulfil your vows and help her? Because if not, you will surely be at fault since, whatever you may think of me or my brothers – and yes, I am who you think I am – *she* has done nothing to deserve your distrust and enmity."

"Very well." The healer lowered her eyes and tucked trembling hands in the wide sleeves of her robe. "You may bring her within." Her blue eyes flashed a warning. "Just you, mind! And only for as long as it takes you to settle…" Guyard thought she hesitated but the pause was so infinitesimal he might merely have imagined it. "Mistress Rowena. Then you must leave." She regarded him steadily before finally adding in steely tones. "*Sir.*"

"I am quite well aware of the terms under which the Grey Sisterhood lives and provides aid," Guyard answered, his tone still curt. "The men and I will ride on to Blackoakleas and trouble you no more. But mark this well, I will return every day for tidings of La… of Mistress Rowena." Turning to the men he raised his voice slightly. "Wait for me here. I will not be long." And to the silently watching healer. "Well, *Sister?*"

At his reminder of her calling her whole face seemed to change before his eyes, settling out of its very visible, if unspoken antipathy, into a hard-won mask of serenity.

"If you come with peace in your heart, enter now and be rested."

The formal words of invitation given, the Sister of Mercy stepped back from the gateway, allowing Guyard to ride inside, whereupon the gate closed behind him and other silent, grey-robed figures emerged from the circle of huts. One laid a hand on the bridle of his horse and somewhat awkwardly, Guyard dismounted, the feverish girl held securely in his arms. Refusing the unspoken offer of assistance, he took a firmer grip on his burden and followed his guide across the small open space towards a round, stone-built hut, ducking under the low heather-thatched roof into a fire-lit warmth that smelt of wood smoke and lavender and other herbs he could not identify.

"Lay her down on the bed," commanded the nameless healer.

Guyard obeyed, his fingers brushing rough but clean woollen blankets and wind-crisped linen sheets.

"You may safely leave Mistress Rowena with us and return to your men," she informed him coolly. Adding with that faint trace of irony he had detected before, "You have asked for our help, so you must trust us now to do our work. I will speak with you again tomorrow, if you care to return then."

"Indeed I will," Guyard replied crisply. "Tomorrow, at noon and every day thereafter until Mistress Rowena is fit to be released into my guardianship once more. And Sister, I warn you, the consequences if she is no longer here when that day comes are likely to be unpleasant for all concerned. You obviously know who I am, so you will know I do not speak idly."

A hint of a frown creased her smooth brow and her blue eyes regarded him thoughtfully.

"Despite your gibe earlier, I do not know you, sir." Her voice hardened slightly. "But I would suggest that threatening me is not in your best interest, whoever you may be!"

"I am Guyard de Martine, Lord Joffroi's..."

"Brother," she interrupted him, comprehension darkening her eyes, her tone hardening still further while her nostrils flared as if she smelt something foul.

"That is true, Sister," Guyard agreed, stung a little but holding onto his temper. "But had you allowed me to finish, I was going to say that I am Lord Joffroi's steward. Nor was I threatening anyone. I was merely attempting to assure the safety not only of the young woman in my charge but of all the healers here, you included. Now, good Sister, I will relieve you of my presence and trust that when I speak with you next you will have better tidings for me regarding Mistress Rowena's health."

"We will care for the young woman as diligently as if she were our own kinswoman," the healer replied firmly. "I can promise you no more than that, were you..." Her voice shook slightly, then steadied. "The Prince of Mithlondia himself. Now fare you well, Sir Guyard, Sister Emina will see you out."

Accepting his dismissal with the best grace he could muster Guyard made the customary gesture of respect, hand to heart, and ducked back out of the hut, although not without a final glance back at the girl lying on the low bed, still clad in his brother's mud-stained mantle and his own worn tunic and breeches. He wondered briefly what the disapproving healer – he still did not know her name, damn it, and was not about to risk another rebuttal by asking a second time – would make of her patient's unusual mode of dress but then pushed that thought aside in favour of a swift, silent prayer to the God of Light.

Just let her be well again and safe with these strangers he had entrusted her to and he would ask for nothing more. Could ask for nothing more...

Three days and nights Rowène lay in a fevered dream of pain and misery, where the mists that obscured the future and the memories that tainted the past swirled together in one roiling, turbulent tide. She knew she was not alone but did not recognise either of the faces that hovered over her, coaxing her with a gentle relentlessness to drink their bitter brews. There were other faces but only these two seemed real. One young, freckled and kindly. The other older, more controlled, with cornflower-blue eyes that had a disconcerting tendency to be transmuted by the fog of fever into the indigo blue eyes that Rowène had thought never to see again.

And while it was well nigh impossible at times to distinguish dream from reality, those warm, herbal draughts were real enough. She could feel their healing power even as the under-lying bitterness of them caused her to retch in rebellion against the memory, not only of the foul taste but also the wet heat of a violent man's mouth. Her wits wandering as they were, she did not know whether, in her agitation, she spoke – or screamed – his name but the freckled face blanched and the controlled face softened momentarily. And the last thing she heard, through the drugged darkness that swept over her after she had eventually managed to empty the cup they held to her lips, was one voice, quiet and low, saying sternly,

"You must not speak of anything you might hear, Emina. Do you hear me? This unfortunate girl's secrets are her own to keep or speak as she wills when she recovers her wits again."

"No, Sister, indeed I will not." This was said most earnestly. Then more hesitantly. "But, Sister, when she speaks of this man, this Ranulf. Does she... can she possibly mean Lord Joffroy's brother? You know more of the world beyond these walls than I, Sister, what think you?"

"I think it very likely indeed that it is Sir Ranulf that she speaks of... or calls to... And also that whatever their... acquaintance, it did not end well. I also think that, bearing in mind that the man we speak of is not only brother to Sir Guyard, who comes so faithfully every day to enquire as to Mistress Rowena's well-being, but to Lord Joffroi himself, that is yet one more cause to keep silence. Do you not agree?"

"Aye, Sister, that I do. But do you think..."

But whatever else there was, Rowène did not hear it, sinking back into her fevered dreams, wherein Ranulf de Rogé came to her and forced her to submit to his lust every bit as ruthlessly as he had done once before, only this time taking his assault to its ultimate conclusion...

Then, as is the way of dreams, everything changed. So that it seemed another day, another place, another time...

She was on her way to see someone – she did not know who – only that she went with trembling reluctance, her arms weighed down by some warm bundle, stumbling down an endless, empty passageway she had never seen before; certainly it was not Chartre castle. The stone of the walls and floor was a pale golden-grey, not the red sandstone of her home. Wherever it was, she came eventually to a chamber, recognising immediately the man within. Not by his face, which she never saw, but by the length of the long, barley-fair hair that tumbled down his back, catching the meagre light as, unaware of her presence, he paced the confines of what appeared to be a prison cell, each step accompanied by a metallic chink. Not from his spurs this time but from the heavy shackles about his wrists and ankles. The bundle in her arms stirred but before she could so much as glance down the steady sound of hammering made her look back at the man standing by the narrow, barred window, staring out. As if he knew that the ominous, terrifying beat heralded his death. She must have made some sound… the man froze, his shackled hands gripping the bars. His head began to turn, just as the bundle – no, it was not a bundle of rags, she saw as she looked down in horror but a new-born babe she held in her arms – stirred and began to cry…

She could still hear Ranulf's voice calling her name, even as she awoke, retching and vomiting. Finally she lay back, drained and exhausted, praying for a sleep without dreams…

On the morning after the third night of her fever Rowène opened her eyes and realised with a sense of relief that both the fever and terrifying dreams had finally run their course and that this place smelling of herbs and sunshine, together with the flesh and blood woman who sat beside her bed, were real.

"Where am I?" she whispered. "And who are you?"

"I am Herluva, one of the Sisters of Mercy of Silverleigh."

"Silverleigh? Is that where I am then?" Rowène asked. The name sounded vaguely familiar but she could not place it.

She looked around her again, at the stone walls, the thatched roof above her, the simple raiment of the woman sitting on a stool beside her low bed. Everything seemed incredibly humble yet was scrupulously clean. The walls were free of cobwebs, the rafters hung with what looked like bunches of dried lavender, the earthen floor swept clean, the woman's pale grey robes smelling of fresh air, her linen headrail bleached as white as sun and wind could make it.

"Yes, child, this is Silverleigh," Sister Herluva confirmed. A shadow seemed to cross behind her cornflower-blue eyes. "A place of healing protected by royal decree. Yet for all that, lying within the demesne of Lord Joffroi of Rogé."

"Rogé… Ah, yes!"

Memory returned abruptly. *All* her memories.

"Sister, tell me, was I bleeding?" she blurted out before she could think better of the question or even realise she had meant to ask it.

The older woman – she could see now by the lines and weathering of that beautiful, controlled face framed by stark white linen that she was in her middle years at least – seemed momentarily confused by this blunt enquiry.

"No, child, you were brought here suffering from a fever not a wound."

"I did not mean bleeding from a wound," Rowène sighed. "But you have answered my question well enough for all that."

Weariness and dread swamped her again and she turned her head away, feigning a return to sleep. Indeed it was not difficult; her limbs felt so weak that any movement was an effort. She heard an echoing sigh from Sister Herluva.

"Sleep then, child. I pray the gods will watch over you."

And then, clearly to someone else,

"Sister Emina, please keep an eye on Mistress Rowena whilst I walk down to Blackoakleas with the good tidings that our patient is safely set on the path back to health."

There was a rustle and the sound of a door opening but not closing again. Reluctantly Rowène moved her head against the pillow and opened her eyes. Sister Herluva had left the door propped open, allowing in the bountiful warmth of a summer's morning, with all the sounds and scents thereof. Indifferent to both birdsong and the soft, golden breeze, Rowène lay listlessly, wondering to whom Sister Herluva would be making her report and wishing she had never woken from those fevered dreams. Terrible though they had been, they were still less frightening, less burdensome than the harsh choices she must now confront.

Her hand felt heavy and as if it did not quite belong to her. Nevertheless she moved it so that it lay across her belly. Gods, it must be there, within her still; Ranulf de Rogé's seed steadily growing into his babe. She did not want it. Neither did he. Not least because in the seeds of that new life inevitably lay his own death. Thanks to that dream, fragments of which she could still remember, she accepted now what he must have known all along; that she had the power to bring him to his doom.

Somehow through the damp mists of the journey over the dark moors, the disorientating fog of fever and the illusory reality of her dreams, she had held onto the hope that she might have lost the babe she had realised back at Lac Linne that she must be carrying. She had hoped that starvation and illness would be enough to see it gone but the babe was obviously stronger than she. As its father had been, she thought bitterly.

Her only consolation at the moment was that even if Sister Herluva suspected the truth – and guessed at the man involved – she could not know who Rowène really was; when she had spoken of her it was as Mistress rather than Lady Rowena. By that token, therefore, it might be possible to stave off the inevitable shame that must taint the de Chartreux name when the truth became known. Her father, the gods send his soul peace, had already suffered the agony and ignominy of a traitor's death. Now she was to bear a de Rogé bastard – or rather she would in three seasons' time.

Moreover, she conceded miserably, now that *she* was certain of this disagreeable truth Ranulf would need to be told. Her eye fell upon the cloak hanging from a peg on the wall, the round silver brooch still secure in its black folds. She remembered her dream of him pacing his prison cell while the carpenters hammered outside, constructing the scaffold on which he was to die. Imagined him stepping up onto that high platform, saw the noose placed around his neck, heard the charges read out... and knew suddenly that she could not do it, despise him though she did.

He had watched her father die a worse death. But she could not do likewise to him.

Not that she would not enjoy watching him sweat a little first, taste at least a sip of the wine of revenge...

She was jolted from this macabre reflection by the realisation that she would have to face Ranulf's half-brother first since, with the fever leaving her wits clear once more, she remembered him bringing her to the Sisters, begging their aid and surely it must be he whom Sister Herluva intended to visit in Blackoakleas. Rowène could only pray that the healer would not include in her report any mention of the possibility that her patient was with child. But what in the name of all the gods was Rowène to tell him? The truth, she supposed.

But not yet. Not until she had first told the man who had sired the babe she was now convinced she was carrying. Like it or not – and she did not like it at all and neither would he! – it was his right to know before any other.

Contrary to her supposition, Guyard de Martine did not come at once to see her, although he sent formal good wishes for her full and swift recovery through Sister Herluva. Rowène was at first merely grateful that she would not have to face him until she had constructed a more solid shield around her heart. Then as her strength increased and she began to venture out a little more into the pale moorland sunshine, so did her reluctance to face him, knowing that she was carrying his half-brother's child. Nonetheless, she knew it was inevitable that she would be given back into his charge and so was not surprised when Sister Herluva brought the matter into the open between them.

She and the older woman were walking, as had become their habit in the days since Rowène had recovered enough to leave her bed, in the walled garth where the Grey Sisters of Silverleigh tended their healing herbs, the vegetables growing in a somewhat larger and more open patch of ground on the opposite side of the enclosure. It was obviously difficult soil to work but still that small, sheltered spot was a peaceful and productive place and Rowène enjoyed the time she spent there, breathing in the scent of the herbs, learning their uses...

"Child, you will have to leave us soon."

The sun was high and the warmest she had yet experienced in Rogé, the breeze light with the now familiar tang of bracken and heather, the bees busy among the flowers of thyme and marjoram at her feet. They had been walking between the beds of feverfew and lavender, fennel and rue, hyssop and lady's mantle, Sister Herluva pointing out their properties. So that, even though she had been expecting the words for some time, still they came as a shock. Stopping, she turned a startled face in the healer's direction.

"But, Sister..."

"You are cured of your fever, your headaches gone, your strength returned. I can no longer hold Sir Guyard at bay and he is insisting you be released to his guardianship."

Recovering her fragile composure, Rowène gave a tiny shrug.

"I do not hold you at fault, Sister, nor expect you to withstand a demand from the Steward of Rogé. For all that, though, I shall miss this place." She looked up at Sister Herluva and attempted a smile. "My sister and I were talking once... about betrothals and bindings and..."

"And babes?" Sister Herluva finished gently when she paused. Rowène sent a swift, suspicious glance towards her companion but came to the conclusion that the older woman had not made that remark with any pointed intent, for she was smiling quite serenely, her blue eyes softened by memory. "Yes, child, I too once sat with my sister and spoke of such things."

"You have a sister?" The words came out with what Rowène could only feel to be astonished discourtesy. "I am sorry, that was rude of me."

"But natural for all that," the healer replied, still smiling, clearly having taken no offence. "I was young once, like you, with a family, a home, a sister I loved and with whom I gossiped and giggled, wondering what our lives would be like when we were grown."

"And did you always wish to be a healer? I told J... my sister I would rather become a Sister of Mercy than wed with a man I did not care for. That was a foolish and rash thing to say since I knew nothing of that calling. Yet even so, part of me wishes it could still be so since I have little hope of wedding a man I can love."

"A healer's life is hard," Sister Herluva pointed out. "And largely thankless. And you are young yet to turn your back on men and the possibility of love."

Feeling suddenly tired, Rowène sank down onto the rough wooden bench set beneath the birch tree that grew in the centre of the garth.

"The man I thought I could love betrayed me," she muttered, her fingers plucking at a loose thread of the borrowed grey robe she was wearing. She looked up into those cornflower-blue eyes. "And although I no longer blame him for what he did, still we cannot be together, even if he felt about me as I do about him. But it was not he but another man who took from me any chance of either an honourable binding..." She touched very briefly the silver bracelet she still wore. "Or even the life of a healer."

"This other man..." Sister Herluva started to ask but Rowène, fearing that if she spoke further of this matter, she would reveal too much, stood abruptly and said,

"Tell me more of the herbs, Sister. If I must leave this place soon, I wish to learn as much as I can before I go. What is this one?" She knelt and touched a tiny green plant covered with small, white daisy-like flowers. Gently crushing the soft, almost feathery leaves to release their aroma, she brought her fingers to her nose...

And promptly recoiled, the blood leaving her face so suddenly that Sister Herluva started forwards in concern. Rowène allowed herself to be guided back onto the bench and then turned a blanched countenance towards the older woman.

"What is it?" she asked again, her voice scarcely above a whisper. She sniffed again, more cautiously this time, seeing not the flickering green leaves of the birch tree or the blue sky beyond, but a hard face flecked with glinting stubble... blue eyes darkened by desire and some maleficent draught... long, tangled hair the colour of barley tails. Smelt again the aroma of sweat and some pungent herb...

"It is chamomile," she heard a woman's low voice say and came back to the sunlit garth to find Sister Herluva regarding her with concern and dawning comprehension. "You drank it as a tisane, along with an infusion of other herbs, when you were ill. I remember that it seemed to do more harm than good, making your stomach rebel where it should have soothed."

"It made me sick, you mean?"

"Alas, yes. Neither Sister Emina nor I could understand it at the time but now..."

She left the thought trailing and Rowène seized the opportunity to ask,

"Does this herb, this chamomile, have any other uses, Sister? Is there any way this..." She gestured with her fingers before wiping them fastidiously on the skirts of her robe. "This aroma might find its way onto a man's... anyone's..." she added hastily as she saw Sister Herluva's eyes sharpen still further. "Skin or clothes?"

"Well, yes," the older woman agreed. "You must understand that I am but lately come to Silverleigh myself but Sister Emina tells me that part of the quarterly tithe we pay to the Lord of Rogé is in the form of soap and packets of sweet-smelling herbs to combat the odours of castle life and which the steward, in his generosity..." Here Sister Herluva's tones took on a distinctly ironical tinge. "Is prepared to accept in lieu of hard coin."

"The steward? You mean, Guyard de Martine?"

"Apparently," Sister Herluva said slowly. "As I said, I am new to Silverleigh and had not met him until he fetched up here with you a se'ennight ago. He is not," she added thoughtfully, "What I would have expected from a brother of Black Joffroi of Rogé."

"He is only a half-brother," Rowène defended him. "And believe me, Sister, Lord Joffroi's true-born brother is everything – and more – you would expect of him."

"Oh, I am sure he is." Sister Herluva's voice was distinctly grim now. "Indeed, my dear, I never doubted it for a moment."

"He is a murderer, a drunkard and a... a womaniser at the least," Rowène said fiercely, although she could hear the tears behind the fire of her words. "As to what else he has done... to my father... to my sister, my brothers...me..." Her voice broke under the threat of tears.

"I know what he did, child." Sister Herluva reached out and drew her into her arms, holding her close against her lavender-scented shoulder. "To your father at least."

"How can you know?" Rowène wept, close to hysteria. "You do not even know who I am."

"I do know who you are, child. And as to your father, I know because I was there, the day Louis de Chartreux died a traitor's death. I saw the cruel pleasure and satisfaction on Black Joffroi's face and in that moment knew beyond all doubt that he was responsible for bringing that doom to your father. I marked also the man who stood beside him, as broad of shoulder and even fairer of hair than the man who brought you here."

"Ranulf!" His name tasted as bitter on her tongue as the man himself. "Tell me, Sister, did you not see the same expression on his face as you saw on his brother's? That tells you what sort of man he is!"

"I confess it was little enough heed I paid him but I think he took no pleasure from what he witnessed. Or perhaps it was merely too much bad ale that caused him to vomit so violently." Then without altering her tone. "Is it *his* child you are carrying then? He forced you, did he not?"

Rowène froze, then looked up in shock, as belatedly she realised the significance of everything Sister Herluva had said to her.

"What! How did you..."

"Know? About the babe? Or that it was that particular de Rogé who had misused you so viciously? Or that one of the reasons you wish to learn of these herbs is because you seek the one that brings death, not healing? It is over there, by the way, that small plant with the greyish leaves and blue flowers."

Flowers, Rowène saw when she looked in the direction indicated, that were the self-same colour of Ranulf de Rogé's dark blue eyes! Would the child, if she permitted it to live, have eyes the same colour as its father's?

*God of Light have mercy on me for even considering... what I am considering.*

Rowène forced herself to look steadily at the deadly herb before returning her gaze to the older woman's carefully calm face and compassionate gaze, feeling her heart shudder into life again.

"Tell me," she croaked. "Not about the herb. Not yet at any rate. But everything else, yes, tell me, if you will."

Sister Herluva sighed.

"Very well but I beg you not to reveal to anyone what you will hear. It is my life I am giving into your keeping, as you will see."

"If it were not for your aid, Sister, I do not think I would be here to listen to you today," Rowène said quietly. "And I give you my word that whatever you choose to tell me now will remain secret."

"Well then... my name is not Herluva, as everyone here in Silverleigh believes, but Héloise. Or at least that is the name I took when I put on the robe and took up the vows of a Sister of Mercy... oh, nearly a score of years ago, I suppose, putting aside the name I was given at birth and carried through into womanhood and motherhood... yes, I have a son, do not look so startled, child. Celibate I may be now but I once knew the passion of a lover's touch though never, I must confess, the weight of a binding bracelet..."

Rowène swallowed and tried not to look either startled or judgemental. God of Light, who was she to judge any other woman? At least Sister Herluva, or

Héloise or whatever her true name was, had appeared to love the man whose child she bore. Thought of her own unborn child's father prompted her to ask, with some delicacy,

"Your son, do you see him at all? Does he... know you?"

"Yes, I see him, on rare occasions. *He*, however, believes his mother to be dead. It would never occur to him that Sister Héloise of Vézière is the woman who was once his father's mistress."

"You did not wish to take the binding oath with your lo... your son's father?"

"There was never any possibility of that. The man I loved was already bound to another woman."

Rowène looked into those wistful, distant, cornflower-blue eyes.

"Did your lover acknowledge his son?" she asked, unwilling to pry but curious nonetheless. Almost without volition, her hand spread over her belly.

"What?" Sister Herluva... Héloise... seemed to return to the present with a start. "Oh... yes, he did. And loved him and took pride in him until the day he died."

"He is dead then, your lover? I am sorry."

"He is dead, yes. But never my love for him. Life, however, continues for me, and will do so as long as there are folk in need of healing."

"Yes but..." Rowène frowned. "Why here? In Rogé, I mean. I thought you said you came from Vézière?"

"Therein lies the darkest part of my tale. I can say without vanity that I am one of the most skilled healers, certainly at Vézière, probably in neighbouring Mortaine and possibly in all of Mithlondia. Or so they told me when they sent me to Lamortaine to tend Prince Marcus..."

"God of Light! Surely you were not the healer brought in to tend him?" Rowène interrupted, her voice rising in incredulous shock.

"I was indeed but how did you come to hear of it?"

"From Black Joffroi's own lips. When he told of Prince Marcus' death. He accused you of poisoning the Prince; you and my father together." Her voice shook slightly. "Gods above! Is that why my father died, a regicide and traitor? Because of you?"

"Because I could not heal the Prince? Or because I deliberately poisoned him? Is that what you believe? Merely because Black Joffroi accuses me of such a crime?"

Rowène made an impatient gesture and wiped away the sudden rush of tears.

"No, I do accuse you of deliberately poisoning Prince Marcus! Nor would I take the word of a de Rogé that the sun will rise tomorrow! I do not think you could ever have healed the Prince, no matter how skilled you are in the healing arts. And however he died, I know my father would never have been permitted to live once Black Joffroi or the Winter Lady marked him down for death. But how did you escape?" She had a sudden thought and said urgently. "I must warn you that they mean to hunt you down as my father's accomplice in crime, I heard Black Joffroi say so myself."

"I do not doubt it. I am innocent and he knows it. But as to how I escaped? When it became obvious to us that Marcus would not live out the night, your father sent me away from the palace. I begged him to leave too for we both knew what would follow. But even as I spoke I knew it was useless, that your father would stay until the end. He was not of a mind to allow his prince, his sword-brother, to meet his death alone, even though it meant his own death by staying. So he ordered me away and, to my shame, I went."

"Why should you have stayed and died too?" Rowène asked, a shade bitterly. "For the sake of a dying prince and a nobleman who was doomed? What were they to you that you should die for them? Better surely to live and heal others?"

"Perhaps. I did not feel so at the time but your father certainly did. He wanted no healer's death on his conscience, he told me. So I left the palace at his command but I could not leave Lamortaine while either Marcus or Lu... Louis yet lived."

"Where did you go?" Rowène asked, frowning a little at the familiar way her companion spoke of the Prince of Mithlondia and the Lord of Chartreux. Then forgot it as Sister Héloise continued,

"I hid myself in the Marish..."

"What is that?"

"The Marish is the poorest, seediest quarter of Lamortaine," the healer explained. "Every depravity known to man is obtainable there, even those vices otherwise outlawed in Mithlondia. There are more taverns and brothels in the Marish, catering for all predilections and purses, than in the rest of the city together and any man who goes in there is like to come out with his guts turned to water or a pox on his private parts."

Rowène winced as she remembered her derisory remark to Ilana about Ranulf being poxed. Had he visited the brothels of the Marish whilst he was in Lamortaine? Knowing what she did of his appetites and habits, it seemed only too likely but she hoped he had not. Or that if he had, he had managed to escape unscathed – although not for his own sake. She half thought of enquiring further of the healer but Sister Héloise had not noticed her distraction and was still talking.

"One day, if the gods are with me, I mean to return there and see if I can mayhap do something to help those poor broken women and their diseased and suffering children, pitiful creatures as they are; ignored and kicked aside by those very men from whose careless seed they sprang."

Gods! Rowène gripped the edge of the bench and felt a trickle of sweat run cold down her backbone as she heard again that rough voice from her memories.

*If you wish, I will acknowledge the child and support it for as long as I am able...*

Ranulf, at least, did not mean to abandon his child, even though it meant his own death. But would it? Despite the implications of his words and the fading horror of her dream of the prisoner awaiting execution, she still did not quite believe it would come to that.

"Sister Hé... Herluva?"

"Yes, child?"

"What is the penalty for... for rape? For a nobleman, I mean, not a commoner? Or is such a proceeding against a nobleman unheard of in Mithlondia?"

The older woman pursed her lips.

"It is a difficult proceeding, child, but yet not unheard of either. Although admittedly it is almost as rare an occurrence as sight of the Moon Goddess of the Faennari blushing the colour of a wild rose."

Rowène felt her own moon-pale cheeks flush pink at this unexpected allusion but kept her gaze dispassionate – she hoped. Apparently she succeeded for Sister Herluva did not pursue the matter of the rose-pink moon and the events of that night.

"The difficulty, of course, lies in finding a nobleman willing to impeach another. On that sort of charge anyway, although the gods know they are free enough with other accusations. And unfortunately it is only the High Counsel that can pass judgement in such a case where one or other parties is of noble blood. Indeed I can only recall one other instance in my lifetime."

"What happened?"

"Gérard, the youngest son of the Lord of Lyeyne was accused of ravishing Sir Heribert de Lacey's daughter Agnès."

"Lyeyne... de Lyeyne? Now where... Oh, I know. Would this Gérard be some kin to Lady Rosalynde of Rogé?"

"Yes. Lady Rosalynde was mother to both Joffroi and Ranulf. She was also sister to Henri and Gérard of Lyeyne, who, it was said, bore a reputation that was almost as black then as that of the present de Lyeyne brothers and their de Rogé kinsmen, although I never heard any ill spoken of the Lady Rosalynde, other than that her very gentleness made her no match for the charming but feckless nobleman to whom she was bound."

"Was Lord Jacques so charming then? I confess I have seen no sign of that – or Lady Rosalynde's gentleness – in either of their sons!" She curtailed any further bitter remarks and said instead, "You were telling me about Lady Agnès. What happened?"

"Incensed at the assault on his daughter, Sir Heribert laid a formal charge of rape against Gérard of Lyeyne which, much to everyone's surprise at the time, Prince Marcus upheld, this resulting in an unprecedented and very public trial. Fortunately there were several witnesses to Gérard's violent attack so Lady Agnès was not forced to stand before the lords of the High Counsel alone and testify to the particulars but it must still have been a terrifying ordeal. So much so that, with the evidence given and whilst the Counsel deliberated, Lady Agnès sought refuge with the Grey Sisters at Vézière, being much overset by the whole affair. From what she told me I cannot think the Counsellors were particularly gentle in their questioning of her. Nor are they likely to prove any more compassionate under Prince Linnius than they were under his father. Indeed, it is not a situation which any woman of any age would find easy."

"And Gérard de Lyeyne?" Rowène asked, absorbing the implicit warning in Sister Héloise's words but ignoring it for the moment.

"He was found guilty."

"And?"

Sister Héloise seemed all at once reluctant to continue.

"And? Please tell me the end, Sister."

"The lords of the High Counsel asked for clemency to be shown on the grounds that Lady Agnès had admitted to not fighting to the end and that the witnesses must have misinterpreted her initial struggles. A term of imprisonment in Lamortaine's dungeons, or better yet at his own home in Lyeyne, they considered most fitting."

"All of them?" Rowène asked, appalled. "Even my father?"

"No, not all of them. And not your father. He and four others, the lords of Vézière, Marillec, Valenne and Veraux called for a more severe penalty but were outnumbered. It was at that point that I was sent from Vézière to Lamortaine with the tidings that Lady Agnès was with child. Gérard was called back before the High Counsel and apparently displayed such arrogance in his refusal to accept responsibility that Jacques de Rogé, who had formerly abstained on the grounds of it being his own wife's brother on trial, was so enraged that he reversed his decision and threw in his lot with the two men in Mithlondia whom he would normally oppose, on any matter off the battlefield, out of sheer bloody-mindedness."

"My father, I suppose? But who was the other?"

"Lord Gilles of Valenne. There was ever trouble and dispute between Valenne and Rogé, though no-one has ever claimed to know the root cause."

"And so, what happened next?"

"Seeing the flow of the tide, four more Counsellors chose to change sides, so that the numbers were equal and Prince Marcus held the casting vote. I cannot think that anyone was surprised when he aligned himself with your father. I *do* think they were surprised at the sentence he passed."

"Yes?" Rowène felt breathless. Not on some unknown ravisher's account, but for the sake of the noblewoman he had so callously ruined and the man who now stood in such similar circumstances and who was, by some ironic quirk of fate, Gérard de Lyeyne's blood kin.

"Are you sure you want to hear this?" the healer asked quietly.

"Yes."

"Well then... and bear in mind this is not gossip. I was there, first as witness for Lady Agnès' condition, then as messenger to carry back word of what followed."

"And what did follow?"

"At Prince Marcus' command they shackled the condemned man, right there in the Counsel Chamber, and then dragged him away, still protesting his innocence. Meanwhile your father sent for carpenters from the town to build a scaffold in the practice yard just outside the condemned man's cell."

Sister Héloise broke off at Rowène's gasp and glanced at her. Remembering her dream of the man in the condemned cell, Rowène fought the sudden panicked belief that she might indeed be the witchling Ranulf had called her. Was it possible that the man she had seen in her dreams had been Gérard de Lyeyne? That what she had seen had not been a vision of the future but a glimpse of the past? And yet...

"You knew this Gérard by sight, Sister?"

"Yes, child, but why..?"

"I know this must have occurred some years ago but do you remember what colour his hair was?" Rowène interrupted.

Her companion regarded her rather as if she thought she had taken leave of her senses but answered her anyway.

"He was as dark of hair and eye as Black Joffroi himself. Indeed most high-born Mithlondians tend towards raven rather than fair. With a few notable exceptions, of course, Lord Jacques of Rogé being one of them."

"And his two youngest sons," Rowène murmured distractedly. Gods help her, it *must* have been Ranulf she had seen in that terrifyingly vivid dream. There was no mistaking that fall of pale hair, glimmering in the diffuse light of that squalid cell. But was it a true vision of what was to come or merely what might be? Pulling herself together, she said grimly,

"Finish your tale, please, Sister."

The cornflower-blue eyes regarded her with deep concern then the older woman sighed,

"As I was saying, rather than send a nobleman for public execution in the city, Prince Marcus decided it would be more discreet to conduct it within the palace grounds. It took the carpenters the best part of two days to build their scaffold and when they were done they brought Gérard forth, naked save for his breeches. He was not so arrogant by then and cursed the Lady Agnès with language most foul until Lord Jacques pushed his way through the crowd and, leaping upon the scaffold, silenced his wife's youngest brother with a blow that caught all present by surprise. Gérard turned on his brother-by-binding then, cursing him too for betraying both his blood and his station. I truly thought Lord Jacques would strangle him then and there with his bare hands, so enraged was he and I well remember what he said. *If you were my own son and had done this vile deed, still I would treat him as I will you.* And with that he snatched the knife the executioner had ready and slicing through the cord of the condemned man's breeches so that he stood naked, emasculated him then and there..."

"Gods!"

Rowène struggled against the twin daemons of faintness and nausea, and barely won.

"Then what?"

"Then the executioner took over, placing the noose about his neck and finally it was over. It was a terrible and bloody day but I truly believe justice was done."

"And Lady Agnès, what happened to her?"

"Lord Jacques rode with me back to Vézière. He knew neither Gérard's father nor his brother would take over his responsibilities towards the child Lady Agnès was carrying. He meant to offer to take the child when it was born in the belief that Lady Rosalynde would rear it. She was already raising one of his illegitimate sons alongside the two legitimate sons of their union and would, he thought, make no fuss at taking in another child, more especially as this one would be of her own blood."

The healer stopped and sighed again.

"He meant well and it was probably the only time in his life he acted out of pure intent towards a woman. But it was all for naught. By the time we reached Vézière the Lady Agnès was dead. She had begged for a draught of the blue-flowered bane to rid herself of Gérard de Lyeyne's child and it killed both the child she carried and herself as well." She paused and then added softly. "Do you truly wish to take that path?"

There fell a terrible silence between Rowène and the woman who had once been Sister Héloise of Vézière. Rowène gripped the bench so hard her fingers ached but she only said stiffly,

"The gods have pity on her, poor lady. And I promise I will think carefully on what you have said. *All* that you have said. But... you still have not told me how you came to be in Silverleigh or any of the rest."

"You are a stubborn child," Sister Héloise replied. "Mayhap you have it in you to weather this particular storm better than the Lady Agnès did. As to your questions, I fled to the place where I believed Black Joffroi would least expect me to take refuge; under his own nose so as to speak. Also, and in spite of my oath to do no harm to any and to help all who ask my aid, I thought too that if I were here, in his own demesne, I might find some chance to seek revenge for the deaths of Prince Marcus and your father." She smiled sadly at Rowène. "So I too have weighty matters to consider. Do I break my oath of healing and pursue revenge? Or do I let Black Joffroi sleep easy in his bloodstained bed and pursue my calling? I do not know... the gods I serve must be my guides but they are silent now and do not speak to me. Perhaps because I come to them with darkness in my heart." She turned to look at Rowène, regarding her closely.

"Come, I have wearied you with such grim tales. You need to sleep again and when you wake 'twill be time for the evening meal."

Rowène rose to her feet, somewhat shakily.

"It is true, I am tired. And confused. And filled with sorrow afresh at the thought that I will never see my father again. But as we walk, will you not tell me how you recognised both me and..." She smiled humourlessly. "My condition? I should not have thought it obvious, it is not even a full month yet since... since that day."

They walked in silence out of the herb garden but it was the silence of confidences shared and trust given rather than tension. Only when they reached the small stone hut that smelt of wood smoke and fresh air, lavender and that something else that Rowène now recognised as chamomile, and Sister Héloise had seen her settled onto the bed and laid the black mantle over her body for a blanket, did the older woman finally finish her tale.

"Close to the end, when Marcus was too weak to move from his bed, your father scarcely left his side. They would talk over times long gone, battles once fought..." Her mouth lifted in an oddly uncondemning smile as she continued, "The women they had once loved, the children they had sired. I do not think they were aware of me... indeed I am very sure they were not." Her smile was tender. "It was not the sort of speech they would have shared in the presence of a woman, and a healer at that."

"Or perhaps they did know you were there, but believed, erroneously, that you would not understand their speech," Rowène said suddenly in Mithlondian.

Sister Héloise did not bother to deny the implication. Instead she replied in the same language, a rueful smile in her eyes,

"I do not normally make that sort of careless mistake. But I have let my guard down too easily in your company." She glanced at the bright hair that Rowène wore in one long, thick braid. "Perhaps there is something in the old legends after all."

"I am not a witch," Rowène sighed. "Although I admit you are not the first person to believe it of me."

"Maybe not, but it was in part the flame of your hair that caught my eye when Guyard de Martine first brought you here. I remembered your father telling Marcus about his two beautiful daughters."

Rowène snorted in rather unladylike fashion at that adjective.

"No, it is true," her companion protested. "In your father's eyes, you and your sister were the most beautiful young women in all the five mortal realms and probably the immortal lands as well. Of course, Marcus swore that his daughter Linette was the fairest of all but that is perhaps the way of fathers. The point I am making is that when I saw the colour of your hair and caught a glimpse of your face I knew whose daughter you must be. Knew too that something terrible must have happened at Chartre for you to be in the keeping of a man whom I had already recognised to be one of Jacques de Rogé's sons.

I just did not know which one." She hesitated and then continued, even more quietly. "As to the possibility that you were with child... from listening to your fevered speech I could guess what Ranulf had done to you and you confirmed it with your first waking words. Now you must decide what you mean to do about it. And its father."

Rowène said nothing – what could she say, when she did not herself know the answer – but Sister Héloise seemed not to expect it.

"By the way, in case you are wondering, I have said nothing to Messire de Martine about my suspicions and Emina, who is the only other one of the sisterhood who has shared the care of you, has promised silence too. And *whatever* you decide, I will do my utmost to help you. If you choose the blue-bane draught, I will brew it for you with the utmost care so that, the gods willing, you do not meet the same fate as Agnès de Lacey. Or if you choose to accuse the man who misused you, then I will support you in that too. It will be necessary, of course, to seek the aid of a nobleman in order to bring that action before the High Counsel... Gilles de Valenne could most likely be persuaded to take up your cause since it involves the possibility of seeing a de Rogé sentenced to hang. But you must be prepared to face the Lords of the High Counsel and their questioning and they will spare you nothing. Or... and there is this third option; you can continue as you are and do nothing."

"And let Guy and the rest of Mithlondia believe the daughter of Louis de Chartreux to be as promiscuous as any Kardolandian courtier," Rowène finished bleakly. "Which given my ten years in Kaerellios is perhaps not so incredible after all. Only Ranulf knows enough to give me the lie and while his pride and his arrogance might have led him to promise to support his by-blow, I cannot see him concerning himself with defending my reputation. Not when he took me in the belief that I was little better than a whore, assuming that if I had lain with his half-brother – which I had not – I would lie with him also."

Sister Héloise made a sound of disgust in her throat.

"And you are prepared to let such a man escape justice? Because if you do nothing... take that third choice... that is what will happen. And what is to stop him then from brutalising other innocent young women?"

"A limp and impotent pri... er... privy member," Rowène retorted with a sudden grin, although she managed at the last moment to change the coarse word Ranulf himself had used. Seeing the older woman blink, she hurried on. "He thinks he is cursed because he took me by force and I am of the blood of the Faennari. And while I do not know how true that may be, *he* certainly believes it. Believes too that, unless I consent to cure him, he is damned to a life of unwanted celibacy until the day he dies which, considering as he is how old...?"

"Not much more than thirty, I believe," Sister Héloise murmured, a frown of consideration wrinkling her smooth brow.

"So… long enough then," Rowène concluded with a touch of malicious amusement. "Especially for a man not formerly known for his abstinence from the pleasures of the flesh."

"A fitting punishment indeed," the Sister of Mercy agreed dryly. "Now, rest, child. Messire de Martine will be here early tomorrow morning. I do not know how easy it will be for us to communicate once you reach Rogérinac but if you have need of a healer, I do not think that he is the sort of man who would deny you my assistance should you request it. He does not appear to be an unreasonable man – for a de Rogé – and he seems genuinely to care about your well-being."

"As his brother's hostage, maybe," Rowène sighed. "Just one more mark in this bloody game of fox and geese which Black Joffroi plays with the lives of the ordinary folk of Chartreux."

"No, I think he cares for *you*," Sister Héloise replied. "It is in his eyes and in his voice whenever he speaks of you."

"And I wonder how his wife will deal with that?" Rowène said quietly. Wondered too, although she did not say it aloud, how *she* would deal with Mathilde de Martine.

# Chapter 8

## *Troubled Road to Rogérinac*

Early the next morning, while the wispy white mists of dawn were still hanging their mysterious veils in the valley depths, Rowène once more mounted the honey-coloured mare and left the serenity and safety of the healers' enclave with feelings of profound regret and not a little trepidation.

Sister Héloise – Sister Herluva, as she must remember to call her – had told her, quite plainly, what choices lay before her. It but remained for her to decide which path she would take, and none of those paths were straight or easy and where any of them might lead her in the end it was impossible to see, disappearing into shadows and darkness as they did. Even so, she knew without a doubt that the Daemon of Death waited beside two of those paths, his icy cold fingers eager to snatch either the tiny life within her or that of the man who had put it there. The third path was no more inviting; bleak and lonely it stretched at her feet, twisting between the leafless thorn trees that grew on a barren moor beneath a cloud-covered moon.

She shivered and shut her eyes and when she opened them again it was to find the sun shining and Guyard de Martine regarding her with a curious intensity as they rode. Beyond a formal courteous greeting she had said nothing to Guy earlier and she did not speak now, merely giving him what she hoped was a reassuring smile. He looked at her a moment longer. Then, apparently satisfied that she could cope with the rigours of travel, turned his attention back to the rough track.

Rowène grimaced and glanced quickly back, wanting one last look, but Silverleigh and its bells had disappeared from sight and the only thing she could hear was the whisper of the wind in the scattered birches and the 'kee-kee' of a hawk high overhead. Already the time she had spent with the healers seemed little more than a fever-induced dream but she knew it had been real. As real as the hawk she could hear in the sky above her, as real as the shabby masculine attire she was once again wearing – cleaned and mended by Sister Emina, bless her – and as real as the man on the big chestnut horse in whose company she must travel the last few leagues to Rogérinac. Alone.

She had wondered, on first seeing him this morning where their escort was, but it was Sister Herluva who had asked the question with a bluntness that bordered on disrespect. Guy had appeared rather taken aback but had answered after a moment or two, his innate courtesy towards the respected healers of

Mithlondia proving stronger than any irritation he might feel. Not knowing how long he would be delayed by Mistress Rowena's illness, he had accordingly sent the men on ahead of him to Rogérinac rather than have them kicking their heels in boredom and creating mischief in Blackoakleas. He went on to assure Sister Herluva, rather coolly, that she need have no fears about Mistress Rowena travelling unchaperoned in his company and that, barring any unexpected problems, they should reach Rogérinac before dark-fall that night.

Sister Herluva had not appeared convinced but had said no more, being well aware that she had no power to prevent the Steward of Rogé from doing whatever he wished to his brother's hostage beyond the rough walls of the healers' domain. Caught up in her own thoughts, Rowène had made no protest either.

In the event it took them the best part of the day merely to descend from the High Moors and they spent the night together after all, alone for the first time since that fateful night at Chartre. Distracted though she was and trust him though she did, Rowène found herself suddenly nervous in Guy's company and keenly aware of everything around them. High overhead the stars were scattered like brilliant flowers and the summer air was soft and sweet. The moon was little more than a pale silver sliver in the sky but Rowène could sense the enchantment...

Obeying an instinct deep within her she closed her eyes and raised her face to the moon, feeling – she did not think she imagined it – the fleeting caress of a goddess's touch. Shivering slightly, she opened her eyes, bringing her gaze back to the mortal man seated on the other side of the fire.

Silence held them both, binding them together with a spell woven of moonlight and starlight and their own secret desires.

He wanted her, Rowène knew. She could see his need and longing as clearly as the flicker and flare of the fire's flames. She felt that same need and longing, hot and bright in her own blood. There was no-one there but them. No-one would ever know if they fulfilled those desires in each other's arms.

Time ceased to exist; the stars paused in their shimmering dance, hearts stilled and the Moon Goddess held the balance in her white arms...

Then Guy dropped his gaze and Rowène looked away.

And a single star sped across the sky in a blaze of scattered silver sparks.

They rose with the dawn after a restless night.

Rowène knew that her companion had not slept well. She had heard him moving about in the night, quiet though he had been, and she had been unable to settle either, disturbed not only by her own feelings towards him but also the knowledge that she was carrying his half-brother's babe and that a decision was hanging over her head, rather like a hangman's noose.

A noose she had glimpsed during the course of one brief, terrifyingly real dream; grim and dark against a bright blue sky, waiting to be placed around the neck of a condemned man. Gérard de Lyeyne, she had thought in her dream, even as she knew it would not be. No de Lyeyne had ever had such long, pale hair. In her dream it lay scattered like straw across the rough boards of the scaffold where the executioner had carelessly dropped it, glimmering gold in dawn's clear light...

No, that must be wrong. Even in her dream Rowène knew that a public execution such as de Rogé's would be, was unlikely to take place at dawn and, with that, finally realised that what she could see between her lashes was the glorious golden glow of a new day. What she could hear was not the muted mutter of an angry crowd or the choking gasp of a dying man but birdsong; sweet and pure and so poignantly alive that she nearly wept. In relief, if nothing else. Her hand went to touch the silver brooch on her shoulder and she looked up to find Guyard de Martine watching her closely.

Flushing a little she took the hunk of bread and cheese he held out to her, ruthlessly pushing aside the last lingering remnants of her troubled dream. She had no wish to spoil this day with thoughts of Ranulf de Rogé, neither his arrogance nor his unexpected vulnerability. Let the future come as it would, today was for her and the man before her.

Indeed the thought came to her several times throughout the day that Guy, too, felt as she did and was intent on taking what pleasure from it that he could. He did not speak of what was waiting for them in Rogérinac, did not speak very much at all, save to point out some view that he thought particularly noteworthy, from the regal rise of the moors behind them to the wooded hills lying before them and beyond that, the flash and glint of silver that was the sea.

The only time he really spoke was when they paused for lunch beneath a flowering thorn tree on the eastern slope of the last stretch of moorland. Sitting there in the warmth of the sun, breathing in the fragrance of the late blossom, he told her of his boyhood and youth, long before he had become steward of the land he so clearly loved, taking care – or so Rowène thought – neither to mention the half-brother with whom he had obviously shared those adventures, or the wife who must be eagerly awaiting his long-delayed return to the place he called home.

Rowène thought she could have stayed there forever on that sunny hillside, beneath the fragile canopy of white flowers, surrounded by clear air and the scent of heather, watching the small brown butterflies as they danced from one tiny pink bell to another. Guy seemed as loath to move on as she and after a while she fell asleep, lulled by the warmth of the sun and the hum of bees in the heather.

She awoke dazed and disorientated, roused by the touch of the freshening breeze that had arisen while she slept and now set the clouds to scud across the sun and leach the silver from the sparkling sea, turning it dull and grey. Her face felt chilled but her back was warm and glancing over her shoulder she found that she was lying curled against Guy's big body, his right arm beneath her neck, his left arm lying around her waist, holding her close against him.

She smiled a little but there was more pain in her heart than pleasure. He was still asleep, she saw, the cooling breeze riffling the short, wheat-gold strands of his sunlit hair. He looked at peace; his eyes closed, the torment she had sometimes glimpsed in those light blue depths hidden. He had discarded his tunic earlier in the day and now the wind lifted his short shirt sleeve, allowing the sunlit to spark off the broad bronze binding ring that circled his left arm, reminding her why they could never be lovers.

She allowed herself the bitter-sweet luxury of watching him sleep for perhaps fifty more heartbeats, then eased carefully out from under his arm. Already missing the closeness, her hand reached out to touch his hair in the gentlest of caresses – she dared not touch his face, fearing he would wake immediately – then swiftly, before she could change her mind, she bent and set her lips to his in the lightest of kisses, feeling his lips soften and mould to hers even as he slept.

She lingered no more than a heartbeat, then drew back so that when he opened his eyes a moment later, she was sitting beside him, a chaste distance between them, arms around her knees, gazing at the distant sea and gathering clouds. She glanced over her shoulder at him as he stirred and said, as prosaically as she could,

"Perhaps we ought to be moving on?"

His eyes went to the eastern horizon and his own smile faded.

"Yes, we must indeed. There is a storm coming by the looks of it. I fear we should not have lingered so long here but you obviously needed the rest. I did not have the heart to wake you when you fell asleep. And then," he grinned a little sheepishly. "I must have fallen asleep too. I trust you will forgive such discourtesy. I only hope I did not snore?"

"It was either you snoring or the bees humming," she replied, putting a little mischief into her voice, not wanting him to suspect either that she had been watching him for some time or how close he had held her in his sleep. "But since I have only just woken up myself I cannot be sure which it was."

Her gaze returned to the clouding sky and she voiced the unease that had been steadily growing in her mind.

"How far away is Rogérinac? Will we reach it before dark-fall or will we have to spend another night... " She was going to say *together* but thinking that too suggestive, amended it to, "Another night on the road?"

Guy looked at her a little grimly but made no reply. Instead he rose to his feet, collecting their cloaks from the ground as he did so. He shook the bits of dry grass and heather from the garments, then handed her the black mantle with a frown. She thought he was worried about the storm but...

"Why did Ran give you his cloak?" he asked abruptly.

She just stared at him, helpless to think of an answer that would incriminate neither his half-brother nor herself; she was not ready for that yet.

"I..."

"And the pin too?" Guy added. "You cannot know, but our father gave it to him the day he died and so far as I know Ran has never been parted from it since. So what is between you and him that he would do this?"

Rowène shivered at the thought of all that lay between her and Ranulf de Rogé, then managed to turn the movement to good account. Rubbing her hands over her bare arms, she said irritably,

"Only the good gods, or rather the Daemon of Hell, can say what was in your cursed brother's mind. I certainly make no claim to knowing what impulses twist his black heart." She felt the damp edge chilling the breeze and continued a little plaintively, "Guy, I am getting cold, it looks as if it will rain again soon and you want to stand here discussing a man I hate and despise. And you still have not answered my question. *Will* we reach Rogérinac before dark-fall?"

"I think we must," Guy answered, the grim note still in his voice. "I cannot risk spending another night alone with you. Your reputation is hanging by a shred as it is."

"Are you really thinking of my reputation?" Rowène enquired sharply. "Or your own? Who would know if you did make me your mistress? Unless you think the sheep hereabouts are clever enough to tell tales?" Her voice softened and she heard herself say. "And it would only be for the one night, after all."

"I have never..." he began and she could hear the iron-cold anger lying just below his surface calm.

"I know, I know!" she interrupted, impatient now to move on and forget this disastrous conversation. "And you are not about to start with me. That being settled, can we please get on our way? You never did say how far away Rogérinac is from here but I imagine from what you told me earlier that it lies on the coast and *that* looks to be leagues away. I cannot think we will get there before the rain comes. I only hope your wife has the wit to organise a bath when we do finally arrive!"

It was a low blow, she knew, to fling his wife in his face, but his unexpected mention of his half-brother had scattered salt on raw places that had never healed and his determination not to spend any more time alone with her than was necessary had hurt her even more.

Riding hard now, they continued their journey down through the lowlands, heading eastwards towards the distant coast and as they rode the land on either side of the track began to change; the rough grass and heather of the moors giving way to treacherous reeking bogs where white tufts of cotton grass swayed in warning above brilliant green mosses and stagnant pools of black water. Pity the unwary sheep or traveller who strayed far from the oozing path! They trod warily here, all their attention given to keeping the horses moving steadily forwards until finally, about mid afternoon, the countryside changed again and they rode through narrow, wooded valleys alive with noisy, rocky streams.

With the sun long since washed away by cold rain, the valleys were strange and gloomy places, nothing to be seen save moss, twisted black oak and sombre holly. Only a light patter of rain disturbed the ominous silence beneath the trees and Rowène, depressed and damp once more, could only pray that they would soon leave these disquieting woods behind.

Even so, it was close to the end of the day before the character of the wood changed again; the moss giving way to bracken and brambles, the stunted oaks growing taller and more upright. The last pallid light had almost gone from the sky by the time they finally emerged to find Rogérinac castle rising before them, the village below already lost in the darkness that rolled in from the east, born on the crashing whisper of unseen waves.

As they rode down into the village Rowène found she could see a little better, enough to glimpse the white-ruffed waters of a dark grey sea and the humble cottages on either side of the track. Now and again a woman peeped anxiously out of a doorway, and a trio of fishermen coming up from the beach stared at her in a way that made Rowène raise her chin defiantly. None of the women spoke, although she fancied she detected both pity and curiosity in their eyes, but one of the fishermen ventured to address a greeting to "Master Guy" which he answered with a tired smile and a comment about the weather and their catch.

It was, she realised, the first time he had spoken since their quarrel – if that was the right word – beneath the thorn tree.

But Rowène had no time to reflect on that. The horses were now making the climb up the stony track that led to the castle itself and Rowène found her gaze drawn upwards towards the looming keep that would be her prison. Unlike Chartre castle there was no hint of warmth or grace about this place, built as it was of some dark granite, the bleak walls squatting menacingly on the very edge of the deep, sheer-sided chasm that protected it on the landward side while the sea must guard its back.

No flicker of light showed through any of the narrow slits that pierced the functional towers and only the glint of mail here and there, high on the outer wall revealed that, despite all appearances, there was life within. Although not large, the castle appeared to Rowène overwhelmingly sinister and grimly unwelcoming, a fitting lair for Black Joffroi and his brother – though she admitted she was biased in the matter. She tried to remember that Guy called this place home, that there had been warmth in his voice when he spoke of it so presumably it must possess some more welcoming attributes.

Not that there was the slightest trace of warmth in his voice as he called up to the unseen sentries. He used the local Rogé dialect so Rowène did not understand the exact words, but whatever he said, it provoked an immediate response and at least two different voices could be heard yelling instructions, presumably at the gate guards below.

"'Tis Master Guy!"

"Get that bloody drawbridge down now."

"And send someone to tell Mistress Mathilde."

Moments later they were clattering over the wooden timbers of the bridge, the hollow sound causing Rowène – much against her better judgement – to look down... and down... into the depths of the chasm from whence a loud roaring rose to echo in her ears. Far, far below she could just make out the flash and curl of the foaming waves as they crashed through the narrow opening between castle rock and mainland.

The hideously long drop to the dangerous water roiling beneath her palfrey's hooves caused her head to swim and she could only hope that, whatever the parlous state of Black Joffroi's finances, the timbers of the drawbridge had been kept in good repair. Indeed, so terrifying did she find that dark drop that it was with a feeling almost of relief that she passed under the sharp teeth of the portcullis and through the threatening maw of the dimly lit gate tower.

Once within the small, square courtyard she was stunned by the sudden tide of noise and light that surged around her. Glancing from side to side, she attempted to separate the confusion into its constituent parts but it seemed to her – weary and apprehensive as she was – that not just the grooms and guards but everyone with any excuse, or even none at all, had come running with torches and greetings, their eyes inevitably slipping slyly from their returning steward to his companion.

Whatever they were thinking, though, one glance at Guyard de Martine's set face appeared to be enough to warn them to keep their thoughts to themselves. Even so, Rowène felt her face burn, finding it easy to guess what the folk of Rogérinac castle must be thinking. Wondered too quite how Guy meant to handle the undeniably awkward situation.

# Chapter 9

## *A Less Than Warm Welcome*

Reining his weary stallion to a halt Guyard dismounted slowly, his whole body stiff with the tension that had held him for most of the afternoon, and handed Fireflame's reins to the nearest groom. Only then did he turn towards the woman he had brought so unwillingly into his home.

With a slight shake of her head she refused his assistance before he could offer it and slipped down from the saddle, wrapping the black mantle more closely about her as she did so; possibly because she was cold, more likely in an instinctive, if futile, attempt to disguise her disreputable attire. Guyard waited only until her feet touched the ground before moving to slip a firm hand beneath her elbow – he was mildly surprised to find she did not pull away from him – and turned her to face him, the bulk of his body some protection between her and whoever might be watching.

"What now, Sir Guy?"

She spoke in common speech – quite deliberately, he guessed – and her voice was steady and cool, faintly derisive even, and gave not the slightest hint to such of the castle denizens who were present, most of whom had no legitimate reason – curiosity did not count – for being there anyway, that they had ever been on more familiar terms than that of gaoler and hostage. Whether she was still angry with him or merely being cautious, he did not know but nonetheless was grateful for the distance her tone established.

Even as he drew breath to answer her, he saw her cast a sweeping glance around the bailey, her delicate nostrils flaring at the pungent odours that wafted from direction of the stables and dung heap. Her eyes met his briefly and she spoke before he could.

"God of Light, Guy!" she murmured in Mithlondian, appalled incredulity all too evident despite her low tone. "I know you said your family were close to poverty, but this? Even my father's swine were housed better! And you call such a midden home?"

Guyard winced at her words – which were, he admitted, quite justified – and wasted neither breath nor effort in arguing. Instead he pitched his voice so that his words could be heard by all and said emotionlessly in common speech,

"Lady Rowena, on behalf of my brother, Lord Joffroi, I bid you welcome to Rogérinac." Then, glancing swiftly around the crowd, he picked out one of the faces he sought, that of Mathilde's serving woman. "Frythe! Where is my wife?"

"I'm here!"

The familiar, temper-edged voice rose above the mumbled mutterings and gawping heads turned eagerly as his wife made her way through the assembled servants. He doubted they had been so entertained since the last time he and Ran had fallen out and resorted to a fist fight in the courtyard to resolve their differences. But he could hardly silence his wife with a fist to the jaw, much though he might wish to prevent her making fools of them all before the servants. Some hope, he thought, as she came to stand in front of him, hands on hips, her once pretty face ugly with belligerence.

"But if you think I'm about to curtsey to your doxy, then you can think again! Think with your head, that is, not your..." She lapsed into an idiomatic expression he did not think a Chartreux noblewoman would be familiar with. Or at least he hoped she had not heard his brother's men bandying it about and worked out to what body part it referred. But he was able to spare only the briefest glance at Rowène before his wife's next words brought his attention back to her. "Surely there are whores aplenty here already. So what's so special about *this one*, that you must needs bring her back with you?"

An awful silence fell as servants and soldiers alike looked towards Guyard, eager not to miss his reaction. Deeply angered though he was, he *could* understand his wife's outrage, even if he was not minded to pander to it. Turning to the woman he must, all at costs, think of only as his brother's hostage, he said quietly,

"Lady Rowena, I must apologise for my wife. If you will come with me I will show you to your chamber." And in a terse under-tone to his wife, "If you cannot be courteous, Mathilde, I suggest you keep silence." He took a steadying breath and continued less harshly, more wearily, "Come, Tilde, let us not quarrel. Not when there is no need. It has been a grim enough errand I have been on without returning to fight with you. Come inside and I will tell you the truth of it. And perhaps then you will not think so harshly of either the Lady Rowena or myself."

That, of course, had always been a forlorn hope and, looking at the stubborn set to his wife's mouth, he could foresee only bitter conflict ahead between himself, Mathilde and Rowène – until such time as Joffroi and Ariène returned to Rogérinac to release him from his charge. Or, against all odds, Joscelin de Veraux decided to claim his bride.

Still hoping to avoid a cat fight in the castle courtyard Guyard turned to look at Rowène. She was standing straight and proud by his side, not deigning to acknowledge Mathilde by so much as a flicker of her eyelashes, though Guyard could see she was growing paler by the moment. One part of him was wondering how any of those watching her gallant bearing and the defiant lift to her chin could doubt that, despite her disreputable masculine clothing, she really was the high-born lady he had claimed. The other part of his mind was reminding him that she had only recently been laid up with a fever and that if he wished to prevent her falling down in a faint he should act now.

*Too late, damn it!*

Even as Rowène's eyes closed and her body went limp, he was reaching for her – just in time to save her from crumpling into the noisome muck of the courtyard. With a grimace he gathered her up into his arms, reflecting that it was just as well that his wounds had now completely healed and that Ranulf was not there to make any clever remarks. Unfortunately Mathilde was still very much present and as he passed his wife, Guyard paused long enough to say,

"Perhaps you would be good enough to remember your duties as chatelaine and order the servants to prepare baths, both for myself and Lady Rowena."

"And just where do you intend to put that..."

"Have a care, Mathilde!" Guyard kept his voice low but it carried a warning nonetheless. "You may say what you please to me in private but in public you will remember the courtesy due to a guest."

Mathilde flashed him an angry glance but chose finally to take some heed of his words and subsided into a seething silence, at least in front of the servants. Seeing that she was not going to venture an immediate response he continued tersely,

"There is a spare chamber in the south-east tower. I will take Lady Rowena there now. If you will instruct the servants accordingly."

"Take her, will you? Shall I then instruct the servants to stay away until you leave?" Mathilde murmured slyly.

Guyard caught the implication but, as he doubted that any of the servants were near enough to overhear the snide words, he chose to ignore them for the time being in favour of getting Rowène to a room she could call her own. She would also need a maid. Though where he was going to find one he could trust to look after her properly he had no notion. Mathilde had, unfortunately, not been far adrift in her scathing description of the castle's serving women; but only in that he did not think either of his brothers had ever actually paid for their services, taking it as their right to bed whichever of the women they pleased, with the possible exception of Kelse the cook.

It being out of the question to remove Kelse from the kitchen, Guyard began to pass under mental review those serving women who were left, all of whom were likely to model their behaviour towards Rowène on his wife's, at least until Lady Ariène arrived. And only the gods knew what that bitch's attitude towards her daughter was likely to be! That, however, was an evil for the future. For now he would concentrate on the problems he could perhaps solve.

He reached the narrow spiralling stairs of the south-east tower and as he began the awkward climb to the top floor Guyard began to sweat, both from physical exertion and a grim determination to find an acceptable solution. He paused a moment on the landing outside the room known as the Steward's Chamber, ostensibly to consolidate his hold on the unconscious woman in his arms but in reality wondering whether he was completely out of his mind to consider keeping Rowène under what would effectively be house arrest so close to the room where he himself worked and had, on occasion, found it expedient to sleep. Then he shrugged. If he was insane, so be it. He would just have to ensure that he kept his distance. And in the meantime he still had to find someone capable of acting as her personal maid. If not within the castle itself, perhaps one of the peasant women down in the village would...

Suddenly a name snagged his attention and a face formed in his mind; young, timid and, as far as he knew, still unsullied. Yes, he was sure she must be, since to judge by his aggressive attitude towards Finn on the journey, Geryth would likely take an extremely dim view of it if any of the soldiers or serving men tried to bed his young sister. As for his own brothers, although Guyard would not have put it past Joffroi to debauch an innocent maid, he had had another prize in sight these past few seasons and Ranulf's preference had always been for women of more experience so her very innocence would have protected her from him.

Confident that he had found an acceptable solution to at least one of the problems besetting him, Guyard settled his burden more comfortably in his arms and continued on up the stairs.

Shouldering open the door to the topmost tower room he glanced around the small, inhospitable chamber, then down at the girl in his arms, relieved to see that her disquieting pallor had been replaced by a delicate colour akin to the palest of wild roses. Her eyes were open now, he saw, and she appeared to be taking stock of her surroundings, unimpressive though they were compared to the luxury of her own chamber in the Lady Tower of Chartre castle.

Or had been until the chamber, tower and almost the castle itself had been consumed by flames, along with her beautiful sister. With an unpleasant jolt Guyard recalled the helplessness he had felt on seeing the desperate fear in the Lady Juliène's lovely green eyes at Joffroi's victory feast when she had realised he could do nothing to help her. And worse than that, his own horror the following morning when he realised she could not escape the blazing tower.

Cursing the futility of it all and his own inability to save more than Rowène's physical innocence from the ruination of lives and property attendant upon her father's attainder, he set her carefully on her feet, waiting until he was certain she was steady before taking a couple of deliberate steps away. The tower room was still in shadow for the shutters had been closed against the night – indeed they had probably not been opened for months – and the only light came from the torch in the bracket in the stairwell. Not that Guyard needed light to read the expression on her face.

He might have said something then, in reassurance or apology he did not know which, when he became aware that Mathilde had followed him up the stairs. Weariness and irritation caused him to address her in a curt tone he rarely employed with any woman, whatever her birth or position.

"Lady Rowena will be needing a personal servant..."

"Well she cannot have Frythe," Mathilde snapped.

"No," Guyard continued with hard-held patience. "I would not ask you to give up, or even share, your own maid. I was actually thinking of Gerde."

Unexpectedly – and incomprehensibly – Mathilde uttered a short laugh and said,

"As you like, Guy. I'm sure they're well suited."

*Now what in Hell did she mean by that?*

Then, with a malicious smile curving her full lips, she laid her hand possessively on Guyard's bare forearm, accompanying the unexpected gesture with a throaty murmur,

"I'm sorry about earlier. That wasn't the way I'd planned to welcome you home, my love. I've set Frythe and Eadwyn to fetching your bath water. You can talk to me whilst you bathe." She slanted a sly, sideways sneer at the woman she clearly viewed as her rival and continued, "Come, Guy, there's nothing more for you here." And, looking up into his eyes, added in a low, unmistakeable tone, "I've missed you."

At these rather surprising words, and even more surprising tone, Guyard gave his wife a jaundiced look, curious as to what had prompted her sudden, and very public, change of heart. Despite the sensual promise of her last words he knew full well that Mathilde was still furious and he could only be grateful that she now appeared to be controlling her anger somewhat better than she had done in the courtyard. He also found it interesting that she felt the need to warn Rowène, who scarcely needed such a warning in the first place, that Guyard was already bound to her and that, as his wife, Mathilde would always take precedence over any chance-come mistress.

All well and good, Guyard thought grimly, except that Mathilde was wasting her effort since Rowène was not his mistress, nor ever would be.

Leaving Rowène in the sparsely furnished chamber, with another apology and an assurance that he would send up a servant to attend her needs as soon as possible, he followed Mathilde down the steps and through the passageways that led to their own chamber – a room that was comfortable only by comparison with the bleak tower room they had just left or the one where Ranulf slept whenever he was home. A large wooden tub, half full of steaming water, stood waiting but Guyard ignored its lure for the moment.

Frythe, Mathilde's tirewoman, was there too, arranging a large ragged square of rough linen and a small dish of tallow soap close to the tub. Having done this she decanted a jug of ale and a pottery beaker onto a clothing chest at the foot of the bed, picked up the tray and was almost out of the door before Guyard spoke,

"Frythe? Would you please find Gerde and send her up to me."

"Now, Master Guy?" Frythe asked, even as she looked at her mistress.

"Of course, now!" Guyard snapped. "Would I ask for her now if tomorrow would do?"

"No, Sir Guy!"

She bobbed a flustered curtsey and sped away. Guyard did not often use that tone but when he did all the castle servants knew it was wise to obey him.

Despite his irritation at Frythe's growing tendency to look to Mathilde to over-rule his orders, Guyard wanted his bath far more than he wanted an argument with his wife. Sitting down heavily on the bed, he began the difficult task of removing his wet and muddy boots. Contemplating their shabby state he wondered grimly whether, now that his elder brother was on the verge of binding himself to the wealthiest noblewoman in Mithlondia, he might soon be in a position to afford a new pair. If, that is, he could stomach the fact that they would be paid for with money stained with de Chartreux blood. No, the boots would have to wait, he decided, as he dropped them on the floor and dragged off his damp tunic and shirt.

A faint scratching sound came from the direction of the door and he looked at his wife.

"That will be Gerde. Can I trust you to deal with our guest's comfort or must I order matters myself?" he queried.

Mathilde shrugged unhelpfully and, with a return to her former waspishness, said,

"You brought your leman here. You can deal with the problems you've made." And in the direction of the door, "Come."

At once the door opened and a young serving girl stepped warily into the room. She had obviously come straight from the kitchens to judge from the grubby linen apron that partially covered her grey woollen skirt, both this and the short-sleeved chemise she wore under a haphazardly laced black bodice showing evidence of repeated darning. Guyard watched as the girl's eyes darted fearfully from Mathilde, standing in the middle of the room, to him, her eyes widening as she took in his semi-naked state. Blushing, she dropped her gaze.

"Master Guy, sir? Mistress Mathilde? Frythe said ye'm wanting to see me?"

"*I* do," Guyard replied crisply, rising to his feet. Sighing, he picked up his damp shirt and dragged it on again, then beckoned the girl closer. She came readily enough now that he was halfway decently dressed again and despite her own somewhat slatternly appearance, he was immeasurably reassured by what he read in the soft brown eyes that lifted to his.

"Now, Gerde, there is nothing to worry about. You have done nothing wrong. But I am sure you have heard that I brought a lady back to Rogérinac with me?"

"Aye, sir."

Observing the flash of discomfort in her hurriedly downcast eyes Guyard assumed that he and Rowène had already been discussed to their detriment in both kitchen and guard hall, and there was a more than slightly grim note in his voice as he continued firmly,

"She is the Lady Rowena of Chartreux, Lord Joffroi's ward, and she will therefore be treated with respect and courtesy while she remains in Rogérinac.

Do you understand?"

"Aye, Master Guy."

This time there was something in Gerde's tone other than apprehension, something that caused Guyard to look at her anew.

"Has Geryth said anything to you about this?"

"Nay, Master Guy, o' course not," Gerde whispered, evidently not wishing to go against the Steward of Rogé but equally unwilling to bring blame to her brother. "He wouldn't tell me naught about aught. He on'y said as least said, soonest mended an' maybe 'twould be best if ev'ryone were ter keep their long noses out o' their betters' business."

Somewhat surprised by this robust declaration Guyard smiled fleetingly at Gerde and continued,

"Well, while she is with us, Lady Rowena will be needing someone to wait on her and act as her tire-maid Do you think you could do that?"

"Me?" queried Gerde in blank astonishment. "But, Master Guy, ye knows I's on'y worked in the kitchens afore. I don't know nothin' 'bout fine ladies an' how they dress."

"Never mind that, I am sure Lady Rowena will help you learn," Guyard reassured her and heard Mathilde murmur, not quite under her breath,

"Well, 'tis not as though Mistress Rowena has many *gowns* to worry about."

"No, something else I must see to," Guyard muttered, misliking the emphasis and reminded of yet another duty towards his brother's ward – it sounded better than hostage, at least! Returning his attention to the young serving girl he said, "Well, Gerde?"

"I'll do me best, Master Guy," she promised. She shot a nervous sideways glance towards her mistress, then returned her attention to Guyard, adding hesitantly, "I's wonderin', sir, what should I be callin' her?"

"You will call her Lady Rowena," Guyard replied firmly. He had not missed Mathilde's slighting form of address but refused to argue about it while the serving girl was still in the room. He could sense that Mathilde's simmering anger was now perilously close to boiling over and with that consideration in mind he dismissed Gerde, deciding that further instructions could wait until a quieter moment.

"That will be all, Gerde. For now, please go and organise a bath for Lady Rowena. And get that lazy scoundrel Eadwyn to do the heavy work while you sort out a clean mattress and fresh linen for her bed."

"Aye, Master Guy, that I will," Gerde replied with a quick bob and a sudden dimpling smile that rendered her rounded, youthful face pretty enough to attract a second glance from most men.

Seeing this Guyard wondered uneasily whether he might, after all, have done the girl a disservice by promoting her out of the kitchens and into the living quarters of a family whose men folk were not noted for their celibacy. But, he argued, Joffroi was scarcely likely to look at another woman once he had made the beautiful and venomous Lady Ariène his wife and Ranulf was at present in Chartre, rutting his way through the wenches there and would probably not be home until winter at the earliest.

Shrugging off Ran's inability to settle down with one woman, be she wife or mistress, Guyard turned his attention to his own comfort, remembering then that the water in the tub was cooling and that he still had many matters to sort out before the horn rang for the evening meal. He also realised that he was now alone with his wife, and likely to remain so for some time.

Rather than welcoming their solitude, however, Mathilde was inspecting him with unconcealed displeasure.

"When did you last wash or shave?" she asked in obvious distaste.

"Properly? The day I left Chartre," Guyard replied mildly, rubbing his fingers wearily over the stubble on his jaw. "I am sorry if it offends you but there has been little opportunity to do either since then." And he had had other things to worry about.

"Well, Mistress Rowena is welcome to your company in your present state. She is obviously more accustomed to the stink of male sweat and wet horse than I am."

"*Lady* Rowena," Guyard corrected her, steel underlying the surface gentleness.

Mathilde shrugged and sniffed ostentatiously at a small bunch of dried lavender hanging from her belt. Taking the not so subtle hint Guyard thankfully removed what was left of his damp clothing. Clambering gratefully into the tub, he scrubbed his short hair and weary body vigorously with the harsh soap before relaxing back, allowing the warm water to lap around him, soaking away the dirt and discomfort of the last month – even if it did nothing to assuage the guilt of blood unjustly shed that still stained his soul.

Without conscious effort his thoughts returned to the woman with whom his name was now irretrievable linked, the woman who would for the foreseeable future be living beneath the same roof as him, albeit in a chamber on the opposite side of the castle from the room he shared with his wife. Would she – Rowène – be lonely without her sister or even him? Frightened by her grim surroundings? Brooding over those whom she had loved and lost?

By now he hoped Gerde would have introduced herself and be preparing a bath for her new mistress, taking steps to set that bleak little room to rights. That was well enough but Rowène would also need clothes; something more fitting for a high-born lady than a harlot's scarlet gown or his own worn garb. Although how he was going to provide such raiment, only the gods knew...

Opening his eyes, he saw Mathilde standing a little distance away, watching him with cold speculation in her dark eyes.

"Well, my lord-by-binding, perhaps now you will tell me what you have been doing? And why you choose to return to Rogérinac in such a way as to cause me the most humiliation?"

Guyard sighed and, taking up his knife, began to carefully scrape away the two-day growth – he *had* made the effort to shave before he left Blackoakleas – of stubble. When he had finished he stood up and reaching for the towel, stepped from the tub, showering scummy water everywhere.

Mathilde took a couple of hasty steps back, almost knocking over the jug of ale Frythe had brought up earlier. Frowning, she poured a measure of ale into the beaker and, stepping warily around the wet patches, offered it to him, affecting a more conciliatory tone,

"Perhaps I should have said it before... but welcome home, Guy."

Guyard dropped the towel on the floor and accepted the proffered beaker. He leaned towards her, thinking he should give her a kiss at least, but she moved away from him abruptly.

"No! Not until you have told me everything. About Chartre. About *her!*"

"Her name is Rowena," Guyard reiterated with grim patience, obscurely relieved that Mathilde seemed not to want his physical touch and at the same time hurt by her reluctance. Obviously his lengthy absence had not warmed her heart towards him. Given the turmoil in his own heart, perhaps Mathilde's coolness was not such a bad thing – although, the gods knew, they still had to live together until such time as death released either one of them...

"And?" she prompted.

"And what?" he asked, momentarily disorientated.

"*Her!* Your precious Lady Rowena!" Mathilde snapped, clearly irritated by his wool-gathering.

"Oh yes, Lady Rowena... Well, she is one of the twin daughters of Louis and Ariena of Chartreux. Her father died a traitor's death in Lamortaine a month ago and her sister, brother and half-brother are also dead, caught in the wreck of Chartre's fall. By now, if all has gone according to Joffroi's plan, he and Lady Ariena will have gained permission from Prince Linnius to take the binding oath. Which means that Lady Ariena is now the Lady of Rogé. And her daughter, as Joffroi's ward, will be treated accordingly."

"So how does this *lady*..." Again there was a certain unpleasant emphasis in Mathilde's use of the term but he chose once again to ignore it. "How does this *lady* come to be riding the moors alone with you, dressed in men's clothing, looking more like some common travelling strumpet than the virtuous gently-bred daughter of the man who was once one of Mithlondia's greatest warlords?"

"Lady Rowena has been brought back to Rogérinac as a hostage for her people's fealty to Joffroi and to wait for her betrothal to be formalised," Guyard replied keeping his tone carefully impersonal.

"Oh, and who is the fortunate man?" Mathilde asked sarcastically.

Guyard did not think she was particularly interested in the answer but she had obviously sensed an opportunity to goad him further. He doubted, however, that she would be prepared for the name he laid before her, as with iron calm he said,

"She is betrothed to Joscelin de Veraux, Prince Linnius's half-brother and also the Lord of Veraux's grandson."

Mathilde's eyes widened a little at this revelation but recovering quickly, she said bitingly,

"It would seem the slut has a taste for bastards!"

Guyard could feel the muscles tightening in his jaw but Mathilde apparently chose to ignore the warning signs, continuing swiftly, now so well launched in her tirade that there was no hope of stopping her. "As for her betrothed, I can only pity him! I hope before it is too late someone will tell the poor man that he will be obliged to take *your* leavings if he holds by this misguided betrothal?"

"My…"

She gave vent to a contemptuous laugh.

"Oh, don't look at me like that, Guy! It is common knowledge that you lay with her! Not only on the night Lord Joffroy took Chartre but every night since then! Or at least that was the gossip brought back by the men whose escort you dismissed a se'ennight ago so that you could have her to yourself without fear of any of them tattling to your wife. But I learned the truth anyway. Which is just as well, since if I'd waited for you to tell me, I'd have waited for ever! Wouldn't I?" She did not wait for his answer but added with ill-concealed curiosity, "There was even some tale going round that you and Ranulf were sharing her and her sister between you!"

"*What?*" Guyard spat the word out in stunned disbelief and glared at his wife, unable to keep his fury from blazing in his eyes and voice. "Daemons of Hell, what sort of unmitigated bastard do you take me for? You are my *wife* and yet you could believe such a thing? Gods above! Even if you have nothing better to do than to listen to gutter gossip, surely you know me – or Ran – better than that!"

His anger was such that Mathilde actually flinched and took a hasty step backwards as if fearing a blow. Recalled to some semblance of reason, Guyard fought to restrain his temper; he had never hit a woman in his life and he did not intend to start now, richly though Mathilde might deserve it.

Instead he drained his ale off and tossed the empty beaker on the bed. Turning his back on his wife he knelt by the clothing coffer at the foot of the bed and drew out a long-sleeved, coarse linen shirt, thick woollen tunic and a much-mended pair of breeches; winter clothing, but all he had left that was clean, dry or yet in his possession.

He thought Mathilde might have been sufficiently shaken by his uncharacteristic outburst to keep her malicious tongue still but as he came to his feet she demanded scornfully,

"So you want me to believe that 'tis not true?"

Guyard finished dressing with quick jerky movements and finally turned to look at his wife, his anger still in his eyes but now under tight control.

"Which part of it?" he queried coldly. "If you are interested in Ranulf's preferences and habits then I am afraid you will have to ask him yourself. If you are asking whether I have ever shared any woman's favours with either of my brothers then I can assure you that I have never, at any time, done so. Even before I took my binding oath to you. And certainly not after. As for the rest?" He hesitated, but even for Joffroi he could not lie to his wife. He could, however, tell it in such a way as to uphold gossip. "Yes," he said finally, "It is true, I did sleep with her..." Slept, not bedded.

"You mean you actually..?" she stuttered into stunned incoherence.

"Yes."

"How many times?" Her voice rose incredulously.

"The night Chartre fell and every night after that, save for the time she lay ill of a fever with the Sisters of Silverleigh. Now, are you satisfied?"

Mathilde stared at her lord-by-binding, unable to speak or even think as the silence deepened between them. Despite the gossip the soldiers had brought back from Chartreux, it was not until this moment, when she heard the words from his own lips, that she actually believed the honourable, tight-laced Guyard de Martine could have deliberately broken his binding oath to her.

A chill shivered through her then at the thought that he might finally have found out about the many times she had been unfaithful to him and had chosen this very public way to be revenged on her. And, if he could do such a previously unthinkable thing as that, what other lengths might he go to in order to punish her? Perhaps even to casting her out of Rogérinac while he set up his doxy in her place as chatelaine of the castle? Surely he would not do that? She did not care one jot that he had finally taken a mistress, but she had no intention of having her power and position stolen from her by some whey-faced, high-born trollop.

The silence continued to tighten between them and she knew that she must say something lest he became suspicious of the reasons behind her apparently tame acceptance of his disgraceful behaviour. Gathering her wits together and quelling her shaking nerves, she said with a fair assumption of hurt,

"Gods, Guy! I know we parted in anger but if you wanted to be unfaithful to me, could you not at least have done it discreetly?"

She saw the anger in Guyard's eyes finally fade away, to be replaced by weary patience.

"Mathilde, our... quarrel has nothing to do with... with anything I might have done with... the Lady Rowena. If you must know, it was only at Joffroi's direct order that I shared her bed. And only then because if it had not been me, Joffroi would have given her to Ranulf or the men of the garrison."

"And that's your excuse is it?" she sneered, more sure of her ground now and certain that he knew nothing of her secret dalliances. "And a pitiful excuse at that, since we both know you've disobeyed Lord Joffroy before and lived to tell the tale. So why not this time? I'll tell you why not! Because you didn't *want* to disobey him!"

She swept another assessing glance over his face and continued with well-simulated anger. "Damn you, Guy, why can't you just admit that your lust got the better of you for once! *That* I might have been able to accept and forgive. Chartre is far enough away, after all. But no, you had to bring her back here. Why? Unless you *wanted* to flaunt your adultery in my face? And now that you have brought her back, will you continue sharing her bed? Here, where everyone will know she is your mistress?"

She knew she had touched him on the raw but he did not allow himself to be provoked into giving way to his emotions again.

"Think what you please Mathilde," he replied with an iron-hard calm. "I know from long experience that you will believe what you wish to, no matter what I may say. But this is the truth and I suggest you listen to it. Whatever there once was between Lady Rowena and myself... whatever we had... you have my word that it is now over. As far as it concerns anyone else Lady Rowena is now Joffroi's daughter-by-binding. She is here in Rogérinac under your chaperonage, awaiting the arrival of the man to whom she is betrothed. She will do nothing to offend you or undermine your position and as long as you can behave with reasonable amity towards her the gossips and scandalmongers will forget soon enough that there was ever anything between her and me. And now, if you have spat out all the poison you have been storing up against my return, I must see to her comfort."

Taken aback by his words though she was, Mathilde still recognised the set look on his normally good-humoured face and knew from past experience that further recriminations on her part would only be met with a stone wall of carefully constructed indifference. She would achieve nothing in that way and, all things considered, the fall-out from this tawdry scandal could have been much worse, and had in fact given her an acceptable excuse to hold him at a distance. Despite this reasoning, however, she could not resist one final barbed remark.

"Just so long as you don't expect me to give up any of my gowns to clothe your whore!"

At these words he stood stock still, then said in the coolly distant tones she hated,

"*If* she were indeed my whore, which she is *not*, I would not expect you to. Courtesy and kindness to an honoured guest is another matter but as you seem incapable of such, I must look elsewhere. I will see you at the meal table, Madam."

With that he picked up his dagger, thrust it into its sheath and strode towards the door. He paused there, his hand on the latch.

"Lady Rowena will be eating in the hall with us – if not tonight then as soon as I can find more suitable attire for her – and I expect you to behave with all courtesy towards her, if only because you are, in the absence of Lady Ariena, the chatelaine of Rogérinac. The fact that you are my wife and the Lady Rowena did, for a few brief nights, bring a long-unfelt warmth to my bed, is completely irrelevant!"

A moment later the door closed firmly behind him and Mathilde found herself alone, torn between fury and a fear that she might have gone too far. But below those emotions was a growing, if scarce acknowledged, desire to go a lot further indeed!

# Chapter 10

## *A Hot Bath, Burned Meat and a Cold Bed*

Left alone in the damp, draughty chamber at the top of the south-east tower, Rowène stood frozen with cold and dread, arms wrapped around her waist, her heart as heavy as the rain-soaked mantle that clung to her shoulders and dripped steadily onto the dusty floorboards. With a disbelieving gaze, she surveyed the dingy little room that was to be her prison for the foreseeable future. Much smaller and darker than the large, light, airy chamber she had shared with Ju in Chartre castle, it was as far removed in terms of comfort and elegance as the stars were from the muddy soil of Mithlondia.

At some time in the long-distant past the bare stone walls had been roughly plastered and lime-washed, but if ever tapestries had hung there they had been removed long ago, leaving only the grey cobwebs and black mould spawned by years of neglect. The only relief from the monotony of the dreary walls came in the form of a narrow window – glassless, but covered by an ill-fitting, broken shutter – and the surprisingly solid door through which she had entered.

The furniture was limited to a single worm-eaten stool and a narrow, curtainless bed upon which lay a tired-looking mattress of such dubious appearance she would have been ashamed to have assigned it to one of the Chartreux serving maids. There appeared to be neither linens nor blankets but that circumstance could presumably be remedied. What she found more disconcerting was the very obvious fact that there was no privy in the vicinity and she wondered just how Guyard de Martine intended to resolve that particular problem, for surely he would not want her wandering willy-nilly about the castle.

Assailed by a sudden restlessness Rowène paced over to the window and peered through one of the shutter's many gaps, but the last dregs of light had been swallowed long since by black night and although she could hear the waves crashing and churning below she could not see the water; as much because her eye was watering from the blast of fresh salt air as from the impenetrable darkness outside. Not that she minded that lack of sight over-much; the sea presently battering the coast beneath Rogérinac castle sounded so wild and fierce as to be a completely different entity from the warm lagoons of Kaerellios or the gentle waters of Chartre Bay that had been her only experience of the sea thus far.

Catching back a sigh, Rowène turned away from the window. Her wits returning from their wandering, she rubbed chilled fingers vigorously over her bare forearms, trying to form some sensible solution to the problems that beset her.

First, and most pressing, was the need to get warm and dry again; a change of clothes and a hot meal would be most welcome too.

At the same time decide how best to deal with that jealous harpy who was currently chatelaine of Rogérinac castle.

If that were not enough, she must find some way to get Geryth sent back to Chartre so that he might return the silver brooch to its owner. And while this was the least imperative of her problems, it was also likely to prove the most insoluble. But in any event she could not send for Ranulf until she had decided what to do about his...

A soft thump on the door made her jump and sent her thoughts flying out into the night.

"Who is it?" she called, hoping it was the promised servant and not the harridan returned, although she would welcome almost anything that took away the necessity of thinking about Ranulf de Rogé and the...

"Guyard de Martine, Demoiselle," came the formal reply. "May I come in?"

Straightening her shoulders and striving to eradicate all thoughts of his half-brother's hell-spawned − and she meant that quite literally − babe from her mind, Rowène crossed the room and opened the door. She lifted her chin as Guy flicked an impassive glance over her grubby, rumpled attire, noticing with a surge of resentment that his hair was damply clean and his face free from the dark blond stubble he had acquired over the past few days; obviously *he* had taken the opportunity to bathe and don clean clothes while *she* had been left to moulder alone in this depressing room.

"What do you want?" she asked abruptly, aware that her tone was unnecessarily brittle but too cold and uncomfortable to care.

Guy remained standing on the threshold and, although he shot what she thought was a rather bleak look over her shoulder at the dark chamber behind her, his tone reflected little beyond a strained courtesy.

"Forgive my intrusion, Demoiselle, I merely came to assure myself that your tire-maid and bath water had arrived."

"A tire-maid and a bath?" she echoed with a scathing lift of her brows. "Well, as you can see, Messire, I have neither. Although I perceive you have been more fortunate, with the bath at least! As to the other comforts your wife or the serving maids might have provided you with I would not care to guess. But tell me, does Madame Mathilde still believe me to be your mistress? Or have you told her the truth?"

She thought for a moment that Guy was going to ignore these deliberately provocative comments. Then he said quietly,

"I have appointed one of the kitchen wenches to be your personal maid. Her name is Gerde and although she may appear to you as lacking in either years or experience, she is at least willing to learn − which is more than can be said for the rest of them. However, since it would seem that she has been delayed, I will go and make sure that both she and your bath are with you shortly. As for my wife," he hesitated and then said flatly, "I told her no lies but what I did say was sufficient to convince her that we were lovers."

"Dear God of Light, Guy! What were you thinking?" Rowène exclaimed, forgetting both formality and sarcasm in her shock.

Apparently unaffected by her reaction, Guyard merely shrugged and continued dispassionately.

"My reasons for allowing my wife to believe that I have broken my binding vows are my own. Though I have, of course, assured her that the liaison between you and I is over."

"And what will you say to Joscelin de Veraux? *If* he ever bothers to seek me out?" Rowène demanded, ignoring for the moment any consideration of what *she* would tell her betrothed, if by that time she was visibly swollen with Ranulf de Rogé's misbegotten babe.

"*When* that happens," Guyard replied grimly. "You have my word that I will tell him the full truth. Now, Demoiselle, by your leave..."

Without waiting for her formal permission, he made a slight bow and disappeared back down the shadowed stairwell, leaving Rowène alone once more and wondering whether, even if the promised hot water did arrive, she would ever be warm and clean again. Shivering in the sibilant draught that came spiralling up the ill-lit stairway she firmly closed the door. It was only then that Guy's words concerning her new attendant impacted on her consciousness.

A kitchen wench, he had said. Gods help her, would this... Gerta, was that her name... prove to be another Ilana? Almost certainly, she concluded, if the slatternly women she had glimpsed earlier among the rag-tag bunch of servants crowding the castle courtyard were anything to judge by.

Unaware of her new mistress' pessimistic conclusions but anxious to perform her new duties to the best of her ability Gerde made her way down to the kitchen, well aware that she could expect little by way of assistance if, by ill fortune, Frythe had already preceded her. In which case the best she could hope for was that the other girl would keep her spiteful tongue to herself for once, since then she would only have to deal with the raucous, but not completely unkind, ribbing of the other servants.

Feeling rather queasy at the thought, Gerde slipped into the hot confines of the kitchen and found to her dismay that Frythe was already there, casually ensconced on the lap of one of Commander Ranulf's soldiers. From this position she was busy regaling the assembled servants with some of the juicier details of the as yet unmended quarrel between Master Guy and Mistress Mathilde. A situation which, according to Frythe, could only have been made worse by the arrival of a person she had no hesitation in proclaiming little better than a common strumpet – a case of the pot calling the cauldron black if ever there was one, Gerde thought indignantly.

Nevertheless, general opinion appeared for the moment to be on Frythe's side and, in the way of such beliefs, was being very loudly expressed by all those present, which included the cook, her two underlings, the spit boy, the dairymaid, the laundress, two serving wenches, three men servants and the soldier himself.

Finn was quite clearly carrying a grudge against the Lady Rowena and in pursuit of this was only too keen to recount his version of the night the ladies of Chartreux had fallen into the hands of Lord Joffroy and his brothers. Those assembled must all have heard it before, Finn having returned some days ago, but this did not seem to dim their enthusiasm to hear it again. Gerde, who had not appreciated the tale the first time – finding nothing amusing in the thought of either Commander Ranulf or Master Guy forcing themselves on any woman – could not repress a strangled sound of distaste.

It was at this point that one of the other servants noticed her hovering in the doorway and drew Frythe's attention to the newcomer. As soon as Gerde realised this she took a deep breath and despite her doubts, both as to her own fitness for her sudden elevation to personal servant and as to whether Lady Rowena really was – or had been – Master Guy's leman, took a hesitant step forward into the largely hostile atmosphere.

Abruptly the noise died away and under the barrage of eyes she somehow found the courage to ask Eadwyn for a tub and hot water to be taken up to the south-east tower room. Far from leaping to his feet and attending to the matter with all haste, he merely stared at her, an unpleasant sneer marring still further his pock-marked countenance, then hawked noisily and spat, close enough to Gerde for the spittle to touch the ragged hem of her grey gown.

"An' 'oo d'ye reckon ye be?" he demanded roughly, "Givin' orders like Lady Muck 'erself!"

"Master Guy bade me attend Lady Rowena," Gerde replied, raising her chin and staring as bravely as she could at him.

She could only pray fervently that he would not guess at her knowledge of his illicit relationship with Mistress Mathilde during Master Guy's absence, else her life would not be worth so much as a bronze farthing! At the same time she wondered how any woman could welcome Eadwyn's touch in preference to Master Guy's. Shuddering, she wrenched her thoughts from the scene in the stable she had so nearly stumbled into, doing her best not to show her fear and nausea as Eadwyn spat again and growled,

"Aye, Frythe heard tell what Master Guy had ter say 'bout that. Reckon the man's losin' it! Allus said his wits were as feeble as his cock!"

Ignoring as best she could Eadwyn's shockingly disrespectful comments and the fact that his sister had evidently been listening outside the door, Gerde flushed and returned her attention to Frythe.

"Look, Frythe," she said placatingly. "Ye must know I didna ask fer this position but Master Guy *is* Lord Joffroy's brother an' Steward here. I can't not do what he orders. An' he said fer Eadwyn ter take hot water an' the bathing tub up ter Lady Rowena's chamber."

Eadwyn muttered something under his breath, but she was less worried at the moment by Eadwyn's covert antagonism than by Frythe's overt opposition. There was a nasty gleam in the older girl's eyes and in desperation Gerde sent a hunted look around the kitchen but even Kelse the cook, who was normally the least malicious of the servants, knew better than to interfere between a hell-cat like Frythe and the hapless mouse caught in her claws. All of a sudden Frythe gave a cruel little smile. Seeing this Gerde felt her legs begin to shake and it was as much as she could do to remain standing as the other woman pushed out of her intimate position between Finn's thighs. Putting her hands on her ample hips Frythe strolled closer and gave Gerde a mocking inspection,

"So now ye thinks as how ye're goin' ter be a lady's maid? Reckon that makes ye better'n the rest of us, do ye? An' 'tis *Lady* Rowena, is it? Sure 'bout that, are ye? 'Cos from what Finn told us, seems her's just as much a whore as ye are!"

"I bain't no whore," Gerde protested, her face reddening still more. "An' neither is she. Geryth says..."

"Oh aye! An' we all know as how the sun shines out o' yer brother's arse!" Finn interrupted, his coarse jibe causing Eadwyn to chuckle and Frythe to grin even more maliciously.

Gerde had long known, of course, that Frythe had a grudge against Geryth and suspected it owed something to the fact that her brother had refused the other woman's advances. In light of that knowledge, she guessed that given half a chance Frythe would seize, with relish, the chance to get back at him through his sister. Numbly, she waited for the blow to fall, certain that when it did it would hurt Geryth at least as much as it did her.

"So ye don't reckon as how ye're a whore?" Frythe demanded.

Gerde shook her head but did not trust her voice to deny the other's ugly words. She could only hope Frythe had not guessed the truth she had been so desperate to hide. She flinched instinctively to see the savage light that glittered in Frythe's feral brown eyes as she glanced from Gerde to the avid faces of the other servants and then skittered over Gerde's shoulder as someone came into the kitchen behind her.

"Well then," Frythe continued, more than a hint of malicious triumph in her voice, "Since ye've on'y been liftin' yer skirts fer *half* the household, rather than *really* whoring like the rest of us, I reckon as how ye'll be gettin' one of yer lovers ter put a binding bracelet on yer arm as well as a brat in yer belly!"

"*What!*"

Gerde had thought the hell she had been living in could not get worse... until she heard her brother's stricken tones behind her. Slowly she turned but she could not meet Geryth's blazing eyes for more than a moment. But even as she dropped her shamed gaze she felt his hard hands gripping her upper arms. Felt too his pain, his disbelief, his denial, his rage.

"Damnit, Gerde, tell me that slut is lying!" he rasped. "Tell me ye'm not breeding!"

"Of course 'tis true," Frythe answered him smugly. "The on'y doubt is who the father is."

"Shut yer foul mouth, ye filthy bitch," Geryth snapped. "This is 'twixt me sister an' me..." He sent a scorching look at the circle of watchers, resting in turn on Eadwyn, Hakon, Wulfnoth, Aeldred and finally Finn before finishing savagely. "An' the whoreson bastard what did this ter her."

At this direct challenge Finn pushed off the table he had been leaning against and strolled across the kitchen until he was within a yard of Gerde and her brother. Then, hooking his thumbs in his belt, he rocked on his heels, spat casually at the other man's feet and said mockingly,

"I allus thought ye a fool, boy! But are ye truly so daft as ter think yer slut of a sister'll be able ter say which of us fathered her brat! Fer all her knows, it might be any of us in the castle – from me all the way up to them loose-breeched lechers upstairs."

Geryth made a choking sound in his throat and Gerde, daring to raise her eyes once more to his face, thought for one moment he might be about to throw up. Mastering himself with an effort he flicked a glance in her direction.

"I'll talk ter ye later, Gerde," he rasped. "Fer now, jus' tell me that whoever else ye may have been with, ye've not laid down with this scum!"

Gerde flinched from the fury in her brother's eyes and said helplessly,

"I... he... yes... but it was not..."

Geryth had been angry enough before but at her halting admission he tightened his grip so painfully that she broke off with a gasp. She had meant to tell him that it was not what he was thinking, not with Finn anyway, but he gave her no chance to explain as he thrust her aside and glared back at Finn, his eyes narrowed to slits of blazing brown.

The other man merely grinned and, ignoring Gerde completely, remarked tauntingly,

"As I see it, Geryth, ye've got two choices. Being the gutless fool ye are, ye could go whinin' ter Master Guy an' leave it ter him ter sort out. Though given what he had ter say last time one o' the castle wenches got wi' child I wouldn't like ter count on his bein' so soft this time! Better jus' ter send her down ter the hag in the village soon as ye can an' gi' the old besom sommut ter get rid o' the brat."

Gerde could not withhold a small moan of distress at these brutal words and, whether it was this or some other cause, her brother's temper finally snapped. With an oath as foul as Finn's suggestion, he drove his fist directly into the other's face. Bone crunched as Finn's nose broke and he staggered back under the assault. Catching his balance he barrelled back into the fray, fists flailing, blood, spittle and curses dripping indiscriminately from nose and mouth. Frythe took a couple of hasty steps back out of the way but her eyes were alight with glee as she shouted encouragement to her lover.

Momentarily stunned by the violent tussle that had erupted so suddenly, Gerde gave a whimper of pure fright and turned to the nearest of the watching men servants, an older man who was usually carelessly tolerant of her.

"Hakon, can't ye stop this?" she begged.

"Not bloody likely," the other replied, although not unkindly. "Those two've been spoilin' fer a fight fer months now. 'Tisn't just ter do wi' the bairn, lass."

"No, I know... oh, it doesn't matter," Gerde replied distractedly. She winced as Finn managed to get a blow past her brother's guard and then moaned again as Geryth doubled over and collapsed to the floor. "Oh gods, I've got ter do something. Finn'll kill him else."

"Bollocks!" Hakon replied calmly, eyeing the straining, sweating, swearing pair struggling on the floor. "More like Geryth'll break his bloody neck. An' not a bad thing at that!"

"But then he'll hang," Gerde moaned.

Desperate to prevent such a terrible outcome she bolted towards the door, only to recoil as she collided with the heavy-set man just stepping from the shadows. He caught her before she could fall and she looked up in surprise, almost weeping with relief as she saw who it was – although she should already have known from his actions.

"Oh, thank the gods 'tis ye, sir! Ye've got ter stop them!"

Guyard cast a swift look over the scene, snapped a curt order to the two men closest to him and waded into the fray. Grabbing Geryth by the back of his gambeson he dragged him bodily off the man upon whose chest he had been kneeling, leaving it to Hakon and Wulfnoth to haul the blood-splattered, half-strangled Finn to his feet. Obviously not realising the identity of the man who was restraining him, Geryth continued to struggle and swear until Guyard gave him a rough shake and said brusquely,

"Be still, man!"

Evidently recognising the voice of the man behind him and belatedly taking in the alarmed expressions on the faces of those watching him, Geryth stood still while Finn leant against the nearest wall, gasping noisily for breath as blood dripped down his jerkin.

"Now, tell me, what is the meaning of this disgraceful behaviour?"

For a moment no-one dared respond to that clipped question although more than a few of those present shuffled uncomfortably. Guyard allowed a hint of his impatience and anger to show in his level tones.

"I asked a question. I expect an answer! Finn? Geryth? Why were you fighting? And what in hell's name were either of you doing in the kitchen in the first place?" He glanced at the vast hearth which was now gushing black smoke and added irritably, "For pity's sake, young Will, get that spit turning again else we will all be eating scorched meat for supper. Again!"

At this pointed reminder the boy shot back towards the hearth and coughing against the reek, hurriedly began to turn the spit once more while Kelse pushed the outer door open. Guyard gave a grimace of relief and turned his icy displeasure back towards the two bruised and bloodstained men.

"Well?" he queried with deceptive quiet.

Geryth flushed and mumbled an indistinct apology while Finn merely shook his head and spat out a mouthful of blood. Guyard regarded them both with cold eyes, then gave a low-voiced order to Aeldred who hastened out of the room.

"What, nothing to say?" Guyard asked, irony heavy in his tone. "It is not like you, Finn, to pass up the chance to stir up trouble."

"Nubbing ter say, sir," came the indistinct response.

"Geryth?"

"Misunderstanding, sir," he muttered. "Got outta hand. Sorry."

"Too bloody right it got out of hand!" Guyard snapped. He did not normally swear at the servants but tonight his nerves were so taut it would take the simplest thing to shatter his control completely and he was in no mind to tolerate a brawl in the kitchen between two men who had no business there in the first place. Certainly not if it meant burnt meat for supper! Fixing the two soldiers with a cold glare, he folded his arms and waited for the arrival of the acting garrison commander. It did not take long.

"Sir? Aeldred said you wanted me."

"Ah, Edwy! Take these two in charge and put them in the stocks. Maybe a few days standing in the rain and mud will teach them both that such undisciplined behaviour will not be tolerated – whatever the reason behind it! And you two, just count yourselves lucky to have escaped a flogging – at least for the time being!" he added, a warning note in his voice.

Hearing a choked sob from one of the women nearby, Guyard glanced around for the source, his steely gaze softening slightly as he realised it was Geryth's young sister. He could sympathise with her distress over her brother's punishment but compassion was largely outweighed by annoyance that he had found it necessary to come seeking her in the first place.

"I thought I asked you to attend the Lady Rowena?" he said sternly. "Yet when I spoke to her a moment ago she had not so much as seen you, let alone the bath I ordered."

"Aye, sir, an' I'm right sorry 'bout that. I come straight down ter see 'bout the bath just as ye bid me but... but..."

"But what?" Guyard queried, keeping his tone as unthreatening as possible – he did not want to scare the girl any further – but Gerde merely stood there looking at him helplessly. She was clearly nervous, either of him or her fellow servants, and he doubted he would get a true explanation as to what had caused

461

the delay, though he thought he could make a tolerably accurate guess given what he knew about the unsavoury antics of the Rogérinac castle servants. This in mind he rounded suddenly on the startled Eadwyn and said coldly,

"You, Eadwyn! Did Gerde not tell you to take hot water and the bathing tub up to the Lady Rowena's chamber?"

Eadwyn gaped at him, then glanced around at the other servants. Plainly he would have liked to deny all knowledge of Gerde's request but knew better than to lie, when likely everyone in the kitchen had heard her.

"I were just about ter do it, sir," he said sullenly. "Then those two started..."

"Not good enough!" Guyard interrupted. "Edwy! Take this one out to the stocks as well. A lesson in obedience for him — and for anyone else here who feels disinclined to obey my orders or tarry over-long in carrying them out. Gerde!"

"Aye, sir?"

"My apologies to Lady Rowena and tell her that her bath will be with her shortly." He continued pointedly, more for the benefit of those listening than for Gerde's. "And, as you are now Lady Rowena's tire-maid, you will obey her as you would me. Now go."

Gerde gave him a strained smile, bobbed a quick curtsey and fled from the kitchen.

"Hakon!"

"Aye, Master Guy?"

"See to the hot water and the tub. Immediately." He turned his head to address the soldier. "Edwy, you can remove these three wastrels now and get them settled in the stocks. As for the rest of you..." He raked them with a narrow-eyed glare. "I want supper on the table in a candle-notch. And it had damned well better not be burnt!"

These terse instructions provoked a chorus of assents and a burst of movement among servants and guards alike and, satisfied that matters would now begin to move in the right direction, Guyard turned on his heel and left them to it.

A short while later Rowène looked up from her uncomfortable perch on the side of the bed as a soft knock sounded on her door. Her gaoler returned? The kitchen wench turned tire-maid perhaps? Her bath water even? Or the evil-tongued harpy herself? Well, there was only one way to find out.

"Enter," she called firmly.

Tentatively the door creaked open and a nervous-eyed girl clad in drab servant's garb slipped into the room. Gulping a deep breath of air, the girl bobbed a curtsey and said in softly-accented common speech,

"I'm Gerde, m'lady. Master Guy sent me ter attend ye. If'n ye please, m'lady."

Rowène gave her a wary nod, somewhat relieved by her words, if taken aback by her youthful appearance; Guy had been right – she was very young.

The girl took another breath, her fingers knotting in her apron as she continued carefully,

"Master Guy's ap... apologies, an' yer bath will be with ye shortly." She glanced behind her and said in a rush of relief, "An' here's Hakon now."

Rowène found that she could indeed hear sounds coming from the other side of the partially closed door; a shuffle, a grunt, a heavy thud and a heart-felt curse. The next moment a middle-aged manservant lurched into the room dragging one end of a heavy wooden tub. The man – Hakon presumably – muttered something incomprehensible in what she was beginning to recognise as the local dialect and lumbered back out of the room, leaving Rowène once more alone with the girl.

Still sitting on the bed she made a discreet appraisal of her new servant, silently thanking the gods that the girl displayed neither open hostility nor resentment – and could actually converse in intelligible common speech. Furthermore, Rowène sensed that, far from being belligerent, the younger girl was desperately unhappy. Her clothing showed evidence of much hard wear and looked as if it had been made in the days before her body had become that of a woman. One work-roughened hand rose to push back a wisp of brown hair that had escaped from under her grubby linen headrail to straggle beside a pale, dirt-smudged cheek. Otherwise her face was round and quite as unremarkable as Rowène's but saved from utter drabness by a pair of huge and beautiful brown eyes that were enhanced by the most wondrously long, dark lashes Rowène could ever remember seeing.

Even her sister would be jealous of them, she thought with an inner smile. Then wondered suddenly if the relationship between herself and Ju might have been less loving if she had had the sort of looks that would have made them rivals for the attentions of the men they had known in Kaerellios. Or whom they might have met at the royal Mithlondian court if their lives had not been torn beyond all mending by the combined efforts of the de Rogé brothers.

Pushing aside that oddly disquieting thought as irrelevant and a sign of her own disordered emotions, Rowène took another look at the girl, noting the marks of dried tears that tracked her cheeks, and wondered with a frown what had caused the girl's distress. Could it be that she was not here by choice and had been forced by the Steward of Rogé into the invidious position of waiting on the woman everyone in the castle must believe to be his mistress? Or was it nothing connected with her at all, but rather something in the girl's own life?

Whatever it was, she reminded Rowène in no way whatsoever of her former tire-maid and, for the first time since she had ridden into Rogérinac castle, her heavy heart lightened a little. Coming to the realisation that her new maid might be finding her fixed stare more than a little disconcerting, Rowène ventured a small smile, to which the girl responded with a tentative twitch of her own lips.

"An' it please ye, m'lady, what would ye have me do now?"

Before Rowène could answer, however, the man Hakon came back with two buckets of steaming water which he carefully tipped into the wooden tub before retreating again. Rowène looked at the water, then back to the waiting girl.

"Gerde? That is your name?"

"Aye, m'lady."

"Do you think you could find me some soap and a towel?" She cast a deprecating glance behind her. "And some bedding if possible?"

Gerde frowned in confusion then, inspiration visibly dawning, said hastily,

"Aye, I reckon I can do that." She turned to go, then hesitated. "Ye wants me ter go now, m'lady? Or wait fer a bit?"

"Now, if you would, please," Rowène answered, grateful that Gerde seemed so amenable. Perhaps they would deal well enough together after all.

With the serving maid gone there seemed nothing left to do save wait for Hakon to return with more water. He said nothing to her on his various trips, but she did not feel threatened by him despite his silence and unprepossessing appearance; the eyes under shaggy brows were curious but not unkind. Finally the tub was full and Hakon let himself out, with a nod and a rather gruff, totally unintelligible comment. She hoped it was something like *enjoy your bath, mistress* rather than *I hope you drown, you worthless whore.*

Barely had he gone when Gerde returned, happily brandishing a small chunk of greenish soap and a large, if worn, square of rough, unbleached linen. Triumph overcoming her shyness, she said with a smile,

"See, mist... m'lady, I mean... I found a towel *an'* some soap. 'Tis probably not what ye're used ter but I couldn't get at the good stuff 'cos Mistress Mathilde keeps that locked in a chest in her own room."

"I am sure what you have will do me well enough," Rowène answered firmly, although privately she was not so certain. She eyed the soap with some misgiving but only said, "Believe me, anything is better than what I have become accustomed to since I left Chartre."

Gerde's lovely brown eyes widened as she goggled across the gently-steaming bath water at her.

"Ye've really come from Chartre then, m'lady?" She made it sound almost as unbelievable as if Rowène had told her she had walked the moon's silver path down from the sky. "Is't true the lordly ones there eat off of gold platters an' that the sun shines every day?"

"Ah, no," Rowène replied, unable to prevent a faint smile. "Although I think it is true to say that it does not rain *quite* as much in Chartreux as it seems to here in Rogé. As to golden platters, I have to confess that I never saw one, let alone ate from it."

"Well, fer sure ye'll not be finding no gold here, m'lady," Gerde warned her.

"I shall just be grateful for something hot to eat and a roof over my head," Rowène replied. "Chartre is not that far away but it feels as if I have been sleeping under trees and surviving on soldiers' rations for ever. I will have time for my bath, will I not, before the evening meal is served?"

"Oh, aye," Gerde agreed with a heavy sigh, her tone suddenly subdued. "Supper'll be ready... soon but there's time aplenty fer yer bath. I don't reckon Master Guy'll let them start servin' 'til ye're ready anyhow."

"Well, I do not want to keep anyone waiting. Or is it normal for Lord Joffroi and his brothers to eat this late?" Rowène asked. Was this something else to which she would have to become accustomed or had the preparations for the evening meal merely been disrupted by their arrival so close to dark-fall?

"Oh no, m'lady, we usually eat jus' gone sundown," Gerde hastened to reassure her. But then her eager tone grew noticeably more muted. "'Tis just there's been a bit o' trouble in the kitchen ternight..."

Her voice trailed off and Rowène looked at her, curious as to what had caused the girl's obvious misery. She did not feel, however, that she would make the situation any better by asking further questions so instead she hastily divested herself of her disreputable masculine attire and clambered into the tub of deliciously warm water.

*Ah, what bliss!*

Settling herself as comfortably as possible in the confined space, she allowed herself to relax and enjoy the heat of the water while Gerde guarded the door. Torn between hunger and the undoubted luxury of the bath, she soaked only for as long as it took to warm up again, then scrubbed herself and her long, tangled hair with the rough soap Gerde had found, the pungent herbal odour of which caused her nose to itch and her empty belly to churn in a most unpleasant fashion. Remembering what Sister Héloise had said about tithes paid in kind to the Lord of Rogé, Rowène was almost certain her conclusion was the correct one but still found herself saying,

"Gerde, this soap..?"

The girl glanced back up, a look of blushing wariness touching her faintly freckled features.

"Doesn't ye like it? I'm right sorry, m'lady, I'd 'a got ye somethin' better if'n I could ha' done."

She seemed close to tears and was twisting her fingers in her apron.

"No, it is not that at all. It is just... well, it does have rather a... distinctive scent," Rowène said. "It reminds me of the herb I found in the Grey Sisters' garden at Silverleigh. Chamomile, perhaps?"

"Like enough, m'lady, though I don't know no names. An' bein' as I couldn't get ter the other soaps, the ones what smell like flowers, this was all I could find an' then I had ter take it from..." She seemed to hesitate for a moment before continuing with a deeper blush. "From Master Ranulf's room."

"Ah, I see," was all Rowène permitted herself to say but she regarded Gerde's hot cheeks with something close to depression.

*God of Light, surely this girl is not another of Ranulf's doxies?*

But then, considering the man's reputation, she knew she would be fortunate indeed if she did not make the acquaintance of many more during her time in Rogérinac. The castle and nearby countryside probably abounded in accommodating women who had serviced the needs of one or other of the de Rogé brothers over the past twenty-odd years – Ranulf and Guy were in their early thirties by Sister Héloise's reckoning and Joffroi correspondingly older – not to mention their father before them. Not that it made any difference to *her* who Ranulf de Rogé had slept with – or perhaps *coupled with* might be a better description of his casual liaisons – and she certainly did not want to make an enemy of the very girl Guy had chosen to be her tire-maid and companion in this courteous form of imprisonment she had been placed under.

She glanced again at Gerde, trying to picture the doe-eyed and dainty young serving girl in any man's bed, while the thought of Gerde having to endure Ranulf's brutal intimacies caused her belly to cramp completely. Disgusted, she allowing the soap to slip from her fingers, then rinsed in the cooling water, wishing she could as easily wash away all her memories of the man.

Standing, she shivered as the cool, salt-laden breeze swept across her wet skin. Grabbing the ragged piece of linen that Gerde shyly offered she hastily wrapped herself in it, rubbing vigorously against the chill that raised goosebumps all over her, wishing it was only the dank caress of the cold night air she fought against and not her bitter memories of the past or her fears for the future.

Having dried herself and her long hair as well as she could, she turned her thoughts once more to the subject of suitable clothing. Matters being as they were, she could hardly go down to the hall and parade herself under the interested eyes of the household in her 'lover's' easily recognisable garments and she had already resolved never to wear the scarlet silk again. Perhaps Gerde could lend her something? But she did not ask, as further consideration raised doubts as to whether the younger girl possessed so much as a spare shift let alone a gown, and even if she did she was so much smaller than Rowène it would never fit.

Still pondering this problem, she looked up to find Gerde staring fixedly at the pile of clothes Rowène had tossed across the bed before taking her bath and muttering to herself. Catching a whisper of a familiar name, Rowène listened a little more keenly.

"...Master Ranulf's...? An' fer sure that's his pin..."

There was a perplexed frown on the young servant girl's face and something else Rowène did not really want to put a name to. That being so, she thought it better to pretend she had not heard the girl's words. But then Gerde herself made that impossible. She lifted the black cloak and stared at it for a moment before looking up. Her face wraith-white in the flickering candlelight, she blurted out,

"Is he in love with you?"

Rowène blinked in sheer astonishment – both at the notion and the fact that Gerde had asked the question in the first place.

"*He?* You mean, *Ranulf?*"

The incredulity in her voice should have said it all but Gerde nodded anyway.

"Aye, Master Ranulf."

There was such a note of deep hurt underlying the simple words as to cause Rowène to regard her new servant with renewed misgiving and a blinding sense of irrational anger towards the man who was obviously responsible for putting that pain there.

"No, Gerde, he is not in love with me," Rowène said, temper making her tone tart. "In my opinion your Master Ranulf is utterly incapable of falling in love. And judging by his vile behaviour at Chartre castle, no woman with any sense would fall in love with *him!*"

"Why? What...what did he do?" Gerde asked, her big brown eyes filling with tears once more.

Rowène regarded her helplessly. She guessed the girl to be no more than fifteen summers old and so innocent and vulnerable that she made Rowène, scarce her senior by three years at the most, feel thrice her age.

"Are you sure you *really* want to know?" she finally asked when Gerde continued to stare mutely at her, tears slipping down her cheeks.

"Aye." She must have seen Rowène's hesitation because she scrubbed a hand over her face, sniffed and said, "I know what he's like, m'lady, truly I do, but I reckon whatever he did, I'd rather hear it from ye than that cow, Frythe."

"You... have... feelings for him, do you not?" Rowène asked quietly, pity filling her heart for the unhappy girl before her. Her own desires regarding Ranulf de Rogé were far from gentle however. *The gods damn you to the darkest pit in Hell,* she thought vengefully. Not for the first time since their initial meeting when she had looked up to see him sitting his stallion in all his arrogance, his dark blue eyes mocking, his hard, weathered features framed by barley-fair braids.

"Feelings?"

Gerde blushed as red as the crimson roses in the castle garden at Chartre, then went as white as winter snowflowers as something that looked like fear shot through her tear-wet eyes.

"O' course not!" A pleading note entered her voice. "Oh, why would ye be thinkin' such a thing, m'lady? Master Ranulf, he's one o' the lordly ones. 'Tisn't fer such as me ter have... *feelin's* fer the likes o' him. 'Tis jus' that... that fer once I wants to know what he's been about afore the rest o' the folk in the castle gets ter hear about it."

Rowène stared at the girl a moment longer, then sighed and said as gently as she might,

"If you know what he is like, then you really do not need me to tell you the details. Suffice to say, he... um..."

*What? Took my former tire-maid up against the wall of a public passageway?*

Oh yes, she had heard the soldiers who escorted her through Rogé talking and knew what he had done that evening. And that was before he had spent the night with her sister, his disgusting actions finally reaching a peak the following morning. But she could not tell Gerde any of that. Or at least not in such explicit terms. Yet there seemed no way of softening those sordid encounters without lying. She hesitated a moment longer but Gerde was still regarding her with painful appeal.

"Well, Gerde, if you must know, it was not just one woman at Chartre with whom your Master Ranulf became... involved."

"Who... who were they, do you know?" Gerde asked, clearly bent on punishing herself still further.

"One was my tire-maid, a slut named Ilana," Rowène said flatly. "You need not concern yourself about her. She meant nothing to him. The second one, however, was my sister, the Lady Juliena."

"An' is that all?" Gerde asked, hope mingling with despair in her voice.

Rowène hesitated but it would do no-one any good at this stage to mention that he had forced her to yield her body to him.

"Is that not bad enough?"

"Aye, I reckon." Gerde regarded her with a woebegone air. "I'm thinking yer sister must be very beautiful?"

"Yes, she is," Rowène agreed. Then realised what she had said. "I mean, yes, she was. She is dead, you see." She saw Gerde was looking shocked and that Ranulf's name was again hovering on her pale lips. "No, no," she said hastily, not knowing whether she was trying to relieve Gerde's anguish or attempting to defend the absent man's non-existent reputation. "Her death was nothing to do with... um... what happened with..."

"With Master Ranulf?"

"No. He may have forced himself upon her but..."

"Master Ranulf wouldn't ha' done that!" Gerde gasped, the expression in her brown eyes midway between denial and confusion

"Well, he did," Rowène snapped, patience momentarily deserting her.

"Nay! Master Ranulf, he'd not ha'... ra..." she halted, choking on the word. "Done such a terrible thing. Not ter yer sister. Not ter any woman. Beggin' yer pardon, m'lady, but ye don't know him, not like I do. Ye must believe me, he's got no need ter take any woman by force."

"No, perhaps not here in Rogé," Rowène conceded wearily. "But Gerde, you have to understand, in Chartre he is regarded as the enemy and most women will not... lie with him... willingly." Then, in deference to the look of utter devastation on the girl's face. "I am sorry, Gerde, but it is true. And I am afraid you will just have to accept that, for once, he... lost control of himself."

"But ye said as how he didn't ha' naught ter do wi' yer sister's death?"

"No, I know she was alive when he left her bed," Rowène said dully. "But there was a fire that morning, and in all the confusion my sister was lost." A sudden flash of inspiration burst into her mind. "And that is when Sir Ranulf gave me his mantle. I was cold and... not very well dressed for such a nasty, misty morning, you see?"

It was clear that Gerde did not see but she nevertheless looked a little happier and said with renewed confidence,

"Still, whatever ye say, an' not meanin' ter be rude about yer sister but ye wasn't there, so mebbe she went wi' Master Ranulf willingly enough. I tell ye, he's not the sort as would hurt a woman, either in bed or wi'out. Not like some as I could name," she added bleakly, her eyes darkening with some unpleasant memory. Then, a little awkwardly, "But fer all that, I'm right sorry 'bout yer sister, m'lady. I reckon as how you must miss her, bein' sent away from yer home ter where ye don't know nobody."

"Yes, I do," Rowène admitted, with a wistful smile, adding more grimly. "I lost my father and both my brothers as well as my sister, thanks to Lord Joffroi and Sir Ranulf. But we all have to go on. So now, Gerde, I want you to wash your face before the water gets too cold and then..."

"Aye, m'lady. An' then I've got ter find ye some clean bedding. An' then..."

At which point Rowène's stomach growled quite audibly. Gerde looked a little shocked, as if high-born ladies should not have belly grumbles, then gave a subdued giggle as her own stomach gurgled in return. Watching as Gerde rubbed a hand gently over the offending organ, Rowène lost any trace of her own amusement in a sudden drenching shower of cold horror... and prayed to the gods that she was wrong in her first leaping assumption.

"Yer right, m'lady," Gerde agreed with a grin. "I'm that hungry I could eat a horse meself." Then she saw where Rowène was looking, flushed again and snatched her hand away. "'Tis not what ye're thinkin'!" Then she flushed an even deeper shade of pink and with a hasty "I'll go find yer beddin' now," she fled from the chamber before Rowène could say anything more.

But Rowène made no attempt to prevent the girl leaving. Instead she wandered over to the bed and picked up the mantle, slowly unpinning the brooch from the wet, mud-stained folds. Her hand dropped to her own belly and she sighed. She *must* come to a decision soon and – in accordance with the promise she had reluctantly made him – somehow let Ranulf know what that decision was. Or at least she must let him know if that decision was likely to lead to his being arraigned before the High Counsel of Mithlondia on the same charge as his mother's brother had been.

Gerde was gone for some considerable time. Long enough in fact for Rowène to come to a decision about what she was going to wear, even if not what she was going to say to Ranulf de Rogé if, the gods forbid, she ever saw him face to face again.

Looking up as Gerde let herself back into the darksome chamber, her arms piled high with crumpled linens, what looked like a worn wolf-skin, the whole topped off with a half dozen thick candles, she saw that the girl appeared a little more composed than she had been when she had left. Indeed considerably more composed than Rowène felt, even now.

"Got the sheets, m'lady, an' a good thick fur ter keep out the chill. Master Guy, he give me some more candles fer yer room. Look, good beeswax ones, the ones he uses when he needs ter see ter do his scribing. An' best of all, Master Guy sez ter tell ye as how he'll sort somethin' decent fer ye ter wear in the morning. Oh, an' supper's almost ready, thank the good gods."

She dropped her bundle on the mattress and laying the candles on the stool, began to make the bed. Rowène eyed the sheets dubiously but forbore to ask if they were clean, thinking it highly unlikely from what she had seen so far of this wretched household. She only hoped that Gerde had not pulled them off either of the absent de Rogé's beds.

At that moment Gerde looked up and saw her expression.

"Oh, 'tis all right, m'lady, the sheets is clean enough. Master Guy left orders as how we was ter wash all the linens in the castle once him an' Lord Joffroy an' Master Ranulf had left. Back in the spring that were an' though it took us a while, mind, ter get everything washed an' dried, 'tis all done now an' fresh as can be."

"Mmm," Rowène agreed. Then, unable not to ask, "And the fur?"

"Master Guy sent that one up fer ye. He's takin' right good care of ye, m'lady."

There was something in the girl's tone that made Rowène look at her sharply but she said nothing. She was only too grateful for Guy's continued protection to protest against it, especially if it made life easier between her and Gerde.

"M'lady?"

"Yes, Gerde?"

"Beggin' yer pardon, m'lady, but surely ye're not intendin' ter wear them clothes down ter the hall fer supper? 'Specially if I'm right an' that's Master Guy's tunic an' breeches ye're wearing. Mistress Mathilde'll cut up right rough 'bout it an' make yer life an' Master Guy's a misery. Mine too, like as not," she finished dolefully.

"Unfortunately, as I have nothing else, we will all have to put up with Mistress Mathilde's bad humour," Rowène replied.

"But surely ye must ha' somethin' else, m'lady?" Gerde asked, her eyes huge in her pale face.

"No, but for the moment this is all I have," Rowène explained patiently. "Except," she added with a flicker of a wry smile, "For a gown that would only confirm Mistress Mathilde in her opinion of me." She saw Gerde was looking bemused again and added, "Where is the nearest brothel to here? I cannot think the village below the castle is big enough to boast such an establishment."

Gerde blinked, blushed, then answered.

"That'd be in Sarillac, m'lady. Down the coast aways."

"And have you ever been to Sarillac?" Rowène asked. "And seen those unfortunate women and how custom dictates they dress?"

Gerde looked deeply uncomfortable and shook her head.

"Nay, m'lady, I ain't never been there but I'm not so stupid as I don't know what a whore looks like."

"Well, Gerde, if you know that, you can imagine why I am not going to wear the only gown left in my possession. Everyone in this castle may believe me to be Sir Guy's mistress but I am not about to confirm that opinion by dressing the part in a gown that would not look out of place in a Sarillac brothel!"

Gerde seemed not to know what to say to that but eventually smiled a little shyly and said,

"I don't mind if'n ye *are* Master Guy's mistress, m'lady. I reckon ye'd make him happier than Mistress Mathilde ever could, even if she tried. Which she don't!" Then, realising what she had said, clapped a hand to her mouth. "Oh, the gods save me! I shouldn't ha' said that, she'll have me beaten fer sure."

"Well, *I* will not tell her you said it," Rowène said firmly. "Nor will I let her beat you. But I do think, Gerde, it might be better if you did not say such things again, even to me. Hmm?"

"Oh no, m'lady, I won't," Gerde promised. Then, on a rush of friendly feeling. "If'n ye've naught else, I could mebbe lend ye my spare kirtle. That is, if 'n ye'd not mind wearing servant's stuff."

"That is very kind of you, Gerde," Rowène said, touched by the other girl's impulsive offer. "But you are such a little thing, I doubt it would fit me anyway." Her gaze returned in a circumspect appraisal of Gerde's straining bodice. "Indeed, now I come to think about it, when did *you* last have a new set of clothes?"

Gerde shrugged and frowned uncertainly.

"Don't know, m'lady. Must ha' been a good couple o' years ago now... I know! 'Twere my feast day when I turned thirteen. Geryth saved his pay 'til he could buy me a length of cloth. 'Twere a lovely shade of green..." Her voice softened and, recognising both the name and the emotion in Gerde's voice, Rowène asked quietly,

"Geryth?"

"Me brother, m'lady," Gerde replied, her eyes filling suddenly with tears. "He's one o' Master Ranulf's men, rode wi' ye an' Master Guy as far as Silverleigh, so he tol' me. Said as how he was sent home special-like by Master Ranulf."

Rowène did not understand the tears but she smiled at Gerde as she said,

"I know Geryth. He..." She hesitated, trying to think of something encouraging to say to the sister who so plainly adored him. "He... seems different to the rest of them. Kinder. Certainly nicer than the one called Finn."

"Aye, he is that," Gerde agreed. Then with suppressed violence, "I hate him! Finn, I mean! He's mean an' cruel an' there's nought he won't do to cause trouble fer Geryth, even... aye well, I'm sorry, m'lady, I'm sure ye doesn't want ter hear 'bout my troubles." Her voice broke completely and Rowène laid a tentative arm around the girl's thin shoulders.

"Ah, Gerde, I wish there was something I could do to help you, if you are indeed in trouble... of any sort," she added as delicately as she might.

"'Tis kind of ye, m'lady," Gerde sniffed. "But there's nought ye can do." She was sobbing openly now and Rowène noticed that her hand was once more held over her – slightly swollen? – belly. God of Mercy, perhaps she had been wrong in her first assumption. Perhaps it was not Ranulf's child that the girl carried but Finn's. And by the sound of it the begetting of it had not been of Gerde's asking. Nor had it brought her any pleasure.

But before Rowène could say any more there came a knock at the door. Gerde was in no fit state to open it or be seen so Rowène walked over and opened it herself. Outside was the bearded serving man she had seen earlier, a heavy tray in his hands.

"Supper, Mistress, fer ye an' the lassie there," he said gruffly, in common speech this time. "Master Guy said fer ye to eat in yer room tonight. Said too as how he'd see ye termorrow, first thing, in Steward's room. Gerde knows, her'll show ye where ter go."

"Very well, set the tray down on..." On where? There was no table and but one small, unsteady stool. "On the bed," she decided. "And you may tell Sir Guy... No, on second thoughts, I will tell him myself in the morning."

The serving man regarded her straggling wet hair and masculine garments for a moment – doubtless thinking she looked nothing like a nobleman's mistress – then, to her complete surprise, contorted his upper body in something that was a bow only in the loosest sense of the word and trudged back down the stairs, leaving Rowène and Gerde alone with the tray, from which arose a satisfying aroma of cooked meat, herbs and warm bread. Rowène felt her mouth water even as she moved to sit on the bed, motioning Gerde to a place on the other side of the tray.

"Come, Gerde, there is more than enough for both of us."

Clearly nervous at the prospect of sharing a meal with a proper high-born lady, Gerde sat stiffly on the very edge of the bed and reached out a hand for one of the bowls of dark broth, only to jump to her feet again as Rowène, having taken a bite of the meat, began to cough.

"M'lady? Gods save us, what's wrong?"

"It is all right, Gerde," Rowène said hastily. "Sit down. I just... er... burnt my mouth."

"Here, m'lady, have a drink. The wine will sooth the pain."

"Pray to the gods that is so," Rowène muttered to herself.

Bearing in mind her experience with the meat, the sip she took of the thin red wine was tentative in the extreme. She found her caution well rewarded as she tasted the vile stuff. Dear God of Light, if this was the sort of vinegar they usually served in Rogérinac, perhaps it was no wonder that Ranulf had drunk so much of the rich and potent Marillec wine that night at Chartre, with such disastrous results.

She took another wary sip of the so-called wine, wondering if the water from the well she had seen in the courtyard was clean enough to drink, and slanted a sideways glance at her companion, tempted to ask her if she thought Mistress Mathilde capable of using poison against one she perceived to be her rival. But Gerde, evidently reassured that her new mistress was not in any danger or discomfort, had resumed her seat and was eating with every appearance of enjoyment from the very same dish that Rowène had just sampled. So, not poison. It was simply that Rogérinac castle could provide no better!

"Um... Gerde?"

"Aye, m'lady?"

"Do you know what this meat is?"

Gerde chewed thoughtfully.

"Well, I reckon 'tis venison, m'lady. Leastways the men brought a deer with them when they come back from Chartreux. Said as how they had Master Guy's permission ter go huntin' on their way back down from the moors. Reckon he knew there'd not be much left in the larder wi' Lord Joffroy an' most o' the men away."

"Indeed. But it has a... unusual flavour, do you not think?"

"Oh!" Unaccountably Gerde reddened. She put down her spoon and bit her lip. "I did tell ye, m'lady, as how there were a... um... bit of a disturbance in the kitchen earlier. Young Will, the spit boy... he forgot ter keep the meat turning an' it got a bit on the burnt side."

"Yes, I remember, you did mention it. So what was this disturbance?" Rowène asked, her curiosity aroused anew.

"'Twas nobbut a bit of a brawl," Gerde replied reluctantly. "Master Guy, he sorted it out, put them as was fighting in the stocks. An' Eadwyn too fer not bringing yer bath quick enough." She glanced fleetingly up at Rowène but would not hold her gaze, continuing hastily, "Kelse – that's the cook ye know – did her best but I s'pose 'tis not what ye're used ter. The sauce is right tasty though," she finished hopefully.

Rowène did not have the heart to disillusion her. With an effort she forced another mouthful down and gave her companion what she hoped was an appreciative smile.

"Yes indeed, the sauce is... most tasty."

"Aye, onions an' early 'shrooms an' some herbs from the garth. Oh, an' some o' that wine I think," Gerde replied with a frown. Then, proudly, "I picked the herbs meself this morning, thyme an' sage, would it be?"

Distracted from her suspicions regarding the identity of at least one of the brawlers Rowène looked up again.

"Garth? The castle has a garden? With herbs? What sort of herbs? Are they just for cooking or for healing too. And what is more important, is it on this side of that horrible chasm?"

"Don't know nothin' 'bout no chasm, m'lady," Gerde replied indistinctly. She chewed hard, swallowed what appeared to be a particularly gristly mouthful and continued more clearly. "The garth now, tha's jus' below us. 'Tis mostly overgrown now so I don't reckon no-one really knows what's growing there an' what's not. Lady Rosalynde used ter tend it, or so Kelse says, but her's been dead fer more'n a score o' years now. Lady Rosalynde, I means, not Kelse."

"Lady Rosalynde?" Rowène queried. She knew quite well who Lady Rosalynde had been but was curious to hear what Gerde might have to say on the subject.

"Lady Rosalynde were Lord Joffroy an' Master Ranulf's ma. The place han't been the same since her died, Kelse says. Mind I reckon as hers the on'y one o' the servants as can remember her ladyship now."

Kelse seemed to spend more time talking than cooking, Rowène reflected, and wondered what that worthy might have had to say about her! Gerde, however, was still chattering on so perhaps the cook had not made any such pronouncements yet.

"Lord Joffroy were near 'nough a man full grow'd when her ladyship passed on but Master Ranulf were on'y a boy. I reckon he must ha' missed her somethin' sore." A hint of a blush warmed her cheek but her tone was steady as she continued. "Him an' Master Guy both. Kelse sez as how they was allus so close, more like twins than half-brothers, what wi' Lady Rosalynde treating Master Guy like he were her own, rather than the old lord's... um... son." She looked directly at Rowène then. "Mebbe I shouldn't say this but I've allus been frighted o' Lord Joffroy. He's got a black temper on him, he has. But his brothers now... I know what ye said 'bout Master Ranulf but he's never hurt me, nor any other lass as fer as I know, an' as fer Master Guy, fer all he's only the old lord's by-blow, he's as good a man as his brother..." Gerde hesitated. "If not better in some ways. Well, stands to reason, he'd have ter be ter put up wi' Mistress Mathilde wi'out takin' hisself a... um... you know... before now."

Clearly Gerde was not going to be shaken in her belief that Rowène was Guy's mistress and at the moment this was of less import to her than the possibilities contained within Lady Rosalynde's abandoned garden. She had no idea how close Guy intended to keep his brother's hostage but common sense dictated that he must hold her within the confines of the castle walls at least. But surely he would not keep her immured in this small, dank chamber by day as well as by night? The garden would be a compromise. She would not be able to escape but from there she would be able to see the sky and feel the breeze. As well as search among the herbs for the one Sister Héloise had shown her... the one with small flowers the same indigo blue as Ranulf de Rogé's eyes.

But first she must obtain Guy's permission without letting him suspect why she wanted to go there.

Her appetite now gone completely, she nevertheless took up her spoon and forced herself to eat sufficient to quieten her empty belly and mollify Gerde's obvious anxiety.

Some time later, left alone again when Gerde took the tray back down to the kitchen, Rowène knelt on the bottom of her newly-made bed, elbows on the narrow window sill, careless of the damp grittiness of the mouldy stone abrading her skin. Discovering that the wind had dropped, and needing to ease the caged feeling that had been growing steadily within her ever since she had crossed over that appalling chasm, she had flung back the shutter and was now taking deep breaths of the night-scented breeze as she gazed out across the black and silver sea.

The moon was rising in the east, a huge pale golden orb in the star-strewn infinity of the sky; the Goddess' light laying a path to freedom along the dark tossing waves of the sea below. Overwhelmed by the sheer other-worldly beauty of the sight, she did not at once realise that the faint strains of music she could hear were not an integral part of the magic shimmering around her and that the haunting melody was definitely of earthly origin rather than some eldritch music summoned by the will of the Moon Goddess of the Faennari.

Nevertheless once Rowène had identified the sound of a plucked harp, she knew who must be playing it since, as far as she knew, Guyard de Martine was the only person within Rogérinac castle – and probably the entire benighted province – with any appreciation for the gentler arts. The music in itself was no surprise since she had heard him play before. What was disconcerting was how close it sounded, almost as if he were...

"M'lady!" Gerde's shocked voice abruptly interrupted her thoughts. Rowène twisted away from the window to see the servant girl's horrified expression. "What are ye about, m'lady? Ye'll be letting the night spirits in if'n ye're not careful. 'Tis dangerous ter open the shutters on a night when the moon's full, everyone knows that. The feys, they'll steal yer soul an' make ye do what they wants ye ter do. An' 'though it don't make no never mind ter me if'n ye are Master Guy's mistress, ye don't want no-one saying as how ye're one o' them as worships the Moon Goddess! Now, let's get that shutter closed quick."

"What do you know of the Moon Goddess?" Rowène asked, lowering her voice instinctively.

"I don't know nothin'," Gerde replied firmly. "An' I don't want ter neither. I only know as wi' hair like you've got, m'lady, begging yer pardon an' all, ye don't want ter give no-one the excuse ter call ye fey or witch."

These words reminding Rowène all too unpleasantly of Ranulf's warning that terrible morning at Chartre, she shivered despite herself and made no demur when Gerde banged the rotten shutter closed.

"There, tha's better." She turned to look at Rowène. "Will ye be going ter bed now, m'lady? 'Tis late an' the candle's nigh on burnt to naught."

"I suppose I must," she agreed reluctantly. She glanced around the bleak little chamber and at the narrow bed with its unbleached linens and grey wolf's pelt, then back at the servant girl, making up her mind about something. "Gerde?"

"Aye, m'lady?"

"Where do you normally sleep?"

"Wi' t'others in the women's chamber on the east side, m'lady. Why'd ye ask?"

"And would anyone mind if you were not there?" Rowène continued.

"Oh no, m'lady, most nights one or t'other of them's missin', 'specially when Lord Joffroy or..." She swallowed. "Master Ranulf's home. Long as they'se back by morning, Kelse don't fuss nor report 'en to Mistress Mathilde."

Ignoring Gerde's stumbling reference to Ranulf's nocturnal activities, she said,

"Do you like it there, with the others? Or..." Catching the look that flitted over the girl's face. "Or is there some trouble between you and them? Or you fear there might be? Because you have been assigned to look after me?" Gerde said nothing, either in confirmation or denial of this guess but she would not meet Rowène's searching gaze. "Would you rather sleep here? It is probably no draughtier than you are used to and it would be company for me. I have always had my sister until recently..."

"Oh, d'ye mean it, m'lady?" Gerde asked, her face brightening. Then, with an anxious look, "Oh, but what about..." She stopped and cleared her throat uncomfortably. "I mean, perhaps I ought ter ask Master Guy first?"

"That would probably be best," Rowène agreed solemnly. "But I cannot see him refusing. It is in his own interest after all," she finished on a more cynical note.

Gerde looked puzzled by this but Rowène did not elaborate; if the girl had not worked out that she would be playing the part of chaperone and could testify to the fact that Guyard de Martine was not sleeping with the woman gossip had already pilloried as his leman, Rowène saw no reason to enlighten her. Nor was it a lie when she had said she would be lonely during the long hours of darkness in this unfamiliar place. She was accustomed to company, her sister's for most of her life, more recently that of the man by whose side she had slept nearly every night since she left Chartre.

"Shall I go ask Master Guy now while he's still down in steward's chamber. There... can ye hear his harp, m'lady?"

"Yes, I thought it sounded close. So where is the steward's chamber exactly?"

Gerde gave her a look as if to say that everyone in Rogérinac knew the location of that room.

"'Tis the chamber below this'un m'lady." Then added inconsequentially, "His an' Mistress Mathilde's room's over on the far side of the castle, near the main gate."

"Very well, Gerde," Rowène replied. "As you say, it is getting late and Master Guy will no doubt be retiring soon. So perhaps you had better run down and ask him now."

"Aye m'lady." Gerde bobbed a curtsey and was gone.

She returned with Guyard de Martine scant moments later, the latter looking weary, dishevelled and – if Rowène had not known him better – the worse for too many cups of vile wine. His light blue eyes held a thousand shadows but his speech was reassuringly untainted by wine or emotion.

"Lady Rowena." He bowed. "Gerde said you wished to speak with me. Is there anything more I may do to ensure your comfort tonight? Tomorrow I will see about a brazier at least. And something more appropriate by way of clothing, of course. But we can discuss your requirements in that respect tomorrow when we are both less tired."

He was being formal in the extreme, even though he kept to common speech, presumably for Gerde's benefit, and Rowène thought it wiser to follow his lead.

"Thank you, Hakon did give me your message earlier," she murmured. "For now, Sir Guyard, if you would give your permission for Gerde to sleep in here by night, that will suffice. I believe her fellow servants may be tempted to be unkind if given the opportunity."

"Of that I have no doubt," Guy replied grimly. "Between them, Frythe and Finn have already done much to distress her. If you think it will help, of course she may bring her pallet up here. She will also be able to show you where the privy is. I am afraid Rogérinac castle does not offer the same level of comfort as Chartre."

That was an understatement if ever she had heard one! Nevertheless she contented herself with a murmured "Thank you." But then she hesitated, wondering whether to wait until their meeting in the morning but the matter was too important for her to sleep on. "There is one other thing. I would ask that you grant me the freedom to walk within Lady Rosalynde's garden when the weather is fine."

He looked a little surprised by this request but answered readily enough.

"Certainly you may do so, if you wish. But I warn you the place is sadly overgrown. Nor are you a prisoner here."

"Am I not? So if I wished to walk down to the village or along the cliffs, no-one would stop me?"

He looked at her, his jaw tightening.

"That may be a little more difficult. You will need to tell me when and where you wish to go and I will arrange an escort for you."

And he had the gall to say she was not a prisoner!

"But as I said, within the castle walls you are free to go where you will. Though I would suggest that you take Gerde with you at all times and stay away from the stables, the garrison's quarters and training ground and the west side of the building where my wife has her room."

"And what about the steward's chamber?" Rowène asked, with a touch of irony. "Is that out of bounds too?"

She thought Guy tensed even more at this question but his voice remained calm and detached as he said,

"If you have a problem or a concern, my lady, my door is always open to you. I would merely ask that you think carefully before seeking me out. Gossip flies swift in this place, as I am sure you are aware, and I would not be the cause of any further conflict between yourself and my wife. Now, if that is all that will not wait until the morning? Good. Come then, Gerde, we will go and collect your bedding and explain matters to Kelse so that she is not worried by your absence. Lady Rowena, I bid you good night."

With that he bowed once more and walked from the room, leaving Rowène feeling more alone than at any other time since leaving Kaerellios.

# Chapter 11

## *Lady Rosalynde's Garden*

The next day, after a near sleepless night, Rowène rose, almost wearier than when she had lain down, just as the first light of dawn trickled through the holes in the broken shutter. Pushing back the battered wooden barrier she leaned out, eager to see what had been invisible the night before. For a while she was content to watch the white sea mews as they wheeled around the tower and fished in the white-maned, greenish-grey water that crashed at the foot of the black cliff, then cast around for any sight of the promised sanctuary. Craning her neck she could just glimpse the beaten earth of what must be the garrison's training ground but nothing resembling a garden, overgrown or not.

Behind her she heard Gerde yawn as she stirred, followed by a sharp gasp and a mumbled apology as the girl ran from the room, presumably making for the privy. Had she been suffering from an urgent need to relieve her bladder or was she afflicted with the sickness that plagues pregnant women in the mornings? Rowène did not know. Nor did she ask when Gerde eventually returned to the chamber, bearing a pitcher of water and Rowène's scanty pack of belongings.

She washed her face in the tepid but clean water and, with Gerde's help, tidied her tangled hair with the bone comb Sister Héloise had given her. She left Gerde engaged in ordering her own wispy curls and headed down to the steward's chamber where she found Guy waiting for her, looking strained and unshaven.

The ensuing discussion was brief and conducted in formal terms, with the door open. It covered little that Rowène had not expected, in essence detailing the same boundaries upon her freedom that Guy had laid down the previous night. In return for her undertaking not to leave the castle without his knowledge and permission he gave his word that she would be kept safe and treated with honour until such time as Joffroi and her mother sent word, or Joscelin de Veraux arrived to take his betrothed into his own keeping.

Guy concluded by requesting that she keep to her own chamber until such time as he had managed to find more suitable attire for her – it would not, he promised, take long – but, unwilling to remain shut in that grim little room with nothing to occupy her dark thoughts save the terrible decision she must soon make, she begged leave to visit the garden, promising to keep her unconventional garb hidden and to do nothing that might reveal the fact she was not in fact dressed as a lady should be. For a moment she feared Guy meant to

479

question her again concerning the circumstances surrounding her acquisition of his half-brother's mantle but in the end he merely gave her a look that mingled exasperation and sympathy and nodded reluctant acceptance of her terms.

Finding Gerde waiting on the step outside the door, he accompanied them to the hall where the dawn meal was being served by a couple of yawning menservants. The meal was slightly more palatable than the previous night's supper, consisting as it did of the perennial oatcakes and gritty brown bread, accompanied by some strong white cheese flavoured with what Rowène took to be herbs but could just as easily have been mould. Last night's vinegar was replaced by ale which, even though she normally disliked the brew, proved more potable than the wine had been.

Even so, she did not believe she could stomach it at every meal and, in any event, thought she would do better to request milk for surely Rogérinac castle, poor though it might be, would have its own small herd of milch cows, for butter if nothing else. That said, she had to admit that butter had been conspicuously lacking so far and the cheese was obviously made from goats' milk. Ah well, even goats' milk would be better than beer or wine. And there was also Gerde's unborn babe to consider, since Rowène was almost certain she was right in her guess as to her tire-maid's condition. As to which of the men of Rogérinac castle had sired the child, that was no concern of anyone save Gerde and the man concerned.

Much to her relief, Mathilde de Martine did not make an appearance in the hall that morning and over the days to come Rowène had little direct contact with her. But what little she did have was sufficient to give her a deep dislike of the woman. Indeed the more she saw of her, the more she despised her. Not so much because of her common birth or the deficiencies in her housekeeping skills but for the appalling contempt with which Mathilde treated the man who, save for that one false confession of faithlessness, had remained stubbornly loyal to the woman he had wed.

The dawn meal over that first morning, Rowène and Gerde left the hall together, heading for Lady Rosalynde's garden which, as Rowène now discovered, lay at the southern end of the tiny island on which Rogérinac castle was built. It was sheltered from the brisk easterly winds by high walls on three sides – the practice ground she had glimpsed earlier lying beyond the eastern wall – and the dark bulk of the castle to the north, so that when the sun shone, as it did that first morning, the garden was a warm and peaceful place, despite the weeds that crept, straggled and tangled riotously over the plants that had once rightfully grown there.

Seated on the fallen trunk of an old apple tree, her cloak held tightly about her, Rowène looked around with an odd sense of near happiness, tempered immediately by sadness that a once lovely garden had come to such a state. She smiled at Gerde's eagerness to show her where she had found the herbs for the stew, but made no attempt to look for the particular plant she had thought she might find here. Not only because it seemed an offence against the lady whose garden this had once been but also because she defied even Sister Héloïse to find one small, grey-leaved, blue-flowered herb amidst such a wilderness of neglect.

Tomorrow, she thought. She must look tomorrow. But for today she would be content to just sit, feeling the sunshine warm upon her braided hair, the breeze from the sea dancing lightly against her skin. Closing her eyes and listening to the harsh calling of the sea mews, she might have been seated atop the Lady Tower of Chartre castle rather than lost and adrift in the weed-choked ruin of a long-dead woman's garden.

Indeed so acute was the sense of her presence that she could almost see, behind her closed eyelids, the wraith of a dark-haired, dark-eyed lady working among the marigolds and lavender or gathering the small blush-pink roses that clung to the grim grey stone walls. A woman who must surely have been as unhappy in her way as Rowène was now; repeatedly betrayed by her charming, faithless lord, forced to raise his by-blow in her own household. Yet everything anyone had said about the Lady Rosalynde pointed to the fact that she had overcome her pain and indeed had loved Alys de Martine's child as much as she had loved her own younger son.

Perhaps the two boys had been in the habit of playing together in this garden, Rowène mused, in the days before Lady Rosalynde's untimely death. They had only been eight when she died and would surely have spent more time with her than the men of the castle. On that thought the wraith of the dark-haired lady looked up, smiling, as she was joined by the shimmering images of two sturdy, fair-haired, blue-eyed boys, one brandishing a wooden sword, the other riding a hobby-horse, both laughing, both brimming with life and mischief...

Abruptly Rowène opened her eyes and, dazzled by the sparkling sunlight that flooded her unguarded vision, could almost have believed the illusion of the past more real than the babe growing within her. Then she blinked, the laughter died, and the world steadied once more. Her throat tightened as she remembered that Rosalynde de Rogé was twenty-five years dead, and those boys had long since grown to manhood and other, less innocent, pursuits.

Indeed she doubted whether either of them took any thought for their mother's garden now; Guy because the demands of running his half-brother's fief kept him too busy, Ranulf because the simple peace to be enjoyed in such a place would be beyond his comprehension. Nevertheless, it was impossible not to wonder whether, in a few years' time, his own child might play here in all innocence, as he had done...

Somehow though that picture would not form in her mind as the other image had done. But why was that? Was it because Ranulf's child was destined not to be born? Or because its mother would no longer be living in Rogérinac? Or perhaps they would both die – as Agnès de Lacey and her child had done.

Shivering at the thought of how close she had come to slipping into the dark waters of the past, Rowène pushed away any suggestion of similarity between Gérard de Lyeyne and his sister's son, and fell instead to chewing her nails, concentrating on the decision that lay before her and grimly determined not to meet the same fate as Agnès de Lacey. Even so, she was still lacking a coherent conclusion by the time Gerde trod through the tangled grasses to tell her that the horn announcing the mid-day meal had just sounded.

Rowène might not have managed to find a satisfactory answer to her own problem, but as she and Gerde ducked under the wild tangle of roses and honeysuckle that sprawled over the entrance to the garden and began to walk back across the courtyard towards the keep, she saw something that might go some way towards explaining Gerde's woeful countenance.

On the eastern side of the cobbled yard, between the stables and the reeking midden heap, three men had been locked in the castle stocks. Rowène had barely noticed them earlier but now her gaze was drawn inexorably in their direction. All three were covered with mud and filth but she rather thought she recognised two of them.

She shot a sideways look at the girl walking just behind her, taking note of Gerde's white face and averted eyes. But she scarcely needed that confirmation; she had already guessed that Geryth had been one of the brawlers who had disrupted the meal preparations the night before and it was surely no surprise to find that Finn had been involved as well; she remembered the other soldier's persistent attempts to goad the younger man into losing his temper. It was all too evident that he had finally succeeded, the only consolation – if a poor one – being that Finn was sharing his suffering.

She sighed a little, wondering how long Geryth's punishment was due to last and hoped that he, if not Finn, would be released soon, both for his sister's sake and, more selfishly, her own; she had not yet decided whether she should tell Ranulf about the babe, but if she did, she needed Geryth free to leave Rogérinac.

Or should she view this as a gift from the gods; a little more time in which to make what was becoming an increasingly difficult and stomach-churning decision. Her life? Ranulf's life? Or their child's life?

She thought again of the alternatives Sister Héloise had laid out for her – indeed she had done little but think of them! One thing she was certain about was that she did not want to bear Ranulf's babe. Did not want to be bound to him by something as tangible as a child when, the gods knew, her memories were troubling enough. Yet she did not think she could take the blue-bane draught, even if Sister Héloise would brew it for her.

Nor, having had more time to think about it, had she changed her mind about Ranulf's fate. She lacked the will or the courage to give evidence in front of the High Counsel of Mithlondia that would condemn him to the same prison cell... the same bloody end on the scaffold as his mother's brother had suffered.

Gérard de Lyeyne had been guilty of rape and abandonment. Ranulf was not. Or not entirely. And he *had* said he would acknowledge and support the child she was increasingly certain he had seeded in her. She hated him, despised him... but not so much that she could perjure herself to send him to his death.

So what was left? She saw no alternative other than to bear the child but tell no-one the father's name. It would be well known that she had come straight from the licentious atmosphere of the Kardolandian court so she would let it be believed that she had taken a lover there. Ranulf was the only man in Mithlondia who would know for certain that she lied but she doubted he would say anything to contradict her. He would probably be so relieved to escape both justice and fatherhood that he might even convince himself that she had not, after all, been the virgin he had taken her for.

Of course, there was the indescribably depressing thought that, if she chose this path, she would be declaring herself no better than a whore. But at least no-one would be dead because of her. It was at this point that a venomous little voice whispered in her mind that if she meant to think of death, this was her chance to take revenge for her father, her brother and her half-brother; two dead beyond recall, the other in all likelihood condemned to live and die still wearing the shackles of a slave. Ranulf de Rogé deserved to die for his part in her family's fall, she knew he did. And yet...

No, perhaps it was just as well that Geryth was not free. She had another day of grace before the gods required her decision.

It was the following morning before Guy came to her chamber with the news that he had managed to locate both cloth and the wherewithal to convert it into suitably feminine attire, at the same time apologising for the drab colour and poor quality of the material, this turning out to be two lengths, one of linen, one of grey homespun; something a servant, but certainly no noblewoman, might wear.

Rowène, however, was in no case to complain and anything was better than her present choice of clothing. Nor would she be sorry to put away the mantle that far too many people here in Rogérinac castle clearly recognised as belonging to their garrison commander. She did not mind being considered Guy's mistress but she cringed from the possibility that anyone might suspect her of succumbing willingly to Ranulf's dubious charms.

Even if countless others, including Gerde, had! But that was conjecture only, she reminded herself as she and Gerde settled to sewing in her draughty, ill-lit chamber, by tacit agreement avoiding all mention of any of the four men who touched their lives at present. It seemed to Rowène a bitter jest that scarcely a season before she had sat sewing new clothing with her sister in the comfort of their own sunlit chamber in Chartre – though even in that warm, faraway spring, there had been unhappiness and secrets shadowing their lives, just as there were on this cool summer day in Rogérinac.

The only diversion during that long, tedious day of cutting and stitching had been caused by Rowène's insistence that one of the sets of garments they were sewing would be for Gerde herself. The girl had been first disbelieving, then bemused that this should be so, before finally gratitude and a new devotion to her mistress had taken over. Quietly amused by the former and wholly embarrassed by the latter, Rowène had disclaimed all thanks on the grounds that it was a noblewoman's place to take care of her dependants and that it was long past time when Gerde should have been provided with new clothes; a duty of care that was actually Mathilde de Martine's responsibility, although Rowène forbore to point this out.

She also refrained from mentioning that whilst the newer, looser clothes might conceal the servant girl's swollen belly for a few months longer, Gerde's secret could not remain hidden forever.

As if the gods had finally decided to take a hand and return the troubled seasons to order, the weather took a definite turn for the better and the sun shone every day from a sky of sweet summer blue, giving Rowène and Gerde plenty of opportunity to escape the damp-ridden, grim grey castle to work in the sunshine and fresh air of Lady Rosalynde's garden.

Nor were they the only ones to take advantage of the improvement in the weather, Guy using this welcome burst of fine sunshine to conduct his summer tithe-collecting visits. While his absence during the day meant that Rowène need not make any special effort to avoid him, she found herself missing his presence in the castle. Although she refused to ask, she knew from Gerde's chatter that while Guy might leave the castle early he never rode very far, confining his journey only to those hamlets that lay within an easy half-day's ride from Rogérinac. She suspected this was due, in part, to his unease as to how his wife would treat his erstwhile mistress once his back was turned but whatever the reason she felt more vulnerable than she would admit to during his absence and was always relieved when, in late afternoon or early evening, she heard his voice in the courtyard, talking either to the groom who came to take his horse or the soldiers guarding the gate.

Once assured of Guy's safe return Rowène had formed the habit of retreating to her tower chamber. There, after washing away the dirt of the day, she would eat whatever Gerde brought up for her supper, declining to dine in the great hall, thinking – with a pain that told her how much she had come to care for him – that Guy might wish for his wife's company without the necessity to contend with the embarrassing proximity of the woman with whom he was believed to have had a carnal relationship.

It was an arrangement that seemed to be working to everyone's satisfaction until, perhaps a fortnight after Rowène had come to Rogérinac, the strained state of truce that existed between Guy, his wife and his putative mistress finally shattered.

Gerde having predicted that the forthcoming day would be the hottest of the summer so far, Rowène had chosen to miss the morning meal in favour of slipping out to the garden before the sun became too warm – if it ever did in Rogé, which she could not quite believe despite her tire-maid's assurances. She worked steadily for some time, weeding the neglected herb beds, fingers busy, struggling to come to terms with the decision she had still not made, keeping half an eye on Gerde about whom she was becoming increasingly worried.

Abruptly abandoning both her wayward thoughts and her futile tussle with a particularly recalcitrant dandelion root, she sat back on her heels, directing a considering look in the direction of her companion. Gerde was not weeding or clipping or indeed working in any way. She was merely standing under one of the fruiting apple trees staring blindly at the grey stone wall that separated the garden from the practice yard. Rowène was not sure but she thought Gerde was crying; silently, desperately, her arms folded around her waist as if to keep her misery locked within her body. Or maybe, Rowène thought uneasily, to protect something within her body, though after that first morning there had been no obvious signs that Gerde might be with child; no swooning, no sickness, just that unspoken fear in her eyes that contrasted so sharply with the healthy bloom on her cheeks.

Yet surely there was no valid reason for Gerde's fear. There were not many children in the castle, it was true, but there were a few, resulting no doubt from the various casual liaisons within the household. She winced as she remembered that she had caught herself searching among the children for any resemblance to Joffroi de Rogé's fair-haired, blue-eyed brothers. Not that she really believed that Guy had lied to her nor that he would break his binding vows with any of those women who served him nightly at table but the more she saw and heard of Mathilde de Martine, the more she wondered that he had not. As for Ranulf, she had no belief at all in his restraint; what he wanted he took, and he had been either incredibly lucky or incredibly careful not to have been caught before now.

Her darkening path of thought was abruptly broken when some sound she was not even aware of hearing made her look up to find Guyard de Martine approaching, booted and spurred, a cloak thrown over his arm, his sword once more at his hip. He was clearly attired for travel and, clad as he was in the gold-embroidered green tunic – now cleaned and mended, presumably by his loving wife – he looked, save for the incongruous nature of his cropped hair, every inch the nobleman he was. Personally, Rowène preferred him in the shabby garments he normally wore. But perhaps the unexpected but welcome heat of the long-delayed summer had rendered the thicker, winter clothing he had been wearing since his return to Rogérinac too impractical, or else his errand called for something more formal and richer in appearance and so he had chosen to wear the glittering garments that had taken shape under the Winter Lady's white hands. Rowène wished he had not.

Struggling to contain her disquiet and not a little curious as to where he might be going clad in such a fashion, she rose to her feet, brushing the dirt from her fingers. Then waited, a quiet dread gathering about her heart, to hear why he should seek her out now, when it seemed to her that he had done his best to ignore her very existence since their arrival.

Coming to a halt about three feet away from her, he dropped the cloak he was carrying over the trunk of a fallen pear tree and made her a bow.

"Good morning, Lady Rowena." He spoke in common speech, not Mithlondian, she noticed.

"Sir Guy," she responded in the same language, dropping a slight curtsey. "To what do I owe this unexpected honour?"

He looked momentarily uncomfortable and cast a glance at Gerde, who obediently wandered out of earshot, although she had the sense to remain close enough that anyone looking out of the castle windows along the south-east range could see they were not alone. Apparently satisfied that he could not be overheard Guy abruptly abandoned formality in favour of blunt speaking.

"I wanted to tell you that I am leaving Rogérinac and will be gone for at least three days. I have to visit the villages of Blackoakleas, Sutton and Longthorne. I should return on the fourth day but if you have any need of me before then, send Geryth and I will come as soon as I can."

"Three days?" Rowène echoed, wondering whether this was a sign from the gods that her time was up? That the decision hanging over her must be made now. It seemed they were even providing her with the means to send Geryth back to Chartre...

"Yes, I am sorry but I cannot leave it any longer."

Startled from her guilty thoughts, she glanced up at her companion, only then noticing the tension in the line of his jaw, the wary uncertainty in his eyes.

"Something is troubling you about this journey," she said slowly. "Surely you do not think you will be in any danger?"

"No, of course not."

"Then why tell me exactly where you are going?"

"Simple courtesy."

"And Geryth? Why are you assigning Geryth to me?"

"He is a messenger I can trust," Guyard replied simply, then added. "He will also be your guard. He and Bran – the one they call The Bear. And yes, he is one of my brother's men but he was not part of the pack that accompanied Ran to Chartre."

Ignoring this little attempt at diversion Rowène allowed a hint of anger to creep into her voice.

"So this is what you think of me, that I will try and escape from here the moment your back is turned? When I am a hostage for my own people's safety? I thought you knew me better than that!"

"You misunderstand me," Guyard said dryly. "I am leaving them here to protect you! To keep you safe from harm! Not to further curtail your freedom!" He took a step towards her and although he kept his voice low, his eyes betrayed the depth of his feelings. "God of Light, Rowène! Do you not think that if I could get you out of this vipers' nest without causing a bloodbath in Chartreux I would do so? But I know you would not buy your freedom at such a cost!"

"No, nor at the risk of your life either," Rowène said firmly, closing the distance between them by another step, looking up into his summer blue eyes, wishing with all her heart that she was not carrying his half-brother's child, that he was not bound to a woman who did not love him.

They stood then in silence, one step apart, only their eyes meeting... until the distant ring of iron-shod hooves against the cobbles of the courtyard broke the connection between them.

"I must go. The sooner I go, the sooner I will return."

"Yes, you must... May the gods go with you, Guy."

"Fare you well while I am gone," he murmured.

He lifted his hand and for one moment Rowène thought he meant to caress her cheek. Then, apparently remembering the many eyes that might be watching them, he stepped back again and catching her hand, bent and lightly touched his lips to her dirt-stained fingers. He inhaled slightly,

"What is that scent? Some sweet-smelling herb is it not? I remember my m..." He broke off then started again. "It reminds me of Lady Rosalynde."

"Lavender." She looked around. "This must have been a lovely garden once."

His lips curved in the faintest of smiles as he followed her gaze.

"It was. Ran and I used to play here. When we were children." He cleared his throat. "Lady Rosalynde would be pleased to see what you are doing here."

The next moment he released her hand and was gone, leaving Rowène to bring the fingers he had kissed up to her own lips, her eyes never leaving his departing figure. Silently chastising herself for a moon-struck idiot, she watched as he walked away, the sun dappling through the leaves to glint on his hair, the spurs on the heels of his riding boots and the hilt of the sword at his hip. And knew this was how everyone in Rogérinac, and indeed the rest of the province, must perceive Guyard de Martine; as the high-born Steward of Rogé, the illegitimate but beloved son of the old lord. She only knew that she had loved him long before she learned the truth of his birth, in the days when he wore a harper's rags rather than the trappings of a nobleman.

Before she had allowed his cursed half-brother to force himself upon her, leaving his seed to take root within her. The decision must be made. She had three days.

No, she had tonight. For tomorrow she must send Geryth on his way. Either to Chartre with the silver brooch. Or to Silverleigh to beg for Sister Héloise's help. Otherwise it would be too late and she would be left with the final choice.

Ranulf's life?

His child's life?

Her life?

Rowène worked with Gerde in the garden until mid-day, by which time the girl was showing unmistakeable signs of suffering from the heat; her hair sticking to her damp forehead and her nose growing steadily pinker. She looked tired beneath the flush of heat, her hand going more often to her belly and the last thing Rowène wanted was to cause Gerde to become ill. She refused to even think the word *miscarry*. Just as she refused to consider from whose seed the child – if there was one – had sprung. *That* was none of her affair. Her servant's health *was*.

Retreat into the cool shadows of the castle was definitely in order, although how she was to occupy herself for the rest of the day she had no notion at present. Perhaps if Gerde could find some embroidery silks – unlikely from what she had seen of Rogérinac castle so far – she might embellish her very drab gown. A pointless enough task but one that would, at least, keep her hands busy while her mind would be free to consider the choice she must make. Failing some suitably ladylike occupation for her hands, she supposed she might help Gerde with the refurbishment of her chamber. So far with hot water, rags and brushes they had managed to clean the cobwebs and mould from two walls. But Gerde, she reminded herself, was clearly tired and needed to rest, not wash walls. And *she* needed to think!

Having decided to leave the garden Rowène was immediately made aware of the new arrangements Guy had put in place. As she and Gerde ducked past the trailing roses into the courtyard Geryth pushed away from the wall where he had been loitering and with a respectful "M'lady" and a baffled look for his sister followed after them as they made their way through the castle to the south-east tower. Arriving at Rowène's chamber he took up a position outside the door, with the obvious intention of remaining there.

Gerde waited until the door closed behind him and then whispered,

"M'lady? Why's Geryth doin'... what he's doin', follerin' ye about like?"

"Sir Guy's orders," Rowène replied. She gave her fidgeting, red-faced maid a considering look. "Have you and Geryth spoken at all since his release?"

Gerde flushed an even deeper shade of pink and shook her head unhappily.

"And are you going to?" Rowène asked.

She was not surprised when the girl shook her head again.

"I can't, m'lady."

"Then there is no more to be said," Rowène sighed. "But you are going to have to talk to him some time, Gerde. He is your only kin and I do not believe he likes this coldness between you any more than you do. Or... you could tell me what is troubling you." Then as Gerde remained miserably silent, she attempted a yawn and said, "After all that weeding and fresh air I think I shall take a rest. And perhaps you should do the same, Gerde. I do not think you slept well last night."

The girl gave her a hunted look but said nothing. She waited until she thought her mistress asleep before collapsing on her pallet, quite clearly overcome with fatigue and fear. Rowène lay on her own bed, awake but with her eyes closed, wondering what, if anything, she should tell Ranulf – either about herself or Gerde.

To her surprise she slept, waking late in the afternoon with her mind still unclear and troubled by thoughts of both Guy and his half-brother. Finding herself stiff from her earlier exertions in the garden and still grubby, she sent Gerde to order a bath and hot water and was surprised to find both arrived promptly.

By the time Rowène had finished her leisurely ablutions and had coaxed Gerde into washing her own face and hands and allowing her mistress to tidy her hair, it was almost time for the evening meal. While Gerde went down to the kitchen to fetch it, Rowène returned briefly to the garden. Not to work but to think and unwillingly remember Guy's words.

*Ran and I used to play here. When we were children.*

Now that she knew what she was looking for she could see them easily through the golden shadows of late afternoon... two boys aged about five or so with their wooden toys. Except this time something was different... ah yes, they were both riding wooden horses and it would have been difficult to tell them apart, save that one had fine, flax-fair hair - much lighter in colour and less coarse than that of his adult counterpart - while the other's soft curls were touched with a bright gold which maturity had muted somewhat. They were watched by the same dark-haired lady as before and although Rowène could not see her face, she knew she would be smiling lovingly at her sons, even as she worked amongst the flowering lavender. Suddenly Lady Rosalynde seemed to hear something for she straightened, her feet wreathed in a silvery mist, her hands full of mauve and purple flowers, to look straight at Rowène, her dark eyes widening in her pale face...

"M'lady?" It was Gerde's voice, familiar but with a rising note of panic. "Lady Rowena!"

Rowène started and blinked and in that instant the wraith woman was gone. Yet by some strange magic – she glanced instinctively up at the sky and saw that the moon had indeed risen – she could still hear a faint echo of the boys' laughter, shimmering like crystal bells in the heavy golden air; carefree, innocent, poignantly vulnerable.

Rowène swallowed against the dryness in her mouth and shut her ears to the sound.

"Yes, Gerde, what is it?"

"Beg pardon, m'lady, but the horn call's gone fer supper. Are ye all right?" the girl added, peering anxiously at her. "Ye look as if ye've been walking wi' a wraith!"

"No... I was just... day-dreaming and did not hear the horn."

She rose from the fallen pear tree with what composure she could muster and walked back towards the castle, very conscious firstly of Gerde's watchful eyes and then her bodyguard's presence when the bear-like soldier fell in behind her as she left the garden.

Dragging her thoughts away from that odd, heart-quickening experience in the garden and anchoring them to the heavy tread of the guard at her heels, it occurred to her to wonder why Guy should feel such anxiety over her safety. Was it simple duty to his lord? Or could it be something else? Something he felt for her? Not love, no, though she knew he had once desired her and she could only hope he might still retain some warmth of feeling towards her, even if it was by nature protective now rather than passionate.

But, the gods help her, she wanted more, including all the love and passion he could never, in honour, give her. Wryly she acknowledged that she would count her own honour well lost for one night in his arms. But that could never be, since not only did he already have a wife but she had allowed his hateful half-brother to take so brutally what she would have given freely to him.

Her mind tumbling into the dark depression that always engulfed her whenever her thoughts slipped towards Ranulf de Rogé and the invidious position into which he had forced her, she found herself by some logical progression – after all the man had been intimate with them both – considering her sister's plight.

But Ju had escaped, she reminded herself, taking comfort from her last sight of her sister; heading up-river in that peculiar little boat. Away from Chartre, towards freedom. Rowène had no idea where Ju and her companion had been going but she trusted that they had found refuge somewhere. Certainly she did not believe that Ju was dead.

Nevertheless, Rowène had the crawling sensation that things were not going as smoothly for Ju as that initial escape from Chartre had led her to believe. Sensed also, now that she was concentrating, the ripples of fear and anxiety that disturbed her sister's mind. Sending up a quick prayer to the God of Light to continue to watch over Ju, she looked up to find Gerde waiting to serve her supper.

"Sit an' eat, m'lady. I got ye fish, knowing as how ye likes it best," the girl was saying as she placed a platter of bread and herring on Rowène's lap. She was obviously much restored after her nap. "Kelse got it fresh in the village this morning."

"And what have you got for yourself?" Rowène asked, eyeing the wooden bowl Gerde was holding with mingled interest and amusement. It constantly amazed her that Gerde could eat, with apparent relish, anything Kelse the cook produced. But then the girl was surely eating for two.

As was she, Rowène reminded herself, feeling that cold spear of dread pierce her belly once more while Gerde – apparently untroubled for once by thoughts of her absent lover – dug her spoon into the brown sludge and fished out a small, solid ball of dough.

"Coney stew, m'lady," she replied triumphantly. "Wi' dumplings."

"Ah, yes indeed," Rowène agreed blandly, turning with relief to her own dish. A relief that proved to be short-lived.

She had not supposed it possible that Kelse could ruin something so simple as baked herring but she had to admit to under-estimating the cook's destructive capabilities. Despite the fact that for once the fish appeared to be cooked to perfection, there was something definitely amiss and after a couple of mouthfuls that left a strange, unpleasant after-taste Rowène pushed it away, much to Gerde's distress.

"Oh, m'lady, ye'll starve ye will. Ye don't eat enough ter keep a mouse alive an' Master Guy'll not be best pleased if'n he comes back ter find ye've made ye'self ill."

"I will not be ill," Rowène assured her worried maid. "But I cannot eat it, whatever Sir Guy may say on his return."

"Aye, but it do seem a shame ter waste it," Gerde said, eyeing the nearly untouched fish.

"Well, you have it then and welcome," Rowène offered.

Gerde gave a shudder.

"No, thank ye m'lady. I doesn't like fish at the best of times an' wi' that there eye staring up at me... well fair gives me the willies it do."

Rowène laughed and, putting aside the fish dish, reached for the chunk of rye bread, asking hopefully,

"Butter? Honey?"

"Sorry, m'lady, Mistress Mathilde were down in the kitchen when I went ter get yer meal an' no way was she goin' ter let me take anything extra. Ye know how she feels about the both of us."

"Well, it has not lost me any sleep yet," Rowène grinned. "And although honey would have been nice, I can live without it if I have to."

"It'll be better once Master Guy's home," Gerde said, a knowing look on her face. "He'll make sure ye gets the best o' what's goin'. He knows what ye likes all right. That being so, I reckons on the fourth day from now ye'll be havin' honey wi' yer mornin' porridge... if not earlier."

To which Rowène did not even attempt a reply.

# Chapter 12

## *The Malice of Mistress Mathilde*

Rowène woke from a troubled sleep somewhere around midnight, soaked in a cold sweat, her stomach an excruciating mass of roiling agony. She rolled onto her side and made a grab at the basin perched precariously atop the stool. Water splashed in all directions but Rowène was past caring as she leant over and brought up what felt like a belly-full of searing bile.

Alerted by the noise Gerde scrambled up from her pallet and after a moment of startled dismay came to hold her mistress's shoulders as Rowène shuddered and retched, helpless to withstand the racking spasms and wondering if they would ever stop. They did, but only when she had been wrung clean of every last drop of vile-tasting vomit, by which time she was so weakened and sore that all she could do was allow Gerde to lay her back against her pillow, whispering her grateful thanks as the girl gently wiped her tear-stained face with a cool cloth.

The vomiting had been horrific enough but, as Rowène discovered, there was worse to come.

Finally, towards dawn, just as the eastern sky began to lighten to lemon and apricot and silver, she found herself lying alone in that grim little chamber, silent tears slipping down her cold cheeks.

She *thought* she wept from relief that the decision had been taken from her but could not be sure. She was certain of nothing by now, save that the frail thread that bound her to a man she loathed had been severed and tonight another tiny star would glitter in the sky...

Gerde cast another anxious look at her mistress, her face so whitely pale in the eerie dawn light it appeared almost green against the lank strands of damp, red-bronze hair. She was lying so still that for a moment Gerde thought she must be dead. Then she gave a soft sob of relief as she saw the slight lifting of the covers that lay against Lady Rowena's pale breast.

A knock on the door had her stumbling to open it, her tears almost blinding her to the man standing on the threshold. Geryth took one look at his sister's face and, grabbing her shoulders, shook her roughly,

"Gods above, Gerde! Don't tell me Lady Rowena's dead! Master Guy'll kill us both! An' if he don't, Commander Ranulf will."

Gerde stared at him for a moment, frowning in puzzlement and a sudden, gnawing jealousy.

"Why would Master Ranulf be angry? Does he... did he..."

"Did he what?" Geryth demanded impatiently. "Want her? Bed her? Not so fer as I know. But if'n he did, why would ye care? Ye know well he's a lecher as'll lay anything in skirts."

"Aye, I knows," Gerde muttered. "An' I don't care what he does. I just wondered why ye'd think he'd care if aught happened to her." She drew in a deep breath. "Anyways, I reckons the worst's over. She's just sleeping now... I think. But, Geryth..." Her panic was returning. "What'll we do if'n she do die?"

"Run!" Geryth replied tersely. "For now, the only thing we can do is beg the gods to keep her alive. Ye stay here an' look arter her as best ye can. An' I'll ride out an' find Master Guy. Sooner he's back, sooner he can find out how this happened and stop it happenin' again. I just hope it don't take me too long to find him."

"The God of Light ride with you," Gerde said earnestly. "An' keep us all safe."


It was late in the evening, although not quite dark, when Guyard returned to Rogérinac castle and found the guards had already secured the castle for the night. He had had a hellish ride, in more ways than one and his heart was beating both painfully and erratically in his chest as guilt, remorse and outright anxiety took their toll. By the time his stallion set foot to the chasm bridge he was wound to such a point that the sight of the closed gate was sufficient to cause him to curse the startled guards who appeared in answer to his horn call with such vitriol that they momentarily mistook him for their commander.

Then the portcullis was creaking upwards and the gate swinging open, allowing both horse and rider entrance. The weary stallion coming to a halt of its own accord, Guyard flung himself to the ground and, with a terse order to the nearest guard to send a groom and a spare horse immediately out towards Blackoakleas, set off for the door into the keep at a pace that was only just short of a run.

Ignoring his wife, who had evidently been drawn from her meal in the great hall by all the commotion, Guyard ran through the dim passages and took the spiral stairs of the south-east tower two at a time, only coming to a halt when he reached the door where Bran stood on guard, his spear already levelled and ready. When he saw who it was, Bran immediately grounded his weapon and reached behind him to push open the door.

"'Bout time too," the big man growled under his breath. And called over his shoulder to whoever was in the room, "All's well now, 'tis Master Guy hisself."

Guyard grunted a combined thanks and greeting to Bran as he passed, then hesitated on the threshold, suddenly overcome with fear of what he might find. As he stood there, frozen, the two women by the bed looked up from their vigil, their expressions identical; a combination of relief and latent anxiety.

"Oh, Master Guy, thank the gods ye've come."

Gerde burst into overwrought tears but Sister Herluva rose calmly to her feet and stepped aside, giving him clear access to the bed and the woman who lay so still upon it.

Disregarding everyone else, Guyard took the few paces necessary to reach the bed and as he looked down at Rowène, lying so pale and still, he thought his heart was surely going to stop. Unable to hold his feelings in check any longer he dropped to his knees by the low bed and tentatively reached out to touch her face. Finding it warm, he did not even think to prevent the incoherent endearments that spilled from his lips.

Dimly he sensed that both women had backed away, unwilling to intrude upon this very private moment. Nevertheless the movement, slight though it was, gave him the necessary impetus to bring his fear and guilt under some semblance of control. And to lock away the love he should never, ever, have spoken out loud.

Taking a deep breath he touched his fingers lightly to the place where Rowène's life-force pulsed in her neck and sighed in relief to find it still there, albeit alarmingly weak. He dragged himself off the floor and collapsed onto the stool by the head of the bed, forearms braced on his thighs. Then, striving for an appearance at least of calm, he looked first at the semi-hysterical servant, then at the pale but composed healer and said quietly,

"Please, one of you, tell me what happened."

He listened carefully as Sister Herluva told him all she had been able to glean from Geryth, Gerde and Bran; the herring that Rowène had barely tasted – thank the gods she had eaten no more than that first mouthful – and the three castle dogs found dead the next morning, presumably after finishing the fish Kelse had thrown out onto the midden. The healer went on to describe in exceedingly blunt detail just how ill Rowène had been and how, after waking once at dawn, had spent the rest of the day in the state between unconsciousness and sleep that Guyard could observe for himself.

Gerde had finally stopped weeping by this time and plucked up her courage sufficiently to ask as to whether he had seen her brother. Guyard made an attempt at a reassuring smile and wearily told her of her brother's tribulations, adding that he rather thought Geryth's feet would be in need of some loving care from his sister on his return. Gerde had looked rather nervously at him at this but, too tired to probe any deeper into the antagonism he had already observed between Geryth and his sister, Guyard simply shrugged her uncharacteristic behaviour aside and reached out to touch the back of his hand to Rowène's brow and cheek.

Belatedly aware that he had probably betrayed himself again, he glanced briefly across the room at the two women.

"You look as if you could both do with some rest. I will sit with Lady Rowena for a while if you wish to go down to the hall and get something to eat. After which I suggest you catch some sleep if you can."

Gerde nodded and sniffed.

"Aye, sir. Should I bring up something fer yerself by way of food when I come back up?"

"Some bread and cheese and ale would not come amiss," Guyard replied. "Oh and make sure that whatever you eat or drink comes from the same platter and pitcher as everyone else is using. Mind that, Gerde!"

"Don't ye worry, Master Guy," she said quickly. "I won't be making that mistake again."

Observing that the healer showed no signs of moving, Guyard said firmly, "You too, Sister."

She looked at him for a moment, a long, level look, then bowed her head in acquiescence and turned to go.

Guyard waited until the door had closed behind the women before he returned his attention to the bed. Knowing himself unobserved, he yielded to temptation and clasped the hand that lay pale against the rough blanket. Uncertain whether he was imagining the faint tremor that ran through the slender fingers at his touch, he brought the hand up to his mouth for the gentlest of kisses before holding it close to his stubbled cheek. And when he spoke his words were barely louder than a hoarse whisper,

"My love, my love... do not leave me..."

When the God of Light finally swept Rowène back from the endless dark sea of eternity and laid her gently on the shores of reality she awoke to find her senses awash with a roiling tangle of impressions that only gradually separated into recognisable form.

The first thing she felt was the cool breeze of freedom silky on her face.

The first thing she heard was the harsh cries of the great white sea mews as they rode the airs above the eastern seas.

The first thing she smelt was the clean and soothing essence of lavender, underpinned by the faintest hint of chamomile.

The first thing she saw as she opened her eyes were the dust motes shimmering in the sunlight that streamed through the open shutters of her room.

Slowly she turned her head on the pillow until she could see the stool beside her bed.

It was empty and for one long, numb moment she wondered why in the name of all the gods she had expected to find either Ranulf de Rogé or Guyard de Martine there!

Yet... they had been present in her dreams, that much she was sure of. Amidst those dark wanderings the two men had seemed at least as real as the looming daemons who had lined the endless shadowy road that led to Hell. But it had been Guy who had reached past the daemons to take her by the hand when she had lost Ranulf somewhere in the black mist... Guy who had held her hand and kept her walking until finally they were both standing in the light again.

So... had it been nothing more than a dream?

No, she would not believe that. He could not have been anything but real.

Even now, if she closed her eyes, she could feel the callouses on his fingers, the tender warmth of his lips, the rasp of stubble on his cheek. She could still hear the whispered echoes of his voice in her mind; he had called her his love and begged her not to leave him. While the indefinable but unmistakeable mix of horse, leather and male sweat, untainted by chamomile, that yet lingered in her nostrils convinced her that she had neither imagined his presence nor mistaken his identity.

But if Guy had been there before, he was certainly not here now.

Nor should he be, she told herself. She had caused the man more than enough trouble without expecting him to sit beside the bed of a woman who was neither mistress nor wife!

At the thought of Mathilde de Martine she felt her mouth twist in a grimace of self-disgust, wondering how she could have been so stupid as to ignore the woman's potential for malice? Naturally Mathilde had seized the opportunity presented by Guy's three-day absence and Rowène's own well-known preference for fish to attack one whom she perceived to be her rival. The only doubt in Rowène's mind was whether Mathilde had meant to murder her outright or had merely wished to give her a few hours of gut-wrenching agony and humiliation.

And surely she could not have known about the other... the tiny seed of life she had managed to destroy... the babe Rowène had lost in a welter of blood and pain.

Almost, Rowène could find it in her to be grateful for Mathilde's jealousy and spite...

So why then had she wept in the darkness of the night? Assuredly Ranulf would feel no such grief. *If* she ever told him. And she rather thought she would not. Not now it was over.

It was only some time later that it occurred to her that while Ranulf de Rogé would inevitably die – from a barbarian arrow, on an outraged father's blade, by an assassin's noose or any number of other horrible ways – at least he would not go to his death because of her.

# Chapter 13

## *Unexpected Consequences*

"Oh, m'lady, ye're awake!"

Gerde's glad cry interrupted Rowène's grim musings and brought her head around sharply. Seeing the unfeigned happiness lighting the serving girl's sun-freckled face Rowène managed a smile of greeting as she struggled to lift herself on her elbow. She tried to say something but her throat was still too raw to allow speech and all that came out was a croak.

"Don't try ter talk, m'lady," Gerde said hastily. "Here, drink this... slowly now... ye'll feel better in a bit."

Made cautious by recent events, Rowène cast a dubious look at the glazed pottery beaker in Gerde's hand. Following the direction of her eyes Gerde said hastily,

"Don't ye go worritin' yersel' 'bout that. 'Tis on'y honey water. I drew the water from the well meself while Master Guy went an' got the honey."

"Guy?" Even as she whispered his name Rowène could hear the tremor of hope and joy in her voice. "He's here then?"

An uncomfortable silence was her only reply. Glancing up as she took a sip of the blessedly cool sweet water, she saw the consternation on Gerde's face. Needing an answer, she rephrased her question carefully.

"Master Guy *is* back from his trip to the villages?"

Slowly, and with obvious reluctance, Gerde nodded, her fingers pleating and repleating the material of her apron, a nervous action Rowène had not observed in the serving girl since that first night. Regretting that her questioning was causing distress, she yet persisted.

"How long have I been ill, Gerde?"

"One night ye was sick, m'lady. So sick I thought ye'd die of it. An' all the blood ye lost. Sister Herluva says the poison works that way sometimes."

So Sister Héloise had been here too and had had the presence of mind to explain her miscarriage away as a side effect of the poison. But Gerde was still talking.

"The rest o' the time, all day yesterday and last night, ye've been sleepin'."

"So Sir Guy returned early?" Rowène asked, curious as to the reason behind her maid's obvious reluctance to speak about what had happened. "And Sister H... Herluva was here too?"

"Aye, m'lady an' that were a piece o' luck and no mistake. Come ter bring some more soap, or so her said, but I reckon as how 'twere the gods sent her here jus' when we needed her. We was that worried 'bout ye, Bran an' me, what wi' Geryth gone off ter fetch Master Guy. An' then Master Guy come back an' he were almost beside hisself, he were so angry."

"Not with you surely?"

"Nay, m'lady! Not wi' me nor Geryth. I think he fair frit Mistress Mathilde though. I didn't hear it meself but Kelse said as how Frythe tol' her that arter Master Guy'd finished wi' her, Mistress Mathilde were shakin' like a leaf in a storm an' the word is that her's kept ter her room ever since."

There was more than a hint of satisfaction in Gerde's voice but Rowène was not particularly interested in Mathilde de Martine at the moment; the woman might be shaken now but the gods knew she would not stay cowed for long. That Rowène knew, as surely as she knew the sun rose every day out of the eastern seas.

No, what Rowène craved – although she knew very well that she should not – was some sign that she had not dreamt Guy's presence by her side or the words he had spoken. She knew now that he had returned early from his trip but how he had spent his time since then she did not know. And now that she was freed from any necessity to communicate with his hated half-brother, perhaps she might pursue whatever it was that lay between herself and Guy.

She took another sip of the honey water and lowered her gaze, feeling that her stare was probably exacerbating Gerde's discomfort and making it less likely that she would tell her what she wanted to know.

"Thank you, Gerde, that is much better," Rowène said gratefully. "Now, you were telling me... about Master Guy."

"I was?" Gerde sounded flustered again.

"Yes. You said he returned early when you sent your brother to find him."

"Oh yes." There was relief now in Gerde's voice, a relief that was short-lived as Rowène continued.

"And what did Master Guy do on his return?"

"Well, he came ter see ye m'lady, ter make sure ye was all right. An' he went to talk to Mistress Mathilde o' course. Only that were afterwards..."

"After what?"

"Well he... Master Guy, he... he sat by yer bed fer a bit!" she finished in a rush. Then, having gone that far, Gerde obviously decided she might as well finish it. "Well, ter tell the truth, m'lady, he sent Sister Herluva an' me off ter get some food an' then told us ter get some rest. An' he stayed up here wi' ye."

Guilty at the rush of sheer joy that coursed through her, Rowène lay back against the pillows and closed her eyes.

"How long did he stay here?" she whispered.

"All night, m'lady. From dark-fall 'til dawn. Oh but m'lady, ye mustn't tell him I told ye. He said ye weren't ter know. Nor no-one else in the castle neither, 'cepting me an' Bran o' course. But 'specially Master Guy said as how he didn't want ye ter know."

"No, I do not suppose he would," Rowène replied. She opened her eyes and forced a small smile for Gerde's benefit. "Do not worry, Gerde, I will not say anything to Master Guy about it."

"Thank ye, m'lady," Gerde said earnestly. Then the worried expression left her eyes as she remembered her errand. "So, now ye're awake, do ye feel up ter something ter eat? It'll have ter be something simple though 'cause Kelse's in the stocks fer lettin' Mis... someone poison yer fish an' I'll have to prepare whatever ye wants meself." She gave a quick grin. "Ye can have anything ye wants, so long as it's got oats an' milk an' honey in it!"

Rowène gave a little chuckle that hurt her throat but still made her feel better.

"A bit of milky porridge and honey will do well enough," she decided. "If you can manage that."

"Aye, tha's easy enough," Gerde replied. "Ye bide here while I goes an' gets it. An' don't ye worry none. Geryth's back on duty now an' he won't let no-one in but me."

With those words Rowène felt her little glow of happiness slip away. Not that she was not grateful for Gerde's devotion or Geryth's protection but...

"Where is Sir Guy now?" she asked abruptly.

Gerde paused with her hand on the door, clearly startled by the question.

"He's not far away, m'lady. Jus' catchin' up on his sleep in his room."

"What, the room below this one you mean? The steward's chamber?"

"Aye, m'lady, that one. He's not slept in his old room... I mean the one he shared with Mistress Mathilde... well, he's not slept there since he brought ye back ter Rogérinac. Everyone in the castle knows that! I thought ye did too."

"No. I did not know," Rowène murmured, more to herself than to Gerde. "I merely wondered..." And that was a lie she told herself. She had not merely wondered − she had actively hoped that Guy was sleeping alone. Now the certain knowledge that he had not shared a bed with his wife since his return from Chartre racked her with guilty satisfaction and left her wondering whether she was more like the scheming, cold-hearted witch who had given her life than she would once have believed possible.

Guyard looked up, eyes burning with fatigue, as a knock sounded on his door. He had scarcely slept for the past two days and the night in between and the strain was beginning to tell on him.

"Not another bloody interruption!" he muttered as he flung down the quill and scrubbed at his aching eyes.

He had been trying to work all day but had little to show for it save a pounding pain in his skull, a stubble-rough jaw and eyes so blurred he could scarcely read what he had written. The gods knew some days he wished he was merely a wandering harper – plain Guy of Montfaucon once more, with no money save what he earned by his skill and, above all, no bloody responsibilities! Instead here he was, Guyard de Martine, Steward of Rogé; his task, to hold together his elder half-brother's lands. With bloody little by way of thanks and absolutely nothing by way of assistance, monetary or otherwise.

So why did he stay? Because he was a fool! And because he would not betray the trust of the man who had sired him, the father who, unable to give his bastard son his name, had given him everything else it was possible to give; love, respect, a sense of purpose and, damn it all, an unbreakable sense of loyalty to his two half-brothers.

Or it had been unbreakable until the events of this summer. Now he was not so sure. He only hoped neither Joffroi nor Ranulf did anything else to test his forbearance.

Gods, but he was tired! And the palpable air of tension in the castle and the very real danger posed by his wife to his brother's hostage did nothing to ease the pain either in his head or his heart. If only Rowène could have stayed in Chartre under Ranulf's protection perhaps his life might not be so bloody complicated now!

Completely forgetting that someone was waiting outside his door, he picked up his quill and looked back down at the parchment on which he had been listing the tithes he had levied on the villages he had already visited this summer, then grimaced at the far longer list of those he had yet to see. Far flung villages all of them but which he would have visited long since had not other circumstances – in other words the bloody distractions caused by Joffroi's insane and obsessive desire to legally bed Ariène de Chartreux – thrown his normal summer routine into disarray.

The knock sounded again and Guyard threw down his quill, with another curse and a splatter of ink.

"Bloody Hell, what is it now?"

The door opened part way to reveal Geryth's wary countenance.

"Yes, Geryth, what is it?"

"Lady Rowena's here, sir. Said ye sent for her."

Muttering another curse, he cast a quick glance around his room but he had stowed the pallet and blankets he had purloined from the guards' quarters out of sight as soon as he had arisen. There was nothing to betray the fact that this had become his bedchamber as well as the room where he had spent years struggling to keep Joffroi's lands and vassals from descending completely into poverty and ruin.

Looking up he found Geryth still blocking the door and said impatiently,

"Well, do not just stand there, man, show her in. Then wait outside. And leave the door ajar."

Geryth gave him a quick frowning look. Then, comprehension evidently dawning, nodded and stepped aside.

"Lady Rowena, sir."

Taking a deep breath Guyard snatched those few moments to bring his emotions under control. He set his hands on the table and was preparing to rise to his feet when he looked up and saw Rowène standing in front of his parchment-laden table – and his fragile control shattered like the icicles of Hell! His heart wrenched painfully at the blank expression in her grey eyes; eyes that glimmered against the extreme pallor of her face like two icy pools in a snowy wasteland. And then felt his breath freeze in his chest as his bemused gaze focussed on the black mantle that covered her from neck to ankle.

"Why in Hell are you still wearing Ranulf's cloak?" he snapped, completely forgetting both his manners and what he had meant to say. "Or do you love my bloody brother so much you cannot bear to be parted from that damned rag just because he once flung it to you in a fit of misguided pity!"

Something flickered in her eyes and her pale face went whiter yet.

"I thought you knew by now that I hate your brothers impartially. As for my reasons for wearing this *rag*, I thought it preferable to everyone in the castle knowing that I had visited the steward's chamber attired in nothing but my shift!" she said coldly, twitching the edge of the cloak aside far enough for him to catch a glimpse of her thin linen undergarment. "I apologise for the lack of proper clothing, Messire, but Gerde has not yet managed to launder my outer garments. Then again, I suppose I could have come to your chamber arrayed in scarlet silk like the whore both your wife and your brother believe me to be!"

He felt himself flush and one of Ranulf's more vicious profanities rose to his lips but he retained sufficient presence of mind not to utter it.

"No, of course not. Forgive me. And please, sit down. You look..."

"Ill? Exhausted. As white as a wraith?"

"Yes, all of them," he assured her, coming around the table and offering his arm, looking down into the grey eyes that regarded him with such a palpable mixture of pain and pride that Guyard thought she would refuse even the minimal contact he had offered. Then, apparently thinking better of it, she placed her hand on his arm but as they walked the few paces to the window embrasure he realised that she had accepted his offer not from reluctant courtesy but out of simple necessity.

Observing the relief that flickered across her thin, white face as she sank down onto the unyielding stone window seat, he felt his gut twist into a painful knot of anxiety. She was obviously much weaker than she would have him believe and he knew with complete certainty that she should not have risen from her bed today. And probably would not have done, save that he had requested that she come down here to speak with him as soon as she felt able to.

Why had he done that? Simply because he had not wanted to risk any more gossip by visiting her in her room when everyone in the whole damned castle was watching his every move. And now he was compounding his error by making her sit on cold, damp stone when she had so recently been desperately ill. His fault again; he should have protected her better. But even he had not thought his wife so viciously jealous as to poison a guest – his elder brother's ward no less – under their own roof.

Turning away, he grabbed the lightweight woollen cloak hanging from the peg on the wall and, hastily folding it up, held out his hand to help her rise.

"Here, sit on this."

He waited until she was seated again and then retreated a few paces to rest his buttocks against the edge of the table, folding his arms across his chest. He said nothing for the space of ten heartbeats but used the time to trace every line of her face, measuring every tiny expression that flashed through her clear grey eyes. Despite that initial brief flare of hostility she now appeared too tired to resent either his presence or his intrusive study but merely sat there, staring blankly back at him. Indeed he doubted that she was even aware of the cool sea breeze that danced through the unshuttered window, rippling through the long glowing tresses that flared as red as flame against the black wool of his brother's mantle.

Reminding himself that he could ill afford to waste this precious time he had with her, Guyard tore his eyes away from his visitor and shot a quick look at the door that gave out on to the landing, assuring himself that Geryth had obeyed his earlier instructions; closing the door far enough to ensure them a certain amount of privacy but leaving a sufficient gap to counter any accusation that Guyard might be indulging in an immoral liaison.

Only then did Guyard speak, calmly and quietly as if what he had to suggest was a normal daily occurrence in the life of a Mithlondian noblewoman, rather than a desperate measure of well nigh scandalous proportions.

"Demoiselle de Chartreux, please accept my apologies for the conditions you have been expected to endure since you left Chartre. I only wish I could assure you that matters will improve. But I cannot. All I can do is give you my word that your life will never again be put at risk."

"Thank you, Messire de Martine," she replied with a frozen courtesy and formality that matched his own.

Gods, what he would not give to hear his name on her lips again, spoken with the warmth and trust she had once shown him. Those days were long gone however and while he was no longer her groom he was nevertheless all that stood between her and danger. And, judging from her recent experiences at his wife's hands, he had made a far more competent groom than he did a gaoler. The thought occurred to him, not for the first time, that she would have been safer staying with Ranulf; at least Ran had only wanted to bed her, Mathilde wanted to murder her!

Shaking off this terrifying conclusion he continued in a dry, even tone,

"As you know I am in the process of visiting the outlying villages and levying the tithes based on this summer's harvest. Unfortunately those villages that remain to be assessed are situated a considerable distance away and will take me away from Rogérinac for the better part of a month. And in the light of recent events I dare not risk leaving you and my wife here together under the same roof."

"So take her with you," Rowène replied, a certain amount of impatience marring the impeccable indifference of her previous tone. "You surely do not think I will regret her absence? Or yours!"

Ignoring the stab of pain her final words evoked, Guyard continued evenly,

"No, I do not think you would miss either Mathilde or myself. But that is beside the point, since I have no intention of leaving you both here in Rogérinac."

"Then what do you intend?" she queried, her copper brows lifting.

Guyard regarded his ink-stained fingers for a heartbeat, then looked up to meet the dawning comprehension in her grey eyes. Carefully keeping all emotion from his tone he said,

"I intend to take *you* with me."

A stunned silence was his only answer. Then with a sudden violent surge of movement Rowène came to her feet.

"God of Light, Guy! Have you gone completely insane!" she hissed, thankfully keeping her voice as low as her obvious exasperation permitted. "Can you not see the folly in what you are proposing? If you do this, it will be tantamount to giving your wife leave to drag your reputation through the gutter! Again! You know what she will say – as loudly and as publicly as possible – if you ride out of Rogérinac with me, not to return for the better part of a month!"

"Calm down, Demoiselle, and at least listen to my proposition in its entirety rather than letting fly before I have finished."

"Very well, Messire," she replied icily, retreating again into formality even as she resumed her seat. "Tell me."

Guyard cast another harried glance at the door and then set out for her consideration the only half-way feasible plan his tired mind had been able to come up with.

"As I was saying, I cannot in all conscience leave you here in Rogérinac and although it is true I could take Mathilde with me, she does not ride even half as well as you, nor would she be able to cope with the difficulties of living rough, as we shall undoubtedly be doing. And unfortunately for you, despite your noble upbringing, you have proved yourself to be more than capable of surviving long days in the saddle with poor or non-existent accommodations at the end of them."

Rowène made a very unladylike sound that indicated she was at the least wryly amused by his assessment. Slightly encouraged by this reaction he continued more confidently.

"Of course, if we were truly to be alone together for the better part of a month, I would be the first to own myself a fool. But we will not be alone. I will be taking Geryth along for added protection while you will have your maid for company... What?" he asked sharply, standing up straighter. But before he could define the expression that flitted over her face she turned her head away, ostensibly staring out of the window at the tangled green of the garden beyond. The place where he had, on more than one or two occasions, found himself watching as she and her maid worked to bring order back to his mother's – or the woman he thought of as his mother – garden.

"Rowène, what is it you are not telling me? Is there some problem with Gerde accompanying you?"

She glanced back at him, a frown in her eyes. Then asked,

"Can she ride?"

It was a reasonable enough question but Guyard had the distinct impression that this was not the root of her obvious unease.

"She need do little more than sit on the quietest horse in the stables. And if even that proves to be impractical, she can ride pillion behind Geryth."

She nodded her agreement but still looked unconvinced.

"Do you have any more objections?"

"Plenty," she muttered. "But none you are likely to take any heed of, stubborn man that you are."

Guyard bit back a grin. He did not think she was likely to appreciate anything he might say to that.

"So, now we are agreed, it but remains to set a day for our departure. I have put this task off long enough already and I should prefer to go within the next couple of days but I will not leave until you feel able to travel."

"Really?" she queried, more than a hint of sarcasm in her voice. "Well then, shall we say the day after tomorrow?"

"If you are sure?"

"I am sure," she snapped and rose somewhat shakily to her feet, evidently feeling their meeting was over. Guyard, however, had not quite finished. Pushing off the table he took a step closer to her.

"In that case, I shall get Geryth to escort you back to your room. Rest if you can. I will see you at the evening meal."

"But..."

"No buts, Rowène," he interrupted grimly. "From now until we leave Rogérinac you will take every meal with me, in the hall, eating what I eat, drinking what I drink, and be damned to castle gossip!" And without giving her a chance to argue, raised his voice in a shout, "Geryth!"

"Sir?"

"Escort Lady Rowena back to her chamber and see that she stays there until the supper horn goes. Then you will bring both her and your sister down to the hall for the evening meal. Is that clear?"

"Aye, Master Guy!" Geryth responded to his curt tone with an instinctive salute before, rather uncomfortably Guyard thought, turning his attention to the slender, black-cloaked noblewoman standing a few paces away. There was a puzzled look in the young soldier's brown eyes but he merely murmured, "Lady Rowena..."

Guyard more than half expected another sarcastic comment but Rowène merely nodded at Geryth and, with one last frowning look over her shoulder, followed the man-at-arms from the room. As the door closed behind them Guyard let out the breath he had not realised he was holding and reached blindly for the goblet of watered wine one of the serving wenches had brought up earlier. Carrying it over to the window he slumped down onto his crumpled cloak and drained the goblet's contents.

*Thank the gods that is over*, he thought. She had taken it better than he had expected but then he had caught her at a vulnerable time. Probably had she not just recovered from being poisoned, she would have put up a far more stubborn resistance to his plans.

Not that he had any proof that Mathilde had deliberately poisoned her but the look on his wife's face when he had cornered her in their bedchamber had told him all he needed to know. He wondered what deadly herb she had used and where she had obtained it from. If it was from the old hag who lived in the village nearby – surely it could not have been from the healers of Silverleigh, Sister Herluva would have said – both of them would bear careful watching.

At this reminder of the lethal properties of certain otherwise innocent plants, he lifted the goblet he had been drinking from earlier. He sniffed suspiciously at the dregs – it had tasted foul but no worse than any other flagon of wine from Joffroi's cellar – but he did not really think it had been poisoned. Mathilde might be sufficiently foolish as to believe that she could, with impunity, harm the woman she believed to be his mistress but she was not a complete fool. Jealous vindictiveness towards the daughter of the disgraced Lord of Chartreux was one thing. Poisoning the man who was brother to both Joffroi and Ranulf de Rogé would take a colder courage than Mathilde possessed and she must know it would be little short of suicide to attempt it.

Hence Guyard's decision to command Rowène's company in the great hall. She might have no desire to be put on public display but like it or not, he would keep her safe by whatever means at his disposal.

# Chapter 14

## *South to Sarillac*

Two days later the Steward of Rogé rode out of Rogérinac, accompanied by a pale-complexioned noblewoman, a baffled but obedient man-at-arms and a frightened looking maidservant. Having handed over temporary command of the castle to Edwy – who in the absence of both Ranulf and Guthlaf was acting as garrison commander – Guyard had bidden a coldly courteous farewell to his wife, Mathilde responding with the briefest of curtsies and one of the sourest smiles he could ever remember seeing on her face.

But Guyard did not care. The prospect of freedom from the castle, not to mention release from the tension and bitterness that permeated every chamber, was far more powerful than his anxiety as to Mathilde's activities in his absence. And the fact that he would be with Rowène only added to his well-concealed sense of exhilaration.

As they rode out from under the dark gateway he directed a discreet sideways glance towards the young woman riding the honey-coloured mare. She had kept all trace of expression from her face during the formal farewells in the courtyard and he admitted to an underlying anxiety as to her fitness to travel; her face still seemed much too pale. But now that they were away from the castle he could see her eyes beginning to sparkle in the sunlight, could almost see her returning to life with every breath she took. She must have sensed his intense study because she turned her head, meeting his gaze before he could look away.

For a moment she just stared into his eyes. Then her lips curved into a smile, offering him all the joy and trust and warmth she had once shown him. He had not expected that she would ever forget his betrayal of her friendship at Chartre. Nevertheless her smile gave him cause to believe that she now understood that whatever he had done, it had been to protect her. And he prayed to the gods that, in time, she might learn to forgive him.

Although if she did, he knew that he must take heed not to betray himself, particularly during the days to come. The quickening of his heart, the singing in his blood, his reaction to her smile, all told him he must be very careful if he should chance to find himself alone with her. Nothing could change the fact that he was bound until death to Mathilde or that Rowène was – in the absence of any formal notice otherwise – still betrothed to Joscelin de Veraux. That being so, Guyard would dishonour neither himself nor her with an adulterous liaison.

But God of Light, it would prove to be nigh on impossible to keep his distance if she continued to smile at him like that!

His fingers tightened involuntarily on the reins, causing Fireflame to toss his head in response. Dragging his gaze away from the soft laughter in his companion's eyes Guyard focussed instead on the wind-blown strands of chestnut mane that flowed over his thighs; strands that were nearly the same colour as Rowène's flame-red hair. Gods and daemons! But he would truly go mad ere this trip was over unless he could keep his mind on the task in hand.

He was not here to seduce Rowène de Chartreux! Or, conversely, to allow her to seduce him, should such a thought occur to her.

He was here to levy Joffroi's tithes and, as a first step to that laudable goal, he returned his attention firmly to the road ahead. Finding they had reached the crossroads, he called to his companions and guided Fireflame off to the left.

"We go this way."

Rowène shrugged her indifference as to their direction, her face still alight with joy in her freedom. Then, evidently feeling she should show some interest, she glanced around and asked vaguely,

"Surely this is not the road to Blackoakleas? But I thought you were not finished there?"

"No, but we can return that way," Guyard replied. "I thought it would be easier riding for you if we rode down to Sarillac to start with, then along the south coast. After that we can follow the Larkenlye north, over the moors and come back down the east coast. We can be in Sarillac by dusk today, spend the night there and start afresh in the morning if you feel up to it."

She regarded him for a moment as if wondering what he was not telling her. Then she shrugged as if to imply she had little choice but to agree and turned her face up to the sun, obviously grateful to feel its warmth, while the teasing touch of the sea breeze brushed a little more colour into her disturbingly pale cheeks.

Sitting her mare high on the gorse-topped cliff, Rowène found herself looking down onto the town of Sarillac-on-Sea and drawing in a breath of sheer amazement. After the grim grey castle of Rogérinac and the pitiful fishermen's huts that huddled on the rocky shore beneath it, not to mention the wretched moorland villages, as exemplified by Rushleigh, she had formed the impression that there were no towns of any size or prosperity anywhere within the province of Rogé. The bustling town she could see below convinced her that she had been wrong and Guyard's dry tones close beside her confirmed it.

"There is wealth in Rogé, Demoiselle, if you know where to look for it. Sarillac and the towns of the south coast are the gems in Joffroi's treasure chest. And even Rogérinac, grim though it now is, was not always like that. Certainly, I do not remember it being so while my... Lady Rosalynde was alive. But after so many years with no chatelaine, we – Joff, Ran and I – became accustomed to it as it was. And, of course, in latter years there was no money to waste on soft furnishings or fine hangings."

"No doubt that will change now that the wealth of Chartreux lies within your brother's grasp. Black Joffroi might not care for luxury but I cannot envisage my mother consenting to live in such squalor," Rowène commented, her dry tone a perfect match for his as they continued to make their way down the steep roadway. But for all that the remark lacked bite since she was more interested in gazing down the narrow cobbled streets that twisted off on either side and the sturdy dwellings rising above their heads than scoring points against the de Rogé men. In some odd way the town reminded her of Chartre, although probably only because of the presence of the big sea-going galleys in the harbour, and because it was clearly a town of some substance rather than the poor fishing village that had grown up on the sea strand below the castle of Rogérinac.

From what she could see, Sarillac had a variety of craftsmen's shops, taverns, storehouses and the inevitable brothels, together with many well-kept dwellings, most possessing a second or even third floor, built so that they overhung the cobbled streets beneath. Without exception the buildings appeared all to be of sound construction, with sturdy wooden beams and painted plaster – a warm ochre rather than the white of Chartre – while the roofs were tiled with dark grey slate rather than red clay. Nor were there any of the pots of trailing red and pink geraniums that provided such a riot of colour to delight the eye in Chartre.

But for all that Sarillac still struck her as much the cheeriest place she had seen in that wild and rather bleak province. Of course, the fact that the sun was setting in a glory of gold and the water in the harbour was a lustrous, molten blue probably had much to do with it. Seen on a rainy day with the wind raging in from the east and whipping up white crests on the grey-green waves it would be a different matter. But for the time being Rowène could not fault Guy's description.

Yet even as they were making their way down through the town, under the curious eyes of its citizens, Rowène could not help speculating as to their ultimate destination. The chestnut stallion and its rider being some paces further ahead, she muttered a question to Gerde but the girl merely shook her head, her brown eyes wide with fright as she clung even tighter to her brother's belt.

The shadows of evening were swooping in by the time Guy led the small party towards a modest house, set in its own small patch of garden, well-tended and abounding with a fine variety of vegetables and culinary herbs. There were even flowers – dainty pinks, bright lupins, tall yellow hollyhocks – which served no useful purpose at all as far as Rowène could see, save that they delighted the eye with their brilliant splashes of colour.

Curiosity overcoming discretion, she had nudged Honey closer to the big chestnut stallion which, in default of any instruction from his rider, was munching enthusiastically on a patch of greenery overhanging the fence while Guy sat unmoving, a troubled expression in his light blue eyes. Rowène allowed him the courtesy of some moments alone with his thoughts, which were obviously not entirely pleasant, but when he showed no immediate signs of remembering his companions, she decided enough was enough.

"Messire de Martine!"

"Mmmm?"

"This place, this is where we will be staying?"

Perhaps it was the calculated sharpness of her tone that caught his attention but Guy finally dragged himself from his reverie. Rowène caught his apologetic glance before he swiftly swung down from his saddle. She watched as he looped Fireflame's reins over the low fence surrounding the garden and then came to stand at her stirrup, looking up at her. She could not read the guarded expression in his light blue eyes but she realised all too well that he was waiting to help her dismount, a service he had performed for her so many times before when he had acted as her groom in Chartre.

For a moment she hesitated, then reading a trace of impatience in the set of his mouth decided not to argue. Dismounting easily was an impossibility as the simple gown she was wearing had not been patterned with riding in mind. Her movements hampered severely, she nevertheless managed to move into a position where all she had to do was slide down into his waiting arms. She stumbled slightly as she landed but although Guy caught her in a firm grip that evoked a sudden, extremely unpleasant memory of his half-brother, he did not prolong the contact any longer than necessary and as soon as she was steady on her feet he turned away without a word.

Unnerved by that sudden, unlooked-for memory and more exhausted by the day's ride than she knew, Rowène felt her temper fray. Reaching out, she caught Guy's arm before he had taken more than a pace away and, too courteous to pull free, he turned back to face her. Nevertheless, the hard edge to his tone carried its own warning; as she had discovered since leaving Chartre, his tolerance had limits and she had no desire to push him beyond them.

"Demoiselle?"

"Forgive me, Guy," Rowène said softly. "It is just you have said so little today and this is no public inn. What are we doing here?"

"I never said we were going to take rooms at an inn." He grimaced at a thought he clearly did not wish to share with her. "This is the home of a woman who was in service at Rogérinac, many years ago now. Lady Rosalynde brought her in as a wet nurse for Ran and myself when we were but squalling brats in the cradle and Hilarie stayed on at the castle until we were both full-grown. Joffroi gave her a generous settlement and she moved back to Sarillac to take care of her brother, who was by then one of the most prosperous merchants of the town, and his daughter. Her brother is dead now and his daughter has no need of her any longer, so Hilarie spends her time growing vegetables and flowers to sell in the market and takes in the occasional lodger. And speaking of lodgers, I had better go and see if I can prevail upon her to give us house room for the night, else it will be a public inn for us all."

Somewhat bemused by this unexpected flood of information Rowène merely nodded and meekly followed him up the path. She could not help wondering, however, what he had *not* told her that would explain his obvious reluctance to impose on his former nurse. Perhaps it was just that he was worried about an old woman's ability to provide accommodation for four unexpected visitors. Or...

Before she could complete the thought, the door flew open and Rowène took a sudden step back, bumping into Gerde who was right on her heels. Gerde gave a squeak and the woman on the doorstep gave what could only be described as a gleeful chuckle.

"Well now, here's a thing! One of my lads comes a-visiting. An' wi' company, no less. So who is it ye've brought ter see me, young master? A wee mousie an' a fine strapping young man. An' another lassie yet. Nay a mousie, though, but a red vixen mebbe..."

The old woman was plainly a little touched in her wits and as she stepped forwards and squinted up into Rowène's face, she was hard pressed not to take another step backwards. She glanced at Guy but he merely shrugged and mouthed unhelpfully,

"Humour her."

Thus adjured, Rowène returned her attention to the elderly nurse. In appearance she was a well-rounded, harmless old soul, white curls bobbing beneath a neat linen cap. But Rowène, looking into those deep, dark eyes, knew suddenly that Guy had been right to be wary and that she, for one, might have found a public inn easier to deal with. She watched uneasily as the old woman flicked another approving look over the 'fine strapping young man' and a knowing one at the 'wee mousie' before turning back to Rowène.

"Aye, humour me, like my lad sez! So tell me, Mistress Fey, who and what ye three may be."

Rowène knew she was gaping idiotically but she could not seem to help herself. She knew what people thought when they looked at her – seeing not *her* but only the dark fire of her hair, a flame that was muted to copper in her brows and lashes – but most would not dare to speak of the Faennari to her face. Only this old woman, and the man who had called her a witch.

"My name is Rowena. Rowena of Chartre," she said shortly. "And this is my maidservant, Gerde and her brother Geryth, who is one of Sir Ranulf's men."

The old woman smiled benignly at this mention of her other nursling and directed a searching look at the one who stood before her.

"An' how does yer brother, Master Guy? Not seen him round here since the gorse came into bloom an' now 'tis harvest time already. I reckon he's still awa' wi' the rest o' the Prince's warriors? Or else drinkin' in some dark den down by the harbour wi' a wicked doxy on his knee?"

"Neither, Hilarie," Guy answered patiently. "He is in Chartre, at the moment. I'll tell you about it later, if you will let us stay."

"Chartre, eh? An' there's a lassie from Chartre here in his stead? Huh! Somethin's not right there. An' ye, Master Guy, what might ye be a-doin' in Sarillac, seeing as ye've never been one fer the brothels?"

"Nothing to worry yourself about, Hilarie," he replied soothingly. "I am on my way to assess the harvest tithes. And am come to beg a night's lodging for myself and my companions if that is possible. If needs must, Geryth and I can sleep rough but Lady Rowena and her maid need rather more comfort than an inn can provide. I will be gone again tomorrow but I had it in mind to leave Geryth and his sister here until I return to Rogérinac. I thought you might be needing some help in the garden and the house before the autumn gales come."

Although this change of plan came as something of a shock to Rowène she managed, by good fortune or the grace of the gods, not to betray her surprise

"So... that is well enough," Hilarie agreed slowly. "An' grateful I shall be fer the help... But what about the fey one? Your Lady Rowena?" the old woman asked, a troubled expression on her face.

"She is not *my* anything," Guy said curtly. "But no, she will not be staying. She goes with me and before you accuse me of any wrong-doing, Hilarie, it is not what you think."

"Since ye doesn't know what I thinks, Master Guy," she replied sharply. "I'll thank ye not ter be puttin' thoughts in me head nor words in me mouth." Then, with an abrupt change of subject. "I've no lodger fer the nonce so 'twill be no trouble ter find room, providin' ye an' the lad doesn't mind sleepin' on the floor. Now then, ye... Geryth, is it? Ye take yon great beasties round ter the shed at the back o' the house, though I'm thinking they'll mebbe find it a tight fit. Ye two lassies come ye in an' make yourselves ter home. I've nay doot ye're hungry an' ye both look as if ye could do wi' a good rest. Not been taking enough care, eh?" she added with a glinting sideways look that made Gerde blush and Rowène cringe.

There was no telling whether Hilarie was alluding to Gerde's slightly swollen belly or Rowène's poison-induced pallor – God of Mercy, she only hoped the old woman had not guessed at her miscarriage of Ranulf's child – but this was definitely not the time or place to discuss it, not with Guy following hard on their heels.

"Here ye are then, my lassies. Sit ye down an' Hilarie shall fetch ye some sweet cider ter cool yer thirst."

This she did, bustling from what was obviously the main living room into the kitchen and back again, carrying a tray with five glazed pottery beakers and a sweating earthenware pitcher containing the promised cider. By this time Rowène and Gerde had found stools, leaving the rocking chair by the hearth for the old woman. Guy remained standing near the door, his shoulders propped against the wall, his face enigmatic in the soft golden shadows of early evening.

Rowène promised herself a few words alone with him. She was still brooding over his fleeting comment as to what would happen when he left Sarillac and she very much wanted to know what had occurred to change his original plan. That would have to wait until later however.

Having served the cider, Hilarie settled herself comfortably in her chair. Then, raising her cup towards her unexpected guests the old nurse offered the conventional greeting.

"Health an' good fortune," she said and took a hearty swig. Then she set the cup down and, fixing her nursling with a gimlet stare, said pointedly,

"An' now ye can tell me what mischief my precious niece has been working. An' just why the Steward of Rogé finds it necessary ter go riding aboot the countryside wi' another woman at his side? One moreover who looks as if she should still be lying on her bed, wi' a hot stone at her feet an' a healing posset for her belly!"

Rowène felt her cheeks warm at the implication behind the old woman's pointed words, then froze as she belatedly made the connection between Guy, Hilarie and...

"Your niece?" she whispered, hoping desperately that she was wrong. The old woman looked at her and laughed, the dry sound holding not the slightest hint of humour.

"Aye, me brother Harold's darter. Did Master Guy not tell ye? Me niece, Mathilde, is his wife!"

That shock aside, the following days – Guy's original estimate of departure having been extended by almost a se'ennight – passed without too many ripples of ill feeling.

Rowène had spent the time gathering her strength and waiting for the bleeding caused by the miscarriage to lessen. Gerde had obviously told the old woman something of what had happened at Rogérinac – although thank the gods she could not have known, or told, of Ranulf's part in it – and Hilarie had roundly informed her former nursling that his lady would leave her care only when *she* decided the Lady Rowena was fit to leave.

Guy had agreed, perforce, and although Rowène had made the most of the period of rest, she was ultimately more than glad to escape from old Hilarie's knowing dark eyes at the end of it. She suffered more than a slight qualm at the thought of leaving Gerde with the old woman, not knowing how the girl would fare or what secrets she might unwittingly give away, but there was nothing Rowène could do about that; Gerde could not accompany her around the province, even without her delicate state of health, and if she were honest Rowène did not want her maid's restricting presence.

She did not know what, if anything, might develop between her and Guy once away from the constraints of castle life but she viewed the coming days as a gift from the gods; an utterly unexpected chance to taste a freedom that would never be hers again, whether her betrothed decided to formalise their binding or not. Yet if Joscelin de Veraux represented her uncertain future, Ranulf de Rogé was nothing more than a fading shadow in her past. The present was all that mattered, a present to be lived in the light of the last of the summer's sun; a golden goblet filled to the brim with a rich and heady wine and she intended to taste every last bitter-sweet drop of it.

# Chapter 15

## *The Heady Taste of Freedom*

Rowène sat her mare on the cliff top a league south of Sarillac, exhilaration setting her skin prickling while the very air she breathed seem to sparkle in the sunlight. She felt alive and free, a sea bird riding the ocean breeze...

This illusion of freedom – and she readily admitted it was only that, even as she drank in deep gulps of the bright air – was no doubt aided by the fact that she was once more clad in masculine attire; the ragged shirt, tunic and breeches she had worn before and boots that Guy had had made for her in Sarillac while she sat with Gerde and Hilarie in the old woman's garden breathing in the mingled scents of stocks and lavender, thyme, marigold and chamomile – the latter for once not rendering her instantly nauseous.

Despite the nature of her garments – which she assumed Guy had intended to mask both her identity and her gender – she made no attempt to conceal her femininity, her long dark red hair being bound into two thick braids that hung down over her shoulders. Let the peasants of Rogé think what they would, she would not impugn Guy's reputation so recklessly. Better that the folk of village and moor should believe that their Steward had finally, and very publicly, broken his binding vows by taking a mistress than have them suspect him of taking another man to his bed. The Kardolandians might ignore or even indulge in the practice but the Mithlondians had never done so. Better for Guy to unjustly bear the name of adulterer, she thought, than an S branded onto the flesh of his cheek; his reputation he might salvage at a later date, the brand he would wear for life.

Such dark reflections, however, were no match for the more vibrant emotions coursing through her just now. Refreshed by her stay in Sarillac, washed by the radiance of the early morning sunlight and invigorated by the sparkling sea breeze, she felt an impulse to laugh aloud with sheer joy. She glanced at her companion, wondering whether he shared her sense of freedom and although she did not speak his name aloud, he turned to look at her, almost as if he *had* heard. A moment later his mouth curved in a smile, his eyes the gentle summer blue that had always warmed her heart.

"What?" he asked, his voice quietly amused.

"You feel it too, do you not?" It was not the question she had meant to ask but it slipped out nonetheless. The harper he had once been seemed to appreciate what she meant without further elucidation.

"The sudden sense of freedom?" he asked. "That is what you meant?" She nodded and watched as he took a deep breath of the summer-scented air. "Yes," he said simply. "For the first time in a long time I feel free. Free of my responsibilities for Rogérinac, free of guilt for the havoc I have helped wreak in your life, free to..." He stopped abruptly and his eyes suddenly lost their whimsical softness as his jaw hardened. "Not, of course, that it is a freedom that lasts," he finished. "Come, we should be moving on."

Gathering his reins, he spoke to his horse, nudging the stallion forwards with the lightest touch of spurred heels. Following his lead Rowène eased the little mare forwards but, since he did not immediately pick up the pace to a speed where conversation was impossible, continued to talk to him.

"Guy?" She wondered for a moment whether she should try to keep to the formalities but nothing in his demeanour seemed to indicate he was annoyed by her use of his given name.

"Yes?"

"Do you think Gerde will be all right with Hilarie?"

"Of course she will. And she has Geryth with her."

"That is what I am worried about," Rowène commented, far from reassured. "You must know that they are at odds over... something that must have happened whilst Geryth was away from Rogérinac and can scarcely bring themselves to speak to each other?"

"And you know what that something is?" he queried.

Grimacing inwardly, she shook her head.

"No, Gerde would not tell me but I know she is troubled by it."

"Well, I would not worry," Guy replied. "I warrant by the time we return to Sarillac Hilarie will have sorted them out." He grinned suddenly. "She never let Ran and I be at odds for more than half a day without intervening, mostly with a hazel switch!" Then, more soberly, "Not that I expect her to do anything so drastic with Gerde and Geryth, although something will have to be done if there is to be any peace when we return to Rogérinac." He frowned. "But do you really have no notion what has caused this coldness between them? In all the years they have been at Rogérinac I have never known them to be like this with each other."

"As I said, Gerde will not talk about it to me," Rowène answered warily. "But possibly Geryth might confide something to you?"

"Hardly," Guyard snorted. "If he had a problem he would go to Ran."

"But your brother is not here and even if he were..."

"What?"

Guy glanced at her, obviously waiting for her to finish. Rowène bit her lip and looked away. After all, she did not know for certain that Gerde was pregnant, and even if she was, Rowène had no proof apart from her gut feeling, which was scarcely reliable, that Ranulf de Rogé had been involved in any way with the girl, let alone sired her putative child. Nevertheless Guy must have been able to deduce something of her thoughts. Either that or he was a better judge of his half-brother's behaviour than she was ever likely to be.

"I see!" he continued with a sigh, obviously feeling the burden of his responsibilities again. "You think Ran might have... er... been intimate with the girl and that Gerde is afraid to tell her brother, lest it cause trouble between him and his commander?"

"Something like that," Rowène admitted.

"Yet even if that were true – and I am by no means convinced it is, since Ran does not commonly seduce innocents into his bed and it is just as likely that it was Joffroi who bedded the girl – do you really think that Geryth does not know what my brothers are like? What happens to any maid who comes to Rogérinac castle, sooner or later?"

"So you approve of your brothers debauching innocents?" she queried, a colder note seeping into her voice.

"No, of course I do not approve," Guyard snapped back. "But neither can I stop them." He took another deep, hard breath. "In any case, there is nothing either of us can do for Gerde until we return."

"No, I suppose not..."

But her mind was no longer focussed on her tire-maid's problems or Ranulf de Rogé's iniquitous behaviour. Her attention had been caught by the narrow, black-hulled ship making its way up the coast under oars, its sail a red warning; a slave ship from the Eastern Isles. Disjointed memories flashed through her mind; the bloody shambles in the courtyard of her burning home, a line of broken bodies who were beyond further pain, the wounded prisoners who were not. The voices of two men arguing above her, as she lay, barely conscious against a broad, mailed chest...

Tearing her eyes away from the slave ship, she stared with appalled comprehension at her companion, Luc's name rising to her lips, but it was Guy spoke first.

"It was the only way to save your brother's life. Him and the others who survived that day."

"Save his life! Is that what you call it? As I remember, there was some mention of the profit to be made from such a transaction. So just how much did your hell-spawned brother get for selling *my* brother to the galleys? Enough mayhap to buy himself a whore to warm his bed that night?"

It was difficult to say whether disbelief or disgust were uppermost in her voice.

"I do not know, I did not ask him!" Guy snapped. "But I doubt he enjoyed the part he was forced to play in that debacle any more than I did. And whether you believe it or not, it *was* the only way I could see of saving your brother and his men."

"But why would you even want to? Our families have been in a state of enmity for the past score of years, if not longer..."

516

"And so you think I should take pleasure in your family's downfall?" He sounded completely bemused but anger was beginning to bubble behind. "I thought you knew me better than that! Gods above, to accept that Joffroi had had your father arraigned for high treason was a bitter enough draught, to then be forced to fight against men with whom I had no quarrel was even worse. To watch as your home and your sister perished in flames... Do you really think I would then knowingly hand the brother you loved – your only surviving male kinsman – over to Joffroi to be hanged? Damn it, Rowène!"

He gathered up his reins, made to ride on.

"No, wait! I am sorry... Please Guy... just stop a moment."

Grudgingly he reined to a halt and sat there looking at her, an unyielding set to his mouth, an uncharacteristically steely glint in his light blue eyes.

"Well?"

She shot another look over her shoulder at the galley still labouring up the coast and sighed before returning her gaze to her companion.

"I accept that *you* meant it for the best, though nothing will convince me that your half-brother saw it as anything other than a means of raising some ready silver." She saw he was about to turn away again and said hastily. "No, please, Guy... just tell me how you think selling Luc into slavery could have saved his life? I have seen the slaves in the market in Kaerellios, seen the pirate galleys they row until they die. And I cannot accept that sending Luc into that life, wounded as he was, would have bought him an easier death than hanging would have been."

"Possibly not," Guy admitted wearily. "But if I, or Ranulf, had given him over to Joffroi... and I think you will find that Ran knew well enough that it was Lucien's body he showed you, though I doubt he would admit it even under torture..."

"*Ranulf* knew?"

She had a sudden memory of his voice, harsh and impatient, his stance bored and indifferent, cleaning his fingernails for gods'sake! And the swift viciousness of his anger when she had vomited over his boots...

And he had known? All the time? That it was Lucien, not Luc, who lay dead and savaged at his feet? Surely not.

Another, more disturbing, memory edged past the others. Of Ranulf holding her afterwards, her tear-wet face turned into his shoulder so that no-one else might see her distress. She had been barely conscious at the time but now she experienced a fleeting recollection of him holding her in his arms as he bore her away from that place of death. At the time she had despised herself for her weakness in submitting to him again, even as the stink of sweat and metal had nearly caused her to vomit over the expensive mail shirt against which she had been pressed so painfully.

But that had been then. Now, with the fresh, salt-scented breeze clean in her nostrils, she remembered only the solid strength of the man as he held her;

supporting and shielding her, despite his own injuries and the weariness he must have felt.

She might not want to accept what Guy had told her but she could no longer deny that Ranulf had known what his half-brother was doing and had even helped him do it. And if their elder brother ever guessed that they had removed Luc from his bloody vengeance...

She shuddered and returned to the present, hastily picking up the thread of Guy's words; he was still talking about Luc.

"If either Ran or I had given your brother up to Joffroi it would certainly not have meant a swift death. Joffroi would have had him tortured first, then hung up to die as slowly and painfully as could be contrived. And you would have had to bear witness to it all, to listen to his cries when the pain became more than he could bear, to watch him dying, breath by tearing breath. Do you think I wanted that for you? Not when I had served you so poorly already."

Rowène felt herself flush with a sort of shamed gratitude, an emotion that was not meant solely for Guy, but which she also extended very reluctantly towards his half-brother.

"I am sorry, Guy. As you said, I should have known better. But, God of Mercy, you took a risk, did you not? What would your brother have done – or indeed do – should he ever learn what you and... Ranulf have done?"

"He will be furious. And well within his rights to be," Guy replied grimly.

A shiver came over her, like the shadow of a cloud across the sun and for a disorientating moment she smelt sweat and dust and blood.

"Furious enough to have you punished?" she asked unsteadily. "Flogged, as he threatened?" She caught another scent, this time sun-warmed bracken and pine. But there were neither on this gorse-topped headland. Dread pooled cold around her heart and she could barely bring herself to mention his other brother's name. "And... Ranulf? Would he fare the same as you?"

"Probably," Guy admitted, then gave her a fleeting smile. "Do not trouble yourself. It would not be the first time Ran or I have been flogged at Joffroi's order, although admittedly we were much younger the last time he had a lash put against our hides. But better, I thought, to risk a flogging than stand by and do nothing. Nor do I regret what I did, save in so far as I did not want to involve Ran in something Joffroi is bound to see as deliberate treachery but he involved himself anyway. I know you cherish no warm feelings towards Ranulf..."

"With good reason!" she interjected.

"I do not doubt it," he replied. "But at least remember that he risked his skin – literally – in that venture."

But she did not want to think of Ranulf de Rogé. Instead she fixed her salt-stung eyes on a patch of bright yellow gorse and concentrated on watching the butterflies and bees going about their business, letting Guy's words wash over her, bringing renewed grief but also a thread of hope.

"Yes, your brother will probably die on the rowing benches. But on the other hand, he may not. If I read him right, Luc de Chartreux would sell his soul to the Daemon of Darkness and crawl out of Hell on his hands and knees for the merest chance of vengeance against my brothers and myself."

She glanced back at him then, just in time to see him flick a glance at the now empty stretch of sea, a quick grimace crossing his face.

"For your sake, I hope he gets that chance, even though it means Ran and I are unlikely ever to sleep sound in our beds again." Then his voice altered, the darkness fading from his humour. "Come, we have lingered long enough here. We have a province to ride, my lady, from sea to moor and back again. And the sun will not shine forever, not in Rogé anyway."

In the event Guy was proved wrong and the sun continued to shine, golden and glorious. They were gone for more than a month and by the time they returned to Rogérinac the purple haze of heather on the high moors was fading and dark gold had already begun to gild the leaves of black oak and silver birch that grew in the narrow wooded valleys that ran down to the sea.

Despite the long hours riding the rough paths and the uncertain accommodations along the way it proved to be almost a happy time for Rowène. By night she was too exhausted to suffer the disturbing dreams that had haunted her sleep since the fall of Chartre and by day she fell back into the easy companionship she had once shared with Guy of Montfaucon, before she had discovered that he was Jacques de Rogé's bastard son. Not that the illegitimate nature of Guy's birth had ever been a consideration but the fact that he was Ranulf's half-brother continued to trouble her.

Not that she did not have plenty of other things to occupy her mind as she and Guy journeyed around the province, and although she would have considered almost anything an improvement over her life as a hostage in Black Joffroi's stronghold, Rowène found herself genuinely interested in the task at hand. Observing Guy about his business, she was quick to conclude that he levied as fair a tithe as was possible in the circumstances and that despite his blood kinship with Black Joffroi – a man the peasants of Rogé clearly both hated and feared – Guy was at least treated with respect, if nothing warmer. It was only when they came to the farthest reaches of the fief, almost within touching distance of the forbidding mountains that rose high and blue-shadowed between Rogé and Vitré that Rowène noticed a difference in the manner in which Rogé's steward was treated.

Here at Mallowleigh, the most northerly point on Guy's circuit, the villagers were still harvesting. Leaving Rowène with the women by day, Guy went out into the fields himself, stripped to the waist and working alongside the village men, too restless by far to wait for them to finish.

Between them Guy and Beowulf, the headman of the village, made the decision that for the few days they would remain in Mallowleigh, it would be best if Rowène lodged with one of the village woman rather than in the headman's hut with the Steward. This young woman, Melangel, had had the misfortune to spend some years at the castle in Rogérinac and was therefore able to converse with her guest in common speech rather than the local dialect which was all the other village women knew.

Over the following days Rowène found herself forming an unlikely friendship with the other woman. Melangel was only a few years older but already had two small children clinging to her skirts and no man in her home to care for them although, as Rowène was quick to note, Beowulf appeared to do what he could to help, if in a brusque and grudging sort of way.

Rowène found herself wondering at the situation but did not feel her position as Melangel's guest gave her any right to enquire beyond what the other girl had told her. Nor was there much time for idle chatter. Melangel was kept busy with the demands of her young family and those of the harvest, at which every one of the villagers, whatever their age or condition, helped in whatever way they could. Even Rowène found herself joining in.

As irked by inactivity as Guy, Rowène had mingled, tentatively at first, with the other women, doing what she could; mostly carrying jugs of watered ale out to the men labouring in the choking wheat dust and summer heat and later with the preparations for the final celebration feast which would take place by the harvest fire when all the work should be done. The harder labour in the fields was beyond her capabilities, not that she thought Guy would have permitted it even had she wanted to try.

This consideration towards herself she did not find surprising but when she accidentally witnessed Beowulf protesting vehemently to Melangel against her determination to join the women in the fields, it made her wonder anew about the relationship between those two. Admittedly her grasp of the Rogé dialect was very hazy but such had been her impression of the heated debate conducted in front of her and the two wide-eyed children who had sought refuge in their mother's skirts, although it could just as easily have been about something completely different. Whatever the subject, the argument had come to an abrupt end when the protagonists had suddenly become aware of their audience and lapsed into an awkward silence. Moments later, with a shrug of his ox-like shoulders, the headman had growled one final prohibition and stamped out of the small, one-roomed hovel leaving Melangel to flash an awkward glance at her guest before bending to comfort her crying children.

Rowène did think about asking Melangel what that exchange had been about but decided against it. It was, after all, no affair of hers and she did not wish to set at a distance one of the few people in the province who had shown her a friendly face and who had been neither openly shocked by her witch-red hair and masculine attire nor covertly curious about her relationship with Guyard de Martine. It was a pleasant change and one she meant to make the most of.

At the end of the third day of harvesting, with the last of the corn safely gathered and stored, came the celebratory harvest feast. Guy had not stayed long enough at any of the other villages to take part in this event and Rowène sincerely doubted whether Black Joffroi's half-brother and his doxy would have been welcome anyway. But here in Mallowleigh Beowulf had freely invited them to share in the celebrations and Guy – as dusty, sweaty and sun-browned as the headman himself – had accepted for them both with clear pleasure.

Rowène had been pleased by Guy's decision but found herself irrationally irked by her own appearance, to the extent that with some willing help from Melangel, she appeared at the harvest fire clad once more in womanly fashion, her long hair brushed free of her customary braids to cascade like living fire over her borrowed garments; a full skirt of blue homespun, worn with a bodice over a shift of unbleached linen. The skirt was rather revealing by court standards – Mithlondian court standards that is, not Kardolandian – showing as it did her ankles and a goodly glimpse of calf, and once Melangel had laced the bodice sufficiently tight, the shift proved to be even more revealing.

Rowène knew what the effect must be but found she did not care in the slightest if she looked like a peasant wench out to snare herself a nobleman's interest. Most of Mallowleigh believed her to be Master Guy's leman anyway, even though it must be common knowledge that she did not share his humble bed in Beowulf's hut. Nor had he ever so much as touched her in public. Nonetheless, she knew – because Melangel had told her – that the majority of the village folk believed their Steward merely to be discreet rather than innocent.

That being so, she thought rebelliously, did it matter if she dressed the part of a nobleman's doxy? And Guy might even be sufficiently shocked by her appearance into betraying his awareness of her as a woman. He had been courtesy itself during their travels but at odd moments she had surprised a look in his eyes that her body recognised.

Certainly the sudden hot flare of approval that flickered in his gaze when he first saw her in the light of the harvest fire was more than adequate recompense for her efforts.


As for Guyard, looking up from his desultory conversation with Beowulf he had suddenly seen the illusion that haunted his dreams transformed into a flesh and blood woman and, despite himself, he felt his blood heat and his loins tighten.

Aware as he was of his companion, the curious eyes of the other villagers and the binding band about his arm, he fought to keep from openly betraying the desire he thought he had subdued, if not completely conquered. All the time he and Rowène had been away from Rogérinac he had retained a rigid control over his emotions but now she had thrown him desperately off balance and he did not know what to say. His only coherent thought, apart from how much he desired her, was that he must not let anyone – least of all her – know how he felt. So rather than doing as he wanted and taking her into his arms he forced himself to take up his interrupted conversation with Beowulf.

Then cursed himself as he saw how keenly she felt his perceived rejection. His mask of indifference melted like ice in the sun and as she turned away he caught her arm, unable to withstand the temptation to spend some at least of this harvest fire feast night with her.

"No, do not go! Forgive my discourtesy but, in truth, you took me by surprise. I was not expecting to see you tonight... or at least not dressed like that! Stay and eat with me. Please. We must head south towards Rogérinac in the morning but tonight... well, I doubt it would be accounted a crime if we were to join Beowulf and his folk in their merriment."

Rowène hesitated a moment, possibly wary of the restrained fire in his eyes, and then nodded. Without asking permission, Guyard took her hand and drew her with him into the firelight. He caught the knowing looks the villagers exchanged but for this one night he did not care what mischief the gossipmongers made. He only knew that Rowène was beside him, that she had not withdrawn her hand from his and that she was smiling up at him once more.

Later though when the sun had set in a blaze of incandescent gold and a million glittering silver stars had taken its place, Guyard cast a glance around the hollow, noting the increasingly wanton nature of the celebrations. Putting down his empty drinking horn he pulled his companion to her feet. Which proved to be a mistake as it brought Rowène very close to him, close enough that he could see the hint of laughter in her sparkling crystal eyes.

"Do you mean to join the harvest dance?" she offered impishly.

"I do not," he replied, more harshly than he had intended to. "And neither will you. In fact I think it is time you were safely back at Melangel's cottage. Trust me, things are going to get more than a little wild from now on."

Rowène frowned up at him, the smile dying in her eyes.

"You think I have not seen worse at the court in Kaerellios?" she asked. Then, obviously reading correctly the set look to his face, conceded defeat. "Oh, very well, Guy. But will you not walk with me back to the village?"

Guyard felt his throat constrict and he forgot to breathe, recognising the invitation in her apparently innocent words and the still more eloquent one in her eyes. At that moment he knew, without a single shred of doubt, that if he escorted her back to the village it would not be to the chaste safety of Melangel's cottage but to a molten coupling in his own bed in the headman's hut.

And gods, how he wanted that night of lovemaking with her! And he could have it, he knew, but at the cost of Rowène's honour and his own...

With an effort he wrenched his thoughts away from temptation and, glancing around, saw Melangel lingering nearby, a wistful look on her face as she watched Beowulf join the chain of dancers cavorting around the harvest fire, one of the other village girls clinging, laughing, to his arm. Suddenly she seemed to become as aware as Guyard that the nature of the festivities was degenerating quickly and began looking around for her children with the obvious intention of whisking them off to bed. Seizing his last chance like a drowning man Guyard almost dragged his companion over towards the other woman.

"Melangel! Wait!"

And as the peasant woman turned a startled look in his direction, continued in a quieter voice.

"See, Rowène, she is returning to the village too. You will be able to walk back together." He grimaced a little at her straight look and added by way of explanation, "Not all the women stay until the fire burns out at dawn or take part in the harvest dance." Only those young, unbound women who desired to embrace the wild fertility of what was a dance only in the loosest sense of the word, a dance between a man and a woman to their own silent music.

"And you?" she asked, her voice as low as his, her eyes a dark, shadowed grey.

Surely she did not think that he wished to indulge in the harvest dance? The truth was, of course, that he did. Not with some nameless peasant lass but with her. Swallowing down the words before he blurted them out, he tried to shrug off the tension that held him, hoping his other aches might likewise ease once she had left him.

"I will stay a little while longer, share one last drink with Beowulf. But I will not be late seeking my bed. I told you, I want to make an early start. Rogérinac is several days' hard ride away and we still have a few villages to visit, not to mention collecting Gerde and Geryth from Sarillac."

"Very well, Guy. I will see you tomorrow then."

She managed a smile of sorts but it almost broke his resolve when she lifted her hand to cup his cheek. For those few precious moments when they touched skin to skin, soft to rough, he could feel the warmth of her living flesh and the beat not only of her blood but his own. And it was as though she were the other half of his heart.

"At dawn," he agreed hoarsely.

Only after she had disappeared into the moonlit darkness did he relax sufficiently to mutter his thanks to the gods that once again he had managed to retain his grip on his increasingly precarious self-control.


Back at the cottage Melangel settled her sleepy children in the bed and then dropped onto a stool before the banked fire. With a gently teasing look at Rowène she said,

"So then... I half thought Master Guy would ask ye to stay wi' him tonight."

Rowène could only count herself fortunate that the unlit darkness of the cottage hid her fierce flush of shamed disappointment.

"And what makes you think I would have stayed with him, even had he asked?" she asked, her voice revealing more than she would have liked.

Melangel laughed softly, although there was no unkindness in it, rather a hopeless sympathy.

"Because I knows ye feel the same way about Master Guy as I once felt fer Beowulf."

Rowène did not waste any effort in a denial of her feelings although she was driven to defend Guy's honour.

"Whatever I may feel, Melangel, you can be sure that he does not think of me in that way at all. We are by way of becoming kin through the binding of Lord Joffroi to my mother. And even if there was not that between us, there is still his wife."

"That bitch!" Melangel exclaimed. "Ought ter ha' bin drowned at birth, that one."

"Melangel!"

"Well, 'tis true. An' don't pretend ter be shocked. I'll warrant 'tis not jus' me as thinks Master Guy deserves better than ter be tied ter that cold-hearted whore," the other woman continued unrepentantly. "Ye know, when I first seed ye wi' Master Guy, I thought as maybe he'd come ter his senses at last an' found hisself a lass as 'ud give him what that bitch can't."

"Like what?" queried Rowène flatly. "I may not like Mathilde but she is still his wife and Guy..."

"She may wear his bindin' bracelet," Melangel interrupted. "But her's no true wife ter him. Ye're forgettin' I spent two years in that black castle an' I could tell ye things about her as'd make ye puke, preferably all o'er her best gown... An' 'tis not jus' that her's the worst slut in the whole castle, though the gods know her is. But if'n Master Guy hadna managed ter get me an' the bairns away from that place, we'd all ha' been dead by now, pushed o'er the cliff belike. Or poisoned mebbe."

"But why?" asked Rowène, her disbelief not as strong as it might have been before her own poisoning at Mathilde de Martine's hands. "I have no wish to offend you Melangel but why should she take against you?"

"Ye mean because I'm nowt more'n a peasant lass what Lord Joffroi took ter warm his bed?" Melangel asked bitterly. "An' no better'n any o' them other whores there?" She caught the expression on Rowène's face and said stubbornly, "I knows what I knows. An' she knows I know the truth about her. That's one o' the reasons why her hates me so much. As for the rest of her spite, I reckon that's down ter her not givin' Master Guy the bairn he should've had. That an' the fact that both my bairns carry the blood o' the Lords of Rogé. Put those reasons tergether an' 'tis enough ter make her spit any amount o' poison. Fer mesel', I'd rather 'most any other man than Black Joffroy fer their da. Even his brother 'ud be better. But Sir Ranulf were allus too careful ter be caught like that!"

*Not always*, Rowène thought grimly as she pulled her gaze away from the pain on the other girl's face. Resisting the temptation to touch her now-empty womb, she asked softly,

"So Linnet and Wulfric, they are not Beowulf's children? I must admit I did wonder."

"Nay, they'm Lord Joffroy's," Melangel admitted. "The gods pity 'em, poor wee bairns. Everyone in Rogérinac and Mallowleigh knows it, so I thought ye must too. But then ye're new come ter the castle from what ye say." She considered the matter for a moment and then continued. "Mayhap thas one reason Master Guy didna ask ye ter lie wi' him ternight. He's trouble enough, I reckon, looking after his brother's..." At least Rowène assumed she meant *brother's,* not *brothers'.* "Bastards without risking any of his own."

But she did not ask and after a moment or two Melangel said quietly,

"Aye, well, if ye've nothing better ter do wi' yersel' this night I'll tell ye about it, if ye like. Mayhap 'twill save ye from making the same mistake as me if Master Guy should happen ter change his mind about takin' ye ter his bed. Or," she added, more harshly. "Against the time his cursed brothers come home."

"But surely you do not want to drag the past up again," Rowène demurred. "Having experienced just how vile Black Joffroi and his brother – his legitimate brother that is – can be, I cannot think it would be other than painful for you."

Melangel shrugged.

"I'd rather ye heard the truth of it from me. Here, d'ye want some more heather beer? Beowulf dropped a skin off earlier, knowin' as I'd not stop late by the fire." Her mouth twisting into an unhappy grimace at some thought she did not share with her guest, she poured a generous measure of the potent brew into two wooden mugs and then started her tale, her voice far more composed than Rowène's would have been had she been called upon to tell Melangel of the lessons she had already learned under Ranulf de Rogé's brutal tuition.

"It must ha' been three... no, four years ago now," Melangel said in a low voice, darting a glance at the bed-place to make sure the children were asleep. "'Twas autumn an' Lord Joffroy an' his brothers were up this way, huntin' deer in the hills, up towards the border with Vitré an' it chanced they come riding through Mallowleigh just afore dark-fall an' decided ter bed down here fer the night." She smiled without humour. "Well, ye can guess what 'twere like that night, wi' the women more flustered'n a bunch o' hens wi' a fox nearby, e'en them as was old enough ter know better. 'Tis not ev'ry day three noblemen drop by an' I weren't the only woman in the village ter act the fool that night."

She looked at Rowène then, her brown eyes dark in the flickering light of the rush dip and although it was impossible to see clearly, Rowène thought the other woman had coloured painfully.

"When I realised Lord Joffroy wanted me ter spend the night wi' him I did try an' tell him I were already betrothed but he wouldna listen. So I went wi' him, thinkin' 'twould be jus' fer that night an' mayhap Beowulf wouldna hate me too much fer it, though 'twere a wicked thing I'd done ter him. Nex' thing I knows, 'tis morning an' his black-hearted lordship's telling Beowulf as how he's takin' me wi' him, back ter Rogérinac. Beowulf could see as how I didna want ter go an' e'en though he were hurt an' angry wi' me, he still stood up ter Lord Joffroy."

"That was very brave of him," Rowène murmured. *If foolish,* she added silently. Melangel apparently had no difficulty reading her thoughts.

"Aye, well, it didna do no good an' Lord Joffroy would ha' gutted him in his rage at bein' crossed but fer his brother..."

"Guy managed to stop him?" Rowène interrupted.

"No," Melangel replied, a bleak note in her voice. "He'd already left, sent on ahead by Lord Joffroy fer some reason I dinna remember now."

"So it was *Ranulf* who intervened?"

"Aye, damn him, fer his own reasons."

Rowène blinked, startled by the other girl's dark vehemence even though it mirrored so faithfully her own feelings towards him. Struggling to be fair to the man who had risked a flogging to save her brother from hanging, she said quietly,

"But surely, he saved Beowulf's life. Why would you damn him for that?"

Melangel gave a harsh laugh.

"Because I knew how that lecherous cur would expect me ter show my gratitude!"

"And did he?" Rowène asked, trying to quell the sudden nausea in her belly.

"Oh aye, he did. An' I hated him fer it," Melangel spat out, her tone as bitter as the bile that rose in Rowène's throat. The other girl's voice shook as she continued, "But at least I knew Beowulf was alive, even if I never saw him again. An' when I got to Rogérinac, once those black walls closed around me, I knew I'd never leave. That was how my life would be from then on, passed between Black Joffroy and his brother until one or both of 'em tired o' me. The following summer Linnet was born an' I thought mayhap that would ha' been the end of it. But no, Lord Joffroy kept me still, though that other cold-hearted whoreson had long since lost interest. Ne'er takes a woman ter his bed fer long, that 'un! A night, two at most, then he's done. Best thing ye can say of him as he takes more care in his whoring than Lord Joffroy..."

Although she was not aware of doing so, Rowène must have made some small noise or movement at that because Melangel's abstracted gaze sharpened into a question. Rowène swallowed and said,

"Cold-hearted I grant you, but care.... That does not sound much like the man I... met."

Melangel shrugged and struggled for words to explain.

"Not care as in caring. Jus' care not ter leave his doxies wi' child. Allus spills his seed outside like. He's well known fer it. An' another thing, I never saw any woman he'd been wi' showing bruises nor any o' the marks like his brother'd leave. Black Joffroy," she explained in answer to Rowène's look. "Deals in pain. He needs it ter make him hard enough ter swive a wench. An' ye say yer ma's ter wed him?"

"They deserve each other," Rowène muttered viciously. "And as for Ranulf, perhaps he is more like Black Joffroi than you think!" She hesitated and then said. "He raped a woman while he was in Chartre."

Melangel regarded her in considering silence.

"Did he now? Well, I've never heard o' him doin' such a thing afore. But I suppose none of us in Rogé really knows what he's like when he's away from here. I've heard that men do terrible things when the fightin's done an' their blood still runs hot." She smiled grimly. "So, there's another woman as hates his guts. But better that way than fancyin' hersel' in love wi' him. An' the gods help any woman as finds herself swellin' wi' his child fer she'll get nay help from him."

"No, I do not suppose she will," Rowène murmured, thinking with pity of Gerde, who quite possibly *was* swelling with Ranulf's child even now. Thank the gods she herself had been spared that fate! At the same time she shuddered at the thought of what Melangel must have gone through as Joffroi's mistress. She had thought those brief moments of pain and the bruises she had earned under Ranulf's hands had been nightmare enough but they had been nothing compared to Melangel's experiences. How long had she remained in Rogérinac, suffering pain and loneliness?

She became aware of Melangel's voice, speaking almost in answer to her thoughts.

"I truly think I would ha' gone mad in that evil place if it hadna been fer one o' t'other lasses there. Gerde, her name was. Her brother was one of Sir Ranulf's men an' I suppose because she'd grown up in the castle those lechers hadna yet thought ter turn her inter a whore like the rest of 'em. Or at least they hadna done so by the time I left."

Rowène managed a wintry smile.

"Yes, Gerde is still at the castle but I very much fear that someone..." She stopped at Melangel's derisive snort. "Very well, either Lord Joffroi or Sir Ranulf has taken away her innocence. But even so, she is still not like the rest of them."

"I pray her never do become like them," Melangel muttered. "But her will, if her stays there." Then as if coming to some decision, continued more belligerently, "Tell her, will ye, when ye gets back, if her ever needs help, ever wants to get away from that place, ter go ter Master Guy an' beg him ter send her here, ter me. I don't have much, 'tis true, but then again I knows what 'tis like ter have nowhere ter go, no escape from that den of whores and lechers."

"I will tell her," Rowène promised, her heart lightening a little. "And is that how you came to return here? With Sir Guy's help?"

Melangel nodded.

"Aye, 'twas simple enough in the end. Lord Joffroy was called away ter court an' whilst he were gone I found out I was goin' ter have another bairn. I went ter the old hag in the village but I'd left it too late an' her couldn't do aught."

Rowène narrowed her eyes at this reference, suddenly remembering Ranulf's blanched face when she had assured him there would be no child, but she said nothing and Melangel continued,

"So out o' desperation I went ter Master Guy. I couldna talk ter him in the hall wi' ev'ry ear flappin' so I went ter his room when I knew he were working up there an' asked ter speak ter him. By some ill chance he weren't alone. Master Ranulf was wi' him an' o' course they guessed what I'd come ter say afore I'd got out a word. I s'pose 'tweren't difficult seein' the state I were in. Master Ranulf he just stood there an' shrugged it off as if he'd never taken his pleasure o' me. But Master Guy, though I could see it ha' put him in a temper, he didna take it out on me. He gave me a choice, ter stay in Rogérinac or go back ter Mallowleigh, with the risk that I might lose the bairn on the way or find myself outcast when I got back here. But I couldna stay there, whate'er the risk. So Master Guy he fetched me home hisself, somehow made it right wi' Beowulf, made it plain that the bairns an' me were under *his* protection an' by next harvest Wulfric had been born. Master Guy sends a bit o' silver every quarter fer us an' tha's enough ter remind Beowulf of what happened e'en if he wanted ter forget."

Melangel fell silent and Rowène could think of nothing to say to break the aching quiet. At last she said tentatively,

"So how is it between you and Beowulf now?"

Melangel sighed.

"'Tis not good but then 'tis nay so bad neither. He did what he could fer me when I first come back. Reckon Master Guy didn't give him no choice. Or mebbe I'm being too hard on him – Beowulf, I mean. He makes sure I has a roof o'er me head an' that neither me nor the bairns go hungry. Which is probably the best I can hope fer. An' after he was all but forced ter take me back an' expected ter look arter another man's get inter the bargain, I'd be surprised if he felt aught but disgust fer me."

"But you said you care for him still?"

"Did I? Aye, mayhap ye're right," Melangel admitted sadly. "An' I know 'tis right I should pay the price fer my folly. But Beowulf shouldna ha' to pay that price as well! I should ha' begged Master Guy ter take me anywhere but here. But Mallowleigh's my home an' I thought by then Beowulf would ha' forgot me, taken some other lass ter wife. An' I could ha' lived with that, truly I could! But he's not taken the binding oath, even now."

"Perhaps he still wants you?" Rowène suggested. "And has forgiven you for something that was not wholly your fault."

"Not he!" Melangel laughed harshly. "Have ye no seen him when he's wi' me? He willna even look at me straight, let alone talk ter me, unless he must. Oh, he's done as Master Guy ordered, helped me find me place in the village again but he canna forget that I was Lord Joffroy's mistress, Sir Ranulf's doxy, borne two bastard brats. Aye, tha's what he calls 'em, my poor bairns what ne'er asked ter be born. I s'pose I canna really blame him fer feeling that way but 'tis tearing me apart. One day he's goin' ter take the bindin' oath but even wi'out that I know he takes other women ter his bed when he feels the need. An' ternight, bein' the harvest fire an' him the headman o' the village, 'tis tradition that he sows the seed fer next year's crop. Not that I'd want another bairn but e'en so I wish 'twere me wi' him."

Rowène grimaced and heard herself whispering,

"As I wish I could be with Guy. But it cannot be."

In the silence that followed these words she knew that Melangel was staring at her. As well she might. God of Light, had she really spoken those incriminating thoughts out loud?

She looked up, meaning to say... she knew not what... but Melangel spoke first.

"D'ye really want ter find out what he'd do if ye went ter him ternight?"

"Oh, I know what he would do," Rowène replied, entirely certain that she should not be having this conversation. "The same as he did when he shared my bed in Chartre. Absolutely nothing."

Melangel gaped at her.

"He shared yer bed? An' didna touch ye? Yet I've seen the way he looks at ye. I know he wants ye. But ye're saying ye're a maid still?" She pursed her lips. "That could be tricksy to manage."

Even as the ice of memory seeped through her body, Rowène could feel her cheeks burning and could only be grateful for the lack of proper light as she said unsteadily,

"Not so tricksy mayhap. I... ah... no, I am not a maid. But Melangel, that is a secret known only to... the man who took my virginity. And now you."

Melangel's gaze sharpened and for one horrible moment Rowène feared she was going to drag Ranulf's name back into the conversation but all she said was,

"Nay then, I'll not tell no-one."

She eyed Rowène with speculative interest for a moment or two and then said,

"Can ye talk ter the Moon Goddess then?"

"What?" Rowène did not know whether to be outraged or dismayed. Certainly she was taken aback by the question.

"Well, I jus' wondered like, what wi' yer hair an' all, whether ye might be able ter."

"You don't mind that I'm a..." Nothing would induce her to allow the word 'witch' past her lips so she settled on the less evocative, "Fey?"

Melangel chewed her lip.

"Well... I ain't never met a fey afore but then there's feys and feys, if ye knows what I mean. An' when all's said an' done, I reckon as how we could both of us do wi' some help ternight."

# Chapter 16

## *An Excess of Heather Beer*

Dawn had long gone by the time Guyard awoke.

He lay still for a moment, caught in the fading mists of a dream... of silver moonbeams glimmering softly on white limbs... the faint fragile scent of the Moon Goddess' own flowers... tiny white lilies and pale star drifts that sprang up where the fey women of wood and water danced in the moonlight...

He stirred, stretching stiff limbs and with the memory of that elusive white scent still in his nostrils slowly opened his eyes, expecting to see... He was damned if he knew *what* he expected to see! The Moon Goddess herself perchance... or a slender wood spirit slipping away with the dawn to her home in a silver birch...

Good God of Light, what was he thinking? He did not believe in the Moon Goddess! Nor, he assured himself, did he place any credence in the notion that spirits of any sort might be living secretly in the trees and quiet pools of Mithlondia, even if he did find them wandering through his dreams!

He rolled over, meaning to sit up, but instead gave a groan and clutched his head, hoping thereby to ward off the blinding pain that had exploded inside his skull with the sudden movement and the fierce onslaught of bright light.

Gods preserve him from all the daemons in Hell! Had he really drunk so much the previous night as to leave him feeling so ill this morning? He had not thought so at the time; his memory was intact enough for him to know that he had been sufficiently sober as to ensure Rowène's safe return to the village with Melangel and after her departure he was sure he had drunk very little more, aware that he needed to make an early start the following day and having no desire at all to appear the worse for drink in front of the villagers – any of them that were sober enough to take any notice of him, that is.

Be that as it may, something must have happened to subdue his good intentions, if the vile taste in his mouth and his bursting bladder were any indications. Pushing up onto his knees with an effort, he sent a bleary glance over the tangled bodies sprawled in haphazard abandon around the smouldering ashes of the harvest fire, noted that none of them appeared to be stirring, and – as he really had no choice in the matter by then – relieved himself of what he could only conclude had been the most potent heather beer he had ever drunk in his life.

Feeling somewhat easier he sank back down with a muttered oath onto something he belatedly identified as the mantle he thought he had left in Beowulf's hut, together with other assorted items of crumpled clothing he should by rights have been wearing. Gods above! How had he come to be in such a state? Not that he did not usually sleep so in the summer – possibly as a defiance to the Rogé winters when folk, whether of cottage or castle, tended to sleep in as many layers of clothing as possible – but, despite the hot weather, he had made a deliberate decision not to sleep naked whilst travelling the province in company with Rowène de Chartreux.

So what in name of all the daemons in Hell had he been doing last night?

Hearing a croaking curse from just behind him he turned his head to find Beowulf stumbling towards him, looking almost as stale drunk as he felt.

"Bloody hell!" Beowulf groaned, dropping to the ground beside him, his hair and clothing all anyhow. "I mus' be gettin' old! I need ter wake in the comfort of a wife's bed, not arse-naked an' alone on the bare ground."

Guyard essayed a grimace of agreement but found it hurt too much. He dropped his aching head into his hands and said,

"Next harvest feast keep me away from the heather beer! I swore after last year not to touch the damned stuff again and that was nothing compared to how I feel now!"

He scrubbed his face, his unsteady fingers rasping against the stubble on his jaw and, as he looked around again, came to another belated realisation and swore in irritation.

"Hell and damnation! It must be mid-morning at least. I wanted to be back on the coast road just after dawn!"

He cast about for this discarded clothes, found his breeches and boots and pulled them on – even though the effort involved made his senses reel. Finally after some deep breaths and further frantic fumbling he found his shirt. Or thought he had until Beowulf broke into a ragged laugh.

"Looks like I'd best keep ye away from the lasses as well as the beer!" His broad, sun-browned forehead creased in a frown. "Mind, from what I could see, ye didna ha' more'n a horn or two." The frown deepened into a scowl. "No offence, Master Guy, but we've enough o' yer brother's misbegotten bastards in the village wi'out none o' your'n!"

"Damn it, Beowulf, watch your tongue!" Guyard snapped, stung on raw nerves. "And since last night's rutting is bound to produce a goodly enough crop come next summer, including a brat or two of your own get, you are scarcely in any position to carp at Melangel's offspring! Add to which, I was still sober enough last night to send away the only woman here I would want to bed!"

Beowulf's head jerked up at this and Guyard knew he had betrayed himself but all the headman said was,

"Tis no secret ter me how ye feels about... the lass an' 'tis fer certain I willna go flappin' me tongue ter anyone else." He hesitated and then continued with a frown, "But beggin' yer pardon, Master Guy, if 'twas not *her*... who was it ye lay wi' last night? 'Cause fer sure that rag ye're holdin' ain't your'n."

"What?"

Dropping his gaze Guyard found that the crumpled linen garment he had taken to be his shirt was in fact a woman's shift. A single shocked expletive left his lips and he wondered for a moment if he really might vomit. Swallowing down his self-disgust with an effort, he glanced at the other man, expecting condemnation but Beowulf was merely looking uncomfortable.

"D'ye want me ter find out which o' the lasses that belongs to. Or would ye rather not know?"

Guyard shrugged, sick to his stomach and trying vainly to come to terms with what he had apparently done.

"Gods help me," he muttered. "I *should* find out. But, if I am honest, I really do not want to know. And there will be no child, Beowulf. Not of my seed. But if there was, you must know I would... acknowledge it and... do whatever is customary in such matters." His mind felt like an empty hole and he could not even begin to think straight. One thing he did know however. "Beowulf, I do not want my wife or R... anybody else knowing about this. Not unless it becomes unavoidable."

"Oh I'll not tell Mistress Rowena!" Beowulf hastened to assure him. "An' I doubt gossip'll fly so far as Rogérinac." Then in sudden doubt, "Mind, ye'd best hope that the lass – whosoever it were – doesna mean to make claim on ye by makin' a show o' returning yer shirt when ye leaves!" Then the headman gave an irrepressible grin as his gaze travelled over Guyard's body. "Must have been like mating wi' a wild cat. Marked ye good an' proper, she did!"

"Damn it, Beowulf! What in Hell do you mean?"

Still grinning, Beowulf described what Guyard could not see; the bruises flowering on his neck and the scratches across his back and shoulders. A wild cat, in truth... and what little he dimly remembered seemed to substantiate Beowulf's assessment. Yet that was in complete contradiction to the soft-fingered sylph who had drifted so gently through his dreams.

Shaking his head and thinking himself in danger of going mad – moon mad they called it, and with good reason apparently – he pushed to his feet, waiting until Beowulf had done likewise.

"Aye well, as ye say, 'tis late, Master Guy, an' we'd best be makin' our way back ter the village. There's a stream on the way an' ye can make yerself as presentable as ye can afore ye meets Mist... anyone else."

"Before I meet Mistress Rowena you would say," Guyard commented bleakly. Then his cool, hard-won control cracked. "In the name of all the gods, Beowulf, how am I going to face her? The last thing I said to her before I sent her away with Melangel was that I would have one more beer with you and then go to bed." He gave a mirthless laugh. "Alone!"

"Well, ye were alone when I found ye," Beowulf pointed out. "An' I doubt she'll ask. From what ye told me, she's a noblewoman, aye, an' such things are beneath their notice?"

"Yes," Guyard agreed with a sigh; certainly the Lady Rosalynde had turned a blind eye to his father's fornicating.

Now he knew they were there, the scratches across his back and shoulders seemed to burn intolerably. His whole body ached from the night's unaccustomed activities, his heart felt like a stone in his chest and the gaping grey hole in his mind was filled with mist instead of memories. Even so, he had the disconcerting feeling that he had enjoyed those wild, moon-drugged moments of sweetness and fire far more than he should have done. Cursing himself for his weakness, Guyard collected his crumpled tunic and mantle from the ground and fell into step beside Beowulf, so that they made their way back towards the village together.

They knelt briefly on the bank of the shallow, alder-fringed stream to splash cool water over aching heads, rising somewhat refreshed but in no better frame of mind. For though Beowulf would never have admitted it, Guyard doubted that he was alone in regretting his actions of the previous night, having some reason to believe that Mallowleigh's headman still had feelings for the woman to whom he had once been betrothed.

Having dried his face and hair on his tunic, Guyard dragged the increasingly disreputable garment over his head, cursing silently as he did so. The tunic could not be fastened at the neck and lacking any shirt beneath, he did not see how Rowène could possibly believe he had not spent the night tumbling some woman and it was obvious from Beowulf's face that his thoughts were the same.

So be it. Did the woman – and he was not thinking of his wife – expect him to be a paragon? Made of stone? He was a man, for gods'sake. His restraint over his bodily needs had limits. And last night he had passed them. It would not, he swore to himself, happen again.

Jaw set tight, Guyard raked his damp hair back from his face and strode off in the direction of the village. They were just approaching the gap in the thorn hedge and Guyard was already bracing himself for what must come next when he heard Beowulf mutter a curse.

"By the gods, now we're in fer it."

Looking up, Guyard felt the headman was probably in the right of it. Besides the two tethered horses, two other figures stood in the shade of a rowan tree that grew just outside the protective hedge; a peasant woman in rough homespun, a linen headrail over her dark braids, standing talking to a lad in a pale blue tunic, faded breeches and good quality boots. No, not a lad. No man wore his hair *that* long or in such a fashion and when she moved the sun set a bright fire dancing along the length of flame-dark braids. She said something to her companion, they exchanged a quick hug, and then Melangel – for it could be no other – called to her children who had been playing nearby, gathered the younger one into her arms and walked in through the gateway, pointedly turning her back on Beowulf.

Turning to untie the horses, Rowène de Chartreux swung lightly up onto the golden mare and trotted down the track towards them, leading the chestnut stallion. Despite her masculine garb, Guyard could never have mistaken her for anything other than a woman. No, he amended, not even a woman; a girl as fresh and sweet as a wild rose with the dew still on it. One moreover who had clearly spent the previous night in chaste and sober repose. Unlike himself! Gods, what would she think of him when she realised what he had done?

Then she was reining the mare to a halt beside him and Guyard forced himself to stand still, enduring the casually assessing glance she swept over him. As she turned to look Beowulf over, he found his eyes drawn, despite himself, to the hands folded about the leather reins. The fair skin had been burnished from its normal pale gold to a shade only slightly darker by the summer sun and her fingers remained smooth and slender, tapering to the unexpected ugliness of short-bitten nails.

He experienced a moment of mingled disappointment and relief as he realised that she could not have been the woman of wild-fire and moonlight who had marked his skin and left him with such ragged memories of pleasure. Nor – and he was certain of this, strange though it seemed – had she been the lissome, white-limbed witch lying amidst the lilies and star flowers of that other dream.

With a supreme effort Guyard locked away any lingering thought of the night before and forced himself to meet Rowène's clear gaze as she greeted him.

"Since it is surely too late to bid you good dawning I must content myself with wishing you both good day. Sir Guy. Beowulf."

It seemed to Guyard that her cool, faintly mocking tones must surely be a mask to hide her embarrassment at their undeniably disreputable appearance and it made him both uncomfortable and uncharacteristically irritated.

"You did say, did you not," she continued. "That you wished to make an early start this morning? I was beginning to think you must have changed your mind and decided to stay in Mallowleigh for another day."

"No, I have not changed my mind," he said, somewhat tersely. "But since I am now here and you are obviously ready, we may as well leave at once."

"Certainly, if that is your wish."

She appeared to look rather more closely at him than she had done until now and a shadow darkened the clear grey gaze as her eyes came to rest on the bruises that marked his neck – and it occurred to him, in a flash of unwelcome memory, that he had likewise left the evidence of his own passion on the woman he had lain with. She did not mention the blood-bruises, however, merely asked with a rather chilly formality,

"Forgive me for asking, Sir Guy, but what have you done with your shirt?"

"I lost it!" Guyard snapped. Then as her copper brows lifted in enquiry he added in the same savage tone but in Mithlondian, "The gods know I am not proud of what I did last night but neither am I answerable to you for who I slept with! You are not my wife, nor even my mistress! So for pity's sake, just leave well alone!"

With that he turned abruptly away from her and, dragging himself wearily into his saddle, gathered up his reins, bade a curt farewell to Beowulf and headed back towards the coast and the road south to Rogérinac, wondering how in Hell he was going to get through the next few days alone with the woman with whom he had managed to build a tentative trust and friendship but who must now regard him as a true son of Jacques de Rogé in all the worst ways.

They travelled steadily southwards over the next few days, moving between the coastal villages and those that edged the high moors to the west, taking full advantage of the fine weather to travel swiftly. It was a journey made mostly in silence, both being occupied with their own thoughts. Rowène could not tell what Guy might be thinking of – whether it was the way in which he had broken his binding oath or just the more mundane problems associated with the harvest tithe – but for her own part she found herself returning again and again to the outrageous way in which she had behaved at the Mallowleigh harvest fire.

What in the name of all the gods had driven her to do what she had done? There were no fine words that could disguise the wanton behaviour in which she had indulged. Encouraged by Melangel, she had deliberately set out to seduce a man who was already bound to another woman, causing him to break vows he clearly held dear, tearing asunder the very integrity that made him the man he was. Moonlight had beguiled her, muffled the voice of her conscience, lit a spark of desire in her blood that only the touch of one man could ease.

So they had become lovers under a harvest moon and although she was very sure that Guy had not been blinded by drink, something... some silvered enchantment lent by the Goddess of the Night... had caused him not to recognise her. Not at first. Initially he had taken her for one of the village women and had ordered her away. It was only later, as he laid her down on his cloak and took her into his arms, finding her mouth with his own and joining their bodies as one, that he had whispered her name into the quiet of the night.

She had crept away in the gold and rose of dawn's first light – sanity returning to her with the waning of the moon – fearing to see the desire and need in his eyes change to hatred and contempt when he recognised what she had bewitched him into doing. Yet, by some last grace of the Goddess, when they had met in the full light of the following day, it had become clear to her that whatever spell had bound him to her during the moon-silvered darkness, the shreds of that enchantment still remained, dimming and distorting his memories of the previous night.

Why, she wondered, had the Moon Goddess – if she existed and Rowène was rather afraid that she did, given the evidence of that night at Mallowleigh

– chosen merely to blur some of his memories and not just wipe everything from his mind? It was clear from his demeanour that he knew he was guilty of breaking his binding oath by tumbling some wench by the harvest fire. Nor could Rowène claim innocence in that; by leaving her shift and taking his shirt – gods, why had she done such a foolish thing? – she had made it impossible for him to remain in ignorance of his adultery, even if he never knew that she was the wench involved

Nor would he never know, she promised herself. There was no power, earthly or eldritch, that could induce her to tell him and – unlike that hideous encounter with his half-brother – there would be no child to brand her a witch, him an adulterer. Irresponsible she might be but not so irresponsible as to seduce a man without thinking of the consequences. But Guy had told her in Chartre, and she had seen for herself during her time in Rogérinac that he spoke truth, that his seed was barren.

Time and distance, she hoped bleakly, would amend all. For the present, she would just have to learn to live with the fact that she was more like her accursed mother than she would ever have believed possible; the woman she hated and feared even more than she had once – and still did for the most part – loathed and despised the man who had forced her to submit to his bestial lust.

At one time she had desired nothing more than to see Ranulf bleeding, broken and begging for mercy at her feet. Now, with the loss of that small spark of life he had set in her belly, the hottest fires of her hatred had been doused. The wolf could live, she supposed, just as long as it was far away from her.

But if she did not want to see Ranulf de Rogé ever again, at the same time she did not much want to be with his half-brother either. She had thought that taking Guy for her lover would allow her to forget the vile things Ranulf had done and said and so she had – for the space of that one moonlit night. But inevitably morning had come and with it the grim realisation that what she had done to Guy was scarcely less forgivable than Ranulf's more forceful abuse of her.

And just as Ranulf could not change what he had done to her, neither could she amend her actions. All she could do was make sure that Guy never learned that he had been bewitched into breaking his binding vows. But guilt and regret proved a heavy burden on her heart, and during those last few days of deceptive freedom she could scarcely bear to look him in the eye, for fear that he might suddenly see there the truth of that night by the Mallowleigh harvest fire.

Indeed, and incredible as it seemed on the surface, she was actually eager to return to Rogérinac, the place that would continue to be her prison until such time as Joffroi de Rogé and the Winter Lady chose to release her – or Joscelin de Veraux came for her.

# Chapter 17

## *The Mermaid of Black Rock Cove*

It took them the best part of a near silent se'ennight to make the journey down the eastern coast and another day after that to reach Sarillac and collect Geryth and Gerde. Rowène was relieved not only to have the company of others again but also to discover that brother and sister had patched up some kind of uneasy peace in her absence. In return, Gerde was unfeignedly pleased to see her mistress and when they stopped to make camp for the night a league or two short of Rogérinac, took the opportunity to confess that she had told Geryth everything. Or nearly everything.

What she had not told her brother – what she still refused to tell Rowène – was the name of her lover, who was assuredly also the same man responsible for the child Hilarie had told her she was carrying. Not that Rowène had really needed confirmation of that circumstance. She was only grateful that Guy, clearly preoccupied with other matters, had not realised anything was amiss. Not that it was a condition that could remain hidden much longer, either from the Steward or the other members of the Rogérinac household but by the time it did become noticeable Rowène hoped to have found some way to help Gerde.

She slept fitfully that night, her last night of freedom before returning to that grim grey fortress on the black isle, finally rising just before dawn and, without waking any of her companions, walked down to the foaming sea. There she found an uncomfortable seat on a jagged ridge of black, barnacle-covered rock and watched the sun come up in a silent and glorious blaze of light that flashed across the restless dark waters in a glitter of green and gold and blue. It was a moment of poignant beauty, power and enchantment and quite literally took her breath away.

Still in that odd state between beguilement and awareness she rose from her rocky perch, and without further thought, stripped off her travel-stained clothes and walked naked into the rippling waters, half-gasping, half-laughing at the silken – and unexpectedly icy – embrace of the sea. Taking a breath she dived under, revelling in sensations she had not succumbed to since leaving the far warmer waters of Kaerellios. Rising to the surface she pushed the long, dark-red strands of hair from her face and, once more aware of her surroundings, looked around to make sure that she was still alone.

The grey-pebbled beach was empty, thank the gods, although she thought she could detect some movement in the shadows of the black oak trees that grew above the shoreline. But it was probably only the horses. They had been tethered there the night before since there was grass to graze and water from the small stream that ran noisily down to the sea from the wooded valley behind. Squinting a little, she just made out the shape of a man kneeling beside the stream... fetching water perhaps? Then the dawn light reached into the dark recesses of the cove, glinting on the blade in his hand and brightening his fair hair to gold. Not Geryth fetching water then, but Guy about his morning ablutions.

For perhaps two score wary, heartbreaking moments she watched him at his task but she was not yet ready to leave the water and did not think he had seen her anyway, concentrating as he was on removing the previous day's growth of stubble. She would wait until he had finished, she decided, then swim to the shore and retrieve her clothes – she grimaced at the thought of dragging them on over wet skin – and return to the camp before any of them became too anxious over her absence. She had obviously not yet been missed and a few more moments would surely not matter.

Turning away from the shore, she swam a little further out, the sun glinting so brightly against the dancing waves that she was nearly blinded. Glancing aside and blinking to clear her vision of the disorientating whorl of black and gold sunspots, she saw... no, she could not really be seeing what her dazzled eyes told her was there... such creatures did not exist, save in myths and minstrels' tales.

She blinked again, rubbed salty fingers across her stinging eyes and stared until her eyes ached. But it... *she* was still there.

There! On the black rocks at the mouth of the cove, the figure of a woman, naked from the waist up, her legs covered by some supple... skin? Shimmering green and silky smooth, it glinted with sapphire, amethyst and silver as the woman moved. Her hair was long and wet and as shining black against the pale skin of her back as the glittering, spray-splashed rocks she was sitting on.

As if sensing her presence, or her amazed disbelief, the woman turned her head to look at her. Rowène held her breath and waited for the sea-woman's eyes to widen in startlement as the wraith-woman's had done that day in the castle garden. But they did not. Instead the jewel green eyes held a disconcerting look of recognition and a depth of knowledge that was even more frightening, as if the other could see into the most secret shadows of her heart...

Rowène thought she saw the pale lips move, half-heard the sound of a man's name whispering along the waves... Then the creature was gone, slipping back into the sea with scarcely a splash.

Truly shaken, Rowène swam back to the shore, fear and amazement lending her speed. Had that encounter really taken place? Had she really experienced that moment of kinship and silent communion with what could only have been one of the Fae? No, she would not believe it! It had been the glitter of the waves, the salt in her eyes, the susurration of the sea as it swept against those glistening black rocks...

Shivering uncontrollably now, she stumbled up the pebbly shore to the place where she had left her clothes, uncaring now whether Gerde or either of the two men saw her.

Scrambling into her clothes proved a battle in itself. Her fingers were shaking, her skin was wet and clammy cold. The wool of her breeches felt unbearably rough against her legs and the worn linen of her shirt only slightly less so. She tied the laces at her cuffs and throat as best she could for her trembling, then reached for the familiar black mantle, wrapping it around her shivering body, before sinking down onto the grating, treacherous pebbles to pull on her boots...

Then just sat there, hands clasped around her knees, looking out over the gentle swell of the glimmering green sea.

*Dear God of Light, Sweet God of Mercy, it cannot be true! There are no such beings as...*

"Mermaids!" a familiar voice said lightly. "Did you know, they are supposed to live in the sea hereabouts. My brother told me once that he had seen one. Here, in Black Rock Cove."

She started violently and glanced around as Guy dropped down onto his heels beside her.

"Wh... what?"

"Truly." He grinned at her, the first time he had smiled without constraint since they had left Mallowleigh. "Ran and I used to come here as boys, whenever we could slip away from the castle, to swim and explore the rock pools. And as we grew older, we still came. Although not so often and not together. I came to listen to the music of the sea and Ran..."

He hesitated and Rowène shot him a sideways look.

"Came here with whichever woman he was dallying with at the time," she finished for him, still shaken enough by her experience to let her bitterness show.

"Ran's reputation being what it is, you can be forgiven for thinking that," Guy said, his half smile fading into a frown. "But in all truth I do not believe he ever brought a woman here. He came, I think, to be alone, away from the treacherous under-currents of castle life. We never talked about it much, either his reasons for coming or what he did here. But he did tell me about the woman he saw here once. On the rocks, just out there..." He pointed to the single black rock that rose, sharp as a blade against the blue of the sea, a froth of white about its feet. "A mermaid he said... although he was more than half drunk at the time, else I do not suppose he would have told me at all," Guy finished wryly.

"Are you sure he was not completely drunk?" Rowène asked scornfully, refusing to look at the rock he was staring at, the rock where..."The fey women of the sea are as much a part of myth as any flame-haired witch or guardian of the wooded hollows," she added sharply when he did not respond to her gibe. "Tales for children and fodder for minstrels."

"You are telling me the Faennari are not real?" Guy said, his voice level. "That the Goddess they serve breathes not, save in myth or harper's song? How does it go... something about a perilous path through the argent night... the silvered light of her star-strung hair... when the Moon Goddess shines bright, let mortal men beware?"

"I... no... I do not know." She struggled to collect herself. "I have not heard that song before."

"No, I do not suppose you have. Hilarie used to sing it as a lullaby when Ran and I were small."

"Oh!" She looked at him, disconcerted. "As to the Faennari..." Rowène looked out over the dancing waves of the eastern seas, no longer an enchanted – and enchanting – wash of green but an innocent, sunlit blue, almost the colour of the eyes of the man beside her. "Yes, I suppose they must have been real once, those that walked the land, with their hair like dark flame and their jewel-toned eyes – is that not how the legends go? But dryads and mermaids... no, I do not think there are any such folk."

And yet... she *had* seen a woman out on the rocks where no mortal woman should be, a woman with a shimmering green tail where her legs should have been. And Ranulf had apparently seen something similar. But then he had obviously been drunk at the time.

She saw that Guy was looking at her quizzically and put an edge into her voice as she said,

"If I drank as much as your debauched brother does, I might think I was seeing things too."

"Ran was not drunk the day he saw his mermaid," his brother defended him. "He was barely fifteen at the time and Father would have whipped him soundly if he had discovered him the worse for drink."

"You said he was half drunk," Rowène reminded him.

"He did not tell me about it until some time later. And, yes, he was well on his way to being sodden drunk then. A not uncommon occurrence for him in the days after Father's death. He would not listen to me and Joff did nothing to stop him. If anything," Guy's thick, fair brows drew together in a scowl. "He encouraged Ran to drink himself into a stupor, to wench to excess."

"He did not try to do the same with you?"

"No. Joff is fond of me in his way but he rarely allows himself to forget that I am his father's by-blow, his half-brother only. Add to that the inescapable truth that my skills lie with quill and harp rather than sword and spear and he had little interest in forging me into his idea of how a de Rogé should be. For which I can only be grateful, although perhaps if he had divided his attention between us, Ran might not have run so wild. I may be wrong," he finished, picking up a handful of small pebbles and tossing them into the sea. "But it seems to me that on those rare occasions after Father's death when Ran managed to get away from the castle and came here, to Black Rock Cove, it was to escape from

Joffroi and his expectations as much as because he believed he might see his mermaid again."

"In the depths of his wine cup perhaps! How else could he look out there..." Despite the scorn in her voice, the hand with which she gestured seaward was not entirely steady. "And see anything other than sunlight on water, seaweed on rock?"

Guy returned her gaze gravely, a hint of curiosity glimmering in the light blue depths.

"I know you do not like the man my brother has become but at the time I speak of Ran was little more than a boy on the edge of manhood. Yes, he was thoughtless as all such young men can be, myself included. But he was never knowingly cruel to either man or beast and treated all women with a decency..."

She started to say something but he overrode her.

"Yes, I know what you are thinking. But when I say *all* women, that is exactly what I mean. And yes, if you need me to put it bluntly, even the whores whose services he availed himself of so frequently in the days after our father's death."

That *had* been what she meant but his uncompromising words made her flush nonetheless. She glanced back out to the empty rocks, trying to still her nausea. But Guy had not finished.

"Whatever he has done since, the boy he was does not deserve your disdain. Indeed, if you had known him then, you might even have found something in him to like."

"When your brother was fifteen years old, whether he was bedding whores or imagining mermaids, I had not even been born," Rowène said tartly. Then bit her lip, remembering too late that Guy was the same age as Ranulf, a fact that made them both old enough – just – to have fathered a child who would be her own age now.

Pushing aside this depressing thought, she tried for a smile and a slight change to the subject of their conversation, a twist away from the man she did not want to think about and towards the woman he thought he had seen.

"Never mind whether I could have liked him or not... did he tell you what this mermaid looked like?"

"After a fashion," Guy admitted wryly. "He was not quite sober, remember, but together we managed to capture her likeness in a song. I played it once at Chartre but it is not something I sing often and never in Ran's hearing unless he has been drinking heavily. Then he might ask me to play it for him. Stone-cold sober, he is as scornful of the experience as you are."

"So even he thought it was illusion," Rowène attempted a light laugh but all she managed was a painful smile. Her gaze was still fixed on the rock where she thought she had seen the mermaid. "An illusion with long black hair, the colour of wet sea wrack and eyes the green of the sea at dawn, sitting on a rock with the water foaming about her tail... at least according to Ju."

She looked at him, brows raised.

"Yes, I did tell her that," Guy answered, an odd note in his voice. "When I played for her and your mother in the garden of Chartre castle, I admit I did give the sea-woman some of your sister's attributes…"

Her gaze sharpened and he answered her unspoken question with a defensive shrug.

"A harper's instinct to play to his audience perhaps. But as for Ran's mermaid…" He returned his gaze to the black rock at the mouth of the cove, his eyes narrowed against the dazzling early light. "Well… that is another tale. One, perhaps, that I should have told from the beginning." He inhaled harshly. "Not to put too fine a gloss over it, there had been some trouble between Ran and Father. There usually was in those days… those days just before Father's death. They quarrelled even more violently than usual, over what I cannot remember now, and Ran stormed out of the hall and then the castle. I do not know where he went and he would not tell me. I only know he stayed out all night and was on his way back home when, passing Black Rock Cove just as the sun came up out of the sea, he decided to go down to the beach, meaning to bathe and…"

*And wash off the scent of the woman he had been with,* Rowène commented silently to herself. *For surely that is how he had spent the night, forgetting the quarrel with his father in a willing woman's arms! And within days, months at most, his father was dead and at my father's hand…*

"And it was then that he saw her! Out there on the rocks!" Guy's words wrenched her from contemplation of his brother's dubious past and shocked her back to the present.

"Her? The… Fae?"

"Just as the sun came up over the water. One moment she was there, he said. The next he was blinded by the light. And when he looked again, she was gone, in a flash of green."

"Gods!"

Guy did not pause but his voice changed, from awed disbelief to something harsher.

"As Ran told it, her hair was not black as a cormorant's wing. Nor was it the gold of the dawn sunlight."

He turned his head so that his eyes met hers and his final words came slow and almost too low to hear.

"He told me…"

"Told you what?" She was cold, she realised, suddenly; very, very cold. "Guy, you are frightening me!"

Yet fearful though she might be… of the past… of the Fae… of the future… she had to know what his brother had seen… what his brother had told him. She saw him swallow and felt the tension begin to tie her own insides into knots. She laid a trembling hand on Guy's reassuringly warm arm.

"For pity's sake, tell me what he said!"

Although she did not – could not – speak Ranulf's name out loud the taste of it lay dark and bitter on her tongue; chamomile, sour wine and bile. Memories of that mist-pale morning swirled before her eyes, blocking out the vivid blue and green and gold of the sea before her. All she could see was black and white and red; black wool, white linen and livid, engorged flesh. Through the shrieking of the sea mews and the crash of the tide against the rocks she dimly heard Guy's voice, halting, hesitant, the words dragged from him one by one.

"He told me that she had hair as red as dark flame. Witch-fire, he called it."

*Goddess save me!*

"And he swore that one day he would find her again, and that when he did he would prove that she was mortal after all. No longer an illusion born of sunlight on the sea or red wrack on a rock but a warm and wanton woman; one whom he might touch and kiss... and..."

"And what?" She could barely breathe, let alone speak, but she had to know.

But Guy did not answer, only shook his head and turned his face away.

She had her answer nevertheless, borne on the breeze that rippled her drying hair and touched her face in cold caress. The same breeze that had once, long years before, tangled itself in the flax-fair hair of the youth who stood upon the grey-pebbled shore, looking out over the waves towards the red-haired witch seated on the black rock. Dimmed though it was by the distance of a time long gone, still she knew his voice; slightly deeper, slightly rougher than his half-brother's even then.

*I will find you again, somewhere, somehow. And on that day, I swear, I will have you, Fae though you be, even if I die for it.*

# Chapter 18

## *Responsibilities and Duties*

By mid-day they were back in Rogérinac castle and had picked up their former routines as if the past month – and indeed those last strange moments down by the sea in Black Rock Cove – had never happened.

Geryth returned to guarding Rowène's door and Gerde took up her duties as tire-maid and companion while Guy busied himself with the collection and storage of the harvest tithes, the payment of Rogé's taxes to the crown, the settlement of Joffroi's quarterly payments to the mothers of his various by-blows and generally seeming to find reasons in plenty to keep out of Rowène's way – except for meal times. These, he insisted, she must continue to share with him at the high table in the great hall. She had not argued with him.

Indeed Rowène was far too worried about her tire-maid to waste time antagonising the very man whose help she would need if she were ever to sort out the troubling situation Gerde had managed to get herself into. Nor, once recovered from her shock, did she allow herself to consider further Ranulf's odd encounter with the fey woman of the sea – if indeed it had even happened. After all, it had been nigh a score of years ago and he must have long since forgotten both the occasion and the drunken oath he had subsequently sworn in his half-brother's hearing.

Or had he? Surely that could not be what lay at the root of his vile behaviour towards her at Chartre? No, she refused to believe it. He had not been in the grip of a drunken obsession when he came to her chamber, she was sure of it. But struggling against the effects of the Winter Lady's dark herbs... possibly?

Even so, *he* – not some half-remembered illusion from his misspent youth or her own mother's manipulations – should be held to account for his actions then. So why, she wondered, when she was at last released from all need to communicate with him, was she making herself responsible for sorting out yet another of Ranulf's indiscretions? Wary of him though she still was, dislike him though she still did... still she would have to talk to him. And soon. Guy would have to be asked to summon his brother home and then she would once more look Ranulf de Rogé in the eye – and demand justice for Gerde's babe.

Having reached this decision at the end of a long and sleepless night, Rowène rose late and sent Gerde down to the steward's chamber with a request that she might speak with him at his earliest convenience, only to have the girl return a few moments later with word that Master Guy had already left the castle and would not be back until evening.

Irritated that she had lost a whole day, her annoyance was exacerbated still further when she discovered that the weather had broken again and she was forced to keep to her room all day with nothing to do but lean on the window sill and stare at the churning waters that foamed and crashed against the black rocks far below; the chamber's one window looking south over the sea rather than eastwards over the garden.

Finally, just after noon, the faint sound of harp music from the room below caused Rowène to turn abruptly away from the window, listening intently. For a moment all she could hear was the rain and the beating of her heart but then the notes came clearer and she sighed in mingled relief and nervousness. Obviously the bad weather had forced Guy to return to the castle earlier than he had planned and she could not bear to delay any longer. Leaving the window, she took two rapid steps towards the door. Then halted abruptly as she caught sight of Gerde, seated on the chamber's one stool, her sewing untouched in her lap, her face white with dread; she too had heard the music and knew what it meant.

Seeing the tears filling the girl's brown eyes, Rowène went to kneel in front her, taking her cold hands in as comforting a clasp as she could manage and said unhappily,

"I am sorry, Gerde, but I can see no other solution. I have to talk to Sir Guy. And I have to do it now. He is the only person in Rogérinac who can help you. You know that."

"Ye're goin' ter tell him 'bout the babe?" the girl asked, looking fearfully at Rowène.

"I have no choice, Gerde. Surely you can see that."

"Aye, m'lady," she sniffed. "But I wish ye didna ha' ter. He's goin' to cut up rough about it, I know he will."

"Possibly... I do not know. What I do know is that however annoyed Sir Guy is, he will do what he can to help you."

Gerde nodded, not wholly convinced, Rowène could tell. She tightened her grip a little and took a breath.

"Before I talk to Sir Guy, there is one thing you need to tell me. Because he will ask me and I believe the answer will make a difference to what he does then." The brown eyes grew even more frightened, the tears now running freely down the girl's pale cheeks. "Gerde, I am sorry to press you like this but you *must* tell me the name of the man whose child you carry."

"Oh, m'lady, please don't ask me that. I canna tell ye."

"Yes, you can, Gerde," Rowène replied firmly.

"I canna. Ye'll think I'm nowt but a trollop, no better'n the others. An' ye a lady."

"You think *I* would judge *you*?" Rowène asked in blank astonishment. "God of Light, Gerde! I swear, you are no more a trollop than I am."

"But it wasna just *him* I went with..."

"Him? Your lover, you mean?" Rowène interjected softly, even as she cursed the image that suddenly leapt into her mind of Ranulf de Rogé in bed with this girl.

"If'n that's what ye wants ter call him," Gerde said, a trifle bitterly. "When we both knows he didna love me. But at least he were kind ter me when he did take me ter his bed, e'en if he's had other women since. But he was nay the only man who's had me, an' that makes me as bad as the rest o' them."

"If you are talking about Finn, being taken by force hardly makes you a trollop."

"Mebbe not but there's the night I spent wi' Lord Joffroy," Gerde admitted in a whisper. "I didna go there willingly, ye un'erstand, but he insisted and Ma... there was no-one ter say him nay so I went."

*And Master Ranulf did nothing to prevent it.* Rowène filled in the blank space in Gerde's explanation. *Damn you, Ranulf, how could you?* she thought grimly, as she notched up yet another grievance against the man.

"So it might be Lord Joffroy's bairn," Gerde was saying timidly. "Or Finn's." She looked a little sick at that and Rowène did not blame her.

"But you do not believe it is," she said with some force. "Do you? Because if it was Lord Joffroi, or even Finn, you would not hesitate to name him since you know full well that Sir Guy would see you well looked after." She eyed the trembling girl and continued gently more, "I think you will not tell me this other man's name because you have been told he takes too much care in his... couplings not to sire a child. That he has let it be known that he wants no child to hang like a millstone about his neck. Is that it? Gerde?"

Very slightly the girl nodded her head.

"It *is* Sir Ranulf, is it not?"

Again that infinitesimal nod and further terrified tears.

Coming to the door of the steward's chamber she was surprised to find it ajar but, hearing the plaintive notes still coming from within, set her jaw, pushed the door open and walked in without even the pretence of a knock.

She opened her mouth to speak but found her breath catching in her throat. The fair-haired man seated beside the window, his head bent over the harp in his hands was informally clad in shirt and breeches, his wet tunic discarded, his linen shirt damp and clinging to his shoulders.

But even as Guy's name rose to her lips, she knew something was wrong and as he lifted his head and turned to look at her, she blurted out the first thing that came into her mind.

"*You!* Gods above! What are *you* doing here?"

The man regarded her in silence for a long moment before carefully setting the harp aside. Then rising to his feet, he walked towards her. His back was to the window and the rain-grey light, his features illuminated only by a flickering candle on the nearby table but she did not need either in order to identify that hard face with its small white scar below the right eye and badly broken nose. Memories rose, washed over her in suffocating waves.

Caught in a blind panic, she took a step back, grabbing by instinct at the door frame, trying to think calmly despite the terrified thunder of her heart. But all she could do was stand like a mazed coney, staring...

At those dark blue eyes blazing with heat.

At that ruthless mouth whose searing touch she had once felt.

At the long pale hair braided warrior fashion, spilling over his shoulders and halfway down his back; hair that had once brushed against the skin of her exposed breasts with a touch as soft as thistledown...

"Like it or not, Demoiselle, this is still my home," Ranulf said, his slightly hoarse tone sending her memories flying all ways. "As to my purpose here..." His lips twisted in that sardonic smile that was so painfully familiar. "Obviously I am waiting for my brother. I would like to imagine that you knew of my return, Sweeting, and came here to see me. But from the surprise and disgust on your face I do not think I can delude myself so far."

He took a step towards her, his eyes burning with a dark blue flame she recognised.

"As you can see, Guy is not here but you are welcome to wait with me if you wish. I have no idea how long he will be gone but we can perhaps find some way of passing the time pleasurably until his return."

Rowène could find nothing to reply to this – nothing that was acceptable anyway – and she feared if she did open her mouth, she would once more vomit at his feet, spewing up the fresh disgust and renewed hatred she felt for him. He was no longer the laughing boy she thought she had seen in his mother's garden. No longer the youth she might have liked. He was not even the man who had risked himself to give her brother a chance of life. He was what he had been to her in those first moments of meeting by the Liriél; a mocking, lecherous stranger. The man whose rape-spawned child she had carried and, thanks to the mercy of the gods and a jealous woman's malice, had lost.

The same man whose child her maid-servant carried even now. She should tell him, she thought somewhat wildly. Now, when she had the chance, but could not get the requisite words past the bile in her throat.

Not that Ranulf appeared to be expecting any coherent response from her.

"On my arrival," he continued blandly. "Edwy informed me that Guy had taken the road south towards Black Rock Cove. The daemon only knows what maggot has got into him that he must needs ride there." His fair brows lifted. "Is it possible, do you think, that he has taken a leman at last and desires some privacy in which to conduct his clandestine amours?" He grinned. "I always found that particular cove most fitting for such a purpose."

She stared at him, horrified anew by his unabashed profligacy.

"But Guy said you did not..." Then cut herself off. She would not lower herself to discuss his liaisons – past or present, real or imagined – with him. Not now. She just couldn't!

Which meant she could not talk to him about Gerde. Not until she had collected her wits for such a battle. And battle it would be, since she did not suppose he would accept responsibility for Gerde's babe without a fight.

"Did not what?" He had picked up on her broken thought. "Take my doxies out to Black Rock Cove? What makes you think Guy knows the half of what I used to do? Or the women I have bedded?" Mockery glinted in his eyes. "And just as well, perhaps, for both our sakes. Hmm?"

Pinioned by his dark blue gaze, cold, shaking and rendered even more nauseous by his blunt reminder of what he had done to her, she could neither move nor speak. There was only one thought in her head; an overwhelming relief that she lost the babe he had spawned on her. Else she feared she would have been tied to him for ever. This man who had no honour in him, this man who did not know what it was to be faithful to one woman, this man who...

He took a sudden step towards her, his shirt hem stark white against his black-clad thighs, bringing back memories of that earlier confrontation, memories that had never entirely left her, even with the loss of the child.

"Well, are you coming in?" he demanded in a different tone, evidently tiring of baiting her. And with sudden violence, as she continued to cling to the door post. "Hell and damnation, woman! You need not be afraid that I will rape you if you so much as set foot in the same room as me. *You*, of all people, know I can not. Even if I wanted to."

She stared at him, slowly releasing her death-grip on the door jamb.

"You are still..."

"Impotent? Yes," he said curtly.

He returned her gaze, his eyes haunted, his voice low and strained.

"And you, Rowène? Are you..."

"What?" she whispered, feeling herself pale.

"Are you carrying my child?"

Even though she had been half-expecting it, the low-voiced question still sent a hot wire twisting in her belly.

"No."

He closed his eyes, the tension visibly draining from his face, and sighed.

"Ah! Thank the gods." And then, opening his eyes again, continued with a trace of his normal irony, "In that case I do not suppose you could see your way clear to restoring my manhood to me? If not at this precise moment, at least before I return to Chartre?"

She knew she was goggling at him but could not seem to help herself. He gave a deprecatory shrug.

"There is a woman I would bed if I could... a wench who works in a tavern in Anjélais, a village a few leagues north of Chartre. You know it perhaps?"

"Dear God of Light! You vile, whoremongering lecher..."

Abruptly released from the chains that had held her motionless, she swept forwards and brought her hand up and across his face in an open-handed slap that – astonishingly – appeared to catch him off guard. She half expected him to retaliate but he said nothing, did nothing, just stood there looking at her with one weathered cheek rapidly reddening.

A heartbeat longer she lingered. Then unable to face him any longer, turned and fled from his presence, her breath catching in her aching throat. Not back to her chamber where Gerde waited and wept, but down and out of the castle, across the courtyard and into the wind-swept, rain-soaked wilderness of Lady Rosalynde's garden.

"Rowène! Wait!"

But it was too late. She had gone, leaving him alone with his bitter memories and even more bitter thoughts.

*Bloody fucking hell!*

He wished with all his heart that he had not given in to that hell-spawned whim to return to Rogérinac.

Wished he need never set eyes on Rowène de Chartreux again, damned little wildcat that she was!

Wished he had never allowed himself to be bewitched into trying to bed her in the first place.

Wished – when it was far too late – that he had not allowed his turmoil at meeting her again to transmute itself into such crass idiocy as he had just displayed. When all he had wanted to do was make sure that Rowène was not carrying his child and, if possible, lay to rest this terrible, twisting tension that coiled in his gut whenever he thought of her.

Having achieved that – always supposing he could – he had meant to beg her, literally if that was what it took, to remove the curse that kept his prick limp and lifeless, in the hope that he might be able to have some sort of a normal life again.

Instead of which he would be lucky if Rowène de Chartreux ever spoke to him again, either in the protective company of others or alone. As for the chances of her touching his cock with healing intent, he could count himself fortunate if she did not instead take a honed blade to his private parts, rendering him impotent forever.

He turned back to the window, swearing steadily and not particularly quietly. Then fell silent as he caught a flicker of movement down in the weed-choked tangle of the garden his mother had spent so much time tending, and which his father and Joffroi had let run to weed and briar since her death. He pushed open the window and leant out into the slashing rain, the thin linen of his shirt soaked through within moments and plastered to his skin by the raw autumn wind. His hair blew about his face in tangled, wet, rats' tails, obscuring his vision until, cursing again, he dragged it back from his face and peered out again, eyes narrowed against the stinging, salty rain.

No, he had not been mistaken; there *was* someone down there, huddled under the twisted, wind-scoured shelter of an ancient, well nigh leafless, apple tree. He caught a flutter of movement, as of a woman's gown tossed by the wind. A grey gown, he thought. One of the serving wenches perhaps? No, he doubted whether any of the castle servants would be out in this gale or that any of them would enter his mother's garden in any case.

But *she*... Rowène... might well do so. When she had run from him she had been wearing an ill-made gown of grey homespun – he had noticed, of course he had, even as he had silently wondered why in Hell Guy had not contrived to clothe her any better than that – and she had certainly been upset enough to have run unheeding into the teeth of a Rogé gale. Moreover, she was obviously familiar enough with his mother's garden to seek refuge there.

Hell and damnation, he ought to do something. She would catch her death of a chill out there, besides being soaked to the skin. As was he – and *he* was only leaning out of a window, not standing in the dubious shelter of a walled garden. He was in no doubt whatsoever that she would not wish to see him again but he had the authority, and the physical strength, to ensure that she returned inside where it was comparatively warm and dry.

Slamming the window shut, he grabbed his damp mantle from the stool in front of the fire and was halfway to the door when it opened again and his brother stamped into the room, dripping water and curses as he came.

"Guy!"

The other man looked up, eyes wide with shock.

"Ran? What in Hell's name are you doing here?"

Ranulf gave a short laugh.

"I see that is the standard greeting around here as far as I am concerned. As to why, that can wait. I must..."

He stopped, his mind finally focussing fully on his brother's presence.

"Do not uncloak yet."

"Bloody Hell, why not?" Guy demanded irritably. "I feel like a drowned rat and..."

"Because our brother's valuable hostage is *outside* and needs to be brought *inside*," Ranulf cut in.

Guy blinked at him, then his eyes narrowed in suspicion.

"Setting aside the *why* for the moment, just tell me *where?*"

"In our mother's garden, with neither mantle nor hood to protect her from the weather."

Guy muttered another oath under his breath and with a brittle glance that held the barely-controlled promise of violence should he discover the girl had come to any harm of Ranulf's causing, stalked from the room, not even bothering to close the door in his haste.

Feeling as if a fist were clenching ever more tightly about his heart, Ranulf returned to the window, watching as his brother entered the garden and, without any hesitation that Ranulf could perceive, went straight to the place the grey-gowned figure stood. Removing his sodden cloak, Guy draped it around the girl's hunched shoulders. It could not have provided much by way of warmth, Ranulf thought bitterly, but there was love in the gesture – and trust in the way she responded to his brother, damn her!

Unaware of what he was doing, Ranulf unpinned his own mantle, letting it drop to the floor in a soggy heap, and sank back down on the seat. Resting his elbows on his knees, he dropped his face into his hands, his fingers clenching in his hair despite the tight braids at his temples.

How long he stayed there like that he did not know. Did not care. The only thing he could feel was the blood draining from his heart, drop by drop, leaving him cold and empty.

Damn it all to Hell, they were *lovers!* His brother and the woman *he* wanted. There was no longer any doubt in his mind; he could see it in the way their bodies responded to each other, even when they were not touching.

That being so, he had no choice but to finally accept that she would never think of him as anything other than a ravening wolf with neither conscience nor control over his bestial urges.

Slowly descending to his chamber, after having escorted Rowène back to her room and handed her over to the horrified Gerde with instructions to order a hot bath, Guyard was not entirely surprised to find that Ranulf had not waited for his return. Supposing his brother had retreated to change and prepare himself for the confrontation that now seemed inevitable between them, Guyard removed his own wet garments and spent the next four candle-notches drinking vile mulled wine and trying to order his tangled thoughts.

He had spent the day – as he had spent the majority of his time since his return to Rogérinac – riding the wooded valleys between the High Moors and the eastern coast in an attempt to regain his sanity and forget the time he had shared with Rowène on the harvest circuit... not to mention those parts of that shameful coupling that he could remember. The day had dawned fair enough, with just a crisp hint of autumn in the air and bright blue skies above. But one of Rogé's swift gales had swept in from the east just before mid-day, drenching anyone foolish enough to remain in its path. Guyard had returned to Rogérinac with an aching head and a weary resolve to somehow sort out the matter of Rowène's unsettled betrothal.

Quite how he was to accomplish that when he was tied to Rogérinac was another matter, but he was determined that Rowène should be gone from the castle before they were all imprisoned there by the winter storms. He did not think either his sanity or his honour could survive much longer under the strain of having Mathilde and Rowène living under the same roof. As it was he spent as much time as he could outside the castle environs, only returning to eat and sleep, keeping his dealings with Rowène to the barest minimum and conducting those with an icy formality that chilled his soul. The gods alone knew what it did to hers.

His only comfort in this whole bloody uncomfortable situation was that she seemed as intent on avoiding him as he was her. Yet even though he knew that maintaining such distance between them was wise, it was still painful to watch the death of their tentative friendship. Even so, he knew that every time he looked at Rowène there was the chance that he would betray his feelings for her. And Mathilde needed no further excuse to treat both him and Rowène with all the contempt and disgust he would have expected, and deserved, had they in truth been guilty of being lovers.

Except they were not, and never had been.

Or, at least, he hoped the vague recollections that continued to trouble him since the Mallowleigh harvest fire were just that; dreams of something he wanted desperately but could never have, rather than disjointed memories of something he had actually done.

Yes, he had broken his binding vows and that was dishonourable enough. If he had also broken those vows for the sake of a woman under his protection, his brother's daughter-by-binding... the woman who was his liege lord's hostage for the fealty of the conquered folk of Chartreux... he would never live down the shame of it.

Surely it was better for everyone that Rowène should go to Lamortaine as Joscelin de Veraux's bride, leaving him to come to terms with the utter desolation of his life in Rogérinac. That such a binding would also put her beyond Ranulf's reach could only be considered a good thing. Guyard did not know what his brother might have said to send her running out into a howling gale but it was obviously nothing he had any business saying to any noblewoman, least of all this one.

So there *would* be a reckoning between them, brothers though they were, Guyard promised himself grimly.

He emptied the last of the mulled wine into his goblet just as the horn rang out for the evening meal. He hesitated, regarding the murky mixture, then finished the liquid in one shuddering swallow; it was at least warm in his belly and the gods knew he needed something to get him through this evening and night.

Rising to his feet, he pulled a dry tunic – it was the gold-embroidered one of leaf-green wool – from his clothing chest and tugged it over his head, then buckled his belt about his waist, one hand coming to rest on his dagger hilt. His sword he left where he had stood it earlier; he could envisage no circumstance where he would need to go armed into Ranulf's company. Moreover, he had a sudden memory of the occasion on which Lady Rosalynde had gently but firmly expressed her disapproval of the notion that her lord, or either of her sons, or indeed her foster son, should feel it necessary to bring their weapons to the meal table. Not that either Ranulf or Guyard had been old enough at the time to bear arms but he still remembered. Remembered too that his father had humoured his wife's wishes, at least while she was alive, and had ensured that Joffroi – always more reluctant to pander to feminine fancies – complied as well.

Which made it all the more remarkable, to Guyard's thinking, that his older brother was now more than willing to allow the Lady Ariène to order every aspect of his life. Well, the witch was not going to order *his,* Guy promised himself grimly. Neither would Mathilde. Nor even Rowène, he concluded, coming to the top of the spiral stairs and nodding to Geryth to knock on the door and announce his presence.

There followed several moments of uncomfortable silence during which Guyard and Geryth exchanged uneasy glances. Then the door swung open and both men found themselves gaping with dropped jaws at the noblewoman standing there in the full light of the flaming torch fixed high on the wall behind them. Guyard did not think he so far forgot himself as to utter the startled expletive that exploded in his head, although he heard Geryth mutter something indistinct under his breath.

Rowène must have heard it too, if the faintest rose flush in her cheeks was any indication, but she did not so much as flick a glance at the flustered soldier and merely regarded Guyard with a gaze as cool and clear as spring rain. In spite of that betraying blush she appeared quite composed – unnaturally so, he thought, given the current circumstances and in complete contrast to her openly agitated tire-maid – and stepped forwards with a calm,

"Good evening, Messire de Martine." He took it as an ominous sign that she was addressing him in very formal Mithlondian. "I take it you are come to escort me down to the hall for the evening meal?"

"Yes, but..." He cleared his throat. "Do you really wish to go down attired in such a fashion? Bearing in mind that my brother has returned home and..."

"I am well aware of Messire de Rogé's presence," she cut in, still icy cool. "Since I had the great misfortune to meet with him earlier. That being so, and unless you have any further objections, Messire, I find I am impatient for my meal. Indeed I am sure Kelse will have outdone herself in honour of your brother's return."

Faced with such an imperious attitude, Guyard had no option but to stand aside with a courteous bow.

"After you, Demoiselle."

They completed the poorly lit descent in a silence broken only by the whisper of silk against stone, the ring of Guyard's spurs and the clomp of Geryth's boots.

At the bottom Guyard lengthened his stride so as to come level with Rowène and offered his arm. For a moment, as she hesitated, he thought – hoped – that she was going to tell him what this was really all about but then she laid her slender fingers firmly on the back of his hand, lifted her chin and allowed him to lead her down the passageway towards the hall.

It was only as they approached the hall doors that he realised the cold fingers resting on his hand had begun to tremble; very slightly, but enough to consolidate his belief that something was very wrong indeed. A quick glance sideways at his companion informed him that her face was now drained entirely of colour and he came to an abrupt halt.

"Do you want to go back to your room?" he demanded without preamble.

She took a deep breath and braced her shoulders as if about to ride into battle.

"No, of course not."

But her fingers were still shaking.

Guyard glanced around but although he could hear Geryth and Gerde arguing somewhere in the darkened passage behind them, for the moment no-one else was in sight. Gripping her shoulders, he pulled her around to face him, concern crushing the formality he normally tried to uphold, in public at least.

"Gods above, Rowène, tell me what is wrong! What did he..." He doubted he needed to specify which *he* and preferred not to speak his brother's name out loud in any case. Even though he was speaking in Mithlondian, Ranulf's name would be recognisable to any servants who happened to be within earshot. "What did he say – or do – to you?"

"Nothing!" she said sharply. "Nothing! Guy, let me go, please... you are hurting me." And she twisted in his grasp with such desperation that, short of using brute force, he had little option but to release her.

Not a moment too soon. Even as he dropped his hands, the door to the hall swung open and one of the serving wenches came scurrying out. Guyard caught the maliciously knowing glance that Frythe cast at them and scowled so fiercely back at her that she missed a step. Recovering herself, she bobbed a quick, insolent curtsey and continued on her way to the kitchen, leaving the hall door wide open behind her so that Guyard no longer had the option of counselling retreat. Even had he thought the woman he sought to protect would have taken that option.

Head up, shoulders back, her fingers once more steady on his – albeit desperately cold – and a smile on her lips, she was now moving forwards into the hall, drawing him along with her.

Ignoring the combination of damp draughts and Mathilde de Martine's unsubtle attempts to gain his attention, Ranulf lounged indolently in his chair, long legs stretched out under the table, his brooding gaze fixed not on the sensually pouting red lips of his brother's wife but on the dark depths of the wine in the battered pewter goblet he held loosely gripped between his fingers. Revolted by the sensation of something akin to a large, over-ripe fruit pressed heavily against his arm, he shrugged, dislodging the woman, and raised the goblet to his lips once more.

He had swallowed one mouthful of the harsh red wine and was in the process of taking another when a startled hiss from Mathilde caused him to glance up

– to see Rowène de Chartreux gliding down the hall towards him. One slender white hand rested on his brother's arm and she was smiling up at Guy in such a way as to render her rather plain face enchantingly lovely.

*Gods*, Ranulf thought, taking refuge in his wine goblet to hide his pain, *if only she would smile at me like that!*

Then she turned her head, looking straight at him, and instantly the smile was replaced by a straight grey gaze in which he could read nothing but dislike and a determination that he did not even pretend to understand.

Unable to help himself, he dropped his gaze and it finally hit him what she was wearing. At which point he choked on the wine still in his mouth, spraying the liquid indiscriminately over himself, the table and the woman frozen in place beside him. Entirely disregarding Mathilde's startled squawk, he came to his feet – less in courtesy than in utter shock – and, absently swiping the rivulets of wine from his face with his sleeve, stared like a starving man. Or some slavering beast, he thought without humour, as he struggled to bring himself under control.

An impossible task, he discovered, as – helpless to prevent himself – his searing gaze traced every line of that body he had possessed all too briefly. A body clad once more in that clinging, indecently-cut scarlet gown that on any other woman would have looked tawdry but on this witchling served to emphasise every slender, enticing curve he had once touched with hands and lips and tongue. Though surely those white breasts were fuller than he remembered, albeit just as lovely. He itched to touch them again, and with the heady rush of desire through his blood he realised that his manhood was far from dead.

Indeed quite the reverse. With the urgent and unfulfilled heat of lust searing his soul, his cock hardened so quickly and so unexpectedly he nearly gasped from the shock. He shifted his stance instinctively but dared do nothing else to ease his discomfort. Not with Guy glaring at him from the dais steps! He knew that his face was flushed and sweating, but he was incapable of doing anything to hide that either. Not all the time Rowène de Chartreux stood before him as she was; no longer a startled, frightened girl dressed unflatteringly in drab, shapeless homespun but a confident and beguiling enchantress, her dark-flame hair loose to her hips.

He had – rather too late, it was true – acquitted her of flaunting herself the morning he had first seen her clad in that scarlet silk gown. But he could not do likewise now. This time, he was certain, she knew precisely what she was doing, damn her! Guy was blatantly bewitched by her and Ranulf was sufficiently honest to admit that he had no hope of being indifferent. One day in the far distant future perhaps. But, the gods help him, not now!

In an effort to retain some sort of balance he forced himself to remember how she had, if not openly rejoiced, at least taken a subdued satisfaction in his withered manhood; he could still hear her cool voice informing him that a few months of celibacy would do him good. That being so, why in the name of all the daemons in Hell, had she chosen to restore him now? More especially as the arrogance with which he had treated her earlier was scarcely likely to have improved her low opinion of him.

Or – and this was a thought – did she even realise that she had released him from his penance? She had steadfastly refused to touch him again so it was possible that she had no idea of the power she wielded with nothing more than her smile. If that were indeed so, it was scarcely in his own interest to tell her what she had inadvertently accomplished, lest she feel inclined to deprive him of his renewed vigour. And he considered the three months of involuntary celibacy he had already suffered had been torture enough without inviting any more.

Drawn from his sardonic reflections by the sound of booted feet on the dais steps he looked up in time to catch the warning expression in his brother's eyes and, not that he needed the reminder, made a slight but definite bow in the Lady Rowène's direction; a courtesy that caused Guyard's grim look to relax slightly and made Mathilde frown in surprised displeasure. Apparently unable to keep her venomous thoughts to herself she stood on tiptoe and hissed angrily in his ear,

"See, it is just as I was telling you. My lord's doxy, flaunting herself before us all like the commonest harlot. And from all I hear tell, her sister was just such another shameless strumpet. But then I am sure *you* must already know that."

Recoiling from the malicious words as much as the warm breast that was again being pressed against his bare forearm Ranulf regarded his sister-by-binding with an icy stare. Inwardly he was stunned by the force of the fury that ripped through him. That she should dare to utter such accusations; this woman whom he could have in his bed with a single heated glance or the smallest crook of his little finger...

Controlling his temper with difficulty, he took a step away from her and, with frost biting in his every word, said crisply,

"You will refrain from speaking of the Lady Juliena to me. Or to anyone else for that matter. Whatever she may or may not have been to me, she died a horrible death and does not deserve to be reviled now that she is dead. And as for the Lady Rowena, whether or not she is my brother's doxy is immaterial to me. I would, however, suggest that you look to your own reputation before you attempt to blacken hers!"

He heard Mathilde gasp in shock and, glancing at his brother, shut his teeth on a curse as he realised that his angry words had been loud enough that both Guy and the grey-eyed little witchling appeared to have overheard everything. Guy was glaring with dark disgust at his wife but Rowène was looking, not at Mathilde but at him, a slightly puzzled look in her eyes. As if she was wondering why he should bother defending either herself or her sister, given some of the things he had said to her when they had been alone.

Suspecting that his once well-ordered mind had finally slipped over the edge of sanity into the hell of utter madness, he watched as his brother's companion... no, damn it, he would call her what she was, no matter that such acknowledgement stung worse than a lash across his back would have done! So then.. he watched as his brother's *leman* flicked a contemptuous glance at Mathilde, no less lethal for being so fleeting. Then, removing her hand from her lover's arm, she moved quickly along the dais so as to take a seat as far away from Ranulf as possible, dipping him the briefest of curtsies as she passed.

Contrary to what had been the normal table arrangement last time Ranulf was in Rogérinac, Guy did not take the seat beside his wife but went to sit with Rowène, plainly intending to share both goblet and trencher with her, leaving Ranulf to entertain a scowling Mathilde.

*Not likely, brother mine!*

Abandoning Mathilde with the curtest of apologies he carried his goblet around Joffroi's empty chair and dropped into the seat next to it that had once, long years ago, been occupied by the Lady of Rogé. At the thought of his gentle mother's place being usurped by that duplicitous bitch Ariène, he scowled and tossed back the foul dregs of his wine, swallowing both that and all his treacherous emotions with the same grim determination.

He saw that Guy was regarding him with narrowed eyes but his brother made no comment and merely nodded at the waiting servants to begin serving the meal. Ranulf did not even try to make conversation and kept his attention firmly fixed on his meal. Time enough to talk with Guy later and attempt to put things right between them, perhaps over a jug of wine in the steward's chamber. Just the two of them.

And after that, it might be that he would take one of the castle wenches to his bed and seek some ease for his aching loins.

In the event it was much later than Ranulf had foreseen before he and Guy found the opportunity to talk privately. Much to his relief, Rowène, accompanied by her teary-eyed maid servant – what ailed the wench, he wondered absently as he watched them leave – had retired to her chamber as soon as she had finished eating. And she had eaten damned little, he thought grimly.

Unfortunately Mathilde had persisted in lingering until even she had been forced to accept that neither Ranulf nor Guy were taking the least heed of her presence, whereupon she had withdrawn from the hall in a sulk. At which point the two men had made haste to retreat before she could change her mind.

Once settled in the steward's chamber Guy had taken up his harp and was now gently plucking the bronze strings in a melody Ranulf vaguely remembered from years ago. Pointedly ignoring the music, he continued to swill his way to the bottom of the wine flask he had brought with him from the hall, although he suspected that his brother was well aware that his performance was little more than a mask to hide his inner disquiet; Guy knew him too well.

It was only as he stretched his feet out towards the brazier and realised that he was almost at the end of the wine that he remembered that he had meant to pick one of the serving wenches to warm his bed that night. Later, he thought. Even so, he feared his conspicuous lack of interest thus far was sufficiently unusual as to have been noticed by Guy and the household alike. In a probably futile attempt to stave off his brother's suspicions a little longer, he took another mouthful of the throat-stripping wine, choked and coughed.

"Hell and damnation! But this wine is foul!" he muttered.

"You have been living in Chartre for too long," Guy snorted. "Overly easy access to the Marillec vineyards and the company of too many accommodating women!"

"I admit the wine in Chartre is far superior to this stuff but I would not know about the wenches."

The last seven words came without intent and Ranulf winced inwardly to hear them. Then, as Guy continued to concentrate on his music, allowed himself to hope that perhaps his brother had missed his muttered words. It was only as he raised his goblet again that he noticed the openly sceptical look that accompanied Guyard's uncharacteristically sardonic comment.

"What, are there no women in Chartreux willing to spread their legs for their new governor? I find that almost as hard to believe as the notion that you might be turning celibate after all these years. Next you will tell me that you are intending to exchange your sword for the sandals and grey robe of a Brother of Peace."

"Believe it or not, it is close to the truth," Ranulf offered with spurious mildness. "Oh, not that I am hanging up my sword! But in all truth, I have not found any woman capable of arousing me for the best part of four months." He swirled the thin red wine around his goblet, staring blindly into the dark depths. "Daemons of Hell! I must have drunk more than I thought – I never meant to tell you that!"

He could feel his brother's eyes on him but declined to look up, suddenly afraid of what he might see in Guy's eyes. He would face any man, with any weapon, without flinching. But pity, compassion, sympathy or even affection he knew he was ill-prepared to deal with. However, when Guy finally spoke, his voice was carefully devoid of any such emotion. Nor did he make any mention, as Ranulf had half feared he might of the events surrounding Chartre's fall.

Instead Guy said quietly,

"So... tell me, why *did* you come home? You must have had some purpose other than getting sodden drunk – which you can do in Chartre far easier and at less risk – and it is a hellish long ride just to find there is no woman you want to bed here either. Or... have you?"

There was something in his brother's tone as he asked this last question that made Ranulf look up from his wine, heart stilled in his breast.

*Gods, Guy! Surely you do not suspect...*

Abruptly recovering himself, he snapped,

"No, I have not. Unless you suppose I have designs on either your wife or your mistress!"

"I know you would never touch my wife and I do not have a mistress, castle gossip to the contrary. So I will ask you again, why did you come home, Ranulf?"

Slightly surprised that Guy had not hit him but nevertheless noting the warning that came with his brother's use of his full name, Ranulf produced the more acceptable of his reasons for returning to Rogérinac.

"I need your help."

Unexpectedly Guy grinned, some of the tension leaving his face.

"That must be a first! And, as it happens, Ran, I need your help too, so perhaps your arrival is not so untimely after all."

"*You* need *my* help?" Ranulf asked in astonishment. Then he managed an answering grin, although he had the feeling it lacked something of its normal sardonic edge. "But of course you do! And just as you never believed I might stop wenching, I never thought to see the day when you would get yourself into such a bloody thorny tangle – and with not one but two women. No, do not bother to deny it, Guy. Not if you want my help. Although what in Hell you expect me to be able to do... I have already given you access to Chartre's wealth, such of it as is within my control, so it cannot be money you want."

"No, not money. I want you to get word to Joscelin de Veraux for me," Guy replied, low voiced, his light blue eyes uncharacteristically grim. "How you get him here, I do not care, but he needs to come to Rogérinac and collect his bride. Preferably before the autumn is out."

"Daemons of Hell! You do not want much, do you?" He regarded his brother intently. "If it is just a messenger you need I can send Guthlaf up to Lamortaine. The campaigning season will be over soon, if it is not already. But what do we – yes, we, Guy, since I am involving myself in this – say to the man? It will have to be in writing, I suppose... though the gods only know what de Veraux will make of any missive we might send him. And you do realise that whatever we say, he may well repudiate the betrothal completely and challenge the pair of us to trial by arms?"

"Yes, I do realise that," Guy snapped. "I am not entirely ignorant of the risks, Ran. But I need Rowène gone from here before winter closes in."

*Rowène... not the Demoiselle de Chartreux!*

"Why?" he forced himself to ask. "What has happened that you are not telling me about, Guy? Is it as I thought when I saw you together in the hall earlier... that you and *she*..." He could not speak her given name... knew he would betray himself if he did. But neither could he call her Demoiselle de Chartreux, it was too formal. "You and she are... lovers?"

"Damn it, Ran! Of course we are not." Guy opened his mouth as if to say something else, then shut it again.

"Well, you do not look as confident as you sound," Ranulf commented, his dry tone barely serving to mask the pain that tore through him. "Out with it, Guy!"

His brother shot him a look in which shame and something else less readily identifiable were plain.

"If you must know, Ran, I have broken my binding vows. Once only, when I was on this summer's harvest circuit. But it is enough to make me guilty of adultery."

Ranulf could only stare at him, not knowing what to say or even if he should say anything. In the end all he could manage was a whispered name.

"Rowène?" But it could not have been her. The harvest circuit, Guy had said. She would have been in Rogérinac… He cleared his throat and tried again, although his voice was not much louder than the first time. "Well, at least it was not our brother's hostage you dishonoured yourself with!"

"No. Or at least I do not think so… but it could have been."

He regarded his brother narrowly. Guy did not appear to be drunk or out of his wits. Or at least not now. Anger began to flare in the pit of his belly and strength returned to his voice.

"What do you mean, it could have been but you do not think so? Daemon's balls, Guy! How could you not know if you had lain with her? Surely you were not so drunk you did not even know *who* you lay with?"

"No, I was not drunk!" Guy snapped. Then added bleakly, "Or at least not on heather beer. Moonlight and a fey woman's enchantments… perhaps."

Ranulf swallowed against the dark taste burning the back of his throat.

"Fey? A *witch*, you mean. Call her what she is!" He made an effort to wipe the bitterness and disgust from his voice and said more calmly, "Has she said or done anything to make you think it was her?"

He did not need to speak her name. Not again. They both knew who they were talking about. Guy shook his head.

"No. Nothing. But then I suppose she would not, would she? It was just one night of madness beside the Mallowleigh harvest fire. And I cannot remember anything clearly enough to be able to say with certainty that it was her."

The ice around Ranulf's heart cracked fractionally.

"So it might not have been her but still you think it might have been? Why?" His brother neither answered nor met his eyes. He hardened his voice. "Guy?"

Finally the light blue eyes came up to meet his narrowed gaze.

"I feared it was so… but perhaps only because I wanted her so much, may the gods forgive me. And yet…"

"Yet what, Guy? Tell me!"

But even as Ranulf made that demand, he knew what the answer would be and his entrails had turned to ice long before Guy said,

"The woman – whoever she was – *was* a woman. Not a maiden. So it could not have been Ro… her, could it?"

Cold sweat pricked his skin and his mind was numb but Guy was staring at him now, the confusion in his eyes slowly sparking into suspicion. He must make some sort of answer and soon! Striving for a suitably casual tone he finally forced words past the constriction in his throat.

"Well then… it was either one of the village wenches or…" Inspiration dawned and he managed a twisted grin. "Or else Juliène was not the only one to take a lover in Kaerellios."

"No, that I do not believe!" The lingering shame and burgeoning doubt in his brother's eyes was abruptly replaced by a blazing anger. "Neither of them would do such a thing."

"And if I said to you that Juliène was no shrinking virgin when she seduced me…"

A clenched fist on the point of his jaw gave him his brother's answer. Picking himself off the floor, he righted the stool and sat back down on it, warily regarding his brother as he rubbed his bruised chin.

"My apologies," Guy said gruffly.

"Oh, do not spoil a blow like that with an apology," Ranulf replied. He managed a lop-sided grin. "I had forgotten you could hit so hard, brother mine. But perhaps you might like to practice on someone else next time, hmm?" He held up a hand. "No, enough brawling over something neither of us can prove. Tell me instead why R… our brother's hostage was with you on the harvest circuit instead of here in Rogérinac where she should have been?"

He could think of many reasons but none of them came remotely near the one Guy supplied.

"It is simple enough, Ran. I feared to leave her here, lest the next time Mathilde tried to poison her, she succeeded."

"Poison!" Ranulf felt ice spike through his gut again but this time the fear was all for her. "Gods! No wonder you want her gone from here." He regarded his brother grimly. "And I will do all in my power to help you in that aim. Write that letter tonight – your hand is more legible than mine – and I will see that de Veraux gets it before…" He glanced at the unshuttered window where a half moon glimmered balefully in a cloudy sky. "Before the moon is full, if I have to ride to Lamortaine myself." Then, with granite calm. "You do realise that Joffroi will have both our heads – and probably strip the skin from our backs for good measure – when he learns how far we have interfered with his plans?"

"*My* head and *my* back, yes. You keep out of it," Guy replied warningly. "You have problems enough of your own, I think, keeping Chartreux in order. And speaking of that, perhaps it is time you told me what exactly brought you back here, seeking my help?"

Ranulf shifted on his stool, struggling to realign his thoughts. He had no intention of telling his brother that his return to Rogérinac had been, for the most part, motivated by a need to see Rowène de Chartreux. Nevertheless, there were practical problems he could ask his brother's advice on. He shrugged and spread his hands.

"You said it already. Chartreux – need I say more!"

561

He did, of course, and they spent the next hour or so amicably discussing the difficulties that had beset Ranulf in the months since Joffroi had passed the governorship of Chartreux into his reluctant hands, leaving him not only with a castle to rebuild but the normal day-to-day administration of the province to uphold. Neither of which tasks Ranulf's military skills had particularly suited him to – or so he had thought when he had first been forced to accept this new command.

Nonetheless, he had found that ordering a province was not so very different to commanding a garrison or raiding party, although the number of people he had to deal with and the area he had charge of differed enormously. His main difficulty had been adjusting to the fact that he was dealing with money-grabbing merchants and pig-headed peasants rather than soldiers accustomed to obeying orders. Then too, although he could write and tally as well as Guy when he put his mind to it, such skills did not come particularly easily to him. Nor did he have any notion of how to restore the near palatial elegance of a castle like Chartre, only the practical knowledge gained from living in a stronghold that had been threatening to fall down about his ears for the past score of years.

He had been in no mind to be defeated, however, and he had applied himself with iron-willed determination, learning as he went and both he and the province had survived – thus far at least. Even so, there remained one problem that was long overdue for resolving and it was on this matter that he most wanted his brother's advice and experience.

Owing to the turmoil that had beset the realm over the past year, the quarterly revenues due to the crown had fallen into arrears and it had been Ranulf who had received Prince Linnius' bailiff and read with disbelief the amount now being demanded. Giving his word that the money would be sent to Lamortaine by the last day of autumn, he had sent the smirking bailiff on his way, dismissed the white-faced clerk and gone to check exactly how much ready coin he had at his disposal.

A night of counting bronze farthings, silver nobles and gold crowns left him with ink-stained fingers, a monumental headache and the knowledge that there was barely enough in Chartreux's coffers to cover the amount owed.

He had spent the following day and night shut in the solar perusing the various rolls of account, straining his eyes and his wits until finally he had found something that might be an answer. Rubbing his burning eyes, he had pinched out the guttering candle and laying his head on his folded arms, had fallen asleep where he was. He had been woken by a pounding at the door and the news that Prince Kaslander of Kardolandia was down at the harbour and a royal messenger was waiting in the hall.

Thereafter Ranulf had been left with little leisure to worry how he was going to pay his brother's dues to the crown. Nevertheless, even as he had fulfilled his tedious duty of escorting Kaslander through Chartreux, he had continued to consider the conclusions he had drawn from his study of the tally rolls. It seemed to him that although most of the taxes levied on the local knights had been collected, there was a large amount outstanding from one particular landholder. The longer he thought about it, the more it became obvious that somewhere there was a great, gaping hole into which more than just the last two quarters' silver had disappeared. Ranulf did not know enough to be sure whether Sir Girauld was dishonest or merely incompetent, but he had every intention of finding out. And of collecting the missing money before Joffroi learned about the problem and thought to put the blame onto *him*.

The loss of revenue aside, there was also the matter of three patrols decimated and two messengers murdered along the main highway to Lamortaine. Having spoken to his surviving soldiers it became clear that all these incidents had occurred within three leagues of the small village of Anjélais-sur-Liriél. It was possibly only coincidental – although Ranulf had smelt enough rats to think not – that the knight who held these lands was none other than the man he suspected of attempting to defraud not just the Chartreux coffers but ultimately – by default, if nothing else – the royal exchequer as well.

"So, what do you think?" he enquired of his brother when he had told him everything he thought of relevance. Guy regarded him with narrowed, thoughtful eyes.

"So this is what really brought you home. I suppose pride would not let you speak of it to start with." Ranulf met his brother's gaze but did not disabuse him of his error and Guy returned to the matter at hand. "So you have not had a chance to question this Girauld yet?"

"No. I met him, of course, at the Midsummer Feasting when all the knights who formerly held land under Louis de Chartreux came to swear allegiance to Joffroi. It has to be said, I did not take to the man then."

A feeling that was founded on nothing more substantial than the observation that, unlike most of the disgruntled knights who had come so reluctantly to Chartre, Sir Girauld had shown no signs of open hostility towards the over-lord forced upon them by the young prince and had even gone so far as to share a jug of wine and game of dice with the new governor of Chartreux. He explained something of this to Guy and concluded with a question,

"Have you any suggestions as to how I proceed from here?"

"I think you could do worse than to pay him a formal visit," Guy replied. "You are right when you say something does not smell as it ought in all this. Moreover, if you were reading those records right, and I am sure you are, it would seem that it is not just Joff he is chary of paying his rightful dues to. That said, if he has been perpetuating this fraud for some time he must be a very clever thief indeed to have deceived his former lord. Louis de Chartreux had a keen eye for things that were off-kilter, as I know from personal experience. Indeed, I have often thought that if he had not been recalled to Lamortaine before he found the time to interrogate me, matters might have turned out very differently."

"I doubt it," Ranulf commented grimly. "The witch had already put the death mark on his brow long before you went to Chartre. And now we are left to mop up his blood whilst Joff lives a life of luxury at court with that conniving bitch he must needs wed."

"Would you rather be in his place?" Guy asked, brows lifting.

"Not bloody likely," Ranulf growled. Suddenly weary, he rose to his feet. "Daemons of Hell, I must be getting old! Every bone in my body aches. And I have another bloody long ride back to Chartre tomorrow. That being so, I think I will retire to my bed while I am yet capable of doing something with the wench I intend taking there."

Ranulf would have left Chartreux as soon as the dawn meal was done but, to his annoyance, found his intentions thwarted. Initially by the obligation to deal with some matters that Edwy unexpectedly brought before him and then, when he found himself free of that duty, by the discovery that Guy had ridden up the coast to mediate a heated dispute that had arisen between the men of Rogérinac and Noirac concerning wreck rights over the cargo of a ship that had been driven onto the rocks halfway between the two villages.

He had been in a vile enough temper even before these delays – in spite of everything, he had not sought out a woman the previous night and by morning his pent-up frustrations had demanded such urgent release that he had been forced to employ an expedient he had not been obliged to resort to since his long-ago youth – and his tension had now reached such a pitch that he dared not remain within the castle and risk another meeting with Rowène de Chartreux.

Disregarding the spattering rain and tearing wind that was all that remained of the previous night's gale, he had therefore taken a horse from the stable and ridden out, deliberately heading down the coast in the opposite direction from the wreck. He would have preferred to leave Rogérinac completely but knew his stallion was barely rested from the long journey from Chartre. Moreover, he did not know whether Guy had found the time yet to compose a suitable missive to Joscelin de Veraux. On balance he thought not, since he did not suppose that Guy would resort to a blunt, *Come and collect the wench before her reputation is ruined beyond repair.*

Even though, as the gods knew, Ranulf had already accomplished that end himself – with the unlooked for consequence that Rowène had been able to lie with his brother without stirring Guy's suspicions. *If* it had been the Demoiselle de Chartreux and not some enterprising peasant wench his brother had tumbled beside that thrice-cursed harvest fire.

Heedless of the wine-induced ache that still threatened to split his skull, doubt and guilt continued to hammer his mind. If that were not enough, sharp-edged memories of that tower room in Chartre, alternating with distorted imaginings of those moonlit moments on Mallowleigh moor, burned behind his gritty eyes while unfulfilled desire and jealous rage sparked and leapt in his blood. At the same time the wild wind tugging at his mantle reminded him that the witchling was still in possession of something of his – even though that something was utterly unimportant when compared to the child of his siring he had feared might be growing in her womb.

Mundane though his missing possessions were, he supposed he should make some effort to recover them. The loss of his mantle meant little to him but the cloak pin was a different matter. Not so much for the weight of silver it contained or the intricacies of its workmanship but because his father had given it to him on his death-bed and ordered him to keep it safe. And Ranulf had little belief that Jacques de Rogé's restless wraith would regard his son's foolishness in giving such an heirloom to a de Chartreux – to the daughter of the man who had in effect brought him to his death – as fulfilling that command.

Unless – and here was an ugly thought – his father might view it as part of the blood-price his son must pay for raping a noblewoman and unlawfully shattering her maidenhead.

As Ranulf well knew, Jacques de Rogé and Louis de Chartreux had crossed swords frequently, both verbally and physically, but he could not envisage either of them using violence against the other's womenfolk. No, it had been left to him and Joffroi to carry that feud to a more brutal level, and he knew he would never ask Rowène to return his cloak pin. If she kept it safe, he would be grateful, but if she threw it on the nearest midden, so be it. And perhaps his mantle might serve to keep her warm, if she could ever bring herself to wear it again.

With these grim thoughts to keep him company, he came just before midday to the wooded slopes above Black Rock Cove. It was raining steadily by then, falling cold against his skull and although his head-ache was in consequence a little less strident, his temper was still raw. Taking the narrow track that led down between the twisted oak trees, their green leaves now darkened to dull gold, he tethered his borrowed mount close to the rushing stream and made his way over the pebbles, the crunch and slither of his booted footsteps barely audible above the roar of the wind-driven waves.

Coming to the shoreline he stood for a long time, heedless of the wild water crashing and foaming at his feet, staring through salt-wet lashes over rain-grey seas towards the tumble of sharp black rocks, now almost obscured by frothing white spray. No mermaid there today! But then had he truly expected her to be? In all truth, he doubted she had ever been there.

He had not consciously thought of the events of that dawn for fifteen-odd years, more than half his life-time ago. So why should he remember now? More especially as the woman presently haunting his mind bore little resemblance to that wondrously lovely creature he had seen – or imagined he had seen – then. Hair the colour of dark red sea-wrack, eyes the colour of the sea itself... He had had no chance to see more before she had fled from him, even though the boy he had been had meant her no harm.

Yet eighteen years later he had done irrevocable harm to a nobly-born maiden who, by some hell-sent mischance, had the same dark red hair as the sea-woman he had once rashly sworn to claim for his own. He winced, suddenly remembering that drunken boast he had made and then not thought of for years. Gods! What a fool he had been.

Had been? As far as he could see, he still was!

The echo of some distant melody pierced his aching head and, cursing, he stooped to pick up a pebble, throwing it with all the strength of his arm, watching as it fell with a tiny splash just short of those barren black rocks.

Hell and damnation, he needed a woman. Not a mermaid. Not a witchling. A warm flesh and blood woman. That tavern-wench back in Anjélais would suit him well enough, he reminded himself, throwing another pebble with vicious force. This time it struck the rearing rocks, rebounded with the force of the strike and was lost in a towering spume of spray.

Belatedly becoming aware that he was soaked to the skin from rain and sea-water, he shook his dripping wet hair out of his stinging eyes and with a muttered curse turned his back on the past.

It was only on his return to Rogérinac castle that he realised that the Faennari had not finished with him yet.

He found Geryth waiting for him in the stables with the message that Master Guy had returned some time before and was wanting to speak with him as soon as he came back. Cursing, Ranulf ran up to his chamber and hastily changed into dry garments before hurrying through the damp, draughty passageways to the south-east tower, thinking only that Guy had finished his letter and he could be on his way without further delay, rain and wet boots notwithstanding.

Walking into the steward's chamber he was unprepared to find his brother with company. His gaze settled immediately and without volition on the young woman seated in the pale light by the window, once more respectably garbed in drab grey, her fiery braids partially hidden beneath an ugly headrail of unbleached linen. Her face was set and unnaturally pale and her grey eyes, when they met his, as cold as the water that dripped down his neck from his wet hair.

He did not think he blurted out the name that rose to his lips but his heart gave a painful lurch in his chest. He understood neither the reason for her presence nor the bleak manner in which she was regarding him but, as much to give himself time to regain control of his own features as for the sake of courtesy, he made her a bow. Far more composed than he, she rose and bent her knee in the stiffest of curtseys before saying coldly,

"Sir Ranulf."

"Lady Rowena."

He replied by instinct in the same language she had addressed him in, even as he was asking himself *why* they were using common speech and *what* she was doing in his brother's chamber at all. Then he remembered that she had come there the day before, obviously looking for Guy. Were the events connected and what in the name of Hell did any of it have to do with him? Pray gods she had not lied to him about the babe...

"You remember Gerde?" His brother's voice interrupted his thoughts.

"Huh?" Ranulf glanced at Guy with a frown.

Now he had recovered himself somewhat he could see that the servant girl in question was standing huddled against the wall by the door, looking as if she wanted nothing more than to dissolve into the rough stones at her back. The wench really did not look well, he thought dispassionately, her face blotched with weeping, her doe eyes wide and terrified. Almost he would not have recognised Geryth's shyly smiling sister and his own former bed mate in this pathetic, pallid creature. She had put on weight since the last time he had been in Rogérinac and it did not suit...

It was then that it hit him! Not only what was wrong with the girl but why she was here. Why Rowène had been looking for his brother. And why Guy wanted to speak to him.

"Yes, I remember her," he said grimly. "And no, you are not going to put the blame for her swollen belly onto me. Or are *you* the instigator here?" he snapped, temper flaring as he flashed an angry and incredulous glance at Rowène.

"Only because it is true," she retorted and something in her flat tone, some shadow far beyond the surface clarity of her grey eyes convinced him that she, at least, believed what she said.

He glanced back at his brother.

"Are you so besotted with this little witch you believe anything she tells you?"

Guy returned his look steadily, his own anger apparent but controlled.

"No. But I have spoken to Gerde and there seems little doubt that it is your babe she carries. What I want to know is what you intend to do about it?"

"I..."

His words dried in his throat as his gaze returned inexorably to those cool, grey pools. She was regarding him steadily and he saw that she was as aware as he of the words he had spoken to her that bitter morning in Chartre. Words he had meant for her alone; that if she found herself carrying his child he would acknowledge the babe and support them both for as long as he was able.

*Will you do as much for a humble servant girl?* she seemed to be asking. *Or is it only noblewomen and witches for whom your chancy conscience speaks?*

Curbing his temper and his guilt with an effort, he tore his eyes away from her accusatory stare and looking his brother straight in the eye, said curtly,

"I want nothing to do with it."

He heard Rowène gasp and Guy swear, both sounds overlaid by a thin whimper from the pregnant girl. Turning on his heel he snarled at her,

"Did I force you into my bed?"

She stared at him blankly.

"Answer me, damn it!" he demanded, fiercely determined that Rowène should hear for herself that this was one woman he had not raped.

"N... no." It was barely a whisper but it *was* sufficient.

"And did I ever make you any oath? Ever promise you my protection if you should find yourself with child? Well?"

"No, sir," she sniffed.

"And did I not take what precautions I could to ensure this did not happen?"

"Aye, sir. At least... I think so."

"Then there is no more that needs to be said," he snapped.

"I think perhaps there is," Guy contradicted him quietly. "Lady Rowena, I think it best if you leave this matter in my hands now. You must just trust that I will see this right."

For a moment Ranulf thought she would argue, then with a vitriolic glare in his direction, she walked over to her tearful servant.

"Come, Gerde, we will leave this to Sir Guy."

She seemed entirely occupied with helping the weeping girl from the room but even so Ranulf kept a wary eye on her hand as she swept past him, having no intention of granting her the satisfaction of another slap when his face was still bruised from the last time. She made no attempt to strike him however, merely regarding him with a contempt colder than a northern night.

"You truly are a despicable cur," she hissed in Mithlondian. "If I could name you as you deserve without insulting your poor mother, I would."

"I am a de Rogé, Demoiselle," he replied softly in the same tongue. "What else would you expect of me?"

He saw something flare in her eyes then, a hint of doubt perhaps, a flicker of memory of the last time they had had a similar conversation and he added, even more softly.

"But you are right, Rowène, I *am* a heartless, worthless bastard. There, I have said it for you."

Then both women were gone and he was alone with his brother. It was obvious that Guy was still angry but Ranulf was in no mood to fight with him over some snivelling serving wench. Cutting across whatever excoriating words his brother might be about to unleash, he merely said,

"Save it, Guy. I will give you however much silver you think to be fair to support the wench and the brat when it is born. If it looks like it might resemble me I suppose I will be obliged to acknowledge it since Father is long dead and no-one in their right mind would believe it to be yours. But, be warned Guy, that is as far as my goodwill goes."

"And you will set your name to that, on an official deed?"

"My word is not good enough for you?" he asked in stunned surprise. "What in Hell has that little witch been saying to you?"

"Oh, I do not doubt your word but you live a chancy life. The barbarian arrow might not miss next time, some disgruntled Chartreux adherent might stick a knife between your ribs even before you get to the borderlands or I might take issue with you if you persist in calling de Chartreux's daughter a witch in my hearing."

"There is always that," Ranulf agreed with a tight smile. "Very well, write the bloody deed and I will put my name to it."

"It is all ready for you," Guy said, some of the tension leaving his stance. He flicked his hand at a parchment laid out on the table. "I had more faith in your sense of honour than... others do." He looked at Ranulf curiously. "Why did you let them think you would turn your back on your responsibilities? It was unnecessarily cruel to Gerde and will merely confirm Rowène in her poor opinion of you."

Ranulf shrugged and moved to pick up a quill. Dipping it in the ink pot, he scanned the terms of the deed before signing his full name below, an inelegant scrawl but legible enough. *Ranulf Jacques de Rogé.* Then he looked up, only then answering Guy's question.

"Perhaps because she expected me to do just that," he said, and saw in his brother's eyes that they both knew he was not talking of the servant girl. "Heartless, worthless bastard that I am." Then impatiently, "Do you have that letter for de Veraux?"

"Yes, it is here. Do you want to read it?"

"No, I just want to be on my way. Seal it up, Guy, and we are done. Unless there is anything else?"

"No, the gods go with you. I think, Ran, you may need their guardianship more than usual in the days to come."

Ranulf took the rolled, sealed parchment and smiled mirthlessly as he stowed it safely beneath his shirt.

"Keep your sword sharp, Guy, and an eye on that little witch... sorry, the Demoiselle de Chartreux, until such time as de Veraux comes to relieve you of your duty."

"You are very sure he will come," Guy commented, brows lifting.

"He is Marcus of Mithlondia's son," Ranulf replied. "And Guillaume de Veraux's grandson. Of course he will come. He is too bloody honourable not to." He smiled at his brother. "Watch him, though, if it comes to combat. He can fight like a gutter-rat if he sees the need for it."

"And you think I cannot?" His brother grinned suddenly, the last shreds of tension dissipating. "After all, I was not the one who ended up with a broken nose that last time our so-called kinsmen came to Rogérinac."

Ranulf lifted his hand and fingered the ridge across his nose ruefully.

"No, but it was worth it just to hear Father telling old Henri that neither he nor his sons would be welcome in Rogérinac again. Even the whipping he subsequently gave us for breaking the laws of hospitality was worth it."

"I suspect Father knew we were fighting to uphold our mothers' honour," Guy said. "That was the only occasion I can remember being punished in the morning and still being able to sleep on my back when I went to bed. He was remarkably light-handed for a man supposedly enraged by his sons' shameful behaviour."

Ranulf smiled in rueful agreement but as he walked back down towards the stables he did have to wonder what Jacques de Rogé would have thought about his younger sons now that they were both grown to full manhood. He had the feeling that his father would have strongly disapproved of much of his recent behaviour. Promiscuous though his father had undoubtedly been, he would never have forced himself on an unwilling woman, be she noblewoman or servant. Nor would he have contemplated for so much as a heartbeat shirking his responsibilities towards his chance-got offspring.

But if Ranulf had learned nothing else from this affair, it was that if he ever managed to tumble that little tavern wench in Anjélais – or any other woman for that matter – he would be even more careful than he had been in the past that his seed did not take root. The few coins it would cost him to support any by-blow he might sire could undoubtedly be drawn from the Chartreux coffers without Joffroi questioning it but he wanted to give no child the right to call him father. Irrational it might be but such was his conviction; he had seen the contempt with which Mithlondians treated those of illegitimate birth, including his half-brother, and despite being for the most part as heartless as *she* thought him, he would not willingly inflict such degradation on a child of his.

Except that now there was Gerde's babe and he had to admit it probably was his. He could only thank the God of Mercy that Rowène de Chartreux had not quickened with his child. And pray to the God of Light that Joscelin de Veraux would act as soon as he received the letter Ranulf was carrying next to his skin and retrieve his betrothed before it was too late.

Unaware of just how often she walked through his thoughts, Rowène stood on the walkway above the gate and watched as the dark-cloaked man on the black horse rode away from the castle, his long hair a flying tangle of pale braids and coarse flaxen silk, tossed and tumbled by the autumn wind. Shivering in the chill of the approaching storm she pulled her mantle closer, all too aware of the weight of the silver brooch lying heavy against her shoulder.

Relieved though she was to see Ranulf gone she wished he had not left so precipitously, before she had found the opportunity to return his cloak and brooch. But by the time she had realised his intention he had been down in the stables, saddling up his stallion, and she was not minded to seek him out in such a place, more especially as his mood when she had last seen him had been dangerous to say the least.

Whether his continued bad temper was the result of a belated attack of guilt over Gerde, sexual frustration due to his forced celibacy or some other cause

Rowène could not guess at, he was riding as if all the daemons of Hell were at his heels. It was no concern of hers and yet she was aware of the uneasy notion that nagged in the recesses of her mind… that if by some mischance he fell from his horse and broke his neck, she would feel – at least in part – responsible for his death. Damn him!

Damned or not though, at least she knew where she stood with him. Hatred was simple.

Her feelings for his half-brother were far more complicated and she had no idea how she was going to resolve any part of that twisted tangle over the coming months.

# Chapter 19

## *Autumn Storms*

A se'ennight to the day after Rowène had stood on the battlements of Rogérinac castle and watched its former garrison commander ride away, the first dream came.

She had not been sleeping well, anxious as she had been about so many things – Gerde and her babe, Guyard de Martine and her own invidious position in his life being only the more obvious of them – and that particular night had been no exception. Lying in an uncomfortable state between sleep and waking, shivering beneath shift, sheet, wolf pelt and black mantle, a stray strand of silver moonlight had slipped through a hole in the shutter to touch her face, causing her to open her eyes...

To see her sister at the door of her chamber, beckoning. The fact that it was nearing midnight and too dark to see anyone did not occur to her and in her dreaming state she merely felt a great desire to laugh for joy as she followed her sister, content to follow wherever Ju might lead.

That happiness had quickly given way to puzzlement when she found herself in what was clearly a tavern. Larger and more prosperous, it was true, than the ale house she had visited that first day after crossing the Larkenlye but a tavern just the same! Then she noticed that the men gathered around the tables, drinking, grumbling, dicing, shouting, were doing those things in the soft accent of her own homeland, not the harsher one of Rogé. The tavern keeper himself was a solid, amiable-looking individual – or so she thought until she saw his watchful, pebble-hard eyes and recognised in him the man she had last seen paddling a coracle up the Liriél river – and her growing unease was only slightly ameliorated by the presence of a sturdily-built woman with a smiling face who watched with anxious affection as a serving wench moved amongst the men, pouring ale and exchanging laughing banter.

Even in her drifting state Rowène wondered why Ju was showing her all this. Until, with a sense of shock so profound that it nearly jolted her back into wakefulness, she realised that her sister *was* the serving wench. Moreover Ju was clearly in control of herself and the roomful of raucous, rowdy men; teasing them with a smile and a fleeting touch of hand on arm or shoulder yet easily holding their attempts at familiarity at bay.

As far as Rowène could observe – and here the vague notion that Ju was only revealing what she wanted her sister to see began to take form in her dreaming mind – there was only one man her sister treated any differently. A man who sat by himself in the darkest corner of the room, ignored by those around him and arrogant in his solitude. Shadows were gathering at the edges of her vision by then, rippling in waves of dark silence over the noisy men... the watchful tavern keeper... the sweet-faced woman... engulfing them one by one so that in the end only a single flicker of candlelight remained. That, however, was quite sufficient for Rowène to recognise the man Ju so obviously wanted her to see.

For one moment she felt nothing... nothing at all. Then the man looked up from his drink and her heart nearly stopped as those bleak blue eyes locked with her own...

Yet even as she struggled against appalled incredulity and incipient nausea, the one remaining candle flame – as if catching a blast of wind through the broken shutter of a far distant castle – was snuffed out and she was left in oblivion... dazed, disorientated, not knowing whether she was awake or still dreaming but shaking as if her soul had been pierced by ice.

When she woke again it was long after dawn and she had only one coherent thought in her mind. That if Ju were indeed intent on using Ranulf de Rogé for her own purposes – and the gods only knew what they might be – her sister had chosen a treacherous path that Rowène would never have taken, a path that seemed destined to bring nothing but pain to all concerned.

Thankfully, Rowène was not gifted – or cursed – with any further glimpses of her sister for some time after that but, as if to compensate for this lack, Guy began to talk to her of events beyond Rogé's borders. In this way she learned that his half-brother's control over Chartreux was holding, if only by the barest of margins, and she gave thanks to the gods that her own presence as hostage in Rogérinac was apparently serving as some measure of restraint against open rebellion. She wanted no man's blood on her hands, not even Ranulf de Rogé's. Even so she understood from Guy that there had been deaths on both sides and she became increasingly fearful lest Ju be involved in some way, although how or why, she could make no guess.

She was out working in Lady Rosalynde's garden one day, collecting the few wind-battered apples that had survived the summer rain and early autumn gales, when the thought suddenly came to her that her sister and the tavern wench Ranulf had told her he wished to bed must be one and the same. For why else had Ju shown her the Governor of Chartreux drinking in the tavern where she had obviously found refuge?

*Gods, Ju! Surely you are not sleeping with Ranulf in order to betray him to whoever is leading the covert rebellion in Chartreux?*

Or for some other unfathomable purpose her sister had not yet chosen to reveal? Whatever *that* might be, Rowène would really rather not know. As for her earlier conjecture – that Ju meant to take the man as her lover and then cold-bloodedly betray him to his death – just the thought caused bile to rise in her throat.

Unable to contain it, Rowène bent over and vomited up what little she had eaten at dawn. Straightening, she met Gerde's concerned gaze but merely wiped her mouth and shook her head, silently enjoining her maid's silence.

The wild storms that raged along the Rogé coast that autumn soon swept the oak trees bare of leaves and the drab days turned even colder, withering all but the toughest plants and sending the creatures of wood and moor deep into winter cover. Not everything was dying though and, even as Rowène watched her tire-maid's belly continue to swell, she strove to ignore what her own body was telling her.

The darkening of the days had one other, unlooked for, consequence in that Guy no longer spent so much time out of the castle and they often came together, usually – meal-times being the exception – in his chamber, which was considerably warmer and less draughty than the hall. But even there, they were never alone. With Gerde sitting unobtrusively nearby, diligently sewing for her babe, Rowène and Guy had a certain amount of freedom to sit and talk; of affairs of their own realm or of Kardolandia, whilst playing countless games of fox and geese. Occasionally – very occasionally – Rowène would take up her own sewing while Guy played his harp and they lost themselves in their own thoughts.

But for all the superficial harmony between them, it was nonetheless not an entirely comfortable companionship. There was an underlying constraint that often took its toll, to the point that the very air between them became so stretched and thin that Guy would make his apologies and stride from the room, leaving Rowène to question what would become of them both when spring finally arrived. Or wonder whether her growing desperation would lead her to confess her terrible crime and throw herself on Guy's mercy long before then.

Thankfully before she could take such a drastic and irrevocable step, salvation from the unlikeliest source swept into Rogérinac on the wings of what was easily the worst storm of the autumn so far.

Although it was close to mid-day the sky was already as dark as it would be at dusk and in the south-east tower room neither Gerde nor Rowène could see to set a stitch in the baby linen they were attempting to sew. The single candle flame flickered and flattened in the gale that howled around the tower, blasting through the broken shutter, and even though the brazier was glowing red, both women shivered in the damp chill.

For most of the day the only sound had been the howling of the wind and the roaring fury of the waves below but suddenly, and utterly without warning, a shattering crash of thunder resounded with deafeningly force right over the castle.

Gerde screamed and Rowène jumped, inadvertently stabbing her finger with her needle.

"For pity's sake, Gerde, it is only thunder," she snapped. Then, as another crash slammed into the stricken silence, she admitted, "But it is very loud." Sucking her bleeding finger she shook her head slightly to clear the ringing from her ears and asked somewhat facetiously, "Do the gods always play this fiercely through the dark seasons?"

"Eh?"

"The storm," she explained to her quivering maid.

"Oh aye, but they'm not often this bad," Gerde muttered. Then her head jerked up. "What's that?"

Straining her ears over the noise of the storm, Rowène thought she could just make out a few wind-tossed notes.

"It sounds like a horn. But who would be mad enough to travel in this weather?"

To her surprise, Gerde turned a sickly white and her eyes widened to dark pools of dread.

"Gods save me, m'lady, ye don't think as how 'tis Master Ranulf come back? Happen he's changed his mind an' come ter tell Master Guy I'm ter be thrown out o' the castle!"

"No, not even *he* would do such a thing! Nor would Sir Guy let him if he tried."

But even as Rowène attempted to reassure her maid, she could not ignore the appalling possibility that it might indeed be Ranulf de Rogé, or worse yet, his older brother and her mother demanding entry. Set against the prospect of Black Joffroi and the Winter Lady, she would take Ranulf any day! Conquering her surge of fear, Rowène forced herself to say calmly,

"Even if it is Sir Ranulf, did not Master Guy give you his word that you might stay in Rogérinac as my maid at least until the babe is born. And then possibly you can go to Melangel in Mallowleigh."

"An' what about ye, m'lady?" Gerde asked, her tone trembling only slightly. "Will ye stay here in Rogérinac?"

"You know I have no choice," Rowène replied bleakly. "Until your lord releases me I am a hostage for my people's obedience. I must stay here."

"Ha' ye tol' Master Guy yet?" Gerde asked in an apparent change of subject although Rowène knew it was just a continuation of the same theme. She shook her head.

"An' are ye goin' ter tell him?" Gerde continued diffidently.

"No. Or at least not yet."

"Ye can't put it off much longer," Gerde warned. From somethin' Kelse said t'other mornin', I reckon Mistress Mathilde suspects. An' ye don't want her getting' ter Master Guy afore ye can tell him yerself."

Rowène shrugged, all of a sudden weighed down by the exigencies of her situation.

"It does not much matter if she does go tattling to him, Gerde. I cannot tell him the truth anyway."

"Why not, m'lady? He'd believe ye, I'm sure." She obviously thought about that premise a little longer and then added dubiously, "Though I doubts he'd like it much."

"No. I am very sure he would not like it at all," Rowène agreed. "Indeed, I think such knowledge would break him. Which is why I will not tell him. And neither will you, Gerde. Do you hear me?"

"Aye, m'lady," the tire-maid sighed. "If'n ye says so. Arter all, ye knows Master Guy better'n I do."

With which depressing conclusion both young women relapsed into a strained silence that lasted until a fist hammering on the door of the chamber startled them out of their abstraction. After exchanging a wary glance with Gerde, Rowène signalled to her maid to open the door.

"Lady Rowena?" Geryth looked more than a little wild-eyed, as if he had been out in the storm although Rowène knew perfectly well he had been on duty outside her door since dawn. "Master Guy is askin' fer ye ter come down ter the great hall. Right now."

Rowène gave the young soldier a pointed look, spared a fleeting glance at his wraith-pale sister, and asked in a low voice,

"Has Sir Ranulf returned?"

Geryth looked at her blankly then shook his head.

"Nay, m'lady. I reckon the Commander's still in Chartre. All I know is that Master Guy said ter tell ye he needs ye ter come down an' welcome an important visitor. Oh, an' m'lady," he hesitated, flushed and cleared his throat. "He did say as how ye wasn't ter wear the... uh... red silk."

"Did he indeed?" Rowène murmured, a hint of sarcasm sharpening her tone. "Then perhaps he should come and inspect my clothing coffer himself since he seems to think I have such a vast choice."

Geryth reddened still further and muttered,

"I think ye look fine as ye are, m'lady."

Against all odds, Rowène felt a flicker of amusement, but she was touched by his loyalty all the same.

"In that case, Geryth, I am ready. Come, Gerde, we are going down to the hall."

"Oh m'lady, at least let me brush yer hair out an' find ye a kerchief fer yer head," the maid protested. "Ye can't go down ter meet anyone important dressed no better'n me."

"Honestly, Gerde, what does it matter what I look like?" she asked with an impatient sigh. "Whoever this important visitor is, he is not likely to be here on my account."

"M'lady, please..."

"Oh, very well, but hurry. It will not do to keep Sir Guy and this important visitor waiting."

Less than a quarter of a candle-notch later Rowène paused outside the doors of the hall, striving to calm her slightly quickened breathing and slow her racing heartbeat. She had no idea why Guy had summoned her but, despite her defiant words to Gerde, she had the sinking feeling that her situation was about to descend a little closer to Hell the moment she walked through those heavy oak doors. She sensed Geryth fidgeting at the delay and taking a deep breath, nodded to him to open the doors. Gripping her hands in the folds of her shapeless grey gown she waited until he had stepped inside and announced her, then swept past him, head held high, radiating as much regal dignity as Queen Xandra of Kardolandia could have done.

Grimly ignoring the trembling in her legs she forced herself to walk towards the dais with all the grace that ten years at the Kaerellian court had taught her. At the periphery of her vision she noted half a dozen strange soldiers standing in disciplined stillness around the walls, apparently impervious to their sodden state. As she continued to walk down the hall she stole another sideways glance, hoping to determine whose troops these were. But whatever colour their cloaks had originally been the cloth was now black with rain and, even had the light in the hall been bright enough to permit close inspection, any identifying insignia was obscured by the liberal coating of mud they all wore.

Then it was too late. Rowène reached the far end of the hall where three people stood waiting for her on the floor before the dais, their vastly differing figures intermittently touched by the flickering light thrown by the torches high on the walls. Mathilde de Martine was there, of course, simpering up at the tall stranger beside her. Close beside his wife, although not touching her, Guy waited quietly, his customary courteous mask apparently intact. Until, that is, Rowène looked into his eyes and realised that the Steward of Rogé was far from being as composed as his appearance suggested, while the grim set to his normally good-humoured mouth reminded her most unpleasantly of his half-brother.

Who, she wondered with a spark of interest, was this visitor who had the ability to shake Guy's habitual composure to such a degree? Apprehension tempered by curiosity, she glanced at the tall – very tall – stranger standing a little to one side. A nobleman, if the length of his hair was any guide, he had already shed his drenched cloak and was now drawing off his wet riding gloves in a manner that bespoke a marked impatience. He half-turned to toss them onto the dais, so her first fleeting impression of his face was taken in profile.

She had a confused sense of dripping-wet dark hair, braided at the temples but otherwise hanging straight down beside a handsome face hard beyond its years, graced by a long nose that showed the unmistakeable signs of having been broken at some stage. Dropping her gaze she took in the fine mail shirt he was wearing, the serviceable sword and dagger sheathed at his belt and the glittering spurs at his heels. Then shivered as a distinctive metallic chime informed her that he had taken a step towards her, turning so that the wavering golden light fell full upon him.

It was then that she saw plainly for the first time the lines of the creature emblazoned on the breast of his royal blue surcoat; a white horse, mane flying, wings upswept, overlaid by the stark black line of a bar sinister. There could be only one man in Mithlondia who would wear such a device and in that first moment of stunned recognition, she did not know whether to weep with hope or swoon from shock.

Fortunately before she could do either, she heard Guy say with impeccable courtesy,

"Messire, allow me to present the Demoiselle Rowène de Chartreux. Demoiselle, this is..."

"I believe I can introduce myself," the stranger interposed curtly. "I apologise for my tardy arrival, Demoiselle..." Here he took Rowène's nerveless hand in his own calloused fingers and bowed low, his long dark hair effectively hiding the fact that he did not actually kiss her hand. Then he straightened and, surprisingly given his obvious reluctance to touch her, retained her hand as he continued coolly, "As you have undoubtedly guessed by now, I am Joscelin de Veraux. Your betrothed."

Despite her best efforts Rowène could not control the sudden trembling in her icy fingers and she clutched convulsively at his own cold hand as she looked up at him, trying to reconcile the boy she had met so long ago with the tall young man before her. But a seven-year old's memory is hardly reliable and beyond the raven blackness of his hair she saw nothing she remembered, least of all the bleakness of that ice-keen gaze.

He might have grown into a cold and unfeeling man – indeed, she was sure he had, although she admitted he might have good reason – but one fact stood out nonetheless; Joscelin de Veraux had made the long journey to Rogérinac, riding through rain, mire and storm, to make public claim on her as his betrothed. That being so, perhaps there was a chance that he intended to proceed with their binding and in so doing might halt her well-deserved slide into shame.

Alternatively, he might be here merely to inform her to her face that he no longer wished to take the binding oath with her. Given the circumstances – and he could not possible know all of them – she would not be in the least surprised to learn that he had reached such a decision. Although if so she would much prefer to hear the terms of his rejection in private, without Mathilde's sharp eyes on her or the distraction of Guy's presence.

Rising from her curtsey, she looked up to find de Veraux watching her, something about his dark-lashed eyes fleetingly familiar.

"Messire de Veraux, I am... honoured and..." *And what?* "And pleased..." *That is scarcely the right word but it will have to suffice.* "To meet you again after so many years."

"It has indeed been a long time," he agreed, a faint smile finally touching his lips, though his eyes – they were pale grey, she saw now, reflecting all the colour and warmth of sleet – remained distressingly distant. "Ten years, is it not, since you accompanied your father to Veraux?"

There seemed little she could say to that beyond yes, but she did not bother since at the mention of her father his smile twisted into a grimace and his voice hardened, in direct contradiction to his quiet words.

"I did not mean to speak of him so soon but the wraith of Louis de Chartreux must stand between us. I must beg you to forgive me for the part I played in his death, and for my tardy arrival here."

She could not speak for the ache in her throat but he did not seem to expect more than the jerky nod she managed. And after all, what could she say to the man who had – according to Black Joffroi – escorted her father to his death and placed the noose around his neck. She shut her eyes and prayed for composure.

Why had she not realised before that she would be bound to her father's executioner? A man who must surely believe that *her* father had murdered *his*? But the answer to that horrifying question was plain enough. In her desperate desire to escape both Guyard de Martine and Ranulf de Rogé she had quite simply forgotten that...

"Perhaps, Messire de Veraux, you would care to share our mid-day meal?"

Startled from her thoughts by the sound of Guy's level, familiar – and yes, beloved – voice, she opened her eyes just as de Veraux said firmly,

"I am sure my men would appreciate some hot food, Messire, but for myself I would prefer to speak to my betrothed. I will, however, accept your previous offer of some mulled wine. Both for myself and the Demoiselle de Chartreux, since she seems to be almost as chilled as I am. Although, unlike me, she has not been out in the storm. Or at least I assume she has not?" He lifted straight dark brows in Guy's direction. "Well, Messire?"

"Of course she has not been outside in this weather," Guy replied with something of a snap. Then, with a visible effort, he moderated his terse tone. "To my knowledge, Demoiselle de Chartreux has spent the entire morning in her chamber sewing with her maid. A perfectly respectable occupation for a young noblewoman who is a guest in this place, as I am sure you will agree."

"Really?" De Veraux queried, a wealth of disbelief in his tone, his grey eyes as cold and hard as granite under ice. "From the look of that gown I would have expected to find the Demoiselle serving the mulled wine rather than sharing it with me. And *this* is her maid, is it?"

He flicked a dismissive glance at the heavily pregnant Gerde, then around at the drab furnishings of the dark hall before returning his steel-sheen gaze to his host.

"If this is how you treat a noblewoman in your care, de Martine," he continued grimly. "The sooner I obtain her release the better. I only wish my duties had permitted me to come sooner. And now, I should like to speak with my betrothed. Alone, if you please."

It might have been couched as a request but no-one hearing it could suppose it to be anything less than an order.

"So, have you somewhere a little more private? And comfortable?" de Veraux prompted, his tone sufficiently stinging to bring a slight flush to Guy's cheekbones.

"Of course, Messire. You may have the use of the Steward's solar. If you will follow me, I will show you the way. I will also have the wine sent up."

Pausing only to order his wife and the awestruck Gerde to remain in the hall, he walked past de Veraux, heading for the doors. Rowène watched him go, an aching heaviness in her breast.

"Demoiselle de Chartreux?"

Hearing her name, Rowène brought her gaze back to the man who addressed her, trying to calm the erratic and uncomfortably fast beat of her heart.

*This is it then, a few more moments, and I will know my fate!*

"Messire de Veraux?" The words came out steadier than she would have expected.

"Joscelin," he corrected, his voice low. "You should call me Joscelin, do you not think? I know we are strangers but we *are* betrothed."

*Are we? But for how much longer?*

Nevertheless, she nodded warily and in response he held out a mailed arm. Still wondering whether this man was a potential ally, or more probably the herald of her destruction, Rowène hastily recalled her court manners. Placing the tips of her fingers on the back of his hand she allowed him to lead her from the hall, along the dark passages and up the familiar, narrow spiral of the southeast tower, the uncomfortable silence broken only by the chink of both men's spurs.

Finally, just as Rowène thought the silence might drive her mad, they reached the steward's chamber. Guy pushed the door open and then stood aside to allow Rowène and her betrothed to enter.

"Forgive the state of the room, Messire," he apologised stiffly. "I was working up here when you arrived."

"At least it is warmer than the hall," de Veraux commented dryly, glancing around in quick appraisal, before saying brusquely, "Thank you, Messire. You may safely leave Demoiselle de Chartreux in my company." And forestalling any argument Guy might have been about to make. "We are, after all, formally betrothed and therefore permitted to spend a modest amount of time alone together."

"Of course, Messire," Guyard agreed sombrely. "But I would request that you take some consideration for Demoiselle de Chartreux's reputation."

"That is rather rich coming from you, de Martine!" De Veraux's eyes narrowed to shards of flint, his curt tone skimming the ice-encrusted edge of controlled violence. "After I have spoken to my betrothed it may be that I will need to speak privately to you. Best use the time to sharpen your sword, just in case."

580

"My sword is sufficiently sharp already," Guy snapped, his polite façade cracking as swiftly as the other man's. "That said, I would rather not have to cross blades with you, though I will if I must. But first I suggest you listen to what Rowène has to say and have the wit to believe that, rather than gutter gossip."

"You damned...!"

"Not now, de Veraux!" Then in a completely different tone, reverting to the courteous host, "Ah, here is the wine. Just put it down on the table, Frythe. That will be all." He waited until the girl had disappeared before saying, "I will leave you now and hope you will both be able to join us for the noon meal. Messire. Demoiselle."

With that he nodded curtly to Joscelin de Veraux, bowed low to Rowène and left the room, closing the door quietly behind him.

Left alone with the intimidating stranger to whom she was apparently still betrothed Rowène could think of nothing to say. She did not fear the man himself, she thought, eyeing him warily. Rather she was afraid of how deeply he might pry into her dealings with Jacques de Rogé's younger sons. Could she bring herself to reveal her folly to this cold-eyed stranger, risking Guy's life by so doing? Or should she just stick to the incontrovertible truth of Ranulf's brutal rape?

She could not decide and, watching de Veraux watching her, it occurred to her that he seemed almost as wary of her as she was of him, his earlier arrogance appearing to have quite deserted him. Finally after a nerve-racking silence he gestured questioningly towards the pitcher of gently steaming wine.

"Thank you, but no," Rowène murmured. Then felt impelled to add, "And I would advise you against it as well. I am afraid the wine you will be served here is like to strip the lining from your mouth at the very least."

"Nevertheless I believe I will risk it since it does at least appear to be warm," he replied, a faintly rueful smile chasing some of the chill from his cold grey eyes. "I account myself as healthy as the next man but I do not think I have known a dry moment since we crossed the Larkenlye. My throat feels as if I have swallowed a dozen knives and I fear lest I succumb to a fever before we can leave this damned, draughty castle. Tell me, does it do anything but rain in this hellish province?"

"I am afraid that is as normal for Rogé as the execrable state of the wine," Rowène replied, slightly reassured by that smile, albeit she was still wary of what might lie behind the thin, almost imperceptible, layer of frost in his eyes.

She watched as he poured himself a goblet of wine and took a sip. He almost managed to hide the spasm of revulsion that crossed his face but then, to her amazement, tossed back another mouthful.

"I can understand why you would not risk it," he said hoarsely, evidently reading her look. "But I am a soldier not a gently-bred lady and have drunk worse in my time. Although, it must be admitted, not often."

She gave him a fleeting smile and felt the silence fall heavy between them again. Finally, when she could suffer it no longer, she said unsteadily,

"Please, Messire, if you mean to break our betrothal, it is more kind of you to do it swiftly than leave me wondering when the axe will fall."

"Unfortunately it is not that simple," he said grimly. "For the time being, however..."

He broke off and began to wrestle the loose, wet sleeves of hauberk and shirt far enough up his arm to reveal the broad silver band he wore just above his elbow, then picked up her left wrist so that the delicate bracelet she still wore flashed silver and purple in the candlelight.

"See, Rowène, we are betrothed."

"But?" she prompted, certain that there was one.

"Yes, there is a but," he admitted, holding her gaze without flinching. "It is not, however, something that will prevent me from removing you from this outpost of Hell and taking you to a place where you will be safe and, I hope, with time, content."

He took another swallow of the wine, coughed a little and continued with a disconcertingly sharp glance,

"That is, if you truly wish to be rescued?"

She blinked at that unexpected comment.

"Believe me, Messire, there is nothing I desire more than to leave this place. The sooner the better."

He regarded her keenly for a long moment, then bowed slightly.

"In that case, it will be my honour to escort you hence, although we should perhaps wait for the storm to quieten a little."

"That may be wise. Though as you have discovered for yourself, if you wait for it to stop raining in Rogé, you will wait forever," Rowène reminded him caustically. Then, recollecting his sodden state added, "But perhaps you and your men should make the most of the chance to dry out and warm up before setting off again."

"I trust my men are being fed now and we have all survived worse than this before. If possible I would like to be out of this dismal hole before sunset. Will it take you long to pack?"

She could not help the wry laugh that escaped her.

"Messire de Veraux, as I have but two gowns to my name including the one I am wearing and the same number of shifts, my packing can be very swiftly accomplished indeed."

"In that case, I suggest you send for your tire-maid..." The faintest of frowns drew his narrow dark brows together. "By the way, is she a Rogé servant or did she come with you from Chartre?"

"No, Gerde is part of the Rogérinac household. I wish it were otherwise."

He muttered something under his breath that she did not catch, then continued dismissively,

"Well, doubtless I can find you a more suitable maid from among my own retainers."

Despite the firm note in his voice and her own fears, Rowène managed a flash of mild defiance.

"Gerde may only be a pregnant servant girl but she has been my faithful companion since I came to this benighted place. And if I thought she would leave her brother and her home I would *beg* you to take her with us."

"My apologies," he said a little stiffly. "I did not realise. I will ask de Martine to release her from her bond if that is what you wish." He hesitated. "But in all honesty I have to say I do not think it wise for her to travel in her condition."

She looked up at him with a flash of startled comprehension.

"You think she might miscarry?"

He shrugged.

"I am no physician but I would think it more than likely. It is not the gentlest of journeys and…"

There were black spots dancing before her eyes now and her legs felt strange. De Veraux was still talking but she could only hear the slightly hoarse pitch of his voice, not the actual words. She thought she swayed, felt a hand firm on her arm, guiding her to be seated, shivered at the touch of cold stone against her legs, heard the window open and felt the slap of stinging rain across her face.

She flinched, gasped and heard the window close again. Then opened her eyes to meet Joscelin de Veraux's troubled grey gaze. It was the first sign of emotion she had seen in him and she gradually became aware that he was holding her cold, trembling hands in his own firm, calloused grip as he sat with her on the window seat.

"Tell me one thing… just one thing now," he demanded, low-voiced. "All the rest can wait! No, I lie, there are two things I must know."

She swallowed, knowing they were not talking about Gerde now, and nodded, her throat so tight and dry she could not have spoken if she had wanted to.

"Was it rape?"

*Yes, I thought it would be that.*

She thought briefly of Ranulf… of those soul-shattering moments in her chamber… saw again the stark expression in those dark blue eyes…

And shook her head.

She saw de Veraux's lips move infinitesimally although no sound slipped out. His eyes dropped to her waist, coolly appraising. Yet, for all his control, she sensed a host of emotions, raw and ragged, hiding behind the expressionless lines of his lean, handsome face.

"Second question." He spoke curtly.

*He is going to ask for the man's name! God of Light, what do I tell him?*

"I am not going to ask you who it was. The answer to that would be obvious even to a half-wit! Which I am not! But I will ask you again the question I asked

583

earlier. Do you truly wish to leave this place with me, even though what I know must inevitably colour my attitude towards you?"

"Even if you abandon me beside the highway once we are out of Rogé, yes, I still want to go with you."

"In other circumstances, I might be tempted," de Veraux replied grimly, apparently unmoved by her fierce declaration. "But this might just work to our advantage."

"What? The knowledge that the woman you are betrothed to is either a witch or a whore!"

"*I* never called you either!" The grip of his hands tightened painfully and his grey eyes glinted with a cold fury. "But someone obviously has." His eyes narrowed, glittering shards of ice between raven-black lashes. "Is it true? *Are* you?"

"What? Witch or whore?" Surprisingly her voice did not shake although tears did sting behind her eyes.

"No, damn it, of course I do not think you are a whore!"

"Ranulf did!" The words were out before she could stop them. De Veraux dismissed them.

"The man's a fool then!"

"He also called me a witch!" Rowène said softly.

"Ah!" A heart-beat... two... three... of silence. Then de Veraux said, equally softly. "Show me... your hair, I mean."

He loosened his grip on her hands and, feeling rather as if this could not be really happening, Rowène reached up and pulled off the coarse linen headrail under which Gerde had so carefully hidden her hair. Fumbling slightly, her fingers sought the bone pins that secured her braids in a neat coil around her head. De Veraux made no move to help, merely sat watching her, eyes cool and wary, until one after the other the two thick plaits tumbled down over her breast to lie heavy in her lap. She would have untied them and loosened her hair completely but he stopped her with a word.

"No. Leave them bound. I cannot afford to be caught in your net of enchantment too."

She looked up, indignant at that.

"I said *de Rogé* said I was a witch. Not that I *am*! And even if I were, I have caught no-one in my net, as you put it."

"Have you not?" de Veraux asked absently. Almost as if fearful of being burned he put out a hand and tentatively touched the tips of his calloused fingers to one silk-soft braid.

"Witch-fire," he murmured. Then he groaned and dropped his head in his hands. "The gods damn you to Hell, de Chartreux, you *knew* what she was! And still you made me swear!"

She stared at him in confusion.

"Swear what? And how does my father come into this? It *is* my father you were meaning?"

Joscelin de Veraux raised his head and looked at her then, his grey eyes no longer pale and cold but as dark as storm clouds before the lightning splits the sky. He held out his left hand, palm up, so she could see the healing scar that slashed from the base of his forefinger to his wrist, and through gritted teeth said,

"An oath sworn by a bastard to a traitor. An oath to see a traitor's daughters safe. Your sister is dead, I cannot help her. But you... you I must protect or be foresworn and prove myself a bastard in truth."

"I am sorry but I still do not understand..."

"No, how could you!" His voice was low and ragged, burning with some feral emotion she could not hope to identify.

He put a hand to his neck and dragged a small leather pouch out from beneath his mail. Ripping this open he tipped something into her lap. She caught a glint of gold and something dark that slithered in the shadows and her heart froze in her throat.

"Wha... what is it?" she managed to whisper.

De Veraux laughed, harshly and utterly without humour.

"Do not worry. It will not hurt you. Only me."

He moved slightly to one side so that the light from the candle on the table fell full into her lap and her heart began beating again. The golden glint resolved itself into a man's signet ring, about which had been tied a long length of black silk ribbon... no, not ribbon... hair. It was hair! As long and raven-dark as de Veraux's own. She picked up the ring, tentatively edging aside the knotted hair so that she could see the device cut into it. Not that she had any doubt what she would see. Sure enough the graceful lines of a swan swam through her tear-filled vision.

"My father's ring!"

She looked up into eyes that were once more as pale and cold as winter rain.

"Yes."

"How... how did you get it? I thought a traitor's possessions were forfeit to the crown."

"So they are," he agreed, voice level. "I... took it."

"You stole it?"

Something was wrong here, desperately wrong, and she did not know what.

"No." Surprisingly he took no offence at her incredulous accusation. "I took it because your father ordered me to do so."

"Since when does a royal Guardian take orders from a traitor?" she asked, a bitter intonation to that last word. "The man accused of murdering your own father by poison!"

"Since the night before that traitor's execution," de Veraux replied, his voice clipped. "And as little as you, do I believe Louis de Chartreux poisoned his Prince. The man was many things, not all of them honourable, but he was neither regicide nor fratricide."

"Frat... gods above!"

She blinked at the man who sat so close she could see every hard-etched line of his clean-shaven face... the sheen of steel, ice and rain-slicked granite in his dark-lashed grey eyes... anger, bitterness and above all, pain. What she did not see was sorrow. Only a grim determination.

"We are... blood-kin? Is that what you are saying? That is why you were willing to swear that oath to my father? To protect me?"

"Yes."

Just one word, but looking deeper into his eyes she saw it... a sudden glimpse back to that last night of her father's life. He was lying on a bed of filthy straw, so weakened by torture he could barely move but still chained in the darkness of a freezing dungeon. And kneeling beside him, close enough that their raven hair mingled unhindered, a younger man, blood dripping from knife and hand as he swore an oath to a traitor to protect a witch's daughter...

"From others," that young man said now, bringing her blinking and shaken, trembling with cold and tears, back to the present. "And, the gods help me, from yourself!"

*Myself?*

But she did not ask. One day, she hoped, he would tell her the full tale but for now... something else flickered in his grey eyes and was gone, but not before she had seen the one truth he had sought to conceal from her. But why would he hide it from her? Did he think she would recoil from him in disgust? Or was it only because he did not yet trust her?

*Because I am the Winter Lady's daughter...*

"It was my mother who murdered Prince Marcus, was it not?" she demanded suddenly. "Not Black Joffroi. He was merely her tool, her thrall! It was the Winter Lady of the Faennari who brought my..."

She faltered but in the face of his steady regard could not speak the word she wanted to. He must do that himself and on the day he openly acknowledged that truth, she would know he had finally come to trust her.

"Who brought your father to a bloody and agonising traitor's death... yes, I believe it was," he finished her uncompleted sentence. "And it was by her will that Black Joffroi nominated me to escort de Chartreux to that death, to stand upon the scaffold and break his sword in two, to put the rope about his neck, to watch him die... to hear him die... to feel his dying in my own flesh and bone..."

"Oh, Joscelin."

Tears running down her face, she lifted a hand to cup his iron-hard jaw. His granite eyes gave nothing away but the warm skin of his cheek was very slightly damp. After a moment he lifted his hand to touch her in return.

"Rowène, do not weep. He was not worth these tears."

"Joscelin, please do not say such a thing. He was my father and I loved him. And you must have felt something for him else you would not have suffered the pain of his death so deeply."

"You did not know him," Joscelin said, his voice quietly bitter. "Nor did I, as it turns out. Not until the end, when it was too late for anything but the truth. For only with that truth could he hope to wring such an oath from me as he did."

"Very well, I can understand your anger." Rowène wiped her eyes, then her nose, on her sleeve and regarded her companion with a bleak determination. "And I shall not hold you to an oath that was forced out of you by circumstance. Nor will I ask of you more than you are prepared to give *freely*. Break our betrothal when and how you choose. It has to be done. But do not ask me to forget that you are... bound to me by blood. Joscelin, you are all I have left. Luc is alive but sold into slavery. Ju is taking a fey path beyond my understanding. And while I do feel the lure of the Moon Goddess' power, I swear, I will never use either moon-silver or witch-fire against *you*."

His eyes stayed narrowed for a heartbeat longer, then he reached out and flicked one of the braids that lay in her lap. The bitter chill in his eyes retreated a little, to be replaced by a cynical interest.

"Does de Martine know you have been using it on him?"

"No."

"And de Rogé? You mentioned him earlier, except then you called him by his given name." His dark brows lifted in unspoken question.

"Only to distinguish him from his older brother," she replied, her voice as cool as his now.

Two pairs of narrowed grey eyes stared into each other.

"And has he, as well as his half-brother, felt the touch of witch-fire at your hands?" Joscelin persisted. "I think he must have done."

"I healed a wild-cat's scratch on his cheek at Chartre," Rowène admitted reluctantly. She hesitated and then added, "And he also believes I have rendered him... er... impotent."

Astonishingly, at that, Joscelin's eyes widened and lit with laughter.

"By the gods, I cannot wait until next spring and the start of the campaigning season. The man will be like a caged wolf by then." Then his face darkened. "But will he not betray you? Denounce you to the High Counsel?"

"I do not think so," Rowène said slowly. "He seemed horrified by the thought of what would happen to me if... if... I were to be condemned as a witch."

Joscelin regarded her dubiously.

"Even so, I think it would be sensible to keep you out of his way in future, just in case he changes his mind – his horror at your likely fate may well wane under the prolonged strain of a bewitched celibacy. Not that it should prove overly onerous to keep you from his sight. He does not come often to court, save when the army musters in the spring."

"Court?" Rowène echoed. "You are taking me to Lamortaine?"

To her surprise, he smiled. She shivered. It was not a particularly pleasant smile to behold, though she did not think his malice was aimed at her.

"Of course we are going to court," he said. "While on the one hand you could be regarded as a traitor's spawn and I as nothing more than a royal bastard, on the other side of the coin, you are Ariène de Rogé's daughter and I am High Commander of Mithlondia's Guardians. My place is there and yours, for the time being, is with me."

His casual drawl suddenly took on the sharpened edge of tempered steel and his eyes darkened to a stormy, vengeful grey that woke an answering wildness within her. She looked into his eyes and her smile mirrored his as he finished softly,

"It may take years to bring... the Winter Lady, did you call her... and Black Joffroi to justice but I swear by the Gods of Light and Mercy – yes, and your Moon Goddess too – that one day the man who died a traitor's death will be vindicated."

He reached out and touched her hair, lightly but without fear.

"In the meantime though, let us just see what sort of blaze we can light at court with a touch of witch-fire..."